I0781080

First printing edition 2025.

ISBN: 978-1-962891-04-2 (eBook)
ISBN: 978-1-962891-17-2 (Paperback)
ISBN: 978-1-962891-20-2 (Hardback)

Library of Congress Control Number:
2024924163

This book is a work of fiction. Names, characters, places, and incidents are the product of the author's imagination or are used fictitiously. Any resemblance to actual events, locales, or persons, living or dead, is coincidental.

Ashgate Fortress, book two of The Great King and the Seer
Published by Vellichor and More
www.vellichorandmore.com

ASHGATE FORTRESS

THE GREAT KING AND THE SEER
BOOK TWO

JESSICA PIETRO

VELLICHOR AND MORE

To everyone who has faced and conquered the whispers.
And to those who have yet to overcome them.

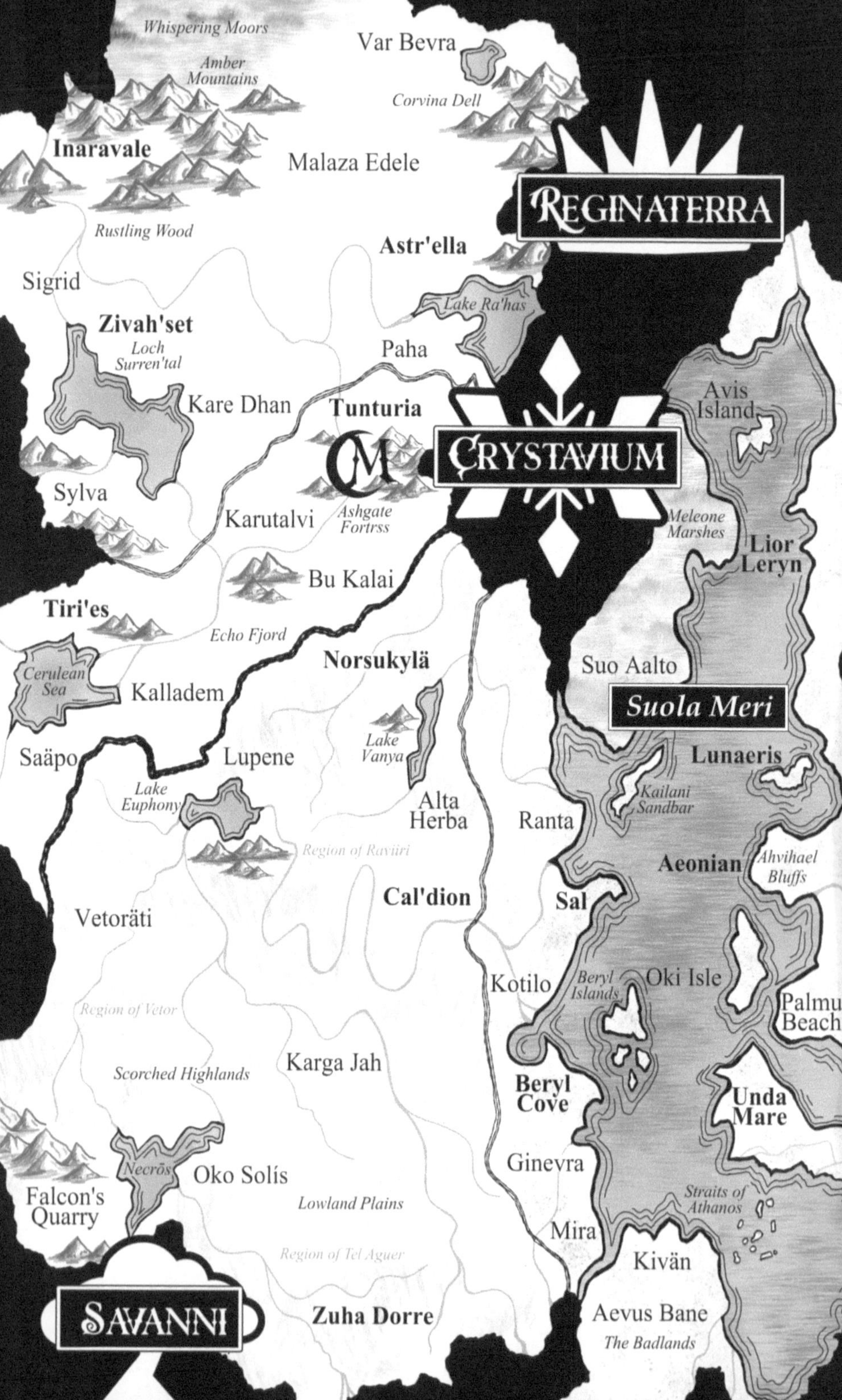

Whispering Moors
Var Bevra
Amber Mountains
Corvina Dell
Inaravale
Malaza Edele
REGINATERRA
Rustling Wood
Astr'ella
Sigrid
Lake Ra'has
Zivah'set
Paha
Avis Island
Loch Surren'tal
Kare Dhan
Tunturia
CM
Crystavium
Sylva
Karutalvi
Ashgate Fortrss
Meleone Marshes
Lior Leryn
Bu Kalai
Tiri'es
Echo Fjord
Norsukylä
Suo Aalto
Cerulean Sea
Kalladem
Suola Meri
Saäpo
Lupene
Lake Vanya
Lunaeris
Lake Euphony
Alta Herba
Ranta
Kailani Sandbar
Region of Raviiri
Aeonian
Ahvihael Bluffs
Cal'dion
Sal
Vetoräti
Kotilo
Beryl Islands
Oki Isle
Palmu Beach
Region of Vetor
Karga Jah
Scorched Highlands
Beryl Cove
Unda Mare
Necrôs
Oko Solís
Falcon's Quarry
Lowland Plains
Ginevra
Straits of Athanos
Region of Tel Aguer
Mira
Kivän
SAVANNI
Zuha Dorre
Aevus Bane
The Badlands

CORDILLERA
GRIM WILDS
Kamari Ravine
Aurora
Jericho
Kovae Saam
Peregrine
Elowen Mountains
Lunalakota Mountains
Lake Lyall
Skull's Gate
Koen Orchards
Lake Tas'kare
Lacuna Kaput Lagoon
Uvelyen
Katutaan
Neoma Dell
'ills Obscura
Vertice Dellalune
Bujarshuri
Region of Sadella
Visk'arus
Region of Vastitas
Werifesteria
Petrichor
Gorge Celeste
Bryä
Ruins of Nefel Ibata
Dysmaa
Villa Montis
Ky'uso
Ame Hana
Ruins of Neoma
Umi Ochrana
Lasskon
Region of Vallemortis
Kesken Ala
Region of Imber
Seigan
Palace of Sateen
Eunoia
Caritas
Region of Pluvina
Sena
METSA SATEEN
ALUNDA
Ferus Basah

THE STORY SO FAR

Six years after abandoning their home for the wilderness of Arkaemor, Foxxglove and Iris Belamour encounter Maeve, a woman who encourages them to search for their missing father and the Sacred Realm of Celestelvyra.

Accepting a destiny bigger than they could imagine, they set off toward the eastern territories.

In the Grim Wilds, Foxx has her first prophetic vision.

After being chased from the desert by the King's Legion, wanted for reasons they can't fathom, they enter the rainforest of Metsa Sateen where they are attacked by a giant nieda. Rescued by a charming stranger named Asher who claims to be searching for the Sacred Realm, too, they agree to join forces and travel together.

While Iris is keen for another companion, Foxx is wary of Asher and his secrets. Still, as the trio traverses the jungle, their bond grows, and Asher slowly reveals snippets of the world he knows, the history of the Monastery of the Morrow, and the Creator Elohim. Foxx endeavors to resist his charms, but the force drawing them together seems unwavering.

In the treetop city of Petrichor, Foxx has her second vision: a city on fire. Iris saw it too, at the Tree of Knowing. Afterwards, Asher at last admits that his true mission is to collect the seven keys that will open the doors to Celestelvyra. Once inside, he will retrieve a magical potion known as Pyhä-ki and return to Arkaemor to slay the Immortal Queen.

Foxx and Iris agree to help Asher on his quest and stand with him against the Queen when the time comes, but before they can move deeper into their journey, Orion and Declan appear in Petrichor and kidnap the girls, stealing them away from Asher.

Little time passes before Orion and Declan's nefarious plans begin to crumble. Though the men seek revenge on Foxx and Iris' father, a former lieutenant who betrayed his team and sent them into exile, the girls watch with wonder as their captors' hearts begin to soften.

Then at Lacuna Kaput, the group is attacked by a lagoon monster, and Iris and Orion are nearly killed. Injured and on the brink of death, Iris climbs the cliffside and shoots the creature between the eyes, saving Orion instead of letting him perish.

Despite this, Orion fights his deepening emotions at every turn, using his anger and vengeance to keep Iris and Foxx at a distance. Iris especially catches glimpses of his true nature and longs to understand him. Her pleasant disposition encourages Declan to open up, too, and she slowly begins to understand the truth of what set the men on this path.

Foxx doesn't allow herself the luxury of looking deeper into the mens' sporadic kindness. Though she grants Declan a fragment of trust in the cave beneath Lacuna Kaput, she keeps her defenses raised.

In Peregrine Manor, she and Iris flee captivity and travel the harsh terrain of Cordillera to the royal city of Jericho in the hopes of locating Asher and the final key.

Around the same time, the Reko Raptors, a group of elite Legion soldiers led by Commander Hector Kayvan, arrive at the city gates seeking Foxx and Iris on Queen Sirena's orders. Orion and Declan make their way to Jericho as well.

It doesn't take long for Sirena to attack, sending her drakinferno to wreak havoc on the city. When Foxx and Iris face off with her, a power Foxx doesn't yet understand courses through her veins, and her fingers grow cold as she and Sirena converse within their thoughts. Foxx pleads with the Queen to let her sister and the rest of the city go free in exchange for herself. When Sirena comments on the darkness in Foxx's heart and invites her to join her wicked cause, Foxx is left disturbed and confused.

Their bargaining is interrupted when Asher approaches the Queen and reveals himself to be her son Alexander Aldrich, the

Prince of Arkaemor. Foxx's heart is torn in two as her previous mistrust is justified. Then Sirena is chased off by a mysterious man who orders her to leave. In her wake, Jericho is left close to ruins.

On the other side of the city, Hector feels called to abandon his allegiance to the sovereigns of Inaravale and assist those devastated by the attack. With the help of the Konungr of Cordillera—a Mad King named Vali—the Reko Raptors and the Jerichonian Guard ignite an uprising like the world has never seen.

Hit by falling bricks in the final blast, Foxx falls unconscious. Despite minimal injuries, she sleeps for days as the city begins rebuilding. Orion has gone missing, and in his absence, Iris and Declan grow closer. Asher, though revealed as the Prince of Arkaemor, continues to go by his alias, rejecting his title and his lineage in favor of revolution against the Thrones.

When Foxx at last wakes, nudged back to consciousness by a strange dream of the Konungr, Asher tells her and Iris everything he's kept hidden, like that he knew their mother when he was a child and that he's been searching for them since her death.

Though still furious with him for all the lies, Foxx agrees to travel back to the Grim Wilds with him, Iris, and Declan where they suspect a doorway to Celestelvyra lies. Her rage continues to grow and fester as more of his secrets make themselves known—like how he knew about barrier jumping, the ability to step through one barrier and out another anywhere in the world.

On their way to the Sacred Realm, they stop in Kesken Ala to check on their friends Rossnetta, Seth, and Mr. Magpie, and learn the devastating truth that Magpie has been brutally murdered for helping them escape the King's Legion all those months ago.

Anguished by his death, Seth pleads that the group allow him to join their mission. The team reluctantly agrees, and they set off into the desert.

When they arrive at the sand-covered Monastery, they make their way into the In-Between, a swamp domain that stands as the gateway between Arkaemor and Celestelvyra. They find Sawyer Belamour trapped within its borders, and Foxx and Iris are overcome with joy at being reunited with their father.

Minutes after they arrive, Queen Sirena appears with two men who are unconscious and on their knees with their hands tied behind their backs. One is Orion, and the other is Declan's brother, Johnathan. Their presence confirms the truth no one wants to believe—Declan betrayed their location in exchange for the lives of his brother and his best friend.

Sirena also reveals that she, like all immortal numinae, cannot bear children and that Asher isn't her son. His true mother was killed at her hands, and soon after, she makes Foxx and Iris orphans too, snapping Sawyer's neck right in front of them.

As chaos ensues, Iris manages to insert the keys into the stone table, and the doors to Celestelvyra open. She, Foxx, Asher, and Seth escape into the most magnificent garden they've ever laid eyes on. As the doors close behind them, Iris watches in horror as Sirena stabs Declan beneath his ribs.

The Queen tries to break through the doors, but Elohim bars her entry. Forbidden from removing the keys from the table, Sirena slaps Orion and Johnathan awake and flees the In-Between, leaving them trapped within its barriers with no memory of how they got there.

Ashgate Fortress

PROLOGUE

STORM 21, 4026

As he approached the iron gates, an unsettling chill tiptoed up his spine. It waltzed across his shoulders, making his neck muscles ache. Though the tundra was certainly one of the most frigid places in the whole of Arkaemor, the biting cold of Crystavium had little to do with his discomfort.

Not many things disturbed Jax Blackmoor, but the conditions in the Prison of the Strayed, deep within the Ashgate Fortress, were diabolical. He would never admit it, but even he'd had nightmares after leaving the premises.

Stopping before the iron bars, he inhaled a breath, dreading the screech of metal that accompanied the opening gates. A glance left offered one last look at the horse he'd left chained to one of the rings screwed into the outer wall. The guards kept a small stable within the Fortress, but Jax preferred a quick exit, just in case. A charcoal stallion with hair as dark as his own, it had a single patch of white above its front left hoof, as if one leg had stepped into a bucket of paint. Another horse stood next to his, indicating a second visitor. His mind cycled through possibilities of who it might be, but since the animal bore no insignia or regimental colors, he wouldn't know until going inside.

Lifting his eyes to the guard tower above, Jax raised a hand in greeting. The men in the tower recognized him immediately and wasted no time opening the gates.

The path leading to the front doors was blood red. Jax had never been sure if this was an aesthetic choice or if the prison's history had permanently stained the concrete. Many stories recounted how the building that once housed the zealous scholars loyal to the Creator had been transformed into the hellish prison standing there today. None were pleasant.

Though, to Jax, what the building used to be didn't matter. All things changed, died, morphed from what was old into what is new. He had a job to accomplish and didn't worry himself with more than that.

He suspected this assignment might take several days, since the rabble-rousers remained tireless in their attempts to cause trouble for the Warden. If he did need to stay, he'd rent a room in Tunturia, the closest city. Beds were made available to the King's Legion in the Ashgate Fortress, but Jax never slept there. Not since that very first night years ago.

The Fortress didn't sit far from the city, but even if it did, the distance was irrelevant. If he had to travel hours, it would be well worth the trip to avoid the nightly echoes of nightmarish screams emerging from the prison below.

PART ONE

IGNITING FLAMES

After they fell and the wall arose, the old god Bryä took a city for his own. He liked the sands best. Not white with salt where the Destroyer would later reign, but red with clay and bloodshed. He called his city Bryä, but even with all his wealth and power, he lacked satisfaction.

He had to beat them. Had to be better than the other numinae who ruled the world. In a fit of arrogance, Bryä twisted the tongues of his people and changed their speech, giving them knowledge of a language all their own.

Soon after, unwilling to be outmatched by their brethren, the gods Vetoräti and Katutaan did the same, one in the grasslands and the other in the misty jungle.

And so the people of these lands speak in these tongues to this day, just as the fallen numinae wished it to be.

~An excerpt from Jumalan Sana.
Recorded in the Book of Histories chronicled by Jaeho the navi.

CHAPTER 1

INTO THE UNKNOWN

Orion's eyes had nearly swollen shut. An array of gashes and varied levels of bruising covered his face and much of his body. The weight of his eyelids fought back against his attempts to blink, but somewhere smothered in drowsy consciousness, he knew he needed to wake up. Taking in the surrounding area through narrow slits, he fought to obtain his bearings. To his right, he saw the ground. Not dirt or grass, but gray bricks. His shoulder tingled from lack of circulation, and his neck felt sore from the awkward angle of his forehead resting against damp stone.

A man's voice spoke Orion's name into his ear, startling him. He endeavored to open one eye wider to get a better look. The opposite eye squinted closed in response.

Orion, you must wake up. Do you know where you are?

Lifting his head with effort, he scanned all he could see. At his best guess, he thought he must be in some kind of jungle, and he wondered if he'd been dumped into Metsa Sateen. The trees growing tall around him looked familiar, but it didn't seem to be raining, a fact he considered a blessing. Still, the air felt muggy like the rainforest, so he expected a downpour would begin at any moment.

He tried to roll onto his stomach and push himself to his knees, only to realize his wrists were bound behind his back, a valid explanation as to why he'd woken in such a strange position. Instead, he twisted his torso and groaned as aching abdominal muscles pulled him into a seated position.

With a better view of his surroundings, he found himself on a platform stained with patches of green moss and dotted with shoots of foliage bursting through fractures in the bricks. Pendulous branches from a tree created a canopy overhead. Above the tree, he saw a colorful, starlit sky.

To his left, another person in a similar condition was dragging himself back to consciousness. He wore the crimson, black, and gray of the King's Legion, and it took Orion only moments to recognize him.

"Johnathan?" The name toppled from his lips as a question, not due to uncertainty but because he couldn't figure out how he'd come to be unconscious on the ground next to his best friend's brother. "Johnathan, wake up."

The sluggish figure didn't respond immediately, his eyelids slowly opening and closing like butterfly wings as he continued to suffer the effects of a backhand to the face and the lingering spell that had kept them dazed.

Orion shifted to rise to his feet. He knew a higher vantage could be invaluable when one found themself lost. When he tried to stand, he sucked air through his lips as the wounds covering his upper body alerted him of their presence. They burned like nothing he'd ever felt. A few had yet to clot, spilling blood down his bare chest. A new piece of the puzzle buoyed up into his memories—the Queen had tortured him.

Brushing recollections aside, he tried again to stand and was met with the cruel reminder that his hands remained secured behind him. Pausing to catch his breath, he fought to blink away the drowsiness clouding his head. Then he rolled back onto his side and struggled to pull his legs through the circle of his arms.

Twisting onto his knees, he tested his balance, which he found to be shaky and unsteady. After a few moments of stabilizing, he lifted a knee and planted his boot flat on the ground. Using the stone for leverage, he pushed himself up until he stood on both feet.

He examined the area and realized he was on a bridge. Swamp water on either side lay motionless, highlighted with lime algae and water-dwelling plants. In front of him, a set of stone steps led to a marshy trail that disappeared into the jungle.

Tilting his head in hesitation, it occurred to him that the world around him was profoundly silent. Metsa Sateen was by far the loudest territory he'd ever traversed. Regardless of day or night, rain or shine, the sounds of Sateen never ended. He lifted his hands to his ear and snapped his fingers, releasing a sigh of relief as he confirmed he had not gone deaf.

So, have you figured it out?

That voice again. He'd thought he had squashed any trace of it long ago. Perhaps he was dreaming.

You are not dreaming. And you couldn't squash My voice if your life depended on it. Not even you are that powerful, Orion O'Connell.

With sudden intensity, the ground rumbled beneath his feet, sending vibrations through the stagnant water. Orion braced himself, spreading his boots and bending his knees until the reverberations passed.

When the world stilled, Johnathan emitted a series of sputtering coughs.

"That's right, Johnathan. Let it all out." With his eyes on Declan's brother, he noticed another body in his peripherals. A hefty man lay in a heap on the ground, his limbs sprawled in awkward and unnatural positions. Crossing to the man in three strides, Orion pressed his boot against his shoulder to roll him over. "Sawyer Belamour?" He bent to get a better view but immediately felt unsteady and straightened. "If you're dead, I suppose my chances of being exonerated are nonexistent. But what are you doing here?"

Orion turned, taking in more of the surrounding area. At the end of the bridge opposite the steps leading into the jungle, he saw a wall with a crescent moon and symbols in a circular pattern. Roots from the great tree framed either side, spilling all the way to the water. His brow pulled together as he debated whether or not he might somehow still be in Jericho. Though, he felt certain there wasn't a single place in Cordillera bearing such ghastly humidity.

Think it through, Orion. You know the truth.

"No one asked for Your help, okay? Not that it matters, since You aren't in the business of helping anyway." Orion had called out to that voice many times as a child, even more so after his mother got sick. The voice had responded often then, and Orion soon learned It spoke nothing but lies. It had promised him everything would be all right, but he'd been far from all right.

Rolling back through his memories, he tried to summon the series of previous events. He knew Foxx and Iris had given them the slip at Peregrine Manor, and he'd been in Jericho with Declan. They'd run into Hector and Raven—two of the current Reko Raptors. Then there was some kind of attack…

The Queen and her drakinferno.

They'd attacked the city, setting it ablaze.

But he couldn't recall what happened after: how he'd made it out of the city and ended up—wherever he was—with Johnathan Declanaire and Sawyer Belamour as his companions.

Off to the left, he saw a stone table along the edge of the platform bridging the swamp. From his position, he could see embellishments on its surface. A cough drew his attention to another prone body drenched in blood. Recognizing his best friend's limp form, he rushed over and dropped to his knees with another wince. With wrists still bound, Orion shook Declan's arm. He squinted an eye again, allowing his other to open wider as he drew closer to the blood pouring from Declan's ribcage. Though he had little medical training, he knew a rib injury was not a good sign. Then he saw a scorch mark high on his chest spreading out from his shoulder like tendrils of spilled ink.

Over his shoulder, he called to Johnathan. "Pull your legs through and stand up. Your brother needs help." Johnathan, who had at last found himself in a semi-seated position, looked around, disoriented. Digging into Declan's boot, Orion found his pocket knife and used it to slice free of the rope bindings. Then he tossed it to Johnathan, who missed the catch. The knife clattered across the ground, and Johnathan crawled after it like a top-heavy toddler.

Orion pulled his hair out of his face, tying matted locks into a bun at the back of his head. Every movement brought with it a brand new torture. He checked Declan's pulse from the point on his throat and could barely detect a beating heart. "Hang in there, bud. We can fix this. I'm going to fix this."

Looking back again, Orion saw Johnathan struggling to cut through his binding. Blood ran down his cheek from a wound on his temple, though he appeared to have far fewer lacerations than Orion.

At last, Johnathan joined them with freed hands, though he'd crawled over rather than trying to stand. "Oh no. Silas." His brow creased with concern as he took in the pool of blood. "Is he going to be okay?"

"He'll be fine," Orion said, unwilling to accept the alternative.

"Quiet a moment, I need to think." He surveyed the area once more: the embellished wall; the lack of wildlife; Sawyer dead on the ground, looking as though he hadn't aged a day and covered in the grime of a man living deep in the wild. Add to that the Creator's voice in his head, and piece by piece, he put together the events that must have taken place. Knowing with certainty where they must be, he swore. Then he pointed down the steps toward the trail. "Go see if we can get out the way we came in."

"What do you mean?" Johnathan failed to restrain his panic. "I don't remember coming here. I don't know how I got here!"

"I think the Queen brought us." If they really were in the In-Between as he suspected, that meant the decorated wall in front of them likely led to Celestelvyra. Orion wondered where Iris and Foxx might be: if Sirena had taken them or if they'd made it into the Sacred Garden. He couldn't imagine the sisters leaving Declan to die. Despite their rocky history, he knew them to be caring and honorable. If they hadn't let Orion be consumed by the lagoon monster at Lacuna Kaput, they definitely wouldn't have left Declan. Unless they'd had no other choice.

Lifting Declan's torso, Orion removed the pack from his shoulders and again instructed Johnathan to go check the entrance. "Just follow the path and find the other door. I don't have time to explain, but I seriously doubt those will be opening back up any time soon." He gestured ahead of them, now seeing the faint line down the center of the wall that proved his theory about them being doors. Another quake rocked the ground, dropping loose twigs from the trees above. "We need to find a different way out. Fast."

Johnathan rose to his feet, holding his hands out for balance. The stone table was close enough for him to grab, but after glimpsing its surface, he didn't touch it. When steady, he followed the steps down to the trail, groaning as his boots squished in the marshy water. After a long moment, he yelled back, "It's blocked."

Orion swore again as a heavier rumble rocked the foundation of the bridge, sending a crack through the stone.

The table, Orion. You must retrieve the keys.

Repeating the words under his breath, he used the table to pull himself to his feet. Stepping over Declan, he examined its surface. Carved into it lay an exact replica of the picture on the doors. He'd seen the symbols before in his father's old books about the

Monastery of the Morrow and knew each represented one of the seven territories.

Increasing trembles sent more leaves and branches tumbling around him. He looked up to see Johnathan hovering on the steps with his arms out and trying not to fall.

"What's happening?" Johnathan asked. This time, the shaking didn't stop. Bricks began to crumble from the building holding the doors, shattering into pieces when they hit the bridge. The leaves of the great tree rattled, dropping sticks and foliage into the swamp.

"We need to get out of here before she buries us under rubble."

"She, who?" Johnathan asked, but Orion ignored him, returning his attention to the table.

The voice had told him to retrieve the keys, though he had no idea why he'd chosen that moment to listen to Elohim's commands when he'd disregarded them so many other times. He ran his hands over the seven symbols, thinking they must be the keys He'd spoken of. They were flush with the stone, but a thin crack outlined each one, as though it might be a separate piece. Again he slid his hand over them, beginning with the crown he knew represented Reginaterra and moving clockwise around the circle until he reached the final symbol—the Jerichonian moon—at the center.

A loud clang echoed throughout the swamp, more metallic than the perpetually falling stones and branches. Then, one by one, the symbols began to rise, beginning with the crown, then the snowflake, and so on, until every stone rested loose atop the surface.

Orion collected them and stuffed them into Declan's bag. "Now let's get your brother." Johnathan helped lift Declan over Orion's shoulder. Another curse escaped his lips as every muscle of his body ached.

Noticing the intensity of his pain, Johnathan asked, "Do you want me to take him?"

Orion hardened his features. "I'm fine. Grab his bag. Let's get out of here." Johnathan scooped up the bag and followed him down the steps to the path, stopping next to him in front of the dark hallway. "This might be uncomfortable. Take a deep breath, and don't stop moving forward no matter what."

"But it's blocked," Johnathan said.

"I don't think it will be anymore. At least, I hope it won't. Stay close to me. Deep breath." Inhaling enough air to fill his lungs to the point of bursting, he stepped across the dark barrier with Johnathan trailing a step behind him. They moved as quickly as they could, pushing through the heavy density of the air and the suffocating lack of oxygen.

Just when they thought their lungs might implode, they stumbled through the barrier and onto the floor. Coughing, wheezing, and gasping for breath, Orion lost his grip on Declan's body, and it tumbled away, landing face down with a cheek smooshed against the floor.

Darkness filled the room but for the beam of moonlight spilling in through the doorway, illuminating the mound of sand and creating a rectangle on the floor in front of them. The entire building rumbled. Sand particles in the wind burned their skin, making it difficult to see and even harder to breathe.

Orion croaked words through a scratchy throat. "If he survives this, let's not tell him I dropped him, okay?" Johnathan agreed without words, his lungs fighting to take in oxygen.

For the first time since waking, Orion heard a second voice in his head, more vicious than the first, telling him he would fail, that Declan would die, and it would be all his fault. He scanned the room, wondering where it might be coming from. Faintly among the shadows, he saw a structure at the room's center and broken furniture around the outer walls. Sand poured in the windows, blocking the moonlight.

Then the first voice returned: *Do not heed the others, Orion. Listen only to Me. Pick up your friend, and escape this place.*

Orion shook his head but dragged himself to his feet. Already he could feel the sand filling the slashes on his chest and arms. For a moment, the pain was too much to bear, and he grabbed hold of a table at the center of the room. "Give me a shirt from his bag."

Johnathan dug through the bag and pulled out a gray tunic, handing it over.

Orion tugged it over his head, grimacing as he gingerly pulled it down his torso. Though loose on Declan, it hardly fit Orion's build. Blood that had spilled from Declan's wound down Orion's torso soaked through the shirt, staining it instantly. "Okay, let's get him."

Johnathan helped push Declan up the sand mound and through the door. They listened as his body rolled down the opposite side and out of sight. Orion helped Johnathan follow his brother, vibrations making it difficult to climb shifting sand. When Johnathan made it free, Orion climbed the mound and tumbled through the door.

The skies of Arkaemor were dark, illuminated only by Ammil's full moon as it slipped in and out of angry clouds. Wicked winds created something like a sandstorm around the Monastery. Orion pulled his shirt up over his nose to block the sand. When Johnathan saw, he pulled off the outer layer of his uniform and tied it around his head.

Peeking out from beneath the awning, Johnathan shouted Orion's name. The tempest swallowed his voice, so he tapped his arm and pointed up. Queen Sirena Aldrich floated above them in a cyclone, accompanied by her drakinferno. Moonlight dancing across her scarlet dress made it shine and sparkle to match Kaen's feathery scales.

Orion gestured toward a stack of rocks to the left, roughly three *sylis* from the building. Grabbing Declan, they darted off into the desert, hoping the storm would be enough to conceal them. Sirena had left them alive in the In-Between, presumably to trap them for the rest of their days as Sawyer Belamour had been. If she discovered their escape, Orion doubted she would let them live again.

Reaching their sanctuary, they dropped to the ground and flattened themselves against the rocks. Kaen released a plume of fire that lit everything in sight with amber radiance. Orion looked out around the rocks to watch the beast plummet toward the Monastery, crushing it to smithereens beneath his enormous body. Another crest of flames, deep orange like the fur of a tiger, set the roof and structure ablaze.

Orion looked away, leaning his weight on the rocks as he tried to catch his breath. Harsh winds continued to howl, assaulting their eyes and orifices with sharp, biting sand, and spreading smoke in all directions.

Then all at once, the whirlwind stilled. Sirena and her dragon vanished, taking the sandstorm with them, and the desert grew quiet but for the crackling fire devouring one of the last remaining Monasteries, slowly but surely dissolving it to ashes.

C

"*This* is Celestelvyra?" Foxxglove, Iris, and Seth looked around, incapable of fully processing the splendor of what lay before them.

A variety of plants and trees lined the trail in intentional, picturesque harmony. The forest wasn't cluttered or disorderly, like the jungle of Metsa Sateen, but instead appeared as if every plant and stone had been placed in a strategically arranged composition.

"This is it." Asher's smile widened up his cheeks, revealing hidden dimples.

"It's a garden?" Iris marveled, lifting her palm as if testing the air. A cool breeze accentuated the comfortable climate, smelling of sweet and fragrant flowers. Blooms of every color, as well as fruit and berries, sprouted from bushes, trees, and vines.

Above the rustling leaves, they could hear water in the distance. Birds sang from the trees, mixing melodies with whistling cicadas and chirping crickets. Two white lepennas, one a full-sized bunny and the other very small, hopped across the path in front of them. They halted to observe the humans invading their garden before pushing off the ground and letting their feathered wings lift them into the sky.

Off to their left, a herd of doe grazed in the tall grass, and in a tree to their right, a brown-feathered barn owl hooted, tilting its head to stare at them.

Iris looked at Asher. "It's magnificent."

"*A land with brooks of glistening water, of fountains and springs, vines and fig trees and pomegranates, a land of olive trees and honey.*"

Foxx regarded Asher with astonishment. "I think I read that in the book I brought along from the Monastery in Metsa Sateen." Taking two tentative steps in his direction, she extended her arm. "This is what your Creator originally intended for the world?"

Asher bubbled with joy. "Brilliant, yeah?"

"What do you think, Seth?" Iris nudged him with her hip, her arm now resting loosely across his shoulder. "You aren't saying much."

A wolf with an elegant coat of smokey fur wandered onto the path. Iris squeezed Seth, and they all froze. Noticing their presence, it approached them, padding right up to Asher and sniffing his pants before raising its head to peer at him expectantly. Cautiously, Asher lifted the fingers at his side, letting his hand hover in the air above the animal's head.

Iris grabbed Foxx's arm as they watched the interaction.

The wolf brushed against his palm, whining as if begging to be pet. Asher dropped his hand lower, and the wolf arched its back.

More secure of the beast's gentility, Asher scratched it behind one ear. Its tail wagged feverishly until Asher finally gave in, crouching face to face with the wolf and using both hands to scratch its ears and neck. After lapping the entirety of his face, the wolf yelped in gratitude and darted off into the trees.

The others gaped as Asher rose from his knee and wiped his face on his shirt.

"What is this place?" Amazement blushed Iris' cheeks. "I've never known a wolf to behave like that." A flock of blue birds fluttered into the air from a tree nearby, and the barn owl's huge eyes were drawn to the sound of flapping wings.

"Everything here, every single living thing, exists together in peace and harmony. Notice how the doe didn't even startle as the wolf ran by? Before the separation of Celestelvyra and Arkaemor, all animals behaved this way. Even those we now consider predators."

Seth cleared his throat so the others would give him their attention. Then he pinched his chin, his brow scrunched in thought. "I guess what I want to know is: are we going to be eating soon? I do love pomegranates."

Asher, Foxx, and Iris burst into laughter, feeling lighter than they thought possible after everything they'd experienced on the opposite side of the doors. The beauty of Celestelvyra had captivated them, its splendor distracting enough to allow them a smidgen of joy. Soon, they would need to wallow in their losses, heal from their wounds, and find a way to fulfill their destinies from behind locked doors.

Until then, they would explore Celestelvyra and discover all it had to offer.

"Shall we have a stroll then?" Asher gestured toward the path ahead.

"Let's stroll." Seth stepped away from Iris and took hold of Asher's hand, looking up at the Prince with a smile that melted Asher's heart.

CHAPTER 2

AFTERMATH

"She's gone," Orion said.

"Are you sure?" Sweat dripped down Johnathan's face, both from anxiety and the desert heat.

The land lay still and quiet but for the crackling fire dismantling the remains of the Monastery. Any creatures living nearby had likely found shelter to avoid the wind and would undoubtedly remain hidden.

"There's sand in my mouth." Johnathan stuck out his tongue. "And my ears. And my eyes." He tried to brush granules from his face, finding the task impossible as they clung to his damp skin.

Orion dragged Declan into the light of the fire's blaze so he could examine him. He held an ear to his chest, hearing the whisper of a beating heart. Then he tapped his face and pried his eyelids open, but Declan didn't respond.

"He's not going to make it, is he?" Johnathan's voice trembled. A coyote howled in the distance, making him flinch as his eyes darted about the landscape.

"He's going to make it." Orion slid Declan's pack from Johnathan's shoulder without his permission and dug through it in the firelight.

"I don't understand what happened. I was on Watchman duty at Castle Solís, then I was waking up in that swamp, and you were there, and Silas was on the ground. I think I remember being with the Queen, but it's foggy. None of it makes sense." He continued rambling, and Orion continued ignoring him as he yanked things from Declan's bag. He kept one eye closed as he searched. The sandy wind had made his swollen eyelids more inflamed, and he longed for a way to cool them.

Johnathan touched Orion's shoulder. "Orion? Please! Tell me what is going on."

"Shut up, Johnathan! Just wait." With an exclamation of victory, Orion pulled out Declan's torch and firestarter and shoved it into Johnathan's hands. "Light this, and hold it for me."

Johnathan did as instructed, holding up the lit torch so Orion could better see into the bag.

In no time at all, Orion found the container of curavenum, healing salve made from a nieda, along with his tin of medical supplies. Unhooking Declan's water sleeve from the pack, he poured some over his face and gasped as the water carved through fresh wounds. Then he took a swig and handed it to Johnathan.

Unveiling Declan's wound, he found it still pulsing blood. The skin above had been scorched, darkened like ash, but since no blood spilled from it, he ignored it for the moment.

Pulling a shirt from the bag, he tore the bottom off in a long strip. After instructing Johnathan to dump water over the wound, he used the top half of the torn shirt to wipe away the blood. Unscrewing the bottle of infection cleanser, he filled the dropper, pulled the wound apart with his fingers, and squirted it into the hole. Johnathan turned and gagged as the glass dropper penetrated the wound. It fizzed, bubbled, and bled even more.

"We have to stop the blood. I'm going to stick some cura in there, and then I need you to lift him so I can tie this around his chest."

Johnathan agreed to the plan, though his face looked pained as he tried to be helpful while averting his eyes.

Orion opened the cura and was disheartened to find it nearly empty. "Damnit, Declan. You always have enough for everyone else, but when you need it, it's gone." He scraped as much as he could from the edges and dabbed it inside the wound. The foul smell had Johnathan grimacing and pinching his nose.

Orion tore another strip from the shirt and rolled it into a ball before pressing it against the hole. Johnathan lifted his brother up by his shoulders, allowing Orion to slide the cloth around his back. He tied the two ends together atop the wad of fabric so it put pressure on the wound until he decided what to do next. "That's all we can do for now. I wish we had more of this." He held up the empty cura container.

"Can we get more?" Johnathan wondered.

"The closest town is a two day journey for healthy travelers. He'll never make it that far, especially if we have to carry him. I may not even make it that far." Orion got to his feet to pace, scratching his chin with stained fingers and mumbling to himself. They'd managed to escape the In-Between and the Immortal Queen only to be stranded in the desert.

Movement in his peripherals caught his eye. He paused to observe the Monastery and saw something shift low to the ground, hidden within the shadows of the structure like a silhouette in the night. As it lurked just beyond the firelight, Orion's hand rose to his hip in search of a weapon, but he found none. Then two eyes flashed in the darkness, reflecting the fire as a wolf stepped into the illumination of the blaze. The animal was large like a timber wolf, but timber wolves weren't native to the Wilds. A stroke of fear sent a current through Orion's body that numbed his fingertips.

"Then you stay here, and I'll go bring some back." Johnathan pushed Declan's hair from his eyes, oblivious to the danger stalking nearby.

The wolf disappeared behind the building. Orion continued to survey the area, wondering if it planned to circle around and attack from a different angle. Johnathan said his name, and Orion spun on him. "He won't make it, Johnathan!" He pulled his bun loose and intertwined his fingers in his hair. Again he looked for the animal without alerting Johnathan of his concern. Running through several options, he tried to come up with an idea to save his friend. The voice he'd heard in the In-Between remained unsurprisingly absent, as had often been the case when Orion needed Him most.

With the amount of blood Declan had lost and their lack of medicine, plus the looming predator on the horizon and their minimal weapons to defend themselves, Orion began to lose hope. He released an emotional exhale and repeated, quieter, "He won't make it, Johnathan."

A woman spoke from somewhere in the dark. "Are you giving up so easily? I had heard better things of you, Orion O'Connell."

It took Orion a moment to realize the voice hadn't come from inside his head—Johnathan had heard it, too. Both men turned to find a figure walking toward them from the depths of the desert. Orion narrowed his eyes to see her clearly, but with them already swollen, it didn't make much of a difference. Johnathan held out the torch to find her suddenly in front of them.

She stood on Declan's opposite side facing Orion, examining them in the torchlight as they examined her. With skin the color of molasses, made even darker by the warm light of the fire and the night sky above, Orion suspected she looked younger than she truly was. Thin wrinkles on either side of her lips and creases shooting out from the corners of her eyes indicated a long and happy life. Her irises reflected the light like mystic topaz, a rainbow of swirling colors.

"Who are you?" Orion's gaze slipped back over his shoulder to see if the wolf had made a reappearance. He wasn't sure how he would manage to protect Johnathan, Declan, and the woman in his current state with only a pocket knife and Declan's pistol on hand.

"My name is Maeve." Her tone remained tranquil, her fingers sliding up and down the length of beaded necklaces that hung all the way to her navel. The olive dress beneath them fit loosely around her body and stopped above bare feet.

"What are you doing in the desert, Maeve?" Orion eyed her suspiciously. She had no belongings: no pack to hold supplies and no sleeve of water. "Are there others with you, or are you alone?"

Maeve smiled and seemed to scan the land behind Orion. Silver hair, thick with curls, bounced as she moved. "I am never alone, but at the moment, there are no others with me."

Johnathan rose to his feet, looking at her expectantly. "Can you help him?"

Orion scoffed and turned from her, resting his hands atop his head. "She carries nothing, can't you see that, Johnathan? How could she possibly help him?"

Maeve took her time answering, watching them in silence. Then her eyes fell to Declan. "I cannot help him, no."

"Then why the hell are you wasting our time?" Orion growled, spinning on her with his fists clenched. "Feel free to run back to whatever cave you crawled out of."

Maeve didn't flinch. "I cannot help him, Orion, but you can. If you can be patient and listen. You want him to live, yes?"

"Of course I want him to live." He looked at his friend's body as he tried to hold his emotions in place. He couldn't lose Declan, he

realized. He wouldn't. With resolve, he decided he would do whatever it took to save him. Whatever this mad woman presented, he
would listen.

Maeve's smile grew. "Your reputation precedes you, Orion. You
are every bit the man they said you would be."

Uncertain whether or not this was an insult, he asked, "Who
said? How do you know me?" A breeze blew through the desert,
cooling their damp skin.

"Those who know things have shared with me what they
know."

"Do you work for Sirena?" Suddenly terrified, he felt foolish for
allowing this woman to come so close without even attempting to
guard against her. Maeve shook her head, and he tried to determine
if he believed her wordless denial. If not the Queen, then who? Who
knew things about him? He ran through the list of people he'd been
close to in his adult life. Declan, of course, Sawyer and the other
Reko Raptors on his team, as well as a few other soldiers years ago,
and Camille. It was a short list.

The cruel voice reached his thoughts again, reminding him how
he'd failed every single one of them.

Maeve's words shattered the malicious accusations. "To save this
man, it will take an act of bravery and selflessness. Are you willing
to do whatever you must?"

"Bravery. Selflessness. Got it. I'm willing. Just tell me what
to do."

Tilting her head, she hummed long and slow. "There are two
paths for you, Orion O'Connell. Two paths running side by side.
You tend to drift back and forth from one to the other, but if you
wish to help your friends, you must choose the path that is straight
and narrow. You cannot continue to walk the line between the light
and the dark. Do you understand?"

His fingers tightened in his fists, nails digging into the flesh of
his palms. "No. I don't understand. Enough with the riddles, just
tell me what I need to do to save my friend."

She smiled wider, his words exactly what she'd expected. "I *am*
telling you." She looked to the south with an outstretched arm. The
fabric of her sleeve belled out beneath it. "Follow the sands in this
direction. When the sun rises, look to the east and you will find
what you need to save Silas."

"Fabulous. Let's go, Johnathan." Orion crouched next to Declan.

Johnathan looked from him to the woman and back again, not moving.

Maeve spoke Orion's name, and it seemed to echo in their ears. He turned to face her, his angry expression melting into captivated uncertainty. "One more riddle for the road: If you seek to save the others, you must search diligently among the briar. Seven no more, but don't lose hope, for all legends are forged in fire."

"Great," Orion said under his breath.

"What will we find in the south?" Johnathan asked, at last finding courage to speak.

"More. But until then..." She knelt to place a hand above Declan's wound, closing her eyes. The air around them picked up, creating a whistling breeze that lifted Orion and Maeve's hair from their shoulders. When Maeve stood again, she took three steps back, her gaze locked on Orion. "This will only last a short while. Silas doesn't have much time. Hurry. You must fly." Dipping her head to him, she offered a farewell. "You will remember the words I have spoken about the two paths. Until we meet again, Orion O'Connell." Then she vanished in a plume of smoke.

"Where did she go?" Johnathan looked around. Orion grew angrier than before, his rage suddenly kindled like a thunderclap of fury. Johnathan said his name.

Letting a wild growl burst free, Orion began pacing again, frantically mumbling to himself. "Go south. What's more? More what? Idiot woman! What can we—" He smacked the side of his own head and yelled, "Shut! Up! I'm trying to think!" Johnathan said his name again, causing Orion to turn and roar, "What do you want?"

Johnathan blanched. "Are you all right? You don't seem... yourself."

"I'm fine, Johnathan. Help me pick him up." He pulled Declan up by his arms, lifting him onto his shoulder without accepting any help from Johnathan. "Grab his bag. You heard the witch. This way." Then he turned from him and the still-burning Monastery, and began walking south across the sandy plains of the Grim Wilds.

C

Candle-lit chandeliers dotted the ceiling, and torches lined every wall in the Hall of Sunsets. With the current time being well past highmoon, the full moon gleamed through the windows behind the thrones, covering everything in a blanket of pale light and casting elongated shadows down the steps of the dais.

King Pollux had heard the commotion from up the hall and rushed in to find Sirena collapsed on her hands and knees atop the crimson carpet. Sputters of anger exploded from her.

Several Watchmen poured in through the doors after him, but none dared approach their sovereigns as blood and tears spilled to the floor, drenching the carpet with evidence of her fury.

Pollux rushed to his wife's side, kneeling next to her. He'd never seen her in such disarray: blood staining her skin and clothes, her hair a mess, the tiara woven into it cocked askew, and her dark makeup bleeding down her cheeks, riding the streams of her tears. Too alarmed by her rabid actions to touch her, he spoke her name. "What happened, my darling?" Silently shooing away the Watchmen to allow the Queen her privacy, he leaned his head lower, trying to level his gaze with hers.

Her eyes, rimmed like flames, snapped to his. "Your. Treacherous. Son!"

"You found him?" Pollux tried to quell his relief.

More enraged by the joy in his tone, she replied, "I found him. Your precious Alexander is a bloody traitor! Do you know where he is right now? He is at this very moment in the Sacred Realm of Celestelvyra." The King's brows rose high on his forehead. "With the Belamours!" She wiped snot from her nose with the back of her hand. "Didn't we send your commander to capture them? He seems to be doing a phenomenal job."

"I'm sure he tried, dear, but they appear to be masters in the art of evasion."

Sirena growled. "Especially now that your spawn is helping them. I should never have let you keep that horrid child. Look what he did to me!"

Pollux's gaze scanned her person, seeing evidence of assault despite the wounds having healed. He reached out to her, but she slapped his hand away.

"Don't touch me." Turning to the door the Watchmen had escaped through, the Queen yelled for them to return. Several tripped over each other to get back into the room, making it obvious they'd been eavesdropping and thought themselves caught. "Someone find Commander Kayvan!" The guards didn't budge, seemingly frozen in place. "Now!" she screamed, and they fled the room.

Her head coming to rest on her husband's lap, Sirena lay on her side with knees curled into her chest, her anger fizzling into sobs.

Pollux, ever the brave and attentive husband, risked touching her again, rubbing the palm of his hand up and down the length of her side in an effort to soothe her.

"How could he do this to us? Didn't we provide him with anything a prince could hope for? We gave him everything."

"I don't know, dear. I really don't know. He is a good boy. He must believe he's doing the right thing."

"By destroying us?" Anger rekindled as she pushed herself onto her hands. "He wants to rule Arkaemor. If he finds a way to get rid of me, the Thrones will be his to take."

"I don't think Alexander wants to rule, my love. He has never shown any interest in the Thrones."

"Because he's a devilish liar! Manipulator! Just like that atrocity in Jericho. Just like Amaryllis." Her eyes widened as if a thought had occurred to her, and the name *Avaline* escaped her mouth in a shallow breath. The thing Alexander cared about more than anything else. His greatest punishment had always been for his sister to be punished in his stead.

The King's face brimmed with terror, but he kept his voice calm and placating. "Leave her out of it, my dear, please. It isn't Avaline's fault Alexander left. If he is in Celestelvyra as you say, you won't be able to use her to hurt him anyway." He waited for her to respond, but she didn't look at him. Her eyes calculated outcomes as she stared at the floor. "She isn't well, my sweet. This has nothing to do with her."

His reasoning didn't alter her vile expression. Without words, she pushed herself to her feet. Pollux rose with her, spotting her for balance. He said her name, trying to draw her back from the edge of insanity, but a grin spread across her cheeks, accentuating the already sinister streaks of makeup. Before Pollux could grab her, she sprinted for the doors and escaped down the hall, cackling with malevolence.

The King called to her, but she ignored him. Switching tactics, he shouted to the soldiers huddled outside the door. "Watchmen! After her!" Some darted off, immediately obeying their King. Others stalled. When Pollux reached the door, he hollered at those who remained, and they jolted into motion, racing down the hall and casting turbulent shadows about the walls as they hastened past lit torches.

King Pollux ran alongside them. "Protect Avaline!" he shouted to the Watchmen up ahead. Other Watchmen guarding the halls heard the commotion and joined the chase, anxious to assist their King.

When they arrived at the Princess's bedchambers, Pollux froze in the doorway. The Queen had yanked Avaline from her bed and was clasping tightly to her blonde curls. Avaline screamed, begging the Watchmen to help, to save her. The King watched as they stood motionless again, caught in the unfamiliar pendulum of deciding which sovereign to heed.

The King had never ordered the guards against their Queen, or vice versa, so they'd never been forced to choose sides, and though Sirena was prone to bursts of outrage, she'd never before behaved so erratically.

"Seize her!" Pollux roared at the stunned soldiers. Four men charged the Queen, two grabbing each arm.

Sirena didn't let go of Avaline's hair, even as the men restrained her. The Princess continued to scream. Tears poured down her cheeks, soaking the hem of her oleander nightgown, but she didn't fight back.

With absolute calm, the King stepped through the doorway and approached them. "Unhand her, Sirena."

"Are you giving me orders now, *Your Majesty?*" She cackled without humor, her fingers squeezing Avaline's locks tighter.

Retaining his composure even as his only daughter struggled and moaned, he replied, "It is not my wish to do so, my love, but you are behaving as a child throwing a tantrum."

Sirena strengthened her grip again, and Avaline released another cry of pain. Pollux said the Queen's name with adamant ferocity. Whether in obedience or defeat, Sirena released Avaline's hair, and the Princess scrambled across the floor away from her.

A young Watchman dropped to one knee to check on her, and Avaline wrapped her arms around his waist and bawled, pressing her face into the front of his uniform. The guard's eyes widened in horror, and he gaped at the King, but Pollux wasn't paying attention as he pinned his focus on Sirena.

"Let's go to bed, my darling. Things will not seem so dreadful when the sun rises, I promise you." He pushed a lock of hair from her face and caressed her cheek. The guards gripping her had pulled her arms behind her back, restraining her from reaching out to him. "Sleep in my chambers tonight, my love. Let me hold you, comfort you. We will figure everything out tomorrow with fresh eyes."

Dark irises bore into his. "I'm not going anywhere with you, Pollux."

Letting his loving countenance fade, he said, "Fine then. Watchmen, take her to her room, and see that she stays there."

Another venomous grin curled her lips. "This is not a wise decision. You will regret standing against me. Just like the rest of them."

"So be it." He didn't break eye contact with her until the soldiers pulled her from the room. Turning to where Avaline had curled around the Watchman, Pollux dropped to his knee.

The man shook his head, frantic. "Lady Avaline just grabbed me, Your Majesty! I didn't know what to do. I didn't want to upset her more by pushing her away. Please don't hang me, sire, I beg you."

The King's gaze remained on his princess. He released a sigh of relief. "It's fine, Thomas. You've done nothing wrong." Scooping her up, he carried Avaline to her bed. She felt so thin and frail, weighing next to nothing in his arms. Though she'd recently turned eighteen, she was a child, her growth stunted by constant trauma. Avaline rolled onto her side and pulled her knees up, her sobs already tapering off into sleepiness.

Without turning from her, Pollux said, "Thomas, I'm placing you in charge of her care from now on. I want extra Watchmen posted outside the door, at least four at all times. You will remain here with her for the foreseeable future. Move your personal belongings into that room there." He pointed to a door leading to Avaline's old playroom. "I will have a bed brought in for you. Find someone you trust to take your place when you need to rest so that she is never left unguarded. Do not let the Princess out of your sight while you are on duty, and tell the man who replaces you to do the same." He pulled the pastel covers up over the Princess, tucking her in, and adjusted her hair so it lay nicely on the pillow. Finally looking over his shoulder at Thomas, he asked, "Do you understand me, soldier? Do you accept this task knowing the responsibility that weighs on your shoulders if you do?"

Thomas gulped, eyes wide, but he held his hand up in salute.

"Yes, Your Majesty. I swear to protect Princess Avaline with my life."

"Am I being entirely clear on what is expected of you, Thomas?"

"Yes, sire."

"Very good." The King kissed Avaline's forehead before leaving her alone with Thomas.

CHAPTER 3

WATERFALLS

S topping often to admire the flowers decorating either side of the walkway, the group in Celestelvyra ambled along the grassy path. Asher pointed out pink hyacinths, purple lilacs, roses and peonies in many colors, stargazer lilies, and golden angel's trumpets, but even he didn't possess the knowledge to name every flower they came across.

They traveled the path to a glittering creek with pebbles of every color dressing its bed. Impeccably placed stones created a bridge over the water, making it easy to cross without soaking their feet. They passed a number of fruit trees, and again Asher named cherry, peach, avocado, pear, and orange.

Eventually, they came to a grassy clearing lined in trees, bushes, flowers, and pathways leading out in every direction into the enchanted garden. In the middle, a waterfall fed a pond filled with lotus flowers dancing above their pads and cattails leaning in the soft breeze.

Iris glimpsed a bush of honeysuckle and dragged Seth over to show him how to pull droplets from the blooms. Foxx explored the edge of the pond, removing her boots and dipping her toes in the cool water. Asher stood at the center of the pasture watching Iris and Seth and glancing sideways at Foxxglove, wondering if it would be safe to approach her.

Despite her seemingly lifted spirits, she'd hardly spoken to him. Before entering Celestelvyra, she'd said nothing remained between them, but he thought her actions told a different story. When they discovered the death of Mr. Magpie, she cried in his arms. When they argued by the fire, her eyes had searched his for truths she yearned to believe, and not being able to differentiate fact from fiction had left her heartbroken.

He'd lied to her, deceived her, but not even that could so easily shatter the bond they'd built. He'd spent six years searching for her and her sister, spent weeks in the jungle endeavoring to win her trust and affections, and let her see parts of him hidden to most. There was absolutely no way he would be giving up her heart without a fight.

However, Foxxglove Belamour might be the most infuriatingly stubborn person he'd ever encountered. The only soul in all of Arkaemor who may trump her was Vali Kirkavall, the Konungr of Cordillera, and Asher briefly wondered what it might be like to see the two of them go head to head in a disagreement.

Figuring he couldn't really damage the situation further, he sauntered to the pond. Foxx leaned back on her hands with her legs outstretched as she gazed at the waterfall. He said her name, prompting her to glance his way, and he found no aversion in her eyes. "Might I have a seat?" Without responding, Foxx turned again to watch the water. Taking her lack of hostility as a *yes*, he shed his boots and slipped his feet in next to hers, though not close enough to spook her, he hoped. "This water is the perfect temperature, yeah?"

She hummed in reply.

"You're always drawn to water, aren't you?"

She turned to him, studying his face as if searching for concealed truths.

A magenta frog hopped from the water and landed between them. Coiled antennas trailed down its spine, jiggling as it moved. It looked first at Asher, then at Foxx. She laid her hand flat in the grass, and the frog hopped over to it. When it landed in her palm, a dragonfly with eight iridescent wings landed atop one of the coils. After a minute or so, the dragonfly rose from the frog's back and landed on Asher's shoulder, fluttering its wings against his cheek.

Foxx chuckled, and the dragonfly flew away, with the frog hopping off after it. Meeting Asher's eyes, she said, "That was interesting."

"Celestelvyra isn't like the world we know."

"Apparently not."

She returned her attention to the water, and Asher surveyed her expression, trying to puzzle out what she might be thinking. For reasons unknown to him, she seemed to be holding an air of friendliness between them. He hoped he wouldn't say something stupid and screw it up.

"I can feel you staring at me," she said.

His eyes snapped away, moving from the pastel flowers dotting the water, to the tall grass and cattails, and then to the top of the waterfall, until finally coming to rest on the ground directly in front of him. A soft wind radiated from the falls, blowing Foxx's white hair away from her face, and he had to force himself to stop admiring her beauty in his peripherals.

"What is it you want?"

Flipping through several truthful answers, he settled on, "I'm trying to decipher what's going on in that pretty head of yours." He released a discreet breath, coaching himself to keep it together.

Seth laughed from across the clearing, pulling both sets of eyes to where he and Iris were goofing around as they snacked on honeysuckle. Asher watched Foxx's expression shift from bland peace to amused joy before dissolving into something akin to moody contemplation, with lines forming between her eyebrows. He said her name, drawing her back to him.

A tear slid from her lashes down her cheek as she tried to force a smile. "I don't know what's happening."

He sat up straighter, yearning to move closer, to comfort her. Instead, he wrapped his arms loosely around his knees. "What do you mean?"

"It's just… I watched my father die. Mr. Magpie is dead. Declan betrayed us? Everything going on out in the world that still needs settled. Everything between us that's such a horrible mess." Her eyes locked on his, and he found more tears brewing within them.

He tried not to feel elated as she referred to the two of them as *us*, but he couldn't deny that it filled him with a small flicker of hope. He nodded in understanding, encouraging her to go on.

"And now we're stuck here for who knows how long. Maybe forever. And I feel it so deeply. It hurts in here." She put her hand over her chest. He hadn't noticed her quivering fingers until the movement drew his attention. "It really hurts, as if my heart has splintered into bits of timber, and someone is using them to light a fire. I can feel it burning me up from the inside. Sorrow and anger in a continuously repeating cycle."

"That makes sense. The last few days alone have been nothing short of devastating."

She nodded. "What I don't understand is that... it hurts—I swear I feel actual physical pain in my chest, but in my head, I almost don't care at all. Like none of it actually matters. I lost my father, but he was gone a long time ago. Everyone leaves, betrays, so that's no unbelievable revelation. And Mr. Magpie... I suppose it just seems predictable at this point. Apparently the Queen will stop at nothing to destroy everything I love, despite me never doing a single thing to provoke her."

Inclining closer, Asher said, "Of course it matters, love. Hey..." Another tear trickled from her eye, and he wiped it away. She let him lift her chin with his fingers. "Sometimes when things become too difficult to bear, there is nothing left to do but shut down for a while. Sometimes our walls go up—even when we don't want them to—to protect our broken hearts. My sister—" The moment the word emerged, he realized he didn't want to talk about Avaline and redirected his thoughts. "Anyway, never mind that. My point is, it's all right to feel like this. I know your heart, Foxxglove. I know how much you care and how much it all means to you."

Foxx's newfound kindness floated away like dandelion seeds caught on a breeze. "It's not all right. And don't say things like that." She drew her feet from the water and pulled her knees to her chest.

"I'm just trying to encourage you. I wanted you to know you're not alone. You're not the only one feeling detached and positively gutted from the horrors of late. You're not the only one afraid of what the future holds."

"I meant don't talk about knowing me. Because you don't." She refused to look at him, resting her chin on her knees and staring into the rippling pond.

Asher looked at his lap, hesitant to respond. He glanced back to Iris and Seth, somehow able to laugh even after everything they'd been through.

"I need to sleep," Foxx said. "I'm exhausted."

"I think we all are." Leaving his boots along the shore, he stood and called to Iris and Seth. They walked over to the pond, each prying the honey from one last flower. "Are you lot tired?"

"I feel like I could sleep for days," Iris said. Seth nodded in agreement, his eyelids suddenly looking very heavy.

Asher rustled Seth's hair. "All right then. Let's go find somewhere to rest."

"Why not right here?" Foxx stood up next to them. "I like the sound of the water." Despite trying to remain neutral, Asher smiled at her words, as they proved his previous statement. She could say he didn't know her, but her declaration didn't change the truth.

"And the birds. I love all the birds singing here," Iris said.

"Young lad?" Asher sought Seth's opinion to ensure he knew its value. He was part of their team now, and what he thought mattered.

"Is it safe?" Seth looked around at the trees lining the field as if trying to discover any ominous dangers that may lay beyond them.

"I don't think there is a single place in the Sacred Realm that isn't safe."

"Then right here works for me."

Unloading their bedrolls, they laid them out in a row off to the side of the clearing, closer to the trail than the waterfall. Seth put his bedroll between Iris and Foxx and hugged each of them with whispers of *merry night*. Embracing Iris last, he confided over her shoulder, "I know we're stuck here, but I'm still happy I came with you. I wouldn't change my mind if I could. And I'm sorry about your father." He paused before adding, "And about Declan." She squeezed him tighter and kissed him on the forehead before helping him lay down, covering him with a thin blanket and tucking it around him so the breeze couldn't creep in.

Asher laid down on Foxx's other side, a few feet to her right. He knew he might be pushing his luck but decided he didn't care. He couldn't give up. What had grown between them was more real than anything he'd ever experienced. None of the feelings he'd expressed had been a part of his deception. In fact, everything that transpired would have been far simpler if he *hadn't* fallen for her.

Foxx rolled to face him and found him flat on his back, looking up into the trees. The sky had darkened with night, painted with auroras and speckled with stars, but the area around them remained as dim as sunset under the Metsa canopy.

Asher felt Foxx's attention and turned his head to face her, wishing for probably the hundredth time that he could read her thoughts.

She sighed and kept hold of his gaze. "I really don't want to hate you."

Her unexpected admission filled him with so many questions he couldn't begin to process, but before he could decide which, if any, to ask, she rolled away.

C

Orion and Johnathan traveled all through the night. Despite the scorching sun slumbering beneath the horizon, the desert heat was relentless. They had long ago finished the single sleeve of water attached to Declan's bag, and neither knew when they'd last eaten. Dehydration and hunger drained their energy more each moment, and carrying Declan made trekking through the shifting sand even more strenuous.

As they walked, Orion sifted through his memories, searching for what happened before he arrived in the In-Between. Small bits of foggy recollections revealed themselves, flashing in and out like the will-o'-the-wisps back in the swamp, but he still hadn't pieced together a clear picture.

He knew he'd been in a dungeon with Sirena, though whether she'd kept him beneath Castle Solís or somewhere outside of Inaravale, he couldn't be sure. He didn't know how he'd ended up in Sirena's possession, nor did he remember leaving Jericho. No matter how hard he combed through his memories, he only managed to dredge up fragmented snapshots of darkness and the most antagonizing sound of dripping water.

He could still hear echoes of those harrowing drips. They'd grown quieter as he'd focused on escaping the In-Between but remained unceasing nonetheless. Now, as they hiked through the silent desert, the sound of falling droplets became blaring, drowning out even the crunch of his boots pressing sand. He continued to scour the landscape, hoping the sound indicated a true water source to quench his thirst, but he saw nothing that looked promising. Glancing sideways at Johnathan, he searched for a sign he could hear it too.

Based on the degree of their injuries, Orion guessed Sirena had held him captive long before she'd retrieved Declan's brother. None of Johnathan's bruises had yet faded to green. Orion's ranged from shades of plum and indigo to lime and pale saffron.

Regretfully, he wondered if he'd somehow revealed Johnathan's true identity. He knew Johnathan had used a false name upon joining the Legion, going by the surname Hughes instead of Declanaire so the sovereigns wouldn't discover his connection to Silas.

Hector mentioned seeing Johnathan in the Hall of Sunsets, so perhaps he'd been the one to tell Sirena. With Hector's past relations to the Declanaire family, Orion figured he'd known Johnathan's identity from the moment the boy joined the Legion. So maybe Sirena had known all along.

As the sun began its ascent into the sky, Orion and Johnathan looked to the east. Casting its golden rays across the horizon, the sun illuminated a hill protruding from the sand. They stopped a fair distance away, not wanting to get close until they had a better idea of what they would find.

"Are they caves?" Johnathan asked.

Orion laid Declan in the sand to examine the dune, though it was draped in shadow with the sun at its back. From what he could tell, the mound bore several holes, each almost perfectly round and likely tall enough for them to walk through without ducking. Three rested ground-level like caves and three more burrowed into darkness above them.

"More." Orion raked a hand through his hair. "More, more, more." He smacked his head again, trying to shake away his inner torment. The voice was especially cruel in his exhaustion, and he reasoned it might somehow be a byproduct of Sirena's torture. He certainly didn't remember being afflicted with malicious voices before.

At least, none other than his own.

Focus, Orion. Ignore her voice and focus only on the task at hand.

"No one is talking to You," he snarled, startling Johnathan from his own silent musings.

"I didn't say anything."

"Not you, idiot."

Johnathan looked around, as though another person may have appeared without his notice. "What did Maeve mean by *more*? What will we find more of in that dune that will help Silas?"

Realization hit Orion like a punch to the gut, stealing his breath like an unexpected fall. He spun to face the mound, his shoulders heavy. "*More.* Of course. Oh, that horrid sorceress."

"What?" Johnathan moved to stand next to him. "Of course, what?"

Orion tangled his fingers in his hair, exhaling as he answered, "It's a hive."

"A hive?" Johnathan drew in a breath. "Of what?"

A grim shadow drew across Orion's eyes. "A hive of niedas."

C

The next morning, Foxx rose first. Digging through Iris' backpack, she found the produce bag they'd purchased in Ataraxia. After dumping the contents back into the pack, she slung it over her shoulder and made her way down the path toward a peach tree they'd passed on their way to the waterfall.

As she walked, her thoughts wandered without restraint. Images of her father's snapping neck made her squeeze her eyes shut. Her chest felt dense, preventing her from sucking in a full breath. Unlike before when she'd had vision-induced attacks of panic, this felt like a steady weight—a tightness, a pressure—as though a hand had wrapped around her heart and was squeezing it close to bursting. Lifting her arms above her head, she attempted a long inhale and was met with lungs unable to fully expand. The failed effort to draw in enough oxygen consumed much of the little energy she had left.

Like her mother, her father was dead—murdered—by Sirena Aldrich. Not with poison, as had been her mother's horrid end, but with a swift twist of Sirena's otherworldly hands. Foxx's palms covered her ears as the crack of his vertebrae echoed over and over in her mind. Darkly, she theorized that if his skin and muscles hadn't been holding him together, his skull would have snapped right off, dropping the rest of his bones into a disheveled pile on the ground. Then the memory of his body collapsing in a heap resurfaced. He hadn't landed properly, his legs and arms contorted in unnatural positions.

And they'd just left him there, left his body to Sirena to do with whatever she wished. Foxx felt a wave of nausea as she brooded on whether Sirena had left him behind to rot in the swamp or had taken his corpse back with her to Castle Solís. When she wiped a tear from her cheeks, she felt the cold tips of her fingers and looked down to find them coated in ice. It spread to her palms, and she shook her hands to dispel the anomaly, but it persisted to her wrists.

She shook them harder, her anxiety escalating as she exclaimed, "What is happening to me?"

Leaves rustled above her, and she glanced up to find a cluster of glowing driädi lingering amongst the branches of a nearby tree. Several drew nearer, close enough for her to see their furry bodies beneath the green light. One slid its foxtail across her cheek before fluttering away. When she looked back at her hands, the ice had vanished. Exhaling a heavy breath, she lifted her chin and continued down the path as if nothing strange had happened.

She reached the peach tree and stopped before it, touching the fuzzy skin of the closest fruit in a daze. Then she slumped down in the grass, turned her back against the trunk, and let her forehead rest in her hands.

Memories of Sirena's words flooded her thoughts. *There is more darkness in you than there ever was in her. It spills from you like a boiling pot about to overflow.*

Then she'd jeered, *That's right, Foxxglove. Protect your lover from the big, bad witch. It's your life's purpose, after all.*

The Konungr of Cordillera had said, *The world awaits your salvation, foxy woman. As do I.*

But how in the world was she supposed to protect and save anyone? She was nobody—nothing. Sirena had called her frail and weak, and Foxx couldn't argue with the observation.

More than anything, she longed to feel the relief of weeping. She'd shed tears after Asher revealed all of his truths but hadn't cried much since. Even her tears for Mr. Magpie and her father had been short-lived. Shoved down. A few trickling drops and then nothing but gouges of pain imprisoned deep inside, fighting to break free like a monster raging in a cage.

Her thoughts slid to Declan and his deception, filling her with a surge of mixed emotions. She reflected on all the evidence pointing to him being an honorable man. Even after he'd assisted in their kidnapping, he always seemed to have their best interests at heart: giving them weapons when in danger; his sincerity under Lacuna Kaput; letting them escape at Peregrine Manor and giving them money to help them travel; and his caring for her sister.

Foxx couldn't figure out what had possessed him to reveal their plans to Sirena or why he hadn't warned them so they could prepare.

First Asher's betrayal, then Declan's.

Her heart kindled with an intense smolder she couldn't snuff out. Her eyes burned with tears refusing to shed, as if a dam blocked the floodgates. The words Asher had used rang true—detached. Gutted.

Fissures all over the dam waited for the precise amount of pressure to collapse the entire structure.

Her brooding continued to spiral with questions about Asher and Declan and the abominable Queen; about lies and deception and heartbreak; family, friendship, and love. Thoughts drifted to Mr. Magpie and his broken body on display for all to see—to send a message about Sirena's obsessive vendetta.

Now that Sirena had killed their father, Foxx wondered if she would leave them alone. Memories of her invitations and declarations in Jericho immediately extinguished that minuscule hope.

Sirena also hadn't found the Artifact, the vial used to transport Pyhä-ki from the Sacred Realm into Arkaemor. Asher had it in his pocket. Perhaps she thought trapping them would be sufficient, since an Artifact full of Pyhä-ki was useless behind locked doors.

Still, Foxx felt certain they hadn't seen the last of Sirena Aldrich.

A wave of anger washed over her, making her shiver. She squeezed her eyes shut, and a familiar picture appeared in her mind's eye: a city on the beach adorned in black clouds and smoke. Certain she'd seen it before, she fought to hold tight to the image, but she could already feel it slipping away. It fizzled from her memories like fog evaporating in the midday sun.

Footfalls sounded on the path, drawing Foxx's eyes open. She lifted her head and leaned forward.

Iris stumbled around the bend, her face a blend of panic and sorrow. She croaked Foxx's name through tears. "Where are you?"

"I'm here." Standing, Foxx stepped from beneath the peach tree and onto the trail. Iris crashed into her, her restraint crumbling in her sister's arms. Foxx held her close, squeezing tight. "I'm here, Iris. I'm right here."

"It hurts so much," Iris sputtered, her nose dripping snot. "It all hurts like nothing I've ever felt, and I can't take it." She balled her fingers into fists.

"I know." At her sister's words and unbridled emotions, Foxx felt her own eyes swell. She longed for the dam to break, for those fissures to at last burst free of the relentless pressure.

As before, only a few trickles wet her cheeks. Not nearly enough to feel any kind of release. Still, she held Iris, devouring her cavernous lament until she'd shed all of her tears and her body hung weak with exhaustion.

Exchanging no more words, they split apart. Iris helped Foxx fill the bag with peaches. Then they linked arms and followed the path back to the waterfall. Deer and zebra gathered to their left, slurping morning dew from tall grass, and to their right, a giant tortoise carried a nest of mice across a stream.

When they entered the clearing, Asher looked their way and smiled. Seeming to notice their flushed faces, he stood in a rush and jogged to meet them. "What happened? Is everything all right?"

Iris nodded, unable to meet his eyes. She released Foxx, pulled the bag of peaches from her shoulder, and started toward Seth to wake him with breakfast. Foxx and Asher watched her go before he asked again, "Did something happen? Something new, I mean."

"Nothing new. Only the people in our lives whom we grow to trust and—" Foxx sucked her lips between her teeth, stifling the word she'd been about to use. "People we grow to care for... betraying us. Lying. Dying. Leaving. It's a lot of torment to carry, even split between two hearts. It's fine, though. We're just working through it together, like we always have. She will always have me, and I will always have her. And that's all we need."

Asher looked struck by an invisible blade, though he quickly schooled his features into patient compassion. "You will both always have me too, love. You can push me away all you want, but I'm not going anywhere."

"Don't you understand?" Foxx reigned in her snarl, but her vehemence endured. "You're already gone. *Asher* is no more. The man I knew him to be was like a fictional character locked in the pages of a book. There to provoke connection and emotion, only to disappear, swept away with the closing of the final chapter and left afterwards to rest on a shelf." She sighed, but forced herself to hold his gaze. "It's Prince Alexander Aldrich who stands before me now, and I have no idea who that man is."

"The name doesn't matter, Foxx. Asher and Alexander are the same man." He took a step closer and took her hand, squeezing it as he brushed her fingers against his unshaven cheek. She eyed the Jerichonian moon at his wrist, tattooed there as a reminder of all he'd known—all he'd been fighting for—long before they'd ever laid eyes on each other. Her gaze returned to his emerald irises.

Emotion ignited the golden flecks within like firecrackers. "The same man who stood with you in the rain. It's me. Why can't you see me, love? I'm right here."

Foxx yanked her hand from his grasp. Her head spun, her stomach sick with conflicting sensations. "Please refrain from touching me in the future."

Asher rubbed his temples with his thumb and forefinger, releasing a sigh as she stepped around him to join Seth and her sister. Crossing the field, he disappeared down one of the paths leading away from the clearing and didn't return for the rest of the day.

CHAPTER 4

THE HIVE

Johnathan gaped at Orion, his nose scrunched with disgust. "A hive of *niedas*? Are you sure?"

"What else could it be? It might be the only thing that can save him. We get curavenum from niedas, don't we? And that's exactly what we need more of." Looking at his friend lying half-dead in the sand, he sighed, resisting his inner foreboding and conceding to what he knew to be true. "It's our only option."

"I've never seen a nieda." Johnathan stared at the hive off in the distance.

"Consider yourself blessed."

After a long moment, Johnathan exhaled a steadying breath. "Okay then." He shifted his weight back and forth and shook his shoulders, chasing away anxiety. "What do we do? You aren't suggesting we walk right up in there?"

From Declan's bag, Orion retrieved the pocket knife they'd used to cut their binds, a larger dagger in a leather sheath, and extra ammunition. He grabbed the pistol from the belt on Declan's hip, decided to take the entire belt instead, and unhooked it from his friend's waist. After sliding it around his own, he handed Johnathan the dagger and kept the small knife for himself.

"This is all we've got?" Johnathan's limbs trembled, and he bit his lip to steady it.

"Sirena didn't exactly leave us with weapons intact, did she? Do you know how to use that?"

Johnathan's eyebrows went up. "Do I know how to use a knife?" he repeated in disbelief.

"The sharp end is the dangerous one. We should cover Declan. I don't want any of these nasty vultures getting ideas." He glanced at the sky in disgust. Tucking the bag next to Declan's body, Orion covered him with a blanket. Then he turned toward the hive and lifted a hand to shield his eyes from the rising sun. "All right, let's go. We should try to draw one out. Walking into one of those entrances would be suicide."

"I am fully on board with that plan," Johnathan said, though the squeak in his voice had Orion feeling skeptical of his capabilities. He wasn't a soldier—not really. He'd always been a Watchmen on the castle grounds. Orion knew he'd been taught to fight like all members of the Legion, but he'd never been a fighter like Declan. He suspected the boy's uniform had never even been half as dirty as it was in its current condition. Until then, it had been kept pristine— a requirement of his royal position.

Johnathan flexed his fingers and gulped. "What if more than one comes out?"

"Then we will most certainly die."

Stopping before the dune, they saw it wasn't a hill of loose sand but a cemented formation. Liquid mixed with sand and cooked by the sun had turned the hill to stone. Orion considered what liquid the niedas might have used to create the hardened sand, and all were unsavory.

"So how do we get one to come out?" Johnathan whispered.

Surveying the hive, Orion chose the smallest hole and approached it. Though smaller than the rest, the ceiling would not have grazed his head if he stepped inside. He checked the clip in his pistol. Six shots. Two more clips in his pockets. A dagger and a small knife. Orion nodded, assuring himself it was plenty of ammunition to kill a single nieda. Possibly two. He looked at Johnathan from the corner of his eye, observing the tremble of the hand gripping the dagger. With a heavy sigh, he retracted his previous confidence and accepted that they were definitely going to die.

Creeping closer to the cave, he spoke into it, low at first, hoping to attract a single creature. "Heeeere spider, spider, spider. Nasty little spider monster, come out, come out, wherever you arrrre." He raised his voice a decibel. "Nieeeedaaaa. Come on, we aren't going to hurrt yoou."

Johnathan looked at him dumbfounded. "I thought the whole point was that we needed to kill one of them."

Orion shushed him. "They don't need to know that!" Johnathan's eyes widened with understanding, and Orion lowered his voice again. "Nieda, nieda, nieeedaa. Come out to plaaay."

A slight rumble shook the ground, shifting loose sand atop the mound. Orion and Johnathan gaped at it. Slowly, Orion raised the pistol, holding it with both hands. Something big moved toward the surface. Sand rained down the hill as a spindly leg with clawed fingers rose from the hole above them. It grabbed the edge, and another followed suit, latching on to the opposite side.

"This is it." Orion locked his knees in a crouch and aimed high. Sore muscles resisted the movements, but he took the pain captive and forced his body to obey his commands.

Two more legs appeared followed by a huge, spherical body covered in coarse hair as red as clay. As it hovered atop the hole, four more legs lifted into view. Pulsing with anticipation, it glared at them through burgundy eyes scattered at random amongst the hair. Orion counted at least thirteen, and most were nearly the size of his own head.

Johnathan said Orion's name, but Orion ignored him, his eyes locked on their impending doom. Johnathan tried again, and Orion couldn't help feeling annoyed at the terror in his companion's voice. Glancing sideways, he found Johnathan staring fixedly to the left of the monster staring them down. Following his trajectory, Orion saw another nieda emerging from a different hole. A wave of panic washed over him as he took two steps in reverse and shifted his gun back and forth between the beasts.

Moments later, another nieda joined the party. Then a fourth.

Four enormous niedas crawled from the hive, climbing down the mound like boulders rolling down a mountain.

Johnathan froze, his voice frantic. "Orion, what do we do?" When he didn't receive an answer, he repeated the question.

Accepting their fate, Orion yelled, "We fight!" He fired three rounds into the body of the nieda still on the mound. It shuddered and fell into the closest hole. Two of the others shrieked, their mouths stretching open to display long teeth. Then they charged.

Orion fired another round but missed.

One leapt on top of Johnathan, knocking him to the ground. It screeched in his face and sank teeth into his shoulder. Awakened from paralyzing terror, he shoved the dagger into its body and pulled the blade toward him with all his strength. Yowling, the nieda backed away, blue ichor pouring to the ground. In moments, it was on him again, spraying blood all over him as he fought to hold it back.

Orion had fallen to the sand. The other two niedas took turns attacking him. One hovered above him, chittering ferociously as clawed fingers pinned him to the ground. The other attacked his legs, angling to yank him away from its companion. Orion kicked, refusing to let it achieve a firm hold. He held his pistol above the mouth of the one straddling him, but the rapid motions made it difficult to aim true. He took a risk and fired. Though he didn't miss, the bullet went through the outer edge of its body and only succeeded in angering it further. It swatted the weapon from his grasp, tossing it to the sand above his head.

Orion swore and punched one of its eyes. It staggered back, bumping into the one attacking his legs. He flipped onto his stomach and scrambled to reach his gun.

Orion, help Johnathan.

Frowning, Orion returned to his feet, pistol in hand, and swung around. Pools poured from Johnathan's wounds. Red blended with the nieda's blue blood, creating a purple mixture that covered his face and torso. He continued to fight, stabbing the creature over and over, but it wouldn't back down. Then the nieda smacked the knife from his hand and pinned both arms to the ground.

Now, Orion.

"I got it!" Orion shouted back, firing a shot as the monster dove in for a second bite. The beast fell back, and Orion dragged Johnathan to his feet. Immediately, the men were surrounded. They stood back to back as the niedas formed a ring around them, stomping their feet and chittering with enthusiasm.

The nieda Orion had shot back into its cave emerged from the hole with no indication it had been injured but for three small patches of blood marring its hair. As it hit the ground, another appeared from the same hole and followed it down the mound. They joined their comrades, ensnaring the men in a deadly circle.

Johnathan fought to keep each monster in his sights. "Orion, what are we going to do?"

"I don't know! I already told you the outcome if more than one came out of the hive. Well, guess what, Johnathan? More than one came out of the hive!" He growled and looked skyward. *Any more helpful hints, Elohim?*

A wolf-like howl erupted into the desert. Then another and another until the sound resembled a pack of wolves. The howling chorus whipped the niedas into a frenzy. Orion had never heard of anything scary enough to spook a nieda—let alone five—and felt certain whatever crested that hill would mean more bad news for him and Johnathan.

Johnathan turned and grasped Orion's shoulder. His eyes were wide with terror, turned down at the corners and surrounded in cyan goo. "What's that?"

"My best guess? The competition. A pack of wolves or lycanox about to take on a pack of niedas—and we're the prize." He scanned the upper ridge of the dune, but the sun had risen higher, blinding him.

To his right, a long spear impaled one of the niedas, torpedoing through the center of its body and pinning it to the ground. Its legs squirmed to break free and its chitters elevated to petrified shrieks. Moments later, the spider stilled, dead. The rest of the niedas skittered frantically toward the hive. Orion thought they might be charging for attack, but when the first made it into one of the caves, he realized they didn't intend to fight, but to hide.

High on the mound, four silhouetted figures appeared—not wolves at all, but humans. Another spear pierced a second nieda followed by two arrows striking a third. The last of the five fled back into the hive and out of sight. The second speared nieda lay dead on the sand like the first, but the one shot with arrows continued to wobble around on unsteady legs. Its sharp cries hurt Orion's ears, making him wince. He shot two rounds into it, and it tumbled to the ground, breathing heavily for a long moment before stilling.

As the desert again grew quiet, the figures descended the hive. Johnathan stepped forward to offer thanks, but Orion grabbed his arm and yanked him back.

"Don't put your weapon down, you fool." He gripped the gun, not aiming it at the people walking their way, but angled to fire if needed.

"But they saved us." Johnathan used his blood-soaked shirt to wipe sweat from his face. His shoulder bled profusely, and he wrapped the opposite hand over his bicep to prevent it from moving.

"Or maybe they just wanted us for themselves," Orion contended under his breath.

When the people reached them, they stopped several feet away and examined Orion and Johnathan from head to toe, sizing them up. One, a woman, appeared unarmed but for a hatchet hanging from her waist, and Orion suspected at least one of the spears belonged to her. Another moment of scrutinizing had him noticing foxtails hanging from the opposite side of her hip concealing a long blade.

The man standing next to her with a torso as thick as a rhino carried a wooden club with shards of metal sticking out in all directions, and the two at his back had bows drawn.

Johnathan spoke first, lifting a hand to show innocence, though it still clutched the sullied dagger, and the warriors' eyes trailed it as he carelessly waved it about. "Thank you for saving us. I don't think we would have survived if you hadn't shown up."

"You would not have," the woman with foxtails said.

The rhino next to her glanced back at the hive. The movement drew a glare to his bare chest, slick with sweat and covered in tattoos previously invisible against his dark skin. "The niedas have been very hungry lately. Food is sparse in the desert." He eyed Orion. "Only a pair of fools would attack them at their home."

"We were desperate," Orion said, though he couldn't deny the man's evaluation. The woman's golden eyes locked on him, and his fingers tightened around the stock of his gun.

"To die?" she asked.

"To save our brother," Johnathan said.

"Where?" Her fingers danced along the hilt of the concealed blade as her eyes scanned their surroundings.

Johnathan threw his thumb over his shoulder. "Back there." His voice seemed to grow more panicked by the moment, and Orion wondered if this was to become a pattern. "Please, he doesn't have much time."

"Show me."

The rhino man spoke sharply to her in Vetoräti, which Orion thought strange given the territory. He wondered if their umber skin indicated origins in Savanni and realized it did look far darker than was usual for the sienna skin tones of the Wilds.

The woman ignored the man's command and followed Johnathan. The other three stayed to watch Orion, who had yet to drop his weapon, though his gaze followed Johnathan and the woman, his feet carrying him close enough to watch over both his companions and his enemies.

When they reached Declan, Johnathan removed the blanket. The woman knelt beside him and examined his body. She leaned an ear to Declan's lips, then checked the pulse point at his throat. "What happened to him?"

"He was stabbed." The blood staining Declan's torso made clear the severity of the injury, despite Orion's attempts to clean and cover it.

"When?" She tugged the shirt higher to look at the scorch wound, running her fingers across it.

"Last night. Someone appeared to us and directed us here. We cleaned the wound and stuck some curavenum inside of it, but it won't be enough. He needs more."

She eyed him curiously. "This is why you attacked the hive."

"Yes. Can you help him? He's my big brother, and I can't lose him again."

The woman looked Johnathan over before looking past his shoulder at Orion. "It is a miracle he lives. Come." She stood and lifted Declan into her arms, struggling only slightly with the weight. Gaping at her, Johnathan offered to help, but she shook her head and started toward the others, laying Declan on the ground before her companions. "Griffin, *iuvo*."

The rhino man crouched next to her, placing his club on the ground before checking Declan's breathing and heart rate as she had. He lifted the bandage out of the way enough to see the wound. After sticking his finger inside the hole, he held the blood and ooze to his nose and sniffed. Then he looked at Orion. "Salve of the nieda?"

Orion lowered his weapon with a sigh. "The last of our supply."

Griffin nodded. Looking at his companions, he gestured to the dead niedas. "Crow, Vera, *vado*." The archers bowed, swung their bows onto their backs, and did as instructed.

"What are you going to do?" Orion asked.

The woman said, "Try to save him. He is your brother?"

"He—we are family, yes." Orion crossed his arms, thinking it was none of her business whether or not blood ran between them.

When Vera and Crow returned, Vera handed the other woman one of the spears she'd collected from the corpses, confirming what Orion had suspected. The woman, frustratingly the only one whose name hadn't been revealed, laid it on the sand next to her with a nod of thanks.

The male archer knelt next to Griffin, holding a shallow bowl shaped of tree bark. He wore a lycanox pelt like a headdress, giving the impression he had ears like a wolf. The snout hung down his forehead as he stirred the indigo liquid in the basin with a whittled stick. Orion thought it must be nieda blood, though it looked too dark to be that alone.

Crow handed the liquid to Griffin, who said, "Iso." The woman put both knees on the ground and lifted Declan's head and shoulders onto her thighs.

"What are you doing?" Orion's fear added more fire to the words than seemed deserved at this point.

The woman smiled at him. "Trust."

Griffin pulled a glass bottle no bigger than his pinky from a pocket on his hip, opened the cap, and held it under Declan's nose. Declan sucked in a gulp of air. His eyelids snapped apart for a moment before closing again. Orion took a step closer, but Johnathan touched his arm to hold him back.

The woman helped Griffin open Declan's mouth and massaged his throat, coaxing him to drink the liquid as Griffin poured it between his lips more delicately than seemed natural for a man of his build. When he'd consumed the last drop, Griffin handed the bowl back to Crow. The woman, whom Orion thought Griffin might have called *Iso*, let Declan's head rest on her lap as she stroked his face and hair. Griffin stood and moved to stand in front of Crow and Vera.

Orion fell to his knees next to Declan. "Will he be okay?"

"Your brother is strong," Iso assured him. "We must let the nieda's magic work."

"How long?" He swallowed, his eyes shifting momentarily with embarrassment. These strangers had saved them from a horde of niedas and possibly saved Declan's life, for no reason at all, it seemed, but human kindness. "I'm sorry for my harshness. I'm truly grateful for your effort."

"I am not always at my kindest when I am worried for my family," she said.

Orion watched anxiously as Declan's breath increased. Holding a finger to Declan's wrist, he could feel the heartbeat already growing stronger, proving that whatever the strangers had fed him seemed to be helping.

Griffin said the woman's name in command. When her face lifted to him, he ordered, *"Tempus vado."* Orion watched her, knowing Griffin had instructed her to leave. He wondered what their relationship might be if Griffin could give such orders.

"Iuvo?" Her face scrunched with uncertainty, but Orion didn't understand her response. He'd spent time in Savanni as a young man and had picked up some of the language, but he wasn't fluent.

Griffin huffed. He glanced from Johnathan to Orion, lingering on Orion a moment too long before returning his gaze to Iso with a frown. *"Advenas."*

Iso's eyes filled with compassion. *"Fidés."*

After another moment, Griffin released a growl. "Aye!" With a slight bow, he spoke again in Arkaen, "It would be my honor for you to join us until your friend is well enough to travel." Without lifting his head, his eyes shifted to Iso, who grinned, obviously pleased to have coerced him. Huffing again, he straightened and stared into the distance in front of him without acknowledging any of them again.

Orion looked back and forth between them before turning to Johnathan, who shrugged and said, "I just want to see Silas get better."

Standing and feeling about as thrilled with the situation as Griffin seemed to be, Orion extended a hand. "That is very much appreciated, thank you." Griffin stared for too long at the hand hanging between them. Finally, he grabbed it with a hard squeeze. Then he turned on his heel and walked between Crow and Vera in the direction of the hive. They turned in unison to follow him.

Baffled, Orion looked down at Iso to find her holding a hand out to him. "I am Isolde. What are you called?"

He accepted her hand, finding it softer than he expected based on her rugged appearance. "Orion O'Connell. This is Johnathan Declanaire, and that's his brother, Silas, but he usually goes by Declan."

"Orion, Johnathan, and Declan." The words sounded strange in her native accent. "Such interesting names."

Orion found himself struggling to tear himself from her golden eyes, a unique hue he'd never seen before and contrasting so intensely with a strip of black paint covering her face from nose to forehead. "Well, you have a friend named Crow, so I'm not sure your opinion is valid on the matter."

Johnathan smacked his shoulder. "Orion! Don't be a jerk."

Isolde laughed. "*Herr* Orion, would you like to carry your brother? I will show you the way."

CHAPTER 5

REPRIEVE

Griffin and the others walked several paces ahead, but Isolde slowed her stride to match Orion's. In less than twenty minutes, shapes came into view on the horizon. As they drew closer, Orion realized the campsite he'd been expecting was nowhere close to the reality of where the strangers had led them.

Though Isolde's company had been a mere party of four, he saw enough tents erected on site to hold hundreds of people. Set up in a wide circle three rows deep, the quaint, nomadic campsite he'd imagined was instead an entire village.

After crossing the village border, Griffin and the others dispersed, leaving Isolde to deal with the men. Tall posts topped with antlers stood on either side of the entrance, and Orion stopped to gaze at the intimidating structure. Leaning inward and intertwined with thorny vines, the antlers met in the middle above his head like an archway.

Isolde watched them take in the intricacies of her home with a smile. "Welcome to Caritas."

Orion shifted Declan's body so it fit more comfortably in his arms. He couldn't help wondering if they would be safe around so many strangers or why said strangers were being so hospitable to begin with. "This is not what I expected when Griffin invited us to join you."

"Do you ever say anything appropriate?" Johnathan asked.

Isolde didn't drop her smile. "Follow. I will lead you to my dwelling."

Orion's brows rose. "You're taking us to your dwelling? Not the village medic or some public tent?" He scanned the crowd as onlookers noticed the presence of outsiders and stopped to stare. Despite his effort to remain focused, whispers clogged his ears above the sound of dripping water.

Isolde's eyes flashed with amusement. "Are you afraid of my dwelling, *herr* Orion?"

"What he means to say is, *Thank you so much for your kindness. Please lead the way.*" Johnathan glared at Orion. "It's been a long time since he's been in the company of others. You must try to excuse his nonexistent manners."

Isolde grinned mischievously and motioned them forward. "This way." Johnathan followed after her, scolding Orion as he passed. Orion spat insults back at him before begrudgingly following Isolde in the direction of her home.

Teepee fire pits lined the inner edge of the homes, and vibrant hues splashed nearly every surface. Bold fabrics hung from lines, and shelves of pottery and other brightly colored handcrafts popped against the desert sand.

People of all ages, most with the same dark skin and wild attire as Isolde, Griffin, and their friends, moved throughout the camp: working, cooking, creating, playing… living.

Elaborate designs decorated doorways to dome-like tents. Isolde's, Orion noticed when they arrived, bore the head of a wolf at its center, with blocky designs that matched the painted tattoos covering most of her exposed skin.

The first thing he saw upon entering her tent was the bed against the back wall. It was unlike any he'd ever seen, draped in pelts, woven blankets, and pillows. More pillows outlined the perimeter of the bed, and rugs covered the rest of the sandy floor. Tasseled fabrics festooned the walls, and lanterns hung from the ceiling. A wooden table with chairs stood to the right of the entrance, and he saw two lounge chairs near the bed; a large chest; a thin desk with drawers; and several slabs of wood seemingly placed at random on the floor.

Isolde told Orion to lay Declan on the bed before exiting the tent. She returned a few minutes later with rags, bandages, and two bowls of water. She set one bowl on the table for Johnathan along with a rag and dressing for his shoulder. The other she carried to the bed and placed atop a wooden plank on the floor.

When she sat down next to Declan, Orion lifted him forward so she could pull his shirt over his head. Then he stood at the foot of the bed with his arms crossed, watching her work. She dunked the rag in the water and began washing away the blood coating Declan's torso. Dreadlocks and braids spilled down her back all the way to the blankets beneath her, and Orion watched in a haze as beads and feathers peeked in and out in time with her movements.

"What happened here?" she asked.

He leaned to see her pointing at the ash on Declan's chest. "I'm honestly not sure. I was unconscious when he was attacked. It looked like some sort of burn to me, but I'm no expert."

Pausing her cleaning, she dropped the rag back into the bowl and retrieved a small tin she'd set next to Johnathan on the table. He had already cleaned the bite wound on his shoulder and was in the process of wrapping it up.

"If you would like help with that, I will assist you when I am finished with your brother. You should have stitches."

Johnathan smiled, his eyes weary with exhaustion. "I can manage for now. Thanks again, Isolde."

Returning to the bed, Isolde popped open the tin and dabbed ointment over Declan's burn. Then she grabbed a needle and thread and stitched the hole in his side. Orion watched her pull thread through tender skin with a steady hand and speculated that she may be the village healer. Perhaps she treated all of her patients in her home, though he couldn't imagine why they wouldn't have a medical tent for such practices. The village certainly seemed big enough to host one.

When she tied off the final stitch, she covered the wound with cura and a bandage. "Help me lift him?" Her request startled Orion from his daze. He circled the bed and lifted his friend so she could wrap a binding around his back and tie it tight over the wound. Then she stood and faced Orion. "Your turn?"

His brow crinkled with confusion. When her eyes surveyed the length of his body, he followed her gaze, remembering only then how disgusting he looked. He'd spent the last twelve hours worrying only about Declan. "I guess I should probably get cleaned up," he agreed.

Walking back to the table where Johnathan now snored within

the circle of his arms, Isolde retrieved another handful of fabric and placed it in Orion's hands. "Pants," she explained in answer to his perplexed expression. "Not like the ones you are used to wearing, but they should do for the night. Change, and we will get those clothes washed for you." Offering privacy, she rotated away. "Whenever you are ready."

Too tired to object to losing his clothes with her in the room, he removed his attire and pulled on the loose-fitting pants. Thin fabric the color of the deep blue sea wrapped around his waist to create wide, overlapping legs. "Where can I wash these?" He held his soiled clothing in one hand.

After peeking over her shoulder, she turned back to him. "I will handle these." Before he could protest, she took the clothes and motioned for him to sit in one of the chairs near the bed. He submitted to her instruction without argument, and the moment his weight settled into the chair, it occurred to him he hadn't sat down since they escaped the Monastery. His head collapsed back against the cushion, his eyes sliding closed with instant comfort. He soaked it in, forgetting his previous concerns in a wave of comfortable bliss.

Feeling moisture on his hand, Orion startled and lifted his head a fraction to see Isolde kneeling in front of him washing blood from his fingers. He observed her, stunned into silence and stillness and wondering for a brief moment if he might be dreaming. She'd ousted some of the lamps at her back, and light from a lamp at his side made her chestnut skin shimmer and glow, adding to the ethereal sensation. Sucking in a breath, he forced his eyes awake and withdrew his hand. "You don't have to do that."

Dunking the rag, she swished it around before wringing the excess back into the bowl. "You have been through a great ordeal. Please, let me aid you." Without awaiting his response, she lifted his other hand and wiped it clean, taking care to wash every finger, his palm, his wrist.

Orion watched her work in a fog, hypnotized by this bizarre stranger's unexpected touch. His body responded despite his exhaustion, spawning unfamiliar sensations in his stomach. It had been quite a long time since he'd been caressed so tenderly.

As a young man, he'd often enjoyed the company of women, but in recent years, keeping people at a distance had been an easier method of pleasure. Dealing with the needs and emotions of others was a heavy burden he endeavored to avoid.

In the cave in Cordillera, Iris had spread curavenum across his many lacerations, and that had felt... monumental. Delightful. Exciting. Her innocence had amazed him, as had her endearing vulnerability. One side of his mouth curled at the memory.

When the pad of Isolde's thumb trailed across the veins of his wrist, a quiver ran through him, and he cleared his throat, helpless to move away. In a whirlwind of imprudent desire, he hoped this peculiar woman would never, ever stop touching him for as long as he lived.

"The pants match your irises."

He pulled his eyes from her hands to look at his legs. Isolde's rag slid up his arm, and his attention was drawn back to her movements. As she squeezed the rag over deeper wounds caked in sand, a dry rag caught the run off. She kept her expression neutral, though the more skin she uncovered, the more her resistance to wincing faltered. Even he hadn't realized the intense coloring of the fading bruises and merciless cuts until she'd begun washing away the dried blood. He'd seen slaughtered animals left for dead with less wounds.

Finding his voice, he said, "I don't think anyone has ever bathed me before."

"You are not sure?"

His eyes fell closed again as her rag washed the fronts of his shoulders and his chest, taking care to wipe close to the open wounds without rubbing over them. If she saw the goosebumps erupting at random across his skin, she didn't say so.

Without his consent, his mind wandered again to Iris. To her fingers delicately gliding over his injuries, making him feel all kinds of heated buzzing. A sickness filled his stomach, and he opened his eyes. Isolde continued to wash his torso, oblivious to his reflective expressions. As she rinsed the rag again, she asked him to lean forward.

He obeyed, resting his elbows on his knees before sucking in a steadying breath. "I have definitely never been bathed by anyone before," he corrected himself, watching the discolored water swirl. "It's... enjoyable." He coughed, holding back all the other adjectives that came to mind. "It would be even more enjoyable if every inch of my body didn't ache." Catching a glimpse of her smile, his attention was drawn to her face—her golden eyes, the streaks of black pulled down her cheek from the wide stripe. Up close, he realized not all of her tattoos were painted. Some had been permanently etched into her skin. A strand of fangs hung around her neck, laying between thick clusters of hair.

"Close your eyes." She wrung out the rag, and when she found him still watching her, she said, "That was not a request, *herr* Orion."

Orion thought she seemed amused but didn't know what he'd done to make it so. "You don't have a husband who might burst in and kill me for this, do you?"

"It seems someone has already made quite an effort to attempt such a feat and has failed miserably."

"She is pretty miserable, yes." He let his lids fall closed and shivered as she tucked his hair behind his ears. The scent of lavender and sandalwood smothered his senses, making him feel even more drowsy, and he was suddenly curious if this was her usual smell or if she'd dosed him with a sleeping remedy.

"A woman did this to you?" She wiped his cheeks before moving upward to clean blood from his brow.

The scent possessed him, making him dizzy. He detected another fragrance: mint, perhaps, but he couldn't be sure. "A queen, in fact."

Isolde paused. "Queen Sirena Aldrich, you mean?"

His eyes opened to find her face closer than anticipated. He swallowed before answering. "The very one."

Isolde's brows pinched together and a trickle of anger spread across her already intimidating features. Examining her expression up close, he tried to unravel what she must be thinking. What kind of woman finds three men looking like death in the desert and decides to bring them into her chambers to wash them?

His consciousness fabricated thoughts of her washing Johnathan in the same manner and a moment of ferocious rage consumed him.

"You must have angered her greatly for her to justify all this." Continuing her service, she wiped under his chin. Then she dipped her finger in the water and slid it across his lips before dabbing them dry.

When she finished the extraordinary exercise of cleaning his mouth, he replied, "Not a difficult task, I assure you." She lifted the rag to the right of his brow, wiping away a patch she'd missed. Unable to handle the intimacy any longer, Orion placed his hand over hers. "*Gratias tibi,* Isolde. I am in your debt, truly, but I think I can take it from here."

Her eyes sparkled in surprise. "You speak Vetoräti?"

He cleared his throat again. "Not much, but some." Dipping her head, she stood and stepped away from him, taking the divine smell along with her. He smiled, cataloging the scent as her own and not the result of some desert sleeping draft.

"There is cura next to the bowl. I can bring you food to hold you over until this evening."

He dropped the rag into the bowl and released an exhalation of breath, his heart rate on its way back to steady. "If I get hungry, I'll pilfer something from my friend's bag. You've done plenty for us already. Too much."

She extinguished another of the lanterns. A second bow had her backing toward the door. "You may rest here until your friend is well. I will return later with nourishment." Then she exited through the doorway without awaiting a reply.

Glancing toward his friend, he saw Declan's chest rising at a normal rate, taking in oxygen better than it had since they'd fled the swamp. Declan's bag lay on the floor at the foot of the bed, and Orion looked at it, ordering his body to stand. Before he found the willpower for mobility, he settled back into the chair and passed out.

C

Startled awake by a shrill scream in his ear, Orion shot upright in his chair and scoured his surroundings to recall where he'd ended up. The ringing *plop* of dripping water resonated in his head without end, and for a traumatizing moment, he thought he must be back in the dungeon.

Then his eyes landed on Declan asleep in a bed. Recent memories resurfaced, and he leaned back in the chair, resting his temple on his fist. He was safe. Declan was safe. Sirena was nowhere in sight.

Across the room, Johnathan and Isolde sat at the table by the tent door, drinking from clay tumblers and chatting quietly. It occurred to him that the scream that rocked him awake must have been a dream—a nightmare. He could still feel her claws cutting crescent moons into his jaw.

Isolde rose from her seat and knelt in front of him like she had the night before. Recollections of her gentle caress and intimacy sent his head swimming. He longed to put distance between them, but as she extended the tumbler to him, her body naturally leaned closer, and her bare ribs grazed the inside of his knee. The unexpected touch felt so intense that he almost leapt from his chair.

"You must be thirsty." She placed the cup in his hand.

He took a few sips without lifting his head from his knuckles, then he allowed the arm holding the cup to rest on the opposite arm of the chair. "*Gratia.*"

"You slept through the night, but you did not sleep well, I think." She scrutinized him as if he must be worlds more complex than he appeared. As if she could sift back through his dreams and analyze every one, picking apart the inner workings of his subconscious and understand all the intricacies concealed there.

Johnathan said, "You make a lot of weird noises when you sleep."

Orion sighed. "Thank you for that observation, Johnathan."

"You have *incubā*?" Isolde asked. "Or, you say, nightmares?"

He wished she'd stop speaking to him in that concerned tone, honey soaked and heady. Swallowing through dryness in his throat, he said, "Apparently so. It's new." As Isolde pulled the empty vessel from his fingers and strode back to the table to refill it, his eyes rose to find the ceiling dyed red with sunlight. "Did you say I slept all night?"

She slipped the newly filled cup into his hand. "Yes, it is now morning. Declan slept most of the night as well. His body temperature rose and fell, but I kept an eye on him, adjusting his coverings as needed."

Orion shook his head. "You've done too much."

She circled the bed to sit next to Declan and tested the temperature of his forehead with the back of her hand before placing a palm over his chest. "He is growing stronger. I believe he will wake very soon." She stood again and moved to the center of the room, facing Orion. "More bedding will be brought in for you and Johnathan after the luncheon meal so you may sleep properly tonight. Is there anything else you require?"

This baffled Orion, and he sat up straight, feeling more awake in his hydration. "We can't take over your entire home, Isolde. Johnathan and I will sleep outside." Johnathan opened his mouth to protest, and Orion eyed him, waiting to see if he would complain so he could slam him for being a wimp. When he kept silent, Orion stood and looked at Declan. "By nightfall, he will be healthy enough to be moved. We don't want to impose on your hospitality any longer than we already have."

"*Ineptia.* You will stay here. I have plenty of options for sleeping."

He said her name with a sigh, and in three steps she stood in front of him, closer than was customary for a woman to stand near a man she barely knew. Orion misplaced his ability to breathe, as well as registering for the first time since waking that he was not wearing a shirt.

One side of her lips curled, her eyes glistening as if entertained by his discomfort. Holding her palm up so it faced him, she said, "*Fidés.*"

He looked at her hand, unable to stifle memories of how it had felt against his skin. Isolde gestured to it, waiting. He lifted his palm and held it in front of hers, but she continued to wait, the opposite side of her lips curving to match the first. Reluctantly, he pressed his palm to hers.

"*Fidés,*" she repeated. "It means *trust.*"

"*Fidés,*" he echoed, still holding his breath. "What is *ineptia?*"

Her smile widened. "You would say nonsense, foolish." Her hand fell to her side. "More bedding will be brought in for you to sleep. Will that be satisfactory, *herr* Orion?"

Griffin opened the entrance flap to find them standing front to front with Orion shirtless and his hand hovering stupidly in the air. The man said Isolde's name, his voice gruff with annoyance. Pulling her eyes from Orion, Isolde turned to Griffin without dropping her smile and said his name in return.

Griffin responded in Vetoräti, and Orion caught a few of the words. Someone wanted to speak with her. A person named Kaat-achi, he thought, unless that was another word he didn't know how to interpret.

Isolde turned back to Orion. "I shall return shortly to check on you. If you do not put the salve of the nieda on some of these wounds by then, I shall be forced to do it for you."

Griffin held the flap open impatiently.

Orion hadn't yet come up with a reply, his mind now manifesting new delusions of what it might be like to feel her fingers on him again. His mouth opened as if intending to speak, but when no words emerged, Isolde snickered and walked away. His gaze trailed her out the doorway, only to land on Griffin, who glowered at him before letting it drop closed.

A barely audible voice behind him murmured, "Oh, my. What have you gotten yourself into now?" Orion spun to see Declan's chapped lips curled into a smile, his eyelids heavy with exhaustion.

"Silas!" Johnathan shot from his chair and rushed to his brother's side, nearly knocking into Orion as he passed. Declan croaked Johnathan's name in surprise, his throat dry like desert sand as he looked him over with cloudy eyes. "It's me, brother. I'm so glad you're alive!" Johnathan helped lift a tumbler of water to his brother's lips, wincing as the movement disrupted his shoulder.

"Am I alive? I'm not sure it feels that way." Declan accepted a few sips of water, holding a hand over his injury as he inclined away from the pillows.

"By all rights, you shouldn't be." Orion tried to shield his happiness so as not to appear as ridiculous as Johnathan. "You're a stubborn bastard, you know."

"I've heard that once or twice." After a failed attempt at sitting up, Declan's eyes scanned the room searching for familiarity. "Where are we?"

Johnathan leaned out of the way so he could take it all in. "Caritas. A small village in the Grim Wilds."

All at once, memories flooded back, and Declan sat up again. His chest ached horribly, and he clutched his ribs. "Where is Iris?"

"Try to stay calm," Johnathan said.

"But where is she?" Declan rasped, ignoring his brother's suggestion. "Is she all right? What of the Queen?"

Orion folded his arms, standing at the foot of the bed. "I can't say for sure. Sirena might have taken her, but I believe she likely made it into Celestelvyra. You'd be there with her if you weren't an idiot." Declan's mortification confirmed something Orion had been wondering. How else would Sirena have known to find them in the Grim Wilds unless someone told her where they would be? And with him and Johnathan being the ones left behind, he'd put it together that Declan might have made some kind of deal.

Johnathan scowled at his rudeness, another pattern Orion thought he would need to get used to. Still, he knew how difficult it had been for Declan to be separated from his brother and felt happy to see them reunited, even if he found the kid incredibly annoying.

Shame reddened Declan's cheeks as his eyes fell closed. "The girls made it into Celestelvyra. Oh, I was such a fool."

"Pretty much."

"Shut up, Orion," Johnathan scolded. Orion shot him a look of discontent, but he didn't back down. "Silas saved us. I've been remembering some things. And I remember Sirena telling me she was going to kill me and you both if he didn't cooperate."

"Better we be dead and he be safe behind those doors," Orion muttered, mostly to himself.

"What about the keys?" Declan asked.

Eyeing the bag at his feet, Orion said, "Left behind. I imagine that means they can't get back?"

"We'll have to go get them." Declan tried to sit up a third time, but Johnathan pushed him back against the pillows.

"You need to rest and heal." Johnathan tucked the blanket around his brother and adjusted a pillow at his back. "You took a knife to the rib cage. It's a miracle you're alive."

"He's right." Orion's agreement surprised Johnathan into gawking. "You need to heal before we can go anywhere. And anyway, Sirena destroyed the building. We can't get back through."

"But Maeve said we could still save them." Johnathan looked at Orion as if seeking confirmation.

"Iris' Maeve?" Declan asked.

Orion shrugged, hating the jealousy burrowing in his gut in response to Declan knowing something about Iris that he didn't. His impulsive notions about going to get her and his obvious misery over betraying her had Orion surmising how things may have progressed between them after he'd been taken by Sirena. He'd long suspected Declan might be concealing blossoming feelings for the younger of the two sisters, and it made sense to think he might have pursued them with Orion out of the way.

He couldn't blame him, really. He'd have likely done the same.

Running a hand over the back of his head, Orion dispelled thoughts of Iris for the tenth or so time since waking in the swamp. "Some mad woman, who knows. Mad Maeve."

"She wasn't mad!" Johnathan exclaimed.

Orion lifted an incredulous brow. "Her riddles led us into a hive of nieda."

"A *hive*?" Declan repeated, his jaw falling slack.

"If she hadn't shown up, Silas would be dead. She saved his life."

"And nearly killed us in the process." Orion turned to pace the front of the bed. The sounds of dripping grew louder, tickling the inside of his ears.

Johnathan scoffed. "A moment ago you said *better us dead and him safe*. You clearly didn't mind running into danger to save him."

Orion turned from them to refill his water, having no argument to Johnathan's claim. He *had* willingly run into danger to save Declan. And he would do it again. A hundred times if he had to. A thousand times.

Declan's eyes flashed back and forth between them, seeming to enjoy their quarrel. "Ri, you guys attacked a hive of nieda to save me?"

"Don't let it go to your head." Orion chugged the water and left the cup empty on the table. "We wouldn't have nearly died at the claws of five nieda if you hadn't been an idiot." Declan's smile vanished.

"You're just mad because you didn't like the prophecy Maeve gave you." Johnathan folded his arms and puffed out his chest, scowling when it hurt his shoulder.

"What prophecy?" Declan asked.

"It wasn't a prophecy. It was a riddle. You know I hate riddles. And it wasn't about me, anyway. It wasn't about anything. Just the ravings of a mad woman." Approaching Johnathan from behind, Orion lifted him up by his arm and shooed him from the bed. "Go tell Isolde he's awake. She will want to check his wound when she's finished with her meeting."

Johnathan gulped. "You want me to go out there? By myself?"

"Yes, *out there*." Orion mocked his dramatic tone and shoved his way into the seat. "Now, move."

When Johnathan finally vacated the tent, taking time to peek through the flap and survey the area before walking out, Declan's eyes trailed Orion's wounds.

"You look terrible. I knew she was torturing you, but I didn't expect it to be… so much."

"You should see yourself," Orion countered, not even close to ready to openly discussing his time with Sirena.

Declan tried to look at his own wound, but every movement produced another shot of pain in his side. "What did she do to me?"

Huffing, Orion answered, "First, she insisted on bringing you in here—to her home—rather than somewhere public, despite my protests. She's been checking on you incessantly ever since and refuses to let us sleep outside and is very bossy and pushy and... bullheaded. You'll no doubt find her fantastic, but I think she's incredibly irritating."

Declan wrinkled his brow, thrown for a moment before grinning as big as dry lips would allow. "I meant the Queen, Ri. What did Sirena do to me? Not the attractive warrior woman whose bed I'm obviously occupying."

"I must confess, I do not find you the most agreeable person either." Isolde's voice shocked Orion into standing.

"That's not what I—" He cut himself off, having no excuse for his harsh words.

She watched him squirm. *"Incredibly irritating,* indeed." Johnathan stood behind her with his hand covering his mouth.

"I thought Griffin pulled you away to see someone." Orion ran his hand down the back of his head, his cheeks and chest warming with mortification.

"I will finish up with Kaatachi after checking on my patient." Setting a bowl on the table by the door, she approached the bed and pressed a palm against Orion's chest to make room for herself. "Hello, *herr* Declan. My name is Isolde."

"Hello, Isolde." Declan didn't attempt to hide his amusement.

"Have they explained your injury? You were stabbed beneath your ribs and lost a lot of blood, but the nieda solution seems to be helping greatly. Your pulse has been stable for hours and color is returning to your face."

"We thought you were dead for sure," Johnathan added.

Declan looked down at his chest. His hand grazed the burn as his expression turned to one of devastation. Then he looked at Isolde and forced a smile. "Thank you, Isolde, for everything you've done to help me and my friends."

"I am going to check your injury now if you do not mind." Untying the wrap, she laid it on the bed on either side of his torso. Then she pulled away the soiled fabric and stood. Leaving him for a moment, she dropped the dirty bandage by the door and grabbed the bowl of water from the table. Returning to his side, she wrung out the rag and cleaned the skin around the wound. "Your friend does not seem to like me very much," she jested while she worked. Placing fresh fabric over the wound, she retied the wrap over it and pulled it taut.

"He must be insane. You seem very likable to me." Declan grinned, and Orion thought briefly about choking him until he passed out again.

"I am inclined to agree with you." She touched his forehead with the back of her hand. "You are much cooler than you have been, but you must be parched. I shall return with some more water and sustenance."

"That would be great. Thank you again, Isolde."

Dipping her head as she stood, she strode past Orion and departed the tent, taking the bowl and dirty bandages with her.

Declan watched his friend's embarrassment and indignation. "I think you might be in trouble, my friend."

Orion plopped back onto the bed with a heavy sigh. "Tell me about it."

CHAPTER 6

CARITAS AND CRUELTY

Orion and his companions spent the remainder of the day resting. Isolde returned a few times with food and fresh water and to check on Declan's wound. Orion had lathered cura over his deeper cuts for fear Isolde was a woman of her word and would do it herself if he didn't handle it. Declan slept for most of the day, and Orion stayed in his chair, feeling something akin to peace while resting in its cushioned solace.

He tried again to convince Isolde to let them sleep outside, but she wouldn't hear of it. She tried to convince him to let her supply him a bed, but he refused. He insisted he didn't want to be near the ground, preferring a view of the whole tent. Specifically—the door. He didn't admit that a small part of him quaked each time the flap opened, and that in his head, he often pictured Sirena standing in the doorway instead of Isolde.

For the second night in a row, nightmares littered his slumber, jolting him awake drenched in sweat. He thought the Vetoräti word for nightmares awfully fitting, given that legends of creatures bearing the same name told of beasts that came in the night and assaulted their victims as they slept.

Isolde had returned Orion's clothing the previous evening, but he'd been too tired to change back into them, a fortunate decision when he woke up soaked. Twice he stood to retrieve a drink from the pitcher on the table, but aside from that, he remained in his chair, tossing, turning, and dreaming of queens and monsters.

C

The following morning, Orion and Declan stirred awake as Isolde entered with a tray of food: flatbread with rich dip, fruit of the prickly pear cactus, and reptile meat. Johnathan remained deep in dreamland.

"The Morrow greets you," she sang, setting the tray on the table.

Orion stretched himself awake and yawned. "Of course you're one of those."

"One of whom?" Isolde was already perched next to Declan and changing the cloth covering his wound. A little more able to lean forward, Declan eyed the stitching with an impressed expression.

"A Monastery of the Morrow lover." Orion sat up and pulled his hair into a bun, his gaze casually raking over her appearance. She'd changed her clothes, but her face and hair looked the same. A fur vest sat atop her shoulders tied together at the center of her chest, and she'd relinquished her fur boots in favor of bare feet. The cluster of foxtails remained at her hip, concealing her long blade.

"Ah. Indeed I am. Are you not? Do you prefer a queen who tortures and kills? Monsters who seek to rule and condemn instead of comfort?" Her hands paused as she looked at him, her eyes roaming his naked torso displaying proof of the Queen of Arkaemor's brutality.

Noting the movement of her eyes, Orion decided he should find his shirt. "I prefer myself. Only I take care of me." To his left he found the blue pants he'd changed out of in the night along with his clean shirt. The reminder of her kindness nearly had him rescinding his statement, but he decided against it and pulled the shirt over his head, biting his tongue to suppress the pain as it slid across cuts and bruises.

"And yet it was I who cleaned your injuries, saved your friend, and provided sustenance." She motioned toward the table. "Was it not?"

He began lacing his boots so he had an excuse not to look at her. "Yes, you. Not some distant Creator or dead scholars and their fanatic beliefs."

"Suppose Elohim drew me to you in your time of need."

Orion barked a laugh. "Not likely. Elohim has never helped when I needed Him before. I'm betting this time was no different. Just some dumb luck."

"Aye!" Isolde exclaimed, sucking in a breath and shaking her head. *"Homo stultus."* Orion's eyes shot to her, his brows raised, but Declan drew her attention before he could respond.

"You have to forgive my friend. He doesn't mean to be such a miserable grump, but he's had a hard life."

"Shut it, Declan."

"As have we all," Isolde reflected, refocusing to knot the fabric around Declan's wound. "When the Creator is ready for you to see Him, you will, *herr* Orion."

"Rion is a tough shell to crack, but he's all gooey in the middle, I assure you." Declan grinned fiendishly, and Orion scowled as he rose from his chair and started toward the table in search of a drink.

Isolde chuckled. "I am beginning to see that."

"Remind me again why I risked my life to rescue you." Orion turned back to face them. "Five nieda. You remember that, friend. *Five.*"

"How are you feeling after a night's rest?" Isolde asked Declan.

He shifted, trying to sit up higher on the pillows, and she helped him adjust the bedding until he felt comfortable. "Better than expected since I hear I was nearly dead."

"You were." Isolde carried his used bandage and empty cup across the room, smirking at Orion as she passed.

"And not only have you been helping fix me up, but you also had a hand in my rescue?" Declan grinned and added, "Drawn to us in our time of need?"

"I did." After refilling the tumbler, Isolde returned to him. "Dumb luck, some think."

Declan laughed, looking past her to Orion who had his eyes closed as he restrained his temper. "Well, I owe you much gratitude, then."

"You are very welcome. Though, I was not alone. I will introduce you to the others when you are well so you may thank them properly."

Declan took a drink and coughed as liquid moistened his throat. "I would appreciate that."

"We serve because He taught us how. We love others because He first loved us." Isolde winked at him and glanced at Orion, who had mumbled something under his breath before sitting down on the opposite side of the bed. "Declan, can you tell me about this?" She touched the scorch on his chest.

Declan looked at it. "The Queen's magic. She struck me from afar with something like black lightning."

Isolde leaned closer, examining the blackened skin. "For now, it seems little more than a burn, but we should watch it in case the sorcery lingers. Does it hurt?"

"Not nearly as much as the hole." Declan chuckled and handed her the empty tumbler before turning to Orion. "So what's the plan?"

Orion leaned back on his hand. "Plan? The first plan is for you to heal. After that we can decide what to do next."

"If Iris and Foxxglove really are trapped, then we need a strategy to save them. And Asher and Seth?"

"Asher was with them too? The man they traveled with before —" Orion swallowed the remainder of his sentence, not wanting to say the word *kidnapped* in front of Isolde. "When they were in Petrichor?"

"Yes. Asher, who, as it turns out, is actually the Crown Prince."

Orion groaned. "I'd hoped the name was a coincidence."

Brightening, Isolde clarified, "Prince Alexander?"

Declan nodded. "They found out when Sirena attacked Jericho. Foxx is furious with him. She was knocked out during the attack, slept for over a week, but she's barely spoken a word to him since waking unless absolutely necessary."

Orion scratched his ear, trying to wrap his head around the news that they'd kidnapped two women from the actual heir to the Thrones of Arkaemor. His eyes slid to his chair, seeking its comfort, but he resisted the pull. "And who's Seth?"

"The young boy from Kesken Ala. Iris talked about him, remember? We picked him up on our way to the Monastery, and he traveled with us through the Wilds."

Orion lifted a hand in disbelief. "Why would you take a kid with you? Especially if you knew—" His words dropped off again as he glanced at Isolde.

When he didn't continue, she asked, "How old is he? Actually, shall I leave so you may speak privately?"

"You're fine to stay," Orion said.

Declan looked momentarily perplexed by his friend's instant trust, but he pressed on before Orion could take it back. "Seth is ten or eleven, I think. His surrogate father was murdered by the Legion because he helped Foxx and Iris escape the soldiers. They beat him brutally and hung him from a wooden cross."

"Oh!" Isolde tapped the bed. "I have heard of this man. His body hangs at the edge of Kesken Ala, does it not? I have not seen it myself, but the reports are graphic."

"Yes, that's correct. The girls were devastated. We took him down and buried him outside of town." Declan shook his head, distant eyes seeming to relive the memory.

Isolde smiled. "At Alexander's will, no doubt."

"You know Prince Alexander?" Orion asked.

"Yes, I have met the Prince on numerous occasions. He is lovely."

Orion's brow furrowed as he tried to figure out how a woman from a tiny village in the middle of the desert could possibly be familiar with the Prince of Arkaemor. Rather than letting his mind run wild with suspicions, he asked, "How?"

Isolde tilted her head. "Perhaps you do not know as much about your prince as you expect."

Orion shared a glance with Declan, who shrugged and said, "Anyway, yes, Alexander did declare the body should be taken down and buried properly. And as for Seth, he had some pretty fair reasons for wanting to come along, so they let him."

Massaging his temples, Orion sighed. "I assume that was Iris' doing? Doesn't seem like the type of thing Foxx would go for."

"Iris did fight for it, yes."

"Typical." Orion knew Iris' heart was simply too big to deny a broken soul's wishes. Especially, he suspected, when that soul belonged to a child. He only wished he'd accepted this truth about her sooner.

Declan's hands rose to cover his face. "I've just remembered Sawyer."

Orion shared in his exhale. "Yes, I saw his corpse in the swamp. Looked like his neck had been snapped."

Declan groaned. "Oh, this is such a mess. She is never going to forgive me."

"Foxxglove or Iris?" Isolde asked, trying to decipher how all the pieces of the puzzle fit together.

"Iris," Orion answered.

Declan looked at him but retreated before their eyes met. "You were right about Foxx though. She wasn't happy about Seth tagging along. Even more so now, I imagine."

Orion fidgeted with the hem of his shirt, distracting himself from the dripping and the nasty voice in his head. Swallowing his pride, he said, "She will forgive you. They both will. But first we have to find a way to get to them. Though, I'm pretty sure they're living much better off than we are right now. If the stories are to be believed, Celestelvyra is a paradise, is it not?"

"The women and the Prince are in Celestelvyra, you say? This is where they need rescued from?" Isolde left the bedside to retrieve flatbread from the table. When she returned, she began pulling the bread into pieces.

Declan nodded. "Did Sirena take the keys?"

Orion's eyes shifted again to the bag on the ground, then back to Declan, avoiding Isolde all together. "No. I assume she tried to remove them, but they must not have risen from the table for her. I'm not sure how the doorway closed with the keys in place to begin with. I would think that wouldn't be possible, though my knowledge on all things related to Elohim is limited to what my father shoved down my throat. And I didn't even know they were keys until..." Orion paused, wishing the conversation were over so he could go back to sleep. Declan waited eagerly for him to finish his sentence, but he moved on without completing the thought. "Regardless, when I woke, the doors were closed, and the keys remained flat in the table."

Frustration stiffening his tone, Declan asked, "So where are they now? Not buried beneath rubble, I hope. Though, would the In-Between be destroyed if a Monastery is? Since Sirena has laid waste to other Monasteries, it must not be affected by exterior destruction. Unless there are multiple In-Betweens." Isolde pressed against his shoulder, encouraging him to rest while she placed bits of bread directly into his mouth so he was forced to keep his arms at his sides.

"It was falling to pieces as we left, but I'm not sure. Either way, the keys aren't buried under rubble, no." After another moment, Orion admitted, "I have them." Distrustful eyes slid to Isolde. He worried he might be jeopardizing their safety by revealing that he held the keys to the magical place of songs and legends. Though she'd been nothing but kind since the moment they met, he'd seen even great men do horrible things in the name of Elohim. "They're in your bag."

"So we have them!" Declan exclaimed. "We just need to find a door so we can get back through. Every Monastery had one. Alexander thought Metsa Sateen might be a possibility."

Watching the tender way Isolde cared for his friend ignited a burning anger in Orion's stomach. He clenched his fingers into a fist. "You need to rest and heal so you can feed yourself. Then we will figure out a plan."

"We can't wait that long. What of Hector and the others?"

Suddenly dumbfounded again, Orion pinched his brow. "What does Kayvan have to do with anything?"

Declan's eyes dropped closed, exhaling slowly as if at last understanding a previous irritation.

"May I inquire about something?" Isolde asked. Orion nodded, seeing no legitimate reason to deny her despite his desire to. He turned to her, and Declan opened his eyes. "How were you able to get the keys from the table, *herr* Orion?"

Orion scratched his head again. "Truthfully? I'm not sure. I heard—" He cleared his throat, thinking to keep all internal voices to himself. "I tried to pry them from the table, and it didn't work. Then I just kind of… rubbed my hand over them and they rose to the surface."

Isolde hummed and stood. "I will leave you gentlemen to talk without my intrusion." Then she strode from the room without another word. Orion watched her go, suspicious of her sudden departure.

Declan tried to raise himself higher, asking Orion to adjust his pillows. When he was as comfortable as a man with a hole through his torso could be, he explained everything Orion had missed when held captive by the Queen.

C

A knock at the door of the King's study had Pollux sighing. He'd just finished his morning tea and hoped it was one of the kitchen staff coming to tidy up the cart. When the door opened, a Watchman stepped in instead, looking fidgety. All the Watchmen in Castle Solís had been on edge since Pollux and Sirena ruled against each other for the first time in over a thousand years. Most respected the King deeply, but all feared the Queen's ruthlessness. Pollux couldn't help but dwell on who might win out in the end.

"Your Majesty, Queen Sirena wishes to speak with you."

Without looking up from his parchment, Pollux asked, "Has she calmed yet?"

Shaking his head, the man replied honestly. "Not consistently, sire, but she seems collected for the moment."

Dropping his quill in the inkwell, the King folded the letter he'd been writing and slipped it into an envelope. "Very well. You will escort me to Avaline first." A single biscuit remained on the ceramic plate next to his teapot, and he glanced at it before looking down at his stomach as if deciding whether or not he needed another one.

The soldier cleared his throat. "Is it wise to keep the Queen waiting, Your Majesty?" Pollux looked at him with a creased brow, and the man hurried to say, "I apologize, my lord. I was only looking out for your best interest and meant no disrespect."

The King murmured a sound of understanding while sealing the letter with wax and pressing the Aldrich crest into it with his signet ring. Then he slid back his chair and stood, his eyes shifting again to the breakfast cart. "Are there others in the hall?"

"Yes, Your Majesty." Moving out of the walkway to the door, the Watchman threw his hand up in salute and waited for the King to pass by. Pollux rounded his desk and swiped the final biscuit. Three Watchmen stood just outside the door. When the King walked by them without a word, they fell into step behind him.

As Pollux had ordered, four guards had been posted outside the door to Princess Avaline's chambers. Knocking once, he entered. Large windows on the wall opposite the door provided plenty of light to the Princess' room, especially in the morning. White paint coated the walls and furniture, and the curtains hanging on either side of the windows were sheer and pastel pink to match her bedspread.

Avaline laid in bed watching Thomas gaze out at the royal gardens below.

Turning at the sound of the opening door, the Watchman said, "King Pollux, a lovely and merry morning to you."

"You as well, Thomas. Is there any news?" The King approached his daughter's bed and sat next to her.

Thomas cleared the gap between himself and the bed in two

strides. "She seems peaceful today, but there have been no developments."

Pollux slid the biscuit into her hand, but even still, she didn't turn to him. "She hasn't spoken to you?"

"No, sire. Lady Avaline remains silent. I have been talking to her though." Thomas smiled at the Princess as if she were the most precious thing he'd ever seen. "Perhaps some day she will respond."

"Was the room next door set up to your needs?"

"Oh, yes, Your Majesty. You've been far too kind."

The King nodded, watching Avaline stare at Thomas with a smile. He touched her face, brushing blonde curls from her cheek and at last prompting her to turn to him. "How are you my sweet girl?" Avaline didn't reply with words, but he sensed something in her expression. "Has Thomas been taking good care of you?" She looked back at Thomas, her thin smile widening. Pollux eyed the Watchman as his face turned a soft shade of pink. "Well done, Thomas. I shall return to check on her soon." Pollux kissed the Princess' forehead and left the room.

His escorts met him in the hall and followed him to the Queen's chambers. The Watchmen guarding her door looked frightened, with quivering fingers and wide eyes.

The King frowned. "Everything all right gentlemen?"

They nodded anxiously, and he theorized their faces might become stuck in a constant state of fear and panic if this madness didn't end soon.

Stepping through the door, he found Renegard, head of the Queen's personal Watchmen, stationed inside the doorway. The Queen lounged on her bed, draped in a gossamer robe and not much else. Pollux stopped several paces before the foot of the bed and clasped a hand over his opposite wrist.

"Pollux, how marvelous to see you. Won't you join me?" The velvet between the gold-lace designs lightened and darkened with the brush of Sirena's hand as she beckoned him closer.

"I shall speak to you from here for now, my dear." The King adjusted his cuffs so they lay correctly on his wrists. "You wished to see me?"

Crawling toward him on her hands and knees, she stopped at the foot of the bed, resting on her stomach with her chin in her hands. Framed in the black poles draped in maroon to match the duvet and back-splashed by the headboard sculpted to mimic the wings of a dragon, the Queen looked viciously tantalizing.

"I was only wondering how long you planned to keep me locked in this room." She grinned, eyeing him through dark eyelashes.

"Until I am sure you are no longer a threat to yourself and others." Pollux appeared unmoved by her sensual provocations. He couldn't deny her beauty or his love for her, but he also couldn't allow the insanity to continue. For years he'd kept his mouth shut. He hadn't protected Avaline the way a father should, but he could no longer stand by and watch his wife rip her apart piece by piece.

And not just Avaline, but the world as well. Provoking the Konungr with her attack on Jericho had been reckless. Pollux didn't know what would come of it, but he felt certain if he didn't get a handle on things—on her—the repercussions would be greater than anything they'd seen.

He'd thought of speaking to the Konungr himself. Though Vali had never cared for him, he'd never been awful to him either, and Ingrid was sweet to all. Still, if Sirena continued on this path, it wouldn't matter what he said to the royals of Cordillera.

"Where is the fun in that, My King? I was under the impression that you liked it when I'm naughty."

He said her name as a warning, in no mood for theatrics.

"What, Pollux?" she snapped, all attempts at seduction abandoned. Pulling her legs around so they hung off the bed in front of her, she yanked her robe closed, covering all the interesting parts. "You don't actually think you can get away with keeping me trapped here. I am mountains more powerful than you. You only live because I wish it so." She snapped her fingers. "That's all it would take for me to end you. Just one single snap."

"Would you prefer the dungeon, my sweet?"

Her face reddened with fury, and she stood, striding right up to him and pressing herself against his chest. "We have played in the dungeons before, My King. Certainly I would be up for it again. Renegard! Send someone to ready the dungeons for the King and I."

"Disregard that order, Renegard." The King lowered his chin in challenge.

Renegard didn't move but for the visible twitch in his hands.

"He is *my* man-servant, Pollux! You may not give him orders."

"It seems I can." Pollux glanced at Renegard. Sirena's eyes

narrowed as she clasped the King's gaze. Then he said, "As long as you can behave yourself, you are free to move about the castle grounds. Your every movement will be monitored, and you will not leave Castle Solís without discussing it with me first. You will stay away from Avaline's chambers, and you will not order anyone to go there in place of you. Is that understood?"

Kaen shuffled his wings within his cage, coughing up a puff of smoke.

Taking a step away from him, Sirena spread her arms wide, allowing her robe to fall open. Without releasing his gaze, she bowed deeply. "As you wish it, Your Majesty."

"Very well." He turned from her and walked toward the door. "You know where to find me if you need, my love. My heart is always open to you." Then the door closed behind him, and the King was gone.

Sirena fell back onto her bed, soaking in her freedom with untamed laughter. Then she sat up so her legs hung open over the edge, the split in her robe leaving her almost entirely exposed. "Renegard? Would you come here for a moment please?"

Renegard's eyes did not stray from her face as he approached. "Yes, My Queen? How may I serve you?"

Curling her index finger, she summoned him closer. When he stood before her, she leaned back, resting her weight on her elbows. Playing with the inner hem of her robe, she dragged her fingers down the edge until her chest was bare. Beneath her breasts, cherry-red scales decorated her skin. They rose and fell across her ribcage like the top edge of a butterfly's wings, with their lowest dip pointed toward her navel. Another patch bloomed on the inside of her thigh. "Closer, Renegard. You may look. I know you want to."

Renegard allowed his eyes to drift lower. She leaned back for him, stretching her arms all the way up into her pillows and lifting her knees so they teased his hips before gracefully pulling herself back to sitting. Slipping her fingers beneath his shirt, she watched him quiver as she caressed his skin. Then she slid her finger beneath the hem of his pants and pulled him up against her, spreading his lips with her tongue and consuming him in a passionate embrace.

His hands slid around her hips as she left a trail of kisses down his throat. "How may I serve you, My Queen?" He leaned back to see her eyes.

"In order to serve me, Renegard, you must obey me above all

others." She drew him nearer, kissing him again. Her lips trailed his jawline to his ear where she whispered, "It seems you are unwilling to do so." Then she slid her blade into his heart. Anguish disfigured his face as blood spilled from his lips.

Wrenching the blade free, she let his body sink to the floor and examined her bloody knife with interest. "Such a shame, Renegard. I really did enjoy your company." Scooting back up on the bed, she wrapped the robe around her body and called for the Watchmen outside the door to come and clean up the mess.

CHAPTER 7

MEETING THE NAABA

"I am blown away to hear that Hector Kayvan is the pioneer of the revolution." Orion paced at the foot of Declan's bed.

"That's understandable," Declan said. "Wait until you see him. He's actually really good at it."

Orion worked through the new information out loud. "So the army is waiting for Alexander to return to Jericho with some poison to kill the Queen. From there, they intend to storm the castle and burn it all down. Figuratively. Except he won't be returning to Jericho, because he's stuck in Celestelvyra."

"Yes, that was the general plan when we left Jericho a few days ago and why it's imperative we get them back as soon as possible. This is the third day since we left the Monastery, correct?" Declan did the math on his fingers. "They will be expecting us to return to Jericho two or three days from now at the latest. I'm not sure how long they'll wait without news before acting, but the plans for a revolution are already set in motion. There's no stopping it now. We should leave today or tomorrow. They need to know what's going on."

Orion clenched his fingers into fists, his steps quickening. "No, absolutely not. You won't be ready to travel for at least a few days. Magic nieda potion saved your life, but your insides still need to heal so you don't risk damaging anything else." He began to ramble with escalating irritation, and soon, the whispers returned. "We don't even know where another door is located." The dripping grew louder, fighting for attention over the murmuring voices threatening his life, questioning his sanity, insulting his identity. He squeezed his eyes shut, trying to block them out.

His aggressive walk roused Johnathan, who sat up from where he'd been sleeping and wiped sand from his eyes.

Orion smacked the side of his head with the heel of his palm, trying to silence the echoing. He yanked the tie from his hair, letting his locks fall free and hoping it would release the pressure crushing his skull. It didn't.

Declan said his name. "What's happening? What's going on?"

Johnathan yawned. "He's been doing that since we woke up in the swamp."

Declan again said Orion's name, but rather than responding, Orion growled and stormed from the room. Outside, he stopped short when the reminder of their current location stared him in the face. Desperate to subdue the noises, he covered his ears and rounded the tent, putting space between himself and the gawking strangers.

Kicking sand in a fit of frustration as he went, he stomped out into the desert, seeking the solace of silence. The whispers continued, growing louder until they became almost deafening as the voice spewed vile words of hate, assaulting the very essence of his being. He didn't know if they were memories of her torture or if she was speaking to him from a distance, but he needed it to stop. He considered firing a bullet into his brain, realized he didn't have a weapon, and groaned at his bad luck.

Climbing the hill outside the village, he froze as familiar chittering reached his ears. He spun to find a nieda standing behind him, covered in blue blood that spilled from a spear stuck through its body at a sharp angle. It screeched and stomped its feet, baring its revolting teeth.

Fear consumed him, and he dropped to the ground, covering his head with his hands. He had no weapon, and he couldn't risk drawing it back to the village, so he accepted his fate and waited for the beast to tear him to shreds. In truth, part of him longed to be put out of his misery.

When nothing happened, he peeked through his fingers to discover himself alone. Standing, he scanned the plains and found nothing but sand. Even the blood he'd seen puddling on the ground had vanished.

The whispers grew loud again, filling the empty space with heinous words.

With both hands grasping his hair, he released a wild roar and screamed at the top of his lungs, "I'm right here, Sirena!" He spread his arms wide, awaiting an answer as though she might appear and smite him on the spot. The whispers laughed, enjoying his agony.

Orion deflated, his hands falling to his sides in despair. "I've had enough of this. Come and get me if you must."

The sound of his name had him whipping around to find Isolde standing behind him, bright eyes turned down with sympathy and concern.

He tried to calm down, knowing he must resemble a raving lunatic. The voices in his head faded, leaving nothing but the faint dripping and his heavy breathing to disrupt the silence. Isolde waited quietly for him to pull himself together, studying him with observant eyes. He noticed she carried her spear and contemplated whether she'd brought it along to protect herself or to gain the advantage as she dragged him back to the village.

It occurred to him then that he may have traded one captor for another.

Over her shoulder, a gray wolf appeared, its head sticking out from behind a rock. The turn of Isolde's head as she followed his gaze distracted Orion's eyes, and when he looked back where the wolf stood, he saw nothing but rock and sand. Squeezing his eyes shut, he fought to keep tears at bay. As far as he knew, gray wolves didn't live in the desert. Certainly not lone wolves who watch from a distance and disappear. The one he'd seen by the Monastery must have been the first sign of his spiraling insanity.

Isolde turned back to face him, clearly trying to decipher what was happening in the world inside his head.

When his heart at last began to steady, he asked through elongated breaths, "What are you doing here?"

"I saw you run away." Her fingers tightened around the spear.

Feeling suddenly caged in the vast wilderness, his face reddened with fury. "Am I your prisoner? Forbidden from leaving of my own free will?"

She searched his ocean eyes for the answers to all of her questions. "You are free to leave of your own will, *herr* Orion." Lifting a hand to touch his cheek, she asked, "Is this her doing as well?"

He averted his eyes, detesting his vulnerability around her and hopeless to understand the agonizing uncertainty in his mind. "I don't know." His dread was made worse by the knowledge of a witness, a stranger viewing the secret horrors that lay beneath his skin. Soon she would run from him, as they all did eventually. As Iris had.

"It fills me with sorrow to see you so lost." Compassion brightened her eyes, making his skin crawl and compelling him to recoil. She had yet to drop her hand from his cheek, and the lavender smell at her wrist made his head spin. Though he found it difficult to retreat, he mustered the strength to sever the connection.

Free of her snare, he took a step back and cautioned, "You should keep your distance, Isolde. I'm not one of the good ones. And not just because of…" He gestured with his hand to his current state. "… whatever the hell this is." Tears burned his eyes, and he wished she would leave him isolated in his delirium and desolation. He sucked in a breath and forced words through a throat tightened with emotions. "I appreciate everything you've done for us. As soon as Declan is able, we will leave this place and not burden you any further."

She inclined her head to the side, irises metallic in the sunlight. He waited for her to react to his words. To flee, as he'd suggested. Instead, she said, "My father wishes to speak with you." Her fingers danced across the hilt of her blade, and he wondered if she intended to draw it on him. Or, more importantly, if he would defend himself if she did. "We will join you in my tent once you have returned." Turning toward the village, she left him alone in his misery.

He watched her walk away, unsurprised by the visual. Though she'd obeyed his wishes, seeing it in action left a hole through his chest he didn't understand. Lifting his hands to his head, he let his lungs draw in the warm, dry air. Once he felt collected enough to converse with strangers, he made his way back to the tent, ignoring the stares of the villagers who'd undoubtedly heard him yowling with hysteria in the desert.

When he passed the threshold of Isolde's tent, he found Johnathan sitting on the bed next to Declan. Both were eating the breakfast Isolde had provided. Remaining silent and avoiding eye contact, Orion crossed the room and collapsed into the chair he'd slept in the night before, resting his head on the back of it and closing his eyes.

"Isolde's father would like to speak with us," Johnathan said.

"Ri? Are you all right?"

Orion could feel Declan watching him. "I'm fine, my friend." He opened his eyes to stare at the ceiling, crossing his fingers over his chest and taking yet another deep breath.

"You don't seem fine. Are you—"

Orion shot his friend a glare. He glanced at Johnathan, then back to Declan, as if Declan should be well aware how much he didn't want to discuss his frailties in front of anyone.

The flap opened, and a man walked in carrying an ornamental staff with the head of an eagle carved into the top and wings spiraling down the shaft to his fingers. A fur headdress, much like the one Crow had worn—though massive by comparison— covered the sides of his face like a lion's mane. Draped in a robe of animal hide, he wore necklaces displaying a variety of teeth and bones. Cherry paint rimmed his eyes, and two lines of coal ran from his forehead, through his left eye, and all the way down to his chin.

Griffin walked in behind him, followed by Isolde, who stepped out around the men and stood on the opposite side of the bed from where Orion sat.

"Father, I am pleased to introduce you to *herr* Orion O'Connell." She gestured to Orion without meeting his eyes. "And his friends, *herr* Declan and *herr* Johnathan." Speaking to the outsiders, she explained, "*Herr* is the formal way to address an unfamiliar man. You would say sir or mister. You have already met Griffin. He is the Abrafo of our tribe. The title Abrafo means *head warrior*. You would call him a commander."

Declan dipped his chin in response to Isolde's introduction. Griffin nodded to each of them, even Orion—though it was swift and lacked eye contact.

"And of course, my father, Naaba Kaatachi, High Ruler of Caritas." Isolde offered the Naaba a small bow, and he returned it in kind.

Orion attempted an air of nonchalance as he processed this news, thinking it made perfect sense for Isolde's father to be the High Ruler of Caritas—Elohim had always enjoyed throwing him off kilter. Though the Grim Wilds remained *terra nullius*, or land unclaimed by the sovereigns of the Five Kingdoms, many cities throughout Arkaemor had rulers outside—and lesser than—the four dominant royal families. Bryä had been ruled by a king centuries ago and was now led by a governor like Dysmaa and Bujarshuri.

If the Naaba was Isolde's father, that made her an heir to his people—her people. Possibly the only heir, since another had not been introduced.

It also meant that the Princess of Caritas had just seen him raving like a mad man.

He exhaled a sigh and unfolded from his chair to greet the Naaba with an outstretched hand. "Your hospitality and the hospitality of your daughter have been instrumental in my friend's recovery. We greatly appreciate it, Your Majesty." He dropped his head, offering the same bow he would King Pollux. He'd long ago learned the ways of kings. Being a member of the Legion had taught him exactly what was expected of the lowly when in the presence of royalty.

Naaba Kaatachi stared at Orion's hand for a long moment, the same way Griffin had. Then he squeezed it between both of his own. "If what my daughter tells me is true, we have much to discuss with one another." His accent was far thicker than Isolde's, clouding the Arkaen words with remnants of Vetoräti mixed in.

"Is that so?" Orion glanced at Isolde with a sinking feeling in his stomach. He'd questioned trusting her from the start. Now he realized she'd undoubtedly told him every single thing she'd witnessed since their very first meeting. Why wouldn't she?

"You seek entrance to Celestelvyra to recover your friends," Kaatachi said.

"That's true, yes." Orion crossed his arms, closing himself off as they created a shield around his heart.

"Sensational. And you have the keys to open the doors, which you yourself recovered from the Table in the In-Between?"

"Also true." Orion sent a sharp glare at Isolde, but she seemed to be intentionally avoiding his gaze, either because of what had transpired out in the desert or because she didn't wish to observe his face as her betrayal became evident.

"I see, I see. Very good." Naaba Kaatachi leaned back to whisper something to the Abrafo.

Orion again glanced at Isolde, but she watched her father and Griffin. His cheeks flared with anger as he fought to maintain his temper. He'd already told Isolde they would be leaving as soon as possible and couldn't understand their need to press for more information. Fanatics wanting to be involved in all things Celestelvyra, he supposed. Perhaps they intended to steal the keys for themselves so they could secure a way through the doors. His eyes shifted to Declan's bag lying unprotected on the floor, and he made a mental note to hide it more efficiently when the conversation ended.

Declan's voice interrupted Orion's racing thoughts. "If your tribe follows the Morrow, would you say that, in the event of a battle, you would stand *with* the King's Legion or against them?"

Orion hadn't considered that they may wish to join the fight, as escaping to Celestelvyra while the world imploded seemed the easier, more obvious choice. Griffin's face contorted, but he kept his lips sealed.

Naaba Kaatachi leaned back again, and Griffin nodded in response. "I would say in the event of a battle, we would most definitely stand *against* the King and Queen of Arkaemor." His features presented no anxiety as he waited for them to respond to this revelation.

Orion knew the Monastery of the Morrow and the royal families had been enemies for over a thousand years. If Isolde's tribe truly did follow the Morrow, he supposed it made sense they would feel called to fight, and the more warriors they had standing against the Queen, the better. "Then it might please you to know there is an army in Jericho at this very moment readying their forces to rise up against Inaravale."

"Yes, I would be very pleased to know that." Naaba Kaatachi turned his head as Griffin inclined forward to whisper again.

Declan added, "The Crown Prince is in Celestelvyra retrieving the only weapon able to kill the Queen."

Kaatachi put a hand on his stomach and smiled wide. "What is the next step in your plan? What do you need from Caritas?"

Orion glanced at Declan. "We need to send someone to Jericho to let them know the reason for the Prince's delay. I plan to take this journey alone." Declan began to interrupt, but Orion's raised hand shushed him. "They are expecting the team in Celestelvyra to return to Jericho within the next few days. We don't want them moving on Inaravale without the weapon if the Prince doesn't return. After that, we need to send a party to Celestelvyra to rescue Prince Alexander and the others with him."

Declan frowned at his friend. "*We* should be able to find another entrance to the In-Between in one of the other Monasteries. We entered previously through the Monastery here in the Wilds, but it has since been destroyed. According to the prophecy, Savanni's was burnt to the ground and Alunda's is under the sea. Cordillera's was demolished in the last attack, so I think Crystavium and Metsa Sateen are the only plausible options."

"Crystavium's Monastery is the Prison of the Strayed." Isolde's lip quivered when she spoke the name, and the tremble drew Orion's attention.

Declan said, "True, but Foxx and Iris stayed in Metsa Sateen's Monastery while traveling through the jungle. I would say that's our best bet."

Orion's eyes drifted to the ceiling. He thought of Maeve's words regarding his two paths. Though he'd assumed Johnathan and Declan were the friends he needed to save, perhaps she'd been referring to a choice between the Monastery in Crystavium and the one in Metsa Sateen. It hadn't occurred to him she might have been talking about saving Iris and Foxx, as he'd never considered them *friends*.

She'd also said: *You must choose the path that is straight and narrow.* He supposed crossing the tundra could be accomplished by walking a straight path, but not a narrow one. The trails of Sateen were often narrow but were almost never straight. He released a frustrated breath as he realized the weight he was placing on the words of a crazy woman.

The Naaba seemed to mull over everything the men had explained. Then, leaving just as abruptly as he'd arrived, he made his way toward the door. "Thank you boys for all of this information. The tribe elders and I will discuss and seek the Creator's guidance. We will meet again tomorrow to go over the plan. Until then, please continue to enjoy the fruits of Caritas. My daughter will take care of any needs you might have." Griffin had already left the tent and was holding the flap open for his Naaba. Before exiting, Kaatachi eyed Orion directly. "We will do what we can to assist you in your mission, as Elohim wills it. Thank you, young soldier."

When Isolde reached the door, she turned back to Orion, meeting his eyes for the first time since entering. "I shall return later with dinner." Then she was gone.

Orion stared at the entrance for a long moment before releasing a weighty sigh. Then he reunited with his chair and turned to face Declan. "You know you won't be going along on this. I can make the journey myself. I'm leaving tomorrow, unless Kaatachi has something else in mind."

"I'll be healed enough to travel by tomorrow. Another night's sleep will be cure enough."

"The cure will be resting as long as it takes for you to heal thoroughly. I didn't drag you across the desert and risk my life saving you so you could mess it all up trying to be heroic."

"But I—"

Orion whined Declan's name. "We aren't arguing about this. I will tie you up and flee in the night if I have to. And don't look at me like that. You know I will."

Declan sighed. "Well, you can't go alone."

"I'll take Johnathan with me." Orion grinned.

Johnathan failed to stifle his terror at the prospect, and his companions laughed.

"Let it go for now, Dec," Orion said. "Get some more rest and let the tribe elders discuss things. Maybe they'll come up with a different solution. Maybe they'll send one of their warriors with me to make sure I don't abandon you here."

"Abrafo Griffin seems like a real treat." Declan looked sideways at Orion to find him putting his head in his hands.

"Oh, please don't let it be Griffin."

After a minute of silence, Johnathan reclaimed his spot on the floor, and Orion suspected he was attempting to offer them privacy. If he'd been brave enough, he would have ventured into the village, but as it was, this would have to do.

Orion relaxed back in the chair with his eyes to the sun-dyed ceiling. Lanterns hung to his left and to his right, though neither had been lit. He wondered if keeping one lit overnight would help with the nightmares, but since he'd never been affected by the dark before, he couldn't imagine it making a difference now.

Exhaling, he said, "So, when we took the girls from Petrichor, they were traveling with Prince Alexander."

Declan scooched lower on the bed and joined Orion's inspection of the ceiling. "That's correct."

Both men had questioned the name Asher when they'd first heard it, but Orion hadn't really believed it a possibility. Why in the world would the Prince of Arkaemor be traveling Sateen with two random women from Alunda?

Considering Sirena had shown up in Jericho to abduct them, as well as reformed the Reko Raptors for the same task, he supposed they must be more important than he'd originally suspected. He'd thought Sirena only sought them to find Sawyer, but as things continued to unfold, he wondered if something else might be transpiring beneath the surface.

I am always working, Orion, whether you choose to believe it or not.

Orion stiffened in response to the voice. He glanced sideways to see if Declan had heard it, too, but his friend continued to stare at the ceiling with increasingly heavy eyelids. He wondered at the reason for Elohim's sudden return and how it related to everything happening around him. Did it have something to do with the revolution? With Sirena's torture or his connection to Iris and Foxx?

All in due time, My friend.

Frowning, Orion growled back through his thoughts, *Whatever it is, I don't want it. I don't want any part in whatever self-righteous scheme You have in the works, Elohim. I'll remind You of what I said long ago: I don't trust You, and I certainly don't need You.*

I could never forget such a painful declaration, Orion. But that does not change what is.

Orion shook his head and returned his attention to the room. Declan's eyes fluttered open at the sound of his cleared throat. "Does he know what we did? Does he hate us for it?" Running fingers through his hair, Orion untangled the knots as he contemplated whether or not they would have handled the situation differently if they'd known. Perhaps they would have tried to join their party as trusted companions instead of concocting some ridiculous plan to take the girls against their will. "Will we be thrown in the dungeons when all is said and done?"

As the word *dungeon* passed his lips, his stomach did a somersault, and his mouth produced the saliva that often precedes the dispelling of bile.

"Well, he doesn't hate me..." Declan said, a smile curling his lips. Then he frowned. "Though he might hate me now, I suppose." His fingers absentmindedly twisted the tip of his bangs into a point as his expression turned pensive.

"Wonderful." Orion dragged both hands down his face, immediately regretting it as he brushed his wounds. "And Hector and the Raptors are leading the revolution. What does Raven think about all this? I assume you spoke to her after we talked in the plaza."

Declan shifted a pillow so his knees bent over it. "She seems to follow Hector faithfully. It was his plan to stay, and so she stayed with him. Same with the others. You know, he confessed everything to her. About us. About my father. I doubt he's ever trusted anyone enough to admit those failings, aside from Jax maybe."

"Wow. I'm sure they will live blissfully ever after." Standing, Orion crossed the room to fill a cup of water, asking Declan if he wanted more.

Declan thanked him but shook his head. "Raven and Hector seem good together. She seems happy."

"It doesn't bother you? Your first love shacking up with the man who killed your father?"

"I'm happy if they're happy. Raven and I discussed it and agreed to let bygones be. The most important thing now is banding together to fix the world."

"I see." Orion sat back down and faced his friend. "And that ease at the thought of their relationship has nothing to do with Iris, I'm guessing." His demand for a direct answer was clear, but Declan pivoted.

"Raven and I have been apart for over six years. I'm just glad she still speaks to me after I left with no explanation. You saw how she acted in the plaza."

"You're avoiding my question."

Declan watched his hands straighten the thin blanket covering his legs. "Because I'm worried you will feel like I stole her from you, and I am not in a position to defend myself."

This pulled a loud and unexpected laugh from Orion, drawing Declan's eyes back to him. "That's true." He cracked his knuckles for effect. "I could kick your ass right now if I felt the need to."

Declan eyed his friend nervously. "I think I might love her, Ri. I know we haven't known them long, but… she's special."

Orion leaned forward in the chair with his elbows on his knees, trying not to reveal the anger he fought to suppress. "Love her so much you betrayed her?" Declan closed his eyes, seeming to feel the weight of what he'd done. Orion turned his head to watch his friend answer. "Why did you do it?"

"I was arrogant. I thought I could juggle it. I thought I could help them and save you and Johnathan. Not to mention all of the soldiers who plan to fight in this war. Everything progressed so quickly in Jericho. Untrained civilians signing up to fight. And there was so much pain and mourning already." He shook his head. "I thought we would get there before her, retrieve Pyhä-ki, and Alexander could run her through the moment she arrived with you two. But the Queen was cunning. She suspected my treachery and arrived earlier than agreed."

"I thought as much." Orion leaned back in his chair, fabricating images of them meeting covertly: Sirena's malicious expression, Declan's desperation.

"I can't say for sure whether I made all of these choices of my own free will, or whether she enchanted me in some way, but it doesn't matter. What's done is done."

"You can never trust the wicked to do what you think they'll do," Orion said.

"You can never trust anyone to do what you think they'll do. People are bound to surprise us when we least expect it."

Orion nodded, agreeing.

"I should have told them so they could prepare. We could have used it to our advantage, planned ahead for this kind of alteration in her schemes. I should have told Alexander the moment she contacted me. She warned me if I told anyone I'd spoken with her, she would kill you. I didn't know how she would know if I talked, but I know she's powerful. Her spies are everywhere, in many shapes and sizes. Everything in Jericho was so fragile and in a state of such disarray, I didn't want to make things worse or further ignite her wrath. Even still, I decided before our final meeting, when I was to reveal the time and location of our destination, that I was going to confess everything to Alexander and Iris right away, but then she brought Johnathan into it. Extra insurance, she'd said. In case my bond with you wasn't secure enough to force loyalty."

Orion speculated whether or not he would have handled the situation the same way if their positions had been reversed and decided he probably would have. "Why Alexander and Iris and not Foxx?"

"Foxx, too, but remember, she was out cold."

"Oh, right. For days though? Why? Is she okay now?"

"Honestly, we are all a little perplexed about the whole thing. She hit her head during the attack, but then she just didn't wake up for over a week. Her vitals remained stable, and we couldn't find anything else wrong with her. Alexander thought she might be hiding in some unconscious misery after finding out his identity, but I'm not sure I believe that. I was worried she would die from lack of nutrition or something, but she barely looked malnourished. When she woke, she was tired and a little dehydrated but otherwise perfectly fine. It's a bit of a mystery."

"Interesting." Orion stewed over more new information. He thought of questioning Elohim about Foxx but quickly decided against it. Then he said, "Iris will forgive you, Declan. Once you explain it to her, she will understand." With a slight chuckle he added, "Foxx might not, but Iris definitely will."

Declan shifted so his head lay more comfortably and closed his eyes. "I'm going to rest now."

Orion got cozy in his own chair, not tired but wanting a reprieve to reflect. When he heard Declan's shallow breaths, he whispered, "Pleasant dreams, my friend."

CHAPTER 8

FIRST DANCE

As the sky darkened, Orion grew bored within the confines of the tent. He decided a walk might be soothing and may even tire him out enough to sleep through his nightmares. Declan was still dozing, and Johnathan sat at the table reading a book Isolde had provided.

Approaching the table, Orion added water from the pitcher to Declan's sleeve.

Johnathan looked up from his book, using his finger to mark his place. "Are you leaving?"

"Just going for a walk."

"What should I say if Isolde comes looking for you?"

Orion pursed his lips. "You can say I went for a walk." When Johnathan asked when he would be back, Orion ignored him and exited the tent.

Teepee fires lit the center of the village as people prepared their evening meals. Several villagers cooked on the stones surrounding the pits. Others worked on assembling a structure across the center of town, stacking wooden crates and stones in a pile. Based on its current progress, Orion couldn't determine its purpose. He sifted through memories of his father's teachings, thinking it may be some kind of ceremonial bonfire or something of that nature, and tried to remember if human sacrifice was part of the Morrow's traditions. Though he didn't think so, he knew some tribes in Savanni practiced it and thought it possible those in the Grim Wilds were the same.

He couldn't see the Naaba or Isolde, but Griffin helped stack piles of wood next to each fire. Orion wondered how they acquired so much wood with very few trees growing in the desert. Most produced olives or pomegranates, things you wouldn't waste on firewood, so he deduced they must haul it in from the Metsa, despite the two day journey.

As Griffin set down a stack of logs, he glared at him from across the yard. Orion waved back politely and heard him growl in return before storming off. No one else noticed as he slipped around the tent and ventured into the desert.

Though the Ammil moon waned, it hung ginormous in the sky, as if it couldn't help but lean in to catch a glimpse of the riveting desert night. It lit his way, brightening the sand so he didn't need a lantern to see.

As before, he realized he should have brought a weapon to defend himself while wandering alone, but after mulling it over, he decided not to turn around and ambled on.

In the silence of the desert, the sound of dripping water echoed throughout his skull, though the whispers had stilled for the moment. As he walked, he reviewed everything he and Declan had discussed.

When he landed on Declan's confession, his body grew hot with sweat. He didn't understand how Declan could possibly claim to love Iris. If he truly loved her, he would be with her now. Had his connection with Orion really been strong enough to prevent that? He'd once told Iris that Declan would never betray him, but he'd been bluffing, dissuading her from trying to manipulate him.

He *loved her*?

Looking back, Declan had stood up for Iris on more than one occasion, but Orion had assumed this the result of his moral compass, not his personal feelings. If he'd truly begun to develop feelings for her, why hadn't he said something?

If Orion had known of his friend's desires, he wouldn't have allowed things to progress between himself and Iris to begin with.

He thought he wouldn't have, at least.

Declan was too important. Surely he wouldn't have let himself flirt with her if he'd known.

His mind swam to their first twelve hours in the cave in Cordillera, caught in the current of all he'd felt: when they'd huddled together for warmth; when her cheeks blushed as her fingers spread cura over his wounds. He hadn't been able to take his eyes off of her, even when she'd scolded him for it, and after she'd screamed at him in the depths of the cave, he hadn't been able to resist the pull any longer.

He'd stolen her first kiss—a fact that had shattered him when he'd realized the truth and now felt even worse knowing it had belonged to Declan.

But he hadn't been able to help it, to stop himself, and when he'd almost lost her to the nieda, the agony he'd felt had paralyzed him.

After that, he knew he couldn't allow whatever had sparked between them to continue. He and Declan had a mission, and that mission included turning in Foxx and Iris' father to clear their names. What sense did it make allowing their bond to grow only to devastate her in the end? Or worse yet, what if he'd fallen for her so thoroughly that he'd chosen her over his own freedom? He'd spent six years fighting tooth and nail for one thing. Allowing her to get under his skin would only prevent the outcome that had consumed him for so long.

He realized now for possibly the fiftieth time what an inconceivable idiot he'd been.

Will you say something? she'd pleaded when they stood alone in their room at Peregrine Manor—the room he'd forced her to share with him. Still, she'd begged, *Talk to me. Let me help you. Whatever it is, we can figure it out together.*

He'd been so stubborn. So unwilling to give up on the plan he'd set for himself. Only over the past few days had he begun to realize it didn't matter at all whether the King and Queen pardoned him. He doubted he would have rejoined the Legion, so why had it felt so important? He could have chosen Iris. He could have put her needs above his stupid, senseless schemes, and maybe she would have wanted him, too.

Again his thoughts drew him back to the tunnel where they'd pressed against each other in the dark, to her confession that he'd claimed the first kiss from her lips. It would never belong to anyone else because he had stolen it without permission, without preamble, after being screamed at within the depths of a monster-infested tunnel. He'd tried to fix it, to kiss her tenderly and make her feel safe in the dark.

Then he'd thoroughly and profoundly screwed it all up.

For a moment, he let his mind wander to how things might have turned out if he hadn't been abducted by the Queen. If they'd met up after the attack, if he'd been the one to find her, perhaps she would have chosen him instead of Declan.

Perhaps he'd never stood a chance.

His stomach hurt with emotions he didn't want to feel, and he forced thoughts of Iris away. He'd never know what would have been, and if Declan really did love her, Orion couldn't take her from him now. He owed Declan too much to try, and dwelling any further on past possibilities would only lead to more pain.

After a while, his thoughts drifted to the voices in his head: one vicious and cruel, and the other... He sighed. Again he wondered what exactly Elohim was thinking talking to him now after all this time. So many times he'd cried out to a voice that didn't respond. Now, out of nowhere, He'd returned. Was Sirena's voice the root of it—two great powers at war inside his head? How could he of all people have become the vessel for such a battle? And more so, how would he ever manage to survive it?

Pulling his reflections from Elohim for fear attention might draw Him to the surface, he thought instead of Isolde and what a strange woman she was. He found her kindness so absurd, he couldn't begin to comprehend it. Warmth seemed to radiate from her, infecting everyone she came in contact with. Even Griffin had bent to her will.

Orion continued on, attempting to shake away thoughts which served no purpose. He heard nothing but the *drip, drip, drip* reverberating as it hit the stone floor. The sands shifted beneath him as he climbed the dunes, irritating his gashes beneath Declan's tight shirt. He didn't relish the thought of traveling all the way to Jericho trapped in the confines of the restrictive material and wondered if he'd be able to purchase something in the village to wear in its place.

He also didn't care for the idea of stepping behind Jerichonian walls in such a weakened position, though he didn't think he had much choice in the matter. Surely Hector would believe his story if they allowed him to tell it. Before being labeled a traitor, he'd been an esteemed member of the Reko Raptors. That had to count for something. And with Hector now a traitor himself, as well as knowing the truth about Orion's innocence in Sawyer's scheme, he felt confident he could win him and his followers over.

Still, he refused to do it in this shirt and resolved to either find a replacement or go without a shirt entirely before arriving.

He continued on for a little less than an hour before turning around and heading back, jogging for some of the time in an effort to get his heart racing. Eventually, he began sprinting, holding the bag of water firmly so it didn't flop around as he forced his blood into motion and blasted out some of his stress.

When he saw the lights of the village, he slowed his pace to a walk. He felt out of breath and ready to get comfortable in his chair so he could drift into dreamland. He'd decided he loved that chair, though it seemed a silly thing to grow attached to. Once they left Caritas, he would never see it again. Still, it was a peaceful place to land for the moment.

As he drew closer, he heard what he thought must be the vibrations of music. Rounding Isolde's tent, he found the villagers gathered in the midst of celebration and drew back to remain out of sight. From the shadows, he saw Naaba Kaatachi seated on a chair above the dancers and realized what the villagers had been building: a stage to hold his throne. Griffin and Isolde sat on either side of him, though not as far from the ground.

Briefly, he wondered about Griffin's role. He'd been introduced as the Abrafo, but did that give him the prestige to sit next to the royals on his own makeshift throne? Warriors seemed highly celebrated in Caritas, so Orion supposed that could be the reason. He might be a relative or even the man chosen as a match for Isolde when it came time for her to marry. Though he didn't know the customs of the village, Orion couldn't imagine Isolde with someone like Griffin. He was far too surly to be with a woman as tender-hearted as her.

Returning his attention to the villagers, Orion noticed a huge fire at the center of the crowd. People danced around it to the untamed melody of the musicians grouped together on the edge of the assembly. Some played instruments of their own. Others lingered around the fringes, eating, drinking, and conversing with neighbors.

All the party-goers had dressed with wild extravagance: faces freshly painted; extra feathers added to their hair; and colorful beads wrapped around necks, arms, and ankles that clinked together as they danced. They sang in Vetoräti with long, drawn out words that vibrated from their throats.

Violet lights flitted about the dancers, and Orion thought they must be henki, though he'd never seen the spirit-fairies of the desert. He watched with interest as they zipped about, seeming to spur the people on with a dramatic dance of their own.

Not wanting to risk being pulled into the festivities by curious strangers, Orion slid around the corner of Isolde's tent and kept to the shadows as he headed for the door. Kaatachi's voice shouting his name stopped him in his tracks. His head fell forward as he breathed, "Almost made it." Then he spun to face the village chief and held up a hand in greeting.

"*Veni! Veni!* Come! Come!" Kaatachi waved his arms to draw him in. Orion eyed the crowd, endeavoring to find a clear route through the horde of dancers. "*Veni!*" Kaatachi called again before addressing his people in their native tongue.

The crowd parted, unceasing in their exotic movements. As he strode the path they created, dancers grabbed him, lifting his arms and spinning him around, enticing him to join their celebration. He smiled and politely declined, using the King's summons to excuse his slight. When he arrived before the throne, he bowed. "Naaba Kaatachi, merry greetings."

Kaatachi laughed. "Indeed my good friend, indeed. We came to invite you to join us, but you were absent from your tent."

Orion thought this must be intended as a question and explained, "I went for a walk. I needed to clear my head." He forced himself to avoid Isolde, focusing only on her father.

"I understand. Many difficult trials lie ahead of you, *herr* Orion, but as they say in my homeland, *At times we drift and wander astray, but to find ourselves lost is to discover the way.*" Orion contemplated whether the Naaba had spoken to Maeve or if he too was prone to prophetic ramblings and complicated riddles. Kaatachi held his tumbler in the air. "Perhaps tonight you will have some fun with us. Relax, eat, drink, and dance."

Despite his resistance, Orion felt captivated by Kaatachi's jolliness. "I think we may have different views on what we consider fun, Your Majesty."

Two women approached Orion from either side and slid a clay cup into each of his hands. He eyed the drinks cautiously and returned his gaze to Kaatachi.

"'Tis the finest wine in all of the Wilds, *herr* Orion. We grow the grapes ourselves, you know. Drink! Be merry!" He laughed from his belly and again lifted his cup in salute. The women helped push the pottery to Orion's lips, encouraging him to taste the delicious nectar of the village winemakers.

"Okay, okay." Orion tipped one of the cups back, drinking the entire contents before returning the empty vessel to the woman wearing a headdress of feathers. Half of her face was painted dark eggplant, and white dots outlined her eyes. Lifting her voice to the air, she howled like a wolf at her victory. Then she grabbed both sides of his face and pressed her lips to his, kissing him passionately. He held his hands away from her, dumbfounded by her unexpected intimacy.

When she released him, she promised, "I will save you a dance, *herr* Orion." Then she whirled away and rejoined the crowd. Kaatachi continued to laugh as Orion turned back to him, raising his remaining cup in cheers to the Naaba.

Sitting to the left of Kaatachi, Griffin looked miserable. Daring a glance at Isolde, Orion found her sipping her own drink, seated in a relaxed position with her elbow on one arm of the chair and one leg crossed over the other. She lifted her drink to him, and he said, "Naabila Isolde, *bonum vos noscere*, officially."

Kaatachi cackled. "Your Vetoräti is not bad, my friend!"

Isolde smiled. "The pleasure is mine." With eyes locked, she and Orion took a swig in unison.

The woman still standing at Orion's side rejoiced. Wrapping her feathered scarf around his neck, she dragged him into the crowd of dancers, rambling words in Vetoräti too fast for him to comprehend. She spun and spun, using his hand above her head for balance. Others noticed the newcomer had finally accepted the festivities and stole him away, passing him from one person to the next. He finished his second drink so he could set down the cup and have another free hand. It was instantly attacked by dancers, now able to share both sides of him.

It had been a long time since Orion truly enjoyed himself. He tried to remember the last time he felt so carefree. Images of Lacuna Kaput flashed into his mind's eye: standing atop the falls, diving in, and Iris diving in right along with him. Though what came after was horrifying and tragic, the experience had been thrilling. Before that, he could remember only a handful of times since their exile when he'd felt so untethered.

No longer needing the villagers' help to frolic, Orion spun of his own volition, tapping his feet and flinging his arms in the air as he switched from one partner to the next. The wine had numbed his wounds so they only ached a little in response to his movements. Another cup landed in his hand, and he drank it down. One woman wrapped her arms around his shoulders, and he spun her in a circle, lifting her feet off the ground. They hooted and hollered and sang and danced until he could scarcely breathe.

As he started to slow, his mind growing fuzzy with exhaustion and spirits, the whispers all at once consumed his ears. Willing them away, he fought to remain unbound. Villagers continued to caper around him, but his vision had gone blurry as whispering echoes drowned out the music. A hand grabbed his, drawing him near. He felt lips graze his cheek before being spun away by an outstretched arm and released. For a moment, he thought he might be falling as the loudness in his head sent his equilibrium out of balance.

When he stopped spinning, he found himself in someone else's arms. One hand held his own off to the side and the other slid around his neck. Vision crisping back into focus, he saw golden eyes glistening before him. The whispers scattered, detonating in all directions until nothing remained but music and laughter.

Licking her thumb, she wiped purple paint from his lips. Shame flooded his cheeks, but she only smiled. "Care to dance with the Naaba's daughter?"

His heart had raced before. His stomach had felt nauseated by the twirling and the wine, his breath thieved by energy and commotion, but none of it compared to the sensation of Isolde standing so close, her skin grazing his.

"I would love to." He couldn't express his gratitude for the relief her touch offered, and he wondered if she possessed some sorcery able to dispel the whispers. The scent of lavender and sandalwood mingled with the smokey smell of campfire and the sweetness of berry wine, and Orion submerged himself in it. Sliding his arm around her waist, he pulled her body against his, feeling the heat of her bare stomach burning through his clothing and the skin of her back scorching his palm. His face fell into her hair as they danced cheek to cheek, moving together around the fire.

Dancers parted to let them pass, making space for their Naabila and her partner. Some extended hands to touch them as they spun by, others bowed or curtsied.

Orion twirled Isolde around his finger, pushing her away from him so their arms spread, then pulling her back into his chest. His heart burst from the thrill of his hands stroking her body and the enjoyment she seemed to be experiencing because of it.

Too soon, the music crescendoed into a finale and climaxed with tremendous howls and praise to the talented musicians. Despite the frenzied fervor all around them, Isolde did not immediately pull away and instead allowed her arms to drape about his shoulders while she caught her breath.

Another song began, causing the crowd to chirp with hysteria, but even as the villagers' jubilation swelled, Isolde and Orion remained stationary. Hooked together, not only by limbs, but through the buoyant and effervescent energy that holds two souls in place following a moment in time so chasmic and significant and radically unexpected that they fail to realize they've yet to let go.

Unable to help himself, his gaze slid to her lips to find the bottom one pinched between her teeth. Before his brain could stop his thoughts from morphing into sentences, he said, "Isolde, I—" But her finger pressed to his mouth before any more words could tumble free.

"Thank you for the dance, *herr* Orion." Without warning, hands grabbed him from behind, causing him to turn from her. The woman with the eggplant face dragged him back into the throng of dancers. He returned his eyes to Isolde, not ready to be pulled away from her yet, only to find the back of her head disappearing into the crowd.

CHAPTER 9

GETTING TO KNOW YOU

Orion stirred awake at the sound of Kaatachi's vibrant exclamation as he entered Isolde's tent.

"The Morrow greets you!" the Naaba cried with as much enthusiasm as he'd expressed the night before.

"The Morrow greets you, as well, Naaba Kaatachi."

Declan's alert voice drew Orion further from unconsciousness, though his drowsiness lingered. It seemed no amount of exercise and exhaustion had been enough to hinder the nightmares. They swarmed his sleep like a disturbed hive of hornets, ruthless and bloodthirsty.

Forcing himself upright, he rubbed his eyes. Sweat had soaked his clothing, and he looked down at himself in disgust. He needed new clothes. If he couldn't get them in Caritas, he would purchase some in Jericho.

If everything went to plan, he would be leaving shortly. For a bewildering moment, the thought pricked his chest like a dozen pins. He kneaded his eyes again, thinking he must still be in that confusing place between dreamland and waking where, despite being stirred from slumber, the world remains sheer nonsense.

Naaba Kaatachi moved to stand in front of the bed. "Young Declan—you do not mind if I drop the formalities, do you? We are all friends now, I think."

"That's fine with me."

"Very good, very good. So tell me, Declan, how are you feeling this fine morning?"

"I'm feeling much better than I did yesterday. How are you? It sounded like you all had an exciting night." His eyes slid to Orion, accompanied by a grin. Orion had refused to divulge the activities he'd participated in the previous evening, though when he entered the tent he'd been grinning like a fool—until Declan pointed it out.

"Indeed, my friend, indeed. My daughter is about to go on a great journey, and I wanted her to enjoy herself before leaving us."

This sparked Orion's attention, and his bleary vision crisped into focus as it locked onto Isolde, whom he'd only then realized stood inside the doorway next to Griffin. The memory of them dancing together sent a flush of heat to his cheeks.

Without looking his way, Isolde crossed the room to stare at his friend's bare chest.

Declan moved his arms, giving her room and watching her as she worked. "You're leaving? Who will tend my wounds when you're away?" Orion considered pummeling him for his grieved charisma. He longed for the days when Declan was silent and broody. When had he become charming and flirtatious? It occurred to him that perhaps Declan really had fallen in love after all.

"I asked Griffin to." Isolde glanced at Declan, a mischievous smile brightening her expression. "But he declined, so Vera will be changing your bandages for the next few days until you can do it yourself."

Declan visibly relaxed. "I'm sure I can manage on my own now."

"I'm sure you could," Orion mumbled under his breath.

Isolde and Declan looked at him as if they'd just remembered his presence. Then they returned their attention to each other. "Because it is under your ribs, I still want someone else checking it for a few days. I do not want you struggling to see it and tearing open the stitches. Infection comes easily in the wild, and once it arrives it can be an unstoppable force. Vera is often not as gentle as I, but she knows how to treat an injury such as this. You will be in good hands." After tightening the tie over the fresh bandage, she stood and joined her father at the center of the room.

As Isolde and his friend separated, Orion suddenly comprehended what the Naaba had said. He sat forward, intending to beat him to the punch, but Kaatachi spoke faster.

"It has been decided." Kaatachi turned to Orion with his arms out, palms up. "Orion and Isolde will journey to Jericho."

Slouching back in his seat, Orion rubbed his temples, willing himself to wake up. The Naaba watched him process the words with a big smile, and Orion realized Isolde learned to smile from her father. Leaning forward again with his elbows on his knees, he looked between them. "No offense, Your Majesty, but I would rather travel alone. I think being responsible for a princess is way above my pay grade." He could barely take care of himself since waking in the swamp with a fun, new talent for hallucinations and breakdowns. He couldn't possibly be in charge of keeping anyone safe.

"I am responsible for myself," Isolde said. When he eyed her skeptically, she put a hand on her hip and cocked it out with an attitude he'd not yet witnessed in her. "Do you doubt me, *herr* Orion?"

Kaatachi chuckled. "While you are in Jericho, you will pass on a message." He slid his hand through the air as if stretching out the words. "Caritas will join the battle." Pausing, he waited to see if Orion would protest. "You will come back by way of Metsa Sateen, free your friends, then return to us. How long will this take you?"

Orion glanced at Declan, who shrugged, looking practically giddy in response to the unexpected turn of events. Keeping Isolde from his line of sight, Orion insisted, "I really don't think this is a good idea, Naaba Kaatachi." Isolde scowled in his peripherals, but he pressed on. "Listen, I am already a fugitive of one Kingdom. You know nothing of me, my past, or any of the things I've done. You have no logical reason to trust me with a task this great. But *I* know me, and I implore you to please reconsider." He waited, but Kaatachi continued smiling without answer. The thought of nights alone with Isolde had Orion's stomach clenching with nervous anxiety, though for entirely different reasons than it had the previous evening. What if he went mad and did something awful to her? What if he lost touch with reality and failed to protect her? "What will my punishment be if I return without her? What will you do to my friends if neither of us return?"

"I am not concerned with such matters. It is all in Elohim's wise hands. We follow His mission and His guidance, and He will make things happen as He pleases."

"Of course He will." Orion grappled for an argument that might convince them, but it seemed the Naaba had no intention of giving in to his request. He couldn't fathom why Kaatachi so adamantly ignored his warnings when he was little more than a stranger to them. At last, he exhaled and worked through the numbers to answer the Naaba's question. "We can get to Jericho in less than three days. Possibly two depending how quickly we travel."

"You are familiar with the leaping of the barriers, then?" Kaatachi remarked. "This magic has been known in Caritas since its inception."

"Have you ever jumped a barrier before?" Orion looked at Isolde for the first time since she'd begun glaring at him.

"No, I have not."

Declan said, "Don't worry about it. I'd imagine it will be as easy as taking a walk for a warrior princess like yourself." Isolde's scowl slid from Orion to look at Declan, her shoulders seeming to loosen in response to his encouragement.

Orion went on calculating. "It's a two day journey between here and the Metsa on foot. Then we'll jump to Cordillera, and it's almost a day's hike to Jericho. Once we check in with Commander Kayvan, we'll return to the barrier and cross into the Metsa. The most time-consuming thing will be getting to the Monastery. If I'm not mistaken, it's a several week journey no matter where you enter the territory. Horses would shorten that time, and Jericho should be able to provide some."

"You will take tryka and reach the barrier sooner," Kaatachi said.

Orion looked confused. "Tryka?"

Isolde said, "They do not do well in the jungle, Father. Their antlers are too large. We will be fine on foot."

"Then it is settled." He smiled at Isolde over his shoulder, but she ignored his excitement and spoke directly to Orion with an edge of coldness to her voice.

"We leave with the rising sun. We will provide you with weapons and clothing for the journey, as you have brought none with you."

"Yeah, Sirena didn't return my pack after all the captivity and torture and leaving me for dead." Orion avoided her eyes, thinking the gold felt vicious when accompanied by that harsh tone. He scanned the ground for his cup of water from the night before and drank it down. Particles of sand irritated his tongue and scratched his throat. Then his eyes left the ground to scan her body, doing his best not to linger on the bare patches of skin. "You're going to need warmer clothes. Jericho is high in the mountains, covered in snow."

"It will all be ready. Vera will look after Declan and Johnathan while we are away. I will come for you when the sun rises." Isolde didn't wait for him to respond before walking past her father and exiting the tent.

Kaatachi watched her go, a proud expression crinkling the skin around his eyes. "My daughter is strong willed. I will not hold you responsible for her safety, but I hope you will look after her while she is in your charge. And I can promise you, it will not be an easy task."

Orion tried not to look annoyed, as he had known this would be the case regardless of what Isolde had declared while asserting independence. With a sigh, he said, "Naaba Kaatachi, I will do my best to safely return your daughter as soon as possible, but I make no promises. The wilderness is dangerous—Metsa Sateen more than anywhere else, in my opinion. I just want to make sure you're prepared for what may lie ahead."

This seemed to satisfy the Naaba, regardless of Orion's lack of commitment. "Spend today resting. You leave with the rising sun." With a bow and wishes of a *merry day*, he and Griffin left the tent.

Orion sighed again and looked at Declan to find him beaming. "What are you so happy about?" He crossed the room, finding a full pitcher of water on the table. With a flicker of irritation, he realized Isolde must have refilled it before he woke.

"You and Isolde are going on a little trip together, huh?" Declan teased.

Orion faced him, finishing his drink before replying. "It's just business. He's worried I'll go off and never return, leaving him to deal with this mess you've gotten yourself into."

"All right, all right. No low blows needed. I'm just ragging on you. At least it's not Griffin, right?" Declan scooted lower on the bed.

"I think I'd prefer Griffin at this point." At least Griffin would have the good sense to run him through, or at the very least, knock him out, should he start raving like a lunatic.

Declan shook his head. "Johnathan and I will head to Jericho as soon as I'm well enough to travel and meet you there when you return from Metsa Sateen."

Johnathan spoke from his bed on the floor. "I'm just glad I'm not the one stuck traveling with Orion."

Orion barked a laugh. "Fair enough."

After a few hours of mulling around the tent, Orion realized he no longer felt comfortable spending excessive time in confined spaces. Declan had fallen asleep again, his body still deep in the throes of healing, and Johnathan, Orion discovered like never before, was the most dull person he had ever met.

Without a destination in mind, Orion stepped out into the sun. The people of Caritas always seemed busy with one task or another: cooking or cleaning, building or creating. The village had no shops, but instead, everyone had their own niche and worked hard to contribute what they could to benefit their neighbors. He wondered if they bartered goods for goods rather than exchanging coins, or if they would even accept his coin if he wanted to purchase something.

They also didn't have pubs or restaurants but cooked and ate together for every meal. Aside from when he'd lived on the Refuge, he'd never been in a place like Caritas. They were a tribe—a family.

Turning right as he exited the tent, he came upon two women sitting cross-legged in front of their home coiling ropes of colorful fabric into baskets. Stopping to watch them work, he asked neither of them in particular, "How long have you been making baskets like this?"

The younger of the two looked at him, and he recognized her as the woman with eggplant face paint from the night before. He hadn't realized her absolute beauty when she'd been splashed in paint and firelight. Now in the sun, he saw skin darker than a chestnut shell and big, brown eyes far lighter than her complexion.

"*Herr* Orion! *Avia*, this is Naabila Isolde's friend. Our fearless Naabila rescued him and his companions from the clutches of the fierce nieda hive." She spoke Arkaen, either because she knew it was Orion's first language or because she preferred it. He suspected the former.

The other woman paused her fingers to gaze up at him. Though her hair had faded to gray and her skin hung in loose wrinkles, she was a near replica of the younger woman sitting at her side. A violet henki hovered in the air next to her, holding the rope as if helping her work. "Pleasure to meet you, *herr* Orion."

"*Bonum vos noscere, avia*," he replied, pleased with himself for catching the name.

Both women chuckled before the younger said, "*Avia* means grandmother. Her name is Marisol. You may address her as *rouv* Marisol, if you did not know. I am Teetee."

"*Nei* Teetee," Marisol corrected under her breath.

"Our lips have already touched, *avia*, so I do not think he needs to worry about formalities." Teetee giggled as Marisol's eyes widened, and Orion blanched. "Do not scold him, *avia*. He did not have a choice in the matter." Fair eyes returned to their guest. "*Tu loqueris* Vetoräti?"

"Some. But maybe we should stick with Arkaen before I find myself even more in over my head." He smiled and reworded his previous statement, bowing to Marisol as he said, "It's a pleasure to meet you as well, *rouv* Marisol." The elderly woman nodded in response, offering him a kind smile before glaring sideways at her granddaughter. Then she returned to her work. The creature at her side bobbed up and down as it fed her evergreen rope.

"*Nei* Teetee, *Gratiias tibi* for encouraging me to celebrate with you all last night. It was enjoyable." Orion noticed Marisol's eyes slide to him with approval and hoped he'd won his way back into her good graces. Though, after feeling this victory, he couldn't imagine why it mattered to him what this stranger thought.

Teetee laughed. "Very good, *herr* Orion. I am certain in time we can teach you the depths of our language. If ever you would like some private lessons, this is my tent." She threw a thumb over her shoulder. Marisol smacked her granddaughter with the rope in her hands and said her name scoldingly. The string of words that followed emerged too quickly for Orion to translate. Then he heard Isolde's name. Teetee looked at him, her head tucked into her shoulders, before continuing her basket-making without another word.

Orion wished the women a *merry day* and moved on, proceeding in the direction he'd been walking. He saw more folks he recognized from the night before and some even greeted him by name. A few more steps brought him to a man sitting before a pottery wheel, forming a bowl with practiced hands. A woman knelt on the ground next to him, cranking a handle to keep the wheel spinning. Buckets of dirty water and shelves of finished or drying pottery lined the clay-splattered rug, and more violet lights fluttered about, sending jingles into the air as they communicated.

One noticed him and zipped over to the woman, seeming to get her attention. When she realized Orion's interest, she waved him closer. Stepping onto the rug, he leaned in to watch the man gently guide the clay to his will. Though the man didn't drop his smile, his eyes looked sharp with concentration.

"That doesn't look easy." At his own words, Orion's face puckered as he questioned where this newfound sense of community had spawned from. His focus on the villagers had quieted the whispers, and even the dripping had faded to a dull hum, so he decided not to overthink it. If socializing was the key to keeping his brain muted, then so be it.

The man looked up from his work, though his hands continued their mission. *"Vis experiri, herr?"*

The words sparked a memory, a flicker in his chest. Elora, a woman he'd met on a farm in Savanni soon after he'd first left home, used to say it all the time. She'd teach him how to accomplish a task, and finish her lesson with, *Vis experiri?* which meant, *Do you want to try?* He owed much of his familiarity with the Vetoräti language to Elora, and despite how things had ended, he'd enjoyed the time he got to spend with her.

Several of the glowing creatures circled Orion in a whirlwind, drawing him back to the present. He responded in Arkaen, hoping they would be fluent, as the other villagers seemed to be. "I appreciate the offer, but really, I would have no idea what to do."

The woman slowed her spinning as the man released the wet clay and stood. Ushering Orion into his seat despite his avid protests, he dipped Orion's hands in a cup of clay-filled water and placed them around the dish. One of the lights landed on Orion's shoulder, and though he could hardly feel its feather-light touch, he knew it must be watching for evidence of talent.

"Nevermind the henki. They do no harm." The woman began spinning the wheel, and the man guided Orion's fingers.

The wet clay felt cooler than he'd expected, especially in the heat of the Wilds. It was a strange mixture, balanced somewhere between a solid and a liquid: firm, but only needing a gentle pressure to adjust its shape.

After a minute or so of instruction, the man released Orion's hands and let him continue sculpting on his own, cheering him on with words of encouragement. A smile spread across Orion's face as he grew comfortable and even mildly impressed with himself.

"It is... *facilis*, yes? Easy?" The man shooed the henki from Orion's shoulder, but it returned in moments.

Orion nodded, afraid speaking might break his concentration. He stared intently at the bowl in his hands, adjusting its circumference with just the slight press of his fingers.

"I did not know you were a potter, *herr* Orion." Isolde's voice cut through Orion's focus. In his distraction, his thumb pushed too hard into the clay and the whole dish smooshed into an awkward shape. The henki leapt from his shoulder and fluttered off as Orion's eyes lifted to find Isolde's hand covering her mouth.

"I'm not." Orion looked at the man apologetically. "Thanks for the lesson. *Gratiias.* Sorry I messed up your bowl."

The man shook his head. "You did well, *herr* Orion!"

Orion stood and circled around to the front of the station so the man could return to his seat. A glance at his hands had him grimacing, and the woman chuckled before pointing to a bucket next to the house.

"You may wash there."

Orion dipped his head. "Thanks again."

The man said, "Come back any time for another lesson."

It took a full minute to wash the clay from his fingers. When he finally rose from his knees, it surprised him to find Isolde waiting for him to finish up. "I didn't expect you'd want to see me, given how angry I made you this morning." He looked her over, his eyes lingering on her hips as he remembered the fire she'd exhibited when he'd offended her. Then he cleared his throat. "Did you need something?"

Isolde gestured as she turned from the potters and began walking the inner edge of the village. Orion fell into step next to her. They passed another two tents before she spoke. "I am sorry to have disturbed your creation."

He scratched the back of his head and realized he'd missed some clay. "I didn't really do anything. He made it, and I was already messing it up before you arrived."

"It did not seem that way to me." She glanced over her shoulder at the potters who had seemed delighted to have Orion with them. "I was unaware you had an interest in such things."

"To be fair, you don't know much about me." He chuckled and picked at the leftover clay on his palm. "And he mildly forced me into it. But it was nice. The clay was smooth like silk, which I didn't expect when he first sat me down."

She made a noise of agreement. "The mūsae seemed impressed by you, too."

"Mūsae! That's what they are." He smiled, and she couldn't comprehend his suddenly joyful expression. "They live in Alunda, too."

"I believe the mūsae of Alunda are slightly bluer than the ones of the desert, but their task is the same: to inspire creativity. Are you very familiar with Alunda? Is it your home territory?"

He looked sideways at her, wondering about her curiosity of his past. "I'm originally from Reginaterra, but I spent several years in Alunda. I love it there. It may be my favorite of all the territories, though perhaps I've simply had the best experiences there, so it only seems that way."

"Why did you leave?"

"Honestly, I was kind of forced to. Not forced to leave the territory, but I was kicked out of the group I'd grown close to. Staying by the sea became too painful after that, so I moved on. I've been back to visit them a few times, but it was never again like it had been." Orion paused by an intense operation, and Isolde stopped with him. Two women dipped fabric into barrels of colored water while another poured wax designs on clean fabric.

"This is called batik." Isolde pointed to the colorful fabric a man pulled from another barrel. Two mūsae helped him hang it on a line to dry. Orion observed the finished work and dipped his chin to the man. As they moved past the dyers, Isolde asked, "What did you do that you were forced to leave?"

"Camille would argue I was *set free* rather than kicked out, but it certainly didn't feel that way. She said it was for my own good. I suppose I'll never know if she was right."

"Maybe someday you will."

Regretting the direction the conversation had taken and unwilling to discuss anything more that would be considered getting to know each other, Orion remained quiet and continued nodding to villagers as they walked past. He couldn't tell if the silence between them was awkward or peaceful, not very familiar with what peace felt like, so he glanced at her from the corner of his eye and attempted to gauge her countenance. She wore her usual expression, tranquil and kind, and it relaxed him enough to speak. "I like your village."

Isolde's mouth fell wide open. "Are you admitting to enjoying the company of actual people, *herr* Orion?"

Her infectious smile spread to Orion's lips. "Perhaps you read me a little better than I'd like to think."

An older man with a long, white beard waved to the Naabila, and she returned it, dipping her head as they walked by. Then a young girl ran up to them and blocked their path. Lifting her fist to Isolde, she uncurled her fingers to reveal a braided bracelet laying in her palm.

"For me?" Amazement brightened Isolde's features. The girl nodded. "Thank you, Ruae! It is lovely." Isolde slipped the bracelet onto her wrist and held it out to admire it better.

"Very pretty," Orion agreed. Ruae curtsied, pulling her dress out to both sides and bowing before rushing off. "See? That was adorable. They all seem so… unburdened. And friendly."

Isolde nodded him onward. "They are unburdened and friendly. It is their Creator within them who makes it so."

"I see." Orion lifted a hand to shield his eyes as he looked up at the sun.

"I think you will see. In time."

Nearly every villager waved or bowed as they passed by. Orion realized how much Isolde's people must love her, and thought, how could they not? She was caring and kind, brave and fierce—everything an heir should be to her people.

All at once, he halted his steps. "This feels weird."

Startled from wherever her thoughts had wandered, Isolde stopped walking and looked at him. "What feels weird?"

"A man, a stranger, taking a stroll around the village with their princess." He scratched the back of his head, suddenly feeling like all eyes were on him. "It might give your people the wrong idea."

"The wrong idea?"

He could tell she feigned ignorance as one side of her lips curled. "You know what I mean. Like I'm some stranger coming to take advantage of you or something."

"Are you?" Her golden eyes flashed mischievously.

Orion scoffed and crossed his arms. "No, of course not. I'm just saying I know how these things work. I've spent a fair amount of time around royals."

"I believe you worry needlessly. Perhaps my people are a kind you have never come across."

"There's no doubting that." Orion scanned the villagers to find few paying attention except to wave in greeting. Isolde turned and cut across the center of the village without explanation. He moved quickly to catch up, not really sure whether he was supposed to or not.

"The sun will set soon."

"That is generally what happens at the end of the day," he mumbled, feeling even more annoyed with her... everything.

"Come." Her pace quickened.

"Where are we going?" he called, thinking he must look like an idiot chasing after her as she jogged between two tents and out of the village.

Turning to him, she jogged backward as they passed through the row of sage dotting a trail around the whole village. "*Fidés*. I want to show you something." As they moved west, her body grew darker, silhouetted by the rays of sunlight at her back.

Orion struggled not to notice her curves as they swayed like the gentle waves of the sea before a storm. "I have a feeling I'm going to regret this."

"Yet you have not ceased following." She turned forward and picked up speed.

They shot off into the desert, running next to each other as if racing. Orion wondered if they actually *were* racing. When he pushed himself harder, she did the same, and he realized she was keeping pace with him rather than attempting to run ahead.

The sun had nearly touched the horizon, casting long shadows behind them. They sprinted toward it as if trying to catch it before it slipped out of sight. Orion had never been to this part of the desert, but it looked the same as the rest of the Grim Wilds: a mixture of sandy dunes and red clay stretching out as far as the eye could see; rocks and tall mesas poking out at random; and spiked cacti of multiple varieties speckling the landscape.

Up ahead, he saw a cave on the side of a tall rock formation. When they reached it, Isolde began climbing up to the cave without pause or explanation, but Orion stopped at the bottom and looked up into the unlit cavity.

"I don't think I like caves anymore." He hadn't known this about himself until that very moment. His throat began to swell, making it hard to swallow as the invisible fingers of fear tightened around it.

"There is an opening on the other side. We will not be in the dark long." Her chest rose and fell heavily from their run. "Want to try it? We can always turn back if it is too much."

He looked from her to the cave and back, finding her hand outstretched. The bracelet Ruae had gifted her decorated the top of her leather cuff. From the compassion in Isolde's eyes, he wondered how much she'd guessed about what he'd been through with the Queen. Did she think him a child afraid of the dark, or did she understand the depths of his terror? Could she even comprehend the pain that pit of darkness triggered in the caverns of his chest?

With a sigh, he accepted her hand and let her help him up the rocks.

When they reached the cave mouth, the blackness inside swallowed everything from sight. With the sun on the opposite side of the structure, even the surrounding stone lay in shadow.

"We must hurry or we will miss it." Without asking permission, she slid her hand back into his, interlacing their fingers together and pulling him forward, coaxing until he trailed after her.

In an instant, smothering darkness devoured all light. His chest, already containing a frantically beating heart, grew rigid as he held his breath. Isolde guided him through the tunnel, knowing exactly where to step to avoid tripping or banging shins. They began traveling up, as if on a set of naturally occurring stairs that curved through the structure, and just when he thought he could no longer hold his breath, he saw a new hue emerging into the abyss. The further they climbed, the brighter it grew until they at last stepped out into the vermillion light of the setting sun. Like a balcony on the side of a building, a plateau stretched out from the cave entrance. Orion peeked out over the edge and shivered.

"You are not afraid of heights as well?" she teased.

"Not of the height, no, but splatting on the ground doesn't sound entirely intriguing."

Chuckling, she released his hand and crossed the platform to sit with her feet dangling over the edge. "This is my favorite spot to watch the sunset. I discovered it long ago when I was angry at my father and ran off into the desert, vowing to never return." Orion moved cautiously to the edge, and she praised his bravery as he sat next to her. "I remained here two whole days."

"Your father didn't send anyone after you?"

"He knew I would return. There are some lessons we need to learn on our own. We cannot always be taught the way."

"I know what you mean." Orion had always been stubborn when it came to being taught things. Camille had seen right through him and worked him to the bone until he surrendered to her instruction, but few others before her or since had been successful. Reminded of Camille for the second time in an hour, he wondered how she and the others might be doing. Perhaps when he'd fulfilled his purposes here, he could make a trip to Alunda and search for them.

The sun looked like a half-circle now, cut by the horizon. It glowed like a bright sunflower, fading into vibrant papaya around the edges. The sky touching the land was splashed with crimson, mustard seed, and magenta, with long wisps of clouds seeming to stretch on forever. Above the clouds, a cerulean sky melted into a deep-ocean blue.

"I jumped off a cliff into a lagoon once," he said. Isolde eyed him with bemused interest. "It was extremely high above the ground, and I wasn't afraid at all as there was water at the bottom to prevent the splat."

"I see." She grinned, letting her feet swing back and forth off the edge.

"Of course, we found out after jumping that the lagoon was home to the most terrifying creature I have ever laid eyes on, with too many eyes and five disgusting tentacles lined with rows of teeth." A shudder moved through him at the memory. Iris' horrified face flashed into his mind, and he shoved it away.

Isolde's eyes ballooned with secondhand fright. "Did you escape unharmed?"

"Unfortunately, no." He remembered the feeling of hanging in the beast's clutches, wishing to die so the agony would cease. Lifting his shirt, he showed her the biggest of the scars. "It picked me up and smashed me into the water until I passed out."

She touched it with the tip of her finger, feeling the ripple that would never smooth over. "And yet you prefer that to a splat in the sand?"

"I think you might be missing the point."

Her finger slipped from the deepest scar to brush another. "I noticed some wounds that seemed weeks older than the others on your first day here."

The reminder of those delectable minutes sent a wave of warmth through him, and he nodded rather than opening his mouth in case something stupid fell out. He let his shirt fall when she moved to graze another mark on his arm, a scar from long before his dive into the lagoon.

Orion ran his thumb across the pale blemish. "That was from a bar-fight in Sal. Glass from a broken bottle." He pointed higher up his arm. "And this one happened in Cal'dion."

"You have so many." Her eyes lifted to his. "Inside and out, it seems."

He hadn't realized how much they'd drawn together until finding her face mere inches from his own. "Yes. I guess I do." An image infected his thoughts: the two of them lying in her bed. He'd show her every one of the marks that blemished his skin, sharing with her the story behind each one. Then he'd explore the valleys and hills of her own body, memorizing every freckle and learning the reason for every scar and tattoo. She licked her lips, drawing his eyes to them, and he leaned closer, swept up in lavender and sandalwood.

A thunderclap had them snapping apart, breaking the heated connection.

"Oh! Look out there." She pointed left with one hand and clutched his bicep with the other. Off in the distance in the dimming atmosphere, bolts of lightning zig-zagged from clouds to earth, creating brilliant flashes of pure white and illuminating the sky in patches of glowing maroon.

He swallowed and straightened, feeling foolish for letting himself become so wrapped up in the moment. "Heat lightning. It's amazing."

"It is," she agreed. "The majesty of the Creator's artistry is unmatched. No potter's wheel nor painter's brush could even come close to the exquisite displays of His design." She glanced sideways and saw his skeptical smirk. "Your unbelief does not affect Elohim's capabilities or dampen His proficiency for magnificence."

"Then I suppose it doesn't matter what I think."

She shook her head and nudged his shoulder. "So stubborn."

He smiled, pretty sure the feeling in his gut might be something close to joy. They had a long road ahead of them, a hard road, but in that moment, he felt relaxed, and he decided to relish in it.

In the morning they would leave for Jericho. Once there, he would have to convince Hector he was on their team. Then he would need to convince the Konungr—a task that might prove impossible. Maybe with Isolde at his side, Vali would find her interesting and friendly and trust Orion for the simple fact that she trusted him. Images of the flirtatious king attempting to woo Isolde filled him with a brief rage that he quickly squashed.

Looking at her from the corner of his eye, he watched her react to each new bolt of lightning. They sat together in silence as the last light of the sun dipped beneath the horizon and out of sight.

With twilight finally upon them, she asked, "Are you ready to go back?"

Orion looked over his shoulder at the mouth of the cave, blacker than it had been his first trip through. "You know, I'm here now, so I'll probably just stay."

"Forever?"

He examined the space thoughtfully. "I think I could make it work. You would have to bring me food, of course. Since it's your fault I'm trapped up here, I hope you will feel responsible for my well-being after you leave." The jest felt unfamiliar on his tongue, as most of his jests were seeped in hostility or sarcasm. Instead, he felt at ease, playful.

Laughing, she stood and extended a hand. "Hold my hand again so you are not afraid."

"I'm beginning to think holding your hand might be far more terrifying than being lost in the dark, Naabila." He took her hand anyway and let her help him to his feet. After one last glimpse at the horizon, Orion inhaled a deep, lung-filling breath, and together they stepped back into the cave.

C

Orion was already standing at the table sorting through Declan's bag when Isolde crossed the threshold at first light. He removed the clothing since it was too small for him and left Declan his pistol and small dagger, keeping the larger blade for himself. Into the bag, he stuffed a torch, the medical kit, minimal food, and a bed roll.

"Are you ready? I brought you some clothing." Isolde set the articles on the table next to him, and he added them to his pack without inspection before strapping it closed and slinging it over his shoulder. Then he changed his mind, dug through the bag again, and pulled out a tunic she'd given him. Isolde turned away to give him privacy without prompting.

Peeling off Declan's shirt, he slipped on the new one. It fit wonderfully and didn't tug at his wounds in the slightest. "Did you pack for cold weather?"

She turned back to face him with another smile as she appraised his new attire. "Yes, *herr* Orion. *Gratia.* Your concern is appreciated." He nodded and scanned the room for anything he may have missed. "I brought food and filled two sleeves of water. If you are ready, we will step into the armory and find you a more sufficient weapon than that itty-bitty dagger." She gestured to the oversized knife at his hip.

For the first time since she entered the tent, Orion turned his eyes to her, and his heart actually fluttered at the sight. She'd cleaned her face of its paint. Only a fresh coating of purple, fading from violet to lavender like the inside of a geode, encircled her eyes and tinted her lips. Her painted tattoos had been washed away to reveal clean, lusciously brown skin. It instantly reminded him of the silky chocolate frosting he'd eaten years ago at that fancy restaurant in Aeonian. Camille had sworn the establishment's chiffon cake was the best dessert she'd ever tasted, and she'd been right. Nothing before or since had compared.

Now his mind fantasized about Isolde's skin, wondering if it might taste even more delectable than that scrumptious cake. His face flushed, and he commanded his thoughts into submission, though his eyes continued to trail an abstract design that disappeared into the hide she wore around her hips. He cleared his throat and returned his eyes to hers. "You washed your face."

"I did not want to appear frightening to your Jerichonian friends." She looked down at herself, adorned in all the same cuffs, jewelry, tails, and boots she'd worn the day they met. She had her long blade hanging at her side, a hatchet on the other, and a spear in her hand, still splattered with the cyan blood of a nieda.

"I'm not sure there's a way around that," he said. It pleased him to see her grinning at the thought. With one last glance at Declan, Orion followed her out into the dim light of a breaking dawn. Only a handful of villagers were awake and out of their tents. A few scattered lights of the henki flitted about, though he assumed most were still sleeping with the humans.

When they reached the armory, Isolde held the door open for him to walk through. On a table inside the door sat a small oil lamp, which she lit so Orion could see his options. Holding it out in her palm, she gestured for him to lead on.

Though most of the weapons in the tent looked primitive in nature, Orion thought it was the most terrifying armory he'd ever set foot in. He walked past maces and bludgeons of all shapes and sizes, including ones with shards of rock and metal exploding from the end. Others had thin handles with rocks or metal shaped into fancy designs, both with spikes positioned at the top. He saw a variety of blades, with sizes ranging from the palm of his hand to the length of his body; hammers and axes, both single and double sided; bows and arrows; spears and staffs; and two daunting scythes.

After browsing the entirety of the tent, he turned to her with lifted brows.

"Impressive, is it not?"

"That's one word for it." He returned to the section of bludgeons. Picking up a few, he tested their weight and the feel of their swing. After choosing a simple club with a curved handle and a spherical rock tied to the end, he moved on to the hammers and axes and chose one fitting both categories.

Isolde handed him a frog holster for each, instructing him to tie them around his hip. When he finished, he held out his hands for her inspection. Stepping up to him, she removed the sheath belt he'd taken from Declan's bag.

"What are you doing?"

Meeting his eyes, she replied, "*Fidés.*"

Orion lifted his gaze to the ceiling and pulled his arms away from his sides. "Right, right. *Fidés.*" Chuckling at his sloppy pronunciation, she lifted the belt over his head so it lay over one shoulder and buckled it together on his opposite hip so the sheath rested at the center of his chest. Looking down at her handiwork, he said, "All right, this will do."

With a nod, she exited the tent, and he followed close behind.

They reached the edge of the village, with the vast desert stretching out in front of them, and he turned to her, holding her gaze so he knew she was paying attention. "Isolde, are you sure about this? I am quite capable of going alone, I promise you. And if

Declan and Johnathan don't make it to Jericho before I return, I will come back for them. I attacked a hive of nieda to save that man. I think you can trust that I won't abandon him here."

"Are you trying to protect me, *herr* Orion? I thought that was *above your pay grade.*"

He adjusted the holsters on his hip. "That is exactly why I am trying to prevent it."

"Is your reason purely concerned with the burden of looking after a princess, or is it that you do not wish to spend so much time in my incredibly irritating company?"

Sighing, he glanced past her shoulder at the desert. "I've no issue with your company, Naabila. I didn't even mean that when I said it. I certainly don't mean it now. Plus, I've seen you in action. I have no doubts about your ability to protect yourself."

Her head tipped as if trying to decipher hidden messages in his words. "So if you do not mind my company and do not consider me someone who needs looking after, why do you question my joining you?"

It was a legitimate question, but what could he say? He didn't have a reason that would be considered acceptable, only a deep knowledge of his own character and the uncertainty of his deteriorating mind. She'd been witness to his recent insanity, and he had to wonder: didn't it frighten her? Nothing at all seemed to deter her from seeking his presence, and he didn't understand why. In a tribe full of warriors, any one of them could have come along to pass on the message to Jericho and make sure he returned for his friends. Why would the Princess be the one chosen to make the trip unless she'd specifically requested the task?

At last, he answered the only way he could—honestly. "I have failed to hide from you the demons plaguing me at every turn. I can't imagine what you must think of the things you've witnessed since meeting me, nor can I understand why you seem so intent on befriending me. You are truly good, Isolde, all the way through to your core. And I am far from it."

Isolde adjusted the bag on her shoulders, her pitying expression giving way to a furrowed brow. "You do not yet know the depths of my core being, Orion. My sins and flaws. My struggles. My scars. Perhaps you judge too quickly."

Orion glanced east, studying the brightening horizon as he fought to quell the tightness in his throat. "Still, I fear my company is not worthy of your companionship." As this truth emerged, his eyes were drawn back to hers.

Isolde didn't reply, nor did she move to walk on. After holding her gaze for far too long, he turned to the east and led off into the open desert, having no idea whether or not she would follow.

CHAPTER 10

GARDEN OF WONDERS

Several days passed as Asher, Foxx, Iris, and Seth grew accustomed to life in Celestelvyra. They explored the paths of the garden, tasted fruit they didn't know the names for, and mingled with creatures of all shapes and sizes. Asher told them they shouldn't eat the animals in the Sacred Realm, and since every animal they'd interacted with had treated them as equals, this had been an easy rule to keep.

As they walked, they searched for the magical fountain, attempting to keep track of which sections they'd already scoured. Despite having no deadline for leaving, they hoped to locate Pyhä-ki sooner rather than later so they were prepared in case someone from Arkaemor managed to rescue them. Elohim had closed the doors to protect them, even though the seven keys remained in the stone table. Surely He could open the doors just as easily when He deemed it time, whether they had the keys or not. At least, this is what Asher assured them. Whenever he pointed this out, Seth was keen to agree, if only to make sure Iris and Foxx kept their spirits up.

Iris seemed more at peace with each passing day, but Foxx's spirits had far from lifted since the moment she awoke in Jericho. Every moment dragged on with cruel uncertainty. Too many unanswered questions and unresolved feelings hung in the balance, and she appeared to have all but given up on facing them entirely.

On their fifth day, they lounged together in the grass near the pond. A pair of tigers lay nearby in the shade, and a herd of goats had gathered around the honeysuckle.

It felt strange not sitting around a fire, but since they didn't need to cook, keep warm, or ward off animals, there was no need to light one.

Iris lay on her back next to her sister, minding her own business and staring up into the night sky. She'd inquired about the mysterious stratosphere the previous evening, and Asher wondered if she continued to contemplate its depths. Neither the sun nor the moon graced Celestelvyra with its presence. The garden shone with natural light that dimmed for them to sleep and brightened when they woke, as if the life in the garden itself was the source of all light. High above them, a galaxy splattered with colorful, nebulous clouds and twinkling stars remained everlasting in the sky.

Seth picked at the grass, his brow wrinkled in thought. "If the animals don't eat each other, and we don't eat the animals, and there are no other people here, does that mean the animals will live forever?"

Foxx laid on her back with the book she'd taken from the Monastery of the Morrow in Metsa Sateen. Its dark maroon cover bore no title, but Asher had known from the moment he'd seen it what book she'd discovered.

Resting it on her stomach, Foxx looked up at Seth. "That's a great question. I was just speculating about the same thing. From what I'm reading in this book, I wonder if the Creator intended for everything He made to be immortal. In the same way Sirena is immortal."

"So only the pure poison water would be able to kill us?" Seth's face lengthened in shock.

"Pyhä-ki." She lifted the book and flipped back a few pages to where she'd left her foxglove bookmark. "But I don't know. It says here that to believe in Elohim is to have eternal life, but it also talks about people dying and going to the After. It's all very mystifying." Foxx crossed her ankle over her knee and pinched her bottom lip. "Perhaps all creatures could still die of sickness or old age?"

Asher longed to join Foxx and Seth's conversation, as he'd spent years studying the book in Foxx's hands, as well as other manuscripts and histories of the world. He glanced at her from the corner of his eye and felt sick to his stomach. They'd barely spoken since their discussion regarding his name. He didn't avoid her out of anger but of a wilted spirit. If every conversation would ultimately lead to an argument, then he didn't have the energy to fight right now. Not with her. Not for her.

He'd prayed for Elohim to fix things: to soften her heart, to ease his pain. He didn't often lack positivity, especially since falling in line with the Creator's plans for his life, but lately he struggled to remain optimistic.

Since learning about Declan's betrayal and the truth about his mother, as well as watching Sawyer die, he'd yearned to commiserate with Foxx. Cry with her. He wasn't prone to loneliness, but the fracture between them left him feeling more alone than ever. He struggled to be near her, as her hatred seemed to emanate from the very core of her being. She'd told him on their first night in the garden she didn't want to hate him, but that desire hadn't changed how she actually felt.

Iris had noticed his gloominess and made an effort to give him more attention—an action that seemed to make Foxx even more cross, though she never spoke it aloud. If it did make her angry, Asher thought that was extremely stupid and selfish. He hoped he'd misinterpreted her grimaces.

Standing, he looked up at the sky, sapphire and bedecked in stars in the middle of the day. "I'm going to have a walk."

Iris met his eyes and read his discomfort. "Want some company?"

His gaze shifted to Foxx, her nose pressed into her book. "Yeah, okay."

Iris told Foxx and Seth they would be back soon. Foxx nodded without looking at her and rolled onto her stomach, holding the book in front of Seth to show him something she'd read.

Iris and Asher disappeared down a trail leading to a grove of cherry blossoms in continuous bloom. "Talk to me, brother." She poked him with her elbow. A stone path led them off the trail and into the grove. It serpentined around the trees, optimally placed so one could walk through the twisted branches without having to duck or maneuver out of the way. As they walked, blossom petals drifted around them like giant flakes of pink snow.

"I was just thinking about my mother." Asher said. Though it wasn't entirely true, it wasn't untrue either.

"Your actual mother? Or Sirena?" Iris' eyes were drawn to a pair of martens zipping up a nearby trunk.

Asher weighed two answers with his hands. "Both, I suppose."

"Hey, you know what I just realized? You have a wicked stepmother, like in some of the old fairytales."

"Ah yes, I feel like a proper fairytale princess, dreaming of meeting a marvelous, charming, and handsome prince. Oh wait—" He directed both thumbs at his own face. "That's me."

"Clearly you're super broken up about it." Chuckling, she nudged him and pointed to a baby black bear sleeping in the crook of a tree up ahead.

They moseyed a spell longer through the cherry blossom grove, stopping on occasion to examine the powder-pink flowers. Kuki swirled around them with wings and feet like a bird and feathers as small as blades of grass. Lights shot from the henki in all directions as their magic helped the buds bloom before their eyes. Iris paused to make a branch sway so more petals spilled to the ground, and one of the kuki zipped around her head, encouraging her to stop.

Asher chuckled before dragging a hand down his face. "Truthfully, I'd prefer not to be a prince or a princess, fairytale or not."

"I've gathered that. Of course you know I'm going to ask why."

He didn't respond right away, running his fingers along a branch of blossoms as they began walking again. At their feet, fiddleheads unfurled into fern leaves. "If we—when we—kill the Queen, someone will have to take her place ruling Arkaemor."

"What about the King? Declan mentioned something. He said some people believe he is like Sirena—immortal, and others think he's human and somehow kept alive by her enchantments."

He scratched the back of his head, fidgeting his hands. "I questioned that as well, but with what we found out regarding Sirena not being my mother, I'm now thinking he's likely human. Unless she lied about him being my true father, though I haven't been able to come up with a legitimate reason for her to do so. If I'm correct and he is human, then I believe when Sirena dies, my father will die with her."

"So not only did you lose your mother, or at least find out you lost her years ago, the woman you thought was your mother isn't actually your mother… and you have to kill her, but you'll lose your father during this whole process also?"

"To rebuild the world, it must first be torn down, right?"

Her feet stopped moving, prompting him to pause with her, and she put a hand on his shoulder. "Prince Alexander Asher Aldrich, I am so profoundly sorry." Then she wrapped him in a hug and rested her cheek on his shoulder.

"You lost your parents, too, Iris." He'd needed the embrace more than he'd realized, and he squeezed her back with fervor.

"But mine were taken from me. You will feel responsible for the rest of your life for losing yours."

"You make a good point." His chuckle surprised her into pulling back to look at his face. He rustled her hair like he would Seth's, and she swatted him away. Laughing again, he said, "Thanks for understanding, Iris. Your friendship means more to me than you realize."

"Foxx understands, too, you know."

Asher recoiled, taking a step back and averting his eyes.

Iris reached out as if bracing to catch a fall. "Whoa, look at you. Talk about murdering your family: no big deal, that's life. Talk about Foxxglove, and you're practically convulsing with discomfort."

"Shut it." He turned from her to continue strolling. "I don't know what to do with her. I don't know how to change her mind or how to make her see." He knew only one Being could open her eyes to the truth, but for reasons unknown to him, Elohim seemed to be keeping His distance.

Hurrying to catch up, Iris fell into step beside him. "Listen. Let me lay some wisdom on you." Asher held his hand out as if signaling for her to proceed. She cleared her throat. "I know this might be hard to believe, but Foxx and I are both pretty stubborn." At his incredulous expression, she scolded, "Shut up." His grin widened, and she continued, waving her hands around for emphasis. "Where I'm emotion and passion, Foxx can be closed off, distant, and even cold. Her walls go up, and it can be really difficult to break through them."

"Don't I know it."

"But we both come to our senses eventually. We figure out what's real and true and logical, and we—usually at least—do the right thing. She just needs more time."

"I can't stand to be around her." His harsh admission staggered them both, but he needed to say it out loud. He'd been bottling it in for days, and he couldn't take it anymore. "It's harrowing. I can't handle the way she looks at me and the ways she doesn't. It hurts, but worse than that, it makes me so angry. How dare she behave this way? Have I not proven myself to her? Have I not done everything I could to make her see?"

Iris sighed. "Then keep your distance for a while. There's plenty to explore in the garden. I don't think we all need to stick together all the time. Unlike in Arkaemor, we're safe here. You can go off on your own, or with me." A flash of inspiration had her suggesting, "Take Seth on a manly adventure. He would love that!"

"That's brilliant actually." Plans for what he and Seth might do together began to manifest in his mind. "Very clever, Iris."

"I know. I'm a genius. I thought that's why you were talking to me."

This pulled another laugh from him, and he thanked her.

"But listen." She busied her hands pulling her hair together and laying it over her shoulder. "Take time away when you need it—don't torture yourself—but also, please don't give up on her. Keep reaching out, keep charming her. You broke through her walls before. I know you can do it again."

"It's not easy being constantly rejected, Iris."

"I actually get that." They'd left the grove of cherry blossoms and moved on to a glade of stone sculptures within a circle of chiseled bushes. Each sculpture displayed a different animal or scene. They saw a wolf howling at the moon, a fox lying within the circle of its tail, and chipmunks that seemed to be pestering a lepenna.

Asher's brows disappeared under his bangs. "Declan?"

"No." Her cheeks flooded crimson. "The other one."

"Orion?" Mouth agape, he exclaimed, "I'm shocked, Iris!"

She punched his shoulder. "Shut. Up!"

His eyes brightened as he processed the information out loud. "Wait, did Declan know? Hang on, are you telling me you fell for both of your abductors? Iris, Iris, Iris." He shook his head in mock disapproval.

"Well, when you put it that way..." They stopped in front of a statue of a stag and stared up at its exquisite detail with amazement. "No, I didn't fall for both of them. Orion was nice sometimes. I mean, he was awful, but he had moments of this astounding passion and kindness. And yeah, it was attractive, okay? I may or may not have kissed him in a dark cave right before being attacked by a giant nieda, but don't tell anyone that! Afterwards, he was pretty much consistently terrible so..." Her sentence trailed off with her thoughts.

Asher's mouth had dropped open into an O.

She punched him again. "Shut! Up!"

He roared with laughter, and she laughed, too. Bluebirds fluttered from nearby trees, chirping as the disturbance sent them flying into the air.

"My point is, I kept thinking he was coming around, and then he would say or do something horrific. It was confusing and frustrating. And very hurtful. So I get how you're feeling." Iris observed the flawless statue with her fingers under her chin. "You don't think the Creator turns living things into stone, do you?"

"I don't think so." Nudging her forward, they passed the immaculate stag and continued on. "But you didn't end up with Orion. You found someone who treated you proper."

Iris let her head fall from side to side. "And then he betrayed us. Let's not forget that. Maybe if I had stuck it out with Orion this wouldn't have happened." Asher eyed her skeptically. He'd only interacted with Orion a handful of times, but his brash demeanor was pretty well known, and he didn't imagine it had gotten much better in exile. "Or possibly I need to stop choosing men because I am apparently terrible at it. Just ignore the point I was trying to make." She sighed as they came to a split in the pathway and pointed down both. Asher gestured left to a trail outlined in white and yellow birch trees. "Hey, maybe when we all move into Castle Solís you can marry me off to a lord or a duke or something."

Asher chuckled again, though the mention of the castle drew a nearly tangible storm cloud above his head. "Who says I'm letting you lot move into the castle?"

Her mouth fell open. "Um. Clearly you need us. You've only been pining for us for like, six years or something? How will you ever manage to rule Arkaemor on your own?"

"*Pining!* Are you mad?" He shook his head as Iris laughed.

"You need us! Just admit it. You want us with you. Besides, I bet I look fabulous in an evening gown." She began striking poses as if she were posh and glamorous.

Asher hadn't let himself consider the prospect of them remaining with him when everything reached its end. At least, not since Jericho. Her unwavering assuredness that they would all be together warmed him from somewhere deep in his chest, spreading out to all his extremities. "You're right, bonkers woman. I need you and want you with me. Whatever happens."

She pushed his shoulder with her own and crossed her arms confidently. "I know it's mainly Foxx you want, but I think I add an interesting and necessary attribute to the dynamic."

"You definitely add something."

Iris smacked him with the back of her hand before stopping in front of a yellow birch. Her fingers grazed the peeling, papery bark. "Did you see this? It looks like actual gold. Incredible!"

"I've seen yellow birch trees. We have them in Reginaterra." At her annoyed expression, he added, "And yes the color is truly incredible!"

Crossing her arms, she said, "Don't patronize me, Prince Alexander. Why does the bark peel?"

Asher shrugged, and she looked appalled. "What? I can't know everything!"

"Just *almost* everything." Iris rolled her eyes and continued down the path. "What's it like? Castle Solís, I mean."

"The castle of Inaravale is an extravagantly decorated prison for the upper class."

Chuckling, she pressed, "I'm serious. Come on. It can't have been all bad. Tell me about it."

Tucking his hands in his pockets, he lifted a shoulder. "The castle is extraordinary inside and out. Outside, the grounds and gardens are kept in pristine condition. There is a huge wall surrounding the entire property that will be difficult to break through even with an army behind us. As well as a secondary wall inside the outer border. Security is very thorough. During our youth, Avaline and I weren't allowed to leave without permission." He lifted a rascally brow. "A rule I broke often."

"Naturally."

"Technically speaking, the only time we would leave aside from visiting the other royals or rulers, was to parade around the city."

"Do the people of the city know how the Queen really is? Do they know anything about her at all?"

"That's a good question. And the answer is: I don't know. They get excited when they see us. Sirena has worked very hard to keep the people of the royal city joyful and blind to the troubles throughout the rest of Arkaemor. I think many within the boundaries of Inaravale might have a hard time understanding why a revolution was deemed necessary. It's only outside the walls where her true nature shines. She has her Legion occupying cities to keep the citizens in line. She controls at least seventy percent of Arkaemor's farming and industry, which means if anyone steps out of line, she can easily cut off their supplies, leaving them to fend for themselves. She takes children as payment for petty crimes, sending them to work the farms and factories, the pleasure houses, or forcing them to join the Legion if they're old enough. Sirena rules with fear, flaunting her power even above the other royals every chance she gets. And my father is a pushover, allowing her to rule as she pleases without opposition."

Iris hugged herself and shook her head. "It's all some genius scheme to keep herself in power as the world crumbles around her. As she slowly infects and destroys everything she touches. Her corruption is so deep it even affects the animals, and I bet most people alive today don't even realize these monsters weren't here at the beginning. All of this evil has become *normal*. Children in pleasure houses? That's despicable. And what she did to Jericho... I can't imagine what else she does behind the scenes. Then she rides around in a wagon waving at her ignorant citizens who don't even know they're stumbling around blind in the dark."

Asher nodded. "Or that the darkness is growing. Imagine generations from now what the world could look like if she isn't stopped. I can't stop thinking about the darkness we saw at the outer barrier. I don't know what it is, but it has to be connected, doesn't it?"

Iris scratched her chin. "What about the other royals? How do they feel about her?"

"Well, I think it's pretty obvious how Vali feels." Asher smiled as he pictured his friend's enthusiasm when discussing the revolution. "The Kirkavalls have hated Sirena for as long as I can remember, and Sirena despises Vali in equal measure. The others though... it's hard to say. I guess we'll find out when it's time to go to war."

"You're pretty close to the Kirkavalls, aren't you? More than royal familiarity. Ingrid said they were anxious for you to return *home*."

"They truly are my family and my closest friends. Vali has been there for me every single time I've needed him, without complaint, question, or judgment. I just hope one day I'll be able to return the favor."

"It pleases me to know you had someone like that in your life." Iris nudged him, and he lifted a brow. "I just mean that, since I've learned who you are and heard your story, it made me sad to think you might not have had anyone looking out for you. I haven't had many people in my life, as you know, but I had Foxxglove, and she has always cared for me above all else, including herself. I'm glad you had someone, too."

Asher looked at his feet. "I honestly don't know where I would've ended up without their love and guidance. Who knows, I may have turned out as evil as Sirena."

"No way. Your heart is much too big."

"Thanks, Iris." They continued forward, exiting the sculpture garden and following the path until they ran into a creek they'd yet to encounter. Celestelvyra overflowed with water sources, and Asher didn't know if the Creator appreciated their beauty as much as humans did or if they were necessary for all the plants to grow. Did plants need water to survive in Celestelvyra? They didn't appear to need sunlight.

Rocks dotted the stream among felled logs, positioned just right for climbing. Iris stepped out onto the closest rock, and Asher followed her. Rather than crossing, they shuffled stone to stone up the center of the stream until they came to a rocky hill. The stream flowed toward them, tumbling down the rocks in miniature water-falls. Iris gestured up the falls, inquiring whether or not he wanted to climb to the top. He signaled for her to go ahead.

When they reached the top, they stood on the edge of a cliff towering above the garden. The stream flowed toward them from the left, turning at a sharp angle along the ridge of the rocky hill and flowing down the way they'd climbed up.

Iris sighed, and Asher lifted a brow, nudging her in question. "I miss him," she admitted, staring off into the glorious distance. They saw mountains and lakes and even a desert off to the left. "I know Declan betrayed us, but... I really miss him."

"I know."

Iris cleared her throat. "I just don't understand. Why did he do it?" Tears trickled down her cheeks, and Asher drew her into his side, rubbing her back. They stood there for a long while, looking out over the land below as she quietly wept in his arms. When her grief subsided, she leaned away from him and dried her eyes.

"I think we need to assume we don't have the whole story, Iris. I'm not saying I'm not angry at him, because trust me—I am. But he couldn't have deceived us all so thoroughly. He was a good man." Asher thought back on their discussion over sandwiches not long after the Queen's attack. They'd talked about Avaline, among other things, and Asher hadn't sensed even a slight deception in him. "But my—Sirena, I mean, is treacherous and manipulative and more cunning than we would like to believe. Perhaps he felt he had no choice. Perhaps she twisted the deal, and it didn't play out as he anticipated. Or he thought we would be there before her and would already have the weapon in hand. There are a lot of possibilities to suggest he was the man we thought him to be, and he just made a mistake."

"A mistake that got us trapped here and him dead. Probably his brother and Orion, too. Not to mention my father."

Asher shrugged. "He may yet have survived."

"If he'd just told us they were communicating, we could've incorporated it into the plan. We could've made sure we had the weapon first."

"She's a dodgy witch with magic beyond our wildest imaginations. Maybe she sealed his lips so he couldn't share, or maybe she hypnotized him and forced a deal. I saw the remorse in his eyes in the swamp. I don't believe things unfolded the way he expected."

"You have an excuse for everything, don't you?" The corners of her lips lifted as she marveled at how he always managed to pull tiny morsels of hope out of every situation.

"I'm simply proposing alternatives. Maybe he was against us the whole time and was conniving enough to trick us all. He did bloody well kidnap you, I suppose." Asher shrugged, truly uncertain himself.

After a long minute of silence, Asher noticed her pinched brow and pursed lips and dragged her from her thoughts. "Now don't you start, too. I can only handle one irate Belamour at a time." Her eyes snapped to him in a fury, but when she glimpsed his charming expression, the anger visibly dissolved. "Wow, I wish it was that easy with Foxxglove."

Iris inclined her head, looking up at the galaxy sky in thought. "You know, you could probably woo her from a distance. If you really wanted to."

Crossing his arms with a raised brow, he asked, "How exactly would I manage that?"

"Just like, never wear your shirt when you're within her line of sight or something. She'll swoon." Iris clasped her hands together and mimicked melting into bliss. Asher bellowed her name in disbelief. "What? I'm just saying, if you got it..." She gestured to his general vicinity before pinching his bicep.

"I can't believe I'm hearing this." Asher rubbed his forehead.

"Oh, come on. No need to play at being coy. What happened to playboy, heartbreaker, Prince Charming? Wandering day-drunk throughout the castle and hitting on everything that walks, I believe you said."

"What?" he yelped. "I never said that!"

She held her fingers to her chin, grinning devilishly. "Oh, perhaps that was Orion describing you. My mistake." Her hand flew to her mouth in mock bafflement. "It's true though, right? Based on everything you did say, it fits the part."

"If I ever see Orion again, remind me to whomp him."

The air filled with echoes of Iris' laughter.

C

Orion and Isolde traveled east without much conversation. The sun seemed way too hot, especially for so early in the day, but Orion hoped it would keep any potential predators hiding in the minimal shade offered by the desert structures.

As they walked, he remained in the lead. It didn't surprise him to find Isolde hanging back rather than keeping pace with him. After his confession, he'd truly hoped to look back and find she'd abandoned him—realized the truth in his words and decided to stay in the safety of her village—but his efforts had been fruitless. So on they walked, trekking across the sand in a silence that had the dry air of the Wilds feeling as weighty as the Metsa.

When they stopped for luncheon, Orion reiterated the plan. "We'll camp tonight and travel the rest of the way to the barrier tomorrow. If all goes well, we should reach Jericho late tomorrow night. It would be best to avoid camping in the snow if we can manage to walk the rest of the way."

"You are the one in a rush." Isolde popped dried cactus slivers into her mouth. "I am content for however long the journey takes."

"You aren't anxious to return to your village?" He broke off bits of the cracker-like bread she'd provided. The sun now shone from high above, beating on their backs with ferocity, though he preferred that to walking directly into it.

"What within the confines of my village could be more stirring than wandering the desert in the pleasure of your stimulating company?"

His brow pinched together, and he wondered if he'd heard her wrong. When he looked up at her, she grinned. "Oh, I see. You're teasing me."

"I would never." She winked. A cool breeze blew past them, and Isolde closed her eyes to soak it in. Sections of twisted hair lifted away from her, allowing the air to reach more of the skin across her shoulders.

Orion pulled his hair away from his face, tying it into a bun. "Trust me, you would not be the first to detest my company." He drew from the water sleeve, taking small sips to conserve it, then handed it to her.

"Why is that?"

"Because I'm an ass."

Caught off guard, a laugh erupted from her chest. She threw her hand to her mouth to keep water from spilling out. Her laugh tugged a smile from his lips, though he hadn't been joking when he'd said it.

"Do you always say exactly what you are thinking?" She wiped water droplets from her chin.

Orion eyed her intently for a long moment, knowing it would be better to lie. Safer. Instead, her golden eyes yanked the truth from him like the wind yanks a sail—forceful and unbidden. "Not always."

Humming a sound of understanding, she closed the water bag and handed it to him. "If we choose, we can camp along the barrier before crossing into Cordillera. Then travel through the snow by day and reach Jericho before sunset."

Orion thought this over, allowing himself to fantasize for a moment too long about what it might mean to spend an extra night alone with her. Then he cursed himself for the inclination. He hadn't even survived one night yet. No sense getting ahead of himself.

On cue, whispers began to manifest, tickling the insides of his ears. Jamming his pinky finger into one, he twisted it around as if he could suppress them by plugging the hole. "Seems like a waste of time to only travel for half a day tomorrow."

"Merely a suggestion. Shall we?" She indicated east, and he nodded, taking the lead.

Foxx and Seth remained as Asher and Iris had left them, laying on their stomachs with their heads hovering over the book.

Alerted by their chuckling as they entered the clearing, Seth called, "You guys were gone a long time."

"The cherry blossom trees are absolutely divine. Asher had to practically drag me away."

Seth and Foxx swiveled their legs around so they sat cross-legged as Iris and Asher approached. "I love the cherry blossoms." Seth beamed as he pictured the tumbling petals.

"I'm going to have a bath." Asher grabbed his bag from where it lay against a nearby trunk and swaggered to the edge of the pond.

Ignoring him, Foxx asked Iris, "Everything okay?"

"Define your terms. What does *okay* even mean anymore?"

"Fair point." Foxx rose to her feet to join her sister, stretching her back by lifting her arms in the air. Perhaps she would take a walk now that they'd returned. Or even a jog to get her blood flowing. It didn't make sense to get lazy and allow her muscles to grow weak just because they lounged in paradise.

Seth said, "I'm going to find some more animals to play with." He trotted off down the path toward the entrance door, giving the slumbering tigers a wide berth so as not to disturb them. The goats had settled, too, and now slept soundly beneath the honeysuckle.

The docile animals seemed to be Seth's favorite part about Celestelvyra. The garden had all kinds of creatures he'd never seen before, and Foxx had noticed him sketching several of them in his paper pad the previous day.

"Don't stray too far," Iris called after him. He waved in reply and continued on. "So, sister of mine, did you find anything interesting or helpful in—" Her words caught in her throat, startled by what she saw over Foxx's shoulder.

Rotating to chase after Iris' observation, Foxx identified the object of her fascination.

Asher stood on the side of the pond bare chested, his arms flexing as he stretched his muscles. He bent down to touch his toes, twisted his torso to one side, held it for a long moment, then twisted to the other side, and lastly stretched his chest, leaning backward with his arms stretched out on either side and his elbows bent.

"What is he doing?" Foxx's narrow eyes inflated to their limits as

Asher bent over to rifle through his bag. Iris couldn't contain her smile.

Hooking his thumbs into his pants, he leaned forward to drop them to the grass, not even attempting to cover himself. Foxx whipped her head away from the spectacle, her hand flying up to shield her eyes as her entire face turned cherry red.

Iris said, "He told us he was having a bath."

Foxx used the book in her other hand to block Iris' eyes, in case she got any funny ideas about taking in the view. "In the pond? When we're standing right here?"

"Apparently!" Iris nodded, trying to stifle convulsions of laughter.

Two of Foxx's fingers split apart, making a crack for her to see through. Asher now stood in the pond with water up to his waist and his back to them. Water glistened off his brawny shoulders and arms, dripped from his sopping hair. For a strange and brief moment, she flirted with the idea of what it might be like to paint him.

"Are you peeking?" Iris cried, louder than necessary, and Foxx's cheeks grew impossibly redder. Hearing the commotion, Asher glanced over his shoulder with a staggering grin. He even had the gall to wave at them.

"Oh my goodness, I hate him." Foxx no longer looked through her fingers.

"I can see that." Iris looked like she might die of amusement.

Foxx huffed and plopped herself back on the grass. Opening her book, she began reading again. At least, she attempted to read. Pretended to attempt to read.

Iris dropped to the ground across from her sister. Using her index finger, she pulled down the top of the book. "So, how's reading going?"

"Why are you encouraging him? You shouldn't be enjoying this. I'm your sister. You are supposed to be on my side." Without meaning to, she glanced over her shoulder to find Asher already moving toward the edge of the pond.

"Did you ever think maybe I am on your side, and that is why I'm supporting him?"

Foxx rolled her eyes and tried in vain to refocus on her book as a shadow appeared above them. Both women looked up to see Asher standing next to them drying his hair, his bicep bulging as it bent next to his head. The tattoo on his wrist peeked through pockets in his locks as he wrung them out. He'd slung the tunic he planned to wear over his shoulder, and every crevice and curve of his torso was exposed for all to see.

Foxx kept her eyes locked on her book, refusing to stare, only glancing up a few times.

"Hey, where did Seth go?" he asked, a picture of nonchalance. "I wanted to ask him something."

Iris pointed in the direction he'd walked. "He said he was going to find some animals."

"Okay great, cheers." Then Asher walked out around Iris, making sure Foxx could get the full view before proceeding down the path to find Seth.

Foxx glanced back to make sure he was gone, then fell forward with her head to the ground, groaning, as Iris gave up the fight to suppress her giggles.

CHAPTER 11

FIDÉS

Orion and Isolde walked for several more hours, roasting under the sweltering rays of the sun. It wasn't safe to travel the Grim Wilds at night, so they endured the sunshine as most travelers did. Unlike Metsa Sateen, with dangers lurking around every curve of the trail regardless of location or time of day, the Wilds were abundantly more savage when night fell. Sleeping within the confines of a cave or high up on a mesa was preferable, but as the sun began to slip below the horizon, they saw none within their sights.

Stopping to make camp, they claimed a patch of hard sand surrounded by scattered rocks and cacti, hoping the small blockade would be shelter enough. With nothing to cook and very little burnable material at their disposal, they decided against building a fire, thinking it would be safer not to draw attention to themselves. Most creatures tended to steer clear of fires as they indicated the presence of humans, but some felt no fear in hunting humans, especially in the desert.

Orion removed his pack and most of his weapons, setting them on the ground before leaning his back against one of the rocks. Doing the same, Isolde sat down next to him.

"You're not much in the way of personal space, are you?" he asked, though he didn't move away. Instead, he sat stone still, letting her upper arm rest against his. He worried if their skin separated, she would think he'd intentionally put space between them, but if their arms remained connected, she might get the wrong idea, as if he were touching her without her permission. Though she always touched him without his permission, so he supposed it was only fair.

"If you are uncomfortable with my proximity, I can move away from you."

Grumbling, he said under his breath, "I'm not uncomfortable."

Sounds ricocheted through the boundless wilderness, too obscure to discern their origin. Though used to the noises of the Wilds, experience didn't prevent the hair on the back of his neck from prickling. He scanned the landscape, trying to glimpse the source, but found nothing more than the broad desert horizon.

"I should have thought to bring sage to deter the sandhaire."

Orion exhaled in understanding. "That explains the plants around the village. I've encountered the sand sharks several times. They are not pleasant." Leaning his head back on the rock, he looked up at a sky permeated with stars, like lunae-lumen scattered across the stratosphere. The third quarter moon shone brightly, glazing the sand around them in its pastel glow. "I really hate the desert, but the sky is gorgeous here. Not as dazzling as Cordillera maybe, but still pretty."

"I would not have taken you for a stargazer, *herr* Orion." She laid her head next to his, her hair spilling across the rock's surface and mingling with his own.

"Drop the *herr*, all right? It's just Orion."

"Orion," she repeated. "I hear the stars are grand from Savanni as well."

"Is that where you're from?" he asked, genuinely interested.

She eyed him skeptically from the corner of her eye. "Are you not familiar with the cultural norms of each territory?" She held her hands out to show off the color of her skin, darker than the crevasses of the kapok tree. In the dim of the night, it looked nearly black.

"Well, yes I suppose, but that doesn't always guarantee birthplace."

She chuckled and lifted her head to pull her hair off her neck. "I was born in the savanna, but my tribe relocated to the Grim Wilds before I was old enough to remember it."

When she'd adjusted her hair and returned her head to the rock, it ended up closer than it had been originally. Orion tried to ignore it. "I did wonder about your tribe speaking Vetoräti."

"How did you become so familiar with the language?"

Sliding a hand beneath his head, he said, "When I traveled through Savanni, a girl who lived on one of the first farms I worked on tried to teach me."

"It sounds like you have traveled all over Arkaemor."

He nodded, though as he realized the conversation had leaned more toward his past than hers, he readjusted. "It's sad that you were born in Savanni but never got to experience it. You're doing a great job at looking the part, at least."

"You think I look great?" she asked, her face tilting slightly toward his.

He held his breath for a moment, catching her smile from the corner of his eye. "I just meant: you look like you're from there. Not just the color of your skin. Your attire as well. Your hair. Your—" Catching himself rambling, he pursed his lips.

"Well, thank you. I am happy to know I am making my homeland proud."

"The friends we're going to save—" He paused, realizing he'd just referred to Foxx and Iris as *friends* for the very first time. Brushing away his fluster, he continued. "The two women with Prince Alexander are sisters, both born in Alunda to the same parents, but they look very different. Foxx has olive skin and narrow eyes like her mother who's from Metsa Sateen. Iris has more of the Alundan features: continuously tanned skin, dark hair, big, auburn eyes." His voice trailed off.

"You like this Iris?"

Again, he could hear the raillery in her voice, and he couldn't fathom why pretty girls seemed to find poking fun at him entertaining. Was there something especially teasable about him, and if so, could he somehow turn it off to prevent future torment?

"She and Declan are… while I was away, I guess they bonded. I think they bonded long before that, actually." Sadness he'd been trying to avoid trickled into his voice, tightening his vocal chords. "I'm happy for them. I didn't treat her the way she deserved. Actually, I was downright horrible, if I'm being honest. Declan deserves to be happy and so does Iris." Sensing his self-loathing, the whispers came alive in his ears. Hateful, spiteful whispers.

Isolde remained silent, mulling over his words or giving him time to let his grief pass, he didn't know, but he was glad for it. He squeezed his eyes shut, moving a hand to cover them as he took long, shallow breaths.

After a few minutes, Orion attempted to speak over the words in his head. "What about you? Griffin seems annoyingly possessive."

Isolde turned to him, lifting her head from the rock. "Are you implying…?" Her mouth dropped open. "Griffin is my brother! The Nabiiga to my people!" She gagged and shivered at the thought.

"Ah, the possessiveness makes sense, then." Despite himself, he felt elated by the information. As quickly as they'd come, the whispers abated, though the persistent water remained, continuing, as always, with its incessant *drip, drip, drip.*

"We do not practice incest in my tribe as is common in others." She shivered again, and he chuckled.

"Good to know. Older brother?"

Isolde nodded. "The true heir to my father's legacy. As to your question, no. Plenty have tried to win my hand, but Father is very picky."

"Fathers often are." Thoughts of his own father's unredeeming qualities entered his mind.

"Whomever I marry would rule the tribe next to me should anything happen to Griffin." She spoke the words with the annoyance of someone repeating a phrase they'd heard numerous times. Then she exhaled and returned her eyes to the stars.

"Ah. Only the best for the Naabila of Caritas."

"Indeed."

Unwilling to allow the conversation to delve deeper, he suggested, "We should probably get some sleep. Tomorrow will be a long day." She nodded and began combing through her pack, pulling out what she needed to prepare for bed. Then he said, "You say your father is picky, yet he seemed determined to send you off with me, a total stranger, a man he knows next to nothing about. So he must not be *that* finicky. Though I suppose venturing into the wilderness isn't as permanent as courting someone who may end up ruling the tribe."

"He likes you." She rolled her eyes. "Though I cannot imagine why."

"Nor can I."

"He could not read your thoughts when we danced at the celebration. Perhaps he would feel differently about you if he had."

"What? No, I—" His brows rose as he turned to face her, wondering for a moment of horror if she could in fact read thoughts. There was all sorts of magic in the world he didn't understand. Currently, he had hallucinations of water droplets and villainous voices. Reading the minds of others didn't seem out of the realm of possibilities. Her lips broke into a smile, and he released a sigh, thankful for the darkness hiding the heat on his cheeks. "Teasing again. Of course."

Unrolling the fabric tied to her bag, Isolde laid it out on the ground against the rock and curled up on top of it. "Merry night and merry dreams, Orion."

Orion placed his bedroll diagonally so Isolde laid between him and the rock. Laying on his back, he continued to stare up at the stars until he drifted into a fitful sleep.

C

A frantic knock drew King Pollux from slumber. Only clothed in his nightdress, he grabbed his robe from the back of a chair and ambled toward the door. A Watchman stood behind Henry, the quiet servant who often brought him his afternoon tea. Tying the belt around his waist, he asked, "What is it, Henry?"

Stuttering, Henry answered, "It's… th… the Queen, my lord." He bowed his head, trembling. "S..so sorry to have woken you, Your Majesty."

Pollux sighed. "Yes, Henry, do spit it out. What is the Queen doing?"

"She's gone mad sir!"

Pollux looked at the Watchman over Henry's shoulder. "Madder than usual?" Both men nodded. With a heavy sigh, the King grabbed the lantern hanging inside his door and followed them into the hall. "Better come along, Thaddeus." The Watchman acknowledged the command and followed behind him. As they drew closer, evidence of the disturbance became clear in the crashing sounds of thrown objects and shrill, angry shrieks.

The Watchmen outside Sirena's door had gone white with horror when they saw the King. Pollux waved them out of the way. "It's fine, gentlemen. Step aside." As he entered the Queen's chambers, he saw broken bits of furniture strewn about the room, the armoire's looking glass shattered, clothing in heaps and hanging from open drawers, and the parchment requesting the whereabouts of the Belamours tacked to the wall and riddled with thin blades.

When the Queen noticed his presence, she lunged at him, pointing her finger in a fury. "This is all *your* fault, Pollux! You promoted that fool!"

"Who, my dear?" He fought to keep exhaustion from his tone.

"You should have never trusted him as your commander. He is a fraud. He has always been a fraud!"

"Hector?" This sparked his attention, drawing him further from sleep, though he kept his voice serene so as to not anger her more. "Tell me what happened, my love."

"This!" She shoved a rolled parchment in his face.

Hector and his Raptors have joined the Morrow. They are stationed in Jericho, and the city has been closed to travelers. I believe they mean to make it the base of a revolt. I am on my way to you now, but we have a long way to travel, so I sent someone ahead to warn you. I don't know what their plan is, but I suggest preparing for a full frontal assault on the castle.

I will be there as soon as I am able.

Your trusted soldier,
General Wraith

The King looked up from the letter. "When did you receive this?"

"Just minutes ago!"

Pollux wished she would lower her voice, though he knew asking her to do so would only make her louder.

"It's dated twelve nights ago!" Sirena began pacing.

"Why wouldn't he have jumped here to warn us right away?" Pollux scanned the letter again.

"He must have members in his group he doesn't trust with the knowledge. He knows to keep it secret unless absolutely necessary."

"Then he must not be worried they would arrive to attack before he returned." He stroked his chin in contemplation. "He would have revealed it to them all if he thought they needed to be here right away. Perhaps he knows they are waiting to attack."

The Queen leaned against the foot of her bed and crossed her arms. "I'm sure they need time to rebuild after Kaen destroyed the city, and we already know they're waiting for that idiot son of yours to return with the only weapon that can destroy us. Now Hector is on their side as well, set on our total destruction, and you have me locked in here like a prisoner rather than your wife. Your Queen!" She stomped her foot, appearing as a child not getting her way.

"I granted you leniency to move about the castle if you could behave. You then chose to stab Renegard—"

"Who was my man-servant and mine to do with what I wished."

The King shook his head, rolling the parchment and taking a step toward her. "You are not well, my love. I think too much time here has worn away at you."

"Do not patronize me, Pollux."

"I do not wish things to be this way." He pulled a piece of her disheveled hair from her face. She didn't appear to have bathed or changed since he'd last seen her. Looking into her eyes, he doubted she'd even slept. "You are a mess, my sweet."

"We are under attack, Pollux. Of course I am a mess."

"We are not under attack *tonight*." It pained him to see her in such a state of madness, especially when he knew he could do little to stifle it. "Let Astell draw you a bath. Or I can draw one for you now if you like. It has been a long while since I've helped you into a bath." Sirena stared back at him, and he caught a glimpse of something in her eyes, though he couldn't find the word to describe it. When she didn't reply, he said, "Get some sleep, my love. I will come back tomorrow to discuss plans on how to proceed."

"I don't need you to make plans." She turned her face from him, and he leaned in to kiss her cheek.

"Get some sleep tonight, my dear. We may very soon have a war on our hands." Then he crossed the room and left her alone surrounded by the chaotic shambles she'd created.

C

Yanked from a horrific nightmare, Orion jolted upright. He thought for sure he'd been dreaming, but the fear was so present he could taste it, and his whispers were so loud, he struggled to drag himself into full consciousness.

The sky above had vanished. Clouds not present when they'd

fallen asleep now blocked out the stars and the brilliance of the moon, blanketing everything in a darkness deeper than jet stone.

He rose to his knees, willing his eyes to see out into the cavernous desert. Fragments of movement caught his eye, coming from everywhere and nowhere in the murky pool of night. His head snapped back and forth, following the static pinpricks of motion and trying to discern if they belonged to actual creatures or if his eyes were catching infinitesimal sparks of light and toying with his imagination.

Isolde stirred. "Orion? What is wrong?" She rose to her knees and faced him before following his line of vision in search of what had spooked him. "What do you see?"

"She's here." His whispered tone held both fury and terror, and his gaze continued to comb the desert as he heaved himself to his feet.

"Who?" Joining him, she scoured the landscape. Orion spun in a circle, his fingers gripping the handle of his weapon as he tried to see everywhere at once. Isolde drew her sword and backed up to him so they covered all directions. After a long moment of searching, Isolde whispered his name, revealing her fright in the tremor of her voice. "It is not the Queen."

His whispers subsided as padding footsteps and shifting sand reached his ears, reverberating unlike any footfalls he'd ever heard. "What do you see? What's out there?"

"Verivaras," she said under her breath. "Blood thieves."

He sucked air through his teeth. "That sounds categorically horrifying."

A chorus of chirps joined the scuffing of movement on sand. "They are vile beasts of the desert. Oversized rodents with wings."

Orion's head whipped to hers. "Wings? Of course they have wings." From above, a verivara dove in front of him, causing him to flail and swing his weapon a second too late. The beast clipped his shoulder as it flew away. Another soared over their heads. Isolde swung her sword above them, catching the creature with the tip of her blade. It screeched and flapped away. More scuttling could be heard as an unseeable number of monsters encircled them. For an agonizing moment, no more attacked.

Orion growled. "I can't see a damn thing!"

"Use your other senses. Hear which direction they are coming from. Feel how close they are. You claim to be the master of personal space. Use it."

"I'd rather use fire." He crouched to rummage through his bag, then lit the end of his torch. Holding it out, he startled as another materialized from the dark in front of him. It stood on the rock with wings outstretched, its wingspan as wide as Orion's own. When it screeched a shrill cry, Orion yelped and recoiled backward, bumping into Isolde.

The bat-like creature bared its teeth, revealing fangs stained with the blood of its previous victim. Orion swung his club, striking it across the head and knocking it from the rock. It ceased movement as it hit the sand.

Enraged by the death of their companion, two more charged them, hopping like rabbits across the sand and leaping into the air as they reached their targets. One vaulted toward Orion's face. The other followed close behind. He hit the first with his club, but the second caught him off guard and scratched his forehead with clawed feet.

Then one dropped from the sky and cracked the torch from Orion's hand. Another tried to grab at the arm holding the club and received a stone to the temple for its efforts.

Suddenly realizing the empty space at his back, Orion spun and shouted Isolde's name into the black night. When she didn't respond, he retrieved the torch and shook it around in search of her. "Isolde!"

"I'm here." Out of breath, she stepped back into the light. The remaining verivaras began chirping mournfully and seemed to be retreating.

Orion gasped at the sight of Isolde's blood-splattered face. Her chest heaved, and more blood dripped from her blade. "Don't do that!" he shouted.

Returning his hostility, she asked, "Do not do what? Defend our campsite? Protect you?"

"Not so far away that I can't see you. And definitely not to protect me." He aimed to contain the anger making his muscles tremble and forced his breathing into long, slow gusts, but it did little to soothe him. When he'd realized her absence, he'd felt fear comparable to nearly losing Iris at Lacuna Kaput. Images of her horrified face seeped into the fringes of his mind, followed immediately by savage manifestations of Isolde, prone on the ground and immersed in blood, her dead eyes hanging wide open as the verivaras tore into her stomach. He quivered, squeezing his eyes shut to dispel the pictures.

"You are mistaken if you think I will run and hide when there is a battle to be fought." She took a step toward him, her determined vexation rising with each word. "I will not."

His fingers balled into fists, one around his weapon and the other around the torch, whitening his knuckles. "I'm not asking you to hide, I'm asking you to be smart and stay safe."

"So now I am an idiot woman?" She took another step closer, raising her voice in his face. "Unable to keep myself from harm unless I am within arms reach of a man?"

"That isn't what I'm saying!" He felt twisted around, lost in how the conversation had ended up there. Blood pounded in his ears, disorienting him, and he couldn't figure out why he felt so irate. She was safe. They were both safe.

"Then what are you saying, Orion?"

Her face looked so unnaturally stern that he considered pinching her cheeks, hoping it might coerce her smile to return, though he knew she would likely pummel him instead.

"I'm saying…" He fought to get his thoughts in order, as well as his breathing. "I'm saying, your father expects me to return you in one piece."

These were not the correct words to defuse the situation. Her eyes narrowed, and the heat of her rage warmed the already hot desert air.

He grasped for the sentiment that would successfully disarm her. "And we are supposed to be a team. So we need to stick together. I certainly can't have anything happen to you while you're off trying to keep me safe." She opened her mouth, but he kept talking, cutting her off. "Not because I have to return you safely to your father, but because I couldn't bear it if you were hurt." The admission seemed to take them both by surprise. Orion inhaled a sharp breath as though he could suck the words back down his throat. Still, the rise and fall of her chest slowed, and he sighed, relieved by her sobering expression.

"Especially trying to protect me," he added. Then he wondered when he'd become a man who deescalated arguments rather than kindling them. "It was in no way an insult, Naabila, I swear. I was just worried. We need to stick together."

Isolde put a hand on the hip she'd cocked out to one side. "Perhaps you are more valuable than you believe yourself to be, *herr* Orion."

He eyed her, wanting to complain again about the formality but deciding against it. "Trust me. I'm not."

She touched a trickle of blood from the scratch on his forehead. "We should clean this up."

"Not now." He pulled her hand away and wiped his face with the back of his own. "See? Fine for the moment. We can look at it when the sun rises."

From their right, a verivara went rogue from the pack and charged them. Isolde released a cry and swung her blade, slicing it down the middle. Two severed halves dropped to the sand with wings still twitching. They surveyed the area, waiting for more to attack, but the verivaras' cries faded into the distance. Isolde ran her blade across her skirt, wiping away the blood before sliding it back into its sheath. "I do not think anymore will be coming back."

Orion failed to conceal his amazement.

Isolde grinned with pride at his expression before searching the sky for the moon, catching a glimpse of it through the clouds halfway to the horizon. "Only a few hours until dawn. I do not think I will manage much sleep after all that."

He nodded and began packing up his bed. With his bag on his back and weapons securely in place, he asked, "Are you ready?"

"Yes, but we will travel without that." She gestured to the lit torch in his hand.

Orion glanced upward. "It's too cloudy. The moon won't light our way. You want to travel in the pitch black? My eyes aren't as sharp as yours, Naabila."

"Your eyes will adjust. I will help you."

"*Fidés.*" He dragged the word out as a long sigh of acceptance. A breathtaking smile spread across her lips as he extinguished the flame in the sand. "And knock that off." She looked a question at him, and he motioned to her face. "All that smiling."

She laughed. "Close your eyes."

He replied, "No," automatically but followed it up with, "Why?"

"*Fidés,*" she insisted.

After another weighty sigh, his lids slid closed. "I have no idea why I listen to you. Declan would be stunned stupid if he witnessed this."

She remained silent for a moment, and he assumed she was testing to see if he would keep his eyes shut. When he didn't peek or press her for further instruction, she spoke. "Now, listen. What do you hear? Smell if there is a scent to catch on the breeze. Feel the movement of the air on your skin. Be aware of the things in your personal space." One side of his lips curled up at her mocking tone.

A nearly imperceptible *swish* sounded by his right ear, and he tilted his head toward it. Hearing it again on the opposite side, he followed the reverberation.

His heart beat elevated with anticipation as he waited for another clue as to where she might be. He could smell her—lavender and sandalwood—and knew she must be close, but he couldn't hear a sound. Standing in the silence, he tried to listen, to feel her presence, the warmth from her body or the gentle breeze changing its course to cut around her. When he still couldn't sense her, he said her name. "You better not have abandoned me in the desert. Especially after making me out the torch."

Then he heard a whispered, "I am here."

He startled, not only from fright but from the tingling sensation filling his veins as her breath tousled the hair at the back of his neck. Fingernails scratched the skin of his left bicep, but he didn't respond immediately, tilting his head in confusion. Then he turned his entire body to the right and opened his eyes to find himself face to face with her. "How am I doing?" His chest felt tight, making it hard to catch a full breath.

"You are a quick study." She turned east, seemingly unfazed by the static energy brewing between them like a lightning storm building in the desert, and strolled away. From over her shoulder, she called, "*Veni.*"

And he did.

CHAPTER 12

ADVENTURES

The following morning, Asher and Seth rose early to begin their manly adventure. Seth was stoked when Asher suggested it and immediately began compiling a list of all the things he wanted to accomplish. Removing most of the things from their packs, they loaded up only what they thought they might need, said farewell to Iris and Foxx, and started off.

They followed the path next to the cherry blossoms, pausing so Seth could run through the tumbling petals. From there they traveled past the building holding the doors to an area they'd yet to explore—a fact that thrilled Seth to no end. "We are going to see things before Iris and Foxx see them. Then we get to tell them about all the awesome stuff we saw."

"They are going to be properly jealous." Asher directed him to go right where he and Iris had pivoted left toward the sculpture garden. Short juniper trees lined either side of the path, rising to Asher's shoulders. A flawlessly sculpted point adorned the top of each evergreen.

Seth touched the prickly needles of the juniper and yanked his hand back. "So jealous. Though I kind of miss them already."

"Me too, lad."

The row of trees broke on their left, creating an opening into a square garden, outlined with the same juniper trees, only these had grown into decorative spirals. A checkerboard garden contained squares of plants, and Seth stopped to smell the first one they came across. "Why does your voice sound like that? It sounds different from mine, and from Iris' and Foxx's."

"Because I'm from Reginaterra."

Seth ran his fingers along the top edge of a hand-painted sign naming the plant *sapphire mint*. "I know different territories have different accents and even other words. My mother taught me Bryä and Arkaen, and I know a little Kaatutan, too. But I have met other people from Reginaterra who don't speak like you do."

Bumblebee lavender came next, and as the sign claimed, bees drifted back and forth between the lavender bush and the mint. Knowing the bees would not sting him, Seth didn't avoid them and seemed amused to see them zip out of his way as he strode past.

Asher bent to sniff the lavender and wondered if Foxx might like the scent. "Well, it also depends on where you grow up in the territory. Or rather, where you spend most of your time. The higher class in Reginaterra have less of an accent, but since I spent so much time sneaking out to mingle with the lower class, I suppose I picked up some words that aren't necessarily universal to the whole territory. I had to blend in, you know?"

Fuzzy sage, royal rosemary, and *lemonade verbena* came next in the line. A spiky echidna sniffed the rosemary, and two red squirrels watched it from behind the sage.

"Mr. Magpie called me lad, too. I wonder if he was from Reginaterra. I never asked him." Seth's face fell.

"Maybe Rossnetta will know. By the way, how are you feeling about all of that? You were pretty broken up when we arrived in Kesken Ala, but you seem much better now."

"I am happy to be with Iris. And with you and Foxx too!"

At the back corner of the garden they found three plants surrounded by butterflies of every color. Chives with long, grass-like leaves and tiny pink buds; yellow fennel, its blooms spraying out from each stem like an upside down ball gown; and soft, green dill filled the three squares.

"You're allowed to like Iris the most. She is very special." Asher stopped to observe the butterflies and lifted his arm for them to land on as they drew near.

"Yeah, she is." Seth mimicked Asher's motion, and several landed on him right away. "I am sad about Mr. Magpie, and I miss him. And I am sad about what happened in the swamp. That Queen is so mean."

Asher's eyebrows rose. "I grew up with her as my mother, so trust me—I know."

"My mother was a lot nicer than that." Seth's smile returned as he thought of her. "She was amazing, like Iris."

"Tell me about her. I should like to hear a tale of a mother who wasn't awful."

"She was an artist, like Iris and Foxx's mother. She liked to paint, and she taught me how to plant things and harvest from the forest and how to cook, a little. We had chickens, and she taught me to care for them and gather eggs. She could fight with a sword, but she never taught me how to do that. She said she would when I was older. She was kind to everyone she met, and everyone loved her."

"She does sound a lot like Iris," Asher agreed, and Seth nodded.

"A lot of people were sad when she died." His chin dipped lower again, though he continued to watch the butterflies take turns tasting his skin. One landed on his nose, prompting him to cross his eyes to stare at it.

After circling the rest of the herb garden, the boys continued down the path of junipers in search of the next exciting thing. They found a stream and followed it, watching frogs hop into the water as they walked along its edge.

"Iris told me it was a nieda that took your mother."

"Yes, it was." Seth kicked a stone that went *kerplunk* when it hit the water.

Asher put his hand on Seth's shoulder. "Niedas are terrifying creatures. Hopefully once we fix everything, there will be no more of them left to hurt anyone else."

Seth considered this with a serious expression. "Are you scared? To fight the angry Queen?"

"A little." The stream led them down a hill. Rocks in the water created miniature waterfalls. Listening to the water roll from one stone to the next, Asher remembered Foxx saying she liked the sound. "I'm more afraid of what comes after, I think. I'll be made king."

Seth's eyes widened at the realization. "Yes, I guess you will. You don't want to be king, Prince Alexander?" He whispered his title and name, as he'd promised to keep it a secret.

"Would you?"

Seth thought it over. "It sounds like a very hard job. You would have to be in charge of everyone in the whole world! And Mr.

Magpie taught me that responsibility is very important." A pair of reptiles flew past them, spiraling around each other as if caught in a dance, their thin tails trailing behind them. Seth pointed. "Little dragons! I've never seen a real dragon."

Asher chuckled at Seth's expression as the dragons swirled out of sight. "Mr. Magpie sounds like a good man."

"He was. He didn't have to take me after my mother died, but he did anyway. He was my best friend." Taking Asher's hand, he drew his eyes to him. "I think you are a good man, too, Prince Alexander. Maybe you shouldn't be so afraid to be exactly who you are. In fact, I think you will make a great king."

Asher didn't have a response for that, so he changed the subject as they stopped by a blueberry bush for a snack. "Did you know I have a younger sister?"

Seth tapped his cheek in thought, crinkling his brow. His finger smudged an indigo stain on his face. "I think I knew there was a princess. I'm not sure. Where is she?"

Asher's shoulders slumped. "She's still at the castle."

"You left her behind?" Seth exclaimed.

"She is… not well. She sleeps a lot."

Seth replied through a mouthful of berries. "Maybe she's just tired."

"Maybe." Asher wiped his stained fingers on his shorts and waited for Seth to finish. "Hopefully you will get to meet her. She's eighteen, so sweet, and very pretty."

"Prettier than Iris?" Seth wanted to know, seemingly unable to imagine the possibility.

"A different kind of pretty. Her eyes are the same as mine, but her hair is lighter and hangs in spirals. She reminds me of Iris, actually. Not really in looks, but in personality."

"Is that why you like Iris so much?"

Asher eyed him, curious about the tone of his question. He wondered if, in some small and confusing way, Seth felt jealous of his relationship with Iris. "I like her because of who she is, but I suppose her similarities to my baby sister made it easier for me to connect with her right away."

Seth nodded. Then he asked a little too quickly, as if it felt awkward to say the words, "Do you like Foxxglove? I mean, not in the way you like Iris. But in the other way." His cheeks blushed a shade of pink matching the rose bushes they'd passed a while back.

Asher scratched his cheek and noticed he still had blue-stained fingertips. "We're barely speaking to each other right now."

"I know, but I can tell you both want to, and you're just being stubborn."

"How can you tell?"

Seth knelt to observe a turtle along the edge of the water. "Because you always look at each other when the other is looking somewhere else."

"She does that?" Asher asked, craving the answer more than he wished. His heart flickered with hope, and he felt tickled from the inside as wings of butterflies awakened.

"All the time." Seth stood and grinned. "And you do too, so don't try to pretend like you don't."

Asher ruffled Seth's hair, pulling him in for a side hug. Then he looked up at the mountain on the other side of the stream. "Want to climb up there?"

Seth's eyes followed the wall of the mountain from bottom to top. "Up there?"

Asher nodded. "Come on, I'll show you how."

The boys crossed the stream over an artfully crafted bridge and approached the wall with Asher giving Seth a lesson on climbing as they went.

C

Having begun their journey earlier than planned, Orion and Isolde reached the barrier to Metsa Sateen not long after first light. Before crossing, they stopped to hydrate and layer up. Isolde covered her thighs and arms in sleeves of fur, asking for Orion's assistance with tying them tight. She wrapped a scarf of foxtails around her neck and offered one to him, but he declined.

He pulled on thick, woven gloves and a jacket made from patches of fur and hide. Then he tied fur around the ankles of his boots. Looking down at the fur and primitive weapons, he said, "I look ridiculous."

"You look like a man from Caritas who is about to walk through snow. Next time, we will cover you in warrior paint as well."

"I'd like to see you try." He lifted a brow, and her grin made it clear she'd accepted the challenge. Turning to face the desert, she stared out into the wilderness. The sun rose behind her, but they stood too close to the tall trees of the Sateen barrier for it to cast much of a shadow. Still, the night sky broke with the colors of the dawn.

"Are you going to miss it?" Orion asked.

"It may be weeks until I see the sand again. The city in the snow, I feel, will be very different from what I am used to."

"It sounds as if you might be nervous, Naabila. I wasn't aware nervousness was in your typical range of emotions." He nudged her, making sure she turned to see his jesting smile.

"It is not usually. But I am."

Orion shrugged. "Well, you shouldn't be. You could run circles around any of those soldiers."

She beamed at his confidence. "A few of them, perhaps, but not an entire city. A city of tens of thousands and tall, stone walls. It is daunting."

Turning to face her, he waited to speak until she rotated to give him her full attention. "You're going to do great, Isolde. You're the fiercest person I've ever met." Her eyes shifted from his, and though her skin was too dark to confirm a blush, he thought she seemed even more nervous than she had before. "Just act like you own the place and everything will be fine. That's what I always do."

With a smile, she turned to face the wall, staring up at its iridescent shimmer as it rose to the clouds.

Orion followed her gaze. "Once we cross over, we'll be walking in snow. Remember to think of Jericho when you step through. Even if you can't picture it, the barrier will drop you off as close as possible. We should arrive at the city by sundown if we can keep up the pace."

Isolde gestured toward the barrier. "After you."

"See you on the other side." Orion pulled the fur-lined hood over his head as he stepped through. Last time he crossed a barrier, it had been the long, suffocating hallway from the In-Between to the Monastery, and he'd been lugging Declan over his shoulder. Jumping from the Grim Wilds to Cordillera felt significantly easier, though the temperature change was still jarring as he stepped from blistering heat into a foot of snow. When his lips broke through the dense wall, the cold took his breath away.

Isolde stepped through right after him, her breath catching in her chest as it was introduced to the frigid temperatures. Her eyes widened as she took in her surroundings. A hand rested on her chest as though it might help her breathe more sufficiently in the higher altitudes. Looking down at her buried feet, she said, "I am not sure I am going to like snow." He laughed, and she shot him a faux glare. Then she looked ahead of them, and her lips parted in amazement. "Wow."

"Extraordinary, isn't it? The view."

"Truly. I have never seen anything like it." She surveyed the landscape from left to right, taking it all in. White-capped mountains reflected the rising sun, and though peaks rose in front of them, she could see glimpses of murky green in the valley stretching down the center of the territory. "This is Cordillera. I have seen mesas and dunes, but nothing like these mountainous summits. They are immense, towering over the land below like giants of tree and stone. It is so beautiful."

"I remember seeing it for the first time years ago. It took my breath away."

Turning around to examine the wall behind her, Isolde found it blacker than pitch and glittering like the stars. "What is this?"

"The outer wall. You've never seen it? I'll tell you about it while we walk." Before he turned away, something caught his eye. Bending down, he saw ground darkening near the barrier, seeping out into the snow more than a foot. "What do we have here?" The grass and dirt looked covered in soot, as if the wall were bleeding darkness into the ground. Tendrils of the black cut into the snow, melting everything in its path.

"It doesn't normally look this way?" Isolde asked.

"Not anywhere I've ever seen." He looked up the wall as he stood, wiping his damp palm off on his pants before returning it to his glove. "We'll bring it up to them when we're in Jericho. Maybe they've already seen it. Are you ready to get moving?" She nodded, glancing sheepishly down the path covered in snow. "All right. This way, Naabila." Then he turned down the mountain pass leading toward Jericho.

C

As the boys embarked on their manly adventure, Foxx and Iris planned to spend the day together, too. They packed, filled their water bags in the falls, and headed off in the direction opposite of Asher and Seth. As a group, they had already traveled some of this path, but Foxx remembered them coming to a Y in the road and turning left. So they decided when they returned to the Y, they would head right instead.

For the first time since entering Celestelvyra, they brought their weapons along with the idea of searching out an interesting place to spar. Foxx hoped she would find somewhere to shoot her bow, as her arms ached for the pull and release of the string.

At the apex of the Y stood an ancient tree. In truth, it looked like two trees merged together: one with bark the color of sand and the other with dark brown, almost red. They seemed to grow from the same roots and twisted together so flawlessly, Foxx thought it couldn't have happened by accident. Since she'd never seen anything like it before, she wondered if it was a species only found in Celestelvyra.

Turning right, the girls followed the path through the wooded area, loving the feel of being back in the woods again. Iris said, "I think Metsa Sateen is my favorite of all the territories so far. I missed the trees."

Foxx gaped. "I'm astounded to hear that since when we were in the Metsa, you whined constantly about all the rain and humidity."

"I know, I know. I hated the rain." She paused to run her fingers across the smooth exterior of a fascinating tree, its bark seemingly painted in streaks of colors. She glanced at Foxx, who also stroked the trunk. When Foxx shrugged, Iris said, "Maybe Asher will know what it is." Then she turned and proceeded to walk the trail. Foxx rolled her eyes before hurrying to catch up.

Iris' fingers brushed the trunk of each tree they passed. "But the trees in Sateen were spectacular. So were all the colorful flowers and the delicious fruits, and do you remember the canopy of birds?"

"How could I forget?" Foxx thought back on how Orion had seemed like an actual human for the first time beneath the canopy of parrots.

"And I like the way the trail forces you to follow its will." Iris gestured to the pathway and the trees surrounding it. "It's sort of thrilling not being in control of where the path is taking you."

"You know, I think Reginaterra has forests, too, but it's far less tropical. Maybe that one will end up being your favorite."

"Do you expect we'll be spending a great deal of time in Reginaterra?"

The question caught Foxx off guard, and she stumbled to get her words out. "Well, if we're attacking Inaravale, then I assume we'll see some of it."

"But we wouldn't be spending, like, extra time there. After?"

"I'm not sure what you're insinuating, Iris, but if you want to spend some time traveling Reginaterra at some point after the Queen is dead and gone, then sure, we can spend extra time there after. I bet Seth will want to see it, too."

They hiked for a while, spending most of the time in silence except when pointing out things along the trail. When they breached the edge of the forest, they took in a panoramic view of the landscape. To the left lay an orchard with apple trees planted in parallel rows. To the right, a cobblestone path led away from their current trail and up a hill toward a structure. It had no walls, but tall columns surrounded in ivy lined the outer edge. The outline of a rectangle rested atop the columns like an open roof.

Iris threw a thumb at the mysterious configuration. "Check it out?" Foxx nodded and strode uphill, following the path to a wide set of steps leading into the building.

Scattered about the platform were large potted plants with leaves that draped toward the ground. Roots had burst through cracks in the pots as the foliage outgrew its container.

"What is this place?" Iris asked, bending to examine one of the pots rising just above her knees.

"It's like a stage? Or an elevated area to host parties?" Foxx did a slow turn. Heaps of stone rubble and knee walls crumbling with age were scattered about. A statue of a man clad in armor and holding the hilt of a sword with its tip touching the ground stood centered on the left side, and on the right stood two more cylindrical columns holding up nothing.

In the middle of the space, Iris found the circular walls of a well, but when she peered into it, she thought it must have dried up. She slid a stone from the top edge and listened as it clattered down into the well, hearing it crack into pieces when it hit the bottom. "It could make an excellent battle ring. Wide open for movement, but with a few challenging obstacles."

"You make a good point." Foxx observed the platform in a new light and soon found a sword drawn at her throat.

"It's a good thing we came to fight then, my lovely sister." Iris stood with her short sword aimed at Foxx. Its sister dagger, Thorn, she held in defense. Foxx grinned at the challenge and shrugged her bow and bag from her shoulders. Iris withdrew and did the same, placing her items along the outer edge of the platform.

Foxx drew her own sword, a dagger sized in between Iris' twin blades, and joined her sister near the center of the arena. They circled each other with weapons raised, taking in the obstacles in their peripherals and waiting for the other to strike.

Iris often attacked first, being the less patient of the two women, but it seemed she planned to take a different approach this time. She stepped out around a small stack of bricks, widening their circle by putting debris between them.

Foxx stepped forward, pressing into the circle Iris had set, and sliced her blade in a diagonal arc.

Iris moved left to avoid the strike. "So I've been wondering, if Asher becomes king, will we stay with him in the castle?"

Foxx stilled, making Iris do the same. Her eyes widened incredulously, then narrowed as she shifted her weight back and forth between the balls of her feet. "Why would we?" They began rotating again, crossing one foot over the other.

Iris eyed her skeptically. "You already know the answer to that question." Again she stepped left to avoid Foxx's attack. Foxx struck, and rather than dodging, Iris blocked the blow with Bloom, sending the ring of metal echoing through the arena.

"I'm sure Alexander will make a fine king, but I see no reason to impose on him by asking to stay there." Foxx moved out around the warrior statue and struck from Iris' right. Iris met her blow with a *clang*. Foxx spun around the sculpture angling to take the opposite side, but Iris ducked and rolled away.

"No reason? Not one single little reason?"

As Iris rose to her feet, Foxx rounded the statue and came at her with swift jabs. Iris countered each one, the metal clanking together with sharp peals.

"I already told you, Iris. It's over between us." Foxx lunged forward, but Iris whirled out of the way.

"That isn't what your face implied when you saw him with his shirt off." A small set of steps leading nowhere rose to Iris' right, and she backed toward it. Foxx rotated, swinging her sword in a wide arc. Iris leapt back, bending her stomach out of the way and ascending the steps.

"Just because I find a male's physique attractive doesn't mean I want to move into his giant castle." In three strides, Foxx stood next to the steps, her blade angled upward.

"Suppose he invites us to stay." Iris flawlessly dodged and deflected each strike.

"He won't." Foxx swung low, and Iris jumped to avoid it. "You aren't even fighting!" Foxx lunged again. Iris blocked. Foxx was already out of breath, her face hot with exertion and fury. She took a step back without lowering her weapon. "Fight back, Iris. You were the one who wanted to spar."

"I am sparring."

Foxx struck again. "You're blocking."

"Blocking is part of sparring. Perhaps he will ask you to be his queen. Then what will you do?"

Foxx raced up the stairs with an onslaught of quick, back and forth swipes. Iris parried and leapt off the other side, but Foxx didn't cease. She chased her, blow after blow, twisting her wrist in a serpentine. Iris stepped to avoid debris and continued to block, though her heart began to race as she fought back against her sister's ferocity. Foxx raised her blade high, bringing it down in a vertical strike that vibrated up Iris' arm.

Iris flipped Thorn around so it pointed out the bottom of her hand and slashed it back and forth, at last attacking back. Their hilts locked together. Iris swung Bloom, and Foxx used her free hand to grab her sister's arm, preventing the blade from getting too close. "Why don't you make it easier on all of us Foxxglove and admit that you are in love with him! It's stupid for you both to be in this much pain when you're perfect together. Don't you see that?"

Foxx pushed to separate their blades and kicked up a pile of brick dust in Iris' face. With a fierce battle cry, she plowed forward. Staggered, Iris fumbled to block, managing to make an X with both blades and catch the attack. She blinked, willing her eyes to clear as she pushed back. Foxx released her, only to strike again, swinging her sword so fast Iris could barely counter it as she retreated.

Something hard at her back impeded Iris' progress, but Foxx continued forward, crossing her blade with Bloom and creating an X over Iris' chest that pinned her to the column. Then she grabbed the wrist holding Thorn and slammed it against the brick above her head.

Locked in place by Foxx's rage, Iris bristled. She looked more aggrieved than afraid. "He doesn't want to be king, you know. I know you think he used us to grab a throne, but if you ever listened to his actual words rather than letting your pain make assumptions, you would know him well enough to see the truth. Not only does he not want to rule, he certainly doesn't want to murder his father and the woman he spent his entire life believing was his mother in the process. Maybe you should try to cut him a little slack, Foxx. He made mistakes, yes, but you surely aren't perfect either." Iris shoved and freed herself. Stepping around the column, she sat down with her back against it and her feet dangling off the edge.

Foxx could hear blood pumping in her ears. A look down revealed her drenched clothing and the flakes of ice receding on her fingers. She slumped on the opposite side of the column, her arms resting on her knees as she fought for breath. Then her chin fell to her chest as two teardrops slipped down her cheek.

CHAPTER 13

BEST LAID PLANS

When the crest of the walls came into view, dense snow began to tumble from the clouds above, and Orion hoped it wasn't an omen signifying what was to come. Isolde held her palm out in astonishment as the flurries drifted around them, and he was reminded of Iris and Foxx's first experience with snow. They'd observed it as if the frozen water droplets might hold some secret mystery of magical riches.

Isolde did exactly the same. "What a sensational presentation." She held both palms to the sky. "I suppose I could come to like snow, just a little."

Orion glimpsed their surroundings, a landscape frosted in shimmering white. It shined with perfection, untouched from a recent coating. It had been years since he'd noticed how extraordinary the sight truly was. Walking the trail from the barrier to Jericho so many times had dulled its splendor. This time he observed the area in a new light. Each summit lay blanketed in snow. Mountain walls between the varied peaks displayed faded violet and powdered ultramarine. Spires of obsidian stone jutted out through the layers of ice, willful bits of land refusing to be hidden or perhaps wishing to take in the remarkable view themselves.

Orion's gaze returned to Isolde, and he found himself unable to look away as she reveled in the new phenomenon. Her dark skin contrasted with the brilliant white in her background, and he couldn't recall a more extraordinary picture in all of his memories. "You're right. It is pretty sensational."

His meditative tone drew her eyes, and she smiled. "Shall we press on?"

As predicted, they reached Jericho right before the sun disappeared behind the mountain ridges. Rather than the iron gates hanging open and guarded by a single soldier in soft grays and bold purples, they found the gates chained shut and three Guards standing beyond the bars.

They approached the gates side by side, and Orion spoke. "Guard, we seek entrance."

"Jericho is not currently open to travelers." The tallest of the three Guards stood at the front, with the other two at his flanks. Though Orion didn't recognize him, he thought the man to his left looked familiar. "You will have to find another location for sanctuary."

"My name is Orion O'Connell. We are here to speak to Commander Hector Kayvan. We have news regarding the team sent to Celestelvyra with Prince Alexander." Orion searched the expressions of the men, seeking evidence that he'd captured their attention.

The Guard up front whispered back to the others. They seemed to mull it over for a long moment, debating whether or not the wildly decorated strangers could be trusted.

"We seek audience with the Morrow," Isolde said, her tone authoritative but kind.

The soldier looked Isolde up and down, then looked at Orion, considering. Whispering again to his comrade, he nodded and began unlocking the chains. "And the Morrow will greet you." Orion lifted his brow at Isolde, impressed to discover she knew a secret password he'd been unaware of.

When the gate doors swung open, the familiar Guard said, "You may wait in here. I've sent someone to retrieve Commander Kayvan for you. Stay in the entrance plaza until he arrives, and don't move out of sight without permission. We have been instructed to take down intruders without question, so leave no opportunity for suspicions." Orion nodded and strolled past the Guard.

"Go in peace." Isolde dipped her chin as she walked by, and all three Guards returned her blessing.

When the clanking of chains and locks sounded behind them,

Orion allowed his gaze to travel the plaza, noting how very different it looked from the last time he'd seen it. All the buildings around the outer edge had cracked and crumbled as if collapsed by an earthquake. The pale stone fountain at the center, once a huge, beauteous ram encircled by a crescent moon, was a heap of toppled stone.

Stopping by the fountain, Orion turned to face her. "How did you know the right words to say?" His eyes continued to scan the area, landing on what remained of the table he and Declan had occupied outside the pub. Fragmented memories of that day began to fill themselves in: Raven had held a knife to his throat before sitting at the table with them. Hector arrived and provoked Declan into lunging at him. Explosions followed, and Hector and Raven had run off. Orion had tried to flee the city, but Declan insisted they find the girls first—find Iris. In reluctant agreement, they'd set out in opposite directions.

"Perhaps if you were a lover of the Morrow, you would know them also," Isolde teased. Her eyes followed the movement of his.

"I need to be more careful what I say around you." His gaze locked on the back alley where he and Declan had stood before splitting up. "You have a habit of returning my words with hostility."

"Most of what you say is hostile to begin with. At least I repeat everything back with sarcasm and a smile."

Pulling his attention from the alley, he refocused. There was no time to explore things now, but perhaps while in Jericho, he could attempt to rediscover what he'd lost. "I can't believe how different this place is. It's only been a few weeks since I last visited." He pointed across the square to the table, on its side now and absent of chairs. "Declan and I sat right there, watching the gate for Iris and Foxx to make their escape."

"Escape?" Isolde asked.

Orion swore internally, cursing for forgetting himself. Isolde didn't know anything about his past or how they'd come to meet Iris and Foxxglove. Her first experience with him had been heroic stupidity. The man he'd been before that sacrificial moment was a stranger to her, and his heart grew heavy at the knowledge of what she would do when she saw him for who he truly was and not who he pretended to be.

In a moment of brave integrity, he turned to face her and took both of her hands in his own. "Isolde. I want you to know, before I reveal this truth and you run from me, that the man you have encountered is far closer to the person I wish to be than the man who existed in this skin before our meeting."

Absorbing his words, she attempted to see into the vast depths of the ocean swaying inside his irises.

He dropped her hands and took one step back, needing space to unleash such an enormous confession. "Please pardon my blunt explanation, but we don't have time for dancing around it. Still, I would rather you hear it from me now while we are still alone. The truth is, Declan and I kidnapped Foxx and Iris in Metsa Sateen. That's how we ended up traveling together." Isolde's eyes grew wide, and Orion glanced around to see if Hector had arrived yet. "We traveled the rest of the way through Sateen and into Cordillera. They left us up the road from here, but we knew they intended to travel to Jericho, so we followed them. We waited by the gate, hoping to catch them on their way out—Declan's brilliant plan." He dropped his head, a pain prickling his stomach as suspicions of Declan's prior feelings for Iris were confirmed. "I know how horrible it sounds. There's no way to sugarcoat it, and I wouldn't want to if I could." He sighed, again scanning the area and hoping Hector would appear before she had a chance to respond. He speculated on whether or not she might leave him right then. Or perhaps inform Hector of his crimes, hoping he would arrest him, lock him up, and throw away the key.

The whispers assured him it was a fate he deserved.

"I'd like to say my reasons were legitimate, and maybe they were, but they're still just excuses that allowed me to justify bad behavior." His gaze met hers, desperate to read her thoughts. "I'm sorry, Isolde. I tried to tell you already: I'm not one of the good ones, and I'm definitely not worth protecting." He couldn't decode her expression. His heart ceased beating as he awaited her response, refusing to resume until it had its answer.

Her eyes found the overturned table, then his own, then the ground at their feet. She bit her lip and looked at him. "There is more to this story?"

"Much more. Years and years more. You really have no idea what you stepped into when you speared that nieda, Naabila."

"I see." Another look of confusion preceded a long moment of contemplation. "Am I safe with you?"

The question pierced his chest, despite its validity. Being not only a woman but a princess, of course she worried about foul play.

She was a princess, and he was a villain.

A monster who'd ripped two innocent maidens away from their prince.

He thought about his answer before speaking. "I mean you no harm, and I never have. I've never lied to you or tricked you. It is my intention to save them from Celestelvyra—not to use them for my own purposes—but so Prince Alexander can lead us to war against Sirena. I guess you could say my allegiances have changed —have been in the process of changing for quite some time, if I'm honest. It just took me a shameful amount of time to realize it."

"Orion O'Connell." Hector's voice had Orion spinning around to find him flanked by Jax Blackmoor, his second in command, and Raven Nightshade, his third. Orion's heart restarted and now pounded so intensely he could feel it in his stomach.

"We thought you might have perished in the Queen's attack." Raven's tone suggested she may have hoped that to be the case. She stood in full gear with two rows of throwing knives across her chest, multiple blades sheathed at her hips, and a broadsword at her back. Orion wondered if she'd been wearing the weapons already or if she'd suited up just for him. Her eyes drifted to Isolde before returning to his. "Where have you been hiding?"

"A pleasure, as always, to see you Raven." Orion noticed the hostility in his voice, exactly as Isolde had pointed out, and attempted to reduce it. "Sorry to have worried you. Queen Sirena held me captive. Then a few days ago, she dropped me at the gates to Celestelvyra and tried to trap me in the In-Between." A swirl of whispers seemed to spiral above his head. His eyes glanced up of their own accord, and he knew he must be imagining actual words floating in the air before drifting away on the bitter wind.

All three looked at him with surprised eyebrows, Jax's bushier than ever as flakes of fresh snow landed atop them. Hector seemed to survey the cuts and bruises covering his exposed skin, and Orion thought he might believe his words on that evidence alone.

Jax surveyed Isolde, taking in her fierce form, wild attire, and the spear in her right hand. "Who's your friend?" His hand lifted to the pistol at his hip.

Orion stepped to the side. "I am pleased to introduce you to Isolde of Caritas, a village in Vallemortis. We have news of Prince

Alexander and a message from her father, Naaba Kaatachi. Naabila Isolde, this is Commander Hector Kayvan, Lieutenant Jax Blackmoor, and Raven Nightshade, of the King's Legion."

"*Formerly of*," Raven corrected.

Isolde dipped her head. "Delighted to meet you all."

Orion continued. "We've traveled a long way. If you would provide us with some food and water, we'll share all we have seen."

Hector's hickory eyes examined him for a moment. Running his fingers across his flattop to dispel the water droplets of melted snow, he glanced between Raven and Jax. "If this is some kind of deception O'Connell, know that every soldier within the city walls, both crimson and violet, are under my command. I will not hesitate to execute you on the spot should you deserve it."

His statement caught Isolde off guard, and her face darkened with protective anger, her hand tightening around her spear.

The movement thrilled Orion more than he cared to admit, as it meant that somehow, something in her still found him worth defending. He grinned. "I wouldn't have it any other way, Commander."

With a final nod, Hector tucked his hands into his pockets, curled his shoulders from their perfect posture to combat the breeze, and said, "This way."

When he turned, Raven followed after him, but Jax extended his hand. "After you."

Orion's gaze met Isolde's, attempting to sort out what she must be thinking. Her returned smile warmed him, and he held out the crook of his elbow. Brilliant smile widening, she wove her arm through his. The feel of her heat drew memories of her body moving beneath his hands at the celebration, twisting his stomach in knots.

C

Foxx and Iris made an unspoken decision not to travel any further into the garden and returned to the waterfall instead. Without a word to Foxx, Iris laid down in the grass and let her eyes fall closed.

Asher and Seth had not yet returned, so Foxx used the opportunity to take a bath. Pulling all the clothing from her bag, she picked what she would change into—shorts and a sleeveless tunic—before undressing and gliding into the pond. It was the perfect temperature: not too cold like most natural water sources, and not too warm either, a blessing since her whole body still felt feverish with anger.

As she waded around in the pond, allowing the water to cool her flushed skin, Foxx reflected on Iris' words. Her frustration toward her sister's pushiness reignited as she played through the scene, and she decided she hated Iris a little for not leaving it alone. Wasn't she allowed to take as much time as she deemed necessary to heal from her heartbreak?

Pink light caught her eye, and she saw several kuki on the opposite edge of the pond, sprinkling magic into the lotus flowers. She immediately worried about the existence of nyädi, and her eyes scoured the depths. No lights shone from below, and she hoped if they did live in the pond, they would be docile, like all the other creatures in the garden. Memories of the lagoon monster had her swimming closer to the shore.

She let her mind drift to thoughts of Asher as the future King. Instead of picturing herself, she pictured another woman, a stranger created by her imagination, sitting on a golden throne at his side. She wore a jewel encrusted crown and held his hand.

Foxx's stomach clenched, contorting into a nauseating spiral of emotion, and she blinked the images away.

She hadn't been certain killing Sirena would also mean killing his father, but hearing Iris confirm it struck a cord of pity in her heart. What a horrible thing for Asher to have to do. She couldn't fathom why his Creator had decided such a task needed to be carried out by the heir. Could they be certain the prophecy about the Monastery of the Morrow came from Elohim to begin with? What if it had been written by a group of old men with poetic aspirations instead? If so, perhaps she could do it for him and free him from the burden of murdering his parents. Though she'd never killed anyone before, she would take the blood on her hands if it would spare him that pain.

A wave of queasiness consumed her senses, plunging her into the water. She fought for strength, pushing herself up into the air, but her breathing was ragged, and her head spun.

A vision, she realized, now conscious of the signs. She rushed toward the shallows to gain purchase and keep her head above water. Consuming images appeared murky and opaque until Iris materialized before her, melting into her vision from the inside out. She wore the most divine gown Foxx had ever laid eyes on: yellow as the morning sun and corseted around her upper body before curving over her chest like the top of a heart. The lower half spilled from her hips, tumbling to the floor like a tulip turned upside down. Crystal jewelry hung around her neck and bedecked the braids in her hair. She looked stunning.

Another girl stood on Iris' opposite side, partially blocked from view. Their arms were comfortably linked, relaxed in the way friends might be. Iris threw her head back in laughter at something the girl had said and grabbed a piece of food from a tray held out to her by a man dressed in a shiny, black suit. He smiled at them, joining in their laughter.

In the background, she saw a doorway leading to a ballroom with extravagantly painted walls, golden decorations, and lavish chandeliers. The room overflowed with people dressed in evening wear.

Then, to Foxx's unshakeable horror, Asher approached the girls in an ivory suit with gold effects and a golden circlet sitting crooked atop his head. He bowed to them like a gentleman and extended an elbow. Iris accepted his arm, and the other girl whirled around him to take the other. As she spun, her face was no longer hidden by Iris' pinned-up braids. Blonde curls framed shining emerald eyes that matched his own.

Not just a girl, but his sister, Princess Avaline.

Not just a party, Foxx realized—but Asher's coronation.

The pictures in her head grew blurry again as the vision melted away like water poured over freshly painted canvas. She found herself returned to the pond, breathing heavily, though not in a full panic as she had been with previous visions. Letting her head rest on the shore, she fought her way back to consciousness. When all that remained was a lingering headache behind her eyes and the tingling of her fingertips, she lifted herself to look around. Iris slept where she lay in the grass, and Asher and Seth remained out of sight.

Thankful no one had been around to witness her convulsing, she drifted back into the deeper water to finish bathing. As she rinsed, she reflected on her body's reaction to this vision in comparison to others. Had it been less challenging because of her location, or had she grown more accustomed to the experience? Perhaps the vision itself wasn't as stressful, and so the physical reaction had followed suit.

Her mother's visions had seemed to grow worse over time, not better, but the more Foxx learned about her, the more she realized how often her mother must have had them. They'd begun long before Foxx and Iris emerged into the world, so perhaps not all produced such heinous reactions. Maybe some simply came and went like a dream.

Submerging her entire body, Foxx separated hair with her fingers as her thoughts wandered further into what she had seen. It seemed a strange foresight in comparison to the others—peaceful rather than scary—and she wondered exactly who decided what prophetic visions she had access to. Could it be a fluke of nature, not driven by any force at all? Future realities compelling themselves into the past in an effort to alter their present? If so, then what had been the purpose of this message? Was she to prevent this outcome?

Replaying it in her mind, she analyzed the girl who could be none other than Lady Avaline. She wore a dress similar to Iris' but brilliant ruby red instead of yellow. Fair skin indicated she may not spend much time out in the sun.

Asher seldom mentioned the Princess. The subject burdened him, though she didn't know why. She thought he'd said Lady Avaline was sick, but the charming girl in the vision seemed fine. Better than fine. She looked vibrant, happy, and very much alive.

Another troubling thing was her lack of presence in the vision. It could have been from her point of view, like the others, but why would she stand there watching him escort Iris and his sister into the room? He hadn't even looked back at her. Did she stand at another's side? Or alone? Or was she absent entirely and seeing the vision through the eyes of a bystander?

Despite what she'd said to Iris, she thought she likely would attend the coronation if invited. It might not be so bad if she got to spend the night dressed up like Iris and Avaline had been.

Perhaps the purpose of the vision was to offer hope rather than prevention. She still had no way of knowing whether her visions were set in stone or mere possibilities, but maybe hope was all it would take to ensure triumph.

Maybe hope was the key to dragging herself from the hole she'd been collapsing into from the moment she'd heard the snap of her father's bones, his body crumpling to the ground right in front of her.

From the moment Declan betrayed them.

The moment Sirena spoke only to her as the city of Jericho crumbled around them.

And from the moment Asher revealed himself to be the future King of Arkaemor.

C

No one carried a torch, as the third quarter of Ammil shined brightly enough to light their way.

At Orion's side, Isolde took in the city, looking disconcerted as they traveled through streets littered with rubble and destroyed structures. Blood stains and black soot soiled buildings and walkways, and she intentionally stepped out around the patches when she could. Leaning closer to him, she asked, "Queen Sirena did all this?"

"With the help of her drakinferno, yes."

"I did not know drakinfernos could be tamed."

Jax said, "I'm not sure if *tame* is the word I would use to describe that beast."

Isolde looked at him over her shoulder. "It destroyed the Monastery here in the city?"

"Killing more than 3,000 people along with it."

Orion squeezed her arm as another flash of anger crossed her features. "She came under the guise of seeking Iris and Foxxglove, but I suspect the Monastery was her true target. From what Declan told me, she found the women soon after arriving but continued her assault on the city anyway."

"That's true." Raven didn't turn to face them as she spoke. "Dom and I watched the whole thing."

Hector slowed to walk closer to Orion, letting Raven walk ahead. "Whether or not she targeted the Monastery, she reacted on impulse. Truthfully, I don't think she knew what she was doing when she showed up here." He shook his head, as if rattling his brain might make the answers more comprehensible. "You knew we came here under her orders in search of the Belamours."

"Iris and Foxx Belamour," Orion clarified for Isolde in case she hadn't yet heard their surname.

Hector glanced back at them with a nod. "But within hours of sending us, she produced a full-fledged blitz on the city. I don't think she would have bothered reinstating the Reko Raptors and sending us here if she already had plans to attack. Especially given what the Raptors represent to her personally."

"You think she was responding emotionally? On impulse rather than because of some diabolical plan?"

Hector shrugged. "I can't be sure. I didn't speak with her when she was here, and I obviously haven't since, but I know she seemed to be losing it the last time I was with her. She was scared. And angry."

"Could we use this to our advantage when we attack?" Orion rubbed his palms together and blew hot air into them. Isolde smiled and followed his example.

Hector said, "I have no idea what state she'll be in when we finally breach the castle walls. I wish we had someone on the inside reporting to us."

"Is there no one you trust still within the castle grounds?" Orion's eyes swept the alley of a cross street, thinking it looked familiar. Scanning the area, he hoped to jog his memories, but things always looked different in the dark, and his efforts triggered little more than fragments of possible recollections.

"Some." Hector mulled it over. "Unfortunately, I brought most of them with me." He glanced back at Jax. "This wasn't exactly a plan. There are some who remain that I've considered reaching out to, but I have no way of knowing whose allegiances might have changed. I doubt most of those who were faithful to me before would follow me into desertion."

When they arrived in the courtyard in front of the Monastery of the Morrow, Isolde looked up at the ruins with unadulterated sorrow. "It is destroyed." She placed a hand over her heart as she whispered a prayer under her breath.

Crates had been stacked against the back wall, with other supplies spread throughout. To the left, they saw rows of injured citizens, and to the right, makeshift beds for the workers beneath a weeping cypress. Above them, a fabric roof spread across the top of the courtyard.

Though the setting sun had sent many home for the evening, evidence of the operation was obvious. The few people still moving about the courtyard paused in their work to observe the newcomers.

"How could she do this to her own people?" Isolde asked. "What kind of queen could do this?"

Hector shrugged. "We are in the process of recovering and rebuilding, but as you can see, there is a lot of work to be done. It was much worse two weeks ago. We've been moving people around as new areas are cleared out. The palace took in a great number of civilians, too. We're rebuilding what is deemed high priority and training new recruits in preparation for what's to come."

Raven whispered something in Hector's ear, and he nodded. After a glance at Jax, she left them, exiting the courtyard through an alley to their right.

Hector watched her go before returning his attention to Orion. "I hope you're prepared for war, O'Connell, because war is what's coming."

"Not until we free Prince Alexander from Celestelvyra. War is pointless unless Sirena can be put down."

Hector glanced at Isolde in distrust. His eyes met Jax, who had already been studying the Princess with a suspicious expression.

Orion noticed their hesitation. Though both were familiar with Caritas, he doubted either of them had interacted with anyone from the village personally, and he knew they must be leery of speaking such secrets with a stranger. "She's with me. She can be trusted. Plus, her father and her tribe want to join us."

"I'm not even sure you can be trusted, O'Connell." Hector scratched his chin, still seeming to consider his options.

Orion lifted a shoulder. "Prince Alexander hasn't returned. It doesn't seem you have much of a choice at the moment."

"We only expected them back yesterday." Jax folded his arms across his chest. He wasn't layered up in battle gear like Raven but instead wore a heavy jacket buttoned all the way up to his chin. "They could yet return. Or perhaps you have thwarted their journey, and that is the source of your certainty."

Orion's brow wrinkled. "What would be my motive in doing so?"

"You were gone when the dust settled. Perhaps you've been in league with Sirena all along."

Feeling the tension build in his shoulders, Orion released Isolde and guarded himself with crossed arms. "So first I'm a traitor to the Thrones, then I'm a spy for them? I'd forgotten how highly you thought of me, Blackmoor." Jax smirked, and Orion gave his full attention to Hector. "They won't return. Not without help. The Prince and the Belamours are trapped, and I think I may have a way to prove it to you, though I would prefer to reveal it in a more secluded location, if you don't mind."

Sparked with intrigue, Hector assessed Orion again, taking in the brutal weapons hanging from his hips. "Jax is right. You could be the reason they haven't returned. How can we be sure you aren't working for Sirena, either of your own free will or manipulated by some spell of the mind?"

"You can't be." Orion looked sideways at Isolde. "But the people of Caritas say *fidés*. It means trust. I guess you have to decide whether or not you want to trust us. Whether it's worth the risk." Next to him, Isolde beamed at Hector expectantly. "We will find Alexander without Jericho's help if it comes to that. We only came here first because we knew you would be waiting for them to return, and we wanted you to have all the information before moving forward without the weapon they went to retrieve."

Hector exchanged another look with Jax, who shrugged. "*Fidés*, huh?" Orion nodded. After a heavy sigh, Hector confessed, "I would really rather not have to kill you, O'Connell."

"I am inclined not to favor that option as well." Orion smiled, certain now that he'd convinced him, at least for the time being. "I know we've been at odds in the past, Kayvan, but it seems new lines have been drawn all around. If you're able to change your ways, why not I?"

Hector reflected on this before calling to one of the workers scurrying about the courtyard and instructing him to bring water and food to the warroom for their guests.

Orion thought of what Declan had said regarding their former commander's talents in Jericho, and he was already of the mind to believe the assessment. He saw a confidence in Hector that rang genuine and entirely different from the man he'd been when commanding the Legion. Cast away was his arrogant and cold heart, a man constantly on edge, and in its place sat a heart more at peace.

"Right. Well, come on then." Hector led them from the Monastery courtyard to a tent strung up in an alley between two buildings. Lifting the fabric doorway, he motioned for them to enter.

Raven stood inside the entrance, and two soldiers from the Jerichonian Guard sat at the long table dressed in uniforms of purple and gray. Both glanced up as they stepped inside.

The space reminded Orion of the warroom at Castle Solís. A

lantern lit a table riddled with parchment and newly drawn maps, and candles on tall stands lined the outer edge of the room. A cabinet rested against the side wall next to extra chairs and a table big enough for two.

Hector gestured to the older man. "Commander Havlar, meet Orion O'Connell and Isolde, of Caritas. Orion, this is Commander Abram Havlar and General Eero Asger."

"Caritas?" Abram smiled at Isolde. "The Morrow greets you, my friend."

"And you as well." She dropped her chin with her usual level of charm.

Hector observed the interaction with interest. Then he took a step toward the table, and Orion, Isolde, and Jax joined him. Raven stayed by the door with her arms crossed and her typical irritated countenance.

Hector tapped the table. "All right, Orion, show us this proof you claim to have, and tell us what you know of Prince Alexander and the Belamour sisters."

Abram leaned forward with intrigue, and Eero set down the parchment he'd been reading to listen.

Orion swung his bag from his shoulder, and the movement made both Jax and Hector flinch. He eyed them with a grin. "Calm down, gentlemen. You should know, I'm not technically allowed in this city by order of the Konungr. I'm meant to be killed on sight, I believe, if the old order stands." He glanced at the Jerichonian commander, who smiled and shrugged. Isolde's eyes were wide, her lips parting in disbelief, and Orion guessed she was reviewing the words he'd spoken in the plaza. "I wouldn't have returned and made my name known to the Guard unless I thought it absolutely necessary. In truth, I'm probably the worst possible person Sirena could use to infiltrate Jericho. If you trust nothing else, trust that."

"He's right, Hector. You remember what he said at that first meeting." Abram looked at Orion. "Your friend was here. Declan. Vali remembered both of you."

Hector nodded. "He called you *that horrid fellow*." Abram chuckled.

"Yep. That's me. Absolutely horrid. However…" Orion pulled the seven keys of Arkaemor from his bag and set them on the table. The others leaned in to get a better look at each stone: an amber crown; a snowflake carved from pink tourmaline; red carnelian in the shape of an acacia tree; a sodalite clamshell, dark blue with white ocean waves; a skull made of crinkled turquoise; an emerald shaped like a raindrop; and a moonstone. "I also happen to be the person in possession of the keys to Celestelvyra. I can only assume Alexander and the others didn't have time to grab them as they ran from Sirena. When I woke in the In-Between, the door had closed, and Sirena was gone. Declan says the others made it through. I retrieved the keys from the table before escaping with Declan and Johnathan." Hector perked up at the familiar name of Declan's brother.

"Why didn't the Queen take them? Or use them to reopen the doors and enter herself?" Jax asked, his expression skeptical.

"That's a good question. And unfortunately one I do not have a solid answer for."

"It is possible Elohim shut the doors to protect them." Isolde wrapped both hands around her spear and leaned against it. "If He did, the Queen would have been barred entrance regardless of the keys."

Abram leaned back in his chair and folded his hands on his stomach. "It is also speculated, though no one alive today can truly be certain, that only some can remove the stones from the table. Anyone can place them, but few can retrieve them once they are molded within. This was true even when it only took one key to open the doors."

"What would be the point of that?" Jax asked. "Why would anyone be able to open the door but not be able to close it?"

"Just because anyone can place the keys into the table does not mean anyone can open the door. The keys are not infallible. The Creator decides when they work and who is allowed to possess their magical faculties."

Orion thought this over, remembering Isolde's strange response when he had revealed his ability to remove the keys from the table. He glanced at her, but her attention remained on Jax and Abram.

Jax crossed his arms. "So if it's all up to the Creator anyway, what is the purpose of the keys?"

Isolde smiled. "If it were as simple as appearing before the doors requesting admittance, anyone could try and seek entrance. Elohim likes to make us work for things. He cherishes our perseverance and uses difficult situations to teach us His ways." Jax pursed his lips but didn't press for more information.

"So what does it mean that you were able to remove the keys from the table?" Hector looked at Orion, who shrugged.

"A fluke perhaps. The Creator needed me to have them so we could save the Prince." He wondered if it would work a second time or if he'd simply been a tool in use. The only person available at the moment. He considered asking Elohim for the answer but feared the truth too much to risk it.

Instead, Isolde answered for Him. "It means he was chosen by the Creator as someone who can open the doors to Celestelvyra."

"Only those with a pure heart, with intentions for good and not harm, are allowed access to Celestelvyra." Abram caught Isolde's eye and gleaned her smile. "It is why the Queen will forever be barred entrance no matter how she attempts to corrupt the system."

Hector scrutinized Orion, who suspected him of trying to figure out how he'd been able to remove the keys if a pure heart was the prerequisite. Riding the same wavelength, Orion scratched the back of his head and stared at the table in deep thought, wondering if this knowledge had played into Isolde and Kaatachi's trust in him.

Then he shook his head. "But if that's true, why wouldn't He have opened the door to free Alexander in the first place. It doesn't seem logical for me to be involved at all." Still, the keys had risen with the touch of his hands, and this, he decided, was precisely why he found all business involving Elohim perplexing and exhausting.

Isolde said, "A true statement indeed. And so there must be more at work here than we yet understand."

Hector cleared his throat. "Regardless of how you got them, you have the keys, which means we will be able to open the doors and set them free. So please, tell us more. Tell us the rest of the story."

CHAPTER 14

RAPTORS AND RAM

Orion gave them a recap of everything he'd experienced since waking in the In-Between. He left out the part about Declan betraying them to the Queen but recounted the closed door within the crumbling swamp, Johnathan and Orion waking to find Declan gravely injured, escaping to meet Maeve who led them to the nieda hive, Isolde and her tribe saving them, and the Naaba's message about joining them for war when the time came.

While he spoke, the man Hector had sent for provisions entered the tent with water and sandwiches. The moment Orion finished the explanation, he sat down and dug into the gifted food while the others thought over everything he'd revealed.

Isolde eyed her sandwich with puzzlement, seeming uncertain how to go about eating it. After watching Orion pick his up and bite into the whole thing from the side, she mirrored his motions and took a bite of her own.

After scarfing down his sandwich, Orion wiped his mouth on his sleeve. "So to summarize, we need to get to a Monastery and find our way into Celestelvyra to set Alexander, Iris, Foxxglove, and Seth free. Hopefully they aren't dilly-dallying in paradise and have actually found whatever it is we need to kill Sirena. Then we can come back here and organize for war."

Hector rested his chin on the back of his fingers. "I agree. We can't attack Inaravale until we have Pyhä-ki."

Jax said, "We are running out of time. Dagon's forces have

already had more than two weeks on horseback to return to Reginaterra. You can guarantee they sent troops ahead to inform the Queen before their arrival. Possibly even jumpers if he trusted any of them enough to do so."

Orion nodded. "Isolde and I can travel to the Monastery in Metsa Sateen and free Prince Alexander. The Monastery is several weeks' journey inside the territory, but if we have horses, we can move significantly faster. You could even provide us with some extra soldiers so we are better protected, if you have them to spare."

"That won't work." Hector's expression glazed over.

"Why not?" Orion inhaled an irritated breath, eyes drifting to the golden owl pinned to Jax's chest. It was the same pin he'd worn when he'd been a Reko Raptor, though his had been bronze. Hector had known the truth of his innocence all those years ago. He'd hoped that would be enough to ensure trust, whether they liked each other or not. "I think I have proven myself. I never would have given you all this information if I planned to betray you. There are countless other clever and effective ways I could have deceived you."

"That's not the issue."

Orion soaked in the perceived insult with pursed lips. It hadn't occurred to him before that moment that he may be pushed out of the mission, though he realized it should have. He'd arrived in a city of soldiers, and it was the Prince of Arkaemor they intended to save. Why would they trust a traitor with such an important task?

As had become the pattern, his whispers awakened with his insecurities. Raising his voice above them, though endeavoring not to speak too loudly, Orion insisted, "Well spit it out then, what is it? What's the issue?"

Abram said, "We received reports from our scouts that Queen Sirena decimated the Monastery in Metsa Sateen. You will not be able to get through that way."

Orion's eyes widened as he realized the reason for Hector's hesitation hadn't been a lack of trust in him, though his elation was quickly swallowed by his terror. "But that means—"

Hector met his gaze. "The only Monastery left standing is the one in Crystavium, the Ashgate Fortress: Prison of the Strayed."

"Fantastic." Orion leaned forward, resting his elbows on the table and rubbing his forehead with his fingers.

"Jax is familiar with the layout." The gears behind Hector's eyes had already begun turning.

"That's true, Commander, but I have no idea where this alleged entrance to the mysterious Celestelvyra might be." Jax scratched his cheek with raised brows. "And on top of that, not many who have attempted a break-in have succeeded, and no one has ever succeeded in breaking out."

Abram said, "It would be kept secure. Out of sight where the guards wouldn't accidentally happen upon it."

"It would be hidden," Orion agreed. "Like the black walls, you would steer away from it without realizing you were doing it. Declan mentioned it was the same in the Wilds. The hallway leading to the In-Between was enchanted."

Raven finally stepped away from the door to join the group, pushing her long braid over her shoulder so it hung straight down her spine. "So the plan is to find an invisible doorway that doesn't want to be found in an inescapable prison crawling with, not only King's Legion guards, but Monastery scholars so corrupted by evil they now do the Immortal Queen's bidding? Not to mention every person who's ever committed a crime despicable enough to land themselves in an Ashgate cell?" A breeze blew the door open a crack and extinguished one of the lamps, sending the sulfuric smell of candle smoke into the air.

"I just love when you join the conversation, Raven. So much positivity." Orion grinned, and Raven glared at him.

Jax shrugged his coat from his shoulders and hung it on the rack by the door. Tugging the fabric closed to prevent more air from leaking into the tent, he said, "If it's true that we need the water from Celestelvyra to kill the Queen—and I would like to put it on the table that I am still skeptical of that—then I think it's the only plan we've got. Otherwise, we call off the revolution now and all go into hiding for the rest of our lives."

"Jax is right." Hector scratched a chin several days past its usual shave. "We have already declared war. There's no going back."

"And if we all die at Ashgate?" Orion asked.

Hector scanned the room, taking in the fearful expressions looking back at him. The weight of this decision was obvious in his eyes, and he rolled his shoulders to ease some of the tension.

Clearing his throat, he answered, "If we die at Ashgate, then the war is already over."

C

After a few closing thoughts and plans to regroup in the morning, Jax sent someone to find Isolde and Orion a place to sleep as Hector waved the Jerichonian commander and general off to bed.

Then Jax called for a meeting of the Reko Raptors. Raven knew where Wyatt and Marshal Hearne and Dominic Ives were currently stationed and hurried to retrieve them as Hector and Jax took a seat at the table.

Jax rolled out a blank piece of parchment and began sketching a map of the prison. After drawing the base outline, he glanced up to find Hector staring off into nothing. "Need to talk it out?"

Hector flinched at the sound of a voice in the silent room. With a weighty sigh, he answered, "I guess I'm… concerned."

"About trusting Orion?" Jax's eyes returned to the parchment. He unraveled a second piece atop the first so he could trace the outline, wanting the maps of each level to be scaled congruently.

"Among other things." Hector rose from his chair and approached the small cabinet against the wall, pulling out two glasses and an unlabeled bottle of dark liquid. "I think at this point, Orion is the least of my worries. Though I have to say, he did seem different from what I remember. And sincere, I think."

"I can agree with that."

Filling each glass two thirds of the way up, Hector carried them back to the table and sat down, setting one in front of Jax and taking a swig from the other. "But breaking into the Ashgate Fortress?" He gestured a lazy hand to the map in progress. "This is a horrible plan."

"We were made for this, Commander. It's going to work." Jax took a quick drink from his glass before holding both parchments up to the metal lantern, double-checking his tracing. Satisfied, he flattened them on the table, using stones to hold down each corner, and began adding the walls for the rooms on the lower level. Though he'd never seen a blueprint of the Ashgate Fortress, he'd spent enough time there to be more than familiar with the layout. "Besides, it kind of seems like it's our only option at present."

Hector lounged back in his chair, resting his elbow on the arm as he took another sip from his drink. Unbuttoning the top two buttons of his uniform, he said, "We could dig through the rubble of a different Monastery and try to find a door that way. With enough hands, it could be doable."

"There is no way we're getting into the one here in Jericho. It's too massive and could take months to get it clear enough to even begin searching. By then, the Queen will have undoubtedly heard about the revolution and will have sent Kaen to decimate what remains of the city, cutting us off at the root. Sateen's has spent the last two weeks saturated with rain, and it was more than likely overrun with plants and vines before Sirena added to its destruction. The Wild's Monastery is covered in sand, and if Orion is to be believed, was completely leveled after they escaped. Though it's still a better option than Sateen, perhaps. Alunda's is at the bottom of the ocean. Savanni's…" He sifted through memories. "Flattened. Burned to a crisp. Could be a possibility if it happened recently, but it's been hundreds of years. It doesn't seem feasible. The Queen was thorough. Her acute demolition is the only evidence that has me thinking this might be a real thing, despite my skepticism."

Hector cracked a smile, pointing at Jax with the hand holding his glass. "You know, for someone who doesn't believe, you sure know a lot about the Monastery of the Morrow's history."

"It was my job to know everything the rebels believed." Jax rolled up his sleeves, revealing a tapestry of black tattoos. Then he swallowed the contents in his cup. "If what Orion said about her enchanting them like the black walls is true, the door will be hard enough to find in a fully functioning Monastery."

Hector leaned his chair on its rear legs, rocking it back and forth. "Harder than breaking into a prison governed by the undead?"

"The amount of time and resources it would take to search through a demolished Monastery plus the probability of actually finding the door within outweighs the risk of coming up with a sound and organized plan to penetrate a location we are familiar with and know for sure will give us access to the door."

"Very logical, Lieutenant." Hector dropped the legs of his chair back to the ground and leaned his elbows on the table. After finishing his drink, he set down the glass and said Jax's name. "Why are you fighting so hard for this if you don't even believe in Celestelvyra or that Pyhä-ki will kill Sirena?"

"I follow you, Commander." His brow lifted as though this should have been obvious. "I always have. If you believe this is what must be done, then I will do everything in my power to see it through, regardless of my personal doubts."

"Just a soldier's work then? Following your leader's commands?" Standing, he retrieved the bottle from its stand and carried it to the table to pour himself another glass. He lifted the bottle to Jax in a silent inquiry.

Jax shook his head, responding to both his questions and his offer. "A soldier follows commands because he respects and trusts his superior. Even if they don't always agree, a soldier relies on those he serves not to lead him astray. You know this, Hector. You're a soldier, too."

Slumping back into his chair, he left the bottle open and drank down half of what he'd poured. Then he ran the pad of his index finger around the rim of the glass, not looking at Jax as he spoke. "I was a soldier who followed the sadistic will of the King and Queen, even when I knew what they ordered was wrong. You were there the day I became commander. You know better than anyone what kind of man I am. I broke the trust of those under me by commanding them to carry out horrible actions, yourself included. I served with selfishness, holding my high-ranked position above all else. I served, not out of respect and trust, but because of fear at what they might do if I didn't obey. I know nothing of what it means to be the soldier you describe. If ever I was that kind of soldier, I have no memory of it."

Jax put his elbows on the table and leaned into them. "It's true. We've all done things under someone else's command that we regret. And maybe you did live a selfish life before, serving and commanding for your own personal gain with little regard for others, but I have also seen you stand up for what's right. I *was* there the day you became commander, and I remember well the reason for Sirena's arguments against Pollux's decision. On top of that, the man you speak of is not the man I see before me now. You made the decision to give up a life you knew—a familiar life, a comfortable life—to be here serving a better cause and fighting for something you believe in. You refused to continue on in blind servitude, and you brought us with you. If anything, that makes you more of a commander than you ever were before, and even more worthy of my trust and respect." Jax tapped two fingers on the table to draw Hector's attention. "Give yourself a little credit, Hector."

"I'm having a hard time with that." He took another swallow

and poured more from the bottle into his cup, spilling a few drops on the table.

"I guess you'll just have to take my word for it then." Jax reached for the open bottle and slid it away from them. Hector didn't seem to notice as his head returned to rest on his fist. It had been a while since Jax had seen his commander even slightly tipsy, but the alcohol already shined in his dazed eyes. "And if I'm proven correct and this is all a huge waste of time, I will be less willing to follow your ludicrous schemes in the future." Without removing his hand from his cheek, Hector looked up at him in surprise. Jax grinned before growing serious again. "But until then, I will follow you anywhere. Into any mission. Into any battle. Even into the hell that is the Ashgate Fortress."

Hector cleared his throat. "Thank you, Lieutenant. That's good to hear."

Jax nodded and looked down at his map. "Do you think what Pollux said that day might have been about what's happening now?" Hector didn't respond, but Jax knew he must be considering it at least a little. From the moment he'd watched his commander lift that soot-covered girl into his arms, he'd wondered if this might be the action that turned the tide, changed Hector's fate, and had the King's prophecy ringing true. "He said one soldier would stand above all others and do great things for the Kingdoms, like none before him. And he believed that man to be you."

Hector hummed and took another drink. "I remember."

Raven appeared in the entrance, trailed by Dominic, Wyatt, and Marshal. Pausing just inside the doorway to take in the scene, she looked from the bottle on the table to Hector's head resting lethargically on his opposite fist. "Oh Jax, you let him into the bourbon."

"I didn't let him do anything." Jax's pencil scratched the parchment, his eyes focused.

"Bourbon!" Dominic hollered. After brushing freshly fallen snow from his ginger waves, his hands came to rest on his belly. An axe hung at his waist, the only weapon he'd carried with him since coming to reside in Jericho. "Pass us a glass, won't ya?"

Raven approached Hector from behind and put her hands on his shoulders, speaking to Jax across the table. "You know he doesn't have the stomach for it."

"He's not my keeper." Hector only mildly slurred his words. Jax cracked another grin. Marshal and Wyatt moved in from the doorway and joined them around the table to examine the maps.

Dominic had already retrieved a glass from the cabinet and poured himself three fingers. "Look at 'im." He cackled as he motioned to their commander.

"A rare sight," Wyatt agreed. Marshal grabbed his own glass, and Dom passed him the bourbon.

Raven reached over Hector and swiped the drink from his hand. "No more for you tonight. We have things to discuss." When she lifted it in cheers to Dominic and Marshal, the men returned her gesture, and they all took a long swig.

"I never get to have any fun," Hector complained under his breath, seeming not one measure like the stoic commander they knew. He squinted a single eye, as if already having trouble seeing through both at one time.

"We'll have all the fun you want when this is over," Jax promised.

"No, no." Hector lifted a hand to the one Raven had resting on his shoulder. "There will be too much to do. A new Kingdom to run. A new king to please." His eyes fell closed. "And we will probably die in Ashgate anyway."

"That's the spirit," Jax quipped.

"He hasn't eaten today," Raven said in Hector's defense. "Wyatt, will you get him something to eat? Something heavy." Wyatt nodded, smirking at Marshal as he left the tent.

Dominic laughed from his belly. "He should know he can't 'old his liquor."

"Not everyone can be as stone-gutted as you, Dom," Raven said.

"You're one to talk, girlie."

Jax said, "He only had two drinks. He was a little heavy on the pour though."

Raven let her arms slide down Hector's chest, hugging him from behind. "Our strong and valiant commander. He deserves to let loose every once in a while. He has a lot weighing on his shoulders."

"Right now you're weighing on my shoulders," Hector mumbled without opening his eyes, sparking a chuckle throughout the group.

Wyatt returned with some bread and a vessel of water from the closest well. After setting the bread in front of Hector, he poured water into a pottered tumbler and handed it to him. When Hector drank it down, Wyatt refilled it.

"Perhaps we should pick this up in the morning," Jax suggested.

"No," Hector said, his mouth full of dry bread. "I'll be fine."

Jax eyed him skeptically, and Dominic laughed again, pouring himself another half a glass. He handed it to Raven, who took a swallow and returned it.

"So what's the plan? I assume we won't all be going to Ashgate."

"Ashgate?" Dominic cried. "Is 'at really what we's meetin' about? That's the plan?"

"Unfortunately." Jax sat back and tapped his pencil on the table.

Dominic looked around wide-eyed. "With the bloody Strayed?"

"That's the one."

"Bleedin' hell." He held his stomach as if he suddenly had indigestion.

"Who's going and who's staying behind?" Wyatt's fingers stroked the fletching on the arrows sticking out from his quiver.

"Opting to stay behind." Marshal held up a hand. "In case anyone was wondering."

"Wyatt and Marshal will stay behind." Hector already seemed closer to himself than he had moments ago. Though his tongue got twisted again as he added, "And Dominic."

"Won't hear me complaining," Dominic said.

Jax looked at Hector, motioning with his finger in the space between the two of them. "You and me?"

"And Raven. If she wants to."

Raven patted his chest. "I'll go wherever you lead me, Commander."

Hector rolled his eyes like a schoolgirl and hiccuped, revealing the liquor's continued influence. "You two," he mumbled. Raven looked a question at Jax, but he shook his head as if they would discuss it later.

"I want to go," Raven declared.

"Then it's done." Jax dropped his pencil into its cup with clang. "Orion will want to come as well, I believe. When we speak with him and Isolde tomorrow, we'll see what he thinks and figure out exactly how many we'll need on the team."

"We're seriously going to trust Orion O'Connell of all people with something this dangerous?" Raven asked.

Hector said, "It was his plan. He showed up here at the risk of his own hide with the intention of finding a way into Celestelvyra."

Jax agreed. "Wouldn't be right to cut him out of it."

Raven sighed, and Dominic chuckled at her.

"Don't get all riled up, Ray. I think you could take 'im out if need be."

"I'm not riled." Raven pushed her bangs away from the sides of her face. "I just don't trust him."

"I trust him." After a moment, Hector seemed to reconsider and added, "I think."

"What about Isolde? We know nothing about this woman."

"Who's Isolde?" Wyatt asked.

"That chick with all the fur and tattoos," Marshal answered, and Wyatt gawked at him. "What? I saw them walk through the court-yard earlier."

Hector lifted his head. "He's right. She did wear an excessive amount of fur. Orion, in fact, was also wearing fur."

Jax chuckled as Marshal added, "She looked pretty scary."

"Really?" Wyatt asked, intrigued.

Jax leaned back in the chair with his hands behind his head. "I don't know what to think about Isolde, but it seems like Orion plans to keep her with him." He didn't know much about the village of Caritas, only that its current leader was called Naaba Kaatachi, and that, though suspicions circulated about them allying with rebels, they'd never done anything to get themselves in trouble with the sovereigns of Reginaterra. "As far as trusting him, I doubt he would do anything to compromise the mission once we're inside. He's too self-centered to put us all at risk if it would put him at risk as well."

"He's arrogant," Raven countered. "Arrogance breeds overconfidence, which breeds mistakes."

"The misses in't wrong." Dominic lifted his glass to her in solidarity.

"He's coming," Hector said, steadfast, and Jax nodded in agreement.

Raven pinched Hector's shoulders, massaging them. "Then if it's decided, I propose we postpone further discussions until we're all together in the morning."

"Here, here." Dominic lifted his glass again before downing the rest of it.

"Sounds good to me." Jax stood and rolled up the maps. "Wyatt and Marshal, you're on night shift?"

"That's right, Lieutenant."

"Dom?"

"Sleepytime for me, sir," Dominic answered.

"All right. I'm off to bed as well." Jax rounded the table to help Hector from his chair.

"I don't need help." Hector stood abruptly and found himself a little off balance. His hand touched the table until the swaying stabilized.

"I'll just walk next to you then." Jax held his shoulder to steady him.

Raven blew out the candles, and they all stepped from the tent into the moonlight and falling snow. Marshal and Wyatt headed back to the courtyard, and the other four walked together up Wayward Street. Dominic wished them a *merry night* as he headed into the Spearhead Tavern where he had taken up lodgings.

Jax, Raven, and Hector continued on to Pinewood Inn. Jax followed Hector up the stairs, covertly making sure he didn't stumble. When they reached their door, Raven used her key to open it. Hector took three strides into the room, laid down on his bed, and seemed to fall asleep immediately.

Raven and Jax stood in the doorway watching him. "Is he okay?"

Jax smirked. "He's fine. He'll sleep it off."

"I mean in general. Not because of the booze."

Jax had known what she'd meant, but he didn't have an honest answer for her. In truth, he'd never seen this side of Hector. While he seemed happy to be free of the evils of the Legion and confident that staying in Jericho had been the right choice, he had also never seemed so terrified of the future.

Shrugging, Jax replied firmly, "Yeah. He has to be."

C

Foxxglove stirred awake with flashes of visions past replaying in her dreams. She'd floated through the doors leading into Celestelvyra to find the white ram waiting for her, just like in her very first visit to the garden. Echoes chimed through her consciousness.

I can see you, too.

A promise of comfort after Sirena Aldrich's torturous storm. Of protection.

Hearing a rustling from somewhere above her head, she sat up and checked on each of her companions, finding them all present and sleeping soundly. Again a swish of movement from behind had her whipping around to see foliage swaying as though something had passed through it.

Intrigued, she stood, quiet as a whispered wind, and crept barefoot toward the disturbance. The grass tickling the spaces between her toes was dampened by a morning dew. The world above was dark and splattered with stars, though the cobalt sky had begun lightening into a bright sapphire, indicating the approaching morning.

Striding from the clearing and onto the footpath, she moved leaves and vines from the walkway as she progressed forward. A bird flapped its wings high in the trees, startling her, and she paused to listen, trying to recapture the direction of the creature she might be following. A small part of her thought herself insane for leaving the sleeping party behind to follow an unknown beast into the depths of an unexplored garden. Out of habit, she reached for her bow, though it didn't hang from her shoulder. In Celestelvyra, there was no need for weapons because there was no danger.

When she reached the end of the path, she discovered a meadow brimming with wildflowers. At its center stood a mammal standing taller than her whole height. Like in her vision, it's thick body wore a coat of white fur. Two enormous horns spiraled from both sides of its head. The summit of the horns towered nearly a foot above its crown and curved down below its shoulders.

It's sheer size had her trembling, knowing it could crush her with little effort. Though it made no indication of aggression, its dark gaze pinned her in place.

I can see you, too.

The words replayed in her head, and she couldn't be sure if she was hearing the memory, an echo of promises spoken weeks ago, or if it—if *He*—was repeating His promise in the present. Taking a hesitant step forward, she tested how He would respond if she drew closer. When He remained motionless, she took another. As she continued to venture nearer, her feet rustled the wildflowers, filling her nose with their floral fragrance. Stopping a few paces away, she lifted a palm, tentatively requesting to touch Him. A final step had the tips of her fingers about to brush His coal-black nose.

He shifted, and she yanked her hand away in fright. Then He lowered His head toward the ground. Foxx thought His neck and back muscles must be incredibly strong in order to hold up such massive horns. He kept His head bowed for a few moments before rising to meet her eyes again. Dipping her head low, she returned His bow.

Less guarded than before, she stretched out her hand. He met her halfway, and she didn't shy from His touch. His fur felt velvety and toasty warm where He nuzzled His cheek within the palm of her hand. His eyelids fell closed, and she watched with astonishment as the wild creature offered her affection.

Other animals in the garden had shown interest, eager to get a glimpse of the intruders. Some had even willingly come close and rubbed against them. None of those interactions had felt as intimate as this.

With her other hand, she stroked one of His horns, beginning where it sprouted from His head above His ear and sliding the length of the spiral all the way to the tip. Delight at her soft touch had His eyes falling closed again. She ran both hands down either side of His neck, and the Ram leaned into her shoulder, sniffing her and brushing His muzzle into her loose hair, nearly the same color as His fur.

Overcome with a wave of emotion like she'd never experienced, tears spilled from her eyes. Not of sadness or sorrow, but of bliss she felt deep in her core. Of trust and love and understanding.

A stir from behind had her turning to find Asher standing on the edge of the clearing, watching them. Several buttons on his shirt hung undone, as if he'd grown warm while sleeping and sought the coolness of the nighttime air. His hair looked a mess, sticking up in all directions. It had grown longer since they'd been together in Petrichor, sweeping across his forehead and covering all but the bottom of his earlobes.

Whispering her name, he asked, "What are you doing?" Her smile never leaving her cheeks, she let go with one hand and waved him toward her. Asher stepped hesitantly into the wildflower meadow and approached, never taking his eyes off of the bighorn Ram. Encouraging him to move closer, she leaned her cheek against the Creature's own, providing evidence of his safety.

Asher bowed, dipping his head low, and when he glanced up, he swore he caught a smile in the Ram's eyes. Then Asher held out his hand, as she had. With the back of his fingers, he brushed the side of the Ram's cheek and received a nuzzle against his knuckles in return.

Foxx wrapped her arms around the Ram's neck, hugging Him and petting His silken fur. Asher stepped out around one of His horns to stroke His spine. The Ram seemed to be thoroughly enjoying Himself.

"He led me here," Foxx whispered, not bothering to wipe the tears from her cheeks.

"How?" Asher kept his voice low, too, as if knowing the Creature was entitled reverence.

"He... spoke to me. Not with His lips. And not today. I don't think so, at least."

Asher didn't press her for more information despite his obvious desire to understand. His eyes drifted to the edges of the wildflower glade where other animals had gathered to observe them.

"When we traveled with Orion and—Declan—" She tripped over his name, the weight of his betrayal hovering over them like a constant shadow no one wished to discuss. Foxx had been the first to trust him. In a way, she'd trusted him from the very beginning; at least enough to keep Iris safe from Orion's destructive behavior. Looking back on all the signs, on all the ways he'd helped them despite the circumstances, she couldn't understand why or how he could have deceived them so thoroughly.

"There was this storm. We later realized it was created by magic and not a natural occurrence. Trees literally crashed to the ground all around us.

"It was Sirena. She pulled me up into the clouds. Well, she didn't really pull me up. It was in my head. Gosh, I feel like my mother. It's hard to explain." She felt pressure against her chest as if it were on the brink of caving in, imploring her to shut down again and avoid the pain by feeling nothing. She resisted, letting the peace of the wildflower meadow and the glorious Ram wash over her.

Asher anchor her to truth. "Try to remember all the things we've learned about your mother. Even when Amaryllis' behavior seemed erratic, even completely mental at times, she wasn't sick, Foxx. Her visions were real."

His intimate knowledge of her mother reignited her feelings

about his betrayal. She brooded for a moment, wondering if there was anyone she could trust wholeheartedly. As if reading her thoughts, the Ram looked back at her over His shoulder.

Asher's words cut through her inner dialogue. "Somehow, she was blessed with the knowledge of things others couldn't see. It was a heavy burden to bear, and perhaps now you must bear it too."

Angry emotions transformed into admiration at his words. The way he spoke of her visions being a blessing—a gift, rather than a curse—was something she had never considered. She thought back on her last vision of Asher's coronation and decided it likely *had* been intended as a gift of hope. Their eyes met, and she considered sharing it with him, but, either to protect him or to selfishly keep it to herself, she didn't. Instead, she returned to her recollections of the storm. "Sirena held me high above the trees so I could see the jungle in every direction. There wasn't a cloud in the sky but for the raging tempest crushing us. I could see Iris and the men below. Declan carried me as they attempted to outrun the collapsing trees. I heard Sirena's voice in my head. She said she could see me and that she was coming for me. Then she dropped me, and I tumbled from the sky."

"That sounds absolutely horrifying, love."

Her fingers danced along the curve of the Ram's horn, stroking the entire scope of the curl. "After I hit the ground, I was suddenly floating in front of those doors." She gestured roughly in the direction of the entrance. "The doors leading us here, to the garden."

He lifted his head. "That's why you said you'd been there before."

"The doors opened, and I floated through them, and He was there at the center of the clearing we've been sleeping in. In my head, I heard Him say, *I can see you, too.* Like He knew what she'd done and wanted to assure me He was keeping an eye on me, as well." Gazing at the Ram with gratitude, she kissed His cheek, nuzzling her nose against it the way He had her hand. "He led me here, I think, or He at least knew I was following Him and stopped to wait for me."

An owl flew across the meadow, hooting as it went, and Asher's eyes tracked the movement. "How did you know you were following Him to begin with? Did He come to the waterfall and wake you?"

"Not exactly. I woke up from dreams of Him and heard a noise on the edge of the clearing. I saw the plants moving near the path you followed here, as if someone had disrupted them, so I came to investigate." Her head burrowed into her shoulders, expecting a scolding.

Asher's eyebrows rose. "You followed an unknown creature into the unknown forest? In a land you have never been to before, with no knowledge of what might dwell here?"

She chuckled. "You said we were safe here."

Her joyous gaiety was infectious, breaking his lips into a smile. "Yes, I suppose I did."

The Ram turned to look at Foxx one last time. After nudging her shoulder with one of His horns, He galloped off. As He fled, His hooves rustled the wildflowers, sending more of their sweet scent into the air.

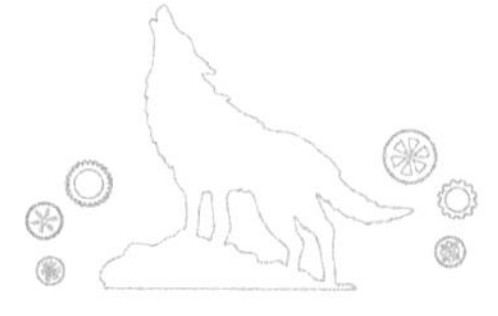

CHAPTER 15

THE OLD, OLD STORY

Foxx stared off in the direction the Ram had gone, lost within a cloud of melancholy. A dull pain prodded her chest as the cosmic tranquility she'd felt in His presence waned like honey dissolving into a steaming mug of tea.

"That was incredible." She used the backs of her hands to dry her tear-dampened face. Replaying the events of the past several minutes, she marveled at the dream-creature brought to life before her eyes. She'd never known an animal to be so... human. No other animal in the garden had displayed the transcendence of the white Ram. None had radiated with such majestic and undefinable power, like ripples emanating a disturbance on the surface of a pond.

Foxx drew Asher's attention, and he turned to her. "I just... What is this place? I mean, I know it's the Sacred Realm of Celestelvyra. But there is magic here, like nothing I've ever felt. I hadn't known sorcery could be anything but evil, like Sirena's sorcery." Her mind flashed to the crystals of ice she'd seen erupt on her fingertips, and a sharp pain speared her chest.

"Don't you think your visions are a form of magic?"

Her brow pinched in the middle as she considered that. She supposed if not magic, then what? "The visions are awful though. Unhelpful, and often painful and exhausting. Nothing like the magic of this garden."

"That doesn't make them evil."

"They tore my mother apart from the inside out."

194

"Maybe." His eyes trailed back to where the Ram had disappeared amongst the trees.

"How can you say *maybe*?" When Asher didn't respond, she looked at her fingers, pinching the tips as if checking them for signs of sorcery. "You say this Realm is what Elohim originally intended the world to be and that even Arkaemor was like Celestelvyra when the world first began." She waited for him to confirm this statement, and he nodded without turning to her. "I'm reading the book I took from the Monastery, but it's so hard to understand. Sometimes it's like my brain can't comprehend the words. Not that I can't read them, but as if they don't make sense the way they're strung together. Like a book of riddles telling a story I can't seem to grasp."

"If it weren't told in riddles, there would be no reason to continue studying it. We learn and grow every single day. If life was simple and straightforward, it wouldn't be as powerful. Or as important."

"Are you quoting from the book? Because that sounded equally baffling."

Finally looking at her, he chuckled. "No, I'm not. Just speaking from experience."

Foxx gestured to the splendor of the garden around them. "If this is what the Creator wanted the world to be, what happened to make it go so wrong? Why does He keep it hidden away while we live out there with horrors and monsters?"

"It is my understanding that long ago when the world was created, Arkaemor and Celestelvyra were one. The invisible barriers separated the seven territories, and the Realm of Celestelvyra encircled them."

"Outside the black walls, you mean?"

"They weren't black then. They would have been invisible just like the walls between the territories and would have led to somewhere in the garden. Now, the world outside the outer barriers is known as the Void. I don't really know how to explain that Arkaemor didn't move exactly. It's still in the same space, but in a different domain. In the Void's domain, I suppose."

"Riddles," Foxx mumbled, and he smiled.

"So Arkaemor and Celestelvyra were one body, one land. People could travel back and forth between them just as easily as we can walk from Cordillera into Metsa Sateen, and everyone and everything lived in harmony, just as you have witnessed since we've been here. The land itself was exquisite and serene, even in Arkaemor, just as it is here."

Asher gestured toward the overgrown footpath that had brought them to the meadow. "Would you like to walk as we talk?" His eyes gleamed with familiar charm.

Foxx knew he was soaking up her attention and worried she might be giving him mixed signals, but she needed answers. He'd spent years researching, and she doubted there were many alive today with as much knowledge about the history of the world as the Prince of Arkaemor.

"Sure." She kept her eyes on her feet, watching as they rustled up the fragrance of the wildflowers. Then she looked back to catch one last glimpse of the meadow before the tall foliage of the path hid it from view. "So, what happened? What changed?"

"Let me try to start at the beginning. The book you got from the Monastery in Metsa Sateen is a copy of *Jumalan Sana*. Within its pages are the keys to the entire history of creation and the Monastery of the Morrow. I know you've been reading through it and struggling with parts, but I've wondered, have you read the book Ah-Luiah gave you? The *Enchanter of Celestelvyra*?"

"I wish we had visited the Ataraxia Mission one last time. With things as they are now, we might never see them again." Her eyes drifted to the beaded bracelet on her wrist as she thought of Chaisai and Tanawat, the brothers who'd made and gifted it to her.

"We'll see them again. There's no doubt in my mind."

"I wish I had your faith." Foxx let her hands fall to her sides. "I've skimmed the book I got from Ah-Luiah, but I've been so focused on studying the other book—*Jumalan Sana*, apparently— that I forgot I had it."

"Well, *The Enchanter of Celestelvyra* is actually a retelling of several of the stories within *Jumalan Sana*. But it was written simpler, so children could learn the stories without having to sift through the riddles."

Foxx's mouth fell agape. "And you didn't think this would be good information for me to have when I was complaining about not being able to understand the book?"

Asher laughed at her expression, prompting the corner of her lips to turn upward. "Honestly, it's been difficult talking to you, Foxx. I've wanted to, but..." He ran a hand over his head.

"I know." Foxx turned her eyes forward and pursed her lips. She wasn't ready to talk about it. She wasn't ready to face it at all.

"Actually, I didn't know how to tell you this, or if I even should, but..." He exhaled and glanced sideways at her. "The copy you have of *The Enchanter of Celestelvyra* first belonged to your mother."

Foxx stopped walking. "What?"

"Well, she gave it to me when I was a child. When I brought Ah-Luiah to Ataraxia, I gave my copy to her. She was so curious about everything. So smart, even at such a young age. I thought she might enjoy the stories. And then she, by some curious and seemingly fateful turn of events, passed it on to you."

Tears burned at the edges of Foxx's eyes, and Asher looked worried, as if he might have said too much. Her mind raced as she processed the news, and a small part of her yearned to rush back to her bag and scrutinize the entire book for clues of her mother's presence within it. A glance at Asher had her sighing and releasing childish desires. "Okay." She lifted a hand, gesturing for him to keep walking, and fell into step next to him.

Asher cleared his throat. "So you can read this story right at the beginning of *The Enchanter of Celestelvyra*, but I'll summarize it for you. Over four thousand years ago, Sirena and other beings like her became jealous of Elohim's love for the humans He'd created."

"Tell me about the other beings. You mentioned them in Petrichor, but we never discussed it deeper. Do you mean there are other immortals? Others with magic?" Her fingers curled, hiding within her fists. The path grew small, forcing Foxx to walk behind him, but this didn't displease her in the slightest, as it allowed her to keep her distance. Walking side by side in a small space had caused their shoulders to bump more times than she liked, each one bringing with it a shiver of warmth.

"Both books refer to the immortal beings as numinae. Whether other numinae still exist, I really don't know. *Jumalan Sana* doesn't say much about them other than what is described in the story about the Deviation. In an act of rebellion, the numinae manipulated many of the humans into joining their quest to take down the Creator—to kill Him. There was a great battle. Human against human, numinae against numinae. When the army realized Elohim couldn't be destroyed, they gave up and fled Celestelvyra, claiming Arkaemor for themselves. It is believed that Elohim was so hurt by their betrayal, He forced everyone out and shut the doors to the

Sacred Realm so none could return. If those like Sirena thought they could do a better job and if the humans preferred their rule to His, then He would let them have exactly what they wanted."

With a contemplative sigh, he added, "I have learned the Creator often allows us to make our own choices, even when He knows we're making the wrong ones. How would we learn from our mistakes if we never made any?"

"Is your father one of the others?"

"I don't think so. Sirena might have been lying in the In-Between, but I don't think she was. Her purpose was to tear me down, to break me with knowledge of things that contradicted what I spent my whole life believing. If she'd killed both of my parents, she would have rubbed it in rather than continuing on with half a charade." Asher swallowed the emotion thickening his throat. Foxx nodded in agreement, though he couldn't see her, and he continued on. "After the barriers into Celestelvyra closed—an act thought to have taken place in year 1, if you didn't know—it took a long time for Elohim to let anyone else back in, though records show He did keep in contact with a select few. More than two thousand years later, He created the In-Between and the stone keys. Then He unveiled the secret doorways to those who remained loyal, and the Monastery of the Morrow was established. He instructed them to build the Monasteries to guard the doors. At the time, the scholars only needed a single key representative of their respective territory to get into Celestelvyra. That's why every territory had its own. It was another thousand years before Sirena destroyed the Monasteries."

"During Arella's Comet, right? Orion mentioned it. The *year of tears.*"

"Exactly. I've long believed she found out about the keys, but when she entered the In-Between, Elohim barred her entry to Celestelvyra. I think the destruction of the Monasteries and their scholars was her revenge. And you're right. She used the comet to do it."

"What do you suppose she did this time when He wouldn't let her in?"

Asher shrugged. "I guess we'll find out when we return to Arkaemor."

When they got back to the waterfall, they found Iris and Seth still asleep beneath the trees. Not wanting to wake them, they strolled toward the edge of the pond, swishing up the scent of honeysuckle as they passed by. The sky above lightened, though the stars never seemed to dim despite the reduction in contrast. When Foxx sat in the dewy grass, she leaned back on her hands and looked up just as a shooting star flickered to life, streaked across the atmosphere, and blinked out of existence.

Asher sat down next to her, keeping a reasonable distance between them. "Do you want me to continue?"

"Yes, please." She wrapped her arms around her knees as she turned to stare at the bubbling falls. Lotus pads floated atop the surface of the pond, and tiny frogs sprang from one leaf to another, causing the flowers to gyrate above the ripples. In the tree closest to the falls, a tiny opossum hung from its tail. "You said she used the key in Reginaterra, but I thought Reginaterra didn't have a Monastery."

"It doesn't. With it being her home territory, the scholars never built a Monastery there, but that doesn't mean the territory doesn't have a door to the In-Between."

"But if she chose to leave Celestelvyra to begin with, why would she care about the doorways or the keys? She got what she wanted, didn't she?"

"From what I understand, the fallen numinae—or Sirena at the very least—have spent a lot of energy fighting to find their way back into the Sacred Garden. The way the Monastery tells it, it only took a few centuries for them to mourn all they'd abandoned."

"I understand their longing to return." Foxx leaned back on her palms again and let her toes touch the water. "This place is extraordinary."

Asher said her name, and she hummed in answer, though she didn't look away from the falls. "If you want any help reading that book, or if you have any other questions about any of this, I'll do my best to help you, okay?"

She nodded.

"And if you ever want to discuss anything else, you know my ears are open and waiting."

Releasing a held breath, she answered, "I know."

They sat together in silence for a long while, both lingering inside their own thoughts. The garden around them continued to brighten. Foxx thought about the Ram, His magnificent beauty, and the sensations she experienced in His presence. She contemplated how anyone could ever willingly choose to leave the wonders of the garden. Celestelvyra was a place of pure sublimity. They had everything they needed to survive, free of pain and monsters and wars. What had Sirena and her companions been thinking to leave its grandeur behind? She couldn't comprehend the thought.

Then she realized with despairing dread—if all went to plan, she and the others would be leaving, too.

Asher noticed the change in her composure and gestured with a finger toward her head. "What just happened in there?"

Meeting his curious stare, she watched one side of his lips upturn to reveal a dimple. Not long ago, she'd longed to share with him all of her thoughts and fears, and had yearned for the day they might find their way back to each other. Even now, despite her anger and resistance, she couldn't deny the magnitude of what she felt being near him. No matter how much effort she'd put into suppressing it, their chemistry had been undeniable since that very first glance in the shadows of Kesken Ala.

As minutes continued to blend together, piling up in stacks of hours that morphed into days of space stretching between the truths he'd divulged and the present, the potency of her anger had dwindled. Though she endeavored to remind herself of all the pain he'd caused her, those emerald eyes expressed so much terrifying emotion, and she couldn't deny the effect it had on the cage barricading her heart.

"You don't have to tell me. I don't want to pressure you."

"Yes, you do," she said, and his smile widened, drawing prickly, treacherous, warmth to her stomach. "But it might be nice to talk about it." Asher agreed.

Avoiding all notions of what leaving the garden might mean, she provided a half truth. "Do you think some places in the garden are more magical than others? I was thinking about what we discussed before: how much everything hurts, but somehow at the same time feels… insignificant. Trivial, even empty. But back in the meadow, my heart thawed. I felt peace there. Not a desolate vacancy or a blatant unfeeling, but a tearful tranquility. Like all of my fears had vanished, leaving only hope in their wake." As they'd departed the meadow, that feeling had withered. Not in a drastic instant, like the sensation of walking through a barrier into an entirely contrasting territory, but like a steady, trickling ebb, as sunshine evaporates morning dew from petals and leaves.

Asher's hand came to rest against his heart. "Yes, I know what you mean. I felt it, too. The Spirit of Elohim resides all throughout the garden, or so it is written, but perhaps when He is truly present with us, His majesty is more formidable."

"So, is it possible for Him to be truly present with us all the time?" She turned to him. "To feel that peace?"

"Well, He is always truly present with those who love and honor Him, but I meant His physical form. When we were in the meadow, the aura surrounding Him was forceful and mighty. Even over-whelming. It brought tears to my eyes as well."

Foxx's mouth dropped open as she processed his words. "Are you suggesting that the Ram was... I mean, you're saying we were with Elohim just now?"

Holding her gaze, he ran his hands along the damp grass. "I believe they are one and the same, don't you? I mean, I didn't realize it at first, though I suppose I should have since a statue of Him sits just inside the gates of Jericho, but after spending only a few moments with Him, I knew with certainty who He must be. Couldn't you feel it? His... supremacy?"

"I don't..." Her sentence trailed off. As his words took root within her, she couldn't imagine how she'd missed it. She'd hugged, pet, nuzzled, and even kissed the cheek of the Creator of the universe.

"It's said He reveals Himself in many forms. Sometimes as a ram or a dragon, other times as a pillar of fire or even a gentle breeze. You said He told you He could see you after the Queen pulled you up into the storm. Then you saw the Ram here by the waterfall."

"So, wait. Does that mean He sends my visions?" Her head spun as she acclimated herself to this new line of enlightenment. Testing the notion on her tongue, she said, "The Ram is the Creator. For months, Elohim has communicated with me through my visions. For years, He did the same with my mother." Allowing her a long silence to take it all in, Asher watched her realizations locking into place. At last she turned to him and asked, "But... why?"

Asher took a long moment to answer. So long, that the move-ment of Foxx tipping her head at him drew him back to the present. "I don't know. Only He knows, I suppose. But I am sorry, love. I thought you knew. He's been with you all along."

Foxx shook her head, shying away from his sincere gaze. Some form of disbelief cut deep into her chest, but she couldn't quite place the emotion. The bighorn Ram was the Creator of everything, and for some unbelievable reason, He saw fit to speak directly to her, singling her out, just as Sirena had in Jericho.

But what was so special about her? What had she done to deserve such a… blessing? Curse?

She drew her toes in and out of the pond, watching as ripples widened before crashing into the waves produced by the falls. A turtle poked its head from the water to her left, bobbing up and down as the undulations disrupted the surface.

Then the invading emotion gouged her, tormenting her heart and scraping it away, as a termite boring through wood. Inadequate. Unworthy. She replayed every moment of the interaction in the meadow, remembering all the ways she hadn't been respectful enough, reverent enough to be in the presence of Elohim Himself.

Finally, she lifted her eyes to Asher and asked again, "But why *me*?"

Asher shrugged. "All I can say is, the Creator does mysterious things to accomplish His works. We can't always understand them, but we need to trust that they're for a greater purpose."

"So if the Creator is really present everywhere in the garden—in fact, you said He is always present, even when we aren't here in Celestelvyra—then why does my chest suddenly feel vacant all over again? Why does He allow us to feel such painful things at all?" Her eyes swelled, and she swallowed past the lump forming in her throat.

Asher sighed. "Another question I don't have an answer for, I'm afraid. However, since we're stuck here for the time being, maybe now is a good time to sort some of it out. Spend more time in the meadow or search for His presence in other places of the garden. Maybe the slight release in pressure will make the process of healing more manageable."

Foxx ran her palms over the grass, letting the blades fill the gaps between her fingers and wondering how it was possible to feel so heavy and hollow simultaneously. She took a deep breath, longing for the weight to lift again.

Looking at Asher from the corners of her eyes, her mind wandered to moments with him when she'd felt the releasing pressure of her burdens. More than once, he'd made her feel like she no longer carried the weight alone. He'd hoisted it up on his shoulder and walked alongside her, bearing half of the load, and she hadn't even noticed it happening until they'd been taken from Petrichor. In the absence of his presence, the undivided force of her and Iris' burdens hung heavy across the back of her neck, yanking her muscles taut and causing her shoulders to pull forward as she tried to support the entirety of the weight.

When she'd been with the Ram, she'd felt the same as she had with Asher—more so, in fact—light as a feather drifting in the wind.

Now, she thought she might crumble until her entire being was crushed beneath the boulder of her sorrow. She considered whether it might have been better never to have known the difference, to have never had the comparison of partnership versus solitude. The shattered trust, broken heart, and empty despair felt far worse than the life she'd known before when it was just she and Iris alone in the wild.

Still, the damage was done. It occurred to her that her only option was to risk loss and disappointment and torment, and strive to trust again. To find her way back to that place of companionship where the burden had lessened. Even if she couldn't trust Asher to remain at her side, surely she could trust Elohim, couldn't she? Perhaps remaining in the meadow, in a constant search of His presence, was the answer.

Asher noticed her intense yet silent thoughts. "What is it?"

Foxx shook away her ruminations. "I was just thinking about trust. Well, actually, about partnership."

"I see. Care to elaborate?"

Sighing, she lifted her eyes to the sky. "I was thinking about Petrichor. Or rather, leaving Petrichor, and how the feeling reminded me of leaving the meadow."

His brows knitted together. "I don't know what you mean."

"It's nothing." Shyness overwhelmed her now that the implications hung in the air between them, whether he could interpret them or not. "I just hate how colossal it all feels with Him gone. It's even worse than before when I didn't know what I was missing. Why does He allow such misery and suffering? If He's really been with me all along, then why didn't He protect us? Protect my mother and my father? Why is there so much trauma and heartbreak, not just in my life, but in the world, when He could stomp his hooves and take it all away in an instant? It seems He could have undone the sins of the numinae immediately and kept the world how He originally wanted it. So why didn't He? Does He enjoy seeing His creation weeping? Does it suit Him to witness our pain?"

Asher took a moment to put his thoughts in order. Then he said, "You just met Him, Foxx. You felt Him. Do you think He enjoys watching your hardships?"

A quiet grumble of frustration rattled Foxx's chest. "No. I guess not."

"I think there are some things we just aren't meant to understand, but I promise you, if you keep reading *Jumalan Sana*, the answers you're looking for will present themselves. It might come slowly, but they will become clear eventually. And even if some things still seem confusing, the trust, hope, and faith that comes from spending time with Elohim will give you peace to combat the confusing stuff."

Foxx hummed and lifted a brow. "And here I thought your ever-present smile was merely an annoying personality trait."

On cue, his lips broke into a broad grin. "Annoying? I'm not sure that's the word you're looking for."

"Yes, annoying. But it's not just your personality, is it?" Her hand flattened on her chest. "There's a peace inside of you. One that doesn't yet exist inside me."

"It's called faith, and it's the only thing that pulled me out of the trenches of the man I used to be and led me here. Without it, I'd still be… well, stuck. Lost. Empty."

"And now you're…?"

"Full, I suppose. Found."

"And adorned in constant smiles." Her eyes flashed to his before returning to the falls, and the brief connection sent her heart aflutter.

Asher chuckled. "Yes, exactly. Just keep searching for Him, Foxx. He's already seeking you and has been for quite some time. You just have to trust Him enough to let Him in."

"Trust, huh? There doesn't seem to be a whole lot of that going around."

"Humans are imperfect. You can't compare your experiences with us to a relationship with Him. I know that's easier said than done, but it might be the most important thing you ever learn."

Foxx wrapped her arms around her knees. A butterfly flew in front of her, drawing her eyes. It was the color of seaweed floating atop ocean waves with details outlined in black. "Speaking of trust,

I feel like I should be honest with you. Earlier when you asked what I was thinking, I lied about the thoughts that changed my expression. In truth, I was thinking about how much I never want to leave this place." In her peripherals, she watched his lips spread into another smile—the visage she both loved and hated.

"Well, we don't actually have a way out right now, so you have some time to enjoy it."

She pushed the thoughts out, knowing by his playful countenance that he had not understood what she attempted to disclose. "That's not what I mean. What I'm trying to say is: Sirena and the others you mentioned chose to leave here, but I can't imagine wanting to leave this place. I don't think I ever want to go back." Her tone shifted from indecisive contemplation to solid resolve. "In fact, I am not going back."

"Foxx…" He seemed to juggle the words fighting for purchase on his lips. "We have to go back. There are people counting on us."

"No one is counting on me." Her tone became suddenly hostile. "Both of my parents are dead. Mr. Magpie is dead. My sister and Seth are here with me, and so is the Creator. I did what I set out to do. I found my father, I found Celestelvyra. My journey is finished." For possibly the twentieth time, she heard the Konungr's words replay through her thoughts. *The world awaits your salvation, foxy woman. As do I.* She looked down at her fingers where they curled around her arms. Then she shook her head. "Now I am here, and you cannot make me leave, Asher. I won't."

He leaned toward her, imploring her to see reason. "What of the others? The people of Jericho? Hector? Rossnetta? What of the children at the Ataraxia Mission? And everyone else who has ever been or will ever be affected by Sirena's wrath?" He watched her, and she knew he must be attempting to decode the thoughts behind her glistening eyes, the pull of her heartstrings as his words rang true. Then he asked, "What if He wants you to leave?"

Foxx contemplated whether or not the Ram might seriously force her from the garden. Would He be angry at her for denying His wishes? After a long moment, she got to her feet. "Saving the world is your destiny, Prince Alexander. Not mine." Then she walked away from him, exiting the clearing through the path leading to the meadow and leaving him alone to analyze his thoughts.

Roused from sleep, Iris rolled over to see Seth snoozing soundly alongside Foxx and Asher's empty bedrolls. He lay on his stomach with his face turned toward her, lips parted as breath escaped in a soothing rhythm.

The gentle boy had seen such awful sights for one so young, and she couldn't imagine how he was dealing with the images floating around in his mind. His arm lay stretched out across the grass between them, and she wondered if nightmares had him reaching for her in the night. Perhaps she could take him to the place she and Foxx had sparred. He'd been practicing with a sword and would enjoy training on the interesting terrain. If they spent some time alone together, he may even be willing to open up about the things he felt beneath the constant joy he displayed.

Sitting up to survey her surroundings, she saw Asher slouched by the pond writing in his journal. She hadn't gotten a chance to talk to him much after his adventure with Seth, and she thought he might know better how Seth was handling things. Standing, she stretched her back, raising her arms to the sky and twisting from side to side. Hearing her movements, Asher glanced back to find her walking his way. He closed the pencil in his book and set it in his lap.

"Merry morning, friend." She plopped down in the grass next to him. "Where's Foxx?"

"Merry morning, Iris. And that is a fair question. Where *is* Foxx?" He began ripping a leaf into tiny pieces, his eyes unfocused as he stared at the ground.

"What's wrong? Did you guys fight again?"

"Again? I'm not aware of a time when the fighting ceased."

Iris tilted her head, offering a small smile, and he sighed.

"No, not exactly a fight." He tossed another flake of leaf to the grass, his eyes landing on the pencil sticking out from the inside of his journal—one in a set of three Foxx had bought for him on a whim in Ataraxia.

Pulling her long hair together, still hanging free of its pony, Iris draped it in front of her shoulder and combed her fingers through it. She'd worn it up in a tail for as long as she could remember, but the night they fled Peregrine Manor, Declan said he liked it hanging loose, and she'd hardly worn it up since then. She'd considered putting it up multiple times since entering Celestelvyra but hadn't yet brought herself to do it. "So what's going on?"

"It's probably better for you to talk to her about it. How did you sleep?"

"Very well! Every night I've slept here has been wonderful." Then Iris fell quiet, her eyes glazing over.

Noticing her blank stare, Asher dragged himself from his own melancholy and turned to face her, crossing his legs beneath him. "So how are you doing with everything?" When she didn't look up or respond to his question, he added, "By *everything* I mean, specifically: Declan and your father."

"I knew what you meant," she snapped, but her tone was playful despite the sadness she felt at his mention of them. Birds chirped from the tree to the left of the falls, drawing her eyes. Without her permission, her mind drifted to Orion and their walk beneath the tunnel of parrots. The thought quickly shifted to memories of Declan in Jericho, then to his betrayal, before landing finally on the Queen shoving her knife up under his ribs.

"Have you thought more about what we discussed? That maybe Declan isn't completely to blame?" A breeze blew by, making their hair sway across their faces.

Nodding, she rested her cheek on her fist with an elbow on her knee. Her opposite hand picked at the grass. "I suppose so. I think I'm more worried about Foxxglove than anything else right now. I don't really remember much of my father. I have some good memories, but he's been absent for so long, Foxx was basically my mother and my father. As long as I have her, I think I can get through anything."

"You should give yourself more credit. I bet even without her, you would shine like a champion."

Iris rolled her eyes, though she smiled. "As far as Declan, I will grieve him in my own time. Since we talked, I've been thinking, what if he really did survive?" The memory of him collapsing as the doors to Celestelvyra closed between them had her feeling foolish for even considering that he might have lived. She shivered and rubbed the tops of her arms to soothe away goosebumps. "I know the chances are super slim, but without knowing for sure, how can I grieve? I feel stuck in the unknown."

"I know exactly what you mean."

She lifted her head from her fist. "But Foxx is an actual mess.

She's either feeling everything too much or burying it and not feeling it at all. Neither of which are good tactics for healing. A fact *she* taught me!"

"Yeah, I know."

"She practically attacked me yesterday." The fear she'd felt in her sister's wrath sent a shiver up her spine. "She's never done that before."

"What do you mean she attacked you?"

"We were sparring and—Okay, I was taunting her if I'm being honest, but she went a little insane, Asher. She's never fought with me like that, with such force and animosity. She pinned me to the wall, and I actually felt frightened. I can honestly say I've never been afraid of her before. Not like that, at least."

Asher straightened. "She pinned you? With her sword? Are you all right?"

Iris grinned at his passionate and loyal response. "Stop getting all protective, big brother. It's fine. She didn't cut me or anything like that. But it did seem like she lost control of herself for a minute. It was… troubling. I saw the moment she realized what she was doing. Something changed in her eyes."

"She is definitely lost." He leaned back on his palms, letting his head fall backward to gaze up at the sky.

"Don't give up on her, Asher, okay? Promise me you won't?"

He sighed. "I can't force her to love me, Iris."

"You don't have to. She already does. All you have to do is not give up." She accepted his absent nod, knowing it was all the confirmation she could ask for with things as they were. "I should go talk to her." Standing, she looked at Seth and said Asher's name. "How's he doing?"

Asher followed her line of sight to the brave, young boy sleeping across the yard. "I think he'll be all right, actually. He's stronger than he seems."

"You're right. He is." Sighing, she touched his shoulder. "How are we ever going to get out of here, Asher?"

He matched her sigh. "We don't have the keys, but that doesn't mean someone on the outside won't save us. Hector maybe? This place is soaked in magic and mystery. Maybe the Creator will show us the way. *Seek His will in all you do, and He will show you which path to take.*"

Iris pondered that. Then with a wave, she left him by the pond and went off to find her sister. Minutes later, she discovered Foxx laying on her back in a meadow of wildflowers. She paused along the outer edge and took it in with awe. Birds filled the trees, harmonizing a wonderful melody, and she breathed in the fragrant aroma of the flowers as she approached Foxx with caution. "May I join you?"

Foxx stared into the galaxy sky without making eye contact. "Did Asher send you?"

"Not exactly. I asked where you were, and he said you went this way. Does that count as sending me?"

Foxx made a noise of disbelief, and Iris took that as an answer in the positive.

Laying next to her, she turned her eyes to the vivid nebulas embellishing the deep-ocean atmosphere. "It's delightful here." She spread her arms through the flowers, stirring up their scent and letting the tall grasses tickle her skin.

"It is," Foxx agreed.

"And these wildflowers smell amazing." Iris closed her eyes and inhaled.

"They do."

Iris rolled onto her side, slid her hands up under her face, and stared at her sister. "So. Do you want to talk about it?"

"About what?" Foxx avoided Iris' gaze, and Iris scooted closer, knowingly invading her space to draw her attention. Foxx rotated her head to look at her, and Iris smiled with victory. "Do *you* want to talk about anything, Iris?"

"So many things."

Foxx mirrored her sister, rolling onto her side with both hands under her cheek, her legs curled so their knees touched between them. "Go ahead."

"Well first of all, there's father."

Foxx's eyes shifted away from Iris' before she fought to draw them back. "He was here all this time. Well, not *here*."

Iris said, "But he didn't abandon us. He didn't even realize he'd been gone so long."

"I know. Neither of them abandoned us."

Iris nodded, thinking their entire lives had been shaped around such terrible lies. "I'm glad we got to see him before…"

"Which brings us to the topic of Declan." Foxx sighed, and it was Iris' turn to avert her eyes. "How are you feeling about it?" She tucked Iris' loose hair behind her ear so it didn't hang in her face. "I like your hair down. It's nice."

"Declan asked me to wear it this way." Iris smiled weakly, almost embarrassed, and Foxx kept silent, dropping her chin and waiting for her to continue if she wanted to. "Asher thinks it maybe wasn't all a lie."

"He would."

A rainbow butterfly fluttered above them and landed on Foxxglove's shoulder. They watched as it rested there, slowly flapping its wings open and closed. Then it flitted off into the trees.

Iris asked, "Are you ever going to forgive him?"

"Are you ever going to forgive Declan?"

"Declan is… dead. Probably, at least. But if he were here…" She thought for a minute, pulling petals off a flower in front of her face. "… I would like to think I would give him a chance to explain, and if he was remorseful, I would try to understand and forgive him, yes."

"We aren't leaving here, Iris." The words flew from her lips without restraint.

Iris drew her head back. "We can't right now, but there is still hope we will find a way. Asher said—"

"You misunderstand me." Foxx's expression became steely and unfeeling. "I don't mean we can't. I mean, even if a time comes when we are able to leave, you and Seth and I aren't going." She squared her gaze on her sister to ensure comprehension. "We are staying here."

This admission shocked Iris into sitting up. Foxx joined her with a countenance displaying annoyance, almost boredom. "What are you talking about, Foxxglove? Is this why Asher is angry at you?"

"I'm angry at him!" Foxx's shout revealed the emotion beneath the surface she'd tried to hide. "What does he have to be angry about? He's the one who ruined everything."

Sitting up higher, nearly on her knees with intensity, Iris argued, "He didn't ruin everything! He was trying to do what he thought was right. He made mistakes, but haven't we all? Like for example: you, right this moment, claiming that you intend to abandon every person you've ever met! You can't be serious, Foxx, no. I don't believe you."

"Entirely serious." Foxx crossed her arms, her eyes hard as the stone wall holding the waterfall above the pond. "We have finished the mission Maeve sent us on. We found our father and Celestelvyra. The rest of the world's problems are not our responsibility."

Iris pressed her fingers into her temples. "Foxxglove, wait. I'm trying to wrap my head around this, because I cannot believe I'm hearing these words—from you, of all people! Pinch me so I can wake up from this insanity."

Foxx shook her head, closing her eyes to block out her sister's ashamed expression. "We've fought enough. We've given enough. We can help Asher find Pyhä-ki, and then he can take it back to kill Sirena. We aren't soldiers. We're just two young women. Hector and Abram have an actual army of trained warriors standing behind them. They don't need us, Iris."

"But we can't just abandon everyone!" Iris' voice cracked, the shriek echoing throughout the alcove of trees.

"It's already decided. We are staying. Seth, too." Foxx opened her eyes but refused to look at her sister, focusing instead on a trunk over her shoulder.

Iris got to her feet, planting them into the ground with fervor. "No. Absolutely not, Foxx. I will not desert our people. You can't force me to stay here." Foxx leveled her with a look of resolve, but Iris continued on. "You can stay. If we find a way out, that means we will have a way back in. I can come back, but I am not leaving Asher and everyone else to fight this battle on their own. I'm not abandoning Rossnetta; or Ah Luiah, Chaisai and Tanawat; Raven, Hector, and the Raptors. No." Crossing her arms, she turned her face away in defiance. "I refuse to do that."

"I'm not letting you go back out into that desolate wasteland of nightmares and monsters."

Throwing her hands out to her sides, Iris yelled, "I'm not a child anymore, Foxx!"

"But you are my responsibility. This conversation is over."

Iris stomped her foot with a frustrated growl that seemed to rattle the leaves of nearby trees. Then she turned on her heel and stormed off.

CHAPTER 16

STRATAGEM

Orion and Isolde met with Hector and his soldiers over breakfast the following day to discuss their scheme for infiltrating the Ashgate Fortress. Abram and Eero joined them, though they wouldn't be traveling with them to Crystavium.

Jax had drawn up three maps the previous evening: two above-ground maps detailing the upper and lower floors of what used to be the Monastery, and one for the underground prison itself.

He'd sketched them thoroughly, indicating what each room was used for, where guards were often posted, dangers and traps he knew of, and possible locations for the door leading to the In-Between.

Hector leaned over the maps like the others, scratching his chin. "The vault seems like the most obvious place."

"Doesn't it almost feel too obvious for it to be in the vault?" Orion stood across from Hector, scrutinizing the hastily drawn yet detailed maps and committing them to memory. Isolde stood at his side, her shoulder touching his, and he couldn't help wondering whether she truly felt so comfortable with him that she didn't notice or if it was simply a trait of her demeanor to disregard all personal space.

Jax said, "I don't—"

Hooves clopping against stone reached their ears through the tented walls. Jax and Hector's eyes met across the table, and everyone stilled, anxiously awaiting the arrival of their unexpected guest.

Abram rose and moved toward the door.

Moments later, the flap opened, and two Jerichonian Guards entered, each carrying a tray between their arms. Without speaking, they circled the table and placed both trays at the end free of maps. One tray held a pot of coffee, exactly enough horn mugs for each person, and dishes of sugar and cream. The other had a mixture of sweet and savory pastries. The Guardsmen bowed their heads to Abram before silently exiting the tent.

"Well, it was nice knowing you all." Orion kept his eyes to the table, leaning on his fists and feeling all eyes turn his way. Isolde's hand contracted around the hilt of her sword at his side.

After what felt like a painfully long time, the flap to the tent lifted, and they heard their guest thank the Guard for holding it ajar. When he stepped inside, Konungr Vali Kirkavall kept his attention on his hands as he pulled his gloves off one finger at a time. He wore bold plum with gray fur draped over his right shoulder and hanging so it nearly skimmed the ground next to black boots. All of his embellishments, including the buttons on his gloves, shined like polished silver.

Abram bowed. "It's good to see you this morning, Your Majesty."

"Thank you, Commander." When he at last had his gloves free of his hands, he slid them into his hip pocket and lifted his eyes to the room, grinning. "Merry morning, all! As you can see, I have provided coffee and breakfast for you to enjoy. Please help yourselves." His gaze scanned the tent, pausing on Jax already pouring himself a horn of coffee. A pastry hung from his mouth as he lifted a hand in greeting. Vali shook his head with amusement and continued his inspection.

When he saw Isolde, his expression brightened. "Naabila Isolde!" Closing the distance between them, he took her hand in his. "How astonishing to find you in my city. To my knowledge, it is your first time, is it not?"

"Indeed it is, and I am humbly grateful to be granted entrance." She bowed with grace.

Vali bent to press a kiss to the back of her fingers before leaning in and pressing another to her cheek. Then he took a step back and looked her over. "What an enchanting woman you have grown into, Isolde."

The Princess beamed. "You are looking wonderful as well, Konungr Vali. Though you do not appear to have aged a day since our last meeting."

"Good genes," he said with an endearing wink. "My lovely Ingrid is the same. Imagine how gorgeous our children would be."

"If you ever get around to having any," she teased.

"Ah, yes. Well, perhaps when this war is at its end, I shall allow my wife to convince me. But what about you? Have there been any exceptional men in your life?"

Rolling her eyes, she chuckled. "You know my father. So I am certain you can guess."

Orion kept his head down, though his eyes were up catching glimpses of the interaction. It wasn't a secret that women often swooned over the handsome and charismatic King of Cordillera, but it hadn't occurred to him that Vali and Isolde might be so familiar with each other.

"Yes, indeed I do." He lifted a shoulder. "I had hoped one day you and Alexander… but, alas, some things just aren't meant to be."

Isolde laughed. "I do not think I am our young prince's type."

"I believe you're correct, my lady. You're far too kind for our friend's tastes. How is your father? I haven't seen him for some time."

"He is very well. I am sure he would adore a visit from you."

"I will definitely make that a priority in the near future, but until then, will you send him my best when you return to Caritas?" At her agreement, the Konungr turned his attention to the others in the room. "Now, Commanders, to business. Would either of you care to explain the purpose of this meeting? Have we heard back from Alexander yet?" Vali's eyes scanned the hand drawn maps with curiosity.

Abram cleared his throat. "They haven't returned, Your Majesty. We expected them back yesterday."

"Something may have delayed them." Vali inclined his head, trying to see what the maps depicted.

"We have reason to believe they've been trapped and need to be extracted from Celestelvyra." Hector accepted a cup of coffee from Raven and took a sip before setting it down next to him. "So we are in the process of putting together a plan to do that."

Vali lifted a brow, pulling his eyes from the maps to look at Hector. "And what is the source of this notion, pray tell?"

Orion straightened at last and made himself known. Vali's eyes widened with recognition as Orion said, "That would be me, Your Majesty." He lifted a hand in a half wave.

"O'Connell!" Vali almost shouted. The soldiers in the room startled, and Raven nearly spilled her own freshly poured coffee. Jax grabbed it just in time, allowing only a few drops to splash from the mug. "How is banishment treating you?" He surveyed Orion, appraising him from head to toe. "Not well by the looks of it."

"It hasn't been terrible." Orion kept his tone even, trying to thwart the Konungr's pleasure at his misfortune.

Vali nodded, though his expression seemed to disagree. "I was fairly certain I gave you clear instructions never to set foot in my city again." He looked up as though trying to remember the details before returning his smug grin to Orion. "Am I mistaken?"

"You are not mistaken." Orion held Vali's gaze, flexing his fingers at his sides and willing away his irritation. Thankfully, the whispers hadn't deigned to surface, and he wondered if they might be hiding in terror of the King of Cordillera.

"Did I specify an amount of time to which this order applied?" Vali placed fair knuckles against his hip.

Orion's gaze met Isolde's as her hand grasped the hilt of her sword, her eyes communicating questions he didn't know how to answer. He drew away from her and looked at Vali. "I believe your words were, *until death takes you and your corpse rots with the worms,* Your Majesty."

Vali cackled, running long fingers through hair as light as pale smoke. "You appear to have an excellent memory, O'Connell. Why have you decided to break this command? Do you have an itch to spend some time with Cordillera's worms? They grow very big down in the valley if you didn't know. Large enough to eat your foot in one gulp. And my oh my, those sharp teeth. Vicious, I say, and ever so hungry this time of year."

Orion fought to stifle a squirm. He hadn't known the worms in the mountain territory to be larger or more ferocious than any of the others in Arkaemor, and the thought made him want to vomit. "No. That's not why I'm here."

"I see. If the worms weren't enough to deter you, I believe you must know I could have you shipped off to the farms in Reginaterra or Savanni as the other sovereigns do with their vagabonds. They'll keep you high on sil ōnni for the rest of your days. A fair trade off, I think. Have you tasted it? It might even be a gift in comparison to your miserable life." Vali chuckled and slipped his hands into his pockets. "You may not be a traitor, but you certainly are a poor excuse for a man. Still, slavery isn't really my style. I prefer to punish with monsters."

Orion drew back his head. "How do you know I'm not a traitor?"

Vali scoffed. "Because I'm not an idiot. And because I'm the one who told Sawyer not to let his team in on our little bargain."

Losing grip on his temper, Orion snarled. "You admit your involvement yet still treat me like garbage under your shiny, pointed shoes."

Vali leveled him with a glare. "We both know my loathing for you has nothing to do with Sawyer Belamour."

"You think you're so much better than me, Vali."

"I *am* better than you, heathen."

"You're a vile charlatan—"

"Charlatan!"

"A corrupt blackguard and a worthless son of a bi—"

"If I may," Hector cut in before Orion could dig himself deeper. Both men burned him with angry stares. "I would like to vouch for this man, sire. He was sent to us by your allies in the Wilds, with the Naabila of Caritas at his side."

Isolde forced a winsome smile in spite of her obvious inner conflict as her history with the royals of Cordillera waged war with her instinct to protect Orion. She released the hilt of her sword, though her fingers danced across the top.

Abram said, "I approved of him joining us, Your Majesty. I knew you would be wise enough to allow it once you knew the truth of his arrival."

Vali lifted a hand, indicating that Abram could be at ease. Then he leaned toward Isolde and lowered his voice, though everyone could still hear him clearly. "Tell me, Naabila Isolde, is it true you've arrived with this scoundrel? Were we not just discussing your father's aversion to the lowly men of this world?" He gestured to Orion, not attempting to hide his grimace.

"It is true, Your Majesty. My father instructed me to come with him to speak to you. I am not sure what issues the two of you have had in the past, but my father is very fond of Orion, as are many of the villagers in Caritas."

The room seemed to share a universal noise of astonishment, and Orion ran a hand over the back of his head. Vali hummed, scrutinizing him again as though attempting see through the mask. His eyes stalled on the wounds laced across his face and arms.

"We need to retrieve Alexander from Celestelvyra before the war begins," Orion said, hoping to move gracefully past Isolde's notations and any questions Vali might have regarding the evidence of Sirena's brutality. "Otherwise we have no hope in taking Sirena out. I do apologize for disobeying your orders, truly, but I know you are an intelligent man, and I'd hoped you would deem saving the world more important than our petty rivalries."

"Rivalries!" Vali cracked. "Ha!"

Orion swallowed, feeling his heartbeat level. "And if I'm not mistaken, I believe you and the Prince are fairly close, aren't you? At least you were at one point. I was hoping your love for him might outweigh your hatred for me."

The others waited silently, eyes flicking back and forth between the two men as Vali deliberated. Jax and Raven nibbled on pastries with gazes entranced by the interaction.

Orion touched the table, his fingers grazing the edge of the maps. "At any rate, once we have this all sorted, we'll be leaving straight away. If we return, it will be with Prince Alexander, and if we fail, we won't be returning at all, and your animosity towards me will be moot."

"How exactly do you plan on retrieving him?" The Konungr again eyed the maps, lips curled as he answered his own question. "This is the Ashgate Fortress." His gaze lifted to Hector. "I thought I was the madman in this lot."

"We believe there is a door to the In-Between in the vault beneath the prison."

Vali laughed outright, longer than seemed socially acceptable given the situation. "It would appear you are correct for once, O'Connell." To Hector, he said, "And it seems you're not as uptight and cowardly as I imagined, Kayvan."

Hector clenched his jaw. "Perhaps we all have much to learn about each other."

"I suppose if you make it out of Ashgate alive, I will consider that notion further. For now, I will allow you the use of my horses to ensure a swift journey. You'll need all of your energy and strength if you have any hope of surviving the Prison of the Strayed."

Hector's eyes tracked Vali as he circled the table. "Thank you, Your Majesty. That would be greatly appreciated."

"When do you leave?" Pausing next to Raven, Vali lifted a savory pastry to his mouth.

"Tomorrow," Hector answered.

After chewing and swallowing, Vali snagged Raven's mug from her fingers and took a sip. Her eyebrows rose, matching Jax's next to her, but she allowed the Konungr to enjoy her drink without complaint. When he returned the mug to her hand, he winked. "Thank you, my dear." Wiping his lips, he rounded the table to stand next to Hector, putting a hand on his shoulder. "Very good. I'll be certain the horses are ready. I sure hope you know what you're getting yourselves into."

Hector exhaled a steadying breath. "It seems the only option since Sirena demolished the rest of the Monasteries."

Abram said, "Do you have any advice for them, Your Majesty? Have you any experience with Ashgate?"

"My only advice is to avoid the Strayed at all costs." Vali scratched his chin. "This will not be easy, but I believe you are right, Hector. It's our only option if we wish to pursue this war. You're all very brave to attempt it. Truly, I salute you."

"Thank you, Your Majesty." Hector slid a hand behind his back and bowed.

"Enjoy your breakfast. I shall leave you to it." Vali spun, his cape splaying out as he did so. After lifting the door, he called back over his shoulder, "You know where to find me should you need anything before your departure. Farewell." With a final flutter of his hand, the door fell closed behind him. Everyone in the room held their breath until the sound of galloping horses reached their ears.

Orion and Hector exhaled a unified sigh and shared a glance. "That could have been much worse, I suppose."

Hector scuffed his jaw. "I honestly can't believe he hasn't locked us both in chains. I wonder what he's planning."

Abram chuckled. "You boys let Eero and I handle the Konungr. Just keep your thoughts and worries on the journey ahead." Eero nodded in agreement.

"He has always been quite a strange man," Isolde said.

"Strange?" Jax took another bite of his pastry and handed the rest to Raven.

"The vault." Hector returned the room's attention to the maps. "That vault is the most protected place in all of Arkaemor. Sirena moved many things there to keep them extra secure after Sawyer Belamour's thievery. She wouldn't have done so if she didn't consider it safer even than the vaults beneath the castle."

Stroking his long beard from chin to point, Abram said, "Even in the vault, the Queen's enchantment will help shield it."

"The Ashgate Fortress is nearly impenetrable. Though most of the time, people are trying to get out, not in, which could be to our advantage." Jax pulled the map of the ground floor in front of him and pointed to the outer wall. "There is a wall, a *syli* thick and more than twenty feet high, surrounding the entire perimeter of the property."

"So we climb it," Raven suggested. "We can manage twenty."

Jax shook his head. "The top is embedded with metal and stone shards. Too dense to maneuver through, too tall and sharp to climb." He pointed to the front gate. "The guards work in month-long shifts. When three guards arrive for their shift, three others go home. I think this could be one way in."

Hector asked, "Swap out? Grab some guards coming in for a switch and go in place of them."

"Exactly. This won't work for everyone though. Hector and I are known at Ashgate, and Isolde would never pass for a guard." He glanced at her, and she smiled with pride.

"You think we should split up?" Raven flipped a throwing knife through her fingers. Standing next to her with his eyes carefully following the movement of the blade, Orion took a step away and bumped into Isolde. She side-stepped to give him space, but barely.

Jax moved to top off his mug before stopping on the other side of the map to point out the area in discussion. "There might be a way in through the back of the building. There is a water source, a small river that flows from outside the wall into the building under the kitchens and drops like a waterfall into the underground prison. No inmate is held above ground in the Monastery. The building is used for guard quarters, security, things like that."

Orion asked, "How far down are we talking for the vault?"

Jax worked through the math in his head. "Twelve levels for inmates, three for the Strayeds' living area. Maybe 150 feet?"

"How sure are we that the vault will hold the entrance to Celestelvyra?" Raven asked.

Hector said, "It's the only place that makes sense. It wouldn't be somewhere the guards could easily access it. I seriously doubt even the Warden's quarters would be considered safe enough to hold it. I'd say the Strayed floors are at the bottom to help guard it. No soldier would dare enter their levels unless absolutely necessary."

"What do they do down there?" Isolde asked.

Abram said, "The corrupt Monastery scholars are known as the Strayed because they have strayed from their mission of serving the Monastery of the Morrow and the Creator. Now they serve the Immortal Queen."

"They're inhuman, difficult to look at, and even harder to kill." Hector grimaced. "They're empty, mindless servants that do not require sleep, food, or water to survive. They serve the prisoners, keeping them alive, but only just."

Jax said, "No one really knows what they do down on their floors, but the guards whisper. Some claim to hear horrific screams coming from below when patrolling the lower levels." Raven shivered. Isolde looked sick. Pointing again to his sketches, Jax continued, "The underground prison is designed like a cylinder with the cells around the outer wall. Grated walkways line the levels, with staircases in between. A never-ending fire surrounded by a moat fed by the falls rests on level fourteen. Thirteen through fifteen belong to the Strayed, and within the final floor is a staircase leading to the vaults."

"Here comes the tricky part," Hector said.

"We haven't reached the tricky part yet?" Raven asked. Hector grinned, the thrill of their dangerous adventure animating him. It drew a smile to her lips.

"The vaults can only be opened by activating a lever in the Warden's quarters on the second floor of the Monastery." Jax cast a glance around the room, gauging reactions. "Once that lever is pulled, there are two more on the first floor that need cranked and held. This triggers a chain reaction of mechanisms running all the way down to the vault door. Outside the vault, another two people must rotate levers on opposite sides of the door until it unlocks."

Orion spread out the maps and pointed to all three. "That's five people in three different places all at one time. Plus someone to enter the vault. How are we supposed to manage all that without being discovered?"

Jax shrugged. "With perfection. It's really our only option. One mistake, and it's over. If anyone lets go before everyone is out of the vault, they'll be trapped inside. Alarms will sound, and we'll all be dead."

"Or worse." Abram moved to pour a cup of coffee.

"Fantastic." A headache had started behind Orion's right eye, and the drips had grown louder since Vali's departure. He rubbed his temples. "We need a sixth player."

"We can pull a soldier from here?" Jax looked from Abram to Eero. "Solvi Brenna maybe?"

"Solvi would be a good pick," Eero said. "She is strong, well trained, and fearless."

"Declan," Orion countered. "He will want to come. We can stop by the village on our way. It'll only add a few days to the trip, and then we can keep Naaba Kaatachi in the loop. I'm not sure he will be pleased with Isolde coming along, anyway." His eyes shifted to the desert princess with caution.

Her mouth dropped open. "You mean to turn me over to my father and not let me take part?"

Orion pulled her aside and spoke low. "I mean to keep you safe at all costs, as I promised him I would. I don't feel right taking you there without letting him know first. There's a big difference between traveling the Metsa and breaking into the Ashgate Fortress."

She crossed her arms, her face washed in a fury she rarely displayed.

He found himself again struggling not to feel enticed by the wild anger directed his way. Glancing at the others, no doubt soaking in every word, he watched as they pretended to stare at the maps and refill their coffees.

Allowing his thrumming heart to settle, he said, "Isolde, it's not because I doubt your capabilities. You are an heir to your people, and that can't be taken lightly. Your father may not wish for you to take part in such a dangerous operation."

"I make my own decisions." She stepped closer, seething through her teeth. "He does not control me."

"He's your father, Naabila."

Isolde scoffed. "I have lived twenty-six years, Orion. I may be a princess, but I am not a child."

Lost again in his desire, Orion felt the room go hot. His palms went clammy as his eyes raked her up and down without his permission, noticing the glistening condensation her emotions created across bits of exposed skin. It was significantly less skin than usually revealed by her attire, and he found himself envisioning the mysteries that lie beneath the layers. The heat of her anger darkened her cheeks, and the gold of her eyes flared like molten flames. He endeavored to abolish sultry imaginings of dragging her back to their shared room. With a hoarse inhale, he spoke through held breath. "Trust me, I am well aware of that." Forcing his eyes from her before he did something unreservedly stupid, Orion returned his attention to the group. "We should stop in Caritas first. Also, did you notice the black ground spilling from the outer walls?"

"There was some darkness at the barrier when we first crossed through," Hector said. "Only a few inches."

"It's almost a foot now, at least where we crossed over. Though if you jumped here, I assume it was the same place."

"A foot?" Jax repeated. "That's a remarkable amount of growth in what?" His eyes met Hector's. "Less than three weeks?"

"What could it be?" Isolde's anger lingered, though it settled to a simmer as she addressed the others. "The barriers breaking down?"

Abram pulled at his beard. "Or breaking in. There are some who believe the world grows smaller with each passing day."

"Actually smaller?" Jax asked. "As in: land disappearing?"

"Swallowed up by the walls. Indeed."

Orion stepped back from the table so he had room to move his feet. "But why wouldn't the ground near the walls have always been black then? If it's been growing smaller all along?"

"Perhaps it is moving faster now," Abram suggested. "Perhaps whatever lies beyond the walls is pushing harder. Or the declaration of a revolution has set things unseen in motion."

Jax said, "Nothing lives beyond the walls."

Abram nodded solemnly. "Maybe, my friend. Maybe. All the more reason to press on, I believe."

Sighing, Jax nodded. "Let's focus on what we can actively work on and leave the rest for another day. We don't need to be adding more to an already full plate."

Isolde said, "Agreed. In terms of participants, Declan will still be injured."

"He'll be well enough." Orion looked at her, but she kept her eyes focused on the others. "And he'll want to come."

"How did Declan come to be left behind anyway?" Jax asked.

Orion kept his eyes on the maps. "Sirena stabbed him."

"So they just left him behind?" Raven's loyalty to Declan surged.

Orion glanced up through hooded eyes. "All I will say is that, yes, there is more to the story, and if Declan wants to share it with you, he will." Declan had not strictly asked Orion to keep his betrayal a secret, but at this point, it was his business. If Iris came out of Celestelvyra and clocked Declan in the jaw right in front of everyone, that was his problem to deal with when it happened. Hopefully, if that was the outcome, she would at least wait until they escaped the Ashgate Fortress.

"So we split into two teams." Raven sighed, flipping her hair to her back so it stopped hanging in the way of the maps. "Orion, Declan, and I knock out some guards, swap uniforms, and walk right through the front gate. Jax, Hector, and Isolde come in through the river, following it all the way down to the prison." Her knife pointed to the locations as she stated them. "Making sure to hop off before plummeting down the waterfall to their deaths. Then you'll head down the levels to the vault. Two of you will hold the door open with the levers while one of you goes in, finds the entrance to the In-Between, and opens the door to Celestelvyra, setting Prince Alexander, Iris, and Foxxglove free."

"And Seth, the young boy they took with them," Orion reminded her.

"Yes, that all sounds right." Jax folded an arm across his chest and rested his chin on his opposite hand. His eyes roamed the sketches.

"How are we going to get into the Warden's office?" Raven asked.

"How are we going to get out?" Orion interjected before anyone could answer. "There will be ten of us, and we won't all be together."

Jax pointed to the falls. "Once everyone is out of the vault, the team in the prison should be able to get out through the waterway, the same route they came in."

"Won't we be swimming against the current?" Orion asked.

"I'm not sure we have much of a choice. The three of you up in the Monastery will make your way down into the prison. The room on the first floor where two of the levers are housed is the same room that leads below ground." Jax pointed to the lines on the map indicating two sets of stairs. "You'll meet us at the top of the waterfall, and we can all escape together. We'll secure a rope outside the wall so we have a way to pull ourselves through the current."

Raven tapped the shape representing the Warden's office. "I'll ask again, how are we getting into the Warden's private quarters? And then hanging out there by the lever until all of this is finished?"

Jax pinched his chin, eyes focused. "The Warden of the Ashgate Fortress isn't known for spending a lot of time away from his chambers except when making rounds. We're going to spread out in three different places, and we can't risk running into him. It'll be too easy for him to catch us off guard if he's roaming the halls, so the only plausible option is to get him out of the building."

Isolde smiled. "We need a distraction to carry him outside. A band of intruders at the front gate?"

"We will be the intruders at the front gate," Orion said.

She pursed her lips. "*Other* intruders. A rebel tribe seeking retribution for the recent destruction of Monasteries, perhaps?"

Orion nodded, tracking with her thought process. "Ah, yes. Griffin."

"Griffin," she agreed.

"Who's Griffin?" Hector continued to watch the two of them interact as if still trying to work out the intricacies of their relationship.

"He is Nabiiga. And our Abrafo, our fiercest warrior. He will take a team to create a ruckus outside the wall."

"He's a bull of a man," Orion said. "Surely scary enough to take on the Warden."

"Are you afraid of my brother?" Isolde at last looked his way and smirked.

"No." Orion folded his arms and avoided her gaze.

Jax said, "It will have to be severe enough to draw the Warden outside to investigate, and the guards will be fighting back." Eying her spear, he emphasized, "With firearms. Some of your warriors may be shot down."

"Thank you, Lieutenant Blackmoor. I am well aware of the

dangers of making war against men with superior weapons who stand on high walls."

Her tone was sharp, and Orion grinned, enjoying the unfamiliar venom behind her words, though his brain involuntarily began creating ways he could redirect it back to himself.

"Still, I'm not sure that will be enough to get the Warden out of his office. Intruders could be handled by the guards. He may not care to bother with it."

Hector agreed. "I was just thinking that. And honestly, I don't want to attempt a full on assault of the building. It would be preferable to get in and out undetected." The group racked their brains to come up with a solution. Then an idea formed on Hector's face. "What if they were turning in traitors? The Warden always oversees incoming prisoners. It may intrigue him to have loyal citizens bringing rebels right up to the front gate."

Jax thought it over. Then a smile loosened the tense skin of his forehead and allowed his bushy brows to relax into a gentle curve. "You know, Hector. That just might work."

PART TWO

BURN TO EMBERS

The fire awaits Surrender. Ferocious flames lick and swarm, cackle and seethe. A warrior of shadow transformed into a servant of light.

But first, the burn, friend mine.

For only in fire can skin be shed, and only one stripped can learn to fly.

Some advice for flight: lowly you must stay, so as not to stray too near the sun, as the man with false wings once tried. And meek you must be, so as not to fall with those who fell before, corrupting nations with their vile greed.

~An excerpt from Jumalan Sana.
Found in the book of Baba the navi.

CHAPTER 17

THE HEART OF A MAN

The meeting in Jericho continued long into the afternoon. They spent hours brainstorming potential outcomes and possibilities while finalizing the details. The plan was to leave the next day bright and early. They would travel on horseback to the black wall and jump to the Grim Wilds, arriving in Caritas sometime late in the night. The following morning, they would meet with the elders, and if Isolde's father agreed to everything and if Griffin was willing to be the distraction as she assured them he would be, they would depart the day after for Crystavium.

When everyone felt satisfied with the proposed agenda, they went their separate ways, agreeing to regroup in the morning by the city gate.

Orion and Isolde departed soon after the Abram and Eero, saying they were going to find somewhere that served hot food. The moment they left the tent, Isolde picked up her pace, walking several strides in front of him.

Orion called after her and jogged to catch up. "Isolde, what's going on?" She paused her steps to glare at him before continuing on, and he realized she must still be angry from their disagreement regarding her father. He'd thought she seemed to be keeping her distance throughout the day, but since her version of *space* mirrored polite etiquette, he hadn't realized so much anger remained. Hurrying again to catch up, he entreated, "Isolde, please don't be mad about this morning. I wasn't trying to exclude you from the mission."

She stopped short, and he nearly slammed into her. "You are right. You are just treating me as everyone does. Like the precious heir who needs protection. I am not even the true heir! Griffin is alive and well!" Crows perched on the crumbling roof of a nearby building squawked and leapt into the air, fluttering away.

"Naabila, I know you don't need protection. You literally saved my life in the desert, remember? Twice. Three times." His brows lifted in question as he took a step closer, not quite invading her personal bubble, but close.

Isolde looked up and to the side, keeping her gaze defiantly away from him. "You are being dramatic."

He moved to stand in line with her eyes, though she averted them again. "I'm not. I'm well aware of your superiority over me, and not just because of your title. You have to believe me when I tell you that, Naabila. I mean look at you." He gestured to her entire person, every fierce morsel of it, but her mood didn't teeter. "I'm only trying to keep my promise to your father. If he doesn't want you to go, I'll do everything I can to convince him, I swear it, but I can't risk something happening to you and then having to slink back to him explaining I led you into possibly the most dangerous location in all of Arkaemor without telling him first."

Narrow vision at last sliding back to him, she said, "So what you are really saying is that you are protecting yourself."

"Exactly! Nothing to do with you. Strictly my own hide I am looking out for."

Rolling her eyes as though she didn't believe him in the slightest, she stepped out around him. "Fine." She continued forward, and he followed her, stopping her with his palm against her stomach.

"So all is forgiven?" He flashed a winning smile.

"Yes, fine, fine. Forgiven."

Orion's grin turned devilish, his voice growing husky in the small space between them. "Though I have to admit, those fiery eyes of wrath were pretty enticing. You're usually so tranquil. I can't promise I won't push your buttons in the future if this vixen is the result of my efforts."

Her smile widened. "You are horrible."

He laughed. "I know. I tried to warn you."

"Speaking of that." She pressed forward, pushing her way through his hand. "We never finished discussing it."

Orion thought he couldn't wait to get back to the desert so she would lose that cold-weather jacket. Snow fell heavier, laying like petals in her dark hair. "Discussing what? How horrible I am?"

"No. Well, yes. You kidnapped those women? The Belamour sisters?"

"Yes." He felt no fear in his heart as he admitted the truth. For reasons unfathomable to him, she seemed keen on sticking with him regardless of past mistakes. He considered how long that might last or if anything he divulged would push her past her limits.

"And it seems Hector and his team were looking for them, too, as well as the Queen of Arkaemor. Who are these women? Why are they so sought after?"

Marshal Hearne came running toward them, his blond curls flopping about. When he saw them, he stopped and asked if they'd seen his brother. Isolde didn't know Wyatt, but Orion said he hadn't. Marshal saluted them before rushing on, heading in the direction of the Monastery.

"Wonder what that's about."

Isolde chuckled. "He seemed very excited."

A sign hung above her head reading *The Speckled Sparrow*, and Orion pointed to the door. She nodded, and they walked in. The pub was like most pubs found in the city, with tables and chairs at its center, booths along the far wall to their right, and a bar with stools to their left. Since it was just past dinnertime and the number of pubs left in Jericho had significantly decreased during Sirena's attack, the room bustled with patrons.

They chose an empty booth, and their weapons clanked against the wooden seats. Isolde leaned her spear against the wall behind them and surveyed the room, pleased to see the citizens looking so cheerful in the midst of all the sorrow bestowed upon them.

Despite the busyness of the pub, only a single waiter scurried amongst the tables, though the bartender stepped away from the bar to help when he didn't have drinks to pour.

Settling into his seat, Orion cleared his throat. "So. Sawyer Belamour, Foxx and Iris' father, was my lieutenant when I belonged to the Reko Raptors. I figure I might as well start from the beginning, right?"

Isolde pulled her eyes from the citizens and gave him her full attention. "You were one of them? Hector mentioned the name, but I did not know what it meant. I noticed the pins—owls."

"They were an elite unit handpicked by the sovereigns for special jobs. After Sawyer's rebellion, the team was abolished. If what Hector says is true, Sirena reestablished them to locate Foxx and Iris. Many years ago, Declan and I were both Raptors. This was before Jax and Raven joined. Sawyer held the same position Jax does now. The golden pin identifies him as the lieutenant."

The bartender, a young man in his late teens, approached the table. He smiled through weary eyes as a bead of sweat dripped down his temple. Then he wiped his hands on the towel slung over his shoulder and greeted them. Isolde ordered water and a salad, and Orion, an ale. When the man promised to return soon with their drinks, Orion assured him there was no rush and he could take his time.

Putting his elbows on the table, Orion intertwined his fingers together. "Long story short, Sawyer stole something from Sirena: an object known as the Artifact. Supposedly, this vessel will allow Pyhä-ki, a magical water, to be transported from Celestelvyra into Arkaemor so it can be used to kill her. The last mission I went on as a Raptor was actually here, in Jericho. Though I don't know the details, Sawyer must have found out something that changed his allegiances. Some kind of plan Vali concocted, it seems. When he returned to Castle Solís he tricked us all into helping him steal the Artifact, and then he fled. The rest of us were charged with treason and sent to find him with the notion that, should we capture him and return him to the sovereigns, we would be pardoned and our positions restored. No longer outcasts."

"So you hunted these women hoping they would lead you to their father?"

The young bartender returned with their drinks and a salad of greens, bright carrots, off-white turnips, and onions. "Finn will come take the rest of your order shortly, all right?" They nodded, and he encouraged them to enjoy.

Orion took a sip of his ale and set it aside. "Not at first, but yes. About five or six months ago, word got around that Sawyers' daughters were searching for him. We thought if they were trying to find him after he'd been gone nearly six years, they must have some clue as to where he might be, so we set out in search of them. We actually met them first in the Grim Wilds and attempted—not very intelligently—to join their party. We should have gone about it a different way, but as I'm sure you've come to realize, I can be quite pig-headed at times." He lifted a brow to her in question.

"I had not noticed." Isolde stuffed a bite of salad into her mouth to mask her smile.

"So we tracked them into Sateen and captured them in Petrichor. Not one of my proudest moments, I assure you. I made such a mess of everything. I was very lost and… grasping so intently on this idea that if I just found Sawyer, Declan and I would be free. Everything would go back to the way it was and this nightmare would be over. It consumed me. It became all that mattered. It was Sawyer's fault we were in exile, and he needed to pay for what he'd done." Orion sighed, taking a break from his story to steal a carrot from her bowl. His heart thrummed as he spoke of past failures, but the loudness of the pub seemed to be drowning out the whispers for the moment.

After another swig, he continued. "So we took Iris and Foxx and forced them to help us, but the more we got to know them, the more tidbits of their story slipped into our conversations. It wasn't long until we both began to realize we were playing for the wrong side." He paused again and leaned back in his seat, grateful Isolde didn't feel the need to fill the space with words. She ate her salad, adding more of the vinegary syrup the waiter had left for her to dress the top.

"Maybe Sawyer didn't betray us to hurt us. Maybe he figured out the necessity of destroying the evils of the world and sought to stand against it. My father was a believer, you know. So I know the history and what you people believe." He frowned apologetically, realizing *you people* had sounded harsher than intended. "And I never wanted to believe it for myself. I never wanted any part of it because… well, perhaps that's a story for another day. But regardless, the longer this goes on, the more I'm beginning to see the method to Sawyer's perceived madness. After Sirena's attack here and her taking me hostage, and after waking in that swamp to find Sawyer dead and Declan on the ground…" He shook his head, dispelling the memory. "I realized with certainty that Sirena needs to be stopped. Whatever it takes."

Another young man approached the table. "So sorry for your wait! I'm Finn. Would you like to hear the specials?"

Isolde folded her hands in her lap. "I would like some soup, I think. I have not been able to get warm since we arrived, and I think some hot soup could be just the thing."

"We have beef vegetable."

"Perfect."

"I'll have the soup as well," Orion said. Finn dipped his chin and rushed away. Orion stole another carrot, more to extract her smile than an actual want of it. "I'm sorry you haven't been able to get warm. Do you want my coat?"

"Then you will be cold."

He shucked the coat from his shoulders and passed it across the table.

Isolde wrapped it around herself, snuggling into it with a blissful expression. "This will help. Thank you, Orion."

Sliding a hand over the top of his head, he sighed. "So all of that to say, yes, I have made a lot of mistakes, Naabila. One of them being the literal abduction of two women who turned out to be—"

Finn returned to the table with cloth napkins and spoons before dashing off again.

The disturbance brought their eyes back together, and though he wasn't necessarily fearful of how she might react to all he'd shared, his shame made him avert his gaze. He busied himself by tucking the cloth napkin into the collar of his shirt. "I spent many years on the run seeking revenge for Sawyer's slight. I didn't care about those women. They were nothing to me. I didn't care about anything but my own freedom. And Declan's."

"Iris changed your mind," she guessed.

Orion blushed. "Iris was special. *Is* special. But I think it was Foxxglove who first had me second-guessing what we were doing."

Chewing the last bite of her salad, Isolde placed her fork inside the bowl and slid it to the edge of the table. After a silent minute, she asked, "What did she do?"

Drawn away from the depths of false memories never to be experienced, he answered, "Foxx was smart. She played me for a fool, honestly." He chuckled. "Iris fought us for days. Declan had to wrangle her like a wild bull. And she *hated* me. She even threatened to kill me in my sleep." When he laughed again, Isolde's eyes widened.

"Foxx was calm, helpful, agreeable—but in this confident way that made it clear she thought she had total control of the situation. Like she wasn't a prisoner at all and helping us was her decision entirely. She spoke to me like I was some foolish idiot she kindly tolerated, and it eventually made me realize how stupid I'd been to think we could kidnap two girls in the jungle and expect them to help us without question or resistance. I'd been so driven by my need for revenge, and she—without even trying or realizing she'd done it, I'm sure—revealed to me how damaging that had become."

Finn returned with two bowls of steaming soup, sliding the spoons next to them. "Anything else for right now?"

Isolde said, "Some more water when you get a chance, please. No hurry." Finn nodded and left the table as both she and Orion leaned over and let the savory aroma fill their noses. Isolde moved even closer so the steam warmed her face. "It smells so good." She picked up the spoon and scooped up a bit of broth to blow on.

Orion stirred his own soup, patiently letting it cool. "When we were attacked by the lagoon monster I told you about, the one from Lacuna Kaput, Iris was injured—horribly injured. The beast pulled her under the surface, and I just remember feeling so terrified when I couldn't find her. It was like the whole world froze or shifted or turned upside down. I swear my heart stopped as the realization that I actually cared about whether she lived or died locked into place. Not because I needed her to find her father, but because I was worried about her safety. That may have been the first time I'd worried about someone other than myself or Declan in years. I was frantic. I knew that deadly monster was in there, but I kept diving under the water trying to find her. When I saw her, she looked so afraid. Blood pooled around her in the water. I managed to get her free and to the surface, and the relief I felt at her safety was inde-scribable."

Orion looked up from his food, realizing for the first time he was practically gushing about another woman while sitting across from the most captivating creature he'd ever laid eyes on. He surveyed her face as she sipped her soup, wondering if it bothered her, but her golden irises were turned downward, so he couldn't be sure what thoughts lay behind them.

"Anyway, the monster pulled me under before I got out, and Iris climbed that damn waterfall, bleeding all over herself, and shot the creature down. She saved me. Which was mind-blowing in the aftermath because if I'd been in their shoes, I definitely would have let my captors die and used that time to flee. But they chose to remain our captives in exchange for saving my life. When I asked her why she'd done it, she said, *I guess, in the heat of the moment, something in me saw something in you worth saving.*" He shook his head, still feeling disbelief at the truths he shared. "I fought with myself a lot after that. Going back and forth between my need for revenge—something I'd held on to, longed for for so many years—and my need for..." His cheeks flushed again. "Connection. Friendship.

"All of that to say, they both helped me see the truth, and that's why I am fighting for them now. I know the others want Prince Alexander back so we can take down the royals, and I want that, too, but I also feel like I owe those girls. And I guess I have this weird desire to show them... I've changed. Or at least that I'm trying to." He looked down at his lap.

Isolde didn't speak until she'd nearly finished her soup. Setting her spoon down, she dabbed her lips with the cloth and reached her hand across the table, placing it on top of his. At her touch, the faint whispers in the back of his thoughts scattered completely. Then she said, "Iris and Foxxglove sound amazing. We are going to get them back."

Orion cleared his throat. "You don't have to worry about..." He stumbled for the words, not wishing to imply anything, but also needing her to know. "Iris and Declan are together. If she forgives him after all this, at least. I think she will. And Foxxglove and Alexander..."

"Are together also?" Isolde sat up straighter. "Is she to be the next queen of Arkaemor, then?"

"I don't know for sure where they stand now, but I would assume as much. If he feels for her the way she does for him, then yes." He smiled, feeling unexpected joy at Foxx's presumed happiness.

Isolde tilted her head, her eyes brightening with her smile. "So you are not interested in saving the Belamour sisters because you hope to confess your love to one of them when they return?" Her breezy tone loosened the tension in his shoulders.

"Definitely not." He chuckled, but as his heart fluttered with weightlessness at her understanding and lack of judgment, the whispers grew tumultuous in his ears, clanging against his eardrums like mallets. They came upon him so quickly and with such astounding force, for a brief and terrifying moment he felt certain he would vomit all over the table. In the days since he'd been Sirena's captive, the whispers had arrived like a breath of air and grown with increasing intensity over several minutes. Never before had he felt such an instantaneous assault on his entire being. His skin blanched, and his face dripped with sweat as the slander consumed his thoughts.

Holding his hands over his ears in a failed attempt to block the clamor, his eyes found Isolde's. Her lips were parted, moving with words drowned out with whispers calling him a coward, incapable of change, a liar, deceitful, despicable, the worst of mankind.

A tear escaped his eye, and he leapt from his seat, nearly knocking over the bartender approaching the table with another water for Isolde. After a quick apology that he might have screamed, he rushed out the door.

C

Isolde stood and grabbed her spear, apologizing to the bartender as she dropped a pile of *metts* on the table and rushed after Orion. Outside, she scoured the street, looking back in the direction of the Monastery and forward toward the inn they'd stayed at the previous night. Orion was nowhere in sight. Only a light dusting of snow coated the bricked street and it was little more than a disarray of scattered footsteps giving no indication of which way he'd gone. She crossed the street and yelled his name as she scanned the area, trying to find any clue that might lead her to him. Up the road on the corner of the next block, a tall plant in a wicker basket had been knocked over, and she ran toward it calling out to him.

A woman turned the corner just as Isolde reached it, and they nearly collided. Seeing her frantic expression, the woman pointed over her shoulder. After jogging the street for two blocks, she stopped short, startled by a figure up ahead. Gray and white with a muscular torso, the wolf stared right at her. She couldn't fathom how a wolf had gotten into a locked city. Jericho was the City of the Moon, so she supposed it might be common for wolves to roam wild in the streets, though she'd never heard of this being the case.

The wolf disappeared down an alley, and some inner tug had Isolde hustling after it. At the entrance to the alley, she stalled again, surveying the thin walkway before her and seeing little more than an empty passage between two disheveled buildings. A cluster of gnonttūs stood to her left, whispering to each other and pointing at something out of sight. She took a few steps forward to better see what they observed and heard Orion whisper her name. He stood in the alcove of a doorway with his back against the wall, his head hanging low, and his chest heaving.

Joining him in the small space, she put her back against the opposite wall and watched as he cried, wishing she understood what triggered these fits and how to stop them. Touching his arms, she said, "Orion? Are you all right?" They were knee to knee in the small space, and she could feel the heat radiating off of him like a tangible aura. She said his name again, and he lifted his eyes to hers, seeming lost within them like a ship forsaken to the depths of the sea.

"I'm sorry." His voice was raspy with tears. "This is crazy. I don't know what's happening to me."

He'd given her his coat, leaving his skin exposed. His scars burned red, highlighted by a sheen of sweat, but the lines littering his face and hands didn't disfigure him. Instead they reminded her of the rings of a tree. Tree rings reveal age, maturity. His lines, both inside and out, were a symbol of all he'd experienced. Everything that made him. The good and the bad. "It is fine, Orion. You do not owe me an apology."

"No, it's not fine!" His palms slammed the wall behind her, caging her within the circle of his arms.

She didn't waver as his body coursed with rage. He dropped his head, and his hair grazed her cheek. He seemed unable to catch his breath, his gasps growing more panicked, so she ran her hands up and down his sides to soothe him. "I mean we will figure it out. Together."

Again Orion lifted his eyes, and she saw anger in them. "*We* will not figure anything out. *I* will figure it out." He recoiled until his back hit the wall, refusing to look her in the eyes. When she reached for him, he smacked her hand. "And *stop* touching me." He growled again, nearly bearing his teeth like a frightened wolf. "You're always touching me, and it drives me *insane*."

Isolde's breath caught in her throat, and she sidestepped out of the doorway. "I am sorry, Orion. I never mean to cause you pain."

His anger dwindled to sorrow. "Damnit, Isolde." The hair in his face dripped with snow and sweat, and his eyes watched the ground.

As her own tears began to fall, she ran from him, and she didn't stop until she reached the city gate.

C

"A storm brews on the horizon. Perhaps the Creator will not allow us to glimpse His spectacular sunset tonight." Ingrid Kirkavall leaned her hip against the stone parapet and looked toward the west. They stood above the city, high atop the palace in their favorite place to observe the firmament. Ingrid had hoped brilliant auroras would tread the heels of a dazzling sunset, but it seemed even the sky yielded to her husband's moods.

"Fitting, is it not?" Vali scratched his chin, his forehead wrinkled.

Ingrid ran the back of her knuckles down his cheek. "My love, what troubles you?"

"This is a horrible plan." He didn't pull his gaze from the darkening landscape and the expanse laden with dense clouds. They hung low and heavy like a brewing storm, oppressive like smoke above a burning city.

"It seems the only plan given the circumstances. The Ashgate Fortress is the last Monastery standing. Surely the mighty soldiers of the King's Legion can handle such a feat."

Vali hummed in reply, his brow clenching into an even deeper crease.

"Perhaps you would find it less horrible if you were going with them." She pulled her stole more taut around her shoulders to combat the chill of the rooftop terrace. It was a full wolf pelt with its empty head resting over her heart. Vali had gotten her several like it over the years, but this particular wolf had been found high in the mountains, so its fur had grown thicker than others she owned. It had also been found close to death and had been graciously put out of its misery rather than being killed for sport.

Vali noticed her adjustment and took a step closer so the tops of their arms shared warmth. "You wouldn't let me go along if I tried."

With a small smile, she concurred, "It's true, I would advise against it. Though, when ever do you listen to me?"

"I always heed your words of wisdom, my darling." One side of his lips curled, and she lifted a brow in disbelief. "I just—on occasion—take the long way around." Ingrid chuckled, accepting this as truth, but Vali quickly returned to his solemnity. "I know you would be right to advise against my joining them, despite the pit of distress tangling my insides. It isn't yet time. However, if Sirena is keen on breaking the rules, why not I?"

Ingrid encouraged him with a nudge, drawing his eyes away from the expanse. "Because you are loyal, and she is not. You must not sink to her level."

His shoulders slumped. "Right as always, my Queen. My going with them would undoubtedly bring to light things not ready to be revealed." Another breeze swept past them, bringing with it a soft flurry that dampened their rosy cheeks and left stardust in their hair. "Though I must admit, I should like to be there when she returns."

Ingrid turned to face her husband, enticing him to do the same. Vali slid his hands around her hips and pulled her up against him. Lifting her arms to his neck, she said, "I know, my love, but you will be seeing her soon enough. We must tread lightly and not interfere with the plans set in place."

"I know, I know. It's just that… we've waited so long."

"And so another few weeks should be no struggle at all."

"It's different now." He released another weighty sigh.

Sad eyes turned down with understanding, though she forced a smile. "Now that you have seen her."

He nodded. "The woman with the white hair. Who would have guessed she would come from Amaryllis herself?"

The moment he'd dropped to his knees on the promenade with Amaryllis' name on his lips and Foxxglove's face in the sky, Ingrid had understood the new obstacles set before him. Obstacles he would have to face whether he liked it or not. Obstacles that might sway his resolve. "I wonder if Amaryllis knew or if it was a surprise for her as well."

"I don't think she knew. It would explain why things changed so drastically after her child was born, and why she never brought her here, never let me see her. She continued to come alone even when it meant leaving her daughters at home."

"Amaryllis certainly would have feared what you would do to her when you found out. Perhaps she endeavored to save her daughter from the heartbreak. Though she of all people should have known we cannot thwart what has already been decided."

Vali was staring off again, only half listening, though he dipped his chin to acknowledge her words.

"She is beautiful," she said.

"Stunning." He looked at her. "But not even comparable to your loveliness, my Queen."

Though her cheeks warmed, Ingrid ignored his compliment. "It will not be easy for you, my King."

"Nothing worth doing ever is. We know that better than most." Leaning in, he kissed her lips, and she responded in kind, her fingers absentmindedly tousling his already windblown hair. "I love you, Ingrid. No matter what happens, nothing will ever alter that."

"Perhaps you will change your mind. Perhaps you will not shatter her heart into a million pieces. And mine."

Vali pressed a kiss to her cheek. He caressed her jawline, sending warm shivers down her spine that melted the bitter chill of the coming darkness. "I must, my love. You know I must."

Ingrid nodded, eyes swelling with emotion. "You will make yourself the villain."

"Every good story needs a villain." He wore his usual mischievous grin. Then he kissed her cheek, catching a tear. "Besides, we both know I have loads of experience."

"You haven't been that man for a long time, Vali."

He burrowed into the crook of her neck and kissed her collarbone. "I will always be that man, my love. He lingers just below the surface, ready to emerge when the situation calls for it. You know this better than anyone."

"And what of Alexander?" she asked. Vali swallowed, inhaling a sharp breath. "He is your dearest friend. Yet you would betray him? Hurt him so thoroughly?"

"*You* are my dearest friend." He pressed a kiss against her temple, pulling her body closer. The wind picked up, and he tugged on her oversized hood so it shielded both their faces. "Now, tell me you love me. Promise me you will stand by me despite what is most assuredly ensuing."

"I thought we would have more time," she admitted, not daring to avoid his gaze despite her stomach willing her to look away. A thousand lifetimes couldn't prepare her for what was to come, and even a thousand more wouldn't be enough time.

"Say it. I need to hear it."

Flipping a stray hair from his brow, she smiled. "I know every one of your transgressions and still, I adore you. Nothing could alter the depth of my love. No heartbreak or villainous deed. No torrent threatening to drown us, nor menacing tempest brewing to overcome us. I am yours, my King, and just as I always have been, so will I always be."

Joy radiated from his innermost heart. "I don't deserve you, but I am ever so grateful you find me worthy of your endearment." As he pulled her in for more heartfelt kisses, the passion of their embrace warmed them both in the midst of the snowflakes. Into her ear, he whispered, "Shall we head to our chambers for the night? I should like to repay you for such a compassionate confession of devotion."

"You have yet to answer my question regarding Alexander." Ingrid giggled when his cold nose tickled her neck.

"You wish to speak of Alexander *now*?" His fingers played at the bow holding the corset tied elegantly up her spine. She nodded bashfully—an emotion not often donning the countenance of the Dróttning of Cordillera. "Alexander will understand in the end, and he will forgive me. He has the heart to do so."

Ingrid hummed, knowing the truth in this statement. "Still, I shall continue to pray for a different outcome. You haven't yet met her. Perhaps spending time with Foxxglove Belamour will change your mind."

"I can't allow it to. My feelings will not get in the way of what must be done. Her blood will not sway my decision. I will shape and mold her into what I need her to be. I will build her up and tear her down until she is exactly the right amount of broken to see it through. I will use the woman with the white hair as I have always planned to, and if destroying all of us is the outcome, then so be it."

CHAPTER 18

COMPANIONS

As the sun began its descent beneath the wall, Hector, Raven, and Jax lingered in the warroom. Two members of the palace staff had arrived earlier in the day to change out their coffee and supply luncheon for everyone—courtesy of Konungr Vali—and had returned again later to retrieve the dirty dishes. Little remained to tidy before calling it a night, but Raven tucked the pencils they'd used into a drawer while Jax rolled up the maps and tied them tight for easy transport.

Candle lanterns kept the tented room fairly warm during the day as long as only a few people came in and out, but as darkness began to fall, the city grew cold. Jax pulled his heavy jacket over his shoulders in preparation for heading out into the night, and Hector did the same, watching Raven as she circled the room to extinguish the lanterns.

Buttoning up the front of his coat, Jax said, "Long day tomorrow. I'm heading back to the inn to get some rest. The others can handle evening duties." Hector nodded, though his eyes continued to trail Raven. "You guys should do the same. Commander?"

Hector looked at him. "Yes, we should,"

"There's no shame in taking the night off. It will be better for those of us traveling with you if you're at full power." Jax extended a hand in farewell, and Hector accepted the gesture. Holding onto it a moment too long, Jax added, "So if you won't do it for your own sake, do it for us, all right?"

Hector nodded again and smiled sleepily. He knew Jax had made a fair point, despite his inner monologue running over the list of things that still needed taken care of before they left. The team staying behind was entirely competent and able to handle the affairs of Jericho for two weeks while he, Jax, and Raven were away. Abram and Hector had been handling most of the plans side by side, and he knew they were on the same page. Considering the Konungr's deep involvement in the affairs of his people, Jericho was sure to be taken care of to the highest extent, and Hector had no reason to worry about anything besides getting his team in and out of the Ashgate Fortress with Prince Alexander in tow.

"I promise to rest," Hector said. Jax dipped his head and released him before grabbing the rolled maps from the table and holding them at his side.

"I'll make sure he does." Raven joined the men by the door, faux glaring at Hector to indicate she had her eyes on him. As she pulled her jacket on, he grabbed the back of it to assist her in slipping the second arm through. Jax watched them, his lips cracking into a wide grin. Raven glowered, and her cheeks brightened with embarrassment.

"And Hector? Lay off the booze, won't you? Raven, you're in charge." Lifting the entrance flap, Jax flashed her a wink.

Hector pushed him through the doorway. "Get out of here." With a final salute, the lieutenant left them alone. Hector turned to Raven to find her smiling. Her loose hair hung in waves, and he couldn't help but reach out to touch it. In all the time they'd known each other, they'd rarely spent time together out of uniform. He found himself wondering what kind of attire she wore at home and if she often let her hair free of its braid when she didn't need it pulled out of the way. She'd been wearing comfy clothing to bed, something plain and cotton she'd grabbed at one of the local shops, and he'd noticed her letting her waves loose over the past few days when they weren't doing manual labor. He decided he could get used to seeing her that way, and his mind created pictures of what she might look like moving around his chambers in nothing but his shirt. His cheeks blushed at the thought.

"What are you so happy about?" Raven lifted a brow. He shook his head, his growing smile the only answer he was willing to share. Then with suspicious eyes and crossed arms, she asked, "Are you going to listen to him?"

Hector pretended to think it over. "Do I have a choice?" She shook her head. "Okay then. I guess you're in charge."

"Good." Taking his hand, she pulled him from the tent. They turned left, moving away from the Monastery and toward the Pinewood Inn, but before they reached it, Raven tugged him down a side street.

"Where are we going?"

Walking backward without releasing his hand, she said, "You'll see."

"Very mysterious."

"It's just a little place Jax and I happened upon the other day. It's not far. Come on." Facing forward, she pulled on his hand. Snow had begun to fall, filling the air with a fuzzy, pale glow and landing in her dark hair, dampening it on impact. Then Raven slowed, and Hector noticed the shift in her energy. He feared he already knew what she wished to discuss, and when she said his name, he hummed in reply.

"What the Konungr said. About the farms."

He cleared his throat. "A cruelty a new king might make an effort to discontinue."

She inhaled a sharp breath through her teeth. "So it's true then? They use sil ōnni on the slaves at the farms? Even the ones I rescue from the dens."

Stopping, he turned to her. "I'm sorry, Raven. I should have told you. There is a great deal of evil tangled throughout the current regime that I wished to shield you from. Far more than Sirena attacking a single city."

Raven nodded, and though she didn't comment further, she didn't meet his eyes before tugging him onward.

The small alley opened up into a miniature courtyard. It was tiny in comparison to the one at the Monastery and shaped like a near perfect square. An evergreen grew tall on the far side of the yard next to a single concrete bench. Bricks creating the terrace encircled its trunk, as if the city had been built around it. The few streets surrounding the yard were fairly empty, though a couple civilians passed by. Raven strolled into the courtyard, pulling Hector along behind her and turning to face him when they reached the bench.

Hector looked around. "What are we doing here?"

Raven wound her dark hair back into its usual braid without

replying. From her chest, she unstrapped her throwing knives and placed them on the bench. His expression remained the picture of confusion as she removed her hip scabbards as well before sliding his pistol from his side and laying them next to the other downed weapons.

The bench had an inscription carved into it, and Hector ran his fingers over the words as he read them out loud. *"I found him whom my soul loves. Mine held onto his, unyielding in the never ending dance of time, and despite our fervent efforts, our souls refused to disentangle themselves from one another."*

"That's a bit depressing," Raven said.

"It's kind of nice though, isn't it?"

She smiled and backed away, stopping when she reached the center of the yard. Then she spread her feet shoulder width apart and raised her fists to guard her face.

Finally understanding, Hector joined her, his face laced with faux disapproval. "Now Raven, what would Jax say?"

"Jax isn't here." She shifted her weight back and forth, bouncing on the balls of her feet and stretching her neck. "He put me in charge, and I owe you." She cracked her knuckles and smiled. "For hiding things from me."

"This isn't exactly resting." Hector began his own set of stretches, opening and closing his fists and loosening his hips.

"You have to get worn out before you relax." Raven taunted him with her fingers, egging him to come at her. Hector bent his knees and lifted his hands into a fighting stance, bubbling with energy as they began to circle each other. "Time to sweat away all the booze you couldn't handle last night," she goaded.

"Oh, is that how it's going to be? I suppose I will never live that one down."

Raven nodded, beaming. He stepped toward her, throwing a quick jab at her head. She dodged, pushing his fist away with the back of her arm. "Moving a little slow, Commander Kayvan? Perhaps you're dehydrated."

He threw another swift punch, aiming at her shoulder, then another to her left. She pulled both shoulders back in time for him to miss, ducking under his arm and elbowing him in the ribs as she passed by. He turned to face her, waiting, deciding a defensive route might be a better option. She wasn't wrong. He did feel slow, his limberness washed from parched muscles regardless of all the water he drank that day.

Raven lunged forward, hitting his hip with her knee and immediately following it up with a kick to his ribs. She threw three rapid punches toward his face, which he blocked with his forearms. Before she could regroup, he punched upward, hitting her high on the chest and pushing her backward. Raven let her head fall from side to side, shaking off the hit with a smile.

"Not as slow as you thought, I suppose."

"We'll see." She stepped around him in a wide arc, and he mirrored her movements. When she punched low, he blocked. When she punched high, he blocked and used his other fist to strike her ribs. She kicked again, striking his back and pushing him off balance. Crouching low, she swiped her leg in an arc to trip him, but he stepped away in time. Following her spin all the way through, she rose into a high kick that struck him across the face.

He pounced on her, moving from left to right to throw her off before grabbing her wrist and twisting her so he held it tightly behind her back. From behind, he spoke low into her ear, "If you're going to keep kicking me, wicked woman, I'm going to get very angry."

"I've never seen you angry. I'm not sure you're capable of such heavy emotions."

He released her arm slightly, and she immediately spun toward him, attempting to strike with her free hand. He grabbed that one as well, still holding the other wrist behind her back and now pulling her chest against his own. "You would certainly recognize the look. You're always angry."

"No, I'm not!"

"Must just be your resting expression then."

Her eyes widened, a glint of fire sparking within dark irises. "Is that so?" Then she smashed her forehead into his, and he released her, stumbling backward. Grinning with pride, she twisted her wrists in a circle, flexing where he'd gripped them. "Had enough?"

Shaking his head, he lunged at her again, wrapping an arm around her waist and lifting her off her feet before dragging her to the ground and pinning her to stone. "Nope. You?"

"Just about." She wrapped her legs around his torso and rolled so she was on top of him, straddling his hips with feet curled up around his thighs and hands holding both wrists above his head. "Now I've had enough."

Hector lifted his head from the snowy ground and kissed her with ferocity she hadn't anticipated. They'd tiptoed around it for weeks now, only sharing that one brief kiss after the revolution rally. They'd slept in the same room, shared meals and jobs, and even casually touched on occasion, but nothing more intimate since that first night after the attack when they'd laid together for warmth in the courtyard of the Monastery of the Morrow.

Raven leaned into him, kissing him back arduously, neither caring what the people walking by thought of them sprawled on the ground tangled in each other's arms. Not caring that the snow fell heavier and soaked their clothing.

His arms wiggled from their trapped position above his head, and he wrapped them around her waist. When she pulled back for breath, his hands tightened around her, gripping her hips with vigor and lifting her off of him while smoothly rolling on top of her. He grasped both of her wrists with one hand and was now holding them captive above her head. His other arm was flat on the ground, holding up his body.

For a moment, she blanched as if questioning everything. Longing to wash away her panic, he kissed her again, more gently than before, and a rapturous smile curved his lips. "We can call this a draw if you like."

She shook her head. "You cheated. I win by default."

"I don't take you as the kind of person to accept that sort of win, Miss Nightshade."

"I'm not." She kissed him again.

A shout of exclamation had them looking around to find Wyatt and Marshal standing on the edge of the courtyard, their mouths showing all of their teeth.

"I thought you said they were fighting!" Wyatt said.

Marshal giggled. "They were! I guess they got bored and moved on to something a little more interesting."

Raven scowled at them, and they skittered away in a cacophony of laughter. From a distance it was difficult to discern which one crowed, "Wait until Dom hears about this."

When she returned her eyes to him, the happiness radiating from her expression filled him with heat despite the freezing ground beneath them.

"Those are the men you chose to join your team of Raptors?" she asked.

"They are the best archers in the King's Legion, and I think they add something lighthearted to the group. Which is important, especially now." His expression turned serious, his forehead wrinkling. "I'm really sorry, Raven. For not telling you about the farms. Your efforts weren't fruitless. Breaking up the dens still helped prevent future citizens from becoming addicts. You still saved plenty of people. It's just that Sirena didn't care to help those already in the throes of addiction."

She kissed the tip of his nose. "Our army needs a name. We can't keep referring to ourselves as the King's Legion."

"We'll come up with something." His eyes shifted toward the evening sky. "Are you ready to rest now?"

A shy smile curled her lips. "Not exactly."

"Want to head back to the room?" he asked, his eyes ablaze. She nodded, and he stood before holding out his hands to help her up. After retrieving their weapons, she slid her arm around his waist and tucked her tiny frame close to his side as they walked from the courtyard in the direction of the Pinewood Inn.

C

After Isolde ran off, Orion let himself drop to the ground, sitting with his legs bent in front of him and his back against the wall. Snow soaked through his pants, but it mattered little. Sweat soaked him regardless.

When his breathing settled and the whispers dwindled, he rose to his feet, leaning against the wall for support as his limbs regained circulation. Stepping from the doorway out into the street, Orion looked down the road in the direction he thought she'd run.

Several gnonttūs huddled together across the alley, frowning at him and whispering amongst themselves in their high-pitched voices.

"Got a problem?" Orion shook snow from his hair and hugged himself, realizing only then why his skin felt so cold despite the fire burning away at his insides—he'd given Isolde his jacket.

Harumphing, the gnonttū in front tugged his pointed hat tighter on his head and stomped a foot. His voice squeaked as he instructed, "Let's go, fellas. Nothing to see here."

Another, seemingly younger despite his white beard, said, "He's right. Back to work!" They scattered, and Orion watched until each of the little men scurried out of sight.

Though he didn't know exactly how much time had passed since Isolde left, he thought he may still have a chance to catch up to her. Up the road a little ways, he passed an elderly woman who eyed him strangely, and he wondered if she'd also been witness to his insanity. Dipping his chin to her, he continued on, heading in the direction of the Inn. He didn't know where else she would have gone if not to their room. She might have returned to the others and expressed her terror at his crazed behavior, but he suspected she hadn't.

When he turned down the next street, he caught a glimpse of a wolf up ahead. Stopping in his tracks in blustering awe, he marveled at the thought of seeing yet another unexpected wolf in his path and speculated whether or not it could somehow be the same one from the Grim Wilds. Had it followed him to Jericho? If so, why? And how had it managed to get past the Guards at the gate?

Unless it was indeed a tortured fragment of his imagination.

The wolf stared at him from several blocks away, observing him with grave intensity. He pressed forward, but when only a block stood between them, the wolf disappeared from sight, moving down a cross street heading west. Sighing, Orion continued forward, stopping at the intersection to search for his imaginary friend. Sure enough, it sat two blocks down the road at the intersection of another cross street, waiting for him.

Orion cupped his mouth and called, "What are we doing?" The wolf pivoted and vanished again. Orion followed. As he surveyed his surroundings, he began to feel a vague sense of familiarity and tried to remember if he'd been there before.

A loud crash reached his ears and the ground beneath him trembled. He ducked and shielded his head with his hands to protect himself from falling rubble, but no assault came. Thinking the city must be under attack again, he scanned the area. It only took a few seconds for him to realize no other commotion could be heard. The two people within his sights hadn't reacted to the racket.

Another loud crack had him pressing himself against a wall. Sweat poured down his face as he tried to settle his erratic breathing. A man up the street peered in his direction, observing him with odd fascination.

Panicked eyes scoured his surroundings. He wondered if the location had triggered memories of the dragon's attack. Had he traveled this street when searching for Iris and Foxx? Had he been there when Sirena abducted him?

He still hadn't wrapped his mind around why she'd chosen him to begin with. Hector and Raven hadn't been phased when they saw him and Declan in Jericho, so Sirena must have known they'd been traveling with the Belamour sisters. Maybe she thought Alexander had been with them, too.

He wished he could remember anything from their conversations in the dungeons. Not that reliving those moments sounded exceptionally appealing, but if he knew the questions Sirena had asked him, maybe the rest of the answers would fall into place.

Focus on looking forward, Orion. Not back.

Orion startled, his eyes wide. Then they narrowed. "And where have You been?"

I thought you didn't wish to hear from Me.

"As if my wishes have ever mattered to You before."

Another loud rattle shook the land, and Orion dropped into a crouch, holding his head. His eyes burned with angry tears, and he wanted nothing more than to scream at the top of his lungs.

A howl drew his attention to the left. Less than a block away stood the gray wolf. It met Orion's eyes and held his gaze for a long moment. Then it howled again and rushed out of sight.

C

When Jax returned to the Pinewood Inn, he'd lingered in the pub for a short while, sipping on a warm mulled cider—a specialty of the establishment, according to the waitress who'd served him.

While there, a woman had approached him, introducing herself as Elizabeth—Eliza for short—and they'd been chatting ever since. They'd chatted at the bar, all the way up the stairs, through the door to Jax's room, and currently laid together on his bed. At this point, they were no longer chatting.

A scuffle in the hallway outside the room distracted them enough to come up for air. Jax's eyes slid to the door, his lips curving into a smile. "I told them to rest."

"Who?" she asked, breathless, her fingers trailing the bulky muscles of his arm.

Jax shook his head and slid a hand around her lower back. Eliza's fingers had already begun pulling at the buttons of his shirt, opening it low enough to slip her hand inside. He sucked in a sharp breath. "That was cold," he whispered into her ear, and she giggled. After lifting a brow at her mockery, their lips collided again more passionately than before. Experienced hands removed her tunic in one smooth motion. Then he rolled on top of her, pinning her to the bed as his eyes regarded the lacy corset she wore underneath.

Three knocks sounded at the door, and their kisses ceased. Jax let his head fall against her shoulder and sighed. Another two knocks had him rising. "Give me a moment."

A young Jerichonian man stood at the door. Seeing the half-naked woman on the bed over Jax's shoulder, Ralph's expression turned instantly apologetic. "Sorry, Lieutenant. I was told not to bother Commander Kayvan and Miss Nightshade, but there is a situation at the front gate I felt I should report. I could tell General Eero, I suppose, or I—"

"Enough. Tell me what's happening at the gate." Jax's hands absentmindedly buttoned his shirt.

"It's the woman who came with the soldier from the Wilds."

"Isolde?" Jax asked, and Ralph nodded.

"She's having something of a fit, I'm told. Kicking the wall. And… yelling at it. I thought you might want to know. Shall I pass it on to the general?"

Jax released another sigh. "I'll handle it. Thank you, Ralph." He closed the door and faced Eliza, who sat propped up on her elbows watching the interaction. "I'm afraid that's the end of it for tonight."

Eliza pouted. "I could wait for you to return."

He shook his head. "No. But perhaps another time." Then he sat down on the end of the bed and began lacing up his boots.

C

Sitting on the ground next to the outer wall, Isolde let her head fall back against cool stone, feeling too drained to keep it upright. Bent knees held up tired arms as she clutched her spear horizontal in her hands, tipping it from side to side.

The guards by the gate eyed her with interest, debating on

whether or not they should be concerned about the outsider sitting in the snow in an obvious state of agitation. She hadn't exactly shown up unannounced as she stomped up to the wall and kicked it several times.

Deciding not to care, she closed her eyes and began reciting her prayers out loud. "Blessed are You, our magnificent Creator, King of all men and Maker of the universe. You are Holy and Just. We ask for guidance and patience as we live out Your will for our lives. We thank You for our constant sustenance and Your inconceivable forgiveness of our grievous offenses. You are abounding in grace and love and kindness for Your people. So be it with peace."

Opening her eyes, she exhaled a long breath and lifted her gaze to the sky. A shadow stood before her with the light of a far off street lamp at his back. She squinted and recognized the black-haired man as one of Commander Hector's Raptors. "Lieutenant Blackmoor?"

Jax stood with a hand in his pocket, glancing at the guards by the gate who made no attempt to hide their stares. "Hey. What are you doing all the way out here?"

"Fuming." She dropped her head against the wall again.

Not having expected an honest response, Jax smiled, though he quickly pressed his lips together in an effort to remain serious in her obvious state of distress. "Want to walk?" He gestured to the city with his shoulder.

Looking at the guards, she exhaled again and pulled herself to her feet using her spear for leverage. Without another word, they fell into step with each other and walked from the entrance square.

Jax cleared his throat, breaking the silence. "You can just call me Jax, by the way." She nodded without looking at him and continued observing the ruins of the city as they passed. "So... are you all right?"

Isolde looked up, but the clouds were too dense for her to see the stars sparkling into existence. Ammil's third quarter rose on the horizon, blocked by the city walls.

Jax rubbed his hands together and blew into them. "The guards said you were kicking the wall?"

Her eyes flashed to him, and it surprised him to feel a brief tremble of fear. Her fingers gripped tighter around the spear, and the fire igniting her irises added to her already intimidating appearance. He considered for a moment who might win should they fight, especially if she kept hold of that fierce spear.

At last, she said, "He is insane. That is why I was kicking the wall."

"Orion?" Jax asked, and she nodded. "Were you imagining the wall as his face, or was it simply collateral damage?"

In defiance of her anger, her lips broke into a smile, and she looked at him. "Surely the walls of Jericho are strong enough to withstand a mere kick."

Jax lifted a hand to a member of the Guard as they passed each other. "I don't know about that. You look pretty strong." Isolde's smile broadened, but she returned her gaze forward without further comment. "Honestly, Orion has never been the easiest person to get along with." He puzzled over how the exiled soldier had managed to find companionship with Isolde in the first place and what he'd done to win the confidence of her father.

"He is impossible." She inhaled again. "One minute he is totally fine, and the next: crazy. He makes me feel so..." She released an angry yell, giving voice to the feelings she couldn't put to words. Then she asked, "Have you known him long? Has he always been this way?"

"I knew him before he went into exile, but we were never very close. Certainly not friends, though I did have many interactions with him as a fellow soldier. Orion has always been difficult and hot headed and intense."

"But deranged?"

"What do you mean *deranged*?"

Her expression turned discouraged before melting into what he thought might be acceptance or understanding. She sighed, and rather than answering his question, she said, "It is nothing. I am just frustrated."

"Did he hurt you?"

Another sigh had her saying, "Yes, he did, but not in the way you imply."

They continued walking in quiet companionship until Jax touched her arm, drawing her from her internal monologue. "I have a room to myself at the Pinewood Inn. You can stay there tonight if you need to get away. Clear your head before we leave tomorrow." A scandalized expression stained her features, prompting him to hold up his palms. "I would obviously stay somewhere else. Hector and Raven room there, too. A few doors down. So you wouldn't be entirely isolated should you need someone."

"I appreciate your offer, but I would not feel right leaving you without a bed."

"It's not a problem. I can easily find other accommodations."

"In a city as destroyed as this, I doubt there are many spare beds waiting to be claimed. The man who found us our room said we were lucky the people staying there had just been moved."

In truth, he'd planned on sleeping in the warroom when he'd offered. Then an idea occurred to him, and he raised a brow. "Well, are you and he—" He paused, hoping she would catch on without him spelling it out. When she didn't, he finished, "I mean, are you two sharing a bed where you're staying?"

Taken aback, she shrieked, "No!"

Jax laughed heartily. "So I'll stay in your room with him. Then you don't have to sleep against the front wall, being gawked at by obnoxious guards. I'm sure Orion will be thrilled to share his room. He is particularly fond of me, if you hadn't noticed."

Isolde smiled. "I do not think that is true, Lieutenant Blackmoor." He chuckled and shrugged, and she looked down at the hand wrapped around her spear. "He will probably hate it, but... I suppose that would be all right."

"He'll be fine. You can make up tomorrow after you've both had a chance to cool off."

"Yes, that sounds fine."

"Well, it's right here." Jax lifted a hand to the building next to them. Isolde's surprise drew a bigger smile to her lips. "I'll walk you up so I can grab my bag, and I'll let Hector and Raven know you're there so you don't have any unexpected visitors."

"Thank you. You are very kind, Jax."

Jax held open the door and ushered her inside. "Not a problem at all."

CHAPTER 19

ACCEPTED

When Hector and his team met at the entrance of Jericho the following morning, Eero Asger and Solvi Brenna were already there, holding the reins of five horses.

Jerichonian horses differed from those of Reginaterra. The Legion soldiers rode larger breeds with sleek, shiny coats. They stood tall, with thin manes, long tails, and muscular bodies. Jerichonian horses were much shorter and nearly as stout as a pony. Their furry coats and full tails kept them warm in the cold weather. A few even had long hair growing on their faces, giving an impression similar to a beard.

Abram arrived to see them off, and when he stopped in front of Hector, he put a hand on his shoulder. "It will be a difficult two weeks, but I am counting on you to return and lead these troops." Salt and pepper hair hung around his shoulders in thick, braided clusters, and two more braids hung in his beard from either corner of his lips. He tugged at one of the smaller braids. "I'm growing far too old to lead men into battle, and Eero will need you as a companion to see everything through."

Hector took in the old man's strong appearance with pride and was startled to find himself yearning to wear the Jerichonian purples rather than the reds and dark grays he'd adorned for so many years. "I feel like I shouldn't be going. I should stay here and help with the training." A truth, though he also felt conflicted about sending his team into such danger without him there to watch their backs.

"Apart from me, you are the only person here who has set foot behind the obsidian gates." Jax ran a hand over the thin hair on either side of his head as he stopped next to Hector. He greeted both men with a nod. "We need you, Commander." He looked up at the morning sky, cloudy, overcast, and about to snow.

"That's right." Abram released Hector's shoulder and placed his hand over his heart. "We will handle everything here until you return, Commander Kayvan. You are leaving some of your best men with us."

Jax grinned with sarcastic confidence. "Exactly. Dom, Wyatt, and Marshal have everything under control." Hector lifted a brow, looking at Jax from the corner of his eye.

Abram chuckled. "They are good boys. We in Jericho appreciate each and every one of the men and women you have brought to us. We couldn't have done this without you, Commander. You must know that. We have an army, but you brought us hope. You brought us the will to fight after everything fell to pieces. You began putting us back together. We will continue to move toward that while you are away."

Reluctantly, Hector nodded. "I will return as soon as possible."

"Go in peace, my friend." Abram bowed to him. "Worry not."

The sound of hooves reached their ears, and they turned to see a carriage approaching, surrounded by a Royal Guard of eight riders on horseback. With a signal from Hector, Jax left them and joined Raven, Solvi, and Isolde by the horses across the square. Orion stood a short distance away from the others, looking at the bottom of a horseshoe as Eero lifted the animal's foot off the ground.

The man at the front of the envoy, head of the Konungr's Royal Guard, dismounted and dipped his head to them before turning on his heel en route to the carriage door. When he opened it, the Konungr and Dróttning stepped down the carriage steps, thanking him as they did so. Viggo bowed deeply in reply and stepped out of their path. Linking arms with his wife, Konungr Vali strode toward the commanders, his cape swaying behind him as a gust of wind blew through the plaza. The silver buttons of his coat glistened in the morning haze. Ingrid slid a hand up the vuokara's single horn and petted its cheek affectionately as they passed by, matching her husband in pale gray from head to toe.

Talking directly to Hector, Vali said, "All ready to depart, Commander? I assume the horses I provided are satisfactory?" He looked past the horses with interest, and Hector followed his gaze to find him looking at Orion and Eero.

"As ready as we can be."

"You will be sure to take care of our horses," Ingrid said.

"Of course, Your Majesty. We won't be in the Grim Wilds too long, but I'll make sure they're properly hydrated. Those coats won't do them any favors in the desert."

"Naaba Kaatachi has always taken care of our horses when we've visited, my dear." Vali pulled his eyes from his observations. "Is O'Connell proving to be everything he claims to be?"

"Thus far. I'll be interested to see how the Naaba interacts with him."

"Indeed." Vali smiled. "Well, we just wanted to see you off and wish you luck." Hector found this admission strange, since Vali wasn't particularly fond of any of them. Then the Konungr added, "It seems the future of the world hangs heavy on your shoulders, Commander. I trust you shall endeavor not to mess it up."

Ingrid looked sideways at her husband, then allowed an apology to slip into her expression. "We wish you the best of blessings on your journey and sincerely hope you are able to return Alexander to us."

"I'll do everything in my power to make that happen, Your Majesty." Hector bowed politely. To Vali he said, "And please know, we greatly appreciate the provisions you've provided, as well as the horses."

"Yes, I believe you would," Vali said.

An awkward silence fell over them, and though it seemed they'd said all they came to say, the sovereigns didn't move to leave. Hector and Abram shared a glance, and Vali looked back at the others, watching from a distance as Jax interacted jovially with the women before returning his gaze to Orion and Eero, who had moved to the side of the horse they'd been discussing. Eero now seemed to be showing him the riding pad, equipped to carry additional gear by the leather cinch holding the pad in place.

Clearing his throat, Vali said, "You are familiar with the Strayed, Hector?"

Taken aback by the hint of concern he detected in the Konungr's voice, he answered, "I have seen them a few times, yes."

Vali shook his head. "But you have never been working *against* them. I urge you to beware. They are deadly beasts, far stronger than they appear and viciously swift. You should avoid conflict with them at all costs."

Hector began to smile, but pressed his lips together. "Thank you for the warning, Konungr Vali. It will likely be Jax, Isolde, and I who encounter them. As we won't be able to sneak undetected through the front gate, we'll be the ones down in the prison. I'll be sure to pass your warning onto them, as well."

"Two weeks?" Vali asked.

"Two weeks."

"Very good. We shall reconvene then." Tipping an invisible hat to them, he spun with Ingrid on his arm and strutted toward the carriage. When they reached it, they turned back around as if they truly planned on seeing the team off.

The commanders faced each other, and when Hector extended a hand, Abram pulled him in for a hug. Again he wished him blessings for his journey. Then he bid him farewell, and Hector started toward the others, passing Eero and Solvi on their way to their own commander's side.

Solvi offered him a quick dip of her chin. "May the Creator be with you, Hector."

"I'm counting on your prayers to ensure He is."

C

Orion remained with the horse he'd been introduced to: a roan whose coat faded from black to gray as if some of its pigment had been splotched away. Isolde approached the horse next to his, and in the name of civility, he extended a hand in an offer to help her up.

She declined without meeting his eyes and swung herself onto its back with fluid grace. Then she leaned forward to groom the beige mane of the skewbald, treating it with all the kindness she offered every other living creature. The mare's coat was white with a few scattered patches of cedar, to include an irregular diamond over its right eye.

Isolde clucked at the beast, cooing words in its ear too low for Orion to hear. She hadn't spoken a word to him since they arrived and had intentionally avoided his gaze.

He hadn't been pleased to find Jax knocking on his door the

night before, especially accompanied by the huge, arrogant grin plastered across his face and Orion's jacket in his hands. But he'd also understood. Again, a nice woman had taken an interest in him, and he'd treated her terribly. Whispers ebbed and flowed, taunting him with possibilities of Jax stealing Isolde away from him like Declan had Iris. He assured himself that neither Iris nor Isolde belonged to him to begin with, and he had no claim on either of them, but no amount of logic quelled his torment.

Grabbing a tuft of his horse's black mane, he pulled himself up onto the roan's back. Jax rode up next to them on a dapple gray with gorgeous silver hair hanging over its right eye, and Isolde nodded to him before trotting off toward the gate. When Jax and Orion's eyes met, Orion thought he caught a glimmer of pity cross his features.

Raven approached from behind them, already having mounted a male palomino. Its light mane and white hair was a stark contrast to her own dark hair and attire.

Hector road up next to her on a chestnut mare. "Ready Lieutenant Blackmoor?"

"As I'll ever be." Jax nodded to the Jerichonians and turned his horse toward the exit.

"Then lead on."

With one last look at Orion, Jax pressed his heels into the steed beneath him and rode off through the open gates with the others at his tail.

C

They reached the black walls a little after luncheon, the horses not struggling as much to trot through the snow as the humans had on their way into the city on foot. Pulling up to the shimmering barrier, they halted to admire the never-ending wall to the sky.

Hector slid from his horse to examine the ground. As Orion had suggested, the strip of black had grown wider than a foot. "Is this what it looked like when you passed through?" He directed his question to both Orion and Isolde.

Hopping from his own horse, Orion crouched next to Hector for a closer look. "It might have been slightly smaller." He looked to Isolde for confirmation, and she nodded.

"I agree. There is more now than before."

Raven said, "Look how the snow melts around it. Is it a substance of some kind?"

"It just feels like ground. Same as before." Hector ran his hand across the dark grass. "No different than the ground next to it."

"It's still wet, as if recently covered in snow." Orion checked his fingers. "Or like it's continuously melting as flakes fall, though it doesn't feel warm." He smelled his hand and found no lingering scent aside from the natural smell of damp earth.

"Whatever it is, it can't be a good sign." Hector stood and dried his hands on his pants. Orion did the same.

"Is it the Queen?" Jax asked.

"I don't know what else it could possibly be." Hector grazed the barrier with the palm of his hand, feeling nothing different about it from any other time he'd touched the black walls. "A problem for another day."

As Hector and Orion remounted their horses, Jax asked, "Think these ponies have ever been through a barrier?"

"Vali said the Naaba cared for their horses when they visited the village, but I can't say for sure that these horses were amongst them." Hector ran a hand down the side of his horse's neck to settle it. All seemed to be feeling the tension brought about by the nearness of the barrier—fidgeting, stomping, and disliking the sinister aura emanating from it.

"Should be interesting." Raven gripped the reins, alert to the stress building in the animal below her.

Jax said, "They may fight it, but you have to get them through. Dismount and guide them if you must."

Isolde cooed softly into her horse's ear as she stroked its mane. "I do not much like the feel of it either. It is only my second time through, so we shall conquer our fears together." The horse breathed through its nostrils and flicked its tail. "Are you ready? Let us show your friends how it is done." Whinnying, the horse reared back in excitement. Isolde clucked her tongue, and the skewbald ran at the barrier, passing straight through without pause. Raven lifted a brow at Orion, who was grinning with admiration at the place Isolde had disappeared.

"Where exactly did you find her, Orion?"

"She saved us from a hive of niedas." Orion kicked his horse into action and followed Isolde through. Raven shared a look with Hector and Jax. With a carefree shrug, Jax trotted after them.

"Last chance to turn back," Raven said. "I know you won't, but you could."

Hector shook his head and looked over the snowy landscape at his back one last time, knowing he might never see it again. "Into the Wilds we go." With a command to his horse, he flew through the barrier with Raven right behind him.

The horses seemed to suffer a mild shock as they stepped from freezing snow into scorching sand, looking around with a glint of panic and stomping their feet. After fussing for a minute or so, they steadied and waited patiently for instruction on what to do next. The team quickly dismounted and removed their cold-weather clothing, stuffing shed layers into their packs. Once ready to face the sun, they shot off into the Grim Wilds toward Caritas.

It was well past highmoon when they cantered through the arched entrance of the village. Not a soul roamed about, as if they'd stumbled upon a ghost town. Hector, Jax, and Raven took in the moonlit village with interest as Isolde and Orion dismounted.

"We need to pen the horses and give them water." Isolde escorted her skewbald across the center of the village, and the others followed. They arrived at a stable near the outskirts with a fenced area at its front. To everyone's amazement, a small herd of tryka rested in the shadows of the shelter.

"There is an empty tent we use for travelers. We will stay there tonight so as not to disturb anyone. Try to remain quiet. Come." Isolde directed them to the tent they would be sharing. It was spacious, with rugs strewn about on the sand for sleeping.

Without complaint or question, everyone found a spot to lay and quickly passed into sleep.

C

Movement in the tent stirred Orion from restless sleep. He had, regrettably, sweat through his clothing again, and he dreaded to think what kind of ruckus he'd made in the dead of night.

To his misery, Isolde had slept on the opposite side of the tent, as far away from him as she possibly could. She still hadn't spoken to him, and he couldn't blame her. The memory of him slamming his hands against the wall and growling like a ferocious bear made his stomach churn as if he'd eaten something rotten.

Catching the tail end of her exit from the tent, he sat up, rubbing the sleepiness from his eyes. Digging through the pack he'd borrowed from Declan, he grabbed a cream tunic, speedily purchased in Jericho, and changed before pulling on his boots. Upon exiting the tent, he found Isolde outside giving instructions to a young man about caring for the horses. Then she sent another to call on her father, letting him know they'd returned and would explain the details of their trip once everyone woke up.

Orion hovered in the doorway, listening to her commanding yet exceptionally kind orders. It was obvious Isolde's people served her in response to that kindness; not only out of duty but out of love for her. He supposed that must be true of Kaatachi as well, since he might be the jolliest man he'd ever met.

Orion considered approaching Isolde when the boy hastened away, but as she'd been giving very clear signals that she preferred he keep his distance, he turned and walked in the opposite direction.

Since the sun already shined on them from high in the sky, a number of the villagers had begun preparing for luncheon. The smell of charred vegetables and roasting meat filled his nose, triggering a grumble from his stomach. As he passed by, many acknowledged him with a smile or a wave, and he returned their gestures in kind, unable to remember a time in his life when he'd been greeted with such familiarity by so many strangers.

Two of the women he'd danced with the night of the big celebration sat together a few tents down looking his way and whispering to each other with obvious giggles. His pride stroked, he grinned, though he immediately dropped his head to conceal it so as not to give the wrong impression. Seeing them sparked the memory of dancing with Isolde, something he would prefer to avoid thinking about, so he turned his attention elsewhere.

He found Teetee and her grandmother Marisol on their carpet creating beautiful, woven baskets. Lights of the mūsae danced in the air around them, and the women dipped their heads as he approached.

"Good to have you back, *herr* Orion." Teetee smiled with her usual coyness.

"Good to be back." He dropped his chin to Teetee and bowed deeply to her grandmother.

"Will you be staying long?" Marisol's wrinkled hands continued to work her craft, undeterred by her attention to Orion. She'd already completed the spiraled bottom of a ruby, saffron, and turquoise basket and had begun moving the rope up the sides.

"Only a couple of days this time, I think." He attempted to ignore the pang in his gut these words produced.

Marisol grinned with a look of wisdom only the elderly can achieve. "Perhaps someday you will come to stay." She glanced past him and across the center of the village to where Isolde stood talking to her brother.

Following her line of vision, he smirked. "Perhaps. Though the odds are not looking great for me at the moment." It amazed him to see an entirely different countenance on Griffin's features. His brows pinched together as he listened intently to whatever Isolde explained, but he didn't look angry, and Orion couldn't help but question whether his disgruntled expression was reserved for him specifically. Perhaps the rest of the time, Griffin was a pleasant and agreeable man.

Letting her weaving hands fall to her lap, Marisol closed her eyes as if reliving an old memory. "Feelings change with the seasons, hearts flutter like the waves of the sea." Opening her eyes, she smiled at him. "But true love, *herr* Orion, is eternal."

Teetee growled at her grandmother. "*Avia*, leave him alone!"

"She's fine." Orion chuckled, enjoying the interaction more than he would have expected, though he did change the direction of the conversation. "I like the colors you're using for that basket, Teetee." It was several shades of brown with pops of daffodil and shards of onyx.

"Why thank you." She looked at Marisol with an expression that had Orion thinking her grandmother hadn't approved of her chosen design. "And if you are to drop the formalities, Orion, I will as well." She winked.

"Are you in need of a woven basket, *herr* Orion?" Marisol's thin smile was playful, and Teetee rolled her eyes.

"I don't think he has any use for a huge basket, *avia*."

"If I ever do come to stay, I'll purchase at least one from each of you. You have my word. I may be very picky with the colors though."

"That would be fine, *herr* Orion." Marisol dipped her head.

Over his shoulder, he heard Hector's voice and turned to find him, Raven, and Jax stepping from the visitor's tent. He wished the ladies a *merry day* and strolled toward Isolde's tent, thinking to warn Declan of the coming company.

When he lifted the flap, he found Johnathan where he'd left him days ago, snoring on the floor, and Declan sitting up in bed. His eyes slid to his chair, and an unexpected feeling of comfort washed over him. The longing to sink into it was so significant, he nearly dove for it. Instead, he calmly stepped into the room and forced his attention on his friend. "Does he ever wake up?" Orion gestured to Johnathan. "It's nearly luncheon."

Declan's eyes brightened. "You're back!" Then his brow crinkled as he put the timeline together. Situating himself higher on the bed and pushing his hair away from his eye, he asked, "Wait, how are you back already? Where's Iris?"

Orion strode to the foot of the bed and smiled in greeting. "It's good to see you, my friend. There's been a change of plans, but all will be explained soon. I came early to let you know you're about to have guests." With the side of his boot, he tapped Johnathan's hip to stir him awake.

"But wh—" Declan's sentence dropped off as a noise at Orion's back drew his attention. "Raven?" he uttered in disbelief.

Raven entered the tent with Hector, Jax, and Isolde behind her. Orion felt the familiar twinge of jealousy bubble in his stomach but did his best to suppress it, crossing his arms and rotating to face them as if he didn't have a care in the world.

"What the hell is going on?" Declan sat up higher again and tried to fold his legs under him, wincing in the process.

Isolde walked around Orion without acknowledging him and sat next to Declan, lifting his shirt to check his wound. "Take a seat if you wish," she told the room without turning to face those hovering by the door. "My father will be here shortly." Removing the wrap from Declan's ribs, she prodded the skin around the opening with her fingertips. "This is looking really good, *herr* Declan. It seems Vera took care of you. How does it feel?"

"Much better," he said, though his face contorted into a grimace of discomfort. "As long as you don't poke it like that."

"You need to heal up soon. We have a long journey ahead of us."

Before Declan could inquire at her meaning, Raven sat on his opposite side and leaned over to examine the wound. Isolde held the shirt out of the way for her. "That doesn't look so bad." Raven's face betrayed her words. In truth, it looked very painful, even with how much it seemed to have healed.

"It will be restored in no time." Isolde replaced the bandage with fresh fabric.

"The stitching looks even better than you would have done, Silas."

"Why, thank you, *nei* Raven."

Declan let out an annoyed breath of air. "You haven't seen my stitches in a very long time, Raven."

Her gaze lifting from his wound to his face, Raven asked, "How are you really?"

"I've been better, but I would really like to know what you're all doing here. Is Iris all right? What happened?" His eyes shifted from one person to the next, imploring someone to give him an answer.

Drawing his attention back to her, Raven said, "As far as we know, she's still in Celestelvyra with her sister and Prince Alexander. The Metsa Sateen Monastery was obliterated shortly after you left Jericho, so we've devised a masterful plan to infiltrate Ashgate and break them out. Doesn't that sound exciting?"

His eyes revealed his dread as they flashed to Orion. "That's the plan? That's why you're all here?"

Orion had given into temptation and moved to the comfy chair by the bed. Exhaling with tangible relief, he propped his elbow on the arm and dropped his temple to his fingers. "It's the only recourse at this point, my friend. It certainly isn't the one we would choose if another option existed."

"Is it even possible?"

Raven said, "Jax thinks it's doable. We already have it all planned out, but if you're too afraid or if you aren't well enough to come, then Isolde can provide us with a sixth."

Declan shook his head. "No way. Not a chance I'm missing this."

Raven smiled with mischief. "I thought you might say that." His serious demeanor softened at her playful expression, and she touched his hand before rising from the bed to join Hector and Jax, who were now seated at the table by the door. Moving to stand behind Hector with her back to the tent wall, she let her hand come to rest on his shoulder.

Moments later, Naaba Kaatachi, Abrafo Griffin, Vera, and a man

Orion didn't recognize entered the tent. Isolde turned around on the bed to face the room. Her gaze immediately met Griffin's. His slid to Orion looking quite at home in her chair before returning to his sister donning an air of irritation. Rolling her eyes, she focused her concentration on their father.

"Daughter." The Naaba wore the same headdress he always wore and carried the same staff decorated with stones, paint, and feathers. Rather than the natural color of animal hide, his robe was dyed dark indigo to match his face paint. His wrists were circled in colorful bracelets, and a beaded necklace replaced the teeth and bones he'd worn before. Orion suspected he'd had the same thought as Isolde of not appearing scary to the newcomers, but he also knew the moment the Naaba spoke, any terror his native attire provoked would be erased by his cheerful disposition.

Dropping her head in return, Isolde said, "*Salve*, father."

"It seems your plans have changed." Kaatachi acknowledged Orion with a nod before taking in the rest of his company.

Hector stood from the table and straightened his shirt before stepping up to the Naaba and extending his hand. "Commander Hector Kayvan of Jericho, formerly of the King's High Legion." He bowed deeply, as was customary when addressing a royal. "It's a pleasure to officially meet you, Your Majesty."

The Naaba accepted his hand and dropped his chin slightly in return. "Naaba Kaatachi of Caritas. I have heard of you Commander Kayvan. I must say, not all of it was pleasant." Jax and Raven exchanged a look of concern, both instinctively shifting their hands closer to their weapons. The movement drew Orion's attention, and he sat forward in his chair.

Hector rocked back and forth on the balls of his feet, fingers tugging at the pockets of pants displaying hints of Reginaterra red. "I believe that, but I was hoping to revamp my reputation. Figured a worldwide revolution was the best way to start." He smiled, tucking his hands behind his back, and Kaatachi laughed. "I'm not terribly familiar with Caritas, but you should know, Sirena has made a point to keep an eye on you as a suspected rebel group for many years now, though you've never done anything to force her into action."

"I suppose that is about to change as well!" Kaatachi stomped his staff against the ground. Taking two steps to the side, he gestured to those standing behind him. "Let us do introductions!

This is Griffin, my son, Nabiiga and heir, and our tribe's Abrafo. These are two of our most trusted warriors, Peiskos and Vera."

"It's nice to meet you all." Hector acknowledged each of them in turn. Motioning to the table behind him, he introduced, "This is Jax Blackmoor and Raven Nightshade, my two best soldiers and closest friends. We have come to discuss our plans to retrieve Prince Alexander from Celestelvyra."

"It was my understanding that was already being taken care of." The Naaba's eyes drifted first to Isolde before he spoke directly to Orion. "Your presence here, and so soon after departing, leads me to believe the first attempt was not successful."

Orion stood and approached the Naaba to explain, ignoring the scowl he received from Griffin. Offering his hand in greeting, he said, "When we reached Jericho, we discovered the Metsa Sateen Monastery had been destroyed as well, so we put together a new plan of action. One that is… slightly more complicated than the last."

Kaatachi's face grew solemn as he took Orion's extended hand in both of his own. "I see you returned my daughter to me in one piece, my boy. I wonder if this plan we are about to discuss will make me fear even more for her safety than I did before."

Orion could feel the rooms' eyes on him, each person interpreting the interaction with acute scrutiny. Kaatachi didn't seem to mind, or perhaps didn't notice, and focused entirely on Orion as though they were the only two in the room. Orion swallowed. "You're right. This plan will be much more dangerous than the last, but Isolde is insistent on joining us. I won't tell you not to worry, Naaba Kaatachi, but I can promise I will protect her with my life if it is in my power to do so." He could hear himself saying the words but seemed unable to stop the vow spilling from his lips. It floated into the room for all to see, though no one dared say a word. He felt certain he could feel Declan grinning behind his back, but since Isolde sat next to him on the bed, he didn't turn and reprimand him for it.

He'd promised Isolde he'd try to convince the Naaba of her joining them, and he'd meant nothing more by his oath of protection. At least, that's what he'd tell himself and anyone else who wanted to comment about it. "So, for whatever that's worth, there it is."

The Naaba gazed at Orion with a minute tilt of his head. "Mere days ago, you would not wish to be responsible for a princess." Orion felt his face warm at the memory of his uncivilized words. "Now you offer your life in exchange for hers? Much has changed in a few days, I see. My daughter tends to have such an effect on people." He released a loud and unexpected cackle. "Perhaps I should have warned you."

"Father," Isolde scolded. "Leave *herr* Orion alone." The sound of her voice had Orion's eyes sliding in her direction, though they quickly skimmed past her, avoiding direct contact, and landed on Declan's face. As he'd suspected, his friend grinned from ear to ear, enjoying the embarrassing exchange far more than any true friend should. Orion added smacking him to the top of his to-do list.

Turning back to Kaatachi, he avoided the eyes of everyone else in the room. "She has definitely had an effect." His hand felt sweaty between the Naaba's, but it didn't feel polite to pull away, so he was glad when Kaatachi finally released him.

Then Kaatachi eyed the weapons hanging from Orion's hips. "I see it is not only my daughter you have developed a liking for, but our brute weapons, as well. I had expected you to trade them for something a little more modern in Jericho."

Orion rested his hands on the tops of the axe and the bludgeon strapped to his hips. "I don't know, Naaba. I think these might be more my style."

"So it would seem." Kaatachi's expression insinuated more than his words, and as Griffin's scowl deepened behind him, the Naaba's smile widened. "Now, explain to me the new plan."

"Lieutenant Blackmoor is actually the brains of this operation, so I'll turn the floor over to him." Orion gestured to Jax, who rose from his seat and joined them at the center of the room, standing between him and Hector.

"It's great to meet you, Naaba Kaatachi." Jax bowed formally, as Hector had. "So, the short version is: we plan to infiltrate the Ashgate Fortress."

With a heavy sigh, Kaatachi said, "I assumed as much. It is the only option remaining with the Monastery in Sateen now gone."

"Exactly. So we plan to send in two teams, one through the front and one through the back. Everything we need to do inside is long winded, but what we need from you, if you would, is a distraction on the outside. A third team: something big enough to draw the

Warden from his chambers and keep him away until we finish the task and escape. We are thinking a faux traitor turn-in."

Naaba Kaatachi eyed Griffin questioningly and received a nod in return.

Hector said, "We would like to give the horses some time to rest before heading out again. We pushed them pretty hard on the journey here, and the tundra is a harsh landscape to traverse. We will leave the day after tomorrow at highsun. That will give the horses a long reprieve and allow you time to get your people ready. We will return to the barrier and make camp in the desert before jumping to Crystavium the following morning. Ashgate is a three-day ride from there."

Jax nodded confirmation, crossing an arm over his chest and resting his elbow on it so he could scratch his chin. "The next shift rotation should happen in six days, around sunset. So we have some time to play with. We want to make sure we're in position soon enough to catch the guards heading into the prison before they're in sight of the towers stationed above the outer wall."

Kaatachi said, "It seems you boys have it all figured out. My son will be ready to travel with his clan by highsun the day after tomorrow. We will provide you beds and sustenance for the next two nights."

Hector shook his head. "We can camp outside the village. There's no need to trouble you with all that."

"It is no trouble for me. Isolde has already shown you to our visitor's tent. If that is sufficient, I see no reason for you to sleep in the open desert. What a tragedy it would be if our heroes were gobbled up by sandhaier as they slept. Besides, I want you all well rested before taking on the tundra, so I implore you, be our guests! And we will talk again in the morning."

"Okay, Your Majesty. Thank you very much for your hospitality."

Turning from Hector and Jax, Naaba Kaatachi said, "I am very pleased to have met you, Orion of Reginaterra. Truly." He gave no further explanation or reasoning, but simply bowed deeply, surprising Orion and the other soldiers in the room with the respectful gesture.

After catching his breath, Orion returned his bow. "I feel the same, Naaba Kaatachi."

"Luncheon will soon be ready. I expect you all to join us." Kaatachi eyed each person in the tent before exiting through the flap. Griffin motioned silently to Peiskos and Vera, and the three of them followed after their Naaba without a word to the others.

When the tent grew silent, Hector eyed Orion with a raised brow.

Orion sighed. "Whatever it is, just say it Kayvan."

Hector's lips spread into a smile, but he didn't reply. Instead, he said Raven's name, prompting her to stand next to him. "Let's go get some luncheon."

CHAPTER 20

WHERE YOU BELONG

Orion remained with Declan as Isolde showed the others to luncheon. Though he hadn't expected her to return so quickly, she stepped back through the flap of the tent only minutes later.

Declan spoke first, moving to sit up the moment he saw her enter. "Isolde, you should take your bed tonight. I will be fine on the floor with the others." He pulled his legs around, but she stopped him with a raised palm.

"No, *herr* Declan. You need two more nights of good sleep before you travel into the wilderness. Please, I insist. It is no trouble for me to sleep elsewhere, I assure you." Before he could object, his mouth hanging open about to speak, Isolde addressed Orion.

He hadn't turned to her when she entered, still feeling a little embarrassed about the personal undertones that took place during his conversation with her father, but at the sound of his name, he rotated to look at her.

"May I speak with you? Outside?"

It took his brain several long moments to comprehend her words —to realize she was speaking to him at all—and then a few more for him to understand that she wanted to speak to him privately. "Yes, of course." Standing, he followed her out the door.

The center of the village was packed with people passing around food and drink and talking amongst themselves. The Raptors stood near the entrance to the visitor's tent holding plates of food and talking to a few villagers Orion recognized but didn't know by name.

Isolde walked out around her tent, past two more rows behind it, and strode off into the desert with Orion following close behind her.

Bright rays of afternoon sun illuminated cloudless, cyan skies. Despite the warm air, a soft breeze blew across the dunes. Orion rolled his sleeves up another fold, hoping she wouldn't notice the change and think he was trying to show off.

Knowing her, he suspected she probably would. And knowing himself, he suspected he probably was showing off just a little.

They walked for several minutes in unrelenting silence before Orion said, "I'm beginning to worry your intentions are nefarious, Naabila." He picked up his pace to walk next to her. "Where exactly are you taking me? I hope I haven't angered you enough to consider murdering me and leaving me to the vultures."

Isolde stopped and turned to face him with her smile returned. It felt so long since he'd seen it, though it had only been about a day. "There are far worse things in the desert than vultures."

Orion looked around as though the mystery monsters with a taste for human flesh might appear. With a nervous chuckle, he ran his hand down the back of his head. She watched him thinking it over, letting the moments pass by in a bizarre silence that felt natural and terrifying all at once.

Finally, she said, "*Salve.*"

He detected shyness in her tone but knew he might be imagining it. Despite his elevated heart rate as he considered what she'd dragged him into the desert to discuss, he took a step closer. "Hello to you, too, Naabila."

Her fingers danced on the hilt of her blade, and he realized this was a nervous habit, something she did when feeling uneasy. She'd pulled her hair off her shoulders and rolled it into a thick bun at the base of her neck, a style he hadn't seen on her before. His eyes followed the line of her jaw and the slope of her throat to her shoulders—parts of her body not often on display.

When Orion registered her long pause, his cheeks flushed with childlike guilt. She'd been talking, but he hadn't heard what she'd said. His eyes focused on hers, making it clear he was paying attention.

Then she said, "I wanted to talk about the Queen. And the after-effects of what she did to you in the dungeons."

His expression hardened as the reasons for her behavior fell into place. He'd severely misread her nervousness and felt a fool for allowing his mind to drift in the wrong direction. "I have to be honest, that is not where I hoped this conversation was going."

In hindsight, she'd barely spoken to him in two days. It had been foolish of him to even consider she'd dragged him into the desert to express affection.

A baffling and irritating smile spread across her lips. "Where had you hoped it was going?" Orion tugged at his ear, his eyes sliding left to a cactus at the top of a nearby dune before returning to her. Her smile deepened. "It was not my intention to mislead you. I only wished to pull you away from those who might over-hear. As it is your business to share with whom you wish." With her other hand, she stroked the foxtails hanging on her opposite hip. Then the fingers of both hands balled into fists before spreading out wide as if she realized her nervous twitch and attempted to stifle it.

"So you didn't share it with Jax? I assumed he let you stay in his room to save you from the ravings of a madman."

A wounded expression crossed her features, though the pain in her eyes sounded like anger in her voice. "Of course not. He was only being kind because the guards at the front gate saw me kicking the wall." This statement left him brimming with curiosity, but he let her continue without interrupting. "I would never expose a secret not mine to tell, and I cannot believe you would think so little of me, *herr* Orion."

Despite his previous attraction to her irritation, he decided he hated the way his name slipped from her angry tongue. And again, he felt like a fool. Of course she hadn't shared his issues with Jax. In just the few days he'd known her, it was obvious that it wasn't in her nature to behave so callously. In defiance of these realizations, his frustration didn't leave his tone. "Well, it's fine. I have it under control." He stepped backward, no longer meeting her eyes.

In two strides, she stood in front of him again, holding his hand. "We will be separated in the prison. I think it may be a good idea for you to share the difficulty with Declan or Raven, so you are not alone if something happens." Her hand fell to her side, leaving the skin of his palm craving the warmth of her touch.

"Nothing is going to happen." He wished more than anything

for the conversation to be over and for the power to rewind time so he could take back the horrible minutes in Jericho when he'd revealed his insanity so thoroughly.

She moved her face in front of his and said his name, forcing him to meet her eyes. "Just days ago you stood right on this spot screaming at no one. In Jericho, you yelled at me. Please understand, I do not say this to embarrass or hurt you."

"But as you have just stated, it is my business to share with whom I wish." The whisper's volume increased in unison with his aggravation. He yearned for her to take his hand again and silence them. He wished he could stop feeling so angry, knowing there was a chance she might be touching him again the moment he ceased being a jerk.

"That is true. I only mean to look out for the safety of the other nine people counting on you while we infiltrate the most securely guarded place in all of Arkaemor aside from Celestelvyra itself." She studied his face with eyes full of concern. "You hear her now, I think. Do you not?"

He tried to determine what kind of signals he gave off to reveal his lunacy so he could try to conceal them in the future. As if someone tapped the side of his skull, the heavy *drip, drip, drip* of the water from the pipe hitting the stone floor echoed throughout his consciousness. Then another voice reached his ears, deep and gentle.

Are you ready to surrender yet, Orion? Or will you continue to fight no matter what damage it breeds?

Sighing a heavy sigh as his mind adamantly defied his denial, he heeded the voice, and yielded. "Okay Isolde. I will do as you ask. I promise. Before we enter the prison, I will tell Declan."

"That would be wise." Again she took his hand and squeezed it tenderly.

The gesture suppressed the whispers in an instant, and he exhaled blissful relief, his eyelids falling closed in his comfort. As if his released breath reminded her of the words he'd spit regarding her constant touch, she tried to pull her fingers away, her expression apologetic. But Orion wasn't ready to be untethered from the lifeline of their connected skin, and he tightened his grip so she couldn't easily slip away. Instead, he tugged her closer, keeping his eyes on hers. "It's settled then."

She dropped her chin in a wordless reply, her eyes glancing at their hands.

"I'm sorry. I'm so terribly sorry for what I said and how I behaved. You did not deserve that. I was… not myself. Though if I'm honest, I've been having a difficult time figuring out exactly which parts of me are truly me and what parts belong to someone else entirely."

"Our traumas shape us, often changing us into something unrecognizable."

He did feel unrecognizable, as if the monster trapped beneath his skin was thrashing and clawing to break free.

Her eyes lifted to his, and she clarified, "But unrecognizable is not always for the worst. We can allow our tragic experiences to help us grow into the people we always wished to be."

"Maybe." The intimacy of the conversation began to overwhelm him, and he swallowed. "Anyway. I'm truly sorry, Naabila."

"I forgive you." Her voice quivered with an unfamiliar anxiety as she added, "And I am sorry for… always touching you. My people are—"

"I know," he cut her off, furious at himself for the words he'd snarled. He felt her pulling her hand from his again, and he squeezed it. "And it's fine. You don't need to pull away. I didn't mean what I said anyway." His brows pinched together. "I mean, I did. But I didn't."

"You are not making so much sense." Her smile returned—to his utter relief. Her thumb trailed his hand, matching his gentle movements with ones of her own.

"I know. I'm sorry for that as well. I'm sorry for a lot of things."

Another glance down at their hands had her promising, "I will make an effort to allow you your personal space."

"Don't!" he blurted. She grinned at his apprehension, and he attempted to reign in his fear. So far, nothing had paralyzed the whispers but the affectionate touch of her skin against his, and he honestly didn't know how he might survive if he lost it. "I mean, I don't mind it. I'm getting used to it." This was both a truth and a lie. As was his previous statement about it driving him insane. "So you don't need to worry about it. Just please, if you can, forget everything I said during that horrible moment. Please."

She nodded and studied his eyes, searching them as if scouring the seas for a lost island of buried treasure.

Since she didn't seem angry anymore—unless he'd misread her again—he decided to test the waters, letting his feelings trickle through his tone with just a touch of arrogance. "So, is that really the only reason you dragged me all the way out here, Naabila?"

"What other reason could there possibly have been?"

He wasn't about to speak his thoughts out loud, so he pinched his lips shut between his teeth to ensure no embarrassing fantasies escaped. Though he couldn't seem to pull his eyes from where they'd landed on her lips, and he knew she couldn't be oblivious to his blatant focus. He busied his free hand running his fingers down the foxtails hanging at her hips, attempting to prevent them from touching anything else. His whole body felt balmy, and he thought she must have moved closer because he caught a whiff of sandalwood and lavender.

After several seconds of heated silence, Isolde stepped to the side and walked around him in the direction of the village. As the distance grew between them, she let go of his hand, and it pleased him to find that the whispers didn't immediately swarm at the loss of contact.

Over her shoulder, she called, "Are you coming, *herr* Orion?"

"I'm coming." Feeling true joy for the first time in days, he jogged her way and fell into step next to her.

☾

The village of Caritas was overwhelmed with intrigue at their visitors. It wasn't often they had so many guests all at once, especially guests so profoundly different from them. They were accustomed to housing nomads and sporadic adventurers traversing the wilderness of Arkaemor and needing solace for a few days, but six former soldiers of the King's Legion was unheard of.

The Raptors sat near the center of the village on rocks used for communal seating. Having finished their meal, they dove into a deep discussion about a game of Hunter's Quarrel played a few nights back. Raven had taken them for all they were worth—despite Dominic clearly and blatantly cheating.

Though most of the villagers let the group eat their luncheon in peace, only staring at them from a distance as they whispered and pointed, when they'd finished eating, people flocked from all sides.

They examined their attire, Jax's tattoos, and asked dozens of questions.

Several women surrounded Raven, interested to know everything they could possibly discover about her. They pointed out the many cuts and scars across her skin, proof of what a powerful warrior she must be, and asked if they could paint her face to look like theirs. Raven gently declined the tattoos but agreed when they requested permission to fix up her hair. She remained perched on a rock as the women unwove her lengthy braid and marveled at her dark, silky locks.

Though used to being fawned over by women, Jax's expression revealed that he didn't know how to feel about the crowd surrounding him. They ran their fingers up and down his arms, admiring the designs and showing off their own tattoos. Others tugged at the hair slicked back on top of his head, debating whether it was long enough to braid.

When Orion and Isolde rounded the corner of the tent, they stopped short to take in the scene. "You don't get strangers often, huh?" Orion laughed at Jax's look of unease.

"Not strangers such as these." Isolde shook her head at her people, though her smile remained. "They are filled with so much love and delight in expressing it."

"I am familiar with the notion. Where is Hector?" His eyes scanned the crowd.

Isolde pointed at the group hovering outside the armory, fighting to stick their heads through the door. "I believe they must have dragged him in there to show off all of our fine weaponry."

"Ah, yes. I bet he's loving that, actually. If memory serves, Hector has always had an interest in a vast variety of weapons. If you noticed, the group he chose when he formed the Reko Raptors use a diverse set themselves. I don't doubt that was intentional."

"Hector formed the Raptors? He does not wear a horned owl like the others."

Amazed by her intuition and how she didn't seem to miss a single thing, Orion shook his head. "He formed them but wasn't technically supposed to become one himself. He put Jax in charge. That's why his pin is golden and the others are bronze. Hector was the commander of the entire King's Legion. He couldn't have made himself a Raptor even if he'd wanted to."

"It seems you are wrong about that."

Orion chuckled and crossed his arms, unable to deny that Hector was no longer the commander of the King's Legion and was instead running around and wreaking havoc throughout the Five Kingdoms with his Raptors. Again his attention slid to Jax: the lieutenant of the Reko Raptors and no stranger to the opposite sex, yet there he stood, blushing and overwhelmed by a group of enthusiastic and tantalizing women.

"He seemed so frightening before this moment," Isolde said, drawing a stark laugh from Orion.

"Jax is frightening, but he's still human."

"Still a man."

Orion nodded. "Even the fiercest warrior can be brought to his knees by a gorgeous woman."

"Indeed. Perhaps we should bring Declan out. Let him walk around a little and stretch his legs?"

"Sure. He could use the fresh air." Orion laughed again as one woman, shorter than the others, climbed atop her friend's shoulders to get a better view of the tattoos peeking out from Jax's collar.

"I will get him." Isolde disappeared from his side before he could turn to protest.

Feeling friendly, especially now that tensions between him and Isolde seemed to have fizzled out, he approached the group, grinning at Raven as the women put all kinds of braids and ties into her hair.

Scowling at him, she snapped, "Not a word, Orion." But her eyes didn't match her grimace, revealing a secret joy in her pampering, even if she would never in a million years admit it.

"You look great," he said, meaning it.

Walking over to Jax and his flock, Orion put a hand on his shoulder. "Ladies, let's give Jax a little break. He isn't used to so much female attention." He smirked, and Jax's expression transformed from gratitude at his arrival to a pinched brow as he registered the insult.

"*Herr* Orion!" Two women appeared at his sides, each grabbing one of his arms. He recognized them as the women giggling at him when he'd first woken. "Bayo and Nabu, remember? Naaba Kaatachi says we may have another celebration tomorrow to see you off." Shorter than Nabu, Bayo had dark, untamed hair coiled with curls and brown eyes surrounded in sapphire paint.

"Will you save us another dance?" Nabu asked, her voice calmer than Bayo's, though not by much. She stood slightly taller than Orion, nearly as tall as Jax, with hair the opposite of Bayo's: smooth, straight, and light brown.

Jax and Raven lifted their brows.

"Or will you only be dancing with Naabila Isolde?" Bayo asked, eyes suggestive. "Do not think we did not notice her keeping you all to herself."

"Have you come to sweep our Naabila off her feet, *herr* Orion?"

"They will fall in love and live happily ever after." Bayo mimicked Nabu's dramatic tone. She held her hands together at her chest and gazed at the sky as though daydreaming of love.

"I think the Naabila may be willing to spare at least one dance," Orion said, not acknowledging any of the other notions they pronounced.

One of the women still hanging on Jax looked up at him. "Do you dance, scary-man?" Jax opened his mouth, but no words came out.

"You can drag him around the dance floor just like you did with me." Orion winked at Jax. "Scary-man will catch on. Though maybe not as quickly as I did. You may have to be slightly more aggressive." Jax pursed his lips, and Raven stifled laughter behind her hand.

The woman on Jax's right shrieked and pointed past Orion. "The stabbed-man has left his tent!" The others fluttering around them made sounds of excitement as they moved their heads out around each other and stood on their tiptoes to see.

"I heard the Queen stabbed him in the chest!" one of the girls cried.

"Our fearsome Naabila saved the day, of course," Nabu said, and Bayo added, "Cheers to Naabila Isolde!" All the women with Jax and Orion rushed to flock around Declan and Isolde.

Orion turned to stand next to Jax, crossing his arms over his chest. "I had no idea you were so afraid of women, Blackmoor."

"I'm not afraid of women. There's just a lot of them. And they are very… friendly."

"Jax doesn't like to be the center of attention," Raven said in his defense.

Orion hummed. Both he and Jax continued to watch as Isolde attempted to shoo the throng of girls away. Declan's cheeks were beet red. "Typical," Orion muttered, shaking his head.

"*He's* afraid of women." Jax grinned.

Raven said, "He's not afraid, he's just shy."

Orion ignored Raven's comment and said objectively, "I think he's prettier than me."

"I'm definitely prettier than you." Jax also crossed his arms and leaned his head to the side to examine Declan. "He's scrawny though."

"He has the pointy hair in the face thing." Orion slanted his own head to match Jax's.

"Is it the freckles?" Jax reasoned. "They certainly don't hurt, I suppose."

Orion turned to scrutinize Jax's face. "You're *not* prettier than me."

"I definitely am."

"You're both pathetic." Raven's hair was still being tied and yanked in all directions. "Hector is prettier than the three of you combined." One of the women behind her paused mid-braid to look at Orion, Jax, and then Declan before nodding in agreement.

"Hector is old!" Orion cried, astounded by the revelation and the other womens' concurrence.

"He's not even four years older than you."

"Stress has aged him."

Raven gaped. "You're insane. Hector is beautiful. He's stoic."

Orion shook his head. "He's uptight. Stiff."

"He is not uptight!"

Jax shrugged. "You may be biased, Raven. He's a little uptight. He was the commander of the King's Legion. You don't get that title by being wild and free." When he noticed Raven's glare, he added, "But being uptight isn't always a bad thing. He's mature."

"I don't think I'm biased, but we can ask the ladies to vote if you would like some proof."

"Pass," Orion and Jax said in unison.

They continued to watch the women fawn over Declan. Then Jax wrinkled his brow. "She called me scary-man."

"You are kind of scary." Orion glanced sideways. "In the prettiest way." Raven couldn't stop laughing, and the women adorning her scolded her for not sitting still.

With excessive effort, Isolde managed to convince the girls to give it a rest for now and wait for the following evening's festivities to become more acquainted with the newcomers. Displeased, but

respectful of their Naabila, they went about their business elsewhere. The women decorating Raven finished up just as Declan and
Isolde joined the group. Declan clenched his entire body as he
walked, though Isolde assured him it would loosen up if he moved
around a little, adding the command to *take it slow.*

"I'll walk the inner circle with you," Orion offered.

Declan breathed heavily, stretching his torso. "Let me catch my
breath first."

"You sure you're going to be up for riding a horse in the next
two days?" Jax eyed him skeptically.

Declan's gaze lifted to him firmly. "Don't worry about it. I'll be
good to go."

To Orion, Jax said, "You know, you might be right about the
pointy hair thing." Orion laughed, and Declan looked confused.

Isolde attempted to shift the attention off of Declan. "There will
be a celebration tomorrow evening. You are welcome to join if you
wish, or you may remain in your tent. Whichever you prefer."

"They'll be there," Orion assured her, grinning. "Jax already
promised several women a dance." Jax scowled. Then Orion
attempted to mimic Kaatachi's voice as he said, "Plus, Caritas has
the finest wine in all of the Wilds."

Isolde chuckled. "That was pretty good. And it is true. We do
have fine wine. It will begin at sundown." Admiring Raven's newly
styled hair, she said, "You look very nice, *nei* Raven. They did a
fantastic job. Perhaps you will ask them to style it for the celebration
tomorrow as well."

"Thanks." Raven blushed, and Jax and Orion's jaws dropped, as
neither had ever seen her embarrassed, nor thought she had it in her
to be so.

"Blood does run through her veins," Orion whispered. Jax
cackled again.

Raven glared at them. "Shut up! Both of you." She scowled extra
fiercely at Jax. Then to Isolde, she asked, "Why do you keep calling
me *nei* Raven?"

Orion explained before she could respond. "She's being respectful. I think *nei* is like miss. Teetee told me to call her grandmother
rouv Marisol instead of *nei,* so I think that would be for someone
who is or was married, like we would say missus instead of miss.
Or maybe it's for someone older than you?" He looked to Isolde for
the answer and found her beaming.

"*Rouv* is a more respectful title, used for a woman who has been married, but you are correct, it can be used for one older than you, especially if you are not sure whether they have wed or not. Do not worry too greatly about remembering these. No one in Caritas will be offended if you simply call them by name."

Orion stepped through the open circle and put a hand on Declan's shoulder. "Let's have a walk, my friend." Declan nodded.

"I'm going to check on Hector," Jax turned from the group without awaiting a response.

"You just want to see all the fancy weapons," Raven accused.

Over his shoulder, he called back, "Pretty much. You coming?" Knowing she would say yes before she answered, he waved her along. Raven said farewell to the others, and the two walked off toward the armory to find Hector and explore the ferocious weapons of Caritas.

CHAPTER 21

MISFORTUNES IN THE DESERT

Orion, Declan, and Isolde watched the two Raptors disappear into the crowd outside the armory. Then Orion looked at Isolde. "You can walk around with us if you want."

"Unfortunately, I have some business to attend to with my father." Pointing at Declan, she reminded him, "Take it slow."

"I'll take care of your patient, Naabila," Orion promised.

Isolde crossed her arms, the look of distrust blatant in her features. "Make sure that you do." With a wave, she left them, heading off in the direction of her father's tent.

Orion stared after her as she strolled away. "She's so bossy."

"You love it."

Clapping Declan hard on the back, he said, "Let us endeavor to remember who is injured and who is not and who could very easily injure the other further to prevent him from traveling with us to Crystavium." Holding his hand out, he gestured for Declan to walk on before falling in line next to him. "You know, you're super annoying now."

Declan exaggerated a scoff. "*I'm* annoying? Try living with you!"

"Oh, I would hate it." He laughed, though a small hole opened in his stomach at the thought. Living inside his own head had become far more trying than Declan realized. This thought triggered the reminder of his promise to Isolde. He needed to share the truth about his dwindling sanity, and though the words lingered on the tip of his tongue, he struggled to release them.

"*Herr* Orion!" A man's voice reached their ears, and both men turned to see the potter rushing toward them. He skidded to a halt and extended both hands toward Orion, a colorful, clay bowl cradled within them. "*Invi! Complevit!* It is finished!"

"It looks great—" Orion paused. "I'm sorry, I don't actually know your name."

"*Paenite,* sorry, *ahmeeka.* I am Ishmael."

"It's a pleasure to officially meet you, Ishmael. This is my friend, my—*ahmeeka*—Declan."

Ishmael laughed. "You are catching on!"

Orion chuckled and gestured to the potter. "Declan, meet Ishmael. He gave me a lesson in pottery making." Declan's eyes widened.

Ishmael nodded with excitement. "This is your dish!"

"My dish?" Orion looked at the dish as Ishmael shoved it into his hands.

"Yes, yes. The one you helped make. I wish for you to have it. So you always remember your first lesson with Ishmael." He tapped his clay-splattered shirt with both hands.

Orion accepted the gift, turning it over to examine it fully. It was an actual bowl, impeccable in shape and construction. The potter had painted it scarlet and decorated it with curly, gold designs. Eyes sliding to Ishmael, he said, "This definitely isn't what it looked like when I finished, but I am honored by the gift. *Gratiias tibi,* Ishmael. I promise to never forget my first lesson with you."

The potter clapped his hands together, grinning from ear to ear. "Come back when you are ready for another round. We will put someone on guard for that pesky Naabila. She is a troublesome one."

"Sounds like a plan." Orion couldn't stop the man's joyous energy from lifting his spirits. "Thanks again." Ishmael acknowledged Declan with a nod and rushed back to his wheel. Orion continued to study the pottery, incapable of comprehending the kindness of Caritas' villagers.

"Seems like I'm not the only one who's different," Declan remarked, startling Orion out of his thoughts. They continued their stroll, waving again to Ishmael and his wife as they passed their home.

"What do you mean?" Orion asked, and Declan gestured to the dish in his hands. Orion shook his head. "That was nothing. I was practically forced into it, anyway."

Declan lifted a hand to coddle his ribs, his face scrunching with discomfort he attempted to conceal. "I wasn't aware you could be forced into anything, Ri. Except maybe by Camille." Orion mumbled something under his breath, but his smile returned almost instantly as they passed another villager who greeted him by name. "You do seem different though," Declan insisted. "Look at you waving at the villagers like you're actually enjoying it. It doesn't seem forced at all."

Orion dropped his hand to his side and broke eye contact with the person he'd been greeting.

Declan stopped walking and grabbed Orion's arm so he would too. "Orion, please don't stop. I'm not trying to tease you. It's nice to see you this way. I can tell you like these people, and they seem to like you, too. That's not a bad thing."

Orion nearly growled his response. "I'm not changed. I'm exactly who I've always been."

"Ri—"

"Just drop it, okay?" Detesting the pity he saw in Declan's eyes, Orion looked across the village.

"When are you going to learn you don't have to do that? You keep everyone at a distance and frankly, it's stupid." Turning from him, Declan snapped over his shoulder, "I'm going to lay down. I'll get up and move around again soon." Leaving Orion alone and without response, Declan ambled back to Isolde's tent.

C

After their disagreement, Orion made himself scarce. In light of the newcomers and the upcoming celebration, the village had grown too loud alongside his returned whispers, so he decided to take another walk.

This time, he remembered to bring his weapons, as well as a skin of water. Before heading out of town, he stopped by Isolde's tent. Johnathan sat at the table, and Declan was back in bed. Orion didn't speak to either of them as he dropped off his pottery and grabbed what he needed.

After filling the waterskin from the well, he began his journey walking north with no destination in mind. He considered heading east and not stopping until he reached the barrier. From there, he could be almost anywhere in the world in just a few days. He could hide in the mountains of Cordillera, catch a ride across the Suola Meri in Alunda, even return home to Reginaterra. He could leave it all behind. Declan and the Belamours and the Raptors—and Isolde.

All of it.

Sirena would never get her hands on him again, and no one would expect anything of him. He would no longer let down the people he cared about or allow his inner torment to seep into their lives. He could disappear on the wind. He could be free.

With all of that in mind, his feet took him north, knowing if he traveled too close to the barrier, he may be more tempted to escape. Meditating on this decision brought to mind Maeve's words about walking two different paths.

You tend to drift back and forth from one to the other, but if you wish to help your friends, you must choose the path that is straight and narrow. You cannot continue to walk the line between the light and the dark.

He reasoned that his current impulses could be what she'd been referring to. His constant battle between staying and going. Should he stay, the road would be hard and long and fraught with danger. Should he go, he would be alone but untethered, no longer shackled to responsibilities, relationships, and inconsistent feelings.

If you wish to help your friends, you must choose the path that is straight and narrow.

Orion looked ahead of him at the vast wilderness. The desert had no paths. Only dunes of sand and long stretches of red clay. If it did have paths, they would be neither straight nor narrow.

The whispers descended, encouraging him to choose the dark; to turn east and head to the barrier; to find Camille and Bellamy and sail the Peril Refuge off into the sunset. Though if Camille ever found out the mess he'd found himself mixed up in now, she'd never let him hide with her anyway. She'd tell him to buck up and get over it.

The Peril Refuge is a haven of safety, a place to catch your breath, but it is not a place to weigh anchor and hide from your problems. The only way to find true refuge is to face the depths of your soul head on and know you were strong enough to survive it.

That's what Camille had told him the day she dropped anchor off the coastline of Sal and gave him until sunrise to say farewell. It was possibly the best and worst day of his life. He brooded over what she might think of him now, wandering the desert hearing voices in his head and contemplating fleeing the revolution and everyone he cared about in pursuit of freedom.

More words from Maeve rolled around his mind like marbles in a tin can. *Your reputation precedes you, Orion. You are every bit the man they said you would be.* He shook his head and said, "Yeah, I bet I am."

A familiar sound reached his ears, and he stopped walking, listening carefully to his surroundings. It was near impossible to detect sounds above the dripping and the whispers, but he felt certain he'd heard something tangible. He scanned the ocean of sand around him, searching for evidence to prove his suspicions true.

Again he heard the rattle and related it to uncooked kernels swished around in a clay bowl. His mother had grown a small patch of corn in their backyard, and he remembered popping dry kernels from the cobs and making an instrument with a bowl and a scrap of fabric.

When he heard the rattle again, louder, closer, his heart jumped, landing somewhere high in his chest. He pulled both axe and bludgeon from their frog holsters and looked south toward the village, but it was long ago out of sight. He was alone.

Untethered, just like he'd wanted.

"I know you're here," he shouted to the open desert. He held his weapons out and continued scanning the surface of the sand. Underneath his breath, he said, "Come out, you slithering beast."

The sand to his left began to shift, spilling down on either side of a rising hill. More sand poured on his right, stopping when its height matched Orion's hips. Horror momentarily immobilized him when he realized it had him surrounded.

At last, the head rose from its hiding place beneath the sand a few feet in front of him, its tan and red scales a perfect blend against the desert landscape. Beady eyes stared down at him from high above. Then the rattle at the back of its tail shook behind him, proving his initial fear: the viparah's massive body encircled him.

Orion kept his weapons raised and bent his knees. He needed to get out of the death circle so he could fight the beast from the outside. Unlike their brethren, viparah hunted for sport. Even the anacondas of the rainforest didn't grow nearly as large or as vicious as the monstrous vipers of the desert. Orion knew it wouldn't be slinking away, and there would be no outrunning it, either. Only death would end this battle, either the snake's or his own.

From above, the viparah opened its mouth to reveal fangs already dripping with sulfur-hued venom. Its forked tongue tasted the air.

Orion took a step closer, and the serpent drew back its head. "Are we doing this? You think you can take me?" It swayed back and forth, vigorously shaking its rattle. To himself, Orion said, "All right. Here we go."

With the axe in his right hand, he swung high, striking the monster's lengthy body. The viparah hissed and rammed its head toward him, hoping to be rid of him in one well-aimed bite, but Orion anticipated the strike and already had his stone bludgeon swinging in the opposite direction. A clang rang out when the stone collided with the viparah's skull.

It scuttled back, and Orion rolled beneath its lifted body, freeing himself from the circular prison. The snake coiled away, pulling its tail behind it as it stared at him.

Orion backed away, putting more distance between them and giving himself more time to react to its swift movements. The snake struck again, and again Orion parried with his bludgeon. It sent two simultaneous jabs toward him, but Orion evaded.

Angered, the serpent dropped to the ground and quickly encircled him again. Orion tried to dodge, but was knocked to the ground. His axe skittered across the sand and out of reach. Enclosed again, now on his back within the monster's grasp, he panicked as the snake lunged for him, holding his bludgeon out in front of his face. It glanced off the viparah's nostril, doing next to no damage, though it did give him a few free seconds to roll out of the way as the snake smashed its nose into the ground. He retrieved his axe and rose to his feet, pausing to take in his surroundings.

Using a rock for leverage, he leapt over the viparah's body, spinning in the air and bringing his axe down hard with the force from his jump. It lodged into the serpent's skin. When he yanked it free, crimson blood splattered the sand, as well as his chest and face.

Orion spat after landing and wiped his lips with the back of his hand. "That's gross." The serpent coiled, pulling its tail out of Orion's reach. "You scared?" he taunted. "It seems like you're scared."

The snake struck, and Orion swung his axe, but missed. Holstering his bludgeon, he hurled a rock gleaned from the ground and hit the snake in the eye. It hissed with rage and struck again, this time knocking Orion off his feet and slamming its nose into his body with two fierce and painful strikes. Orion grabbed his stomach, wincing from the pain as the viparah pulled back, preparing to strike again. It lunged for him with bared teeth, taking another face-full of sand.

Orion rose and regained his footing, remaining in a crouch as he waited to see what the beast would do next. He armed himself with another stone. Rising slightly, he launched the rock, but the snake avoided the attack. It struck again, this time with its tail, and sent Orion flying. He landed on his stomach several feet away, and the viparah slithered after him. Orion dragged himself up again and barely avoided another blow. Then the snake rose above him, looking down at him with its mouth open. It struck, and Orion jumped to the side, swinging his axe. The curve of the blade locked it into the snake's flesh. Using it for leverage, he pulled himself behind its head and mounted it behind the base of its skull. The snake thrashed and pulled free of the axe, but Orion already had his fingers curled into the side of its mouth. He clutched the top of the viparah's jaw behind its fangs and didn't let go.

The snake twirled and swung, but Orion kept his legs wrapped tautly around its neck. Blood poured from its wound, and at last the beast began to grow sluggish. When it slowed enough, Orion struck it through the top of its skull.

Without waiting to discover the blow's efficacy, he yanked it free and struck again, over and over until the viparah's body stilled beneath him, and not even the sound of its rattling tail could be heard in the soundless desert. Orion hastened from its corpse, scrambling across the ground while keeping the creature within his sights. Erratic breathing pained his ribs, and he wondered if they might be bruised. He tried to calm his heart rate as he watched and waited. When the snake remained still, he fell backward to rest in the sand.

In light of his elevated adrenaline, the whispers seemed to have subsided. His eyes found the sun in the sky falling close to the horizon, and he knew he should be getting back. He looked down at himself and found his whole torso covered in blood. He tried to wipe his face, but in the desert heat, the blood had already begun drying to his skin.

A scuffle to his right had him sitting up and bearing his weapon. He caught a glimpse of something sticking out from behind a rock not far off. He squinted against the sun and discovered a wolf eyeing him from a distance—another gray wolf in the desert.

"What are the odds of that?" Orion said out loud. The wolf crooked its head to the side. "What in the world are you? What are you doing in the Grim Wilds? What were you doing in Jericho?" The wolf howled, seemingly in response to words he couldn't have heard. Then Orion yelled, "You could have helped, you know!" He lifted a hand to the carcass at his back.

The wolf held his gaze for a long moment, yelped, and disappeared behind the rock.

Orion leaned over and waited for it to reappear on the opposite side. When it didn't, he pulled himself to his feet, dusted off his pants, and strode over to it. He circled the rock but found no trace of the wolf. Holding his hand to his brow, he surveyed the landscape but didn't see a single paw print.

"So. I'm yelling at hallucinations again. That's fantastic." Holstering his axe, he drew from his skin of water. He held his hand out in front of his face, finding the sun four finger-widths from the horizon. "An hour until sunset. I guess I should get moving." He looked east, again considering running and never looking back.

You did not care to be alone this evening, did you Orion?

Rubbing his temples, Orion groaned. "First snakes and wolves, then gods. What a fabulous outing this turned out to be."

I am the only God, the One that stands above all others, a fact you know well.

"Do I?" His voice rose with each passing word. "Let me ask you this God above all others: what the hell am I doing here?" Screaming now, he asked, "Why is this happening to me? You care so damn much, do You? Then *why are You watching me suffer?*"

Alongside a cooling breeze, the Creator replied, *Like shade in the desert, I am here to offer shelter, protection, wisdom, comfort. You need only ask, Orion.*

"I have asked!" Orion's face had grown red with rage. "I've begged! And where were You? No where. Even now, You're here. You speak. But it means nothing. You do *nothing.*" His entire body vibrated as he fought for calm breath. When no voice answered his

shouted pleas, he swiped away tears with the back of his hand and
started the walk back toward the village.

C

Rossnetta's teapot shrieked, and she hurried over to pull it off the
stove. After filling a cup she'd already seasoned with tea leaves, she
moseyed over to the kitchen table and took a seat next to the
window. The flowers Seth gave her had wilted days ago, but she
hadn't been able to bring herself to toss them.

Being a widow and having lived alone for so many years, she
never expected to miss the company. Over the past ten days since
Seth left with the others, she discovered herself longing for companionship and even experiencing spells of loneliness. She felt
saddened when she considered how long it might be before she saw
him again, knowing deep inside the very real possibility that he
may never return at all. The world of Arkaemor was full of adven-
tures to be had, a fact she knew better than most.

Sighing, she pulled the flowers from the vase and carried them
outside, thinking to decompose them in her garden. In a way, Seth's
gift would continue to feed her flowers and vegetables with fertil-
izer, and would in turn remain with her forever. Thunder crackled
above, drawing her eyes to the cloud-covered sky. She often had a
sense for such things, but she hadn't felt a storm brewing. Though
since she'd spent a better part of the afternoon lost in daydreams, it
was possible she simply hadn't been paying attention.

She watched the clouds, seeming to blacken by the moment. All
at once, three things happened: the clouds burst, allowing torrential
rain to shower the village; a giant, winged creature appeared from
inside one of the ashen clouds, spraying a breath of fire into the air;
and a woman materialized in the middle of the street in front of her
home.

She wore a fancy dress, dark obsidian bleeding into crimson. It
bore no sleeves, but from where the black halter encircled her neck
like a thick choker, red gossamer hung down her body in long strips
that blew elegantly around her in the wind. Despite standing in the
rain, she didn't appear wet in the slightest.

A man emerged behind her, seemingly from an iridescent
doorway in the middle of the street. A hefty man, he looked malicious in a High Legion uniform, and it occurred to Rossnetta that

this woman must be the Queen of Arkaemor. If so, that meant the beast in the sky might very well be the same drakinferno that had attacked Jericho.

A buzzing ring reached Rossnetta's ears, and she winced as the woman's voice assaulted her thoughts.

Kesken Ala. You are accused of conspiring with rebels. I had thought sending a message with the man on the cross would stifle your fire, but I now hear reports of you consorting with other renegade cities. I have come to ensure that you are cruelly punished for your treacherous behavior.

Townspeople began darkening doorways. Some even stepped out into the rainy street, attempting to glimpse the woman speaking into their minds. Many, Rossnetta noticed, already carried weapons. She looked back and forth between the gathering crowd and the Queen, watching anxiously to see what would happen next.

It was one thing to forgive you assisting two seemingly innocent young women. It is another thing entirely for you to directly collude with traitors to the Throne.

The Queen glanced at the man standing at her flank, and he offered a swift nod before moving toward the civilians with his sword in hand. No other soldiers arrived, but the dragon continued to circle above the town.

I made an example of Jericho, but apparently, you need to witness the fire firsthand. The drakinferno spewed more flames into the sky. *You are not the only guilty parties, and you can trust I intend to confront every one of the treacherous rebels scheming against me. It's just your luck I've started with you, the original traitors in this painstaking rebellion. And so, Kesken Ala of the Grim Wilds and Metsa Sateen, how do you plead?*

Several long moments of silence passed. Rain continued to fall, made more oppressive by peals of thunder and harsh flashes of lightning.

At last, a man shouted, "You are not welcome here, Sirena Aldrich."

Hearing the man perfectly clear as though he stood right next to her, Rossnetta gaped and whipped her head around to see Daniel, the weaponsmith, pushing himself to the front of the crowd with a rifle in hand. Two men stood at his flanks. They stepped forward as if separating themselves from the congregation. The Queen's smirk widened with amusement as more and more villagers moved closer.

"You are no longer our Queen," Daniel said. Sirena's catlike expression morphed into a ferocious glower. "Kesken Ala no longer serves you and your King. We stand with Jericho."

In an instant, a bolt of black lightning shot from the Queen's outstretched hand, and without any time to block or resist, Daniel crumpled to the ground in a smoldering pile. Those standing around him peered at his body, awestruck and motionless. Then Sirena screamed Kaen's name, and the dragon descended on the town with fiery breath ablaze.

C

Orion hadn't been paying much attention on his way out and only had a vague idea of how far he'd walked. After an hour or so, he knew he must be reaching the village soon. He paused for a drink and splashed water in his face. The flaking blood had begun to itch, and he scrubbed at it with rough hands.

Glancing toward the sun touching the horizon, he spotted a familiar structure and altered his course. As he drew closer, he realized it was the mesa where Isolde had taken him to watch the sunset before they'd left for Jericho.

Climbing the rocks to the mouth of the cave, he peered inside. His heart raced as he scoured the pitch black he knew would lead to the overlook. His eyes played tricks on him, projecting movement within the darkness that didn't exist. Last time, he'd had Isolde's hand to guide him. Another reminder of what it felt like to be alone made his chest ache. How foolish he'd been to consider leaving everyone behind.

"Don't be a coward, Orion. It's just a cave. You can do this." He put a hand on either side of the entrance and leaned his head inside. As the darkness swallowed his face, a wave of fear threatened to drown him, and he yanked himself back.

"Perhaps you need a hand?"

The cool voice speaking at his back frightened him so severely, he jumped and nearly toppled from his place high on the rocks. He breathed her name with relief and leaned his back against the wall. "You scared me."

"It was not my intention. Though I must say, you looked pretty scared already." Isolde ascended the rocks until she stood next to him at the mouth of the cave.

"What are you doing here?" He still tried to catch his breath, though it seemed to be evading him even more thoroughly in response to her proximity.

"I felt drawn here, and so I followed the pull. It seems you have done the same." She extended a hand to him in an offering of companionship. Orion looked from her face to her hand and back up again into golden eyes glowing brightly in the shadows. He placed his hand on hers, and she twisted so her fingers separated his. Then she led him through the dark, up the spiral staircase, and out onto the landing.

The sun had dropped halfway beneath the horizon, shooting extraordinary colors into the sky. Rather than sitting over the edge as they had before, they stood hand in hand outside the cave mouth. Isolde loosened her grip, but he squeezed tighter to indicate her touch wasn't making him uncomfortable—even if it did make his heart race more than the horrifying darkness at their backs.

"I can't even tell you the last time I held someone's hand." His words drew a blush to his cheeks. He thought for a moment of the girl he'd loved in his youth, Lacy Robinson, and then of Elora, the woman he'd first met on the farm in Savanni. Ages ago. Another man's life.

Isolde's smile widened, though she kept her gaze on the sunset. "I have never." She looked down at their hands, lifting them to get a better view. His fingers, tanned from the sun, wove through her dark ones in a stirring contrast. "Not like this, at least."

He nodded, certain he understood her meaning but too frightened to open his mouth. He wondered what in the world might be happening between them and who in the hell he thought he was holding hands with a princess.

Gently untangling his fingers from hers in a way he hoped seemed natural without offending, he advanced forward to stand closer to the cliff's edge. Isolde moved with him but made no attempt to touch him again. They stood in silence, watching the sun until it nearly disappeared.

"You are a puzzling man, *herr* Orion."

"Just Orion," he said.

"You are a puzzling man, *Orion*."

"You're not the first person to think so."

"Do you torment all women with your indecision?"

Her boldness drew his eyes, his mouth agape. Recovering, he deflected. "Only the really pretty ones."

Isolde chuckled. "I see. It appears a solid tactic."

In unison, they rotated to face each other. "A solid tactic?" He couldn't help but admire the way the remaining sunlight danced across her skin, brightened her irises, and bronzed her cheeks. He regretted releasing her hand, but knew the message it would send if he reached for it again. Instead, he cracked his knuckles with his thumb and endured the temptation.

"For keeping people at a distance." Her eyes left his to survey the blood coating much of his upper body, and her brow pulled with concern.

"Have you been talking to Declan? He accused me of the same thing earlier today."

"Is that why you ran off?" She angled her head, searching his eyes the way she always did, as though hunting for answers his words refused to divulge. The altered position added more shadows to her dark features, making her lips appear fuller and accentuating the sharpness of her cheekbones.

Orion sucked in a breath and forced his eyes to resist perusing. "I didn't run off. I went for a walk to take a breath."

"It was a very long breath."

"Well, I got a little sidetracked. Giant, desert vipers are hard to fight off on your own."

Stunned, she exclaimed, "You fought a viparah?" She examined his body again more carefully, searching for injuries. "Are you hurt?"

"It was fine. No big deal." Despite his efforts, his eyes took advantage of her distracted attention. He wished the sun would finish its descent so the blanket of night would stifle his urges.

Isolde shook her head at the peculiar and concerning man before her. "Perhaps you should not walk and breathe on your own from now on."

Orion laughed and scratched the back of his head. "Perhaps you're right, Naabila." In defiance of his previous wishes, the darkening sky had him giving into the impulse to observe her, deciding he wasn't ready to be blind to her beauty just yet. His gaze lingered on her lips, and his heart ached to close the space between them.

Scolding himself again, he yanked his vision free and wondered if he would ever be capable of controlling himself. Though even if his eyes were misbehaving, he was doing an excellent job keeping his hands in place, and he thought that should count for something.

Not once in his entire life had he felt the urge to touch someone so severely. She was right when she accused him of keeping others at a distance. He'd touched plenty of women over the years but not as a result of anything more than physical attraction mingled with loneliness; very rarely out of comfort or connection. Maybe for the briefest moment, he'd thought it could be more with Camille, but that was just a foolish boy fallen for his rescuer, not to mention far too much Alundan whiskey.

With Iris, he'd felt his desires creeping beyond physical, and it was so foreign to him, he'd smothered it with anger and malice.

Now Isolde stood in front of him, and he had no idea how to suffocate the new things he felt. There was no hope for them. She thought he was confusing, but what about her? What right did a royal have toying with a man like him? Nothing could ever come of it, and even if it could, he was definitely not fit to lead a nation. He wasn't fit to lead anyone.

"What happened?" she asked, keenly observing his eyes.

He rattled his head to shake away the whispers growing louder with each passing moment. He knew touching her skin was all it would take to dispel them, but he couldn't baffle her more with his indecisive actions. Nor could he allow himself even a taste of the pleasure it would bring. "What do you mean?"

"Your face. You were happy moments ago. Now you are not."

Orion turned away from her to glimpse the last remnants of the sun, though it had disappeared beneath the horizon now, leaving only the residual twilight sky in its wake. When he didn't answer, she said his name to draw his attention back to her. "Don't worry about me, Naabila. Everything is fine."

She touched his arm, and he all but leapt from the cliff in surprise. Instead, he caught her gaze. Lifting a hand to his blood-flaked cheek, she said, *"Novi'tueor tuu mielu."*

Though he couldn't interpret the Vetoräti words, he sensed the profoundness of them in her tone, her expression. His breath caught in his throat as he asked, "What does that mean?"

"It does not translate with perfection, but to us it means something like *I see the core of who you are, into the depths of your very soul, and I embrace you. All your yesterdays and all your tomorrows.*"

"Novi'tueor tuu mielu," he repeated, testing the words on his tongue. Isolde smiled. "I have to be honest, Naabila. I don't know what to do with that."

Chuckling, she asked, "Shall we be heading back then?"

"I thought about leaving today." His shame turned his sight back to the horizon. "Actually leaving. Jumping the barrier and never coming back."

Isolde considered her response for several long seconds. "We all think about running away sometimes. Is it not the nature of all living things to fight or to flee rather than look our fears in the face with grace, compassion, and understanding?"

He glanced at her from the corner of his eye, lifting a brow in disbelief. "I don't imagine you ever think about running away."

"Well, I do. Our thoughts do not determine the core of who we are in here." She placed a hand on her heart. "Instead, our actions reveal a reflection of our desires, character, and inner strength. You wished to leave, but you came back. Which of these accurately declares the truth of who you are?"

Orion didn't have an answer. Instead, he swallowed his fears and concerns, and held out his hand. "Lead me back through the dark, Naabila?"

Isolde grinned broadly and dragged him back through the cave.

CHAPTER 22

THE MAGIC OF DANCING

The following day began uneventfully. Orion and Declan were visited early by Isolde who informed them Jax had called for another meeting to review the details of the plan now that Griffin and his team had agreed to join. Rather than cramming everyone into Isolde's home, they met in the tent used for village meetings and gatherings.

A large but vacant tent, it consisted of little more than a few rugs scattered about to create a makeshift floor, lanterns hanging from the ceiling, and wooden stools lined against the western wall for those unable to sit on the ground.

When the company arrived, Griffin introduced his team as Crow, Vera, Jovan, Leone, and Kwame, and Orion introduced everyone else. The new recruits seemed eager to join the expedition, and the young man introduced as Kwame made a comment about it having been a long while since any of them had needed to prepare for battle.

Jax gave an outline of the operation, answering questions and discussing suggestions. Jovan, Kwame, and Vera were very vocal. Griffin shushed the boys more than once with a sharp breath. Leone took in every word with calculating attention, while Crow remained quiet and unmoving beneath his headdress.

When the team felt comfortable with their responsibilities, Jax dismissed them. Then he, Hector, and Raven returned to the visitor's tent, and Declan, Johnathan, and Orion went back to Isolde's.

Johnathan sat at the table as Declan climbed into bed and Orion collapsed into his chair.

They'd hardly spoken since their disagreement the day before. When Orion returned to the village after sunset, Declan was already asleep, and when they rose that morning Orion had kept to himself. Though he'd interacted to the degree expected of him at the meeting, he'd said little more than was absolutely required.

Some time later, Isolde arrived to change the bandage on Declan's wound, but Orion ignored her, too. They'd separated on good terms the previous evening, and he knew his mood must be concerning and confusing her, but he couldn't bring himself to offer more at the moment. His attention had drifted toward her off and on during the meeting, but he'd made sure to look away before she noticed.

Now he sat in the chair by her bed, ignoring her and Declan as they chatted about his wounds. He thought he'd heard something about removing Declan's stitches, but he didn't care enough to verify it.

Then he heard her ask, "Will you gentlemen be joining our celebration this evening?"

"I will probably come out for a little," Declan said. "But no dancing, I know."

"Very good." Isolde chuckled.

There was a long pause before Johnathan said, "I suppose I could come."

Orion hoped that would be the end of it, but when he heard his name, he at last turned his head from the design in the tapestry that held his attention and looked at her.

"Will you honor me with another dance tonight?"

In his disheartened state, he didn't know how to respond. At the moment, he didn't have the desire to flirt nor the energy to smile. Holding her gaze, he finally answered, "If that is your wish, Naabila, I would certainly not withhold it from you." Before she could reply, he leaned back again, resting his chin on his fingers and staring into the wall of the tent.

The whispers taunted him relentlessly. Since a horrible dream woke him before the rising of the sun, they'd persisted without end. On top of it being draining and awful, this fact also meant that Isolde had been right: he wasn't in control of himself at all, and he needed to tell someone before entering that prison and putting everyone at risk. He was a ticking bomb, ready to detonate at any moment, and he considered the very real possibility that it might be better for everyone if he opted out. Wouldn't he be jeopardizing the entire mission by simply being present?

Again, he entertained the idea of fleeing to the eastern barrier and leaving everyone behind. When the battle against the Aldrich's reached its end, maybe he could come back for Declan. Maybe they could find somewhere peaceful to live out the rest of their lives.

Thoughts flashed to Iris, and for a moment, he imagined the three of them living together in Reginaterra. He wondered where Foxx might fit into that dynamic. Perhaps she would be the new queen at Alexander's side. Grimacing, he realized the lunacy of living with Declan and Iris. Surely they wouldn't want him tagging along forever, a constant storm cloud hanging over their heads.

Perhaps he would purchase his own ship and sail the Suola Meri with a small crew of his own. Camille had taught him the ropes, and with a small ship, he would only need three or four others with him. He could drink bourbon and laze on the beaches of Avis Island for the rest of his days.

Memories of his dream swarmed him, and he shoved away all thoughts of being linked to anyone.

In the dream, he stood on a tall mountain, so high he could run his hands through the feathery clouds. Looking out over the land before him, he found himself enjoying the view. He was no longer in the Wilds and thought he might be in Reginaterra, but he couldn't be sure. Something about it seemed different from the Reginaterra he remembered.

Suddenly, shadows shrouded the land. The sky darkened with heavy clouds, and thunder rolled in the distance. He looked around, trying to figure out… something.

The land before him began to die, turning gray as if drained of the luscious colors giving it life.

A hand grabbing his own made him jump, and he turned to find Isolde standing next to him, her face stained with suffering, anger, and shame. Then she pointed down, and he followed the trail of her finger to find a pile of bodies stacked together at the base of the mountain. To his horror, he recognized the mutilated faces. He saw the Raptors, Abram and Eero, Declan and his brother, Iris, Foxxglove, Prince Alexander, Griffin, and all the people he'd met in

Caritas. Even Ishmael the potter and the little girl who'd gifted Isolde the bracelet.

Desperate eyes lifted to Isolde to find her turning gray, bleeding away her pigment until she was devoid of color. The last thing to turn ashen was her glittering, golden eyes.

"You did this." The voice coming from her lips was not her own, but the voice of his whispers speaking through her. Pulling her hand from his, she backed toward the edge of the cliff. "Why did you do this, Orion?"

"I didn't. I didn't mean to." He reached for her, but she stepped from the ledge and plummeted to her death, landing crooked on the pile of bodies below.

Orion shivered in his chair, his body tightening with discomfort. Even a crew of three or four would be too many.

He was better off alone.

C

Declan watched Isolde leave the tent before looking over at his friend, wondering what could be making him behave this way. They'd argued, but he couldn't imagine that had caused this despondent mood. Spending six years traveling the wilderness together, they'd survived countless arguments, many far worse then their spat the previous day.

Johnathan called after Isolde in farewell before setting his book on the table and standing to join Declan on the bed. "How is it?" He gestured to the wound.

"Stitch free." Declan lifted his shirt. Some bruising remained around the edges, but the cut itself had closed in a nice line now in the early stages of a scar.

Johnathan leaned closer to get a better look. "She did a great job. How do you feel?"

"Tired, mostly. The pain's comparable to the after effects of taking a punch to the ribs: sore but not unbearable, but my body feels weak from all the healing."

"It's been working overtime." Johnathan looked at his own wrapped shoulder. "Mine is feeling better, too. Still sore when I move but healing well. If it weren't for all the sand, I'd have unwrapped it already."

"That's good to hear. What will you do when we leave tomorrow?"

"Isolde said I could stay here until you return. I could travel to Jericho, but honestly, I want to know you're okay as soon as possible." He looked down at his hands, seeming nervous. "I spent so many years not seeing you at all. You can't imagine how it felt to wake up in that swamp and find you there in such an awful condition."

"I'm sorry for that." Declan felt heavy with guilt over past decisions. Not only the events leading to the swamp but leaving Johnathan to begin with. More than once, he thought he should have taken his brother with them. He could have protected him. He could have taught him to live in the wild. They could have grown up together, and the Queen would have never gotten her hands on him. Instead, he left him alone, and the moment he was of age, Johnathan joined the Legion too, following in the noble footsteps of his brother and father.

"Hey, why don't you come with us?"

"What?" Johnathan gasped. "I couldn't!"

Orion seemed to hear this and rotated his head toward them. Declan glanced his way, finding his friend's eyes nothing short of haunted.

"Not to the prison," he said to Johnathan. "You can stay at the campsite. We should probably have someone there to watch over the guards we swap places with anyway. And the horses."

"That's not a bad idea." Orion's monotone voice matched his still glazed and distant eyes. "I'll run it past Jax and Hector." He stood and exited the tent without awaiting further reply.

Johnathan threw a thumb over his shoulder. "What's up with him?"

"I'm not sure." Declan stared at the door.

"I guess I could hold down the fort. If Hector approves."

Declan nodded, returning his attention to his brother.

Again Johnathan glanced down at fidgeting fingers. "You know, he's different than I thought."

A short laugh escaped Declan's lips. "You have no idea. I think he's different than anyone thought. Except maybe Raven. She always sees what lies underneath, be it good or bad. Her past made her a good judge of character."

"I used to hate him. I'd glare at him when he came into the Hall of Sunsets."

Declan's eyes snapped to him. "You shouldn't have done that. He was your commander."

"It was his fault," Johnathan argued in his own defense, though rather than anger or resentment, Declan heard the sorrow in his tone. "All of it. Father. You. It was all because of him."

"That's not entirely true, Johnathan. And anyway, everyone makes mistakes, even you, even me." Declan sighed, thinking over his own failures. "Even the commander of the King's High Legion. He did the best he knew how to do at the time. Just like we all do."

C

By moonrise, the evening's festivities had begun. Music played, passionate and unrestrained.

Declan stepped from Isolde's tent followed closely by Johnathan. Seeing Hector, Jax, and Raven standing outside the chaotic dance area, they headed toward them.

"How's everyone doing tonight?" Declan asked when he reached them. A villager approached them with two clay tumblers, slipping them into Declan and Johnathan's hands before hurrying away. The group cracked up, amazed by the villagers' attentiveness.

"They are very adamant about sharing their wine." Hector stood behind Raven, sipping slowly from his cup as his other hand rested on her hip.

"Unlike Raven, who is often stingy with her booze," Jax said.

Raven's mouth dropped open. "I am not!" She swatted his shoulder.

Hector chuckled before asking Declan, "How are you feeling?"

"Much better than I have been." Declan tapped his ribs as proof of healing. "No more stitches. Healing up nicely."

"Nice enough to travel tomorrow?" Jax asked.

"Definitely. You just worry about your part, and I'll worry about mine."

"I'll worry about all of it." To Johnathan, Jax said, "Johnathan, right? O'Connell says you want to come along to Crystavium." Johnathan nodded, looking intimidated. Declan wondered if the two men had ever interacted before that moment.

Jax sipped from his tumbler, as if that were all that needed to be said on the subject.

Hector said, "Having someone stay with the horses is a good idea. I would hate to return from the prison only to find ourselves traveling back across the tundra on foot."

Pivoting subjects, Jax said Declan's name. "Think you'll be joining the Raptors again once you're all healed up?"

Brows rose in unison throughout the group. Declan's eyes slid first to Hector, who grinned, then to Raven who seemed to be intentionally withholding evidence of her opinion. "I hadn't actually thought about it."

"Since the Reko Raptors have never technically been a branch of the King's Legion, your exile means little. Not that it really matters now regardless."

"I think most of us know the truth of that exile anyway." Hector took a longer drag from his wine.

"We'll talk more about it later," Jax said. "If we survive Ashgate."

"Where's Orion?" Raven scanned the crowd.

Johnathan said, "He's grumpier than usual today."

"Is that even possible?"

"He's fine." Declan thought for a moment before adding, "I think he's fine, at least."

☾

When Orion stepped from Isolde's tent, he looked around, saw the other soldiers across the circle, and began walking toward them. Before he made it five steps, Teetee spotted him across the crowd and rushed over, wrapping her arms around his neck in greeting and planting a kiss on his cheek. "Orion! Here, have some wine." She put a cup in his hand and waited for him to take a drink.

She'd styled her hair differently than he'd yet seen it, flipped over so it all laid on one side of her head. In the exposed ear, she wore an earring of feathers that draped down her neck, and painted diamonds decorated her face.

When he finished taking a long swig, she latched on to the front of his shirt. "Do not forget you promised me a dance."

"I wouldn't dare." He grinned and took another drink.

Teetee peeked inside to find it empty and smiled at him mischievously. "I will get you another." She scurried off before he could stop her.

Orion began walking again, but two more girls approached him, stopping him from progressing forward. They also hugged him and kissed his cheeks before talking excitedly, their hands flying about as they talked.

Then Teetee returned, glaring at the others from behind their backs before squeezing between them so she stood in front. Smiling victoriously, she put another tumbler of wine in Orion's hand.

He pointed toward the group of Raptors watching the entire interaction with amazed expressions, and the girls turned to look at the soldiers. Then they danced off into the crowd, waving farewell to Orion as they went. Visibly sighing, his chest rising and falling with heavy breath, Orion continued his seemingly extensive journey across the village.

When he reached them, Hector lifted his cup in greeting. "You're pretty popular here."

"Apparently so." Orion sighed again and looked back at the dancing crowd. "I have literally no idea how it happened, but it's a bit exhausting. I don't know how Isolde manages to wrangle them with such kindness." Thoughts of Isolde had flashes of his nightmare bubbling to the surface. He closed his eyes and took another drink to wash away the images.

"Seems exactly like the kind of attention you would enjoy," Jax said, and Orion didn't know if he'd intended it as an insult or if he was just stating the general knowledge of his personality.

He looked across the crowd at Bayo and Nabu, clearly glancing his direction and waiting for him to join. "You're not wrong. Not long ago, it would have been the perfect recipe for a good time."

"Getting old on us, Ri?" Declan pushed his friend's shoulder.

"Definitely not." Orion downed the rest of his drink. Stretching his shoulders back and inhaling yet another relaxing breath, he turned to face Jax. "So. You coming with me?"

"In there?" Jax pointed to the horde of dancers. The same look of dread he'd worn the day before when crowded by all the women flushed his face. "That's a terrible idea. I don't dance." He stared at the dancers, observing their exotic movements. "At least... not like that."

"It's easier than it looks, trust me."

Jax regarded Orion with an expression indicating he very much did not trust him.

Orion grinned. "If you don't come willingly, I'll send Teetee out here to drag you in. I can't handle them all alone, and Declan is under strict instructions not to dance, and Hector is..." He motioned between Hector and Raven. "And Johnathan is... well, Johnathan."

"Hey!" Johnathan gasped.

"They aren't going to stop gawking at me until I join them." Orion put a hand on Jax's shoulder. "You're my only hope."

Jax took another swig and exhaled. "Which one's Teetee?"

"The girl who brought me the drinks." Orion's eyes sparkled, knowing he'd convinced him whether Jax admitted it right away or not. There was no denying Teetee's beauty.

"How do they make the wine, anyway?" Johnathan examined his tumbler, as if the answer lay etched in clay.

"A vineyard along the barrier of the jungle," Orion answered, eyes still on Jax. "So Lieutenant Blackmoor, are you in or are you out?"

Jax seemed to mull it over before finally succumbing to persuasion. "All right, let's do it." Orion exclaimed his victory, clapping him on the back as he led him into the sea of dancing bodies.

☾

When the men disappeared from view, Declan shook his head. "I've never seen the two of them so cordial."

Raven turned to Johnathan. "I thought you said he was extra grumpy today?"

"He's up, he's down. Who can keep track of his mood swings?"

Hector whispered something in Raven's ear that neither Johnathan nor Declan could hear, and both men averted their eyes from the private moment. Raven looked at Hector over her shoulder with an expression seeming to say, *you can't be serious.*

"Come on, it'll be fun." He pressed a kiss against her exposed shoulder. "And... we may never get another chance." She looked back at him, saddened. Then she rolled her eyes and took hold of his hand, pulling him toward the dancers.

Johnathan and Declan watched them disappear into the crowd. "There goes the last of us."

Declan nodded to the dancers. "You can go join them if you want. I'll be all right alone."

"No way!" Johnathan squeaked.

They watched for a while, enjoying the happy expressions on their comrades faces when they blinked into view. After a long moment, Johnathan asked, "It really doesn't bother you that she's with him?" Declan drew back his head in surprise. "I just mean, doesn't it feel like she betrayed us or something? Being with the man who…"

Declan shook his head. "Hector isn't that man anymore."

Johnathan relented. "He does seem to like her, I guess."

"I think he more than likes her." Declan saw Raven throw her head back with laughter. Hector wore a look of pure pleasure as he watched her enjoying herself. "And no, it doesn't bother me. Raven Nightshade was my first love, and I don't think I'll ever feel nothing for her, but I am happy for them. They both deserve to find love, and so I'm glad they have."

"Did you find love, too?" Johnathan asked.

"I guess we'll find out when we finally get those doors open." Declan looked around. "I wonder where Isolde is."

Johnathan shrugged, joining his brother in the search. "I haven't seen her since she took out your stitches."

Suddenly, the loud and energetic music came to a crashing halt, bringing with it a wave of electric silence.

Naaba Kaatachi raised his hands in greeting from a recently crafted stage, his voice echoing throughout the massive crowd as he shouted a long and drawn out, "Caritas!" The partygoers gathered near the front of the platform, eager to hear what the Naaba had to say. "*Veni, veni.* Gather around. What a wonderful revel we have here this evening. I am very pleased, *ahmeekas*, very pleased. Our magnificent Creator has brought us together tonight, not only to celebrate the making of new *ahmeekas*—or I should say: new friends —but also to wish a fine farewell to my children as they embark tomorrow on a great and trying adventure in Elohim's name. As a special offering in the hopes of a safe journey, Isolde has prepared a treat for you all! Are you ready to see what it is?"

The whole village erupted into howls and applause.

C

Isolde's name caught Orion's attention. Standing near the center of the crowd with Bayo and Nabu's arms slinked through his, he scanned his surroundings for a sign of her. To his right, Teetee had her arms wrapped around Jax's waist, watching her Naaba with attentiveness. Kaatachi stepped off the stage, and the crowd remained quiet, waiting patiently for what would come next.

A voice began singing from somewhere out of sight. Long, drawn out vocals and hums grew louder as if the singer drew closer. The rattle of a beaded instrument began to play along with the voice, and moments later, other instruments joined in.

Two women, wrapped in resplendent dresses decorated in beads and tassels, climbed onto the stage, each holding a huge fan crafted of hundreds of colorful feathers that overlapped in the air between them. As the invisible singer's extraordinary voice crescendoed into a high note, the song cut off, and the musical instruments again fell abruptly silent. The two women on stage rotated their bodies so the fans of feathers opened up like a set of double doors to reveal a woman standing with her back to the front of the stage. A murmur swept over the crowd as the villagers discovered their Naabila hidden behind the fans.

Her dress was unlike anything Orion had ever seen. It wrapped over one shoulder, enveloping her upper body and leaving her other shoulder and a large portion of her back unclothed. Though it appeared gold at first glance, he saw an artful blend of pomegranate, lapis, and fern beads reflecting the firelight, glimmering and sparkling as if she herself was engulfed in flame. The dress stopped mid-thigh, cut at an angle and flaring out loosely around her legs, and her ankles wore a strip of the same cloth above bare feet.

Isolde turned her head to the side so she could look back at them over her shoulder. The sudden and unanticipated movement sparked a jolt of energy, and a low percussion instrument beat a tangible pulse that vibrated through the crowd as she spun to face them. Wild hair sat high on her head, tied up by another piece of the glittering fabric. Charcoal rimmed her eyes, and her cheeks shimmered as if painted to mirror her golden irises.

Staggered motionless, Orion's heart seemed to stop as her eyes found him in the throng of bodies, holding him ensnared and tormented by her enchanting beauty. Her cherry painted lips parted, and she began to sing, releasing him as she spun with her arms in the air. The instruments joined her, fierce and untamed. The two women dancing behind her now held instruments of their own which they shook in their hands to the rhythm the musicians played. Isolde danced as she sang, allowing her body to become one with the music and her voice to belt the words in time with the melody.

The crowd began dancing with her, unable to remain still during such an intense presentation, though they kept their eyes toward the stage. Orion remained frozen solid, blindly unaware of anything happening around him. Isolde found his gaze again and held on to it. Every muscle in his body grew tense as if a bolt of lightning had penetrated him from above.

As she descended the stage, the crowd parted. Her voice continued echoing with song as she sashayed forward, moving in a direct line toward him. His body was on fire. The heat of the desert, of the dancing, of the display, overwhelmed him. Confident in the belief that he had literally ignited, he remained immobile, his feet cemented to the ground as his body burst into flames along with her dress.

By the time she reached him, her singing had faded to a low hum and the musical melody dissolved until the song ended, again throwing the crowd into absolute silence. Total stillness ensued but for the heavy breathing of the dancers and the erratic beating of Orion's heart. He willed himself to breathe in spite of his lung's refusal to cooperate. Dumbfounded and dazed, he attempted to observe the happenings in his peripherals. The women who'd been standing next to him, as well as everyone else in a three foot radius, had backed away to give them space. He could feel every pair of eyes focused entirely on him and the Naabila, and the pressure had his heart throbbing against his eardrums.

Isolde's mouth curled up on one side as she watched him react to the atmosphere. Orion gulped. Holding the side of her dress with one hand, her leg slid back behind her, and she bowed deeply to him.

The food and wine he'd consumed that evening threatened to make a sudden reappearance.

When she straightened, her eyes found him again. Seemingly of its own accord, his body bowed to her in return. He hadn't a clue how he'd achieved it without releasing the contents of his stomach, how he'd managed to do it at all. Never in his life had he experienced anything so overwhelming and profound.

Then she stepped closer to him, taking his hand with the one not holding her dress. His other slipped around her waist. And all at once, they were dancing. The whispers extinguished for the first time that day, gone like pinched fingers devouring a candle's flame.

The villagers watched for a moment before joining their fearless Naabila, dancing around them as the music grew turbulent and exhilarating again, ferocious as a roaring tempest.

Still nowhere near breathing, Orion found himself in motion, his feet knowing the movements required even if his brain felt muddled.

Isolde smiled at him. He smiled back. He thought they might actually be floating above the crowd, but he was too afraid to check, as if breaking the connection might make it all fall apart.

They danced late into the night, partnered with no one but each other. It didn't take long for the people of Caritas to cease keeping their distance and dance right alongside them. Isolde and Orion paused only when absolutely necessary for hydration and breath, never letting go of each other for a single moment.

When the revelry died down and the evening's festivities dwindled, Isolde spoke low in the space between them. "It is time for sleep. We have a long journey tomorrow." She lifted her eyes to the sky to find the waning Ammil moon already descending toward the horizon.

"Not yet." He pulled her closer by the fingers intertwined on either side of their hips. They stood outside the door to her tent, leaning into each other in elated exhaustion. "Let me walk you to where you'll be sleeping." At the tantalized glimmer in her eye, he clarified, "As a gentleman, not because I'm trying to find out where you sleep." Though the idea had crossed his mind once or twice.

"But I have already walked you to your tent," she replied coyly.

Leaning closer to her ear, Orion chuckled quietly from deep in his chest. "But Declan and Johnathan are already in there."

"Griffin went to bed already as well." She smiled, and his eyes widened as he realized the tent she'd been staying in belonged to her brother who would surely kill him without a second thought if he caught him in his chambers with his little sister. She laughed at his frightened expression.

"Let's go for a walk." The husky breath of his words caressed her neck, sending chills down her spine that made her shiver. Noticing her tremble, his smile widened, and he drew closer. "We can go visit your favorite place and stay until the sun rises."

"We will not be able to see the sunrise from the cliff." Her cheeks flushed. "It faces west."

"So many excuses," he chided, his heart aflutter at their playful banter. He took a heavy breath, out of ideas to persuade her. "Fine. But so you know, you're a bit bossy."

She laughed, and he along with her. Then she put her lips to his ear and whispered, "Perhaps when we return, I can show you my favorite place to watch the sunrise."

Overjoyed by this idea, a tremble rattled through his entire being. Hoping to appear unaffected by the sultry voice she teased him with, he said, "Can I tell you a secret?"

"Is it a good secret or a bad secret?"

Orion thought it over, looking to the sky above and reconsidering saying it all together. "Neither. It's just a secret."

"Go on." She rubbed his hand with her thumb, watching him expectantly. He exhaled a long, slow breath, and her smile became rapturous as she sensed his hesitation. "Now I *really* want to know."

"Okay, I'll tell you." He exhaled another breath and whispered, "I'm thirty today."

Her eyes swelled with amazement. "Do you mean to say it is the day of your birth?" He nodded, and she leaned closer. "Why do you keep it a secret?"

"Because I usually hate it. Stuff from my childhood, I guess. It doesn't matter. Also, if you haven't noticed, I don't much like to be the center of attention." He lifted a brow, and her mouth fell open in mock-shock. "I thought your father and the others might go crazy if they found out." Bashfulness transforming into arrogance, he added, "Because, you know, they are so terribly fond of me."

"Indeed they are." Isolde giggled and leaned into him so her head rested on his shoulder.

With her warm body closer, he whispered, "Did I tell you how breathtaking you look tonight?"

"Only about eight times." She shook her head and tilted back so she could see into his ocean irises. "A joyous birthday to you, Orion O'Connell."

"Thank you for making it the best one I've ever had."

Glee painted her expression. "I will see you when the sun rises."

Tugging again at their clasped hands, he pulled her into his chest and placed a tender kiss on her cheek. "Merry night, Naabila."

She stepped backward and their fingers slowly separated. Then she turned and walked away, leaving him melting in the sand.

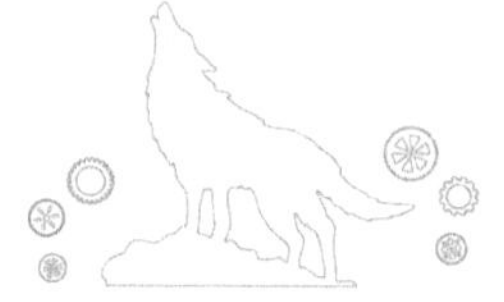

CHAPTER 23

HEIR TO THE THRONE

Several days had come and gone since Asher and Foxxglove's discussion by the pond. Shortly after Iris stormed back from the meadow and plopped herself against a nearby tree, Foxx had retrieved her bag and bed things from their grassy knoll by the waterfall, and she'd yet to return.

Two days later, Asher had ventured the path and found her napping in the midst of the wildflowers with kuki fluttering above her like bees hovering around a bloom. Knowing the Creator was looking after her, he decided to give her the space she needed.

Now, Asher, Iris, and Seth sat in a circle eating a breakfast of red apples from the orchard, seeded grapes from a trellised vine they discovered on the opposite side of the entrance building, yellow tomatoes from a vegetable garden near a stream behind the cherry blossom grove, and peaches, because they had become Seth's favorite and grew close by.

With peach juice drizzling down his chin, Seth asked, "Are we going to adventure more today?"

"Every day until we find the fountain," Asher said.

"I've been trying to put together a map." Iris pulled out her leather-bound notebook, nearly identical to Asher's as both had come from Iris' mother, and opened it to the sketched map of everything they'd seen in the garden so far. "It isn't exactly to scale, but it's something."

"There are herbs here." Seth pointed to the map. "It's shaped like a square with spiky trees all around it."

"Junipers." Asher spit grape seeds into the grass.

"Yes, junipers." Seth watched as Iris added them to the map. When finished, she held the book out so the boys could examine her addition. "Yes, that looks right." Seth let his finger follow the sketched walkway. "The path continues this way to a stream right about here." Iris followed his instructions, and when she finished, Seth gave his approval. "What other additions do you have in there?"

"Check it out." She handed her journal over, and he began flipping through it. She'd already shown him the new monster drawings so he hurried past those, but he paused on the page containing the prophecy of the Monastery of the Morrow and skimmed the words.

"So this is it, huh?" His eyes lifted to Asher, and he held up the page so he understood the question. "This is why you began your journey?"

"That's it."

Seth hummed and moved on to the next few pages. He saw more song lyrics and poems, followed by a few short stories. Then he came to a page listing the monthly moons and began studying them. "Wow, I didn't know some of these! I knew the names, but not the origins."

Iris leaned over his shoulder to look at her notes. "Pretty cool, huh?"

"Rosh for new beginnings. Alyin for the halo seen around the moon. Oh, Sunset is when we see the most beautiful sunsets in the Wilds! Willows bloom in Willow, and even more flowers bloom in Petal, especially in Metsa Sateen. Arctic wolves are born in Susi. Hey, the first Monastery of the Morrow was built in London!" He looked at Asher, who nodded in agreement.

"The word London means *fortress of the moon.*"

"Fitting," Iris said with a smirk.

"What else?" Seth put his nose back into the book. "Storm is the stormiest month in Alunda. Ammil marks the beginning of the cold season in Reginaterra. Reaping for the farmer's harvest season. Then there's Navi." He looked at them. "But this one doesn't have an explanation."

"That one's a bit of a mystery." Iris turned to Asher in the hopes that he might have an explanation.

Asher said, "It's true. Not much is known about the name of the second to last moon. *Navi* was another word for the prophets or seers who lived around the time of the Monastery of the Morrow, but I'm honestly not sure what the significance of having a month named after them is. Just to honor them, I guess."

"Weird." Seth wrinkled his nose. "And Liviana for the white moon. The final moon of the year."

"That's right." Iris rustled his hair.

As the three continued to chatter about the moons, Foxxglove appeared in the treeline, stepping from the path leading to the meadow. Asher saw her first, as Iris and Seth were preoccupied with the book. He lifted a hand to her with a restrained smile, attempting a casual welcome. Iris and Seth noticed his movement and followed his line of sight.

"It's Foxxglove," Seth said. Iris returned to her journal without acknowledging her sister, but Asher and Seth continued to watch her from a distance. Neither stood to greet her or draw her closer for fear they might spook her back into the trees.

A gentle breeze blew past, and Foxx's bright hair moved with it, flying away from her face. "May I join you?" she called when the wind settled.

"Sure!" Seth exclaimed, but even with his permission, she didn't move. Asher looked at Iris to find her blatantly ignoring the situation. He said her name and received an uncommunicative hum in return.

Looking back at Foxx, he waved her forward. Foxx ambled over to them, sitting next to her sister who intentionally kept her eyes locked on the pages of her journal, though she was clearly glowering. Looping her arm through Iris', Foxx pulled her close with the crook of her elbow. "Iris?"

Without untangling from her, Iris set down her journal and crossed her arms, making another disgruntled noise in the direction of the pond. Foxx scooted closer and said her name again, her tone as sweet as honeysuckle. "Please don't be mad at me." Seth and Asher watched the interaction with amusement. "Iris..." Foxx bumped her shoulder into her sister's and wobbled back and forth, cooing her name annoyingly.

Iris finally turned to her and declared, "Well, you're being ridiculous!"

Foxx released a breath. "I'm not being ridiculous." Her eyes flashed to Asher's to find him watching her with a small smile. "Well, maybe I am."

Iris' brows rose high on her forehead.

"But I'm also just… tired, Iris. I'm so tired." Foxx again looked at Asher, and he hoped she could read his understanding and compassion.

Exhaling, Iris said, "I'm tired too, Foxx, but that doesn't mean we can just abandon everyone who needs us."

"But they *don't* need us. They need an army. They need their prince."

Seth's eyes widened as if he couldn't believe Foxx had divulged a secret everyone already knew.

Iris let her head fall against her sister's with a heavy sigh and offered a bite of her peach. "I don't want to talk about this anymore. If you want to stay, fine, but we still need to find the fountain and a way to return our prince home so he can go on saving the world." Iris smiled at Asher, who returned the expression, though afterward, he dropped his head to study the grass.

Seth said, "I like this idea, but can we please eat some more breakfast before we come up with a plan to save the world?"

C

Orion found himself waking with a smile when Isolde appeared in the doorway of her tent. She announced that there would be food and drink served in the meeting tent where they would finalize the plans for the day.

When he, Declan, and Johnathan arrived, she was already sitting next to her brother and his group of warriors. After everyone settled into a seat, Jax and Hector ran through the plans for what seemed like the hundredth time.

Despite Griffin's disgruntled and watchful gaze, Orion couldn't take his eyes off Isolde. Memories from the night before continued to spark joy into his thoughts, prompting him to smile at awkward times: like when Jax was answering Johnathan's unnecessary question about what the Strayed looked like. Declan noticed and eyed him strangely, but Orion shook his head and put his face in his hands to hide his grin. Isolde caught his eye from across the room and smiled along with him, chuckling from a distance as if sharing an inside joke no one else would understand.

Once they had their fill of breakfast and the agenda was set, the group went their separate ways with the instruction to meet at the entrance to the village around highsun.

The horses were delivered freshly fed and hydrated, cleaned and groomed, and decorated with feathers, beads, and braids in their manes. "They need to feel adorned in majesty before heading into battle," one of the villagers explained in response to the group's flummoxed expressions. "They will behave better for you if they feel special."

Isolde and the others thanked them for the exceptional care, and after a deep bow, the young villagers hurried off.

Jax eyed his pony dubiously. He turned to Hector to find him grinning, petting his horse's mane, and showering the chestnut with compliments of its beauty. Raven saw Jax staring and laughed with him at their kind-hearted commander. When Hector noticed their mockery, he straightened, his face turning serious as he mounted.

Declan was up and walking better than everyone expected, with the exception of Isolde who remained resolute in the fact that she knew he would be fine if he took enough time to rest.

Raven pulled herself up on the back of Hector's horse to give Declan his own, as they had only brought five with them from Jericho.

Declan climbed onto the palomino without too much trouble and patted the horse's snow-colored mane so the male could grow familiar with him as the new rider. "These horses are incredible," he said, rubbing his hand over the strange texture of his horse's hair. "They're so furry! Which will be great for traveling Crystavium. The heat of the desert must be hard on them though."

"Abram said they're resilient." Jax mounted his own horse and closely examined the braids and embellishments within its mane. To Isolde, he asked, "My question is: how will your brother and his clan keep up if they aren't on horseback?"

In a perfectly timed response, the team from Caritas came around the outside of the village, each riding a huge, elegant tryka. The elk-like creatures were massive, muscular, and carried racks of antlers from the crowns of their heads to halfway down their backs. The lowest antlers had been sawed off to make room for a rider, and they didn't seem to mind having a human seated on their backs.

"Doesn't it hurt them to remove their antlers?" Raven asked.

Griffin answered, "They fall off and grow back every year. We assist. Not until the velvet has dropped."

Raven nodded in reply, seeming slightly fearful of asking any further questions Griffin might feel compelled to answer.

Isolde said, "We have two more in our village, *nei* Raven. Would you like to ride?"

Raven shook her head and tightened her grip around Hector. "No, thank you. I'll stick with the horse."

"One more," Griffin corrected, and Isolde counted the number of tryka with them. Then the galloping hooves of another approaching reached her ears. Surprising everyone but those in Griffin's clan, Johnathan sat on the newcomer's back, looking nervous but seeming to have the hang of it. Griffin mumbled something that sounded like annoyance under his breath.

Johnathan directed the tryka toward his brother for inspection and nearly fell off as he pulled back on the antlers to halt the animal. "What do you think?"

Declan laughed. "I think it's fantastic."

"*Herr* Johnathan, would you like to trade?" Isolde asked from her mare.

"Maybe." Johnathan looked anxiously at the animal beneath him. "I'll let you know." Declan clapped his brother on the shoulder.

"Iso," Griffin spoke gruffly to his sister. "*Tempus vado.*"

Isolde dipped her head. "*Vado.*" Griffin shot off into the desert, followed by Crow, Vera, and the others of his clan. Isolde clicked her tongue and galloped off after them.

Orion translated for those remaining. "*Tempus vado* means *time to go.*" Then he kicked his heels into his horse and yelled, "*Vado!*" as he raced off.

C

Later that day, Foxx, Iris, Asher, and Seth traveled through Celestelvyra. With the help of Iris' map, they figured out which directions they'd yet to explore and decided to begin their journey at the apple orchard, planning to follow the trail running through it and discover more of what lay beyond. When they arrived, Seth and Asher disappeared between the rows of trees to harvest a few more apples to add to their packs for snacking.

Foxx stood on the trail outside the woods, staring off at the structure where she and Iris had sparred. A muster of storks had invaded the structure and were seemingly in the process of constructing a giant nest.

Coming up behind Foxx and slinging an arm over her shoulders, Iris followed the line of her vision. "What are you doing over here?"

Foxx took a while to answer, lost in regretful thoughts. Letting her head fall against her sister's, she said, "I'm so sorry, Iris."

"For what?"

Foxx gestured to the structure. "For a lot of things, but specifically for how I treated you that day. I don't know what happened, but I should never have fought you like that."

"True. But luckily I was trained by a pretty amazing fighter."

Foxx sighed. "You shouldn't be so forgiving. Especially when people don't deserve it."

"Most people deserve forgiveness. Most people don't specifically set out to hurt you. Maybe they make wrong decisions that affect you. Maybe they have a hard life or they're having a bad day. But most of the time, especially when people seek forgiveness, we should give it." Iris leaned closer for a hug, squeezing her sister tight. "I forgive you, Foxxglove. I love you. Of course I forgive you."

"I still want to stay here in the garden," Foxx admitted, though her voice remained low, as if she didn't want anything lingering close by to hear her confession. Somewhere deep in her gut, she felt guilty for wanting that. She knew it meant abandoning real life for a fairytale, knew it meant giving up, but hadn't she earned the right to do so after everything? Didn't she deserve this freedom?

Iris wiped a tear before it fell from Foxx's eye. "We're going to get through this, okay? We always do."

Asher and Seth joined them on the edge of the orchard and said in unison, "Ready ladies?" Foxx and Iris shared a chuckle, and together they continued on through the garden. They walked under the ceaseless song of chirping birds and bubbling brooks. Iris kept her journal handy and added little notes to the map, planning to go back later and sketch things more accurately.

After an hour or so, Iris said Asher's name. "What if someone does open a door to save us but they aren't coming from the Monastery in the Grim Wilds? How will they know where to find us? Since the Queen was there, there's a very good chance she will have destroyed it, don't you think?"

"If I'm correct, all doors outside lead to that same doorway." He pointed in the direction of the entrance. "The In-Between is unchanging. No matter which Monastery you go through, you will always end up in that swamp in front of those exact doors."

Iris considered this with a wrinkled brow. "I guess that makes it easy. So we aren't looking for a bunch of different doors."

Hearing a scuffle on the edge of the path, the group paused to see a pair of foxes tumbling over each other, playfully locked in a battle to catch the others' tails. It occurred to them, after a few moments of observation, that each fox had three tails instead of one.

Sensing their presence, the foxes stopped and stood next to each other to stare at them. Unlike the black fur of their backs, their chests were white, and their legs looked as if they'd stepped through red paint, dragging the tips of their tails through it, too.

Startled by a sudden sound the humans couldn't hear, the foxes shot off into the trees and disappeared from sight. After chuckling at the animals, the party began walking again, and Iris continued her previous thought. "So we just need to find the fountain and then hangout by the waterfall until someone finds us."

"Correct." Asher's eyes scanned the treeline for more interesting creatures that might be lurking about. "I'm sure Hector and the Raptors are working to get here as we speak."

"I hope so," Iris said, though she had to admit she had her doubts.

Then Foxx said Asher's name, and the sound of it on her lips seemed to stun all three of them into gaping as though she'd said a dirty word. Ignoring their blatant astonishment, she continued carefully. "I also have a question."

Asher momentarily forgot how to speak, taking a moment too long to at last choke out, "Go ahead."

They walked several more paces before she spoke again, keeping her voice level and unbiased. "Iris seems to be under the impression that after all this is over, you don't want to become the king."

He peered at Iris from the corner of his eye, then he inhaled a nervous breath. "That is… not a question."

Foxxglove's head snapped to him, and she felt baffled by the spark of amusement his words produced in her. His eyes found hers, and she quickly looked away. "I guess I would like to know if her assumption is accurate, and if so, why?"

Asher ran his hand through his thick hair and down the back of his head. "Well, I guess there are a lot of reasons." Foxx waited patiently for him to continue, offering no further direction.

"I think being a king would be a very hard job," Seth said, and Asher winked at him.

They walked a few minutes more before Asher finally answered. "Reasons I don't want to be king. Besides the obvious–killing my father and the woman I spent my life believing was my mother– becoming the King is a huge responsibility I don't feel qualified for."

This insecure admittance baffled Foxx, as to her, Asher always seemed entirely confident in himself. She was also fairly certain he would not only succeed, but excel at anything he put his mind to.

Asher lifted his hand to brush the long, thin leaves of the white pine trees along the side of the trail, letting the pliable needles tickle his palm. "Everything I know about ruling came from a black-hearted mother or a subservient father. Not to mention the resistance that will no doubt come with taking over the Five Kingdoms. People have been loyal to the Queen for so long—generations of the royal families, the King's Legion, and other powerful people."

"The Konungr will support you," Iris pointed out. "And I'd wager he's taught you at least a little of what it means to lead, even if you didn't realize he was doing it. Look at how he handled Jericho's recovery. I can't imagine you've spent any amount of time with him without learning something."

"It's true, Vali would definitely be on my side, but he and Ingrid aren't the only royals who could grasp for power. I'm not even thirty, I'm unwed, and most importantly, I abandoned my Kingdom when I ran away. These things will not be taken lightly. There will likely be assassination attempts, people vying for my power, thinking I'm unworthy or simply that they could rule better. All of these things make the prospect of ruling Arkaemor sound, frankly, awful. A very hard job, as Seth so intuitively pointed out."

Seth grinned at the inclusion of his opinions and slipped his little hand into Asher's, holding it as they walked.

"I know you didn't know me when I lived at the palace, but

many others did. I didn't exactly live in a way that proved I was worthy or capable of taking over. Since Sirena is immortal, I never thought I would be taking over. You are right though, Iris. Vali has taught me many things. He and Ingrid both."

"How did you come to be close to them anyway?" Iris asked.

"All the royals know each other. They get together at least once a year for one event or another, so I'd met him many times over the years." Asher chuckled, and the noise drew the eyes of the others. "At one of the events held in Jericho, Vali caught me exploring his palace. I was maybe nine or ten. Close to your age, Seth. I'd gotten bored of the party and snuck away, hoping to find something more exciting. He must have seen me leave because it was only minutes after I escaped that he tracked me down. I'd made my way into one of the guest rooms and was kneeling in front of the fireplace, flicking steel against flint and watching the sparks fly. He said, *Young sire, are you attempting to burn my palace to the ground?* I leapt from my skin, dropped the flint and steel, and threw myself across the floor."

Iris and Seth laughed, picturing the story as he told it.

"Then he asked, *Did your mother put you up to this?* And I answered that she didn't and that I most certainly was not trying to light the palace on fire, and he said, *Well that's a good thing, indeed, because if you were, you know I would be forced to execute you.* I was so terrified, and it must have been blatant on my face because he laughed heartily. He came the rest of the way into the room and closed the door behind him. Then he strode to the hearth, bent down, and started building a fire—something I'd never seen another royal do in my life. I said, *You aren't supposed to do that. That's what servants are for.* He smiled and kept working until the flames crackled. Without a word, he turned toward the door and began to leave, but I called after him, and he looked back at me. Though of course, as soon as he did, I felt too nervous to say whatever it was I thought I might say to the strange King who'd caught me somewhere I wasn't supposed to be and hadn't punished me for it. Perhaps I called him back to remind him that he'd forgotten to reprimand me." Asher shrugged and shook his head at his own foolery. "When I didn't speak, he said, *You may stay here as long as you like, Prince Alexander. Enjoy the fire, steal some sweets from the jar on the dresser. There are staff—not servants—circulating the halls. Feel free to reach out to them should you need anything.* I nodded, stunned silent by his words. Then his eyes glanced around the room with approval as he said, *It seems you've picked a good one. This room belongs to you now, Alexander, and it will be available should ever you find yourself wanting. Do you understand?* I nodded again, though I really didn't understand, and he disappeared, closing the door behind him. I was… dumbfounded. It was years before I returned to the room, but it was ready for me, as he promised it would be; with wood by the hearth, a fresh jar of sweets on the dresser, and even some clothing in the closet that somehow fit just right."

Iris ruminated over the retold events before saying, "Wow, what a strange story. I wonder why he did that. He just gave you a room? Maybe he had a hunch you would need it someday."

"He wasn't wrong."

Seth said, "I think it was because Asher is awesome, and the King could tell right away, just like I could. He must be a very smart king."

Iris laughed and pulled Seth in for a hug. "I think you might be right. Asher is pretty awesome, and we could tell right away, too." She smiled at Asher, and he looked past her to Foxx, who wore a thoughtful expression.

Clearing his throat, he said, "Anyway, back to Foxx's original question. Another reason I don't want to be King is that it would require I spend most of my time at Castle Solís. I want to explore the wonders of Arkaemor. Fight off wild creatures and carry a torch through deep, dark caves. Take a nap on the beach and climb mountains. I don't want to be stuck behind the walls of a castle, under the constant shadow of guards and the continuous watchful eyes and judgments of every single person around me. I have spent a lot of my life rejecting everything the Thrones stand for. The idea of carrying the heavy weight that comes with them…" His words trailed off, and his gaze crossed Foxx's.

She held his stare for a moment before pulling away, returning her eyes to the road ahead. It meant something to her that he felt this way, though she couldn't place exactly what quite yet. He really didn't want to walk the path destiny had lined up for him, so perhaps he truly could empathize with her resistance. He wasn't just being kind or supportive but truly resonated with everything she felt, and if he were more of a coward, he might even choose to stay in Celestelvyra just like she wanted to.

"But I guess we all have to grow up sometime." Asher cleared his throat. "You guys grew up long before I did, and I have eight years on you." Chuckling without humor, he brushed his head again. "So, that is the long-winded explanation of why I don't want to be king."

Foxx thought of her recent vision of him with the golden circlet about his head and considered sharing it with him, though she wasn't sure whether it would inspire him or only serve to increase pressure.

"Those all sound like reasonable motivations to me," Iris said.

Standing on the far side of their line as the trail was wide enough for them to walk next to each other, Foxx said nothing in response to his words, needing time to reflect on them. She looked off into the open field to her right, lost in her thoughts.

Twenty or so minutes later, they stopped at a huge weeping willow, taking refuge beneath its canopy, eating some snacks, and rehydrating. Asher sat on the ground, leaning his back on the tree's wide trunk. Iris laid in the grass looking up into the exotic branches. Seth joined her, laying with his feet facing the opposite direction and the top of his head right next to hers. They spoke quietly to each other, pointing at strange shapes they found hidden within the tree's maze of limbs.

Foxx stood near the outer edge, brushing her fingers against the inside of the draped wall of leaves. Snapshots rolled through her mind of the last few months. Not much time had passed, but so much had happened. Horrible things and hard things and sad things and wonderful things. Enough things to fill a lifetime.

Her chest felt heavy, and her mind flooded with more questions: What was she supposed to do now that she had all of this information? How was she to trust Elohim with her future? With Iris' future? How was she to trust the beautiful prince whose patience knew no bounds?

A breeze blew, its tendrils whistling through the long whips of the willow. She closed her eyes, listening to the sound, breathing in the fresh air, and allowing peace to settle in her heart. Then she looked over her shoulder at Asher, finding him sitting in silence with his head resting against the tree. His eyes were open, but he didn't seem present within them.

Before she could change her mind, she sat down next to him, not close enough that their arms might accidentally bump, but next to him nonetheless.

C

Startled by her sudden appearance, Asher's whole body stiffened. He waited for her to speak if she chose to, and she didn't for a long while. She sat quietly with her arms resting on elevated knees, twirling a willow whip between two fingers.

His thoughts drifted to his and Iris' conversation about moving into the castle. Though he didn't wish for the day's peculiar events to get his hopes up, he couldn't help but wonder what the Creator had planned for his future and how Foxxglove fit into it. Would they simply be companions? Family? Would he always love her as she continued to resist him, or would they eventually be in sync? If their bond did evolve, she might one day be crowned queen. She could rule alongside him and help him maneuver the terrifying waters of kingship.

Without his permission, fabrications flooded his mind of them standing next to each other in the Hall of Sunsets. She wore a gorgeous dress with a crown atop her head, looking fierce and strong as she stared out at her people—their people. Whatever might happen, he'd learned a long time ago to put his trust in Elohim's plans, and he would continue to follow His will for his life, whether it included Foxxglove Belamour or not.

Still, he offered a silent and pleading prayer that it did.

Breaking through his inner monologue, Foxx said, "I think you will make a great king." This bewildered Asher even more than her close proximity, and he wasn't sure how to respond, so he didn't. "You're very personable. Your people will love you. Once you show them the truth of who you are, the castle staff will see your compassion and generosity, and you will charm everyone, like you always do. Even the other royal families, I bet. And you can change things. Change what the Thrones stand for into something you believe in. You don't have to follow your parent's footsteps. In fact, you couldn't even if you wanted to because you're too good." Foxx quivered at the intensity of her own words. Then she added, "And since you'll be King, if you meet any resistance you can just lock those who oppose you up in the dungeons or something."

Out of the corner of his eye, he again noticed her lips curve into a small smile and found himself no longer able to contain his own. It burst free from his lips like a sunbeam, revealing all of his perfectly white teeth. Her words were too kind, too exactly what he needed to hear, though he hadn't known it until she'd said them.

"I think you will end up enjoying it more than you think."

"Perhaps you're right." The conversation stalled for a minute as both reorganized their thoughts. Asher felt elated to learn her true thoughts on the matter. In the name of sharing truths, he said, "I think I liked that you girls didn't know me as the Prince. It meant I could be exactly myself around you." His eyes shifted to her again and witnessed her chest visibly tightening at the memories brought to a head by the admission of his lies. But he needed to say it—to explain not just with the logical reasoning of his plan, his past, and his future but to explain his heart.

"Everyone knows about Prince Alexander and all of his unruly shenanigans. At least, it seemed that way from my perspective. Everyone always expected me to be something: the Prince of Arkaemor, spoiled rotten, a playboy, noble, a troublemaker, prestigious, royal, a brother, a son, the heir. Not many tried to see me for who I really am. They tried to fit me into a box based on who they already thought I was.

"You girls had no reason to expect me to be anything at all besides exactly what I unveiled to you. For what seemed like the first time in my life, I was able to be wholly and entirely myself. Playful without being destructive, flirty without being sleazy, intimate without judgment. I didn't have to push things too far, I didn't have to hide my true nature." He paused, taking in air he hadn't since he'd begun. "We built bonds like no relationship I'd ever experienced with anyone, not even Vali and Ingrid. It's true, they are my family, and I do have ties with them unique to all others. I know Vali loves me, in his own way, but he's also strategic and manipulative. He's a king. And Ingrid loves me like her own child, but she's his Queen. I'm not foolish enough to think pure kindness had him gifting me that bedroom. There was something calculated and tactical behind it that I may never fully understand. Regardless, I'm glad for it, and I feel so blessed by them and everything they have done for me, but it isn't the same as what I felt building between the three of us when we traveled Metsa Sateen. I don't know how to explain it other than to call it true friendship. You didn't desire to be close to me because I was the heir to the Thrones. You just wanted *me*. I know I hurt you with my lies, and I hope my words haven't refreshed your anger, but I still feel the need to thank you for allowing me to be… just me, and enjoying my company anyway."

He thought her eyes looked glossy from the corner of his vision, but he was too afraid to face her directly. Her chest seemed to rise and fall with purpose, as if she fought to control her breathing.

Then she said, "You made it easy," and released a long breath.

When he didn't respond, her chin dropped to her chest, her eyes falling to the ground. Surprising him with her change in subject, she admitted, "It's crazy to me that you knew my mother. I don't know how to feel about it."

"Maybe share the different things you feel, and I can help you piece it together."

She let her head fall back against the tree so she could look up into the willow's branches. "Sometimes my mother was amazing. I know I speak poorly of her because most of my memories come from later years when I was older and she was… worse. But I do have memories of her being the most wonderful mother a person could ask for. She taught me to cook and to braid Iris' hair and to be the very best big sister I could be. She always insisted I look out for Iris—said it was my responsibility. I suppose she must have known what our future would bring.

"Mother told us stories and taught us songs. I remember sitting on her lap when I was very young, I don't even know how young, and she put a paint brush in my hand and let me paint on top of a background she'd already designed. Then she hung it on the wall and called it *Our Masterpiece*." Foxx sighed.

"Amaryllis was an astounding woman."

"But I think I'm jealous of you in a way," she said, and his eyes widened. "Because all of your memories with her are good memories. You don't have any recollections marred with her insanity. You have no memories of hiding in the kitchen cabinets, trying to keep Iris safe while she threw a tantrum and flung things about the house. Or of hateful, awful words tearing apart your character. Or of actual physical violence. Amaryllis always made you feel loved and safe. And while I'm glad you had that, that was not the case for me."

Not for the first time that day, Asher felt at a loss for words. Nothing he said could change the truth. He had known Amaryllis, and she had been one of the few people to love him the way a child deserved to be loved. It pained him to know Foxx had a tragically different experience with the same woman, and it made him wish even more that he'd found her and Iris sooner. If he could have spoken the beauties of their mother into their hearts from an early age, maybe it would have altered their perception of her, and things wouldn't feel so painful now. "Doesn't it help at all knowing her visions were real? Experiencing them yourself and realizing she wasn't actually deranged?"

"A little, I guess. But it also makes my fear of ending up like her even more prevalent. Before the visions began, I worried the sickness ran in the family and might strike me one day. Iris and I both did. In fact, when I had my first vision in the Grim Wilds, I think Iris knew right away what was happening because it looked just the same as mother's had.

"Having the visions is now solid evidence proving I will indeed end up just like my mother. Real visions or not, she had moments of insanity. Times where she lost all control. A sane woman doesn't hurl knives about the kitchen when her daughters are crying in the cupboards. A sane woman doesn't throw enraged force into an attack against her own sister when they're supposed to be sparring for fun." Her eyes shifted to her sister, but if Iris overheard them, she made no indication to reveal it.

"So I suppose the answer to your question is, not really, no. It helps that I know there was some greater purpose to her visions, and hopefully to mine as well. But other than that, it just breeds more fear in me for what my future might hold."

Asher chuckled, drawing her tear-filled eyes. "I wonder if all weeping willows have a little magic in them." He ran his fingers across a strand of leaves hanging near him.

"Why do you say that?"

"We grew closer after our time under the Tree of Knowing in Sateen. Like it opened something inside of us and brought us together." For the first time since she sat down, Asher turned his head to her. "Maybe this willow will have the same effect."

Without meeting his gaze, she said, "Perhaps it will."

"Are you guys ready to move on?" Seth sat up on his elbow and looked at them.

Asher gave his attention to Seth. "I think so, mate. Are you ready?"

"Certainly, lad," Seth replied, mimicking Asher's accent and drawing a smile to his lips. Iris remained on the ground, staring up into the tree.

Seeing that neither sister had moved, Asher stood. "Let's step outside and see which way we want to explore next. What do you think?" He winked, and Seth nodded eagerly, understanding the secret message passing between them. Grabbing his hand, he dragged Asher outside, leaving the girls to follow after when they were ready.

# Chapter 24

A Tale of Two Figs

The sky was spotted with clouds, creating a gradient of shadows atop the sand as Orion and his companions traveled across the desert, not stopping until they reached the barrier to Metsa Sateen. Once there, they found a gathering of rocks to tie up the animals and made camp for the night. Griffin and Vera crossed into the jungle to hunt, hoping to save any provisions they brought with them for their journey through the tundra where food would be sparse.

Orion and Jax built a fire while Isolde got Declan set up in a comfortable spot to rest. Though he insisted it was unnecessary, she wouldn't take no for an answer, saying he would thank her later when his aches and pains were minimal. Johnathan tried to assist her, but there wasn't much for him to do, and he mostly got in the way.

Hector and Raven tended to the horses while Kwame and Jovan handled the tryka. Once the fire was kindled, Jax took over with the horses, telling Hector he needed a few minutes of solitude and that they should go join the others.

Crow and Leone had crossed the barrier to harvest mangos for everyone to share and were in the process of slicing the skins from the juicy fruit. Declan manned the fire in Jax's absence, making sure it stayed large enough to cook a meal over. Orion sat on the ground in front of the fire with Isolde weaving tiny braids into his hair from where she'd perched on a rock behind him.

When Griffin and Vera returned from the jungle, each wearing a tan primate slung over their shoulder, Griffin saw Orion and Isolde sitting comfortably, and his disgruntled demeanor hardened his features. He glared at Isolde from across the fire, and she ignored him. Vera nudged him, and the two approached the others, holding out the slain primates to show off their score.

"Macaques!" Declan said. Griffin grunted and walked away to skin and ready them for cooking. Vera glanced apologetically at Declan, and he smiled. Then she turned to follow the Abrafo.

Isolde said, "Please forgive my brother. He is unhappy about some things, but he will get past them in time. He would not have agreed to come if he did not believe it necessary."

"It's fine." Declan shifted a log on the fire to allow more oxygen into the coals below. "We're all tired and nervous about the days ahead. You can't expect a group of thirteen people to get along consistently."

Orion touched Isolde's hand. "Stop after you finish that one, okay?"

Removing her fingers from his hair, she replied, "All finished."

He stood, brushing her shoulder as he walked out around the rock without another word. Following the direction Griffin had gone, he found him and Vera using a flat rock as a makeshift cutting board and carving into the already skinned macaques. As Orion approached, Griffin held his very large, very sharp machete in the air, about to slam it down and remove the animal's head. Freezing with the knife mid swing, he eyed the newcomer with suspicion.

Though Orion didn't know if the man had simply paused from his work or if his position was intentionally intimidating, he walked up to Griffin with his palms out in innocence. "*Nei* Vera, Abrafo Griffin." Vera nodded and continued working. Isolde's brother kept the bloody knife suspended menacingly as he waited for Orion to speak. "I just wanted to say, I hope there aren't any hard feelings with us dragging you and your clan into this operation."

"I do not fear Ashgate," Griffin replied gruffly.

"Right. I just couldn't help but notice some tension, and I wanted to see if I could do anything to help remedy it." It felt as if someone else spoke through his lips, and he reflected briefly on the extreme changes he'd noticed of late and what might be the cause of this strange and proper man he felt himself becoming.

Griffin slammed the knife into the macaque's neck and left it there as he turned to face Orion. His huge arms seemed to flex as his anger swelled, and his fingers curled into fists as he examined Orion through scrutinizing eyes. "Iso is my sister." His tone was forceful and stern but not unsteady.

"Yes, I am aware of that." Orion studied the bear of a man, confused by the direction the conversation had taken, though he thought perhaps he shouldn't have been.

"And the succeeding heir to my tribe," Griffin added.

"Yes." Orion nodded slowly as his brain caught up.

"This is very important to my people." Griffin's voice became abrasive but low, so as to not be overheard by the others. For reasons unknown to Orion, he didn't seem to mind Vera overhearing, and he wondered about their relationship. Griffin's eyes shifted to Isolde sitting by the fire and laughing over something out of earshot. Without pulling his gaze from her, he said, "Who stands beside her is very important to my people. *Our* people."

Continuing to nod, Orion said, "I think I understand."

"I do not think you do." Griffin's head snapped back to Orion as his muffled tone got away from him. "You do not know her. She is special."

"I know she is, Griffin." Orion's expression transformed from friendly to serious. "I know."

"No, you do *not* know!" Griffin's raised voice drew the eyes of those by the fire, though all but Isolde quickly looked away. Her golden eyes flashed in the firelight as she observed their confrontation.

Vera touched his shoulder, and he growled at her, but she didn't flinch away. Then he turned back to the carcass and retrieved his knife before tossing the macaque's severed head into the sand.

Orion inhaled a deep breath to ensure a controlled tone. "I'm not going to let anything happen to her, Griffin."

Griffin paused again, his russet cheeks darkening with rage. Orion took an involuntary step backward, keeping his gaze on the gruesome knife in Griffin's hand. "*You* have already happened to her."

Vera leaned forward to look into Orion's eyes, wearing an encouraging smile. Since she didn't seem thrown by the things her Abrafo spoke, Orion assumed they'd already discussed it. Perhaps he'd shared his frustrations and concerns with her. Though it seemed she might not agree with his opinion, she stood with him in companionship, and again Orion considered what the man before him might be like to those in his confidence. He seemed so brutish and angry, but perhaps there was another side of Griffin that only a select few were privileged enough to see.

Griffin's vision slid sideways to Vera, and she quickly pulled back, returning to work.

Feeling the conversation a lost cause, Orion pivoted back toward the fire. Before he walked two steps, Griffin halted him, using his name for the first time since the day they met. To his surprise, it didn't sound hateful or stained with malice. Instead, it rolled from his thick tongue like a careful petition. Orion stopped without facing him, listening intently for what the man would say. Several seconds passed, and Orion thought he'd changed his mind about speaking. Then Griffin said, "If you do not feel for her as she does for you, then I would ask you to leave when this mission is complete. And never return."

Having no immediate response to his statement, Orion remained still and silent for a long moment, waiting to see if Griffin had anything left to say. When the sound of a knife slicing flesh reached his ears, Orion returned to the fire, sitting on the ground next to Declan rather than reclaiming his spot in front of Isolde. Though she'd witnessed the interaction, she said nothing to him about it and allowed him the distance he'd placed between them.

After Griffin and Vera set the macaques to cook over the fire, they joined the others. Griffin leaned against the rock Isolde sat on, and Vera claimed a spot in the sand between Crow and Leone.

The atmosphere around the fire grew quiet, as most were lost in their own thoughts and worries about the upcoming days. Hector and Raven whispered to each other, giggling occasionally at things the others couldn't hear. Isolde tormented Griffin, poking him and portraying the cutesy younger sister to try and smooth things over. He pretended to be annoyed, but it was clear he reveled in her attention.

Declan drew on the ground with a stick. Vera laid on her back next to Leone, both women looking up at the bright sunset of colors fading from the sky. Jax returned to the fire walking between Jovan and Kwame. They discussed something about the tryka that didn't make sense to anyone catching the end of the conversation. The men from Caritas joined Leone, Vera, and Crow, and Jax sat down next to Hector.

"Kwame and Jovan were explaining the plan for the distraction outside the gate. After we eat, you should hear what they're thinking and see if you have any suggestions."

Hector agreed they could discuss it after food, knowing everyone grew close to famished.

Orion let his mind meander, blocking out the buzz of the people around him and focusing on the crackling of the fire. The drips in his head elevated, but he hadn't been tormented by whispers for the majority of the day, which he thought must be progress. In light of that thought, he remembered Isolde requesting he speak to Declan about his issues, and his eyes drifted to her. She seemed to be intentionally irritating her brother, with her wrists crossed over his shoulder and her chin resting on her hands so her mischievous grin lingered right next to his face.

Orion returned his gaze to the fire as he recalled what Griffin had observed.

You have already happened to her.

Though he yearned to deny it, he knew the truth. Something immense had sparked between them. Something he'd never felt before.

And the succeeding heir to my tribe.

He mulled over what might happen when the war ended. Assuming they survived, what would be the outcome of whatever he and Isolde were becoming? He didn't know how to play prince, especially to a tribe of people he knew nothing about. Regardless of whether or not the people of Caritas seemed to enjoy his presence, he doubted they would welcome him as a leader. He was a stranger: interesting to study but not someone they would follow.

Who stands beside her is very important to my people.

When they rescued Prince Alexander and the Belamours from Celestelvyra, he would return to Jericho and they would prepare for war. He didn't have high hopes of making it back from that, but even if he did, what would happen then? Would he move to Caritas to be with her? Would she leave her people to be with him? Neither seemed plausible.

He knew he didn't deserve someone like Isolde anyway. She was perfect. Extraordinary. *Good.*

Her eyes met his across the fire as if she sensed his inner turmoil and wished to scold him for it. With the release of her gaze, the whispers began. The noose around his neck tightened as they legitimized how much he indeed did *not* deserve her, cataloging every detail of his life that stood as proof of the notion. They recited to him how thoroughly he deserved nothing but his current miserable existence, insisting he really didn't even deserve that. Above the crackling fire and the mumbled voices of those around him, they grew in volume even louder than the dripping.

Feeling a touch at his arm, he turned to see Declan staring at him, his eyes overflowing with concern. His lips moved, but Orion heard no words. "What?" He twisted his pinky finger in his ear, a futile attempt to clear a pathway to hear above the blaring noise.

At last, he gave up. Shaking Declan's hand from his arm, he stood and walked away from him, from the others, from the light of the fire. He crossed the barrier into Sateen, slumped against a tree in the pouring rain, and wept.

C

When Asher awoke the following morning, Foxxglove was nowhere in sight. Leaving his bedroll, he rummaged through his bag. After changing into shorts and a hunter green tunic with strings criss-crossed loosely between the split hem at his chest, he rinsed his dirty clothes in the pond by the waterfall and left them to dry on a branch. Kneeling at the pond's edge, he splashed water in his face before crossing the field to the path leading to the meadow.

Elohim, please guide me in what to do here. I don't want to push her, but I can't help the hope welling up inside me after our discussion yester-day. Is it time? Is she ready? I will follow where You lead.

When he passed through the treeline into the glade of sunshine daisies, violet bellflowers, crimson poppies, and magenta coneflowers, he didn't find Foxx laying amongst them. Scanning the outer edge of the meadow, he used his tracker's eye to see if she'd wandered further into the wood and saw bent foliage at the back of the circle. Investigating, he found the footpath continuing on through the meadow and out the other side.

Like the path leading to the meadow, a mixture of vegetation and trees lined either side. When passing a plum tree, he plucked a fruit and bit into it.

As he tossed the pit, just before reaching a break in the trees, he discovered a fig tree. Debating whether or not it might be an answer to prayer, he felt warmth blooming in his chest and picked two ripe figs, tucking one into each of his pockets.

Lifting an oversized leaf from the path, he stepped out onto a grassy knoll at the base of a mountain. He took in the beauty of the scenery: the mountain ridges to his right and grassy fields to his left. Another water source cut through the land from a cave underneath the mountain, and the sound of rushing water mingled with morning birdsong.

Looking up, he found Foxx at the top of the waterfall sitting with her feet hanging over the edge. He called her name, announcing his presence, and she leaned to look as he began his ascent.

When he reached her, he sat on her right and hung his boots over the edge next to her bare feet. "Did you climb that wall without your boots?"

Her eyes slid to her feet, and she wiggled her toes. "I didn't plan on coming. I only meant to lay in the meadow, but then I remembered seeing this ridge when getting water from the stream, and I wanted to check it out. I didn't feel like going back for shoes."

Asher followed her line of sight and found himself amazed by the extraordinary view of the garden. From their vantage, they could see far beyond the building containing the entrance doors. They saw more snow-capped mountains, waterfalls, and streams; another orchard of trees in perfect rows off to the right; and endless flowers, trails, and plants of every variety. The herb garden Asher and Seth discovered lay off to the left of the building, as well as the stone wall they'd climbed together. He could also see giraffe heads sticking out above the trees, grizzly bears splashing in a stream, and a herd of cows grazing in a field of grass.

"It seems to go on forever, doesn't it?" Foxx asked.

"It's wonderful. I've never seen anything comparable."

Foxx leaned back on her palms. "And yet you want to leave."

Asher sighed. "How are you today, love?"

She straightened her legs, lifting her feet into the air and looking down at her toes. "I'm not sure. I've been sitting here reflecting on everything that's happened and all the things we discussed beneath the willow. I guess I feel confused. I don't know what to do."

"Regarding what, specifically?" Though he feigned nonchalance, he longed to know how the conversation may have changed her perspective. She didn't seem as distant or as angry as she had before, and he thought she might be reconsidering past decisions.

A siege of white herons flew in front of them, and Foxx paused to watch them descend toward the falls. Two dove into the pond while the others switched directions and followed the falls upward. Wind blew Foxx's hair out of her face as they zoomed past. Though her lips curved into a small smile as she watched them fly off, she said, "How do you heal from a lifetime of pain?"

"Maybe you never really do."

She turned to him, narrow eyes squinting at the unexpected response.

"Not fully, at least. Maybe you continue to grow from everything you've learned and help others heal and grow in the process."

She pulled her feet up, crossing them beneath her and putting her hands in her lap. "I haven't helped anyone heal and grow."

Asher heard the sorrow she tried to conceal. "Sure you have. You've helped Iris, for one. You're helping Seth. Just him being with us is helping him deal with the loss of Mr. Magpie. It seems you helped Declan. From what Iris told me, he was quite different when you first met him." He shrugged and scratched the back of his head. "And you've helped me."

"That was all Iris." Foxx stared at her fingers. "She advocated for Seth to join us. She broke down the walls in Declan's hard exterior. Maybe even Orion's, too."

"And me?"

Foxx's head shifted in his direction, but she didn't meet his gaze. "Iris has been pushing me to forgive you since the day I woke up in Jericho. If it weren't for her, we wouldn't even be speaking right now."

"I don't believe that. And honestly, Foxx, how do you think she learned to take care of people?"

"She was born with an overwhelming love for others in her heart." Her sarcastic tone attempted to mask her jealousy. Her sister had always been full of love in a way Foxx could never comprehend —had envied.

"And you weren't?"

Her chest stiffened. "No, I wasn't."

Asher scowled. "The lies you believe about yourself infuriate me." She turned to him in surprise at his daring words. "Her life could have gone a very different way if she hadn't had you as a big sister to take care of her. You've both told me stories of your childhood. I see and know your heart and your strength more clearly than you do, Foxxglove Belamour."

His assertive use of her full name made her flinch, and again she faced the vast and wondrous landscape.

"And..." His brow lifted with arrogance. "You won the heart of a prince, so you can't be all that bad."

A smile spread across her lips, she muttered, "A foolish prince."

He laughed outright, his hand lifting to hold his stomach. "That may be so."

Another few minutes passed with chirping birds and rushing water as the only sounds breaking the silence. The breeze above the falls felt refreshing and smelled crisp and clean, reminding him of the cool air of Cordillera. Asher thought of the plants surrounding him and realized he could identify vegetation from every territory. What an imagination the Creator must possess in order to design Arkaemor's territories, each with their own specific habitats, plant and animal varieties, and weather temperaments, even as they all blended together here in harmony.

Then he looked at Foxx and considered everything he knew about her: her visions and her strength, her family and her destiny, and the entirety of what had led them to Celestelvyra in the first place.

Amaryllis, her mother, who also had been gifted with knowledge of futures to come, who had set so many things in motion long ago, telling stories and singing songs to Foxx, Iris, and even Asher himself that revealed wisdom they would later decipher. She brought them together, and he even wondered if she'd known what he and Foxxglove would mean to each other, how their destinies not only intertwined for the sake of Arkaemor but coiled into their hearts as well.

Smiling at the thought, he cleared his throat and nudged her shoulder. "Where do we go from here, Foxx?"

Sighing, she looked forward. After a minute, she exhaled a long breath. "Maybe we just let it all go."

"Is that what you want?"

Teeth gnawed at her bottom lip. "What if..." She shook her head and started again. "I just wish I understood what Sirena meant. Why she's so interested in me. And why the Konungr—"

"Vali? What did he do?"

"Nothing, he just... there's just still so much I don't know, don't understand. There's… this darkness. And nothing in you is dark, Asher. Nothing." She released another breath.

"There's nothing dark in you, either, Foxx."

"I just worry I might not be what you think I am."

"What do I think you are?" When she didn't answer, he counted on his fingers. "Strong, beautiful, stubborn, fearless, terrifying. What else is there to know?"

She looked at him, eyes wide. "You think I'm terrifying?"

His grin revealed his dimples. "You scare the hell out of me, love."

She returned her attention to her fingers, tucking them into fists. "What if I'm more scary than you know?"

"I'm certain you are, but it does little to change my mind." He reached for her hand in her lap, chancing rejection with words he hoped would sway her heart. "I want it all, Foxx. All of you. Every broken piece." Her cheeks flamed, and she wouldn't meet his gaze. "Do you remember the lamppost? In Petrichor?"

Her cheeks grew warmer as she slipped her other hand beneath her leg, out of sight. "Yes…"

"It was a mosaic, did you notice? A mosaic of broken glass. And the outcome was exquisite. That's how I see you. Broken doesn't mean ugly. Sometimes stains are beautiful. Sometimes shattered pieces shine the brightest. They catch any glimpse of light in the darkness and amplify it into a flurry of sparkles. Even when the moon is but a sliver, it illuminates the blackest night."

She shook her head, a smile curling her lips. "You talk just like a prince, you know. It's hard to believe I didn't realize it before."

"Well… I *am* a prince. I'd say it's part of my charm, but we both know I'm charming regardless." Releasing her hand, he reached into his pocket and retrieved a fig. "The truth is: I searched you out because I was wondering if we might spark a truce."

Foxx looked at him, then at the fig. By her expression, he knew she was remembering their time together in Metsa Sateen when he'd left them at the Monastery of the Morrow. He'd returned with a plethora of injuries and a ridiculous excuse about an offended fig tree. As proof of his tale, as well as a peace offering for causing them to worry, he'd brought a couple of the figs back with him.

From his other pocket he withdrew the second fig, holding them next to each other. "And naturally, I snagged a second one because big sisters get two." His grin turned rascally as he repeated the words he'd used that day.

Foxx took one of the figs and countered, "One for me and one for you."

Emerald eyes glistened with excitement. "Does this mean you accept?"

She looked him over, seeming to take in every inch of him, to pick him apart piece by piece and discover truths he might still keep hidden. She wanted to trust him, he could tell, wanted to give in. He looked back at her, his eyes roaming the curves of her face, the spirit of inquiry in her expression, and the ferocity of her scar that labeled her a warrior not to be trifled with at first glance, though he knew this to be true even without the visual reminder.

Then she said, "Define your terms." Her voice had turned airy, and she swallowed to adjust it. "So we're both clear on what we expect from one another."

His eyes turned to the fig in his hand as if intently examining its purple skin. "We look after each other. Not just as allies, but as a team. No matter what happens."

Foxx frowned, and the expression lit a flicker of hope in his chest. Was she disappointed by his answer? Had she been hoping for more?

"Okay. Allies. I promised we wouldn't let you fight Sirena alone, so I will go with you to Inaravale. In regards to what happens after this is all over, I can't make any promises."

"I understand." Asher's entire being dripped with glittering charm. "And thank you. I know I said it was too dangerous and I didn't want you to come, but I'm pleased to know I'll have you by my side. We can figure out what happens after when the time comes." He forced away the returned images of her in a crown standing next to him atop the dais, though his smile grew wider regardless, and he thought it lucky she hadn't yet lifted her eyes.

"I'm going to get down now. Iris will be up soon, and I don't want her to worry I've run off again." Twisting her legs up onto the rock ledge, she found Asher already standing with his arm outstretched, offering to help her to her feet. She accepted the gesture, holding his fingers as she stepped out around him.

Right when he was about to release her hand, he squeezed it, stopping her in her tracks. He said her name, and her eyes snapped to him as he took a step closer. "Iris will be fine. I'm… not ready to let go yet." Another step had him saying, "I don't think I ever will be." He waited, his heart pounding like a thundering avalanche. She stared at him, her lips parting as she searched his eyes for answers he wanted to give her.

Lifting his free hand, he ran a thumb down the length of her scar like he'd done when they'd stood together in the rain. He held her gaze, willing her to unravel his true feelings. He'd felt their connection the moment their eyes first met in Kesken Ala, and it had grown exponentially ever since.

"Foxxglove, I—"

Her lips smothered his words.

A rush of frightfully elevating energy surged through him as the incredible truth of what was happening sank in: she was kissing him.

Slipping his arms around her back, he pulled her close, and she dissolved into his touch. Her arms wrapped around his neck, her fingers tangling in his hair as she slid her tongue between his lips. She dropped one hand to wrap around his waist, and he gasped as she clutched the back of his shirt. Her unexpected passion fueled the heat he'd been holding back for months. He radiated bliss, his body vibrating with exhilaration.

Stalling for breath, he pulled back without letting go and observed her dilated pupils, swollen lips, and flushed cheeks.

The corners of her mouth lifted as breath escaped in heavy bursts. "What's wrong?"

Clasping his hands together behind her back, he admitted in a heady voice, "I've dreamt of this moment many times, so I just wanted to make sure I'm actually awake."

"You are. But stop trying to read my thoughts." Her voice was breathless and playful. "They are mine to give you, if I so choose."

"Give me one then." He fluttered a trail of kisses across her shoulder. "Whisper to me sweet nothings, love. So we can both be clear on what we expect from each other."

She smiled at his paralleled words. Leaning into him, she put her lips to his ear, sending shivers down his neck. Anticipation made his heart tumble and skip as her silence lingered on. He held it out to her in the palm of his hand, having no definitive idea whether she would grasp it, hold it next to her own, or slice it in half, letting the pieces topple down into the depths of the falls. He wondered if she felt as vulnerable in his arms as he did in hers.

In reply, she whispered, "You won my heart also." Her lips grazed the soft skin under his ear, sending another wild surge through him. "Foolish prince."

He chuckled, pulling her against his chest so she rested her head on his shoulder. "You have no idea how glad I am to hear you say that, love." He felt so light, he might lift off, floating up into the clouds, drifting into the galaxy above.

Then Iris and Seth's voices reached their ears. "Foxx! Asher! Where are you guys?"

Releasing each other, they stepped to the edge of the falls and waved. "Up here!" Asher called.

Startling, Iris and Seth looked up.

"Whoa!" Seth waved back with glee.

Iris held her hand over her eyes, shielding the sun out of habit despite there being no sunlight to block. Her lips curled with whimsical suspicion. "What are you guys doing up there?"

"We're coming down now," Foxx yelled back.

From behind, Asher put a hand on either side of her hips and spun her into him. Leaning in to drop a flurry of kisses along her jawline, he said, "We don't have to go right this second. They don't know how long it should take us to return."

Letting herself melt into him, she found his lips again, learning them, acclimating herself to the way they moved together with her own. His teeth nibbled her lip, sending a new wave of heat into her core as his mouth moved to her neck.

His name escaped her lips, and he froze. She'd called him *Alexander*, and there'd been no malice or flippancy in her tone.

"I like when you call me Alexander," he whispered.

"I don't think you should hide from it anymore." She breathed deeply, trying to clear the fuzziness from her brain, though new fog continued to manifest with every touch.

"Seth said the same thing." Pulling back, he grinned at her closed eyelids. When they fluttered open, she found him gazing at her and matched his smile.

Then she brushed his hair sideways across his forehead so it didn't obstruct her view of his eyes. "Prince Alexander Aldrich, of Arkaemor." Her fingers lingered on his face, grazing the outside of his cheekbone and sliding down his jaw to his chin. "Someday: King Alexander Aldrich."

"Perhaps." In his head, he thought, *Thank you, Elohim.*

Her hand dropped to his, and she clutched it before stepping out around him to head down the mountain. They followed the pathway back through the meadow and into the clearing where Iris sat cutting into a pair of zucchini and Seth picked through a pile of blackberries.

Iris grinned with pure happiness when they approached, seeming to read the cheerful energy between them. "I hope this means you guys made up."

"Were you still fighting?" Seth asked through a mouthful of berries that had already turned his lips purple.

Asher ruffled his hair. "More exploring today?"

"Seems like you two were already exploring," Iris chided, taking in her sister's wind-chapped cheeks. "But yes, more exploring. Maybe today we'll be lucky enough to be gifted two miracles."

C

"Did you handle it?" Queen Sirena stood on the edge of a cliff looking out over the deciduous forest. There was a chill to the air common for that time of year, and the breeze rustled the leafy trees below. Though in most of the territories, the environment didn't change with the seasons, Reginaterra was special in that as soon as the Ammil moon graced them with its presence, the air turned brisk and the leaves began the exquisite process of dying.

Sirena very much enjoyed watching the leaves change from forest greens to flaxen, papaya, and cardinal red. She felt it confirmed the splendor of death; of the old passing on so the new could take its place. After a few weeks, new leaves would begin to sprout from the empty branches, growing fresh and green once again.

Thoughts of a beautiful death were both bitter and sweet. The concept was not foreign to her as she'd watched many births and deaths over many millennia, but knowing she herself would never get to experience this glory was surprisingly… unfortunate.

Not that she wanted to die, but the art of living, at least in the world as it now was, had become tedious. She reflected on when she'd agreed to this life, surrounded by vile human filth. The splendors of the garden had once been plentiful and hers to enjoy. The perfection of everything Elohim had shaped and formed with His own hands had been gifted to her for no other reason but His incomprehensible kindness.

But she'd squandered it. *They* had squandered it.

They'd only wanted a little more power and the freedom to rule as they pleased. They deserved to rule over the filth, surely. He was the one who designed them to be better, stronger, and more magical than the humans.

Though she ruled over them now as she'd always wanted, this purgatory existence had become... not what she'd hoped. She certainly hadn't expected to live out the millennia alone.

"My men have gone everywhere you instructed, Your Majesty." Dagon knelt behind her with his head bowed.

"And a few others just for fun?" She pulled her long coat tighter around her shoulders to combat the chill. Her scarlet dress dripped to the ground, unsullied by the dirt below her. Her hair was bound atop her head in a crown of braids, the enchantment holding it together unaffected by the blustery wind.

"Yes, Your Majesty." Dagon stood, straightening his uniform and folding his hands behind his back.

She lifted her eyes to the sky, watching as it endeavored to rival the dazzling colors of the changing leaves. "Very good, Commander Wraith. What of the people? Where are they being held?"

"We've moved them all to a building in the valley of the Amber Mountains until you decide what to do with them. One of the old vaults. Even if Alexander does return from Celestelvyra, he won't have much of an army willing and able to fight for his cause. Jericho will stand with him, but their numbers are minuscule compared to ours. Your Legion will overtake them easily, especially if you still plan to get the others involved."

"Ah, yes. The others." The Queen stretched out her arm, letting her fingertips dance along the shimmering black wall at her side. It pushed back, creating ripples in the barrier. Dagon took a step away from the wall, watching from the corner of his eye as the Queen cooed, "Patience, my loves. All good things come to those who wait."

CHAPTER 25

HOPEFUL PRAYERS

Upon waking the following morning, the company in the Grim Wilds packed up their belongings and changed into warmer clothing. Like Isolde, everyone in Griffin's clan had heard about barrier jumping, but none other than Griffin and Vera had actually performed the feat. Jax and Hector explained with confidence that if they kept the Prison of the Strayed in their thoughts, they would all exit the barrier at the same location.

After mounting their rides, they crossed through, stepping out the other side along the eastern barrier of Crystavium. Those new to the practice reacted to the black walls at their back the way most did when seeing them for the first time. Jovan bravely put his hand against the glittering wall, releasing sounds of excitement that he'd survived the task. Kwame gave the wall a wide berth the moment he'd made it through and refused to move any closer, even when the group noted that the discoloring on the ground against the border was just as bad there as it had been in Cordillera.

Permafrost engulfed the outer fringes of Crystavium. In the frozen soil, wild grasses and vegetation grew, long ago adapting to the bitter temperatures of the tundra. The closer one traveled to the center of the territory, the lower the temperatures plummeted, turning the ground into a barren wilderness under ceaseless cover of ice and snow.

Deep in the snowy mountains, a handful of sporadic, indigenous tribes made their homes in igloos and naturally occurring ice caves, but most citizens of Crystavium remained on the outskirts where the permafrost lay.

Caribou, reindeer, lycanox, and grizzlies were but a few examples of wildlife making their homes in the permafrost, and wolves, foxes, and polar bears braved the arctic. Hares and lepennas, snowy owls and other birds, oxen and vuokaras, and a variety of rodents lived throughout the entire territory.

Despite its extensive wildlife, hunting was a challenge for those unaccustomed to the territory. The animals knew well how to hide and even better how to flee when discovered. The team hoped they wouldn't need to hunt at all while there, and if everything went to plan, they should have plenty of food to make it to the prison and back without needing to.

Now feeling the intensity of the cold, everyone added extra layers to their clothing. Orion wore the coat and other cold-weather clothing Isolde had given him before they'd left for Jericho, and Isolde had made sure her brethren brought along appropriate attire to survive the low temperatures.

When everyone felt comfortable and ready to move forward, they raced off together into the depths of the icy desert, with Jax and Hector leading the way.

C

After spending the day traversing the wonders of the garden, Foxx, Iris, Asher, and Seth returned to their home away from home by the waterfall and sat in a circle eating the spoils gathered on their return trip. The surrounding area grew dim as night approached, and a sky smattered in purples and greens and sprinkled with stars adorned the garden from high above.

"How are we supposed to find this fountain?" Iris popped delicious, lime-colored grapes into her mouth. "We've been searching nearly two weeks, but if Celestelvyra is limitless, as you believe it is, we could search for years and never find it."

"Maybe you should ask Elohim." Asher looked at Foxx before biting into a plump berry he didn't know how to name. Pulling off their stems, he bit them in half with his front teeth to remove the pit. Squirrels hovered nearby, watching as he set the pits down at his side in a pile.

"Why me?" Foxx peeled skin from a banana. "You're the Prince He sent on this mission. You ask Him."

Asher set another pit on the pile as a brave squirrel scurried up to him, standing on its hind legs and looking at him curiously. "Because He already speaks to you directly." He kept his eyes on the squirrel, and when it gestured to the pile of scraps, he told it to go ahead, prompting the creature to jolt with excitement. Turning around, it squeaked at the other squirrels on the edge of the field, and they all rushed over, collecting every single pit Asher had discarded. The humans watched the squirrels with fascination, feeling they'd never get used to the atypical behavior of the wildlife in Celestelvyra.

As the squirrels departed with their seeds, Iris refocused. "The Creator speaks to you, Foxx?"

Foxx stared at the ground in deep contemplation and avoidance, and Asher stared at her. Then he said, "He comes to her as the bighorn Ram."

"The Creator of Arkaemor is a bighorn ram?" Seth felt as baffled as Iris.

Asher shook his head. "He's not actually a ram. His form is infinite and can be whatever He chooses it to be, but He portrayed himself as a white, bighorn Ram to Foxx, both in her visions and here in the garden. I met Him, too."

"No way! I want to see Him!"

Iris said, "You mentioned a ram before. After the storm in Metsa Sateen."

Foxx nodded. "I saw Him a few nights ago. He's the reason I found the meadow. He led me there."

"Ask Him, then. Ask where the fountain is because my feet hurt from all this walking." Seth pulled his shoes off and massaged his stockinged toes as if to emphasize his point.

"But I don't know how to reach out to Him. He always comes to me." In fact, Foxx had spent days in the meadow hoping He would return, and He never had.

"He's with you all the time, remember?" Asher lifted her chin with two fingers. "Not only here, but out in the world, too. When He spoke to you after the storm, it was to comfort you, to assure you He was with you even after what Sirena did. So just talk to Him. He will hear you."

"Out loud?" she asked, feeling tense with nervousness.

Asher shrugged. "I'm not sure it matters. Sometimes I talk to Him out loud, sometimes I don't. He is the Creator, magnificent and above all, but He's a physical and emotional entity too, just like me and you."

Closing her eyes, Foxx took a few deep breaths, apprehensive about what she should say and also feeling a little silly. Finally, she thought, *Elohim, if You're listening, we need to find the fountain to fix everything. I think. I'm not really sure if it's what You wanted or intended for Your world, but Alexander seems fairly certain this is the right path. So if You do want this, want us to take down Sirena, I mean, would You lead us to the fountain?*

She waited a long moment before adding, *Please?* Then she opened her eyes to find everyone staring at her.

"Did you do it?" Seth asked, enthralled. "The wind got all weird for a few seconds."

"Did it?" Foxx hadn't realized a change in atmosphere. She looked around to find evidence of Seth's claim, but aside from the growing group of squirrels along the treeline, everything seemed as it had before she'd closed her eyes. "I asked Him."

"Did He answer? I think He breathed on us or something with all that wind. Maybe He was sighing."

Iris suppressed a giggle at Seth's overall adorableness, and Foxx shrugged, returning to her detailed inspection of her fingers. Her cheeks flushed crimson as she replayed her words over and over again in her head, wondering if it were truly possible He might have heard her.

"Give it time." Asher leaned back on his hands and stretched out his legs. The newly arrived squirrels scurried over and scooped up the remaining pits before rushing off again.

"I'm ready to bathe and go to bed." Iris yawned and stretched her arms above her head.

"Me too," Foxx agreed.

"Do I have to take a bath?" Seth asked, clearly hoping the answer was *no*.

"You can wait until you wake up." Iris' words provoked a wide, mischievous grin, as if he'd just swindled them with his amazing negotiating skills.

He stood and gave each of them a hug before curling up onto his bedroll. "Merry night, everyone." Looking up into the starry sky, he cooed, "Merry night, Mr. Bighorn Creator."

Iris smiled, watching him. "Gosh, I love that kid."

Asher agreed. "He's a good lad. Strong. Stronger than he thinks."

Foxx said, "He really is. I'm glad we decided to bring him along."

Iris' eyes grew wide. "What was that? You're glad he's here? Weren't you the one voting against it?" Her mocking grin brightened Foxx's mood.

"I'm not happy he witnessed all the death in the swamp." Foxx quivered as the images flashed through her mind. "But yes, I am pleased to have him with us now. He adds a bit of sunshine to the group, I think."

"I thought I was the sunshine of the group?" Iris huffed, scrunching her nose. Seth giggled from his bedroll.

Foxx rolled her eyes, then realized her thoughts of the swamp triggered a memory they hadn't yet unpacked. Looking at Asher, she asked, "How are you feeling about what Sirena told you? About —" She paused, wanting to soften the blow with words that didn't exist. "Not being your mother."

She wondered if he and Iris had already discussed it. They'd spent quite a lot of time together since arriving in the garden. Though Foxx had felt a tinge of jealousy regarding their bond before, she found no residual pain in her stomach at the notion. In fact, she hoped they'd leaned on each other when she'd failed to be there for either of them.

In that moment, she vowed to handle things differently from then on. She'd had her time to grieve and hide, and maybe when things settled, she could take more time to be sad. Until then, she needed to get it together. Not just for them, but for herself as well.

C

"Oh, that?" It was now Asher's turn to examine the lines and crevices of his hands as he considered Foxx's change in topic. After a long moment, he ran them through his hair. "Honestly? I'm still trying to decide whether or not it's a relief."

"Was she ever motherly to you?" Iris asked.

"Not often, no." He thought of the few times in his childhood when Sirena had behaved as a mother should. Some days they would walk around the massive gardens behind the castle, hand in hand. She'd point out all the different flowers planted there, naming them and sharing details she knew about them. He realized with a mixture of sadness and regret that he'd mirrored her actions when he pointed things out to others, teaching them the names for all the plants and animals they came across both in the Metsa and in the garden.

So many learned behaviors are collected in the span of a lifetime, often without notice of it happening. He tried to think of what else he'd learned from her: how to command those who were below him —and how not to; how to dress in such a way that would give the impression he desired; schmooze others into doing whatever he wished; present himself as a prince to the castle Watchmen and servants, the other royals, and the world.

Though he complied to these standards at a young age, as he grew older, he often chose to disobey rules of propriety in favor of acting out, breaking hearts, and running his mouth. Whatever he could do to anger his mother.

Not his mother—Queen Sirena.

Letting his mind wander, he thought about the other rulers: Dante and Serafina Valentino and the Raja Decha Narong. Governor Campana of Sal, Governor Malik Kane in Lior Leryn, Alta Herba's Chieftain Sarpong, and Naaba Kaatachi of Caritas. Those were only a few examples of ruling powers who may stand against him for ownership of the Thrones.

He wondered which side, if any, those rulers might choose to stand on when the final battle began. Would they take up arms with the runaway Prince, the defector commander, and the Mad King, or would they stick with history and side with the King and Queen reigning from the Hall of Sunsets?

Thoughts of the castle brought with them thoughts of Avaline. He realized for the first time that she too was not a true daughter of Sirena and that he would most likely be the one to break the news. He wondered how she might be doing and whether or not she was being properly taken care of in his absence.

The night Asher left Castle Solís, he'd stopped by her room to say farewell. She hadn't risen from her bed in days, sleeping mostly or laying awake staring at the designs carved into the plaster above her bed. He carried a small torch in one hand as he entered her room and closed the door behind him. The noise roused her, and she turned to look at him.

Sitting next to her on the bed, he said, *Avaline, Avaline, where have you been? Have you been hiding in the garden again?* To which she used to reply, *Alexander, Alexander, surely you see. There's no other place I would rather be.*

He'd made up the rhyme one day during a game of hide-and-seek in the gardens. She'd responded without missing a beat, and from then on, it became their special saying. When Sirena was being horrible and their father oblivious, they would sing the rhyme to each other, both picturing happier times when they'd played together in the garden.

Asher had ten years on Avaline, but from the second he met her, he thought her the most precious thing he'd ever laid eyes on and vowed to protect her forever. He'd since broken that vow many, many times. He'd broken it that night, sitting on the bed and waiting for her to respond with those special words before he left her alone to begin his fated destiny.

Avaline never did respond. Instead, she looked at him with open eyes, but he could tell her spirit wasn't alive within them. It was off somewhere in a garden of her own making, he hoped. He kissed her on the forehead and whispered, "I have to leave, Ava, but I swear on my life, I will come back for you." He waited to see if she would respond, but she continued to stare. Sometimes, he thought she definitely recognized him, but others, like in that moment, she appeared not to have a single clue who sat before her. "I love you," he'd said, and he thought the corner of her lips lifted slightly, but he couldn't be sure.

"Are you mad?" Foxx's question jarred him abruptly from his internal reminisce.

"At least now you don't have to murder your mother," Iris said.

"You're right Iris. Someone already did that." He didn't mean for the words to sound aggressive, but they had, and Iris winced.

"I'm sorry. I should have thought before speaking."

"It's fine." Sitting up, he crossed his legs. "I'm fine. I don't have a mother. You don't have a mother or a father. It doesn't really seem fair to complain to you."

Iris eyed him skeptically, and he knew she was thinking about how they'd already discussed this particular cop-out. Before she could contradict him with the same words she'd used before, Foxx spoke.

"Hey, of course you can. Our loss doesn't render your loss invalid. We are all in this together, remember?"

It pleased him to see her smiling at him again, smiling like she might love him, even if she hadn't said so. Her words echoed back in his head. *You won my heart also, foolish prince.*

"Together," he agreed, taking hold of her hand and sending a flush of heat through her limbs. "I still need to work through the stuff regarding my mother. You're not wrong, Iris. I was concerned about how it would feel to kill Sirena when I thought she was my mother, but truthfully, it will likely still be difficult. Even if she didn't birth me, she was my mother for twenty-eight years. A perfectly horrid mother, but still, she was mine."

"Maybe it doesn't have to be you," Foxx said. "Maybe I—"

Asher interrupted before she could finish. "The prophecy makes it pretty clear it's supposed to be the Prince, and I wouldn't let you take my place in such an incredibly dangerous situation anyway." He tried to soften his hard tone by forcing a smile. "So thank you, but no. It has to be me."

C

Foxxglove went to sleep that night hoping for and anticipating another visit from the Ram. Upon waking the following morning, she felt disappointed that her prayers to the Creator hadn't worked as Asher thought. He encouraged her again to have patience, insisting not everything would happen as quickly as they wanted it to. Elohim had a plan, and He would bring it to fruition when He was ready, in His own divine time.

They spent the next two days continuing to explore parts of the garden they'd yet to venture, utilizing Iris' map to ensure they covered as much ground as possible. Foxx thought it was feasible the Creator would lead them to the fountain a different way, rather than a dream or a vision as He had in the past. Asher continued to embolden her to have faith in the Creator's will. When it was time for them to find it, they would.

Over dinner the second evening, Foxx declared she wasn't going to think about finding it anymore. In fact, she told them, they shouldn't even look for the fountain the next day. They should hang out by the pond, wash their clothing, read together from *Jumalan Sana*, and relax. The others agreed to this proposal and went to sleep that evening prepared for a day of chores and relaxation.

C

The group rode for three days before reaching the outskirts of the land holding the Ashgate Fortress, located in the outer region of the territory's glacial center. The Prison of the Strayed rested within a valley surrounded by hills and mountains on all sides. This far into the territory, the ground was spotted with large patches of ice and snow, but pockets of avocado-, jasper-, and mustard-tinted shrubs endured, dotting the landscape and fighting the frost with persistence.

While the others set up the campsite, Orion, Hector, Jax, and Griffin went to run surveillance on the fringes of the prison. A monumental wall surrounded the building, exactly as Jax had described: huge rocks cemented together, at least a *syli* thick and stacked twenty feet high, and topped with massive, savage-looking spikes. Facing west, they could see the entirety of the front wall and the entrance gate, as well as three lookout towers: one on both the southeastern and northeastern corners and a third stationed to the left of the obsidian entrance, all nesting high above the wall.

"You three will enter through there," Jax said to Orion, motioning toward the cast iron bars.

Orion thought the extravagant designs of the iron gate seemed out of place for the entrance to a prison and wondered if they might be the ones used by the original Monastery. The others he'd seen hadn't been gated, but it was plausible they'd sought extra protection with this one existing so close to Sirena's territory.

"When you approach the gate, lift your faces to the guard tower, and they will let you through," Jax continued.

"Hopefully." Hector crouched lower to become more thoroughly hidden behind the hill they spied from. His obvious discomfort made Orion feel even more uneasy. Hector, like Jax, knew what lay beyond those gates.

Orion wasn't looking forward to finding out. "Is there a chance they won't?"

"You will be unknown faces." Jax shrugged. "The guards don't know every single person who comes and goes from the prison, but they do know many."

"They know me." Hector shivered and pulled his scarf tighter.

Jax said, "You were the commander of the King's Legion. They risked beheading by not knowing you. Or worse. But you'll be in uniform, Orion, so I am fairly certain you'll be safe."

"Wonderful." Orion's sigh dulled his sarcasm. He glanced sideways at Griffin, who seemed to be scrutinizing Hector, likely weighing what Jax had said against the man he had witnessed over the last few days.

"Once you're in, the Abrafo and his team will proceed to the wall with their rebels." Jax looked to Griffin who nodded in return. "Hector, Isolde, and I will be traveling through the back. See that river?" He pointed to the left of the outer wall, far off in the distance from where they crouched. "That feeds the entire prison as its primary water source. There's a well on the northern side, but it's not reliable. The river is always flowing. We'll follow the water until we reach the wall, then we'll be swimming."

"It's going to be freezing." With a spark of concern, Orion wondered how Isolde's body, so accustomed to the heat of the desert, would handle the harsh, icy water.

"It's going to be awful," Hector agreed.

"I have to be honest. I'm not feeling as confident in our ability to pull this off as I was before."

Griffin grunted, and Orion supposed the warrior thought him a coward for saying so, but he wouldn't be going beyond the walls, so he didn't really have a right to an opinion. He also suspected Griffin hoped he would perish inside so Isolde would be free of him, but he kept those thoughts to himself.

"I think we can universally agree that our chances are slim," Hector said, and Jax gestured his agreement.

Orion brushed his hands together. "Let's head back. I want to go over the plan one more time and get some sleep. Tomorrow we're on watch to abduct some guards. Then it's go time."

C

They built a fire atop a patch of solid dirt for everyone to huddle around and keep warm. Personal space seemed to fade off into the distance as the desire not to freeze to death overrode propriety. Thirteen people not being a small party, the circle was wide but smooshed.

Orion shouldn't have been surprised when Isolde managed to squeeze in between him and her brother. He'd only been momentarily perplexed when Griffin sat down next to him before realizing his intention had been to prevent this very thing. In Griffin's aversion to Orion, he had not sat close enough to dissuade his sister.

By a stroke of luck or blessing, the wind was minimal, even as the darkness consumed the landscape. Jax went over the plan in minute to minute increments, hoping to engrain it into everyone's mind so nothing would go wrong. As long as they all confidently portrayed their belonging there, no one should suspect incursion, and they should be able to get in and out without issue.

After the planning discussion subsided, the group grew quiet. Staring into the fire, they sat in silence for a long while. Eventually, Vera and Leone laid down to sleep. Kwame, Johnathan, and Jax went to bed soon after, followed by Declan.

Isolde and Griffin, Orion, Hector and Raven, and Jovan, remained alert, unable to shut their brains off and let sleep take them.

Isolde laid on her back, staring wide awake into the starlit sky. Griffin leaned back on his hands looking up at the stars alongside her. They whispered to each other, pointing out constellations as they spotted them. Orion listened to their banter, not catching all the words spoken but content hearing them interact.

After a while, Isolde asked her brother a question the others didn't hear, and Griffin sighed heavily before sitting up straighter and shaking his head.

Orion glanced between them, discovering a look of victory in Isolde's expression. Then to his unimaginable bewilderment, Griffin began humming a deep and melancholic tune. Isolde's smile broadened, and the others around the fire were drawn to the saturnine and beautifully gloomy words rising from low in his chest.

Long ago in the days of old,
Prophets sang of whispers told.
Their tales foresee a navi soul,
Precious, lost, and white as snow

As Griffin's voice faded into silence, Isolde rested her hand on his knee and smiled up at the sky. The others lingered in the quiet, reflecting on the eerie words the warrior had sung.

Breaking the ominous foreboding, Jovan said, "You had to choose the *Navi's Foretold?* Could you not think of a more inspiring tune to serenade us on the eve of facing such a foe?"

Orion's mouth dropped open. He felt certain the boy would receive a rebuke for speaking so disrespectfully, especially in front of strangers, but yet again, the Abrafo's response left him dumbfounded.

With a big smile that showed his teeth, Griffin chided, "Next time, you shall entertain us, Jovan. I have heard Leone say you have an exceptional knack for storytelling."

Jovan's eyes widened as though in offense and everyone remained silent. Hector grinned, looking back and forth between the gruff Nabiiga and his young comrade. Jovan was slim, almost gangly, with the underdeveloped muscles of a boy in his late teens. He was barely a third Griffin's size in weight and nearly a head shorter, making it entirely possible for him to be crushed within the massive muscles of his Abrafo.

It occurred to Orion as he observed them that Griffin had chosen this young man to be part of his clan. Of the whole village, he'd brought five warriors alongside him, and Jovan had been one of them. Unless there was something really special about the wiry warrior that remained unseen, he thought this must be an indicator of a deeper level to the beastly man's character.

After far too long, Jovan put a hand on his forehead. "Leone hates my stories. She says I could not entertain a toddler." This sent a spark of laughter through the group, and when Griffin bellowed heartily, sounding so much like his jolly father and so far from the grumpy man he usually displayed, Orion couldn't help but laugh harder.

Isolde said, "I love your stories, Jovan! Leone is only teasing you."

Jovan shook his head, thin eyebrows still raised high. "I really do not think she is. She does not have your youthful humor, Iso." Griffin squeezed his sister's hand, his smile widening in agreement.

Silence fell amongst them. Jovan added another log to the fire, and Griffin pressed a kiss to Isolde's forehead before laying down with the others. For a long while, Orion joined Isolde in gazing up at the stars, though he made no attempt to converse with her about them.

Then Hector shattered the stillness with Orion's name. "If you don't mind discussing it, I'm curious about something. Feel free to decline if you wish."

"Go ahead." Orion straightened his spine and scooted closer to the fire, longing for its warmth as a new chill washed over him.

"I was wondering… where were you? From the time you were taken from Jericho and when you woke up in the In-Between?"

All eyes veered to Orion, including Isolde's, who sat up to listen. She didn't move closer, even though sharing body heat would have warmed them both. In defiance of their distance, heat radiated into his skin where just the tip of her knee rested against his leg. Looking around at the expressions surveying him with curiosity, he hesitated. Then he aimed his gaze at the fire to avoid making eye contact with anyone directly, cleared his throat, and stuttered, "As I told you before. I was… with the Queen. Sirena."

Jovan's eyes widened in disbelief. "Why were you?"

"I believe she had me held in the dungeons below the castle, though my recollections of it are spotty at best. She must have spelled me when we traveled, because I have no memory at all of getting there in the first place or of getting from there to the In-Between." This still troubled him, mainly because he didn't care for the idea of things happening to him when he was unconscious.

He'd traveled from one side of the world to the other without a clue as to how he'd even been taken from Jericho to begin with. He'd been running the streets looking for Iris and Foxx, and then... nothing. "And my time in the dungeons is almost entirely cloaked in darkness."

"I suspected as much," Hector said. "I'd wager that was not a pleasant experience."

Orion shook his head, unable to put thoughts to words. He focused on the fire's flames, watching them lick the air as they danced, swayed, and popped. Then he noted how they cast varying hues of amber on the eclectic skin tones surrounding them.

Isolde's said, "When he came to us, cuts and bruises littered his body. Many more than are visible now. I am from a tribe of fierce warriors, and even I have never seen such a thorough display of wounds."

Orion glanced at her from the corner of his eye, teetering between feeling angry for the divulged information and thankful he hadn't needed to relay it himself.

"She tortured you?" Jovan asked.

"She's still torturing me," Orion admitted, surprising Isolde into stillness beside him. Again his eyes slid to her, this time latching onto the shimmer of her golden irises, and she encouraged him with a smile. Emphasizing his distaste of the directive when he spoke the word, he said, "Isolde *instructed* me to inform someone on my team tomorrow what has been happening." He looked at Raven, as she was the only one in attendance who would be venturing into Ashgate alongside him. Raven lifted her head from Hector's shoulder and scrutinized Orion with a calculating expression. "I planned on telling Declan, the obvious choice considering our mutual loathing for one another." He gestured between the two of them, and Raven grinned.

"That's accurate."

"But he's still mildly injured, and I know he will be worrying about Iris." This was partially true, though Orion knew Declan could separate his emotions from the dangers at hand. He'd often thought clearly and reacted calmly in intense situations.

Except when it came to Orion.

For reasons unknown to him, Declan seemed to have a soft spot for his arduous friend. "The truth is, he isn't always as firm with me as he should be. A fact I've no doubt taken advantage of in the past, but also one that could be detrimental to the mission in case something happens." He sighed, hating unveiling his weakness in front of Hector and Raven. But if he stepped into that prison and messed anything up, he needed someone he could trust to set things straight and put the team and the operation above their emotions and loyalties. "All that to say, I think it's smartest, though unfortunate for both of us, that I lay this burden on you."

Raven didn't speak but continued to watch him, waiting to hear what he would request.

As he fumbled for the words to explain exactly what was happening, the whispers, already playing in the far reaches of his mind, crept to the surface in ghostly tendrils, drowning out the constant dripping. He closed his eyes, willing them to cease so he could continue. At his appeal, they dulled slightly but refused to dissipate completely. "She's in my head." Feeling like he may be talking too loud over the whispers, he lowered his voice. "I hear her, sometimes very loud, like waves of whispers in my ears accompanied by a constant dripping. The dripping from the water in the cell where she kept me."

"Is she communicating with you from a distance, in the present?" Hector asked.

"I don't think so." Orion was thankful the darkness and the fire masked evidence of his embarrassment. He knew it would seem less insane if she truly was speaking to him from afar, but it would also elevate the risks of their mission and leave them exposed if she had access to his thoughts and, as a result, their plans and location. "I think she really messed me up. Like I'm going mad or something."

"Thank you for sharing this with us." Isolde's words flowed like warm honey and blocked out the whispers. As she rested her hand on his knee, he exhaled a breath he hadn't felt trapped in his lungs.

"What do you need from me?" Raven asked with sincerity he'd never heard her direct his way.

"Hopefully nothing. I just wanted someone to be aware of the situation. Just in case." He felt his jaw clench as his teeth chattered involuntarily, whether from the bitter cold or inflamed nerves, he didn't know. "If something happens, try to break me out of it. If you can't—and this is truly why I am telling you and not Declan—I need you to knock me out and leave me behind."

"Declan would never allow such a sacrifice."

Orion looked her dead in the eyes with all the sternness he could muster. "I know. And you know me well enough to understand I'm much too selfish to ask you to leave me behind unless it was absolutely necessary." He felt a flush of warmth at his divulgence in front of Isolde. She knew a different side of him than the one the Legion had known. A better version that he someday hoped to be. Clearing his throat, he finished, "But should the worst happen, I'm going to need you to knock him out too, and drag him along with you."

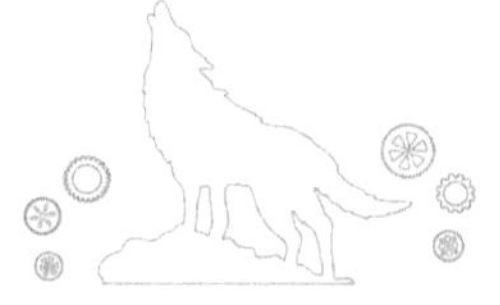

CHAPTER 26

NIGHTMARES AND DREAMLAND

As Foxx strolled through the garden in a shirt too big for her body, bare feet wicked dew from the morning grass. Buttons ran up the front, holding the shirt together, and as her fingers grazed them, she looked down at the strange attire, trying to recall how it had come to be. Upon closer examination, she fought to imagine how she'd come to be in such a state at all. Her knees brushed together, bare like her feet, and a tug at her hair had her hand rising to discover the source of the pull. Flummoxed, she felt something metal encircling it and yanked the object from its resting place. Holding it out, her suspicions were confirmed: it was a crown with a Jerichonian moon at its center, sunbeams shining from the moon, and roses embellishing both sides.

Her heart thudded, and her stomach felt sick. She couldn't fathom why she would be wearing a crown, especially one that looked so different from the thin circlet she'd seen Alexander wearing in her vision. It wasn't even gold, as his had been—but silver.

Though mystified by the discovery, Foxx pressed on, placing the crown back on her head and taking in the scenery. If she wanted to figure out what was happening, she needed to pay attention to things other than her ludicrous wardrobe choices.

The dimness of the garden revealed the time of day to be the very early hours of the morning. Foxx continued to walk, though she didn't know the purpose of her journey or her intended destination. In fact, she couldn't even recall when she'd begun venturing in the first place. It made sense to think the others must still be sleeping if she was heading out on her own, but she didn't know for sure. She peered over her shoulder, wondering if Alexander would materialize as he often seemed to do, but the trail behind her remained empty—a blessing, she thought, since she currently wore a crown and no pants.

She followed the path away from the wildflower meadow to the base of the mountain above the waterfall where she and Alexander had kissed. A flutter in her stomach as the memory replayed had her cheeks flushing. Lifting her hands to hide them despite her lack of witnesses, she found her fingers ice cold. She pulled them away from her face to examine them and saw frost crystalizing on her fingertips.

Frowning, she tried to wipe them on the grass, but rather than flaking off, ice spread across the blades.

Jumping back, she stood and clutched her hands together, trying to warm them. The ice spread up her hand to her wrist and halfway up her forearm. "Stop!" she cried, and the ice melted. For the second time, she looked back to see if anyone had witnessed these peculiarities, but again, she was alone.

To her left, a stream rolled from a cave beneath the mountain. Foxx stopped next to it and crouched on the bank to observe the water. Hills of white foam bubbled up around the cave's edges as the water poured over rocks and ridges.

For reasons unknown to her, she felt certain she should follow the stream, and so she did. She walked along the water's edge, enjoying the view of the miniature falls scattered throughout the rushing waterway. The stream didn't have verdant pads topped with ombré lotus flowers like the pond where they'd made camp but instead was littered with fuchsia petals falling from a dogwood tree in full bloom on the opposite bank.

As she walked, she noticed the world slipping by faster than her feet treaded the earth and thought it strange. She'd never known time to be a fluid substance, to move of its own free will at whatever speed it chose, but it seemed she was mistaken. The garden around her began to blur as she wandered, as if she were flying, though her feet remained firmly planted in the cool grass.

Suddenly, it all stopped, returning again to its usual speed, and she realized she'd reached the end of the stream. In front of her, a building of sorts rose from the earth. Similar to the one that had led them into Celestelvyra, the outer wall was made of mossy and aged bricks, though this building had no door. Instead, the stream slipped under an archway, spectacularly decorated with carvings of suns and moons and stars. She approached the building and found a footpath on either side of the stream traveling beneath the archway. Moving toward it, she reached her hand out to caress the carvings in the damp stone.

Then she sat up in a rush, awakened by an unknown disturbance, to find Seth sleeping to her right and Alexander laying on her left staring at her with an impish grin.

"He spoke to you, didn't He?"

Foxx shook her head, rattling away lingering sleepiness and trying to get her bearings. She thought she'd been walking along a bubbling stream, so how had she gotten back to the waterfall? Her consciousness crisping into focus, it occurred to her that she must have been dreaming.

Glancing down at her attire in a panic, she found she no longer wore the baggy, button-down shirt, and she did, in fact, have on pants. A sigh of relief passed through her lips until she remembered the ornament adorning her head, and her hand flew up to check it. When she found it empty, she sighed again. Asher watched her odd behavior with obvious fascination.

At last, she lifted her eyes to him, only to discover with absolute mortification that in her dream, she'd been wearing the shirt currently covering his torso. Her cheeks flushed and her fingers rose to hide the blush.

Asher sat up on his elbow, riveted. "What? What's happened?"

Thinking she needed to get it together before she made an even bigger fool of herself, she finger-combed her hair away from her face, making sure no strays flew free and looked ridiculous. "No, He didn't, but He did send a message. I think He showed me where it is."

Asher's eyes sparkled with eagerness as he gestured to Iris and Seth. "Should we wake them?"

"No, let them sleep." She laid back on her side, facing him with her hands tucked under her cheek. He did the same, his lips revealing charged delight. "They will be up soon, and then we can go."

Asher nodded and extended his arm between them, letting it

rest in the grass. She removed one hand from beneath her cheek and placed it next to his, grazing his pinky with her own. He slid his hand closer, playing with her fingertips. "You're cold." Tucking her hand into his, he pulled it up to his lips so he could breathe warmth onto her fingers.

"Not really. Just my fingers."

"Too bad." He grinned mischievously and blew on her fingers again, keeping his eyes on her. Her cheeks grew even more heated, but she didn't look away. When he felt he'd warmed them sufficiently, he let their hands come to rest in the grass between them. "Did He show you anything else besides the location?"

Her cheeks flushed yet again as she answered quickly, "Nothing of consequence."

Asher chuckled. "Are you still sleepy or are you ready to get up? Do you want to go somewhere?"

"Where?"

"Anywhere you like."

Foxx glanced back at Iris and Seth before sitting up. "Okay. We can go somewhere."

When they rose, Asher took her hand and led her to the path between the honeysuckles. They moved in silence, with her trailing behind him and doing her best to quell the butterflies erupting in her stomach as they strode alone into the forest.

Last time they'd been alone, she'd thrown herself against him in an absolutely unexpected and embarrassing display of passion. Her mind hadn't stopped replaying the memory of their time together above the falls, reciting words that left her stomach in a constant state of turbulent bliss.

I want it all, Foxx. All of you. Every broken piece.

Her palms began to sweat, and she tried to loose her fingers from his, but he clutched her tighter, glancing back at her with a knowing smile.

The trail opened to a flower garden of dahlias, roses, and giant peony blooms, and the display distracted Foxx from flustering thoughts. "It's beautiful here." She leaned to sniff a peony. Asher nodded, smiling as he watched her enjoying the blossoms. Sticks snapped in the distance, drawing their attention past the garden to the woods surrounding them, though whatever creature had made the noise remained out of sight.

"You're so quiet," she observed, tugging his hand so he would turn to her.

"I'm just taking it all in." His smile radiated like sunshine as he pulled her closer. His fingers fiddled with hers in the space between them.

Since their moment above the falls, they hadn't kissed more than a swift peck on the cheek. Shy eyes left his to follow a pair of bumblebees harvesting pollen from the flowers.

After a quick glance his way, she stepped around him and continued down the path without releasing his hand. He happily followed after her. A few steps later, she paused to smell another bloom, and he stopped behind her with a hand on her hip. Her skin burned where his fingers rested against her, but she kept her eyes trained on the flowers.

"You seem happy today," he said.

"Do I?" She pinched a leaf between her fingers, feeling its texture. The dahlia leaves had zig-zagged edges.

Asher hummed.

"Well, I suppose I am happy. Happier than I've been, at least."

When they reached the wide oak centered between the two rows of bushes, he turned his back to it and pulled her against him. Foxx giggled as she all but stumbled into his arms. The warmth of his body had her heart rate elevating. Her knee had fallen between his legs, and her chest pressed against his.

"Might I take some credit for that?" he asked. "That gorgeous smile and those glowing cheeks?" Her eyes flitted away, though her smile widened despite her efforts to keep it restrained. Asher chuckled and the sound drew her gaze back to him. "Merry morning, love." He pushed hair away from her face and pulled her closer until their lips lingered inches apart. "I've been wanting to do this every moment since we returned from atop the falls."

Her body shivered with heat as her hand rose to his chest. Her heart raced as if she'd been trying to outrun a bear. In a way, giving in to these feelings was far scarier than a hungry mammal. She'd killed bears, but there was little she could do to slaughter the emotions currently pouring from her heart. "Then why haven't you?"

He nudged her nose with his own. Playful, teasing. "I guess I wanted to make sure."

Foxx drew her head back. "Make sure?"

He kissed her cheek. "I know this is a lot. I know part of you is still angry. I just didn't want to push you."

She frowned. "I'm not some delicate blossom that needs protecting, Alexander."

Grinning, he said, "Okay then." He grasped her hips and shifted her against him. Foxx gasped in surprise. "I'll take whatever I please, and I won't worry at all about offending your delicate sensibilities." He kissed her top lip before pinching the bottom between his teeth. Then his hands gripped her tighter as he claimed her mouth with his own.

Foxx's hand rose to his hair, pulling him closer with every breath. Waves of bliss like nothing she'd ever felt washed over her, and for a brief moment she truly wondered how she might ever stop kissing him. It was like moonlight and dancing and bursts of shooting stars. Like the rain on her skin and the wind in her hair and the taste of fruit on her tongue. She rose to her tiptoes, longing to press every inch of her body against his.

She'd been so shocked before. Too overwhelmed to fully appreciate the sensations coursing through her in response to his touch. Now she felt each caress with every fiber of her being. His fingertips grazing the skin beneath her shirt, his breath on her neck, his lips as they nibbled her ear. She wanted to commit each and every new spark to memory so she could revisit them for the rest of time.

After a long and passionate embrace, his fire settled, his lips slowing into a gentle hum.

As conscious thoughts returned, Foxx fought to catch her breath, though her inhale only served to trigger more feverish zest as she breathed him in. His pine scent mixed with the smell of roses, and she drank it in like the most perfectly delicious flavor she'd ever tasted.

She decided then it was her new favorite scent—pine trees and roses. The perfect blend, a composition arranged just for her.

His voice drew her attention back to his eyes. "The others will be up soon. Maybe we should head back?"

Foxx shook her head and leaned into him, turning so her cheek came to rest against his shoulder. "Not yet."

Asher chuckled and clasped his hands together behind her back before pressing a kiss to her forehead. "Okay, love. We can stay as long as you like."

$$C$$

Orion was eight years old when his mother first got sick. His father, a fully devoted follower of the Monastery of the Morrow, was adamant she would recover in time. He'd followed the Monastery since childhood and believed faithfully in their gracious and powerful Creator.

Even as a child, Orion had no heart for fantasies and fairytales, and his father's obsessive ramblings about the Monastery annoyed him to no end. When his mother became ill, Orion was not foolish enough to believe she would magically heal. He saw the reality of the situation better than his fanatically blinded father, even at such a young age.

For two years, his mother grew sicker and sicker. Eventually her body began rejecting food, and she wasted away. When she could no longer keep even water down, Orion knew she had but days.

They lived in the western most territory of Reginaterra, though their tiny cottage in the woods was nowhere near the royal city of Inaravale. It was further south, roughly an hour on foot outside the village of Sylva. They had a few distant neighbors, farmers mostly, but none close enough to know the ins and outs of their everyday lives. If they'd had closer neighbors, maybe one of them would've pushed his father to see a doctor long before his mother got so bad. They had no other family to speak of, so no one knew the severity of her illness.

And so no one but Orion spoke up.

In his mother's final days, Orion begged his father to call for a doctor, but he refused, insisting Elohim would provide a miracle and make her well again if they just held on a little longer, if they had enough faith.

The day his mother passed into the After, Orion cried harder than he ever had in his life. His father cried, too, unable to fathom the inescapable truth as he buried her under her favorite hydrangea bushes.

The following day, Orion stopped crying. His anger at his father and his father's unreliable Creator ignited a fire of rage in him like he'd never believed possible. He hated his father and his romanticized notions of anything the Monastery of the Morrow represented.

As time went on, it became clear his father abhorred him as well. The man who'd raised Orion with such kindness and patience, albeit misguided at times, changed into something unrecognizable. He swore off Elohim and the Monastery of the Morrow, vowing never again to put his trust in fairytales. In exchange for books and prayers and songs of worship, his father delved into booze and tantrums and violence, with Orion as the sole recipient.

One night after Orion turned sixteen, he came home late from a date with a girl from school. Her name was Lacey Robinson, and she was not only the prettiest girl in all of Sylva and the surrounding area but also the kindest person Orion had ever met. He could not comprehend what she saw in him, but he'd asked her out, and by some miracle, she'd said yes.

Four months into their relationship, Orion felt certain he would marry her. Lacey made him feel things he hadn't known could be felt. She loved him. And he loved her in return.

On nights when his father got himself inebriated beyond all recognition or reason, he would beat Orion. Sometimes with a belt, other times with his fist, and once with a frying pan. Orion did his best to keep the bruises hidden from Lacey, but she was not blind to the pain in his eyes. When he curled into a ball on the ground bracing himself for the lashing to come, he would keep her face in his mind, focusing only on her. He would imagine her smell—like lilacs—hear the tranquility of her voice, and picture the pure bliss on her face, the long, tawny ponytail tied up with a ribbon, her beautiful auburn irises, and he would get through it.

He couldn't help but understand his father's rage and the need for release, and so he forgave him, time and time again. He sympathized with the guilt and shame his father felt knowing he had been the reason his wife had died. If he'd only sought medical help rather than trusting in some distant and absent Creator, she might still be alive. He understood his father's self-loathing, because he felt it himself. If only he hadn't obeyed and had run for help on his own, his mother may have lived.

Orion got into fights in town and at school all the time, taking his anger out on the other boys who picked on him for being poor or not having a mother or whatever else they decided deemed him unworthy of their respect, but never had he fought back when his father abused him.

On the night Orion entered the cottage later than his curfew permitted, his father punished him for his disobedience. For the first time ever, Orion fought back. He let it all out, releasing every bit of the fury and hatred he kept boiling inside of him all those years.

He didn't mean to do it, hadn't planned on engaging in his father's tantrum. He couldn't have known how explosive their brawl would become.

When the sun rose the next day and his father still hadn't woken, he put his ear to his mouth to check for breath that would never come. By then, his skin felt cold to the touch, and Orion knew what he'd done. He'd made himself an orphan, and there was nothing he could do to take it back.

Retrieving a shovel from the shed, Orion buried his father next to his mother beneath the hydrangea bushes. Then he left his home, left his town, and left Lacey Robinson behind forever.

C

Yanked from sleep like a shotgun shell blasted from a barrel, Orion shot straight up. Realizing immediately he couldn't take in a full breath, he gasped for air. He wrapped his hands around his throat to check if something physical was choking him but found nothing. His breath came in short, quick bursts; his eyes burned with the tears spilled in his nightmares; and his body felt inflamed, defying the frigid temperatures of Crystavium as he sweated through his clothes.

Sensing his anxiety, Isolde untangled herself from her blanket and rushed to him. Surveying his face, she realized his plight, and with serenity she alone could summon in the midst of chaos, she said, "Orion, you need to breathe. I know it feels like you cannot, but I need you to try. Do it with me." With exaggerated breaths, she acted out what he needed to do, encouraging him to mirror her actions. One long inhale, hold it, then one long exhale, over and over again. Her words were hypnotic and soothing, but his breathing only grew faster and faster, even as he tried to suppress it.

"Orion!" she yelled in unison with the clap of her hands, attempting to shock him out of his fit. Then she reached for him, pressing her body against his and drawing him into an embrace. Her arms wrapped around his shoulders, squeezing him with fervor. The shockwave of the unexpected action and the sensation of her strong body curling around him stole his air. For a long moment, he was entirely still but for the rapid beating of his heart.

Then he exhaled and inhaled crisp, cold air. Tingling arms shook around her lower back as he held her close. His face fell into the nape of her neck, his tears spilling into her hair as he drank in her wild scent, letting it consume his brainwaves. Slowly, his chest settled into a normal pace, no longer crashing against hers, and his heart stopped thrashing in his eardrums. Even the dripping went silent as they sat with their knees on the ice-cold ground, holding each other.

When she released him, she let her arms rest on his shoulders as she looked into his sapphire eyes. "It was only a dream. Was it her again?"

Shaking his head, he tried to draw words from his raw throat. "A memory. From another life."

"Maybe you will share it with me sometime." She smiled, and he thought someday he actually might, though he didn't say so out loud.

"I hope you don't expect me to do that if you freak out in there." Raven's harsh voice abruptly popped the bubble encasing Orion and Isolde. He yanked his arms away from her, his eyes immediately finding Griffin's scowl.

Isolde let her hands slide to his chest, undeterred by the others and looking only at him. "You are going to be okay, Orion. I believe in you."

"You're about the only one."

"Perhaps it only takes one person's belief to manifest something into existence." With a squeeze to his hand, she returned to her makeshift bed and the warmth of her covers.

Only Raven, Hector, and Griffin had witnessed what took place upon waking, though none spoke a word about it. The others slowly roused into consciousness as the sun stretched its morning rays across the horizon.

Orion avoided any further eye contact with Griffin, seeing no point in confronting the glare continually directed his way. He'd never had a sister, so he didn't entirely understand Griffin's possessiveness. However, he knew there was nothing he could do in this life or the next to ever be worthy of a woman like Isolde. On that, at least, they could agree.

As he reignited the coals from the previous night, his mind drifted to Lacey Robinson. He'd never deserved her, either. Certainly not after everything he'd done. He hoped she was happy, wherever she was, and that she'd found a good man to take care of her and help raise a houseful of kids in the countryside, like she'd always wanted.

Orion would never have that life.

In fact, he fully intended on not surviving the battle to come. He would go out of this world fighting, and there was nothing anyone —not Declan, or Iris, or even Isolde—could do to stop him.

C

Foxx shared the news as soon as Iris and Seth woke up. They dressed quickly, excited to finally have an actual destination to search for. They filled their water skins from the falls and left the clearing, bursting with gleeful energy. Foxxglove led them to the meadow, stopping along the edge to observe its beauty.

"This is where you saw the Ram?" Iris asked. A breeze rustled the wildflowers causing a floral scent to fill their noses.

"Yes." Foxx stepped into the meadow, stopping at the center where she'd found Him. "He stood right here." In unison, her and Asher's eyes drifted off in the direction the Ram had run when He'd departed that day, both hoping for a brief instant that He might materialize from the same spot.

"Cool." Seth looked with amazement at the ground beneath his feet. He took several tentative steps until he reached Foxx, and she rubbed the top of his head.

"Through here." Crossing the meadow, Foxx revealed the path leading to the mountain and the stream. The others followed her, and Iris and Seth snagged a few plums and figs along the way.

When they emerged, they stood in awe at the scene before them. Iris said, "I keep thinking I can't see anything more exquisite than I've already seen, but then I come upon a new place, and it astonishes me."

"I know what you mean," Asher agreed.

Seth looked up the mountain. "Is that how you got to the top of the waterfall?"

"Very smart observation, Seth," Asher praised, and Seth beamed at the compliment.

Foxx led them to the left in the direction of the stream, and Seth stopped to marvel at the dogwood petals fluttering to the water and collecting in clusters along the banks. Then they continued on, following the stream as Foxx had done in her dream. She didn't know how far it would be since she'd traveled so fast in her vision.

When they grew hungry and needed rest, they stopped to eat luncheon, enjoying the melody of the whistling cattails, singing birds, and croaking frogs. A family of dragonflies flew around them, seeming to dance in rhythm with the music the garden composed.

Cerulean lights slipped past them beneath the surface of the water, and Iris sucked in a breath. "Are there nyädi here? I hadn't thought they would exist in the garden."

"Not like the nyädi you know." Asher leaned closer to the water, and Seth followed.

"What kind do you know?" Seth's eyes widened as he watched the lights.

"The kind that hold people at the bottom of the Suola Meri until they drown and then gobble them up!" Iris threw clawed hands in the air, and Seth gasped. Then he fell into a fit of giggles.

Asher said, "Yet another creature corrupted by the darkness. The nyädi here will be like any of the other henki you've seen—helpful and nurturing."

"I wonder why only one kind of henki was corrupted," Foxx said.

Asher shrugged. "Only the ones in the Suola Meri are like that, at least from what I've read. I've swam with them elsewhere and they've been perfectly kind."

"Once we find the fountain, what is the next step of our plan to get free of this place?" Iris cut into her papaya with Thorn, the smallest of her sister blades.

"Maybe Foxxglove can ask again." Seth gazed eagerly at the papaya in Iris' hands.

"Let's just figure out one thing at a time." Asher looked at Foxx, and when their eyes met, she smiled at him, grateful he seemed to understand the war waging within her. She wanted to stay in the garden, and every step they took toward the fountain brought them one step closer to leaving.

"How long until we get there?" Seth asked, not for the first time. Before someone could reply, their eyes were drawn to a cluster of mushroom creatures floating past with frills swirling around them like jellyfish in the sea.

Foxx laughed at Seth's amazed expression. "Soon I think. It's a building at the end of the stream. Hopefully it won't take too much longer to reach it."

C

Sirena crossed through the iron gates at the Palace of Sateen. She held her dress off the ground to avoid the overgrown foliage and nets of kudzu that seemed to be taking over the entire region. A rampant tiger with wings stood atop a dried-up fountain, its pale stone speckled with moss.

Following the steps to the entrance, she pushed open the doors without invitation and stepped into the hall. Despite the exterior of the Palace, the inside shined like polished stone. The walls in the hall leading to the throne room depicted grotesque murals of battles long ago. Sirena ran her finger along a particular scene, smiling at the memory before continuing on.

Two guards stood before the throne room doors, shirtless warriors with long swords crossed over their backs. Before she reached them, a woman appeared at an intersecting hallway and spoke her name. Sirena turned and greeted her with a half curtsy. "Puteri Kirana, lovely to see you."

As the woman bowed deeply, jewelry on her wrists and ankles jingled. When she rose, she straightened her crown. "And you as well, Your Majesty. Have you come to speak with my father?"

"Indeed I have."

Kirana crept closer, polished fingers sliding around the corner between the halls. "We've heard whispers."

Sirena pulled her hair over one shoulder, remembering now two of the many reasons she hated visiting Decha at home—the humidity... and his daughter. "I imagine so, being this close to the Cordilleran barrier."

"What do you plan to do?"

One of the soldiers down the hall shifted his stance, and the movement drew their eyes.

Sirena cleared her throat. "What I have always done: whatever I must."

"Won't that prove difficult, given the enemy at hand?" Kirana smirked and twisted a curl around one finger.

Sirena narrowed her eyes. "Which enemy might you be referring to, Puteri?"

Thin brows furrowed. "Is there more than one? More than one that counts, anyway."

"Is your father in his throne room?" Her gaze again shifted down the hall, and the Princess pouted.

"Yes, Your Majesty." She bowed and twirled on bare toes before heading back the way she'd come.

Sirena sighed and adjusted her dress. When she reached the double doors, the warriors stepped aside, allowing her passage through with the drop of their chins.

Decha sat swallowed by his throne, his tiny body no match for the grandeur he wished to present to his visitors. He rose as she entered, wearing an obligatory smile. Before she reached the dais, he descended the steps and dropped to one knee.

"*Selaa, Ōritsuri. Baikchaku.*" He spread his arms wide to indicate the room.

"Such a kind welcome, Decha," Sirena replied in Katutaan. "Please, rise."

The Raja stood and stopped before her. He was nearly a foot shorter than she, and light from the chandelier shined off his bald head. "I know why you have come." He continued on in his native tongue. "Shall we have a drink first? Bintang!" He shouted a command, and a young boy appeared from behind the throne.

Scurrying toward them with his eyes down, he knelt before Decha with his head to the floor. "*Hei, masū.*"

"Drinks for Her Majesty and myself. Now."

Bintang ran off without another word, disappearing down a corridor to the left of the throne.

Decha returned his attention to Sirena, pushing jeweled fingers against his sides. "Now. To business. You wish me to side with you against Valerian and his band of renegades."

Sirena kept her chin high, looking down at the small king over her nose. "Traitors, I believe you mean."

"*Hei.*" Decha grinned. "Traitors, indeed. I hear he stole your commander."

Sirena tucked a stray hair behind her ear and again lifted her braid from her neck. "It was a folly of my husband to promote him anyway. He thought him the commander of legends, but he was obviously wrong."

"Was he?" Decha tilted his head and twisted one of the many

gemstones lining both ears. "Will your commander not be remembered for all time, as the prophets say?"

Angry heat rose up from her core, but she kept it at bay. "Enough of Hector. I am here to discuss our partnership."

"Partnership? Is that what we call it? I hadn't known." He scratched his cheek and gleaned her scowl. "Rest well, *Ōritsuri*. Loyalties remain where they have in the past."

"That is exactly why I have come. Your loyalties have not often been clear, Decha. I know of your friendship with Valerian. I know you and Veronica helped him when he left me."

"That was ages ago, my darling. And you deserved it. You tortured the man! I'm afraid some of us could no longer sit idle and watch. Besides, you're happier now anyway. And so is he. So no harm done." He flourished a hand in the air and began to turn away from her.

"She's here, Decha. The woman in white."

Stopping mid-turn, he looked at her and drew back his head. "You've seen her?"

Sirena nodded and leaned closer, her smile like a cat about to strike. "And so has he. The best part is this: she's Amaryllis' daughter."

Decha swore and pinched his chin, his face scrunching in concentration. "And so navi as well? That is troubling. Amaryllis was very powerful. This woman in white will undoubtedly be a force to be reckoned with." He looked at her, his eyes traveling up and down in examination as he accepted the glass Bintang handed him. The boy bowed and gave Sirena her own glass before hastening from the room. Decha sipped and hummed delight at the sweet liquor. Then he said, "You do not seem concerned at all. You, on the brink of war with Valerian and the Seer hanging in the balance."

"Hence the reason for my visit, Raja Narong. I am hoping to leave here even less concerned than I was before arriving." Sirena sniffed the liquor, attempting to detect any trace of poison before taking a sip.

He shook his head, one side of his lips curling. "I'm not sure that even I could tip the scales in your favor this time, Sirena. Have you visited the others?"

She folded her arms, regretted the immediate heat it brought to her torso, and released them. "You are the first. I'm heading to Aeonian next."

Decha hummed, his eyes elsewhere. "Let me know what they say. Then I will give you my decision."

She said his name, her mouth dropping open. "Are you implying your allegiances waver?"

"The Seer adds a distressing ingredient to the mix. It will be as I said. Talk to Dante and Serafina. Perhaps we should have a Summit."

Sirena lifted a shoulder and took another drink. "Valerian won't come. Not with her in Celestelvyra. He will wait until he has her in his grasp before he makes any moves."

Decha's eyes bulged. "Celestelvyra? You mean to say she has found her way into the Sacred Garden? *Ōritsuri*, this could be the end of everything. You know what the prophets say."

"I don't give a damn what the prophets say!" Sirena's eyes flashed with rage.

"All the pieces are already in play, exactly where the navi predicted they would be. This is very, very troubling. I need to think." Decha turned from her and paced toward his throne. With a hand in the air, he said, "Come back to me after you visit Aeonian. I will give you my decision then."

C

Waiting for the incoming guards to arrive took less time than anticipated. As the team in Crystavium sat around the fire eating luncheon, Kwame and Vera alerted the group that three men had been spotted traveling toward them.

Orion, Hector, and Jax took on the task of disarming and incapacitating the men, hiding behind a boulder in some high shrubbery and waiting for them to pass by. With stealth, they advanced from behind. Hector and Jax wrapped their biceps around two of the mens' throats until lack of oxygen had them passing out. Orion took a different approach, whacking the third on the head with the handle of his stone club. Hector and Jax eyed him incredulously as the man dropped unconscious to the ground.

Dragging the three bodies back to their campsite, they tied them up with their wrists behind their backs and proceeded to rummage through their belongings, hoping to find extra uniforms to avoid having to strip them. Isolde covered them with blankets, not wishing for them to freeze to death while being held captive. Johnathan promised to keep the fire going for them and to monitor their temperatures.

Raven, Orion, and Declan dressed in the crimson, black, and dark gray guard uniforms. They were similar to those of the King's Legion but had an emblem representing the Ashgate Fortress across the chest. It depicted a flame with two points, like that of a candle, and was stitched into the fabric with red thread. Orion grimaced, looking down at himself and thinking he preferred the hide and fur coat Isolde had gifted him. He wondered briefly if it would look too peculiar to wear it over top of the uniform but knew he couldn't risk it.

Raven's outfit was big on her, but she made do, cuffing the bottom of the pants and the sleeves at her wrists. She removed the blades from her waist and back in exchange for a pistol belt taken from one of the guards. Declan and Orion did the same. Hector and Jax were walking in with only pistols as well, and Isolde dropped all of her weapons but for the thin sword hanging at her hip.

Standing in a circle around the fire, Jax gave one final rundown of the entire plan.

Then Hector said, "We all know why we're here and what we need to accomplish. It isn't a stretch to say the entire weight of the free world rests on our shoulders. Without Alexander, we cannot win. Follow your directions with precision, adjust with intelligence as needed, and watch each other's backs. Some of us may not make it out, but as long as we get Alexander and the others free, our sacrifice will be worth it."

"In other words," Jovan interrupted, "If we fail, the world is doomed. So do not fail."

Jax chuckled, and Hector nodded.

"Exactly. Failure is not an option, but should failure find you, be sure to go down fighting."

Griffin said, "A prayer for safe travels." He lifted his eyes to the sky and closed them, prompting the others to follow his lead. "Creator of all. We have accepted this perilous task under Your command. We obediently offer our lives if needed for Your will to be done. Please, protect each of us, especially those moving beyond the gates. Allow Your light and majesty to shine while we infiltrate the darkness within. So be it with peace."

Hector thanked him for the prayer and offered one last farewell before the three teams dispersed toward their proper locations, leaving Johnathan behind to watch over the prisoners and the animals.

C

After Foxx and the others finished their luncheon, they continued following the banks of the stream. Along the way, they saw several species of henki, four lepennas, half a dozen of the three-tailed foxes, a plethora of birds and insects, a herd of doe with tinaeras on their backs, and a pair of wolves.

They walked through another patch of rose bushes, and the scent brought back memories of the morning. When Asher caught Foxx blushing, he squeezed her hand and kissed her cheek. Iris and Seth pretended to be utterly disgusted in response.

An hour passed before the building from Foxx's dream came into view. Shrieking, she cried, "There! There it is!" The others lit with tangible excitement and began running toward it, but she lingered, taking it all in. It was even more extraordinary than she remembered. Not only the building itself, but the entire surrounding area. Flowering trees framed either side of the structure, surrounded by a rainbow of blossoms: morning glories in full bloom despite the lateness of the day; azalea and rhododendron bushes; and stalks of giant sunflowers. They saw leafy bamboo, ivy, twisting vines of verbena, and mushrooms of every size and color littering the grass before the building.

A stone path began along the stream and led them beneath the archway, just as Foxx remembered it would. Her eagerness to see the inside of the building overwhelmed her. The moment she stepped up to the archway in the dream, she'd woken up back at the falls and hadn't had a chance to glimpse what lay beyond it.

The group followed the thin path under the arch to find the building opening up into a wide terrace. At its center stood an immaculately sculpted fountain, unmarred by time and a mirror image of the fountain that once stood in the entrance plaza of Jericho. The stream flowing into the room encircled the fountain like a moat circling a castle.

Gray bricks, aged and spotted with patches of green moss and pastel lichen, made up the floor. The walls matched, each with their own rectangular windows, empty of glass. No roof stretched above them, intentionally left open so the Ram of the fountain could stare up into the starlit sky.

"It's stunning," Iris said.

"Radiant," Foxx agreed.

Asher took a few reverent steps toward the fountain, unable to tear his eyes from the object he'd spent so long searching for, the thing he'd given up his throne for, that Sawyer Belamour had left his young girls to find, and that Amaryllis had died fighting for.

The others stopped, seemingly rooted in place, but he continued toward the fountain. Stepping gingerly across the moat created by the stream, he stood next to the statue, looking up at the grand, bighorn Ram with horns spiraling from the top of His head down to His jawline. It was the spitting image of the Ram he and Foxx had met in the meadow: the Creator, Elohim, sculpted from white stone and standing in the midst of a crescent moon. The moon curved up under the animal's torso, curling around the side of His body and into the space above His head. The outer rim of the fountain stood a little over a foot tall and depicted the phases of the moon.

Drawing his eyes from the statue so he could peer inside, Asher gasped. He reached his hand into the bowl and ran his fingers across the dry stone at the bottom.

"What's wrong?" Iris took a step closer.

Asher turned to face them and pulled out his hand. "It's empty."

"What?" Foxx asked, staggered by his declaration.

"How can it be empty?" Iris rushed to join him. Reaching in, she pulled her hand out and revealed its dryness to the others. "He's right."

"What does this mean?" Foxx hadn't moved from her spot next to Seth, worried proof of their words would be too devastating, especially after witnessing the expression on Asher's face. He walked around the fountain, inspecting it from all sides in a futile hope the water might magically be visible from a different angle. Foxx said his name and repeated her question.

"I don't know, Foxx!" The aggression didn't suit him. All eyes flashed his way, and he placed his hands on his head, looking up into the sky. "I don't know what it means."

"There's something written here." Iris brushed her hands over the top edge of the basin. Asher looked down and glimpsed the letters appearing beneath the dust. Frantically, he joined her in wiping the surface clean, walking the whole circle until all the words were revealed.

"What does it say?" Seth stood on his tiptoes to try and see, though he felt too nervous to draw closer.

Asher stopped across the fountain from Iris as she began reading the inscription. *"Only when the lineage of kings joins with one who is…"* She stopped when she could no longer see the words, and Asher continued from his side. *"… one who is chosen, will Pyhä-ki be received."*

His eyes met Iris' across the basin, and she asked, "Well, we have one from the lineage of kings, but what does it mean by one who is chosen? Chosen for what?"

Asher shook his head and circled the fountain, passing by her as he reread the words to himself. Then he growled in frustration. "We can't have come all this way for nothing." He found Foxx's gaze and held it.

Seth said, "Maybe Foxx is chosen. The Creator did lead her here after all."

Foxx flushed. "I don't think that's the case, Seth."

"He's right." A spark of Asher's enthusiasm returned. "You do have a special connection with Him. Maybe that's all it means."

Foxx shook her head, but Iris waved her toward them.

"Just come over here, Foxx. It can't hurt to try."

Sighing with reluctance, Foxx left Seth and stepped over the moat, joining them in front of the bighorn Ram. She looked up at Him, and though it was carved into His exact likeness, the statue felt nothing like being in the presence of the Creator Himself. Holding her arms out, she said, "I'm here. And still no water." She leaned over to check the basin, just to be sure, but it was as dry as it had been when they arrived.

"What are we going to do?" Iris looked back and forth between Asher and Foxx.

Asher's face scrunched into a look of deep contemplation. "I don't know, Iris." Then he crossed the stream, passed Seth where he stood, and strode from the building.

CHAPTER 27

BREAKING AND ENTERING

Orion, Declan, and Raven ambled in the direction of the obsidian gates. Coming in from the south, they passed under the guard tower on the southeast corner without acknowledging it, as if they'd strolled beneath it dozens of times before. They followed the wall adorned in vicious spikes akin to a nieda's teeth.

Raven's eyes followed the wall up to the murky sky, thick with gray clouds. A bitter wind had Declan flipping up his collar to block the breeze.

Orion brushed off the front of his shirt, as if he could sweep away the Legion colors and all they represented. It seemed so long since he'd worn Reginaterra red, and he wasn't pleased to be wearing it again. If he died inside, it would be the last thing he ever wore. The thought made him shiver.

"Jax said to stop in front of the gate and look up at the guard tower," he said, though the others had heard Jax instruct this numerous times. "Just act like you belong here. As if you've passed through these gates a hundred times before."

Raven glared at him and spoke under her breath. "We get it, Orion. Now stop talking. You're freaking me out."

Declan said, "Actually, talking will look more natural and relaxed than three people walking in silence." Orion held out his hands and aimed a smug expression at Raven. Declan eyed him as if he were behaving like a child. "Remember, we aren't trying to sneak in. We are infiltrating as guards who work here." He adjusted his uniform. "Assimilate."

Orion straightened his own uniform and squared his shoulders, following Declan's lead. Then he looked at Raven again. "So Nightshade, you and Commander Kayvan, huh? I doubt anyone saw that coming." He raised both eyebrows. Raven scowled and thumped his arm.

Declan ran his fingers along the stone wall to his left, seemingly serene. "I think it's great. You guys are good for each other."

Raven sensed an insult. "And why is that, exactly?"

Declan opened his mouth, but Orion spoke first. "Because you're all scary and—" He made a motion with his face and fingers, mimicking a monster. "And he's all stoic and brave. Experienced in the taming of feral things." Raven punched him again, and he laughed, rubbing the muscle. "What? He did work directly under Sirena, so he must—"

Glowering, she punched him three more times, silencing his words in a fit of laughter. "You're a jackass, Orion."

"He has a point though." Declan's statement received an equally threatening glare, and he lifted a hand to halt her angry response. "Listen. I just mean he's like calm water to your fire. It's not a bad thing, despite how Rion described it. You compliment each other. You can give him excitement, and he can give you rest. And you both deserve that, Raven. I'm happy for you."

Shying away from his sincere and tender words, Raven looked straight ahead as they approached the gates. Stopping before the soot-colored bars, the trio looked skyward in unison. Orion lifted his hand to shield his eyes. Up above, they saw two guards leaning over the edge of the lookout tower.

The hearts of the infiltrators spiked as the guards took their time scrutinizing them. One of the guards disappeared from sight.

Declan looked at Orion, who shrugged.

"Should we say something?" Raven asked.

"Not yet." Noticing movement off to the right, Orion turned to look.

Raven followed his gaze. "A wolf."

Orion's eyes widened. "You can see it, too?" The animal looked identical to the wolves he'd seen in the desert and in Jericho—the ones he'd thought he'd hallucinated.

She peered at him oddly. "Why wouldn't I be able to see it?"

Declan said, "You don't usually see gray wolves in the tundra, do you? Arctic wolves dressed in white, but not gray where it's this cold. Only in Reginaterra right? Maybe the lower mountains of Cordillera?"

Orion opened his mouth to respond when the sounds of clanking gears echoed off the walls and the obsidian gates began opening inward. Shaking his head, he took one last glance at the animal before saying, "Never mind, let's go."

Declan lifted a hand in thanks to the guards as he and his companions passed without objection through the black gates.

C

Jax, Hector and Isolde progressed with the quietness of infallible thieves, following the rocky edge of the riverbed as they drew closer to the outer wall of the Fortress. The plan was to stay dry until getting wet was absolutely necessary. The water would be cold as ice, and staying submerged for too long would be dangerous. Once in sight of the guard tower above the southwest corner, swimming would be required to prevent detection.

Using a pile of rocks as a shield, they crouched low. Jax looked over the top to survey the wall ahead. Almost a hundred *sylis* of ground remained between them and the wall, but if they moved any closer on land, the guards in the tower might notice them.

Nervous tension polluted Jax's words as he said, "It's time to go under."

"Are you sure we can't wait any longer?" Hector joined him with eyes atop the rocks. The bitter air had already grown colder as the sun made its journey toward the horizon. " We still have about 600 feet until we reach the wall. The dimming sky should cover us at least a few more *sylis*. We won't have much time in the river before hypothermia kicks in." From their vantage, they could see only one guard up in the tower, circling the edge to see in all directions, but they knew the Warden required two present in the towers at all times, so there was sure to be another out of sight on the other side.

"We can't risk getting closer without staying hidden." Jax searched for more cover, but the land was flat and free of debris between their rocks and the wall. "This plan must be executed flawlessly or it will fail. If we're caught, it's all over."

Isolde said, "We can do it. When we enter the water, the current will propel us forward, and we will reach the wall in no time." Flattening her feet on the ground while remaining low, she secured the strap holding her sword to her waist. "Do not stop until you hit the wall." Then she dove into the river, creating minimal splash.

Jax and Hector regarded each other with eyebrows raised. "You heard the lady," Jax said. Their boots crunched pebbles into sand as they crept toward the water's edge.

Hector grazed the surface with the tips of his fingers and winced. His eyes trailed the rushing current. "As long as we let the river carry us, we'll make it."

Jax nodded, though his real concern was climbing back out. The sky will have darkened completely by then, so they would only need to swim until they reach the outside of the wall. They could have waited until later to begin the mission, but he'd worried the gate guards would be more thorough after dark, which might have meant trouble for those sneaking in the front.

Hector clapped Jax's shoulder. "You first, Lieutenant."

Jax scowled and toed the edge of the river. Taking a nerve-settling breath, he adjusted the spool of rope tied around his waist, securing it so it wouldn't be lost to the current. "All right, let's do this."

"We'll never hear the end of it if we keep letting Isolde show us up."

Isolde rotated in the water to verify they'd followed her and found them crouched on the edge, wading in slowly. "If the rest of the mighty King's Legion turns out to be babies like yourselves, this mission is sure to go off without a hitch." She accompanied her statement with a laugh and turned away from them to continue swimming.

Hector said, "She's right, you know. You are a pretty big baby." Jax grabbed Hector's shoulder and shoved him into the ice cold water before jumping in after him.

C

Orion, Declan, and Raven strode the wine-colored path from the obsidian gates to the front doors of the Ashgate Fortress. Frosty, teal grass lay on either side of them within the confines of the wall. The walkway stretched roughly sixty feet from gate to doorway, taking them less than a minute to reach the entrance at a sluggish pace.

Orion inspected the front of the building, trying to assess what the inside might look like before entering and comparing it with Jax's maps. One hundred feet wide, the structure rose two stories above the ground and was made of twilight-gray blocks blackened with soot from the fires alight around the exterior wall.

The only window visible from their angle, aside from the large circular window high above the entrance doors, was barred with black iron. Sharp spires protruded the top of the building, aimed savagely at the sky. The Monastery in Jericho had spires as well, but in this setting, the spikes on the roof looked menacing.

Wooden doors crafted of dark oak had been stained almost black. Each bore circular handles hanging from an onyx ball. Thorny vines of cast iron decorated the doors without symmetry, as if the metal had grown naturally in whatever direction it pleased.

The trio paused in front of the doors, knowing they had moments until their hesitation appeared suspicious, but none yet ready to grasp a handle.

With a sharp inhale that straightened his posture, Orion said, "There's no going back now. We know what we need to do. Stick to the plan, and everything will be fine." Declan and Raven nodded. Voices shouting from beyond the gate pricked their ears. Resisting the urge to spin toward what they knew would be Griffin and his team in the beginning stages of their scheme, Orion reached for the handle. The door was heavier than he'd expected and required a great deal of effort to pry open wide enough for Declan and Raven to step through.

Before entering himself, he glanced back at the gates. For a single moment, he considered abandoning the mission and fleeing with his life intact. Instead, he whispered a quick prayer to Elohim for safe passage and passed through the door into the mouth of the beast.

C

Foxx explored the walls of the building, looking for clues and lost in thought. Asher hadn't come back since he'd stormed off, but they'd decided to give him time, knowing he would return chipper and ready to press on.

"We can't just give up." Iris and Seth sat on the stone floor, eyes trailing Foxx. They'd stopped searching twenty minutes prior, but Foxx had pressed on.

"When the lineage of kings joins with one who is chosen," Foxx repeated. "What could that mean?"

"Asher has to be the lineage of kings, right?" Iris asked, and Foxx nodded from across the room. "So who is the one who is chosen?"

Seth sat up on his knees. "It has to be Foxxglove! The Creator talks to her, so she is chosen by Him, don't you think? He showed her how to get here." His stomach grumbled, and Iris retrieved a green apple from her bag. He graciously accepted and bit into it right away.

"But nothing happened when I stepped up next to the fountain." Foxx's shoulders slumped in her discouragement. She felt like a failure for not being the right person for the job. With a sigh of defeat, she sat down on the floor between Seth and Iris.

"Maybe you have to say the magic word or something," Seth suggested through a mouthful of apple.

"What's the magic word?" Iris asked.

Seth pinched his chin in thought. "It could be a magical word we don't know. Or something like, *open sesame*! Like in that old story about the thieves." They turned toward the fountain to see if Seth's magic word had worked. When nothing happened, he shrugged and took another bite. "Maybe you should ask the Creator again."

"I have been." In truth, she'd hardly stopped whispering silent words to Elohim since Asher left.

Stepping back through the archway, Asher strode toward the fountain without acknowledging them. He crossed the stream and put his hands on the edges of the basin, leaning over so he could see inside.

Foxx watched him, hearing him whisper prayers to Elohim as he examined the fountain.

"I apologize for my outburst," he said. "But I need Your help, here. What is going on? What do You want from me? Please, show me what to do."

Foxx repeated his prayers in her head, thinking it might work better if said twice.

Iris nudged her sister. "Maybe you should go talk to him."

Foxx continued to observe their friend, thinking she'd rarely seen him so distraught. Standing, she walked toward him so slowly she could have been tiptoeing. When she reached the moat, she stopped and said his name.

Asher lifted his gaze from the basin, his desperation creating a shadow in his usually bright eyes. She yearned to snuff it out like a candle flame.

Elohim had shown her how to get there. Surely He wouldn't have done so if they didn't already have everything they needed. Crossing the moat, she ran her hands along the edge of the fountain before grazing the crescent moon. She looked into the stone eyes of the statue. "What are we missing?"

When no answer came, she returned her attention to the basin's edge and spoke the words Asher and Iris had read. *"Only when the lineage of kings joins with one who is chosen, will Pyhä-ki be received."* As she wiped more dust from the carved letters, her fingers brushed Asher's. He startled, yanking his hand away and standing bolt upright. Drawing back in surprise, she asked, "What is it? Did you figure something out?"

"Didn't you feel that?" His eyes scanned her from head to toe, and she didn't understand the fear she saw in them.

She immediately wondered if he'd somehow caught a glimpse of the darkness Sirena claimed spilled from her like a boiling pot. Her attention shot to her fingers, but they were free of ice. Still, his intense expression had her reeling, and she grabbed the moon for balance. "No. I didn't feel anything."

"What happened?" Iris rose to her feet with Seth next to her.

Foxx and Asher stared at each other. When he extended his palm, she looked at it as though it might bite. "What? What are you doing?"

"It's you."

"What's me?" Foxx retreated, taking two steps back.

Asher moved with her. "Humor me." He smiled wide with every bit of his handsome charm returned and every worry stripped from his expression. She shook her head, and he said her name, raising his eyebrows. "Trust me. You do, don't you?"

She looked from his face to his hand, to the fountain, and back into his eyes. Cautiously, she admitted, "Yes, I do." He moved his hand closer, encouraging her to reach out. With an exhale of breath, she held up her palm, stopping an inch from his.

The air began to swirl, blowing felled leaves around them in wisps of wind. Foxx's hair blew high in the breeze, and Asher's swayed in front of his face. Something ignited in the space between their hands, a density thick and warm like a storm brewing in the jungle. Crystals of ice spread across Foxx's fingertips. Then something like miniature lightning sparked between them, and both yanked their hands from the burning electricity. At their separation, the winds settled and the world grew eerily still.

Asher rubbed his hand and looked at Foxx with jubilation.

"What was that?" Iris stood next to the moat, looking fearful of crossing over to join them.

"It didn't come from me." Asher's entire being seemed to glow. He rocked on the balls of his feet.

"It wasn't me either." Foxx rubbed her own hand, searching for ice that had melted away.

Iris said, "Something was happening. The instruction says the king and the chosen one must be joined. Maybe it didn't work before because you weren't joined together. Do it again."

Letting her head fall from side to side, Foxx stepped forward and held out her hand. Asher did the same. The wind began again. The pressure built between them, but rather than waiting for the electricity to strike, they pressed their palms together. The ground rumbled, and the gale drew them closer. Iris held onto Seth, her feet braced to react.

Asher smiled like a madman. Foxx tried to pull her hand away to see if it was possible, but the swirling energy had her securely tethered. Suddenly, painful ice blossomed on the backs of her knuckles. She winced at the burn, far more intense than before. Fear speared her heart, and she prayed, *Don't let it spread to Alexander. Please, don't let it hurt him!*

Then the sound of pouring water reached their ears, and they leaned to look inside the basin. Glistening water spilled from holes surrounding the circular base that held the bighorn Ram. Asher laughed, and the sound was so contagious, Foxx and the others joined him.

When the water ceased its pour, the wind stilled, and the energy encompassing them diminished. Foxx pulled her hand away and wiped it on her pants, though the ice had already melted, leaving no evidence in its wake but the burning cold.

Iris and Seth jumped the stream to look inside. The liquid was cloudy and iridescent, as if filled with shimmering starlight. It reminded them of the moonstone, opaque with a rainbow flaring within.

Asher pulled the Artifact from his pocket and stared at it in his palm.

Foxx noticed his change in demeanor and touched the hand hanging at his side. "What are you waiting for?"

His gaze lifted to hers. "I've waited so long for this moment, fought so hard to see it through…"

"But you also know what comes next," she said, understanding.

He nodded. "War, death, and in the end, a pair of Thrones." Foxx sucked in a breath, tucking hair behind her ear and fidgeting as she held his stare.

"Do it already, Asher!" Seth's encouraging voice rang out, drawing their attention. "Get Pyhä-ki. You can do it!" Iris chuckled and wrapped her arm around him, pulling him into a hug.

Asher looked back at them and smiled. Releasing Foxx's hand long enough to remove the cork from the Artifact, he dipped the crystal vial into sparkling water. When it filled to the brim, he held it up to examine it, twisting it around and watching it glisten and dance as he released a heavy sigh. He secured the cork without letting go of Foxx's hand, and she laughed at his awkward maneuver. Then he looked around at the group of people who'd become his family, like no family he had ever known before. He held the vial up so they could all get a good look at it, and everyone leaned in.

"It looks like you bottled starlight and rainbows." Iris' fascination had her reaching for the vial.

Foxx took Asher's hand and flipped it over, appraising it. "Your fingers are shimmering where you touched it." Seth stood on his tiptoes so he could see.

"You're right. It's clinging to me." Asher stretched them out.

"So cool!" Seth exclaimed as Asher booped him on the nose with a glistening fingertip. Seth crossed his eyes trying to see if his nose was sparkling.

"I bet if you pour it on a blade, the metal shines the same as your fingers. Douse a sword, then stab her in the heart." Iris made a stabbing motion in the air with her fist. "Could work on bullets too, maybe."

"Or arrows," Foxx suggested with a grin.

"So it isn't a poison she will drink?" Seth scrunched his nose. "In the old stories, they always drank the poison. Or ate it." He rubbed his nose, looking mildly concerned about it being on his skin.

Asher wiped his hands on his pants and returned the Artifact to his pocket. "I'm not sure it matters, as long as it gets into her body somehow. The scribes were never clear on that. I assume they would have been if there was a particular way to handle it."

"It can't poison us though, right?" Seth asked.

"Definitely not."

"Now what? We have Pyhä-ki to kill Sirena, but still no way out." Foxx's lack of fear surprised her, but she truly felt ready to take on whatever awaited them outside the doors. She squeezed Asher's hand, and when he glanced at her, still beaming with delight, she pressed a kiss to his cheek.

Seth made a funny face as if he was partially ecstatic to see them happy but also grossed out by their affection.

Iris slung an arm over his shoulder. "I think we head back to the waterfall and trust our friends on the other side to come through for us. The Reko Raptors will find a way to us when they realize we can't return."

Foxx left Asher to hug Seth and her sister. "Then let's head back to the waterfall. Nothing left to do now but wait."

☾

"It's perfect, Your Majesty. You've outdone yourself."

Konungr Vali stood next to Abram and Captain Solvi Brenna on the promenade at the foot of the palace in Jericho. With crossed arms, he appraised the New Commander's Tent with approval. "I assure you, I did little, Commander. Credit goes to my fantastic wife."

Abram chuckled. "Do give her our sincerest thanks, then. It's far larger and more efficient than the one the Raptors strung up in that alley. I'm certain Hector will agree and be very pleased when he returns."

"I believe you are correct, Commander," Solvi said.

"He'd better." Vali scratched his chin. "You know, I'm really proud of how you've handled working with him, Abram. Truly. You have no obligation to keep him around, and yet you seem to take no issue in working side by side with the man."

Dropping into a small bow, Abram said, "Such high praise, Your

Majesty. And undeserved. Hector is a good man. And a strong ally. He and his team have been a great help to us."

"Even still. Should you change your mind, know I would have him flogged and forced out at your word." Vali lifted a brow, his grin shifting into one of mischief.

A laugh deep from his belly rolled through Abram's chest. "Thank you, but I don't believe that will be necessary."

Solvi tucked gloved hands into the pocket of her coat. "Hector has been nothing but honorable since he arrived. I should think this will continue when he returns." Abram nodded in agreement, and Vali shrugged.

"The others should be entering the Fortress soon, if they haven't already. They will return in a few days at most, if everything goes to plan. I'd like to be alerted the moment they step through the gates." Vali looked pointedly at Abram to ensure understanding.

Solvi said, "The hyvä mon grow restless. It is as if even the wind in the trees can feel the tension building and is attuned to the arrival of something big on the horizon."

Vali lifted his eyes to the mountains outside the walls. "Will they fight with us, Captain Brenna?"

"I believe they will. I think they will gladly fight in your honor, Your Majesty."

"Very go—" Vali clutched his chest, his vision blurring as he cried out. Pressure filled his ears.

"Vali!" Abram grabbed the Konungr's shoulder, and Solvi took his opposite arm to keep him steady. "What is it? What's happened?"

"It's her. Something—" He groaned again, and this time the pain brought him to a knee.

"Her who, Your Grace? The Queen?"

Vali shook his head. Though it wasn't nearly as agonizing as last time, the pain took his breath away. He touched his nose to find blood just below the nostril. Then he looked up as snow began to drift from the sky. Coughing turned to laughter that had the soldiers' eyes widening.

Viggo appeared at Vali's back and looked at Abram. "What happened?"

The commander shrugged, a baffled expression elongating his features. "I'm not sure."

Vali reached up to Viggo's shoulder as he tried to catch his breath. "It's fine, Viggo. I'm fine. It's just that—" He coughed as Viggo and Abram helped him to his feet. Frantic eyes scoured the area. "I felt her. Again. She can't be back already, can she?" He looked at Abram. "The team has only been gone a week. Have any of them returned?"

"No, Your Majesty." Abram looked at Solvi, who furrowed her brow.

"Does he mean Raven?" she asked. "Or the woman from Caritas? No other women went with them."

"No." Vali gasped, his hand rising to his heart. "Foxxglove Belamour."

Viggo tried to keep Vali's attention on him. "The team hasn't returned, Vali. No one has entered the city since they left."

Vali exhaled through a wide smile, continuing to hold Viggo's shoulder for balance. Lifting his face to the sky, he allowed the falling snow to cool his cheeks. "Something must have happened. Her sól is so strong. One might even say unmatched once she learns to use it." He shook his head, baffled. "Incredible."

Viggo leaned closer to the Konungr and cleared his throat. "Perhaps we shouldn't speak so openly, Your Majesty? Let's get you back to the palace."

"Do you need anything, sire?" Abram asked.

Vali shook his head. "No. To rest, maybe." Then he moved his hand from Viggo's shoulder to Abram's, looking him straight in the eyes. "You must alert me the moment she arrives. The moment the team passes through the front gate, I'm to be told. And I'd like to know if the woman with white hair is with them. Do you understand, Commander?"

"Of course, Your Majesty."

Righting himself, Vali brushed his hands down his torso and looked between the soldiers. "Very good. Thank you Abram, Solvi. Viggo, come. We must find Ingrid. We have much to discuss."

C

As Hector, Jax, and Isolde swam with the current, stiffness infiltrated their limbs like a rapidly spreading infection. Their bodies quaked with shivers. They'd anticipated the cold, but none could have prepared for the absolute frigidity of the river.

When they reached the halfway mark, Isolde smashed her knee

on a sharp rock in the riverbed and muffled her cry with a hand. It hurt worse than the aching cold, a pressure point of searing pain.

Soon, rushing water began to feel like thick mud. Their heart rates sank, and their breath escaped blue tinted lips in shallow wisps. They swam close together, hoping each other's body heat might save them. With not a single second to waste, they pressed on, praying they didn't lose total limb control before reaching the wall.

At last, they crashed into the bricks, too weak to stop before colliding with the solid structure. The river disappeared beneath in a bubbling torrent, suctioning them to flat stone and threatening to drag them under. Jax pointed at the shore beneath the guard tower. With great effort, they crawled along the wall and flopped onto the solid ground. The frozen earth felt warm against their ice-cold skin.

Hector and Jax scooted toward Isolde, cocooning her between them. Her knee had stopped bleeding, but her head felt light and floaty. Tremors coursed through them as their muscles fought to raise their body temperatures. Their teeth chattered, and plumes of chalky breath filled the air above.

"Are you going to… be able to swim?" Jax stammered. Isolde nodded, still trying to calm her breathing. The warmth created by their joined bodies had begun to take effect, allowing their convulsions to settle.

"We need to dive… under the wall and the building." Jax cleared his throat, fighting to get the words through freezing lips. "It will not be pleasant. It isn't far, but there will be no… air pockets until we make it through. There is fire on the other side." Hector and Isolde acknowledged him without words.

After several minutes, Hector choked out, "We are running out of time. We need to go." Rolling onto his stomach, he pushed himself to his knees and extended a hand to Isolde. "Are you ready?" She nodded, accepting it, and they stood together. Her knee left her off balance.

Jax sat up and examined the injury, his cold fingers pressing into her skin so he could turn it toward him for a closer look. "Will you be able to walk on it?"

"Can we wrap it up?" Hector checked his empty pockets. "It might bleed again when we get warm."

Jax looked up at her, awaiting an answer.

"I can walk. I will be fine."

"We can wrap it inside if we need to." Jax crawled to the edge of the river and tested a sharp rock frozen into the ground along its bank. He looked a question at Hector, who nodded and moved closer to help unwind the soaked, heavy rope from Jax's waist. Their fingers struggled to secure it with a knot. When they finished, Jax tugged on the rope to test its stability.

"It will work." Hector helped Jax to his feet.

"It better." Jax stood between them, watching anxiously as water vanished beneath the wall. They carried no bags—no water, or bandages, or extra layers—only the clothes on their backs and the weapons at their sides. The plan was to be in and out in less than an hour from the time Orion, Declan, and Raven crossed the threshold at the front gate. It had already been at least fifteen minutes by Hector's calculations. Maybe twenty.

"It's time," he said.

"Isolde first." Jax handed her a section near the end of the rope. "Hold on to this and do not let go. Try to stay near the edge if you can and keep your guard up. The moment you have air above you, squeeze that rope with everything you have and get to the surface. I don't think it will be deep, but we'll be right at the top of the falls. The current will be fierce, and you'll be freezing, maybe even numb. Whatever you do, don't let go."

"Should we tie it around her?" Hector asked, but Jax shook his head.

"If something happens and it gets tangled, I don't want her trapped below the building with no oxygen. She's strong. She can hold it." He looked at Isolde. "Ready?"

"I am ready." She tested her tingling grip around the rope. It felt nearly as cold as the river itself, and the coarse fibers scraped her palms, now raw and sensitive.

"Then dive in. We'll be right behind you."

Isolde dipped her chin and took a step toward the water. Before she could jump, Jax said her name, prompting her to look back over her shoulder.

"Don't let go."

"I will not let go, Jax. I promise." Then she dove head first beneath the wall. Jax followed after her, clutching his own section of rope, and moments later, Hector did the same.

CHAPTER 28

ASHGATE FORTRESS

The entrance hall of the Ashgate Fortress was shrouded in shadow like the inside of a tunnel. Very few windows lined the walls, likely for maximum insulation, so fire was the primary light source. Cast iron chandeliers draped in cobwebs snaked from the ceiling, and the walls matched the floor's ashy stone, embellished with charred patches surrounding the ever-burning torches.

Orion worried about the claustrophobic darkness. Though the entrance hall was massive, he feared what the rest of the building might be like and desperately hoped the close corridors wouldn't trigger his whispers. The stone reminded him of Sirena's dungeon, and he shivered at the memory, willing his mind to focus on the task at hand.

Orion knelt to rifle through his bag, giving them a few moments to take in the space. Two staircases ascended the walls on either side of the room leading up to a second floor landing. Straight ahead they saw double doors beneath it. Stone statues of hideous creatures, the likes of which they had never seen, stood on the end of both staircase railings. They looked like people—almost—with bald heads and sharp teeth that rivaled the horns sticking out from behind their ears. Crouched atop the pillars, their wings spilled down past their feet, nearly grazing the floor. The one on the left had a long tongue hanging from its open maw.

Upon further inspection, they saw several more stone creatures throughout the hall: one in each corner of the ceiling and two guarding the doors leading outside.

A door on the southern wall led to the cafeteria. The clanking metal and loud chatter of the dinner crowd confirmed the map's accuracy. To their right stood an entrance to a hallway bending out of sight.

"Have you noticed the mood in here?" Declan whispered.

"Doom and gloom." Raven watched a few more guards walk by, exiting the cafeteria and making their way back to their rooms. "Everyone seems miserable. It's almost palpable"

"Angry, even."

A guard walked past them and barreled into Declan's shoulder for seemingly no reason.

"Watch it!" Raven snapped. The man turned around and shot her an obscene gesture. "What is wrong with these people?"

"Would you enjoy working here?" Orion asked.

Raven crossed her arms. "They chose to live this life."

Declan said, "We all choose our lives, Raven. That doesn't mean we necessarily end up where we intend to."

A guard rushed in through the entrance behind them, bumping into Raven as he flew past. After a hasty apology, he raced up the steps on the right side of the room. A few guards stopped to watch him go, but most continued about their business without disruption. Another pair of guards walking by, a man and a woman, crinkled their eyebrows at the three of them, clearly questioning why they hovered at the center of the hall.

"I think that's your cue." Orion stood, seemingly finished with whatever he had been doing in his bag. Raven nodded and started toward the stairs.

"Hey." Declan took hold of her elbow. "We'll be right below you. Once time is up, come back down these stairs, and we'll meet you on the opposite side of those doors."

"Don't mess it up." Raven's gaze lingered on Orion, conveying a silent warning. Then she left them in the hall and began her trek up the stairs en route to the Warden's private chambers.

C

Isolde was the first to thrust her head from the water. Certain she had never been closer to death in her entire life, she coughed and choked, letting oxygen flood her lungs. Before breaching the surface, she had but moments left before the sweet bliss of drowning swallowed her.

She clutched the rope and pressed her feet against the ground, now shallow enough to stand. Fighting the current, she made her way to the walkway lining either side of the water. Splashes behind her indicated that Hector and Jax had made it, too. Dragging herself from the river, she rolled onto her back. The men emerged from the water's edge and laid next to her, gasping.

"That is our way out?" Isolde sputtered between breaths. "Will we not have a… child with us on the return trip?"

"We certainly won't be walking out the front gate," Jax said, still out of breath himself. Water dripped from the ceiling of the dark tunnel unlit by torches. The air felt stuffy with humidity, a blessing to combat their frigid skin, though it added to their difficulty in breathing.

Hector coughed. "I will say, that was significantly harder than I anticipated. Fighting against the current will be difficult, but we do have the rope." He held it up as proof of his words, though his tone was laced with sarcasm.

"It's our only option." Jax slicked his hair back and let his hand fall against the ground above his head. "There is no other way except the front gates, and they must be opened from the guard tower above."

As their heart rates returned to normal, they made their way to their feet, keeping a hand against the wall for support. Following the walkway, they stopped at the edge overlooking the prison below.

As Jax had described it, laid out before them in cylindrical form was the Prison of the Strayed. The mouth of the tunnel opened where the river dropped off a cliff, spilling into vertical falls. The diameter across the center was nearly ten *sylis* wide, and levels of cells lined its outer wall.

Isolde's mouth fell open as she took in the view of the massive hole lit from below by a gigantic fire. "This is the prison?"

Hector's shoulders tensed. "This is it. We should get mobile. The others will be in location soon, and we have a long way down." Sitting on the ledge to the right of the falls, Hector jumped to the metal floor running along the inside circumference of the cells. Turning back, he offered Isolde a hand.

"I am not afraid of heights, Commander." Sitting as he had, Isolde hopped down, landing in a crouch next to him. Her knee smarted as it bent and began to bleed again. When she stood, blood trickled down her shin.

"We should wrap it." Jax dropped last, making the jump without sitting first, and crossed the landing to look over the railing. "Thirteen stories until we hit the Strayed levels. The prisoners may try to sound the alarm. Whether or not the guards will heed their cries, I can't say. We'll move quickly and quietly, and when we reach the Strayed levels, it may be wise to draw weapons." He turned to face them, already tearing a strip from one of his shirts to wrap Isolde's knee.

When he finished, they began their descent into the depths of the prison.

C

Raven ascended the steps with the confidence of someone who knew exactly where the path would lead.

The Warden's living quarters were centered against the back of the building, but a wall stood between the landing and the passage that held the entrance. This passage could be reached from either side of the landing, so rather than following the guard through the right door, which she knew led to the armory, a room for guard quarters, and the security office, she took the doorway on the left. Three more rooms used for guard quarters stood before her, and she crossed the hall straight into the second of the three.

It held two rows of four bunkbeds situated against opposite walls for a total of sixteen available sleeping spaces. She knew there to be another two rooms for guards on the first floor, meaning ninety-six guards could reside in the Fortress at any given time, packed in like sardines in a tin.

Four beds in the room appeared empty of personal effects. She claimed the only available bottom bunk and set her stolen bag on the mattress before plopping down next to it.

Of the five guards in the room with her, two were sleeping, one laid on his back with open eyes staring blankly into the bunk above him, and two rummaged through their bags. The staring man in the bed next to her stood to get dressed from a plain shirt and baggy pants into heavier attire. As he stripped off his clothing right in front of her, she found he was not wearing undergarments. Quickly shielding her eyes, she spun her legs to the opposite side of the bed and shuddered. Another man she hadn't noticed sat on the bed across from her with feet planted on the ground and elbows resting on his knees.

Seeing the distaste written blatantly across her face, he peered out around her to see the other guard's bare bottom. "You get used to it." He grinned.

"I'm not sure how."

"You must be new." He extended a hand. "I'm Roger. Naked guy over there is Emery." Hearing his name, Emery turned to face them, bending below the top bunk to wave. His pants had been pulled up, though they remained unbuttoned.

Raven wiggled her fingers at Emery and returned her attention to Roger, though she didn't accept the handshake. "Raven."

She realized too late that she probably shouldn't have used her real name. They hadn't discussed what to do should they need to interact with anyone. Though at this point, she thought it likely didn't matter. If everything went to plan, they would be in and out before anyone realized what was happening.

Roger let his smile drop with his hand, though he quickly replaced it with a new smile that Raven thought seemed artificial. "I'll be here for the next month, but lucky for you, Emery is on his way out. His replacement should be here at some point today, as well as a few others."

Emery waved again and slung his bag over his shoulder, saying Roger's name by way of farewell. The two men who'd been going through their bags left the room with him.

"Unless you're his replacement," Roger said.

"Maybe." Raven glanced at the hall, wishing Roger would stop talking so she could focus on watching for the Warden to leave his quarters. A hand on her knee had her turning back to him, her eyes finding his hand before rising to meet his. His suggestive leer turned her stomach.

"It should be an exciting month. You picked a good room to bunk in, Raven."

Offering him a winning smile, she allowed his hand to remain where it had crept halfway up her thigh and swallowed bile threatening to rise. Though she'd sworn never to allow another man to touch her without her permission again, she also didn't want to cause a scene. "I'm looking forward to it, Roger."

This seemed to boost his confidence since his right hand joined his left and began making circles on her other thigh. "So how did a pretty bird like you end up in a place like this?"

"The Legion sends us where the Legion sends us." Raven scrambled for a plan. She couldn't risk leaving the room and having Roger follow her. His persistence had her suspecting he might track her down the moment she walked away. She considered knocking him out but worried the close quarters might prove a difficulty, and even if she did manage to render him unconscious, she couldn't guarantee he would land quietly on the bed.

Leaning closer, she lowered her tone. "Tell me, Roger, where do you guards generally sneak off to when you want to have a little fun? It must be hard if all the bunk rooms look like this one." She glanced around at the cramped space.

Roger snickered. "There are a few places to get away. I can show you if you like." His hands crept higher, and she pictured stabbing both of them with the daggers she'd smuggled in beneath her shirt. Her face revealed a flash of discomfort, and Roger didn't miss it. He drew back, though his hands lingered. "Raven isn't a very common name. Have you been with the Legion long?"

"A few years." She swore at herself and tried to regain her composure, smiling again as she tucked hair behind her ear.

"I heard about a Legion soldier named Raven who defected recently. Along with Commander Kayvan and a few others. Word travels, you know? Even in this desolate place. I was never a fan of Hector, anyway. Personally, I hope the Queen finds him and gives him the punishment he deserves."

Hoping the dull light of the room hid the heat rising to her cheeks, she cleared her throat. "Yes, I heard about that also. I guess you never really know people, huh?"

"I guess so."

Despite Roger's words, Raven could see the gears turning in his eyes and knew he must be cycling through suspicions. She scolded herself again for using her real name. She'd been in plenty of undercover situations, and she knew better.

He opened his mouth to ask another question, but Raven held her finger to his lips, thinking she may just cut off that finger later.

She felt confident she would never be able to fully wash away his filth from her skin.

Astonished by her intimate touch, Roger grinned again.

Raven rose to her feet, pulling him with her and leaning into him so his back pressed against the bunk. "Have you ever thought of having a little fun in the Warden's chambers? I just saw one of the guards scurrying up there. Apparently there is some commotion outside the walls." She slid her finger down his chest and bit her lip, glad no one was there to witness her crude behavior. Declan would mock her forever if he saw, but she knew there was no way she could leave Roger alone now.

"We'll be hanged if we're caught," Roger said, though he didn't seem to be rejecting the idea.

Raven leaned forward so she could speak alluringly into his ear. "Oh Roger, that's what makes it fun."

Looking thrilled, he placed his hands on her hips, eagerly pulling her against him. "You're a naughty one, huh?"

Raven thought he might actually be drooling. "Let's go. We won't have much time." She turned from him and strode toward the hall with him at her heels. They stopped in the doorway. "When the Warden comes out, take that door. I'll meet you on the other side." Then she winked and crossed the hall to the landing. She could feel his stare at her back and again choked down vomit. As she reached the door on the opposite side, the frantic guard shot out from it, nearly running into her again.

Behind him strode an older man, distinguished in his polished uniform. Similar to the guards uniforms, it bore shiny silver emblems, buttons, and stitching. The flame symbol worn by the other guards was stitched across the back of his coat, and he held a cane in his right hand, though he didn't appear to need it for walking. Atop his head sat a wide, plum hat with an oversized feather billowing out its side. If she hadn't known him to be the Warden, she might have thought the prison invaded by a pirate commodore.

His eyes met hers, and he dipped his hat, the picture of calm as he followed the distraught gentleman down the stairs.

Exhaling a held breath, Raven continued through the door, turning left and then immediately left again and opening the door she knew would lead to the Warden's hallway. Jax and Hector had told her the landing and the hallway were originally one space. When the current Warden moved into Ashgate, he had a wall built through the center of the landing, separating his rooms more thoroughly from the entrance hall and allowing himself privacy he didn't have when the door to his chambers was out in front for all to see. Architecturally, it didn't make a lot of sense, but at the moment, it suited Raven's needs just fine.

Entering the empty hall, she closed the door behind her with total silence. A door mirroring the one she'd just entered stood at the far end. Halfway down, two torches framed a set of fancifully decorated double doors with silver handles. Approaching the doors, she gave the handles a tug, but they were locked. She inspected the hole and found it to be the home of a mortice key.

The door at the opposite end of the hall opened, and Roger's ugly face peeked through. Hurrying inside and closing the door behind him, he met Raven where she stood. "It's locked," she said as he situated himself behind her, again placing his hands on her hips.

"I know of somewhere else we can go," he whispered, moving his body closer. She could feel him pressed against her, and it took every bit of her willpower not to lash out. His palms slid over whatever parts of her he wished to touch. Memories clouded her thoughts as the action stole her breath. She closed her eyes. Then a sound drew their focus down the hall: men laughing on the other side of the door.

The distraction had her refocusing, and she winked at Roger over her shoulder. "Let me handle it." Pulling two rods of bent metal from her pocket, she slid one into the keyhole and felt around until she lifted the lever inside the mechanism.

"You were pretty prepared for this."

Again she heard the suspicion in his voice and knew she needed to get him on the other side of the door fast. If he sounded the alarm, it would all be over. Luckily, Roger seemed to be the kind of man who didn't think with his brain but with another body part.

Pushing up on the lever, Raven pulled back slightly until she felt resistance, making it easier to hold the first rod in place while she inserted the second. When she secured it beneath the first, she twisted it clockwise until she heard the telling click of the deadbolt.

A grin lifted her cheeks. It wasn't the first time she'd used her burgling skills since leaving Tunturia. Rather than selling her body, as many girls from the slums had done, she'd begun pilfering wares for resale in her father's pawn shop at a very young age. When her mother died of a virus that rolled through the slums and her father fell deep into a sil ōnni addiction, she'd been left to support them all on her own. Several small mishaps had led to a very big mistake, and failing the wrong criminal had almost lost her everything.

Still, it pleased her now to see her talents being used for good.

Looking left and right one last time, listening intently for the echoes of footsteps, Raven twisted the handle and pulled open the doors.

Roger whistled. "That was sexy."

Raven took one of Roger's hands from her hip and ushered him inside, locking the doors behind them. She closed the distance between them and smiled up at him with as much seduction as she could muster in her repulsion.

"Where did you learn to do that?" He slid his hands around the small of her back and pulled her up against him.

"You pick up a few tips and tricks here and there."

"You really seemed to know how to handle those rods." Roger grinned at his own innuendo.

"And that's about as much as I can take." Raven slammed the side of her hand into his carotid artery, and Roger's body slumped to the ground.

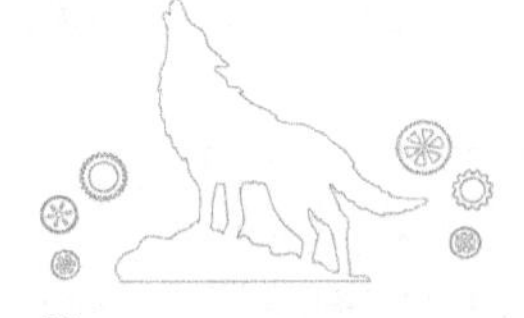

CHAPTER 29

THE DESCENT

Each floor in the Prison of the Strayed had a single set of stairs leading to the one below, and with each passing level, the staircases were placed a quarter of the way around the circle in a clockwise pattern. If the door leading above ground was positioned at midnight on a clock, the first set of steps descended to level two at a quarter after, and the waterfall plummeted into the cavern at the center of ten and eleven.

Four torches on each floor offered little light for the prisoners to live by. Every cell had a rickety, metal bunk and an overflowing bucket in the back corner. The smell lingering in the air was the most atrocious thing Isolde had ever had the displeasure of encountering: rotten flesh and sun-cooked feces; moldy feet and unwashed armpits.

She counted the barred enclosures and found 32 cells on each level. Thirteen floors added up to 416 cells. Accounting for the entrance, which took the place of three cells on the top floor, and a lift that seemed to pass through every level, she thought there must be about 400 chambers available for prisoners. Even if a few scattered stalls had been converted into storage and the like, at two prisoners per cell, the maximum capacity for the Queen's penitentiary was nearly 800 inmates.

Jax, Hector, and Isolde had dropped down onto the metal walkway with the falls on their left. Turning right, they moved counterclockwise around the circumference of the top level en route to the first set of steps. As they crept down to the second floor, their boots rattled the planks. From there, they switched directions and traveled another quarter of the way around until they reached the six o'clock position.

So far, none of the prisoners seemed to have noticed them. Jax and Hector wore the colors of the Legion, so even if their uniforms were slightly different, it was doubtful the inmates would notice the distinction. Isolde, however, was dressed in animal skins and fur, a variation that was sure to draw attention.

Level three looked just the same as level two, though a pair of guards stood near the railing, surveying the scope of the prison. Jax and Hector crept through the shadows and grabbed them from behind, wrapping arms around their necks and holding them stiff until they passed out. After dragging them beneath the stairs, they continued around the circle and stopped just before the falls, directly under where they'd first dropped down.

The flowing water echoed throughout the cavern like white noise, growing almost deafening as they drew nearer. Though the sound of the falls dampened the reverberations of their footsteps, the stairs still creaked beneath their boots.

On level five, a prisoner's dirty fingers wrapped around the bars of his cell. A bone rod pierced his septum, and a thick layer of grime coated his skin. He watched as they strode by without acknowledging his presence and proceeded to level six.

Rounding the bend not far from the next set of steps, Hector grabbed the back of Jax's shirt and held an arm out to stop Isolde. Then he pointed at the backs of two more guards up ahead.

Again they crept through the shadows, but as Jax grabbed the one standing closest to them, the guard several feet away was alerted by their footfalls and spun around.

"Hey, what are you—"

Hector darted past Jax and lunged to punch the man between the eyes. The guard's body tumbled to the ground in a heap.

Isolde and Jax jogged to him, arriving as he stood from his crouch. "Impressive. I am now beginning to understand how you became the commander of the King's Legion."

"You questioned it before?" he asked. She lifted a shoulder and walked past him in the direction of the steps, with Jax following close behind her. Hector whisper after them, "I'll just drag the bodies out of the way myself then!"

Jax cracked a grin over his shoulder but didn't turn back to help. He stopped against the inner railing and looked at the floors below. Prisoners had begun to notice the presence of invaders. Some made noises in their cells, alerting and summoning others to their gates with pounding hands and random shouts of greeting and curiosity, but no drastic sound of alarm had yet been made.

Isolde appeared at his side. "Do you think the guards above know the conditions these prisoners are made to live in? How does the Queen get away with such an atrocity without her entire Kingdom revolting?"

Hector joined them on Jax's other side. "All the guards who work here bunk upstairs. I'm not sure how many patrol the prison regularly, but it's the majority for sure."

"We knew," Jax admitted, his voice low with shame.

"And you were able to continue living your lives knowing people were barely existing like this?" Isolde asked.

They began walking again. A filthy man, not much more than skin and bones, sat against the bars of his cell. Urine and feces coated the floor around him, as if he'd not moved from that spot in ages.

Hector held a finger to his nose as they passed. "The corruption of the Five Kingdoms runs deep. We're doing our best to turn things around. To make up for old mistakes."

Isolde peered into each cell as they walked by. "I know it is our reason for coming. I meant no accusation. Only that I did not expect it to be so horrible. *Animus fractus*." She touched her chest. "My heart, it breaks for them."

A hand extended from between the bars of the closest cell and grabbed Isolde's fur boot. Stopping, she saw a woman not much older than herself. Despite her young features, her skin looked gray with malnutrition. Her hair was such a nest of gray filth, Isolde couldn't determine its color. High, severe cheekbones framed a long, thin nose that tapered to a sharp point.

She wore little more than a long tunic that hiked up as she stretched out her arm in desperation. "Please. Please help me."

Isolde turned to Hector, then to Jax. Her stomach churned with more disgust.

"I didn't—" The woman paused to cough against the floor. "It was… Sirena. I didn't know."

"Do you hear this?" Isolde asked. "Can nothing be done?

Hector shook his head, appearing disheartened.

Jax said, "We have to stay on task. I know it's heartbreaking, but this mission has to be more important. When the Queen is gone, we can work on fixing the rest of the world."

"You mean… to kill her?" The woman inched nearer, pressing her face against the bars. "I can help. Set me free, and I can… help."

"We have to get moving." Jax's eyes canvassed the surrounding area.

Isolde knelt, and the woman released her boot. Up close, she was startled by the color of the woman's eyes: one jet black and the other dark maroon. "I cannot help you today, my friend, but when this is all over, I promise we will come back for you."

The woman's body slumped in defeat, though her eyes remained fixed on Isolde. "I shall be waiting."

With a heavy exhale, Isolde stood and faced the men.

"I'm sorry," Jax said.

"I understand, Lieutenant." Isolde didn't meet his gaze. "Lead on."

The platform holding the fire was located on level fifteen, resting in the middle layer of the three floors allocated to the Strayed, but the tips of the fire's flames rose six or seven levels above the base. The closer they got to the fire blazing at the pit, the worse the atmosphere became. On top of the mind-disorienting smell, the dense, muggy air of the lower levels was sweltering. Even used to the heat of the Wilds, Isolde had no idea how the prisoners tolerated such extreme temperatures.

When his feet touched down on level nine, Jax held out a hand.

Still halfway up the steps, Isolde ducked to see past level eight's floor and wiped a bead of sweat from her brow. Two scraggy figures moved around the level pushing a cart with an uneven wheel along the grated floor. The wheel on the opposite corner spun horizontally, creating a crude squeak as the balance of the cart shifted. Rather than the crimson and gray uniforms of the guards, they wore dirty robes covering their arms and hanging all the way down to their ankles. Their feet appeared bare, though so blackened with dirt it was hard to know for sure.

When her eyes found their hideous faces, she fought to suppress a gasp. The Strayed worked, spooning sludge into each cell with a large ladle. The fingers holding the handle of the ladle were almost completely empty of skin, with only darkened bone and bits of tendons visible. Both faces were contorted in agony and horror, as if they'd been tortured so horrendously for so long, their faces had frozen that way. Misshapen skin exaggerated their expressions, hanging as if making an effort to pull away from their skulls and escape the terrors it no longer wished to endure.

Isolde recoiled, one foot backing up a stair as bile rose up her throat and spilled into her mouth. She wished to spit it out, but her only option was to swallow it back down.

Though the creatures didn't seem to notice their presence, the prisoners in the cells nearby were not so unmoved. Making more of a commotion than those of the upper floors, they began banging on the bars and shouting at them. When those above heard the disturbance, they joined in the noisemaking.

They'd taken out four more guards on their venture down the levels and hoped no more would come despite the prisoners prattling. However, they knew there would be more Strayed than the two before them. Though not very smart creatures, they were trained to attack anything that didn't belong.

As the Strayed continued ambling from cell to cell, spooning food between the bars, Jax stood still, waiting. A full minute passed before a man in the cell closest to the Strayed finally yelled the word that got their attention. "Intruders!"

The Strayed turned to face them, and Isolde realized for the first time that their eyes were smokey, as if grayed by blindness. The creatures stared at them for a long moment, likely confused since the soldiers standing before them wore Legion colors. At their blank expressions, Isolde wondered whether they might actually be blind.

Jax tested a stride forward, letting his foot drop away from the step and onto the metal floor. They needed to walk past the two Strayed to reach the next set of stairs but weren't entirely certain they could safely traipse right by them without triggering an attack. The Strayed didn't fear the guards, though they usually didn't bother them, either. Isolde, however, was clearly not a guard.

Jax moved another pace closer.

The Strayed continued to stare, flawlessly unmoving as if turned into statues carved in stone. Hector followed Jax onto the metal walkway, then Isolde. The prisoners grew louder than ever. Even the floors below had joined in the ruckus.

The Strayed on the right tilted its head, and Isolde swore the skin hanging from its bones leaned with the shift in gravity, sliding further from its skull. Then both eyes widened along with its mouth, filled with broken and blackened teeth, and it shrieked, feral and ravenous, like a bird of prey about to dive for a meal. Its ladle clattered to the floor, flinging slop through the metal grates, and it charged them, moving faster than seemed possible considering its scrawny and decrepit form.

Jax pulled his pistol and smashed the butt into the Strayed's forehead, causing the creature to slump to the ground. Eyes snapping back to the second Strayed, Jax didn't wait for it to catch on. "Run!"

Blasted into motion, Hector and Isolde followed Jax past the Strayed just as it turned to attack. Isolde ducked under its swing, smelling the foul scent of decaying flesh as she slid under its outstretched arm. A glance back told her the one Jax knocked down had already returned to its feet. Both raced after them.

The prisoners were now in total uproar, enjoying and encouraging the excitement. They shouted to get others involved, hoping to alert the guards above and make things more interesting.

When Jax reached the steps leading to level eleven, he paused at the top, letting Hector and Isolde run past as he planted his boot in the chest of the nearest Strayed.

No longer attempting stealth, their boots rattled every stair they touched, sending echoes of metal ringing throughout the cavern. The piercing cries of the pursuing Strayed penetrated their eardrums like serrated knives, and the shouts of the prisoners grew louder as they continued sprinting the curve of each floor.

Jax swore, and Isolde looked back to find three more following them, gaining quickly and moving impossibly fast. One grasped the back of his shirt, and he yanked forward, throwing an elbow to bat it away. The Strayed stumbled but didn't let up, its bony fingers continuing to slash at his shoulder blades and the back of his arms as he ran.

Jax yelled Hector's name. Hector skidded to a stop, spinning to face him with his pistol raised. He fired on the one closest to Jax, and the monster rolled backward from the impact.

The blast from Hector's pistol echoing throughout the chamber made Isolde flinch as she ran past. She spun with her blade drawn and planted her feet. "Are we fighting or running?"

Free of his tail, Jax braced himself as the other Strayed barreled toward them. "Fight!" One of the creatures slammed into him, teeth bared. He took the hit and hit back before wrapping his arms around the monster and slamming it against the metal floor. Another lunged for him, but he dropped low, and the creature careened over him, landing on its stomach and flailing as it tried to stand. Hector shot the downed Strayed in the head as Jax continued to wrestle the other.

Isolde was caught in her own battle, sparring with a Strayed who wielded a long metal rod broken to a sharp point. For seemingly mindless creatures, it fought her with unexpected skill.

Jax shot his opponent in the forehead, and it ceased movement. "Let's go!" Isolde eliminated her Strayed by cleaving off its head. Hector had been pushed against the guardrail by two more. They grabbed at his throat and arms, cutting scratches into his skin as they tried to throw him over the ledge. Jax hastened toward him, grabbing the foot of one and flipping it over the rail. It grabbed on, managing to cling to the thin, metal bars. Its legs swayed as it tried to climb back up, but Jax crushed its fingers with the butt of his gun, and it finally let go.

Evenly paired now, Hector punched the one remaining, an act that distracted it enough for him to slip sideways. He pushed the Strayed up against the rail and pummeled it again and again until it finally toppled toward the pit. Its high-pitched squawks rang through the cavern until it was engulfed by the flames below.

Joyous sparks burst from the menacing furnace, as if appeased by the offering it had received.

C

Orion and Declan found a room with two empty bunks and made themselves at home, dropping the bags not their own next to the beds. Other men lounged in the room with them, but they'd so far paid them no mind. They'd stood in the hall to watch an immaculately dressed man follow the anxious guard down the steps and out the front door.

Griffin's part in the scheme was to turn over Jovan and Vera—alleged rebels against the King and Queen—to receive punishment for their crimes. They only hoped the process took long enough for everyone inside to complete their tasks and get out.

Orion and Declan were to give Raven exactly five minutes before entering the double doors below the landing in the entrance hall.

Lucky for Orion, Declan had an impeccable knack for keeping time, and so Orion could occupy himself worrying about other things that might go wrong. He mulled over the possibility that the Warden might return sooner than expected, the levers might not work as they'd originally thought, or that they might be caught sneaking into the double doors.

"One minute." Declan's demeanor had returned to the serious and broody man he'd become while in exile. Orion realized he didn't look nervous in the slightest. Though he rarely did, one would think breaking into a maximum security prison would spark at least a small amount of anxiety.

It didn't. Declan had one goal, and nothing would deter or distract him from achieving it. Seeing him so serious and stiff made Orion realize he actually preferred him jovial and annoying, though he would never admit that to him.

"Now." Declan stood and moved toward the door. Orion followed.

"Hey, new guys." The stranger's voice stopped them in their tracks.

Orion turned, unable to keep the malice from his face though managing to force nonchalance into his voice as he replied, "Yes?" Declan faced the man as well, his expression cold as the stone color of his irises.

"You can't leave your crap on the floor in the middle of the walkway. It goes under the bed if you're bottom bunk or in the chest if you're top."

"Of course." Orion exhaled with immense relief. "Apologies." Returning to the beds, he kicked the bags underneath.

"Won't happen again," Declan added with the dip of his chin.

"Yeah, it better not."

Back in the entrance hall, they approached the double doors. Orion kept his eyes on the winged statues as they passed between them, a small part of him worrying they may awaken if he got too close.

Two guards walked through the hall in deep discussion but didn't seem to notice them. Once they were gone, the hall was momentarily empty. The large room on the opposite side had grown quiet as most of the guards had finished their dinners. With any luck, most were already lounging in their beds or bathing away the grime of the day, and little attention would be paid to two men disappearing behind the doors.

Orion glanced over his shoulder one last time. "Ready?"

Declan's hand went to the pistol at his hip. Orion had left his brutal weapons behind, opting for a more inconspicuous pistol as the others had. Though at the moment he envied Isolde, knowing she'd refused to come without her sword. His left hand grasped the stock as his right reached to twist the handle. It rattled, but didn't open. "It's locked." He tried again to be sure. "Unbelievable."

Declan seemed utterly unfazed as he stood with his back to the doors. "It actually makes sense for it to be locked."

"What do we do now?" Orion snapped. He turned to face the front entrance, standing shoulder to shoulder with Declan. Another guard passed through the room moving away from the cafeteria and up the left set of stairs. He glanced their way and dipped his head in greeting before continuing on.

"Ask someone for a key?" Declan suggested.

"Did that knife to the chest affect your brain, Declan?"

Declan frowned. "Or I'll trade places with Raven, and she can open it. Apparently she's an expert lock-pick, did you know? I didn't."

"She's a woman of many talents."

"I know how much you'd love to have her by your side. So I'll go get her for you." Declan grinned at the distaste visible on Orion's face. "Go back to the room and lay down. Three minutes." Ascending the stairs, he exited the room through the doorway on the right.

Orion turned toward the hall they'd come from, but rather than reentering the room with the man who'd scolded them, he turned left, deciding a trip to the washroom was a better idea. The washroom was at the end of the hall, and when he entered, he found it filled with more guards than he would have liked to see, especially since most of them wore little to no clothing. Since it would look too suspicious for him to leave the room immediately after entering, he strode toward a stall and closed himself inside.

He only needed to stand in there long enough for it to seem normal, and then he could make a quick exit. But the moment he closed the door to the darkened stall, his head began swimming with whispers. He spread his arms, flattening his palms against both sides and tried to steady his breathing.

"Not now," he commanded under his breath, willing the whispers to obey. Claustrophobia began to set in, and he thought for an excruciating moment that the walls were literally closing in on him. Tremors shot through his veins, leaving him lightheaded.

You are safe, Orion. I am with you.

Growling, Orion thought back, *I can handle this on my own.* Lifting his eyes to the ceiling, he watched the light from the torches flickering above, inhaling and exhaling more long breaths just as Isolde had taught him to do.

You prayed for safe passage as you entered the Fortress, yet now you reject My aid?

Orion ground his teeth and let his head fall forward. His neck ached with anxious muscles. *I don't know why I did that. It was foolish and pointless. Just leave me alone.*

The answering reply sounded miles away. *If that is what you truly wish.*

Orion looked up again, straightening his spine. He pictured Isolde's arms around him when he'd woken up from his awful dream unable to breathe. She'd walked him through it and held him rigid until he calmed down. If he tried hard enough, he was sure he could imagine her arms around him and dispel the whispers on his own.

Though it felt terrifying to do, he closed his eyes and forced himself calm, feeling her hands on him, feeling his palms touching the skin of her back, hearing her voice over the whispers instructing him to breathe in and out.

Orion knew for sure his three minute time frame had passed. Despite the tingling in his fingers and the dripping in his ears, he opened the stall door and stepped back out into the washroom.

CHAPTER 30

STRAYED

Jax, Hector, and Isolde allowed themselves little time to pause for breath before continuing onward. They knew the noise had alerted more predators of their invasion. The prisoners continued to shout, and they could hear the clamorous shrieks of more Strayed heading their way.

The walkway of level eleven appeared empty, but they couldn't risk taking their time. Moving quietly but quickly, they hurried around the circumference. Then Jax caught sight of something up ahead and stopped them. A few of the cell doors hung open with no guards in sight. They could be empty, but Jax knew the usual procedure was to lock every cell regardless of occupancy.

Hector looked leerily through the grated floor above their heads. "We have to keep moving." A squeal from somewhere far out of sight had them scanning the level behind them. Sweat dripped into Isolde's eyes, and she wiped it away, her heart lurching with every new sound. Sticking to the inner railing, they sidestepped toward the open doors.

Jax approached the first cell, peeking around the corner to get a glimpse inside.

A hoarse voice from the cell next door rasped, "Don't do it. Don't go in there." Jax looked into the locked cell and saw a man leaning against the wall next to the bars. What little hair he had left was frosty gray, and an untrimmed beard covered his face. A skeletal arm reached for the bars, and Jax took a step back. The man pointed a scraggy finger at the cell next to his. "Don't."

Hector touched Jax's shoulder, and he flinched so violently he almost punched Hector in the face. Swearing at him under his breath, Jax crept closer to the open cell and peered inside. Foggy shadows formed in the blackness as his eyes tried to focus on the scene.

Hector grabbed a torch from the wall and joined him at the door. Accepting the torch, Jax held it inside. His regret was instantaneous. The ground flashed in the firelight, wet with dark liquid that coated the concrete floor. On the side of the room opposite the bunks, a shape lay against the wall. Jax took another step into the cell to extend the light. He pinched his nose to stifle the horrid smell of the dismembered corpse. A second carcass stuck out from beneath the bottom bunk.

Hector's silhouette appeared in the doorway. "What is it? Is anyone in there?"

"Both dead." Jax leaned over to get a better look at the first body. "And not because of malnutrition." Though it seemed one solid lump at first glance, closer examination revealed it to be a pile of pieces all stacked together: severed arms and legs, organs pulled from their place within the torso, and bones licked clean. Flies buzzed around the pile, devouring its spoils and laying eggs in the crevices, instinctively providing nourishment for young maggots to feast and grow.

"What do you see?" Isolde whispered from behind Hector.

Jax straightened. "Don't let her in here." He moved toward them, freeing himself from the gruesome images but not the heinous stench.

Hector stepped out of the way as Jax looked into the next cell, finding it the same with little investigation needed. Hector moved ahead, exploring two more open cells of his own. "What are they doing? *Why* are they doing this?"

"They're depraved." Jax ushered Isolde away from the cells, though she attempted to look over his shoulder and glimpse it herself. Drawing her eyes with his sharp tone, he said, "You don't want to see it, Isolde. There's no reason for you to." He held her gaze, willing her to obey the command. "Hector, let's get moving. There's sure to be more coming."

Hector agreed and moved on from the room, walking past the last open cell without looking inside.

Isolde clenched her teeth. "You do not need to protect me."

Jax said, "I'm a soldier who spent most of my service doing the Queen's bidding. But soldiers are supposed to protect people, aren't they? Let me be the kind of soldier I wish to be." Isolde's eyes remained locked on his until Hector hurried them onward. Jax gestured for her to go ahead of him, and though she scoffed, she did as he requested.

Footfalls on the metal walkway had Jax looking over his shoulder, though nothing chased them on level eleven yet. As he passed by the last open cell, another sound reached his ears, and he paused, trying to place it. It sounded wet, like slurping soup rather than running water. A shuffling sound had him backing away, but the creature inside had already spotted him.

It leapt from the darkness into the firelight, slamming into him so they both fell to the ground. The torch rolled away and over the balcony edge. Patches of long, stringy hair swung back and forth against the Stayed's face. Its teeth thrashed as Jax pushed against its torso.

Isolde yelled his name as three more appeared from the dark, their faces twisted in hateful wickedness. They attacked her and Hector before either could help Jax. Footsteps rattled the stairs. Another handful appeared, swarming the thin walkway and overtaking them.

Isolde defended with her sword, but they'd managed to push her backward, separating her from the men. Hector had been taken down and was wrestling three on his own.

The one on top of Jax stopped struggling, its dead eyes seeming to glisten with joy as it lifted fleshless fingers to reveal a knife. Another Strayed arrived, hoping to join in on the tussle, but the first thrust its blade up through the other's chin and made quick work of tossing it away, unwilling to share its prize.

Jax tried to push the monster off with hands around its neck, but it was too strong. It toyed with him, pretending to slash his throat. He winced as it ran the ragged edge across his forehead, too soft to break the skin. Releasing a loud screech, it swiped the knife across his bicep, cutting through the uniform and tearing into muscle. Jax cried out, and again moments later as it carved a gash across one of his bushy brows. Blood poured into his eye, blinding him. He yelled for Hector, but his commander had his own monsters to contend with.

The Strayed pried one of Jax's hands away from its throat, holding his wrist at a painful angle. It grinned, revealing rotten teeth and breath, before slicing the knife across his fingers. Jax screamed as two of them went flying. The creature watched the fingers tumble away and scrambled off of him, endeavoring to catch them before they fell through the grated floor. Jax rolled onto his side, gripping his hand in agony. The monster hunched nearby, gnawing on his severed fingers, chewing away muscle and slurping the blood with delight. Jax grabbed his pistol from where it had clattered to the ground and shot the Strayed in its temple. Then he rose to his feet and kicked its limp body off of the walkway, watching through one eye as it plummeted.

Snapped back into action, he raced for Hector, who had managed to shoot one of the three attacking him. It lay prone on the floor at his side. The other two remained on top of him, fighting over who would get the next bite. One was bald with splits and tears in his skin that revealed an eggshell skull underneath. The other might have been female in its previous life.

Jax thrust his boot into the empty ribcage of the bald one and shot the other in the head. It slumped next to the first. The one he'd kicked rolled into a crouch and stared at him. It shrieked and lunged, but stalled midair as Jax shot it between the eyes.

Dropping next to his friend, Jax looked over Hector's wounds. Isolde continued to fight on the opposite side of the level. He knew he needed to help her, but Hector had stopped moving. The monsters had been feasting on him. A section of flesh had been eaten away from his forearm, his thigh, his chest. "Commander," he breathed, tapping his shoulder and trying to rouse him. Hector didn't move, and Jax swore.

He stood and yelled for Isolde. He could see her across the cavern, still on her feet and fighting, and he ran for her. Coming up behind her attackers, he shot two, and she decapitated the last.

The obnoxious calls of the prisoners echoed throughout the vast cavern alongside the sharp clangs of metal against metal. Those close enough to have witnessed all the downed Strayed booed and complained that the excitement had ended so quickly.

"Where is Hector?" Isolde looked over his shoulder, trying to spot him.

"Come on." Jax grabbed her hand. "We need to hide. They'll never stop coming if we keep fighting." They ran the circumference back to Hector. Jax's injured hand throbbed, and his head began to feel foggy, but with Isolde's help, he dragged Hector into the closest open cell.

The floor was slick with blood, making them slip as they pulled Hector to the back of the room. Jax slumped against the wall, and Isolde crouched next to them.

"Is he going to survive?" They heard movement coming their way, and Isolde scrambled closer to Jax. Then she grabbed his hand and whispered, "Elohim, keep them blind to us, I beg you. Let them move past as if we do not exist. Let them return to their tasks with no memory of intruders. Please, Elohim, keep us safe."

A group of Strayed came into view outside the cell. They looked around, noticing their downed comrades with building frenzy. One turned and gazed directly into the cell, though it made no indication that it could see them. Squeals and yowls from far away drew their attention, and the Strayed returned their call before racing off.

Jax and Isolde released a breath and relaxed against the wall, safe for the moment.

C

Declan entered the hallway leading to the Warden's quarters and closed the door behind him. When he reached the double doors, he turned the handle and found it locked. Knocking quietly, he whispered, "Raven? Raven it's me."

Seconds ticked on with no reply. A sound in the direction of the door he'd come through drew his attention. Keeping his eyes on the distant knob, he said her name again before hearing the bolt unlock.

Peeking a single eye through a slit in the doorway, she whisper-yelled, "Silas! What the hell? You scared me half to death!"

"Let me in."

Raven stepped out of the way and let him pass before closing the door behind him. "What happened? This wasn't the plan." She blanched. "Is Orion all right?"

Declan's forehead wrinkled. "Why wouldn't he be?"

Exhaling a relieved breath, she waved off his question. "What happened?"

"The doors to the prison entrance are locked. We need to swap out."

Raven's head tipped to the side. "That's strange."

"It actually makes sense. Why does everyone think it's weird for the doors leading to the underground prison to be locked?"

She smacked his shoulder with the back of her hand. "I mean it's strange Jax wouldn't have known or would have forgotten to tell us. I could have taught you how to pick it if we'd known."

"I agree, but he's had a lot on his mind." Looking around the room, he surveyed the Warden's decor, thinking it extremely bizarre. Then he saw a guard on the floor with his hands tied behind his back and a gag in his mouth. The man stared at Declan in desperation. "Who's he?"

Raven crossed her arms and kicked the man's thigh. Tears soaked the fabric that held his gag in place. "Silas, meet Roger. He's slimy and vile, so don't pity him. And don't ask how he got here because we don't have time."

Declan twisted the tip of his bangs. "Okay, back to the door. Let's consider it a lesson in thinking on our feet. It's all going to be fine, but we need to readjust. Did you find the lever in here?"

She pointed across the room toward an open door. "His bedroom is through there. The lever is next to the bed on the right side. I was just about to activate it when you gave me a heart attack."

He grinned. "Orion will meet you by the doors."

"Lovely. Party time with Orion."

Chuckling, he pushed her toward the door. "Get going."

"If I lock you in, you'll be stuck. So I'm leaving it unlocked. Watch your back."

"You too."

"And keep an eye on him." Raven eyed Roger, who was still squirming with mild hysteria. Then she crept back into the hall.

C

Raven passed a few guards, but if anyone questioned her exiting the Warden's chambers, they didn't express it out loud. A man leaning against a doorframe barked at her. When her eyes found his in the dim corridor, he scanned her body from head to toe and back again with unsavory concentration, sporting a foul grin.

"Not a chance," she said, and his grin widened as if accepting the challenge. Scoffing, she passed through the doorway and onto the landing. She didn't have time to fend off another creep and decided if he chose to follow her, she would knock him out right away, regardless of the consequences.

Traveling the steps to the entrance hall, she rounded the staircase to the double doors. She glanced up in search of the guard, but he didn't appear to have followed. With no witnesses in sight, she picked the lock. A hand grabbed her shoulder from behind, and she bit her tongue to suppress a shriek. Whipping around, she yanked one of the hidden knives from beneath her shirt and pressed the blade against her assailant's jugular.

"It's me." Orion's eyes were wide. He held his hands up, realizing what he'd done. She mouthed his name in a silent shout, and he dropped his head into his shoulders. "Sorry."

Swallowing the blood leaking from her tooth-pierced tongue, she rolled her eyes and returned the knife to its hiding place.

"You weren't supposed to bring those." Orion's grin had her sensing approval rather than reprimand. Jax had told her to leave all weapons behind but for the pistol retrieved from the kidnapped guards, but she preferred her blades and the level of stealth they provided, so she'd brought them along, too.

"I feel safer when I have them. Keep your mouth shut about it." Then she turned back to the doors and pulled them open.

C

Isolde didn't know how long they sat there in the dark waiting for the prison around them to settle. Hector still hadn't stirred, and now that Jax's adrenaline had fizzled out, he'd begun to shake in his agony.

Isolde heard him suck air through his teeth and looked to find him clutching his hand to his chest. "You are injured. What happened?" Jax shook his head, but she wasn't as blind as he was in the dark and could read his pained expression easily. "Let me see." He held out his hand, his whole body trembling, and she winced at the sight. "Oh, Jax. We need to stop the bleeding." He nodded as she scrambled for a plan.

"Use my shirt." He tried to undo the buttons of his jacket, but Isolde swatted his hand away, already on her knees in front of him.

When she finished with the buttons, he leaned away from the wall and attempted to shuck it off his shoulders. It was still wet and clinging to his skin. His undershirt had already been torn to wrap her knee, and the fabric was softer and more pliable than what made up the jacket.

Jax hissed when her fingers grazed his skin as she pulled the shirt up over his head. Tearing a strip from the bottom, as he had done, she reached for his hand.

"I can do it," he said, but she ignored him, pulling his hand closer and wrapping it in the fabric. He swore. "I might pass out." She told him to rest his head against the wall, and he did, closing his eyes and trying to control his breathing. His head slid to the side, his lips parting, but she continued to work.

When he jolted awake, she encouraged him to remain calm, promising she was almost finished. He nodded, and the motion mixed with the pain had his stomach churning. He turned to the side and vomited onto the floor. Isolde held tight to his wrist so he didn't injure himself further and used her other hand to rub his back. He coughed, dry heaving until the convulsions settled.

When he leaned his head back against the wall, she said, "Hopefully this helps until we can get out of here and wrap it properly. Hold it above your heart if you can." She felt his forehead with the back of her hand, but with how hot the room was, it was impossible to tell if she felt a true fever. "We have medicine back at the camp."

Jax nodded, and she encouraged him to breathe each time he began to hold his breath. The foul odor of copper and filth assaulted their noses, making them choke and gag as new waves wafted through their nostrils.

When his breathing began to settle, she leaned closer to look at the cut above his eye. She used the shirt to wipe it clean, but it continued to bleed profusely, spilling into his eye and down his cheek to his neck and chest. "It is a blessing. Any lower would have blinded you."

"It will clot on its own eventually."

"You have already lost so much, and the head always bleeds more. I can wrap it."

"Exactly, so it likely looks worse than it is." Jax inhaled and coughed. "Check on Hector. He still hasn't woken."

Isolde scooted sideways, her knees sliding in the blood that drenched the floor. She stuck two fingers against Hector's pulse.

"He lives." Moving closer, she examined his wounds. The worst was on his arm, where flesh and muscle had been torn down to bone. Ripping another section from Jax's shirt, she wrapped the wound, tying it tighter above like a tourniquet to help stifle the blood. Blood soaked his thigh, so she tied that wound up as well. Then she ran her fingers down the side of his face, enticing him with gentle words to wake.

His eyelids fluttered, and he startled in a panic.

"Calm, Hector. We are hidden for now. You have both lost a lot of blood, but we need to be moving on soon."

Hector inhaled a sharp breath and bit his tongue to stifle a cry as the pain in his body finally registered. He tried to lift his arm to look and found it bandaged, though the thin shirt tied around it was already saturated. He said Jax's name.

"I'm here, Commander."

"I want to sit up," Hector said, and Isolde helped him lean forward and rotate so his back was to the wall. "Where are we?" His own choking gag answered his question.

"It was the only option. Everything out there seems to have calmed down." Rising to her feet, Isolde turned toward the cell door, but Jax grabbed her fingers.

"Wait. Let me go."

"Hush." She pulled free and moved to the entrance, peeking out and scanning everything she could see. Some of the prisoners continued to express their disappointment, but most had quietly returned to their incarcerated misery. No Strayed lingered nearby, and she didn't hear movement on the metal walkways. "I think we are safe for now."

She returned to the men and helped Jax up first, holding his jacket open so he could slip his arms back into it. When he turned to face her, she began buttoning it closed before he could protest.

Together, they helped Hector off the floor. His injured leg made him unsteady, as did the blood loss, but they had to move forward. There would be no escaping until they'd completed their mission.

C

On the other side of the double doors, Orion and Raven found themselves in a dimly lit chamber, darker even than the rest of the flame-lit Monastery.

Someone unseen spoke from the other side of the room. "Hey, what are you doing in here?"

In a flash, Orion crossed the space, slamming the butt of his pistol into the man's temple. The guard dropped instantly as another man tried to attack him from behind. He slammed his elbow into the man's nose, and he fell just as quickly as the first. When no others appeared, he scanned the remainder of the room before turning back to Raven. "All clear."

"Savage." Raven's eyes widened. "Silas probably has the lever activated by now."

Orion had already crouched to tie the mens' wrists together with strips of fabric he'd had stuffed in his pockets for this very occasion. "The gears are there." He pointed to either side of the staircases wrapping the outer edge of the room and leading into the prison below. Red carpet ran the length of the steps, and a cast iron chandelier matching those in the entrance hallway hung above them, swaying eerily in the windless air.

Orion approached the set of gears on the left side, and Raven went to the right. Four gears of varying sizes were set into the wall, and the one on the outside had a handle.

"How will we know for sure if it's time?" Raven asked.

"Because Declan is punctual. I assume if he hasn't yet, the gears won't turn for us."

"Fair point." She wrapped her fingers around the handle. "Do you think the others are in place yet?"

"Should be soon." Drops of water grew louder in his head. He hadn't realized they'd been silent since the mission began and wondered if they came from a true source rather than from his memories. He looked around. "Do you hear that?"

"Hear what?"

Orion couldn't see her expression in the dim light, but her worry was clear in her tone. His eyes scanned the dark space. "The water? Dripping water?"

Repressing a concerned sigh, she answered, "No, Orion, I don't. Are you good?"

Orion shook his head, attempting to expel the sound. His heart sped up, but he willed himself to remain calm. The room looked like the dungeon, but he'd expected it would, and he'd prepared for it. He'd made it out of the bathroom stall, and he could make it through this as well. A bead of sweat dripped past his eye. "I'm good. Ready?"

"Yes."

"Then spin."

They grabbed their respective handles and cranked them clockwise. The first gear began to rotate, and the others followed suit. Then a chain reaction of clinks and clanks began reverberating behind the wall and below them. When they could spin the gears no further, they held them in place.

Exhaling another heavy breath, Orion said, "If you have any kind of faith, Raven, I'd say now is the time to start praying."

C

Isolde led the way around level twelve until reaching the set of stairs that would lead them to level thirteen.

Stopping at the top, Jax looked down into limitless darkness. "This is it. Be ready."

Isolde grabbed a lit torch from the wall and held it over the staircase.

A prisoner in the nearest cell noticed them stop and prepare to enter the Strayed levels. Realizing that they must be the cause of all the commotion up above, he began to shout. Jax raised his pistol at the man's head. Immediately silent, the man backed away from the bars and out of sight.

Hector started down the stairs into the pitch black, one arm grasping the railing for balance. Isolde followed after him, and Jax followed her. When they reached the bottom, only their torch provided light to the corridor. Hector looked pointed to the firelight. "Won't that draw more to us?"

Jax said, "They can see in the dark, and they can smell us. We got away with it upstairs because they wouldn't have questioned the human stench. We won't be able to hide so easily down here, and we won't survive totally blind."

Needing no further convincing, Hector reached for the torch. The ring of Isolde's sword sliding from its sheath sounded in the silent hallway.

Hector held the fire forward, casting the area in front of them in a vibrating hue. This, they came to realize, was an unfortunate circumstance, as the contents of the hall revealed it to be a torture chamber. Iron rings hung from the wall, and they didn't have to guess at their purpose, since several still held bodies hanging limp with arms stretched above their heads.

Isolde's hand flew to her mouth, and she turned away, squeezing her eyes shut to block out the image. "Oh my word," she breathed, her voice tight with emotion. "I can never unsee that." Jax put his pistol arm around her, allowing her a moment to soak in the comfort of his shoulder. She inhaled a deep breath, finding the air in the room even more atrocious than it had been near the cells. She choked and pinched her nose closed. "I might be sick."

"I vomited just outside the wall the first time they let me in the prison," Jax admitted.

Slowly, she rotated back around to find Hector holding the torch up to a corpse, surveying the intricate ways the body had been mutilated. An obscene amount of cuts littered the corpse, and dried blood covered every inch of exposed skin. Something long hung from a laceration near the man's stomach, dangling down his body until it coiled on the floor. Several fingers and teeth were missing, as well as an eyeball. The other eye hung wide open along with his mouth, as if he'd died in the middle of a petrified scream.

"We should probably move faster." Hector pulled the torch from the mangled carcass, and rested a hand against the opposite wall to steady himself. Yanking his hand away with a grimace, he revealed a slimy substance tainting his fingers.

Jax gestured for Isolde to walk in front of him. They followed Hector along the rounded corridor with blood, guts, and entrails strewn about the walls and floors. Their boots squished against the stone floor, but none looked to see what they stepped in.

The base of the fire lay on the other side of the wall, making the chamber's heat unbearable, even oppressive. Their thick, cold-weather clothing stuck to them like sopping masses of heavy mud.

As they reached another set of stairs, a body hanging from the wall next to them shifted, causing them all to leap from their skins. Isolde grabbed Jax's shirt and buried her face in his shoulder again, only to quickly move away when her senses returned to her. She'd never been the type of person to scare easily, and certainly not one who needed to hide in another's arms to feel safe, but being in such a gruesome place had all of her emotions heightened and her senses overloaded.

A groan escaped the man's lips, and Isolde cringed toward Jax again, though she didn't touch him. "He is alive," she gasped into her hand, turning back to look at him. She kept her fingers near her face so she could shield her eyes at any moment.

"Barely." Jax clutched his pistol between his ribcage and his arm so he could reach two fingers to the man's throat to check his pulse. Though his condition looked similar to the first body, wet blood dripped from his lips. Jax withdrew his hand and wiped his fingers on his pants. "He's close to death. He suffers."

Isolde shoved her sword up into the man's chest, holding it there for a moment before pulling it free. As if exhaling the remains of his life force, the man's body sagged with dead weight. "He suffers no more." Wiping the sword on her clothing, she walked past them down the next set of stairs without another word.

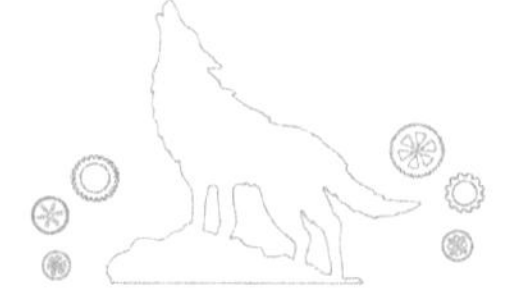

CHAPTER 31

LEVEL FIFTEEN

The second level belonging to the Strayed curved like the one above. Instead of a torture chamber, it was lined with tools, weapons, cleaning materials, and the like.

Hector said, "When we reach the next level, it won't be a hallway but a wide open space."

Jax nodded. "The stairs are dead center under the floor. There will be Strayed down there, so we will likely need to run." He looked at Hector, who tapped his leg and smiled.

They passed rows of folded but dirty fabric and piles of cut wood, and a few crates shuffled as they walked by.

Alerted by a freakish wail, Hector and Isolde whipped around to see a Strayed with its arms wrapped around Jax's shoulders. The tone of its shriek revealed its possible femininity, even if its face did not. Jax twisted and shoved at the monster's hands where they'd latched together on his chest, but with only one hand, his strength was insufficient against its grip.

Hector pushed Isolde out of the way and shot a bullet directly into the creature's forehead, silencing it instantly. As it released Jax, the Strayed slumped to the ground behind him, and he scurried away. They waited soundlessly to see if anyone nearby had been alerted by the noises.

When nothing came, Jax turned to Hector and said, "Thanks, Commander."

"How did it manage to sneak up behind us?" Isolde asked.

"They seem rabid and brainless, but they're actually devious and crafty." Jax let his head fall to each shoulder, cracking his neck as his heart settled. "Once we're in the room holding the vault, we'll bar the door. Hopefully any chasing us will have grown bored by the time we come back up through."

"Hopefully?" Hector echoed.

Jax nodded. "Either that or we will be fighting off a horde of flesh-hungry undead while scrambling through the dark in search of the way out."

"*Hopefully.* Got it."

When they reached the top of the steps, Jax asked, "Ready?"

Hector coughed. "No."

Isolde straightened her spine and twisted her sword. "We are here to save our prince. We can do this. Lead the way, Lieutenant."

"She's kind of a show off, isn't she?" Hector said. Jax grinned, and Isolde's mouth dropped open in offense.

At the bottom of the stairs, the firelight previously illuminating the walls dispersed into an orb that stretched out into the room before being swallowed up by darkness.

"How will we know where the center is if we can't see anything?" Hector whispered. On the outskirts of the light, shuffling noises sounded, seemingly all around them. Detectable movement filled the dark.

Jax took a small step in reverse. "We guess. A headshot won't kill them, but it subdues them the longest." His words came out in a stutter as his chest tightened with fear. A Strayed stumbled into their aura of light, wobbling as if unsteady on two feet. A patchy scruff of hair grew from its chin. Slowly, it drew closer, its ghostly eyes shifting between them.

Hector held his hand out, hoping to halt the creature as he'd been taught to do. Though to his knowledge, that tactic had only been tested in the upper levels. The Strayed paused momentarily, studying his hand in confusion. Crossing one foot over the other, Hector side-stepped, making sure to continue facing the monster as he moved. Jax and Isolde followed suit, holding their weapons at the ready but moving cautiously toward what they hoped to be the room's center.

Another came into their orb of light, moving more aggressively than the last. As it walked, its left foot dragged behind its right, causing it to hop. The monster bared its teeth and screamed, lunging despite its crippled ankle.

Jax fired his last shot into its forehead and made quick work of trading out the empty magazine. Movement ceased momentarily as the Strayed hiding outside the circle of light digested the scene. All seemed to realize their fallen comrade simultaneously, and the horde ascended. Pistol shots hurt their eardrums, echoing harshly throughout the chamber as they ran through the screaming crowd.

The room's center was their destination, but the room wasn't empty. Tables and crates and all kinds of debris littered the floor, making a straight run across the space trickier than anticipated. They ran forward, all attempting to stay within the orb of firelight in Hector's hand. To his left, he felt bony fingers encircling the arm holding the torch, and he fired a shot. His hip crashed into a table, and he rolled over it, dropping the torch. Jax avoided the table and hastened to help him up, returning the torch he'd scooped off the ground as they regained their footing and continued onward.

They moved much faster now, dodging and maneuvering the multitude of scattered objects as quickly as possible. Isolde kicked a piece of furniture into an oncoming Strayed and stabbed another through the eye before leaping over a table. Another coming at her from the right grabbed her hair, yanking her backward. Her eyes widened as they met Jax's, and she dropped into a crouch in time for him to shoot it in the temple. Fingers released her as the assailant fell.

A Strayed nearly ran through her en route to Jax, but she rolled out of the way. They picked up their pace, continuing to head toward the center of the room. Several more shots echoed around them over the high-pitched screams of the undead closing in from all sides.

Isolde spun in a circle, releasing a wild battle cry as her long sword decapitated three in one swing.

"Decapitation may work better than headshots," Hector called, a hint of impressed satire bleeding into his tone. "We should have brought swords."

"I'll remember that for next time." Jax tripped over something and tumbled. Grasping around him, he found the handle to the door and quickly lifted the floor hatch to reveal a set of hidden stairs. "It's here. Let's go!"

Hector arrived first, and both men turned back to observe Isolde howling as she wielded her weapon like the desert warrior princess she was. Jax called her name, and she ran to them, swinging one last time to strike an attacking Strayed before hurling down the steps with Hector and Jax leaping in behind her. Jax pulled the door shut, sliding the metal locking rod in place. They collapsed on the cramped stairs, heaving breaths of relief as the creatures banged on the metal plate above their heads.

Isolde winced with each new smash. Hector let his temple come to rest against the cold, stone wall.

Jax pointed at Isolde's leg, drawing attention to the bandage ripped free in the scuffle. "Your knee."

"It will heal. I am more concerned about you." She gestured to his wrapped hand saturated with blood. Then to his tanned cheeks looking pale even in the amber torchlight. "And him." She nodded to Hector breathing heavily against the wall. His arm had fallen to his side on the steps, though it still clutched the torch.

Jax said his name, drawing hazy eyes.

"I'm with you." Hector's bandages were just as bloody as Jax's, the thin fabric of the shirt doing little to suppress the wounds. The rest of their uniforms were drenched in blood from the floor in the cell, as if they'd bathed in it.

After a long minute, Isolde stood and helped Jax to his feet. Then they both grabbed Hector. The steps trailed downward in a spiral leading to a tiny room, only big enough to hold ten or so people if everyone stood squished together. Light gray walls framed a checkerboard floor, empty but for the door and two huge gears attached to the walls on either side.

"The vault." Hector hobbled toward the door, holstering his pistol. His hand slid across the carvings cut into the metal, trying to decipher the image displayed there. Stepping back, he held the torch further away so he could take in the whole picture.

The scene on the door showed the Queen with one arm raised in victory and the other at her side, palm up with a black orb of magic hovering above it. Below her feet lay a pile of corpses, mangled in indescribable ways. Hector shivered, pulling the light from the door and aiming it instead toward the gear on the left wall. Clearing his throat, he stabilized himself with a hand. "Each of you take a gear. Theoretically, if they've been activated from above, they should spin with no problem. Fingers crossed that the others were able to get in place and remain there."

Isolde tried to argue that she was the least injured and should be the one to search the vault, but Hector refused.

Jax grabbed a handle. "You need to be quick. If something happens above and one of them releases a lever, it'll all lock solid, and you'll be stuck."

Hector put his hand on Jax's shoulder, grinning. "I have the keys. If something happens, I'll join the Prince in Celestelvyra, and you can rescue us via another route."

Jax's reply wasn't as calm as Hector's. "If there was literally any other option besides this one, Commander, we would have taken it. We can't mess this up."

"If the worst happens, I'm sure you'll think of something, Lieutenant." Hector looked at Isolde, and she nodded, confirming she was ready. Jax did the same, and Hector stepped up to the door with the torch in hand.

Jax and Isolde began to spin the handles in a clockwise circle. Though nothing seemed to be happening at first, when the gears could be cranked no further, mechanical sounds clamored throughout the tiny room. After a long, loud moment, the door began to swing open.

"Wish me luck." Hector tapped the keys filling his pockets. He mused internally on whether or not he would be able to remove them from the table in the In-Between after the others escaped. Abram had said only those with a pure heart could lift the keys from their holes, and he truly had no idea if his would be deemed worthy, as Orion's had.

The room grew silent as the door ceased moving. Jax shifted his weight to better hold his lever in place. "Be aware of your senses. If it seems like you shouldn't be looking at something, force yourself to anyway."

"The vault isn't that big. I'll be out in no time." Hector stepped through the door, and all at once, torches lining the walls immersed the room in firelight. He looked back to make sure the door remained open behind him, as he'd been mildly concerned it was a trap to snare anyone who dared enter.

Then he began circling the outer edge of the room. He ran his fingers along the exterior of the space, feeling no resistance, nothing encouraging him to shy away. Chests littered the floor, a large painting of the Immortal Queen leaned against the back wall, and gorgeous, shimmering jewels filled rectangular cases. Hector wasn't sure exactly what he'd expected, but he definitely thought he would find far more heinous things than artwork and *gemma*. Lifting the lid of each chest, he found clusters of scrolls; *faeru*, *terras*, and more gems; and a bunch of magical tools, like wands, potions and powders, and dried flowers. A creepy row of jars stood on a shelf near the room's center, each filled with various liquids. When Hector realized one of the things inside resembled a human heart, he shied away from the rest and continued searching elsewhere.

He tilted the painting away from the wall, checking behind it and feeling the surface of the front and back. He fingered the outer edge of the wall, looking for anything that might reveal a hidden door, but nothing in the vault seemed like it could lead to a doorway. No invisible barriers. No feelings of nausea encouraging him to look away. Nothing. It was simply the vault of a wealthy witch. He knew there must be things of value he didn't understand, but there was definitely not an entrance to the In-Between.

Surprising Jax and Isolde, Hector exited the vault and said, "It's not here."

Jax's eyes widened. "What do you mean? It has to be."

"You look." Hector offered to relieve Jax of his handle. "I couldn't find anything."

Jax rushed in to scour the vault. Isolde and Hector leaned back far enough to peer through the doorway at him and watched as he mimicked Hector's every motion: feeling the walls, moving the picture, opening the chests. He lifted and moved and poked, hoping a secret entrance would open up, but there was nothing. Finally, he gave up and exited the vault looking bewildered. "We have to get out of here."

Isolde said, "But wait. It must be somewhere in the prison, right? Where else can we look?"

"I have no idea. There is nowhere in this entire building more fortified than this vault." Hector let go of the vault's gear, prompting Isolde to do the same, and the sound of retracting cogs filled the room. "Even the Warden's chambers aren't secure. The very fact that we made it in there proves Raven was able to break in with a simple lock pick. They don't fear intruders or even betrayers amongst their guards. The punishment is too severe."

"Would it be hidden somewhere else on the Strayed levels?" Jax scratched his head as he paced.

"They do cower from Sirena when she approaches." Hector

continued thinking it over. "Perhaps? We won't be able to search them with just the three of us, certainly not in the conditions we're in now. There are too many of those monsters up there." His eyes shifted to the ceiling, and he shuddered.

"I don't know about that," Jax said with a playful smile that didn't fit the situation. "I think Isolde may be able to hold them off while we explore."

"It won't be safe," Hector said, knowing they would need more weapons, more torches, and more people to fight off the Strayed. "We barely made it to the door, let alone taking the proper time we would need to search for something intentionally and magically hidden."

Isolde nodded. "We need the others. We can regroup with them at the top of the waterfall and travel back down."

Hector shook his head. "It's a miracle we haven't been discovered so far."

Jax said, "Your brother and his team will be rushing away from their meeting with the Warden any minute, if they haven't already. The plan was to escape before he got his hands on Jovan and Vera. We are out of time."

"It may be our only option." Hector fought to think up another solution. "It will be near impossible to plan another break in, and as we've already discussed, finding an invisible door beneath a pile of rubble isn't a reasonable solution either."

"We can sneak back in through the river. If we are only searching the Strayed levels, we will not need to be above ground like we did this time." When they didn't seem convinced, Isolde said, "Prince Alexander is trapped. We need to figure this out. There must be a way."

Jax sighed. "Let's meet them at the top of the falls as planned and decide then. We can let the others weigh in."

Hector and Isolde nodded. With a signal from Jax, they began their ascent up the spiral staircase. When they reached the door, it sounded quiet on the other side.

Isolde held her ear flush with the metal, listening for movement. "There are some noises, but they sound distant. I think we are safe to go through, but we are not using the torch this time. Put it out, and let your eyes adjust to the blackness. We know the steps to the next level are straight from this door. If we move quickly and quietly, we may have a better chance of getting there without having to fight."

"They can see in the dark," Jax reminded her.

"So can I. Stay close to me."

Hector ousted the torch and let it clatter back down the stairs.

Isolde waited a full minute to let their eyes adjust to a world without torchlight. Then, sliding the bolt away from the door, she lifted it open with undiluted silence, somehow even preventing the rusted creak. Letting it rest in its upright position, she crept up the steps, poking her head out to look around. A lot of Strayed filled the room, but all seemed busy or distracted. Some worked, filling pots with slop or stacking buckets. Others wandered the floor aimlessly, but none had noticed the opening door.

Her footfalls remained undetectable as she stepped from the hole in the floor with her sword raised and ready to strike if needed. Jax and Hector followed her, leaving the door open so as not to risk it making a sound. Sneaking across the level, they moved as quietly as prey avoiding predator. They maneuvered the debris, finding a path through the scattered furniture that didn't require them to climb over anything. Two Strayed stood next to a cart, leaving little space between them and a pile of boxes. Isolde rotated her body sideways and stepped past them, keeping her eyes on them as she went. Jax and Hector did the same. One of the Strayed turned just as Hector was walking past. He leaned back to avoid the creature's elbow. It seemed to survey him, but as Hector kept moving, it returned to its work.

They had almost made it to the steps when a single Strayed, seeming to amble around with no destination in mind, stopped next to them. It angled its head as if contemplating their existence, the skin of its face hanging way too low and dangling below its jaw. Its eye holes sagged to reveal cheekbone. Then its face seemed to reflect an expression of recognition, and it screamed.

"It was fun while it lasted." Jax shot the monster in the head before it lunged at Hector. "Now run!"

C

In a glistening bubble of glee, Foxxglove, Iris, Asher, and Seth returned to their waterfall. Asher fell into the grass on his back with his arms outstretched, seemingly unable to refrain from smiling.

"You're practically glowing," Foxx chided, sitting down next to him.

"I feel like I've finally accomplished what I set out to do. I know the hard part hasn't started yet, but this?" He tapped the pocket holding the Artifact. "A small part of me thought, what if it isn't real? What if there is no fountain, and I'm not the chosen prince? What if I'm just an arrogant sod?"

"Well, you are that."

He grinned. "True. But not *just*. I'm also smart, charming, devastatingly handsome, and princely, as well."

Foxx laughed. "Not to mention modest."

His face revealed an expression of total offense. "I would never claim to be that."

She rolled her eyes, lifting them to the sky. The galaxy above was brightening as the world around them dimmed. The day had grown late, and Foxx thought it must be nearly past sunset in Arkaemor. Asher's hand rose from the grass and landed on her knee, prompting a tremble to roll through her. Their casual contact was a new development, yet his hand rested there as if it were the most natural thing in the world. She hadn't realized her stare until his words invaded her thoughts.

"What are you thinking about?" He tapped his fingers on her leg.

"Nothing."

He smiled. "We're stuck here. You don't have to feel rushed." His other hand slid under his head.

"Someone could come through that door at any moment." She forced her eyes to glimpse the trail leading toward the door, though they found their way back to his beautiful physique almost instantly. "I feel like I don't know what to do. Part of me is preparing, the other is pleading to relax, and I feel stuck in between."

Letting his hand drop from her knee, he snaked it around her back, propping himself up on his elbow. "I wonder if I might help with that." His grin was impishly splendid, his voice low and throaty and mischievous.

Her heart quickened while her stomach performed a full set of somersaults. Glancing around him, she saw Iris and Seth disappearing down the path that led to the entrance. Her eyes again found his, and she shouldn't have been surprised to find him watching her, but the realization provoked another wave of tingling.

Some unintentional fear must have been written across her features because his brow crinkled as his head dipped to one side. "Please don't pull away from me, love." He scooted closer. "Not when I finally have you. Don't ever pull away from me again."

His words caused convulsions in her chest, and she wished he would stop doing things that made her body respond so intensely. "I'm not pulling away," she promised, finding it hard to draw words from her constricted throat.

"Then why does your face look like that?" One side of his lips curved to reveal his hidden dimple.

Her smile matched his. "I thought you liked my face."

"I love your face." He caressed her scar, and her skin prickled with delight. "It's the most stunning face I've ever laid eyes on."

"Stop saying things like that." Her eyes fell away as her cheeks flooded with heat.

"Never." He kissed her before she had a chance to shy away. His lips moved against hers with such tenderness she thought she might melt from the inside out. Though nothing like the heated passion from before, it felt a thousand times more intimate. Her body leaned into his, drawing him closer, her fingers grasping the bottom edge of his shirt before slipping underneath and dancing across the soft skin of his side. His breath hitched, and he laid her down next to him in one smooth motion. She was flat on her back, her fingers toying with his hair. His palm slid up and down the curve of her hip, her thigh, and across her stomach.

She felt dizzy with pleasure, her whole body tingling with electrical sensations as she lifted herself closer, wrapping an arm around his neck.

"I guess you were right, Iris. They really have made up." Seth's voice broke through their consuming embrace, and they tore away from each other. Foxx looked up to see Iris and Seth standing at the end of the path with four peaches in hand. Iris grinned, and Foxx dropped her head back to the ground with a heavy breath. Asher let his hand rest on her stomach, chuckling at Seth's hilarious expression. Then he leaned over and pressed a kiss to Foxx's forehead, sending another flood of color to her cheeks.

CHAPTER 32

THE NOT SO GREAT ESCAPE

Orion and Raven stood quietly, listening to the sounds of the guards throughout the mansion.

"How much longer?" Raven asked.

"Declan is the time keeper, not me. Just listen. We heard when they activated the gears below. We'll hear when they release them." He leaned his ear to the wall, trying to perceive any kind of commotion. The stone felt cold and damp against his cheek, just as it had in the dungeon when he'd smashed his face into the floor after a heavy smack from his torturer—a memory he hadn't recalled until that exact moment. The torch directly above him cast strange and swaying shadows on the wall, and he moved his face away, turning to look at Raven and hoping to distract himself before any whispers threatened.

"How are you doing?" Raven eyed the door anxiously as his brows furrowed, her sincere tone surprising him again.

"Don't use my issues to distract yourself from your worries."

She turned to him, and their eyes met. "Truthfully, Orion, I'm far more afraid of being trapped in here with you than anything on the other side of that door."

"I'm fine. I already told you."

She scrutinized him, eyes sliding from his tense brow and sweat beading on his forehead to the quake in the hand not holding the gear. "I mean with the voices," she clarified.

"I knew what you meant," he snapped. His eyes scanned the

room again, looking at the men he'd knocked out, the door, the creepy chandelier hanging above them. Then he scowled. "The voices are quiet. For the moment at least." Pressing his ear to the wall again, he attempted to ignore her questions only to be reminded of the dungeons a second time and quickly pull away.

"Does that mean something?" A noise outside the door drew their heads. After several seconds of silence, she added, "Are they somehow blocked in here? Or does she know we're here and is on her way, too busy to bother with making you crazy?"

"I don't know, Raven." His temper rose, and he fought to contain it. "I heard them before, when Declan went to get you, but I managed to silence them. So no, they aren't blocked in here. Aside from that, I really don't know."

A spider slid from the chandelier from a single strand of web. Raven backed closer to the wall.

Orion's lips quirked at her obvious fear of a tiny bug. Not that he could comment after finding himself afraid of tiny bathroom stalls. "I doubt she even knows I'm hearing voices," he said, trying to distract her from the tiny monster hanging between them. It climbed back up the string a few inches before dropping low again, and then repeated the process several times as though trying to discern the superlative place to hang.

"And they aren't constant, so maybe I'm not hearing them now because I'm just not. Or possibly I'm so focused on the task at hand I'm able to drown them out." He shrugged. "The more we discuss it though, the more my attention sways, so can we stop?"

"Sorry. Good point." She put her ear to the wall as he had done, listening for the sound of turning gears below. "So, what's with you and Isolde? Her brother seems super fond of you." His eyes snapped to her, and she grinned.

"I don't want to talk about that either." The words didn't come out as harshly as he'd meant them to. In fact, her chuckle lifted the corners of his lips.

The sound of cogs turning and teeth knocking sounded beneath their feet. "They did it." Orion's expression shifted from mild annoyance into hesitant relief. In unison, he and Raven released their levers and watched them turn in reverse. Then he met her at the center of the room, his gaze following her steps as she intentionally gave the dangling arachnid a wide berth. "Declan will be down any minute."

She nodded and jogged to the doors, putting an ear to the wood and listening for him to arrive. Looking back at Orion in horror, she said, "Orion, he's returned." Ear to the door again, she specified, "Not Silas. The Warden."

C

Declan stood in the Warden's bedroom with his hand on the lever as he took in all the ridiculous things the man kept on hand. One wall of his office was bedazzled with fancy hats in every color, each with a huge flower or feather—or both—pinned to the brim.

A desk far bigger than any desk had the right to be held little more than two stacks of paper, a bottle of ink and a quill, and a wooden structure which seemed to have no identifiable shape or purpose.

In his bedroom, nine pairs of the exact same high-heeled boots lined the wall, each shiny and black and tall enough to cover the ankle. A velveteen coat hung from a hook by the door, and a grand armoire sat against the wall with a looking glass big enough to see at least three people standing next to each other at once. A bed sized for a king was draped in a comforter of deep maroon, embroidered with silver thread, and above the bed hung a portrait of the Warden himself, dressed to impress in one of his ginormous hats. A similar painting hung in his office behind the desk, though in that portrait he wore emerald instead of eggplant.

Declan startled at the sound of rotating gears. When the noises quieted, he released the lever, hoping the sounds meant the job was done and not that something had gone wrong. With no way of knowing for sure, he headed for the door, ready to be free of the bizarre room.

To the man tied up on the ground, he said, "Roger, I'm sure you'll come up with some kind of explanation as to how you got this way, but whatever you do, you should probably leave us out of it. Otherwise, Raven might come back someday and get her revenge."

After offering the man a polite salute, Declan turned toward the exit. As his fingers grasped the handle, the door swung open, and a man in a wide hat filled the doorway.

"Who are you? What are you doing in my chambers?" His heavy heels clopping against the floor, the Warden stormed into the room and towered over Declan with cheeks already flushed by rage. "You there! What is the meaning of this?" His eyes shifted between Declan and the man tied up in front of his desk.

Declan leaned back. "Apologies. In truth, I arrived with the intention of requesting a transfer." He tapped the Legion colors on his uniform. "But then I caught a glimpse of your terrifying display of hats, and I've since reconsidered." Without a moment's pause, he punched the Warden square in the nose. The man stumbled, and Declan took advantage of his unbalance, shoving his entire body weight into him before bolting out the door. The Warden hollered after him, alerting the guards of an intruder.

Declan raced down the hall, his hand putting pressure on the still healing wound beneath his ribs. As he reached it, the door swung open to reveal three guards with weapons drawn. Declan held up his hands, his face painted in innocence. He threw a thumb over his shoulder to indicate the intruder was behind him.

The guards looked him up and down, seemingly confused by his uniform. One asked, "What's going on?"

The Warden clambered from his chambers yelling, "Arrest him!"

Two of the guards leapt forward, and Declan drew his pistol, firing off a shot into the closest man's thigh. The guard behind him tripped over the tumbling man but regained his footing in time to grab Declan's arm and slam it against the wall. Declan's pistol clattered to the floor. The third guard entered the hall and grabbed his other arm, pinning him.

Seconds later, more guards flooded the hallway. Two stood behind the Warden with guns in hand. Another two picked up the man Declan shot and helped him limp away.

The Warden approached Declan. His already crooked nose dripped with blood, and the pockets below his eyes were turning a hue that rivaled his hat. Bloody saliva spewed from his lips as he snarled in Declan's face. "I asked you a question, *boy*. Now tell me, what the hell is going on here?" Declan kept his lips sealed, leveling the Warden with a stony glare. "Who else is with you? What were you planning to do?" His face grew redder and his tone more fierce with each word he spit. When Declan remained silent, the Warden spoke to the guards holding him. "Take this man to the cells. Maybe a few days in lock up will loosen his lips."

"Hey you, with the ridiculous hat." A voice from beyond the door reached their ears, followed by two guards tumbling to the ground as they crossed the threshold. "What do you think you're doing with my friend?" Orion stepped into the hall and over the men, his pistol in one hand and a confiscated one in the other.

Declan grinned at Orion and returned his cool gaze to the Warden. "I tried to leave before this happened." He smirked, and Orion put two bullets in the men holding Declan's arms against the wall: one in the hip and the other in the shoulder. The Warden backed away as the two guards at his flanks crossed in front of him, though they seemed just as confused as the others had. Both observed the newcomer's uniform, uncertain as to whether they should be shooting him or not.

Declan had already reached for his pistol and was rolling out of the way as Orion sent two more bullets flying.

Finally awakened, the guards in front of the Warden aimed and fired, their bullets lodging in the concrete walls. Another shot grazed Orion's hip, and he cried out before sending two more bullets down the hallway. Declan was already out the door incapacitating someone in the next hall as Orion backed away from the Warden and his guards. He ducked to avoid another shot and pulled both triggers again. One bullet hit a guard in the chest and the other created a sizzling hole through the top of the Warden's hat.

Out in the hall, he glanced sideways at Declan to see him aiming at a guard wrapped in a towel and holding up his hands. Deciding their next move without words, Declan and Orion sprinted from the hall and down the stairs. Other guards had been alerted by the disturbance, but no one seemed to be following what was happening.

Rounding the staircase, Declan pounded on the doors, calling for Raven to open up while Orion stood at his back with double pistols in the air aimed at anyone who might think it intelligent to join the party.

Raven opened the door to find Declan grinning and out of breath. His hand cradled his ribs as heaving breaths caused more pain than he'd felt in days. "The charade is up. Time to go!"

She moved from the doorway, and both men ran inside. Seeing the guards in the entrance hall, Raven pushed the doors closed and secured them with the deadbolt.

C

Orion bolted down the left staircase, taking steps three at a time, and Declan and Raven followed. The stairs spanned the back half of the room and followed the right angle of the far corners, meeting across from each other on a lower landing. Only one door stood between them and the prison below.

Raven pulled out her metal rods and began picking the three locks lining the right side of the jam. "Did the Warden catch you? What took so long?"

Declan said, "Orion was late." Orion's mouth dropped open, and Raven laughed. By the time she finished, footsteps from the room above alerted them the door was no longer secured. Guards shouted to each other as they tried to assemble and apprehend the intruders.

Yanking open the door to the underground prison, the trio charged over the threshold only to halt abruptly in their tracks at the sight of the massive cavern. Together, they scanned the cells surrounding the huge gap in the center before moving forward a few steps to get a glimpse of the intense flames raging below. When his amazement subsided, Declan pulled his hidden pocket knife from his boot and jammed it into the crack separating the frame from the door.

Raven brought her fingers to her nose. "It smells horrendous."

"This place is huge." Orion leaned over the railing to take in the levels below. "The waterfall is there. Let's move." Raven and Declan followed as he began jogging down the metal walkway.

The prisoners' uproar echoed throughout the cavern. Nefarious laughter and rattling bars filled their ears, growing louder by the second as more joined in.

Above the commotion, Orion heard Isolde's voice shouting his name. He skidded to a stop and leaned over the guardrail again to find the source of her cry. Eight rows down, he found her running at top speed with Jax and Hector at her heels. Behind them, a horde of humanoid monsters chased with unbelievable agility, screaming horrifying shrieks that clattered against the cavern walls.

Declan and Raven joined Orion at the railing and immediately noticed their low numbers. "Iris and Foxx aren't with them." Declan's voice filled with dread. "No one is."

"They're hurt. Look." Raven pointed at them. "Wrapped up and bleeding everywhere."

Isolde cried out again. "Orion! It was not in the vault! The door was not there!"

Orion strained to comprehend her words over all the noise and stimulation, but the stress of the situation spawned the whispers. He grabbed both sides of his head, closing his eyes, trying to think. It had to be in the prison. If not the vault, then where?

Somewhere hidden. Somewhere others wouldn't want to search.

He considered the cells but quickly realized Sirena would never leave something so important to chance.

His whispers were raucous and grating, made infinitely worse by the screaming of the Strayed, the guards banging on the door behind them, and the bellowing prisoners making noise for no reason other than elevating their own entertainment.

All at once, the riddle Maeve had spoken to him in the desert consumed his thoughts, and he heard her words in his ears as if she stood right next to him speaking them again.

If you seek to save the others, you must search diligently among the briar. Seven no more, but don't lose hope, for all legends are forged in fire.

Awakened from the memory, Orion heard his name over the tumultuous clamor just as a brain-jarring slap cracked across his jaw. His eyes opened to find Raven's mouth agape, and he realized she looked terrified rather than irate. Her dark eyes pierced his as she yelled, "Orion, come back! We need you!"

As if the slap had rattled everything into place, the meaning of Maeve's riddle crisped into focus. He knew what he had to do. He leaned over the railing looking straight at the roaring flames. "It's in the fire!" His voice was drowned out by the chaotic sounds and tormenting whispers.

"What?" Raven and Declan bellowed, their eyes alight with a new level of horror.

"The door. It's in the fire. There's nowhere else it could be. Where better could Sirena hide a doorway to the Sacred Realm but in a fiery death trap at the bottom of a hellish pit of her own making?" He evaluated the two paths Maeve had spoken of: between the light and the dark, between the selfish and the selfless. One path makes a failure, the other—a legend.

"You're insane!" Raven shouted. Orion took several steps back from the railing.

"Rion, what are you doing?" Declan approached his friend with arms out as if soothing a feral animal.

"It has to be." Orion's whispers grew louder, outweighing the shrieks from the monsters below. Even that felt like a confirmation that he was on the right track: they were trying to stop him from doing what needed to be done.

"Orion!" Raven yelled as he planted his feet and lowered into a slight crouch, preparing to run. "You have to stop! You're not thinking straight."

Isolde was shouting his name, her voice breaking through the roaring volume of the whispers even from several floors down.

Frantic, Raven asked, "Can you hear her now? Is Sirena making you do this? You can't listen to her, Orion! Orion, answer me. Please!"

With a heavy sigh, his body and mind fully accepting what he had to do, he wrapped his fingers around her upper arms and fixed her with the most serious expression he could muster. "Yes, Raven, I can hear her, but she's not telling me to jump. You just have to trust me. I'm right about this."

"I don't trust you!" she screamed.

"Orion, please," Declan entreated. "Just wait. We can figure this out."

"There's no time!" Orion released Raven and stepped as far from the railing as he could. "You just worry about getting everyone out safely. I'll find Alexander and the others and bring them home." He bent his knees, readying to charge. With one last glance at his friend, he added, "And Declan? If this doesn't work, try not to miss me too much, okay?"

Then he bolted for the railing. Wrapping both hands around the metal bar, he vaulted over, throwing himself from the walkway into the wide open cavern. Declan tried to reach for him.

But he missed.

And Orion plummeted.

Isolde careened to a stop as she caught a glimpse of his falling form.

Hector and Jax each grabbed one of her arms and dragged her with them.

Orion's body dropped like a meteor, plunging into the massive flames. The last thing he heard before being entirely consumed by the blaze was Isolde screaming his name.

Part Three

Rise From Ashes

In the garden of wonders, sacred and holy,
A truth will be revealed.
one path chosen, another forged.
One to live and one to die, one to fail and one to rise.
But there is hope.
As hope is all that lifts us up on wings like
Eagles soaring through the bright blue sky.
Carries us over oceans, enduring tempests and violent waves.
He will lead the way, in His mighty plans,
He will make the path straight.
Though darkness threatens at every turn, seeking to devour.
Though lions roar and serpents bite,
All will be consumed in light.

And even as the Destroyer reigns,
Seeking to kill and shred and maim;
And even as chaos rules this world,
When the red moon rises and the sun fades;
And even as all hope smolders to dust,
And the dark Queen takes her place;

Two will stand. Two will fight. Two are needed.
And in the end,
Light.

~An excerpt from Jumalan Sana.
Found in the book of Baba the navi.

CHAPTER 33

OUT WITH THE OLD

Hector, Jax, and Isolde met up with Declan and Raven on the top level. As they passed by the door leading above ground, the guards broke through just in time to converge with the Strayed. Distracted and needing to defend themselves, the guards lost sight of the escaping intruders climbing the wall to the top of the falls and disappearing from view.

Above the waterfall, they jogged parallel with the river, searching for the rope they'd left behind. Isolde said Jax's name, and Hector thought she must have realized in that moment what he'd figured out himself—there was no way he and Jax would be able to pull themselves against the current with their injuries.

An unexpected *bark* had them looking around in search of its source. To their astonishment, a tunnel materialized against the wall where Isolde, Jax, and Hector had first pulled themselves from the water and lay thawing out on the concrete shore.

Several *sylis* into the tunnel stood a gray wolf.

"Another wolf?" Raven and Isolde shared a glance Hector didn't understand. Before he could question it, the wolf barked again and turned from them, disappearing into the darkness.

Hector made the snap decision to chance the wolf and mysterious tunnel rather than risk the river, and the others followed without question. When everyone stepped inside, the entrance to the tunnel closed up before their eyes, plunging them into darkness. Seconds later, the ceiling lit with thousands of tiny lights.

Raven reached for Hector's arm. "Lunae-lumen."

"Moonflies." Isolde lifted a hand, and a swarm of the glowing insects swirled around it.

Jax touched the block wall where a doorway had existed moments before. Then he looked at Hector, his brow pulled together.

"This way." Hector limped between the others and led them through the passage. They walked for several minutes until reaching a set of steps that led up to a hatch laying flush with the ground above. Finding it unlocked and easy to open despite the frigid temperatures of the landscape, they emerged from the door into a land barely lit by the recently new Reaping moon.

More than one hundred feet from the prison wall, they could hear the alarm sounding within the Fortress. Hector looked around, thinking no one could have expected them to exit where they'd surfaced. He hadn't known such a tunnel existed, nor had Jax, despite their thorough knowledge of the Prison's interior. By the time the guards corralled the Strayed and caught up to them, they would be long gone.

Plus, if blood loss hadn't caused a hallucination, he'd seen the door disappear into a solid stone wall. He felt certain the others had too, but weariness continued to siphon his senses, so he didn't waste energy asking.

The wolf never reappeared, but no one spoke on that either.

They began their trudge toward camp, each consumed by their own thoughts and worries. Hector walked next to Raven with his arm slung over her shoulder for balance. He tried to comprehend her obvious anger and sorrow. She and Orion had always butted heads. The way she told it, she'd seen what an arrogant idiot he was the moment they met, so he couldn't understand why she seemed to be taking his loss so hard.

After giving up on dissecting her emotions until they could discuss it, Hector's own failures swallowed him. They hadn't saved the Prince, and he had no clue how they would succeed without him.

He looked past Raven to Declan, longing to comfort them both. Orion had been Declan's best friend—his brother, his sole companion for so many years, and Hector saw the weight of that loss in his downturned gaze.

It took them just over half an hour to return to their campsite. A dull relief settled over each of them as the smell of burning fire alerted them they'd made it back to the others.

Johnathan raced toward them, his face dropping when he saw their low numbers and dejected expressions. "What happened?"

No one responded as they walked past, though Declan paused and put a hand on his shoulder. After shaking his head to indicate their failure, he proceeded toward the fire.

Griffin rushed to Isolde the moment he saw the blood drenching her clothing. At the sound of her name on her brother's lips, she crashed into him and crumbled into a fit of tears. Confused and worried, he wrapped heavy arms around her and let her cry. His eyes scanned the crowd for Jax, finding him sighing and shaking his head, expressing the disaster of their mission in his woeful countenance.

He tried to pull Isolde back and ask what happened, but she wouldn't stop crying.

Hector spoke a low explanation at his side. "The door wasn't in the vault as we expected. And Orion—" He glanced at Isolde. "Well, he jumped into the pit of fire at the base of the prison. We aren't really sure why."

"He thought that's where the door was hidden." Raven left Hector and stomped toward the fire. Seeming to teeter back and forth between grief and rage, she plopped next to Declan, who sat cross-legged on the ground with his head in his hands.

Griffin's eyes scanned Hector, taking in his injuries. "You need cura. Vera, *iuvo.*" Vera appeared at his side, and when she saw Hector's bandages, she hurried to grab her bag. Griffin nodded for Hector to follow her before returning his attention to Isolde. "*Homo stultus,*" he snapped like a curse under his breath.

Isolde yanked back, her expression of grave offense. "No! *Fortem!*"

Griffin spouted more aggressive Vetoräti. Then she yelled back a single, irate word before rushing away into the darkness of the icy wasteland.

"*Femina stultus!*" he shouted after her before returning his axe to his hand and chopping a chunk of wood in half.

"Someone should go after her." Declan looked at Hector, then at Jax. "It isn't safe for us to be separated."

"We need to get moving soon," Hector said.

"I'll go." Jax made eye contact with Hector, a silent communication passing between them. Then he walked off after Isolde.

☾

Jax found Isolde weeping on a rock several *sylis* from camp. Approaching slowly, he spoke her name, pulling her attention to him. Face obscured with tear-streaked paint, puffy eyes, and the blood from the cell, she looked years younger and nowhere near the scary warrior he knew her to be. Standing before her, he waited for her to convey what she needed.

"What was he thinking?" Another sob emerged, and she covered her mouth with a hand.

"I don't know. I don't understand what happened." His temper kindled, not toward Isolde, but toward the idiot who'd leapt to his fiery death. He'd never cared for Orion, but Isolde clearly did. How could he do this to her? Though Jax had made many women cry himself, none had been women like Isolde. None had even come close.

This thought caught him off guard, and he winced as wrinkled skin pulled at the gash above his eye. Before he could examine it further, Isolde rose to her feet and turned to him. She attempted to wipe tears from her cheeks but only succeeded in smearing the muddled paint and blood. When she at last lifted her eyes to his, he asked, "What can I do, Isolde?"

More tears spilled down her cheeks as her forehead fell against his chest. Jax wrapped his arms around her and let her cry, seeing no other obvious course of action. His rage toward Orion swelled, fueled by the cadence of her sorrow. He decided then that if that arrogant jackass somehow managed to survive, he would be the one to beat him senseless for making Isolde feel such agonizing grief. Then he continued rubbing her back, allowing her to rest on him as she wept over the loss of Orion.

☾

Iris threw a peach to both Foxx and Asher, and they dug in. Peaches had become their favorite thing to eat, and they ate them almost every day. Iris thought no peaches outside the garden would ever taste as rich and delicious as they did within the boundaries of Celestelvyra and wondered if that might be true of everything they'd eaten since arriving. "You guys look entirely too happy," she chided, nibbling away the final flesh clinging to the crevices of her peach's pit. "We're still trapped here, you know. No need to get *too* blissful."

"I have many reasons to feel excessively happy, Iris, and your rubbish attitude shall not deprive me of them." Asher squeezed Foxx's knee and winked. Iris stuck her tongue out at both of them and sat down in the grass. Night had fallen, and the stars above sang with colors and glittering light. The grassy field grew dim enough for sleep, and the air warmed to the optimal temperature for relaxing.

Seth giggled and plopped into the spot next to her. "We could be trapped in a really scary place though. With nieda and other monsters." Then his eyebrows flew up as if something had just occurred to him. "Wait, there aren't monsters here, are there? We haven't seen any, but that doesn't mean they don't exist. Maybe they are just really good at hiding."

"No monsters here. The Creator wouldn't let them in. Trust me. And soon there will be no monsters out there either." Asher pointed toward the entrance, and Seth's eyes widened. "I'm not sure if they'll die with the Queen or if the Creator will restore them. Or maybe they'll die out over time with no new ones mutating. Either way, the world is going to begin looking very different when this is all over."

Seth considered this information with a look of deep contemplation.

"I would like to discuss something." Iris tossed her peach pit into the treeline where two squirrels waited patiently for them to finish up, hoping to glean any remaining tendrils of flesh before cracking them open to devour the smooth seed within.

Asher and Seth eyed her expectantly. Foxx stared at the grass.

Iris continued, "We obviously need to revisit the fact that the enchantment guarding the fountain was unraveled, not only by the Crown Prince, but by my lovely sister, who is apparently *chosen* by the Creator himself." Three sets of eyes turned to Foxx, who had set her half-eaten peach at her side in favor of picking at the grass.

"We already knew she was special." Asher smiled.

Foxx lifted her eyes to him before rolling them dismissively. "I'm not special."

"You must be!" Iris shoved Foxx's shoulder. "Did you see what happened in there?"

Shaking her head, Foxx lifted her hands to dispel Iris' words. "Whatever magic happened back there was triggered by the fountain or the enchantment connecting us, not by me."

"I'm not entirely sure that's true, love. Your—"

The scream of a man falling from the sky cut Asher's sentence short. The man landed hard in the grass directly in front of them with a loud *thump*. Asher and Foxx leapt to their feet, and Iris squealed, clutching Seth with both arms.

The squirrels from the treeline took advantage of the distraction and rushed over to snatch Foxx's discarded peach, working together to roll it out of sight.

The man attempted to sit, but found his back stiff, making it difficult to lift his torso off the ground. He wore a disheveled uniform similar to the King's Legion garb but displaying an unfamiliar emblem on its chest, like that of a flame stitched with red thread. Opaque smoke rose from his skin in thin wisps, and his long, dark hair hung in his face. Still, there was no mistaking him.

"Orion?" Iris gaped.

Sitting up with effort, Orion O'Connell held his hands out in front of him, first examining his palms, then turning them over to look at the smoldering skin covering his knuckles. He wiggled his fingers and clenched his fists before moving to touch his legs and knees. Then he rubbed his chest, patted his face, and pulled his hair. "I'm alive," he whispered. "Actually alive."

"I think you may be wrong about the Creator not letting monsters into Celestelvyra." Iris glanced at Asher, only half joking, but Orion wasn't paying attention.

Asher hurried to offer him a hand.

Orion groaned. His hand found a bleeding wound above his hip, and he swore. When he pulled it away, blood stained his fingertips. He looked around, scanning the lush scenery of the garden and seemingly trying to get his bearings. Then he rubbed his tailbone and frowned. "That really hurt."

"How did you get in?" Asher asked. "You didn't come through the door. What happened?"

Orion scratched the back of his head, again surveying the area.

Then he looked up at the galaxy sky free of the moon's ivory beams. "Where am I?"

Asher kept his hand on Orion's shoulder. "You're in Celestelvyra, mate."

"You fell from the sky!" Seth exclaimed.

The unfamiliar voice drew Orion's eyes to Seth. Then he lifted them to the sky again, and the others followed his gaze, as if the answers would be written in the stars.

"I guess it worked." He ran both hands down his face. Asher let go of his shoulder as Orion began to pace and mumble. His words were low and indiscernible, but he seemed to be working out some difficult calculations. They watched him for a long moment, baffled.

When she could no longer wait for him to get a grip, Iris took a step closer and said his name, prompting his eyes to snap sharply in her direction. "What are you doing here? How did you get here? Tell us what's going on!"

He stopped pacing and faced her, though the gears behind his eyes continued to spin with fervor. "I jumped into the fire," he said, only managing to confuse them further. "We went to the prison to find another door so we could get you out of here, but it wasn't in the vault like we thought. So I thought maybe the fire…"

Asher blanched. "The prison? You mean the Ashgate Fortress?"

Orion nodded without diverting his attention from Iris, though she sensed him staring right through her. She couldn't remember a time when she'd seen him so dazed and out of focus. He'd been forever intense and attuned to the world around him. Now he seemed lost in the labyrinth of his thoughts.

Asher tried to draw him back. "Why were you there? Were you being held there? Did you escape?"

"The Monastery in Metsa Sateen was destroyed. It was our only option for getting to a door. Strange I ended up here and not in the In-Between, don't you think? I'm talking too fast." He paused and took a long, slow breath. "But I don't even have the keys. Hector has them. I probably should have thought of that before jumping…"

Asher stepped out of the way as Iris placed herself directly in front of Orion. She spoke with concern and kindness, hoping to soothe him so they could get some logical answers. Saying his name, she leaned closer to grasp his eyes with her own.

At last, his gaze truly latched onto hers, and his expression softened with relief. His lips curled, and a twinkle returned to his eyes.

She'd forgotten the enchanting sapphire. So captivating. She tried to decipher what thoughts might be swirling within them. Then a yelp of surprise escaped her lips as Orion wrapped his arms around her and pulled her into a tight hug. Shocked by his closeness and the intimacy his expression displayed as he'd reached for her, she stood stone stiff.

"Am I having a vision right now?" Foxx asked Asher under her breath. "Am I dreaming?" She tilted her head to the side as if changing her perspective might help her make sense of it.

Asher chuckled. "If you are, then I am too."

"Me too." Seth folded his arms over his chest with indignation in his brow. "Who is this guy?"

Orion nuzzled his face into Iris' hair and breathed her name. "I'm so glad you're all right."

Yielding to his explicit emotions, Iris slipped her arms around his waist, her body slumping into his warmth. Sturdy muscles tightened around her, holding her with such strength, she thought she'd never felt so safe or secure. A heavy exhale escaped her lungs, and she squeezed him back with all her might, clutching her fingers around the wrist of her opposite hand.

Orion groaned as she pressed against his wounds, but he didn't pull away.

Tears streamed onto his shoulder, soaking his shirt. Just when she began to feel embarrassed by her unkempt emotions, she realized tears poured from his eyes, too, seeping into her dark hair as his heart became unshackled in her arms.

It was too much for her to handle. Orion there and Declan gone. Not only was Orion there, saving them, jumping through fire—apparently—but she could already sense that the man with his arms around her was the man she'd only glimpsed a few times. One filled with kindness and compassion, emotion and humanity.

The last time she and Orion had interacted, he'd been entirely inhospitable. As well as nearly every other time they'd interacted. But Iris had a soft spot for him in her heart. A tenderness she didn't quite understand. She'd felt it when he taught her about the birds and when they saved each other from the lagoon monster. When he opened up about his father and in the warmth she sometimes caught in his eyes.

Something existed in the space that stretched between them. It was unusual and perplexing and… sweet.

Orion pulled back and searched her eyes. He let one arm drop to her lower back and used the other to wipe tears from both their cheeks. Still embarrassed despite his own bared emotions, Iris kept her eyes to the ground, hiding the windows to her soul with damp eyelids. Orion whispered her name and tapped the bottom of her chin. "Iris, look at me, I have to tell you something."

Wiping the remaining tears from her lashes, she sighed with exhaustion. "What is it?"

Orion looked down and saw blood from his bullet wound on her shirt. Touching it, he said with a small chuckle, "Sorry about that."

Iris shook her head, unconcerned by her marred clothing. "Are you okay? Does it hurt?" She lifted his shirt to see blood seeping from the gash in his skin. Now more focused on his body, she saw the cuts and bruises in the process of healing. Scars littered his torso, his arms, and even his face.

Orion sucked in a breath as her fingers grazed sensitive skin. "Someone shot me. Of course it hurts." Her gaze found his, and his smile widened. Then he grabbed her shoulders to focus her. "Iris. Listen to me: Declan is alive."

Round eyes swelled with emotion, and a slice of physical pain cut through her chest like a knife as she choked out, "What did you say?"

Looking nervous, as though perhaps he'd made a mistake, he said, "I thought you might think him dead if you saw Sirena stab him. It was a really bad wound." When she didn't react further to his words, he continued, "But maybe you didn't see that, and I'm scaring you for nothing?" His arms had dropped to her waist as if not ready to let go yet.

His mind seemed to wander as he looked her over, his attention so intense it made her blush. She wondered what he must be thinking, wondered what his words could possibly mean—how they could possibly be true.

Then a proud, teeth-revealing grin spread across his lips, a stark contrast to how sorrowful Iris felt standing in front of him.

Her voice drew him back to the present. "I did see him stabbed." She felt her world caving in. Or possibly her chest. Or maybe the sky. Her words trembled with newly falling tears. "I saw him fall. Sirena stabbed him under his ribs. There's no way he survived an attack like that."

"I assure you, he did." Orion wiped away more tears. "What

reason would I have to lie about it? Declan is fine. At least, he was when I left. He was with me and the team at Ashgate."

Suddenly remembering herself, Iris' face ignited with fury, and she shoved him away. "He betrayed us," she snapped, as if just then realizing Declan didn't deserve her tears.

Orion took a step closer, holding his arms up in a petition for her to remain calm. "I know. He's an idiot." Iris looked away from him, turning her head to the side and crossing her arms in defiance. Seth matched her stance and huffed.

Orion said, "Iris. Just listen. Declan knows what he did, and he has spent every moment since waking trying to come up with a way to save you all." His eyes slid to Foxx and Asher. "He isn't even fully healed from his wound, but he took the risk and came with us anyway."

Iris refused to look at him, though even in the midst of her anger, she found his pleading on behalf of his friend mystifying. His tone of voice had shifted into timbres of deep compassion and patience, as though a completely new man wore Orion O'Connell's skin.

"To the Ashgate Fortress, Iris. The scariest place in all of Arkaemor. To save *you*."

An incoherent sound gurgled from her throat, and she took another step back to stand next to her sister.

C

Foxx also didn't know what to think or how to feel about the things Orion shared. She, too, held a deeply rooted anger toward Declan. No matter what he'd done since then, the original betrayal stung like a pulsing blaze in her chest. And though she wasn't particularly fond of Orion either, there he stood seeking forgiveness for his friend.

There he stood—rescuing them.

Bittersweet emotions filled her heart. For a split second, she considered killing Orion right then and there so they could remain in Celestelvyra forever, but as if the Creator whispered words of encouragement into her thoughts, she realized that couldn't be part of His plan for her life. Or Alexander's.

If Orion had truly dropped in from the sky, it wasn't some fluke of nature or cruel trick. It had to be the Creator's doing, and so she would trust Him and follow through with whatever plans He'd set out for her. She'd already made her decision, and even if Orion O'Connell was the herald standing before her, she would do her best to fulfill Elohim's wishes.

"Did you say Hector?" Asher asked. "Who else was at the prison? Are they safe now?"

As if suddenly realizing his disrespect in the presence of a royal, Orion turned and extended a hand. "Prince Alexander. I apologize for my rudeness, Your Highness." He dipped his head, and Asher laughed.

"No need for pleasantries, soldier. We owe you our freedom, if that truly is why you're here."

Then Orion's gaze turned to Foxx. She'd crossed her arms, scrutinizing him as she scrutinized everything. "Hello, Foxxglove."

"Hello, Orion," she replied. "Of all the people I've pictured coming to save us, I never once expected it to be you."

Orion chuckled. "Though now that I've arrived, I fear I may have trapped myself with you. Hector has the keys to the door." His eyes scanned the area as he scratched the top of his head. "I don't know if my team is safe. When I left, half were being chased by the Strayed and the other by the guards."

"What's the Strayed?" Seth asked.

"You don't want to know."

Seth harrumphed again, and Foxx suspected he didn't much care for the man who'd showed up out of nowhere, talking like a crazy person and hugging Iris.

Orion's hands moved with his words. "We had it all worked out, practically down to the minute—Jax is very thorough—but the door to the In-Between wasn't in the vault beneath the prison as we thought it would be. So when we realized the plan had failed, I kind of went rogue and jumped thirteen stories into a raging fire." His voice trailed off as if embarrassed. "Some of the Raptors were with us: Hector, Jax, Raven. Then me and Declan. And Isolde." He paused after her name left his lips. Then he cleared his throat. "Isolde's brother and several of his clan created a distraction outside the walls to get us into the Warden's chambers. It was a pretty extensive operation. But it failed because the door wasn't in the vault."

Catching the unfamiliar name, Foxx asked, "Isolde?"

"A woman I met in the Grim Wilds. A princess, actually. Her father is Naaba Kaatachi." He glanced at Asher.

"Of Caritas," Asher said.

Orion groaned and closed his eyes to combat a dizzy spell. His hand clasped his hip.

Asher again stood at his side holding his shoulder steady. "We should do something about that wound."

Orion nodded. "Isolde, her brother, and two others of their tribe found Johnathan and I in the Wilds…" He paused again, his foolish expression returning. "… attacking a hive of nieda." Chuckling at their horrified expressions, he continued, "I know, I know, but Declan was dying. We needed to save him. They ended up saving us. Isolde nursed him back to health and has stuck by us ever since. Her father has pledged to join us when we attack Inaravale." Sighing and putting more pressure on his hip, he added, "You guys have really missed a lot."

Asher observed the blood spreading across Orion's shirt and the top hem of his pants. "I can't believe you broke into the Ashgate Fortress."

"It seems the plan didn't fail entirely since you did manage to get here." Foxx looked sideways at her sister, finding her intrigue over Orion's explanation outweighing her previous anger.

"Let me get this straight," Iris said. "So you met a princess and for some crazy reason she decided to join you and the Raptors on this perilous mission to break into a prison to find a door to Celestelvyra that you ended up not finding, and so you decided to jump into a huge pit of fire. Am I getting all of this correct?"

Orion grinned. "Well, when you say it like that, it sounds pretty insane. But yes, that about covers it."

Iris' head leaned sideways in unison with the upturning of her lips. "And… you like her," she said. "Isolde of Caritas."

Foxx drew back her head, surprised, then she looked at Orion in an attempt to discover whatever her sister had noticed.

Orion lifted his eyes and looked at Iris through long lashes. "Don't start."

Beaming at his confirmation, she smirked at Foxx, who frowned.

"All those people came to save us?" Seth asked, still eyeing Orion with dubious suspicion.

"All those people came to save Prince Alexander and the magical water." Orion looked at Asher. "Did you find it?"

Asher slipped the Artifact from his pocket, holding the vial out in his palm with a proud grin. "Took us a while, but we got it."

Orion leaned closer to take a look, his eyes widening at the sight of the sparkling liquid.

To their left, a shining light appeared, forcing them to shield their eyes as they turned to see what caused it. When it faded, they saw a woman in a dandelion yellow dress that flowed all the way down to her shoeless toes. Her skin was dark like tree bark, and her silver hair was a wild mess of curls.

CHAPTER 34

CHILDSON

"Maeve?" Asher drew back in surprise as Foxx and Iris exclaimed the newcomer's name in unison. All were baffled to find someone else in the garden. They'd been there two weeks and hadn't seen a single person, and within minutes, two had appeared from thin air.

"Hello children. Alexander, it's lovely to see you, and Foxxglove, Iris, it has been a while since I have glimpsed your beautiful faces. You are looking well. Following your destiny seems to be suiting all of you." Maeve's smile filled each of them with a feeling akin to motherly comfort, warming them from the inside.

Asher was the first to bow. "It's lovely to see you as well, Maeve."

"Thank you, Maeve." Foxx dropped her chin in a slight bow, and Iris said, "It's so good to see you!"

"It is a very good day indeed." Maeve turned her attention to Seth, who clutched Iris' side with one hand. "Young man, I do not believe we have met, but you are Seth Everett, are you not?"

Suddenly at attention, Seth released Iris and puffed out his chest. "Yes ma'am, I am."

"You are growing into a very strong and mature man, Seth. I am proud of the joy you have retained through all you have endured."

Seth smiled shyly as he mumbled a timid *thanks*.

"We're proud, too." Asher's voice drew Maeve's attention.

"Prince Alexander, I see you found them, as instructed." Her fingers slid up and down her lengthy necklaces. "You have done well."

"All thanks to you, Lady Maeve. Your assistance was much appreciated."

"Your diligence and hard work are appreciated. You have taken good care of them." She directed her attention to the last person in the party, tilting her head to study him with a broadening smile.

Orion had been staring at the edge of the clearing pretending not to exist. Though after a long moment of feeling her stare, he glanced her way and sighed. "Hello Maeve." Crossing his arms, he eyed the woman with suspicion. Maeve dipped her head cordially.

"You know her?" Iris asked, bemused by his expression.

Orion glared and gestured to her with his hand. "Maeve is the lovely woman who led Johnathan and I to a hive of nieda."

"Were you able to save your friend, Orion O'Connell?" Maeve asked.

"Nearly died in the process."

"Ah, but you did not. And I believe you even made some new friends. Important friends."

Orion rolled his eyes, and Iris suppressed a grin. Before he could say something as inhospitable as his expression, she asked, "Maeve, what are you doing here? *How* are you here?"

"I am with my Creator, of course." Maeve gestured to the regal Ram suddenly materializing at her side. Her hand stroked the back of His neck as though He'd been there all along.

Everyone froze, staring at the Creature without words. Even Orion dropped his arms to his sides and gazed at His majesty. The Ram nuzzled Maeve's arm with His nose, careful not to graze her with His massive horns.

The area around them brightened, glowing with life in response to the Ram's presence. Birds flew near, landing in the trees above and singing sweet songs to their Creator. Frogs croaked, and crickets chirped. Henki of various colors peaked out from hide-aways within trees and bushes. Squirrels chased each other up and down the tree trunks. A swarm of bees buzzed nearby, spiraling around Him before zipping away, followed immediately by a flutter of butterflies dressed in every color of the rainbow. A herd of doe appeared in the treeline, as did several rabbits, three black foxes, and a number of other animals who lived in the woods.

Even the trees joined in the performance, swaying in the breeze and releasing groupings of leaves that swirled in the wind. The henki began to dance in time with the music the leaves created.

"What is happening?" Iris' mouth hung wide open. "Am I about to wake up from the world's most bizarre dream?"

Maeve tittered and shook her head, scratching the Ram under His chin as the menagerie settled.

"Are you here to let us out?" Asher's eyes shifted between the dazzling animal and the humble servant standing at His side.

"Everything in its time, Your Highness. Orion, your friends are currently escaping the Ashgate Fortress. He has created safe passage for them that will not require swimming through icy water."

Orion exhaled relief, seeming to forget his grumpiness in light of this kindness. He bowed in appreciation to both Maeve and the Ram.

"So we're on the right path?" Asher stood closest to Maeve and the Creator, just a few feet away. Speaking directly to the magnificent Ram, he knelt on one knee. "I have Pyhä-ki now. I'm to kill the Queen of Arkaemor with it? That is what You wish of me, Elohim?"

The Ram held his gaze for a long moment, and Asher felt rigid with anticipation. He'd spent so long preparing for a destiny he believed to be his fate, but kneeling before the Creator now, he felt arrogant for thinking himself so high and wondered if his plans had been self-righteous and misguided.

Without breaking eye contact with Asher, the Ram nudged Maeve, encouraging her to speak.

In her tranquil voice, Maeve quoted the prophecy to them.

> *"All lands come together to repair a grand era.*
> *Each used in the end to unlock the Elvyra.*
> *A childson is needed to do the unbending,*
> *to unwind the history and bring forth all mending.*
>
> *To shred all to ruins, he'll forfeit his crown.*
> *To rebuild the world, it must first be torn down.*
> *When all is restored, we will have but one master,*
> *Living in freedom, peace and joy ever after."*

As her prophetic words faded, the garden erupted with creatures and plants praising their magnificent Creator.

"So that's a *yes*." Those words were the reason Asher had started down this path to begin with. Amaryllis Belamour had embedded them deep in his heart at a young age, and he'd never forgotten them. He turned questioning eyes from Maeve to the Ram. "It has to be me. I have to kill Sirena.

Sadness lurked within the Creator's expression, though He did not answer.

Maeve took several steps toward them, stopping in front of Asher and drawing him to his feet. She placed her hand atop the vial still resting in his palm, dragging the pad of her thumb over the Jerichonian moon at his wrist. "*A childson is needed to do the unbending*. It is true, Sirena must be vanquished with Pyhä-ki, carried from the garden in the Artifact you now possess." The Ram made a noise, stomping His hoof and puffing air through His nose. All eyes turned to Him. Maeve took in their confused expressions with a soft smile. "You must understand, it never pleases Him to lose one of His children."

For a moment, Asher thought she was referring to the child in the poem. Had he missed a clue indicating that the childson would die in the process of killing the Queen? He gulped as his heart rose to his throat.

"Stifle your fears, Alexander. Sirena is His child as well. It grieves Him to lose her to such a horrible fate, despite knowing it is the only way for His world to begin its path to restoration."

Asher looked around Maeve, meeting the Ram's eyes again. Sorrow transformed into resolve, acknowledgment that Maeve's words rang true.

"When this darkness has fallen, Elohim will begin the process of healing. The prophecy must be fulfilled as it is written." Maeve made eye contact with each of them. Settling lastly on Orion and holding his gaze for a long, uncomfortable moment before returning her attention to Asher. "Although, the prophecy does not specify *which* childson it must be."

No one spoke as they attempted to comprehend her words.

Asher repeated the line, his uncertainty making him anxious. "*To shred all to ruins, he'll forfeit his crown*. I did that. I left Castle Solís and betrayed the Queen and my father. I gave up my right as the heir, at least until Sirena is destroyed."

Maeve smiled, the way a grandmother smiles at a young child who gifts her a dandelion. "That is true, son. You did. You have done a wonderful job following Elohim's wishes, and He is extremely pleased with you."

Asher exhaled, elated by the affirmation. Emotion softened his features as he again peered around Maeve to look at the Creator. Though the Ram couldn't smile, the look in His eyes emanated joy and pride. Asher smiled back, and Elohim bowed to him in return.

"However." Maeve quirked a brow as her gaze slipped to each member of the group. "Not all crowns are worn on the head. Some are embedded in our hearts, and we think ourselves lofty. It is only through humility and sacrifice that we are able to fulfill our destinies and the wishes of our magnificent Elohim. In truth, Alexander, either childson will do if the prophecy is to be believed, as it does not specifically say, *Alexander Asher Aldrich*." Maeve sent a joyful glance over her shoulder at the Creator before adding, "And it seems, in the midst of all that has happened, *both* have relinquished their crowns."

"Both?" Asher's thoughts slid to Avaline. Not a *son*, but perhaps *son* only reiterated *child*? Though he couldn't begin to comprehend how Avaline could possibly be responsible for murdering Sirena. Most days she could hardly pull herself from bed.

Maeve watched him with gentle humor as he attempted to grasp her bewildering message. Her eyes twinkled gleefully as if about to reveal a secret. Removing her hand from Asher's, she extended it toward Orion standing just two paces behind him.

Orion accepted her hand, allowing her to tug him closer and watching intently as she placed his bloodstained fingers atop the vial within Asher's palm.

With her hands encircling theirs, Maeve's mystic eyes sparkled as she at last spoke the word that spawned a new wave of gasps from the collective. Asher's face contorted, and Orion stiffened at his side. "Brothers," she breathed, soft and tender. "Both childsons to the King of Arkaemor. Both heirs to the royal Thrones." Maeve's lips cracked open to reveal beautifully white teeth. "*Both* capable of fulfilling the Monastery of the Morrow's prophecy. Either will do. Or perhaps both, together."

C

Orion recoiled, though his hand remained where Maeve had placed it between Alexander's and her own. His whole body felt stunned into a hardened clay, heated until solid by a fiery furnace.

"The King has had many dalliances in his time," Maeve explained. Orion and Asher dropped their hands the moment she released them, both taking a small, involuntary step away from each other. "In all his years, many heirs were conceived. Few made it to childbirth. Even less survived after. Sirena is very skilled at stamping out opposition, as you will soon learn first hand.

"When Orion's mother discovered her maternity, she ran from Sirena without telling the King, fleeing Inaravale with her fiancé." A cycling plethora of emotions distorted Orion's features, and Maeve nodded as if reading his thoughts. "Your father suspected, but never knew for sure. Regardless, he married her and raised you as his own."

The Ram behind her breathed through His nose again, drawing Maeve's attention.

Looking over her shoulder, she dropped her chin before turning back to the Princes with a consoling expression. "Your father was so lost, Orion. He never fully understood what following the Creator truly meant. But despite his misguided notions, he did love you and your mother very much."

Orion stood rigid, staring straight ahead without meeting Maeve's eyes. A tear slipped down his cheek and dripped off the edge of his chin. Contradictory to what this tear revealed, his expression was livid. "And you know what happened to him, don't you?" He directed his snarl over Maeve's shoulder.

The Ram held Orion's stare, unaffected by his aggression. *You are forgiven.*

Orion's chest tightened, a cobra constricting his lungs. Finding it impossible to draw breath, he could no longer hold back his tears. They spilled down his face like a roaring torrent as he endeavored to harness his temper. *Forgiven? There is no forgiveness for patricide.*

Elohim stomped a hoof. *You don't decide such things, Orion O'Connell. Only I can decide what is and what is not forgivable.*

"Enough," Orion snapped.

Asher turned toward him, and, sensing the movement, Orion glanced his way from the corner of his eye.

"Shall I continue?" Maeve asked.

Squeezing his fingers into fists, Orion grunted his approval and gazed off into the landscape at his side.

"Very well. For years the King pleaded for Sirena to allow him children. He knew of her disposal of the heirs and begged her to permit him just one. He explained how much the Five Kingdoms would benefit from having an heir to spoil and how children would bring much needed joy to Castle Solís and the royal city. Other stipulations were made, but Sirena, at last, agreed." Maeve was looking at Asher now. He matched his brother by clenching his fists and lifted his eyes to hers as tears threatened to pour free.

"At first, your mother worked as a maid in the castle. Pollux had always been particularly fond of her. She was sweet, charming, and all who met her, loved her.

"After you were born, Pollux was very persuasive in his request to keep her alive. You needed to nurse, after all, something Sirena was unable to provide. Rather than hiring someone in the city and risking the exposure of Pollux's affair, Sirena allowed her to stay and look after you. In fact, she remained with you for much of your childhood."

Eyes wide like a startled deer, Asher shook his head in disbelief.

"You knew her as Alice, your nanny. When she became pregnant with your sister, she was locked in the dungeons, and after your sister was born, Sirena had her executed. Pollux was forced to watch the horrific display. Many in the castle were. I would prefer to spare you the details." Maeve's eyes dropped apologetically.

Asher looked as if he might fall to his knees, and something in Orion had him longing to console the man at his side, though his feet failed to obey. Saving him, Foxx appeared and took Asher's hand. The touch had him turning and burying his face in her hair as he wept.

After a long, quiet moment, a gentle breeze blew through the clearing, cooling the emotions alight in their hearts like a caressing embrace. Orion released a heavy exhale. Asher wiped his cheeks and faced forward again, clutching Foxx's hand tightly at his side.

Maeve clasped her hands together. "This is a lot to take in, but your fight is not over. There is still much to be done. Take time to grieve, to refocus, to heal. But when you leave this place, you must make fulfilling your destinies your utmost priority." Her eyes slid across each of them before returning to Asher and Orion. "There is still much to be discovered, but you have plenty of time to unearth what is to come, to grow what needs to be grown, and to love where love will conquer." Taking a step closer, she placed a hand on each of the mens' shoulders. Then she returned to her place by the bighorn Ram, running her fingers down His neck once again.

"What do we do next, Maeve?" Iris joined her sister, and Seth followed along.

"Your Creator will open the door for you. You will arrive at the campsite in Crystavium and travel back to Caritas with your comrades. From there, the journey is up to you. The best advice I can give is this: no matter what occurs next, do not rush hastily into this battle. You may have procured a necessary ingredient, but remember to use all resources wisely. There is still much to do before the darkness breathes its last."

On the side opposite the Ram, a wolf strode into view and stopped next to Maeve. "Ah!" she exclaimed, patting the animal on the head. "It seems your friends have escaped safely, Orion. All went well, Rejio?" The wolf nudged her leg with his jawline in answer. "You see? All is well."

Orion's attention locked on the wolf, knowing it must be the same one he'd been seeing and again feeling astonished to discover it hadn't been a hallucination. "You," he said, eyes marveling at the sight. The wolf lifted its head in greeting and yipped a soft cry. "Friend of yours?" Orion looked from Maeve to Elohim.

Maeve chuckled and stroked its thick coat of gray fur. "Rejio is a good friend, indeed."

C

While the others focused on the new arrival, Foxx felt Elohim's gaze fix on her. She'd noticed Maeve's acute attention when she'd spoken about there being much to discover, and it terrified her.

She would like to think all the peculiarities she'd witnessed so far had been entirely the result of her presence in the garden and being so close to Elohim and His magic, but she couldn't deny the moments when she'd caught ice crystalizing on her fingers outside Celestelvyra. Add that to the visions, her mysterious connection with the magnificent Being before her, and Sirena's direct focus on her, and there was no way to avoid the truth. She'd been chosen. For what purpose, she didn't know.

She thought of her visions of the Konungr's face, both on the mountain pass and again as she'd slept in the city. When she'd seen him at the revolution rally, he'd singled her out. As if in that enormous crowd of faces, her attendance had somehow been significant.

Silently, knowing He would hear, she said, *What is Your plan for me? What is my purpose? Who am I to You, Elohim? Who am I to them?*

Elohim spoke back so only she could hear. *All will be revealed in time, My child. I know you are hesitant to leave, I know you fear what is to come, but I would ask you to trust Me, if you can. I promise you will return someday to this glorious garden, but for now, I still have need of you out there. There are still many of My people to be saved. Will you help Me save them, Foxxglove?*

A tear slid down her cheek. Her breathing grew shallow as she nodded in response.

Iris wrapped an arm around her waist and pulled her close. "Are you ready?"

"No," Foxx replied honestly. Continuing to stare into the Ram's eyes, she added, "But yes." Elohim dipped His head, acknowledging her agreement.

Maeve held out her arms as if she could wrap them all in one big hug. "We will see each other again. Continue walking your paths." Suddenly, she gasped and clapped her hands with one, loud smack. "I almost forgot! I have one final gift for you, Orion O'Connell." She appeared in front of him in a flash, and he stumbled back. Two fingers against his forehead sent a pulse of energy throughout his entire body. "Remember the words I spoke to you in the desert."

Then, as before, she disappeared in a puff of smoke, and the Ram and the wolf vanished with her.

CHAPTER 35

COMING TO GRIPS

Orion prodded his head where Maeve had touched him, trying to figure out what she'd done. *A gift,* she'd said, but he had no idea what kind of gift might come from such a strange sensation. He hoped he wasn't growing horns or something. Turning to look at Iris, he pointed to his forehead, and she shrugged, indicating she saw nothing out of place. Orion sighed relief before lifting his shirt to inspect the hole in his hip. What minutes ago looked discolored with bruises was now his usual skin tone. The brown scabs from Sirena's torture and dried blood of the bullet wound were reduced to pale scars, as if they'd been healing for years. *A gift,* he thought with a small smile.

Asher stood next to him staring at the ground as if utterly lost. Orion opened his mouth to speak, but no words came out. Hearing his breath, Asher met his gaze with his own uncanny expression. Neither knew what to say, so neither spoke.

Then Orion spit out, "I need a minute." After another glance at Iris, he hurried down a trail on the outskirts of the field.

C

Iris touched her sister's arm, motioning toward where Orion had run off, and Foxx nodded. Before leaving, she stopped where Seth had slumped onto the grass and knelt beside him. "Are you doing okay, buddy?"

As if she'd startled him, Seth exclaimed, "I'm fine!" His eyes landed on Foxx wrapping Asher in a hug. Then he looked around the glade. Many of the animals had dispersed, though two owls remained and the squirrels had gone back to picking through their peach pits. "Everyone else seems so upset. I don't know what to do."

"I know. Why don't you try to relax for a little bit until we figure some things out, okay? Go nibble on some honeysuckle or play with the frogs in the pond?"

He nodded sadly but remained in his spot.

Iris rubbed the top of his head. "Maybe you can talk to Asher after he's calmed down. I bet you would be great at cheering him up." This idea lightened Seth's mood, and after a final wave, she promised to return soon.

She found Orion in the grove of cherry blossom trees seated against a trunk and staring up at the petals falling around him. Approaching carefully, she ducked beneath one of the low-hanging branches. "Hey, what are you doing over here?"

Releasing a heavy sigh, he replied honestly, "Watching these weird petals that never seem to stop falling."

"Care if I join you?"

He tapped the ground next to him.

"They're cherry blossoms." She pulled her hair together in front of her shoulder and adjusted her shirt, which had ruffled awkwardly as she sat against the trunk.

"They turn into cherries?"

"Not cherries you can eat, but they produce little cherry-like berries that are super gross, though the birds seem to like them." Gazing with him up into the trees, she twisted a section of white hair around one finger.

The movement drew his attention, and he looked at her. "Your hair is down."

With a touch of embarrassment blooming on her cheeks, she stopped playing with it and wrapped her arms around her knees. "I leave it down sometimes."

"Not really." He squinted as if trying to unravel her strange reaction to the mention of her hair. "Only after you've been swimming or sometimes when you've just woken up."

"You don't know everything," she grumbled, shifting her eyes from him and resting her chin on her knee.

He lifted both eyebrows and sighed. "More and more it feels like I know very little," he said, sounding wiser than she remembered him ever sounding before. Holding out his palm, he let a few of the blossom petals land on his hand, then he turned it sideways so they could continue their descent to the ground. "Prince Alexander is my brother." He frowned, as if unsure. "Alexander is my *brother?*"

"So it would seem." Iris mimicked him catching the petals and played with the ones landing in her palm. "How does that feel?"

"I have no idea." A dole of doves flew into their line of vision and landed high in the tree above them. Orion and Iris watched for a moment as they seemed to settle in, getting comfortable in the tree's crooked branches.

"I guess you've already figured out that you're older than him."

At her words, his eyebrows pinched together as if he didn't understand how that bit of information was relevant. "Yeah, I guess so."

Iris pressed, "Asher is twenty-eight, I think. You're almost thirty, right?"

"A few days ago, yeah."

"Your birthday was a few days ago?" she exclaimed, and he nodded. "Orion! Merry birthday! Did you celebrate?" A small smile curled his lips. His eyes looked caught in a dream. When it was clear he wasn't going to answer, she asked, "Well, you know how family lineage works with royalty, don't you?"

Expelled from his daze, his eyes snapped to her. "What are you saying?"

Iris reconsidered her words, thinking maybe she didn't want to be the one to reveal the information he hadn't yet realized. She'd assumed it was the reason he'd looked so distressed before fleeing. When he continued to stare, his expression growing more irritated as he waited for her to make her point, she exhaled. "Well, if you're older, that means... you're the true heir to the Thrones of Arkaemor."

A terrified expression consumed his countenance, leading her to believe that he had not, in fact, figured this out.

"No." He shook his head feverishly. "I can't be." Iris nodded, assuring him of the truth. He looked at the palms of his hands, tripping over his words. "No, Iris. Alexander is going to be king. He grew up in the castle. He's the Prince!"

"That's true, but we now know you're a prince, too. An older prince. That's not something we can all just ignore, Ri."

"Maeve must be mistaken." Orion dropped his head in his hands. "This can't be happening. It can't be real, Iris."

"I don't think Maeve is in the habit of getting things wrong." After another minute of awkward silence, she added, "If it helps, I'm sure Asher is feeling the exact same things you're feeling right about now."

"Of course he is! He just learned I'm the one in line to be king! He's probably contemplating my assassination." He cackled madly. "This is unbelievable. You know, I thought I was doing a good thing for once, putting others above myself. Taking the correct of the two paths, or whatever. Risking my life to set things right for the Prince, for the world. For you." His eyes slid to her. "This can't be real."

Iris didn't know what to say, so she didn't say anything. Instead, she lifted her hand to catch more petals. One of the miniature dragons they'd seen throughout the garden soared past, disrupting the petals as they fell. Its pink scales matched the trees surrounding them, and it appeared to have actual flowers growing down its back. Landing in the next tree over, it curled into a ball and rested its head on its tail.

Orion didn't notice their guest. He remained lost in his thoughts for several minutes before finally saying, "I'll step down. Abdicate. He can have it. I don't want it. I can't."

"Maybe Asher doesn't want it either. It's a weighty thing to accept." She knew this to be true but didn't think it was something she should divulge as fact. Images of Orion wearing a crown flashed through her consciousness, and she tried not to reveal her smile. She decided he would look exceptionally handsome as a king, maybe even more so than Asher.

"Why do you call him that if you know who he really is?"

"It's what he wants to be called. He feels like he gave up his right to rule when he left to head out on this quest, so I guess this is his way of separating himself from that life."

"Well, he doesn't have a choice. He spent twenty-eight years preparing for that life. It's his responsibility." Orion let his head fall against the trunk of the tree. "I've no idea what it means to be a king, Iris. I can't. And you can't honestly tell me you think I'd be anything but awful at it."

Turning to him, she scrutinized his expression, though she

waited to speak until his breathing seemed to settle. "Why do you think you would be awful at it? You keep saying *I can't*, but it feels like there's something beneath those words that—"

"You're damn right, Iris. I can't because... well, look at me!" Turning to her, he held out his hands, eyes wide, as if his person should be explanation enough. "You know me. I'm—" He shook his head, seemingly unable to finish the thought out loud.

"I guess that is something you're going to have to figure out, Orion. You and Asher together."

"Me and Asher together," he repeated blandly. "No, not Asher. Prince Alexander."

"Prince Orion and Prince Alexander." Iris grinned as she released her knees and tucked her feet beneath her. "I like the sound of that."

Orion groaned and dropped his head in his hands. "Don't ever call me that again," he whined.

Iris chuckled and patted his head. "For the record, I don't think you'd be awful at it. But I see things in you that you don't allow yourself to see."

He grumbled but didn't comment further.

The blossoms continued to drift down around them, coating the ground in a soft layer of pastel pink. She looked at him again, studying the panes of his face, the scruff on his chin and cheeks, the long hair hanging into his eyes. "Thank you, Orion."

Drawing back his head, he looked at her. "For what?"

"I guess for..." She paused, thinking it over. "For jumping into fire for us. I mean, I don't entirely understand everything you explained, but I can at least comprehend *jump into fire*." She nudged his shoulder, willing him to loosen up. "So... thank you."

Exhaling again, he said, "You're welcome. And don't you dare say that was a very princely thing to do, or I swear, Iris." Her mirth became evident, as that was pretty close to what she'd been about to say. "You're incorrigible." The slightest grin finally curved his lips.

She felt a warmth in her chest as she discovered her continued ability to cheer him up. To break down his mean, angry shell and find the squishiness beneath. He truly was different now than he had been before. It was apparent in his entire state of being. His demeanor, his expressions, his words. Even his anger didn't emanate from him in the same way. With her shoulder against his, their first night in Cordillera fluttered up from her memories.

They'd sat together in much the same way, comfortable somehow, like old friends.

The last time they spoke, they'd been in bed at Peregrine Manor. He'd drunkenly apologized for treating her so poorly and promised her things would be different. She'd snapped at him, unwilling to believe words that had never remained true before.

But she saw it now—the difference in him. He truly did seem profoundly changed. Perhaps he'd fallen in love with this princess he'd met in the desert, and it had softened his heart like nothing but love has the power to do.

C

Orion let his head fall back against the tree, taking in the extravagant wildlife of the garden. After sitting quietly for a long while, listening to the birds, the crickets, and the breeze, and watching the kuki fluttering about making flowers bloom, both he and Iris opened their mouths to speak. After a soft chuckle, Iris encouraged him to go first.

Swallowing, he exhaled. "I'm truly sorry, Iris. For what I did to you in that cave."

Iris flushed. "It's fine."

He looked at her. "No, it wasn't. You were… a child. And I knew better. I crossed a line. And on top of that, I was horrible to you after. You must have been so confused."

"I'm not a child, Orion. I'm eighteen. And I've survived in the wild for years. I can kill and skin an animal, cook it over a fire I built myself. I can—"

"You are a child when it comes to this. Or am I mistaken in thinking it was your first kiss?"

Blushing deeper, she shook her head, eyes lifting to the falling petals. "It was."

"Okay, then. We don't have to talk about it if you don't want to, but I need you to know how sorry I am. How much I've regretted treating you the way I did. Everyday since the moment I woke up in Peregrine to an empty bed. Even before that, if I'm honest."

Humming in reply, Iris sighed. "Tell me about Isolde."

He glanced at her from the corner of his eye, unable to stop himself from smiling as thoughts of Isolde penetrated his mind. Suddenly feeling lighter, though he tried to suppress his glee, he thought back on what Maeve had said about them having safe passage from the prison. Isolde was safe. He exhaled a breath of relief. "What do you want to know?"

Iris shrugged. "I don't know. Anything. What is she like? Why do you like her? Does she like you? What's her father like? Is she really a princess?"

He chuckled and shook his head at her stream of questions, resting his arms on lifted knees. His stomach felt sick again for reasons he didn't entirely understand. Answers to her questions surfaced as images in his thoughts. Isolde washing him that first night, yelling at him in Jericho, dancing with him at the celebrations, holding his hand as she led him through the dark cave to watch the sunset. The moment they shared outside of her tent on their last night in Caritas. Another wave of nausea erupted from his stomach. "I don't think I can talk to you about this. Not now, at least. Not yet."

"Why not?" She wrinkled her nose before asking in a teasing voice, "Do you love her or something?"

His eyes met hers with intensity, hoping she would understand the things he refused to say. New images appeared in his thoughts: Iris screaming underwater and his panicked need to save her; the closeness they'd shared in the cave in Cordillera; their passionate and tender kisses in the dark—the first ones she ever gifted to anyone; and her begging him to open up in Peregrine Manor.

The memories had unexpected emotions rolling through him like gusts of wind rolling across the savanna. Regret and longing and hope and fear and tender affection.

He let his mind drift to how things may have turned out if instead of remaining silent and pushing her away at Peregrine Manor, he'd apologized right then for all the things he'd done and shown her he could be different. Revealed the man he wished to be.

Perhaps she wouldn't have left him that night. They could have entered Jericho together. Sirena would never have gotten her claws into him, Declan wouldn't have revealed the location of Celestelvyra, and all of the events that transpired afterward would have never come to pass. It was incredible to think a single moment could have changed the course of events so considerably.

But he hadn't done that. He couldn't have, because he *hadn't* been different then. He hadn't been able to be the man he longed to be, no matter how hard he tried. Everything that occurred after that moment had led him to this one, and looking back now, he wouldn't change any of it. Things had played out how they were meant to. He'd been humbled by the darkness that is Sirena Aldrich, he'd met Isolde, built new bonds with the Raptors, and, despite all odds, come out the other side of a blazing furnace.

Isolde's face flashed through his thoughts, and he tried to imagine what she might say when she found out the truth. Not just that he'd made it to Celestelvyra—but that he was a prince.

Suddenly, Iris' shoulder felt very warm next to his own, and he wished he could pull it away. At the same time, a small part of him still didn't want to. His eyes glanced at her hand, now resting loosely on her knee, and he wondered what she would do if he reached for it. Curling his fingers into fists in his lap, he cleared away foolish thoughts. He'd tried to force Iris away using every method he'd acquired over a lifetime of keeping others at a distance. Before her, only Declan had remained at his side regardless of his cruelty.

Orion knew where Iris' heart belonged, and it wasn't next to his. Declan held it captive, and there was nothing he could do to steal it from him, even if he wanted to. If losing one might mean losing both, he wasn't willing to take that risk. "You should forgive Declan. He's an idiot, for sure, but one that deserves forgiveness."

Iris looked up into the misshapen branches of the tree. "He killed my father."

Orion's eyes widened, and he jolted forward, turning to her. "What do you mean?"

"He brought the Queen to the In-Between, and she snapped his neck right in front of us." Her fury at Declan rekindled with her spoken words, and angry tears pricked the insides of her eyelids.

Shoulders relaxing, Orion returned his back to the tree. "He could never have predicted that, Iris."

Her mouth dropped open. "He could have predicted that working for the Queen was stupid and selfish and put every single one of us in unnecessary danger."

"You're right. His actions were misguided, but he did it to save me and his brother." He pulled his hair back into a bun and tied it, for no other reason than the need to busy his hands. "It was a huge mistake. But he has a good heart, and I think you know that."

"Why are you defending him?"

"Because he is my family, Iris. Because I love him." His answer caught them both off guard. It occurred to him that he had never used the word *love* in reference to a single person since Lacey Robinson, and he had certainly never thought of his friendship with Declan to be rooted in it. Saying it out loud now, he knew it to be true without a doubt. "I may have just discovered a new connection to a blood brother, but Declan and I have a brotherhood bond thicker than blood. It's why he risked everything to save me. Why I would have done the same thing if the story were reversed." He shrugged, realizing it was also why Declan, above all others, had stuck with him all this time—because in their hearts, they really were brothers.

Her anger fizzled out in response to his sweet words, and she smiled at him as if wanting to poke his gooey center. "Love certainly changes people. It softens them."

"Oh, I am well aware. He is a ridiculous sap now, and it's all your fault." He pointed a finger in accusation.

"I wasn't talking about him." She frowned, likely not ready to unpack the implication in his words. "I'm sensing a significant amount of sappiness all around."

"I told you not to start. I thought you were here to comfort me. Thus far you've mostly been obnoxious and annoying."

Laughing, she nudged his shoulder again. "I never said I was here to comfort you. I simply asked if I could join you, and you said yes. I made no promises, and you gave no prerequisites."

"I thought it was implied." He joined her laughter, though his eyes drifted to the path he'd used to get there. He thought of Isolde, of her voice screaming his name as he plummeted toward the fire. "How long do you think I should wait before trying to talk to Alexander?"

She tilted her head back and forth, following his gaze as she contemplated his question. "I think you should do whatever you're comfortable with. Go talk to him right now if you want to. Or wait a while longer. I'll sit with you amongst the petals and pain as long as you need me to."

He smiled at her. "Truthfully, I really want to get out of here and check on my team, but talking to Alexander seems like something that should probably happen first, even if it sounds like the worst conversation any two people could possibly have. The single worst conversation in the history of conversations."

"Good gracious, you're dramatic." Then she challenged with blatant insinuation, "Just your *team*?"

He shot another annoyed smile her way. "Yes, Iris. The *whole* team. Twelve of us. Well, thirteen if you count Johnathan, which I don't."

"Thirteen!" she exclaimed.

"I told you it was a serious operation. It's no minor feat to infiltrate the Ashgate Fortress."

"Wow, that's remarkable."

"And I'm thinking some of them, though not many if we're being honest, but some, may be worried about where I ended up." His chin fell to his chest. "Since they all witnessed me jumping into a pit of fire, they may even suppose me dead."

"We should get moving as soon as possible then. Come on. Let's go figure out a plan to get you back to your princess." She stood, extending her hands to help him up. "I mean your whole team, of course."

Orion rolled his eyes. Despite the heat he'd felt between their shoulders, it felt easy to accept her hands and allow her to pull him to his feet, as if something had shifted between them. Perhaps they could move on from whatever had been and become something entirely new.

"I really appreciate you not hating me, Iris."

Rather than words, she smiled and gave his fingers a squeeze. Then they walked back along the path toward the waterfall.

C

When they returned to the clearing, Iris saw Asher and Foxx standing at the center of the grassy field in a discussion bordering on argumentative. Asher had the fingers of one hand to his temples.

Seth sat by the pond creating ripples in the water with a stick, uncomfortable and avoiding them.

Iris jogged ahead of Orion. When she arrived, Asher sighed and moved away from everyone so he could think. Iris looked from him to Foxx with a wary expression.

"Hey, how's he doing?" Foxx motioned past Iris to where Orion ambled their way, clearly in no rush to get in the middle of whatever was happening.

"Oh, he's a mess." Iris glanced over her shoulder with a pitying look. "But we need to get him back to his group. They probably think he's dead. How's Asher?"

"Also a mess. I'm not sure how he feels about everything. He hasn't been very forthcoming."

"It's a lot to take in. A new brother. And that stuff about his mother is insane. I can't imagine how he must be feeling." Iris rested a hand on her sister's arm. "What about you? Are you ready to leave? I don't want to rush you, but I think it's time."

Foxx looked around the field that had become their temporary home: the pond where Seth sat fiddling with a cattail, the top of the falls where she and Asher had their first kiss, and the honeysuckle bushes that framed the path leading to the meadow. Turning back to her sister, she said, "Yeah, I think I am."

As if in response to this statement, the clank of a locking mechanism and the hinge of a door swinging open with a long creak reached their ears. Asher looked toward the sound, then spun to see if they'd heard it, too.

Seth was already on his feet and jogging toward them. "The door!"

Iris looked at Foxx, tucking her hair behind her ear and touching her scarred cheek with a smile. "Okay then, let's go." She turned to make sure Orion was coming and found him only a few paces away.

"Let's do it," he agreed.

Seth stopped next to Asher, grabbing his hand. "You heard them!" Taking off again, he dragged Asher along behind him until they reached their bags. After throwing on a few extra layers to combat the frigid temperatures of Crystavium, they began loading everything up onto their backs and strapping on their weapons. Orion was instructed to fill the water bags in the falls. When he returned, the company was geared up and ready to go.

They started down the path toward the door, anxiously moving closer. Seth had ceased running, suddenly solemn as he realized they would be leaving the magical land of the Sacred Garden. They paused by their favorite peach tree so he could tuck a few into his bag. Iris and Foxx walked next to each other while Asher kept pace with Seth, and Orion followed behind them.

When they reached the faux building holding the elegantly decorated doors, they found them wide open. A gust of cold air poured in from the darkness beyond and nipped at their skin.

"It's freezing." Seth shivered and scooted closer to Asher, seeking his body heat.

"Ever been to Crystavium, kid?" Orion passed the girls and stopped on Seth's opposite side.

"Never. I'm from the desert! Have you, Asher?"

"I have, my friend. It is not an accommodating place. Especially in contrast to where we're departing." At the mention of their current location, the group looked around, taking in the splendor of Celestelvyra one last time and cycling through their memories of time spent there. When all eyes returned to the open doorway, they stared at it anxiously, each waiting for someone else to move forward first.

Orion said, "It's a three day journey to the barrier from where we're camped."

Asher turned toward the sound of Orion's voice, and their eyes met. Then Seth spoke Asher's name and broke the connection. "What's up, lad?"

"I have a suggestion." Seth's thumb and index finger rolled the bottom hem of his tunic.

"Go on." Asher glanced over his shoulder at Iris and Foxx, who shrugged.

Digging the toe of his shoe into the ground, Seth kept his eyes on the dirt path. "Remember when we talked about Mr. Magpie?" Iris and Foxx shared a glance.

"I do," Asher said.

"About responsibility being important?"

Asher sighed, his eyes meeting Orion's again for a quick moment before returning to his young friend. "I have a feeling I know where this is going."

"Good, then I don't have to say it." Seth grinned up at him. "Sometimes it's hard to say things even when you know they should be said. And sometimes it's hard to do things even when you know they are the right thing to do."

Again looking over his shoulder at the girls, Asher said, "I think we should leave the kid here."

Seth's mouth dropped open in bewildered offense. Iris and Foxx chuckled, though they still didn't understand what the boys were talking about.

Seth huffed. He glanced back at Iris and Foxx for help, but they didn't offer any. Then he turned toward Orion, seemed to regret it immediately, and drew his gaze away. At last, he spit out his words in a rush. "I think we should stop calling you Asher! There, I said it."

Iris and Foxx nodded to themselves, at last comprehending the conversation.

Asher ruffled Seth's hair. "I think you're right, Seth. Thank you for pushing me to do the right thing even when you knew it probably wasn't what I wanted to hear. You're a good friend."

Seth beamed. "Someone really wise once told me that sometimes we need other people to be brave for us." He glanced back at Iris, who clutched her chest, his restating of her own words nearly bringing her to tears.

Foxx's fingertips grazed Asher's side, and he peered back at her with his familiar smile returned. "Prince Alexander it is. Squire Seth has spoken."

Seth's eyes went wide, his mouth dropping into an O.

"I like it." Foxx leaned in to kiss the Prince on the cheek.

"Me too!" Iris agreed.

Orion scratched the back of his head. "I, on the other hand, would prefer to keep the new information regarding..." his eyes flashed to Alexander again, "... us, between the five of us for now. Until I process some things."

"I understand," Alexander said, though Iris thought he seemed to be choking out the words. She wondered how long it would be until the men had the inevitable conversation and if Alexander was just as fearful of having it as Orion seemed to be.

Orion looked back at the sisters.

"Our lips are sealed for now," Iris said. "But you can't hide from it forever."

"Neither of you can." Foxx looked back and forth between them.

"All right. Now that that's all settled, let's get out of here." Seth turned and gazed longingly at the path leading back to the falls. The rest of the group followed his line of sight.

Pulling the filled Artifact from his pocket, Alexander held it in the palm of his hand. "Everything changes now." Again, he met Orion's gaze.

"Prince Alexander? Can I really be a squire?" Leaning his head to the side as he rubbed his chin, Seth added, "Also, what exactly is a squire?"

Alexander squeezed his hand, chuckling. "I'll tell you later."

"Are you ready then?" Seth asked.

After slipping the vial back into his pocket and taking one last look at the rest of the group, Alexander confirmed he was ready, and he and Seth stepped through the door, blinking from sight in a flash of white.

"See you on the other side, ladies." Orion followed them, disappearing as the boys had.

Iris linked her arm into Foxx's. "I know it's hard to say farewell, but maybe someday we can come back. We have the keys now."

Foxx nodded, her damp eyes revealing the heaviness in her heart. She looked back the path once more, and Iris followed her gaze to see the Ram as far away as could be seen. Her breath caught as she stared at Him, and the same happened to Foxx at her side.

He watched them intently, His eyes seeming to twinkle with happiness, or perhaps pride. He dipped His head all the way to the ground and lifted it back up.

Iris startled when Foxx began to speak.

"Thank you, Elohim. I will try my best to do what You've asked and make You proud."

"Thank you, Elohim," Iris echoed. Despite their hushed words, both girls knew the Ram would hear them. Then Iris squeezed her sister's hand. "I love you, Foxxglove."

"I love you, too, Iris. Let's go."

CHAPTER 36

REUNITED

The team remained at the campsite, hoping to rest for a short while before beginning their long journey back to Caritas. They figured they had some time considering how they'd escaped, and they weren't too worried about being discovered yet.

Most sat in a circle around the fire, shoulder to shoulder for warmth as they had before. Crow and Leone sat next to each other in quiet discussion. Kwame was staring at Jovan as he retold the exciting event at the prison from his point of view, though Kwame had been there the entire time and seen everything for himself. Hector sat on Jovan's other side, switching back and forth between listening to Jovan's story and trying to soothe Raven. Her worry at his horrific injuries as she watched Vera treat them had overshadowed some of her anger. Now, with him bandaged and sitting at her side holding her hand, her demeanor had shifted into sadness.

Declan hadn't said a word. Neither had Griffin. Both men stared into the fire, though where Declan felt overwhelmed with sorrow and loss, Griffin was enraged by the foolishness of the man he'd tried to keep away from his sister. Vera stood at his side, his silent companion should he need her, and Johnathan sat next to Declan.

Isolde and Jax hadn't yet returned to camp. More than once, the company heard whispers of her cries on the wind, but no one went after her, leaving the lieutenant to be her unexpected comfort.

Vera offered to go look for them after Hector shared that Jax was injured as well, but Griffin forbade it.

The original plan had been to leave immediately. They needed to release the prison guards still tied up by the fire and knew the Warden would be sending out scouts to find them eventually. Regardless of the dangers steadily drawing closer, no one seemed willing to press forward.

When Jovan finished his story and began repeating the exciting parts, Hector leaned across Raven and put a hand on Declan's knee, getting his attention. Declan lifted his head, his freckled face splotchy with grief and his eyes rimmed red. "If you need anything or want to talk, know you have friends who are here for you. You are not alone."

Declan didn't know how to respond. Their rocky past kept walls between them, even now, and he wondered if they might ever heal entirely from the historic divide. Eyes sliding to Raven sitting between them, he found her smiling in agreement with Hector's words. Declan nodded in thanks to both of them, unable in that moment to properly express his gratitude.

With Orion gone, he was going to need friends. He and Raven had been connected since the day they met, and, despite their marred history, Hector had always reminded him of his father. Their personalities were so similar, it was clear he and Ryder had not only been companions, but friends.

A flash of light snagged everyone's attention, snapping them out of their worries and sorrow. Thinking they'd somehow missed evidence of the Warden's people drawing closer, the entire company jumped to their feet and drew their weapons.

Instead of firelight, the illumination reflected the color of daylight and appeared as a square hanging in midair. The shape grew, spreading out evenly in all directions until it touched the ground.

Griffin frowned, his arm rising to protect Vera at his side.

Hector took a brave step forward, holding his hand up in an attempt to touch it.

Raven sidestepped, keeping the light in her sights as she moved in a circle around it. "It's flat like a doorway. A doorway leading nowhere."

"There's something here," Hector said, drawing Raven back around to the front. A prick of darkness appeared at the center of the light, growing larger as it drew closer. Most of the group took a step or two away, worried something bad might be coming through.

After an agonizing moment, two figures materialized within the illuminated square and stepped out into the Crystavium night.

"Alexander?" Mouth agape, Hector looked back and forth between the Prince and the young boy at his side.

Alexander held up a hand in greeting, wearing his usual charming smile as his eyes adjusted and scoured the crowd for familiar faces. Seeing Declan, he held his gaze before turning his attention to Seth and pulling him out of the way.

Behind him, a man with long, dark hair stepped forth, looking back at the shining light before turning to face the group.

"Orion!" Declan cried.

"What is happening?" Hector put both hands on his head. Raven's lips remained parted in awe.

For a tense moment, no one moved toward the people emerging from the bright light as if fearing they may be ghosts or specters. Then Griffin yelled, "Iso!" into the wasteland behind him.

After the men, Iris and Foxxglove Belamour stepped from the door arm in arm, and the light blinked from existence.

Declan exclaimed Iris' name. At last finding his feet, he crashed into her and wrapped her in his arms. Iris accepted the embrace, standing on her tiptoes to squeeze him tight. Into her hair, Declan entreated, "Oh, my gosh, Iris, I am so sorry. Please let me explain before you decide to hate me. Please. You have to." She gripped him harder, holding onto his shoulders and squeezing with all her might.

Watching his best friend ignore him after Iris had appeared, Orion looked sideways at Alexander. "I see where I rank." Alexander chuckled as Hector approached him with an extended hand.

"Prince Alexander. I don't have any idea what's going on, but I sure am glad to see you."

Alexander grinned with delight. "Glad to see you as well, Commander. I was confident you would find a way to get us out."

"It seems O'Connell is the one who found a way." Hector looked at Orion, shaking his head as he offered a hand. "I don't know what to say except: I'm glad you're not dead."

"Thanks, Commander." Looking over Hector's shoulder, Orion scanned the group for Isolde, feeling a twinge of fear when he couldn't find her amongst the present company. "Sorry for going rogue on you."

"It's good you did, though I still don't really understand how it happened."

"You look horrible, Commander," Alexander said, and Orion joined him in observing the excessive blood tainting his clothing and all the places Vera had wrapped him up.

Hector nodded. "The Strayed. Jax is pretty bad, too."

As if finally coming alive, Raven stomped into the space between them, her boots crunching the frosty ground. She punched Orion in the shoulder, then again in the chest. This continued until Hector wrapped his less injured arm around her middle and pulled her back. Her limbs flailed like an animal fighting restraint.

Iris and Declan separated to watch the altercation. Those from Caritas watched intently, too, attempting to follow along. Jovan grinned with wild amusement at Raven's feral attack. Kwame shouldered him, scolding him for being disrespectful in front of Prince Alexander. When Jovan pointed out that Alexander was enjoying the show as well, Kwame let it go, and his own lips curled.

"You're such an idiot!" Raven shouted. "What were you thinking? You ask me to watch out for you then you jump into a freaking fire fifteen stories down?" Her hair was a mess, sticking to the sheen of sweat permeating her temples as she raged.

Orion couldn't help but laugh at the bizarre circumstances playing out before him. Raven, of all people, was screaming at him for risking his life. Looking at Hector over Raven's shoulder, he smirked. "I have to say, this is not a reaction I expected." Hector shrugged, feeling equally perplexed. Alexander took a step back so as not to be caught in the crossfire.

"If you had died, I would have had to live with that failure for the rest of my life. I can't believe you!" Raven yanked away from Hector and began punching again, spouting insults with every hit. "Stupid! Idiot! Jerk!"

Orion grabbed her wrists to halt her, forcing her to look at him. He repeated her name imploringly until she calmed down and stopped fighting his hold.

Glaring at him, she blew hair from her eyes and snapped, "What?"

"Raven, I'm sorry. I know I broke the plan and put myself in terrible danger. I put that responsibility on you, and I am sorry. Truly."

Raven breathed like a bull blowing steam from its nostrils.

Staring at him, though her anger seemed to be dulling into surprise at his candor, she huffed and exhaled a breath.

"I think you bruised me." He released her arms and gingerly touched his chest. "It hurts."

"It's nothing less than you deserve," she spat, though her venom had dissipated. "I can't believe you jumped into that fire. What an idiot."

Eyeing her suspiciously, Orion chided, "I think this means you would have missed me, Raven."

"Definitely not!"

"Is it because I bared my soul around the campfire or because I saved you from that tiny, harmless spider?" Over her shoulder, he saw Hector suppressing a laugh. Alexander wasn't suppressing his.

"You are the worst." Raven ran her hands down her shirt to straighten the wrinkles and calm her nerves. "I still hate you. I just don't like people dying on my watch, okay?"

"You like me a little bit though." Orion used his fingers to show how much.

"Whatever." Raven crossed her arms, eyes rolling toward the starlit sky.

"But hey, it worked!" Orion gestured to Alexander with both hands. "I jumped into the fire, and I found him." Alexander waved his fingers.

"Hello, Prince Alexander." Suddenly embarrassed by her angry display, Raven dropped her chin. "I'm glad he found you. Sorry for…" She gestured between her and Orion.

"I'm not sure I'll ever be upset to see Orion take a few good punches. In fact, I owed him a couple myself, but I'm thinking you covered it." Alexander winked at Orion, who scoffed, though his heart wasn't in it.

"Foxxglove, you look well." Hector offered a slight bow, though the movement after so much commotion made him unstable, and Raven stepped closer to steady him.

Foxx looked him over again, her eyes lingering on his forearm and the sickly pallor of his face. "You look terrible, Commander. I'm so sorry for the trouble we caused you."

"Don't worry about it. We're all alive, and you all returned. I'm considering this a win."

Alexander wrapped an arm around Foxx's back, hooking his

thumb into the pocket on her pants. Hector observed the gesture and met Alexander's eyes with a smile.

It occurred to him then that if Alexander and Foxxglove remained together, she would become the next queen. The thought made him smile wider. He'd seen the intricacies of what it meant to rule and knew having a partner to help sift through the muck would be beneficial.

Isolde called Orion's name from where she stood on the edge of the firelight, stunned in place as if she'd seen a ghost. "Are you...?"

Jax stood behind her, mirroring her shock as he took in the scene.

Orion ran to her, seeking to catch every tear spilling from her eyes. He enveloped her in both arms and lifted her off her feet. Then his lips were on hers, kissing her feverishly. She responded in kind, her hands wrapping around his head. She dragged her fingers through his hair, slid them down his shoulders, his arms, his back, still not entirely sure he was real.

When she pulled away for breath, she searched his eyes for answers. "How are you here? I saw you...?"

"I'll explain everything later." He pressed his lips to hers again. Enormous and extraordinary feelings flooded his entire being, as if the very stars in the sky had aligned just for them. He realized what a fool he'd been for not doing this sooner. He should have kissed her that night outside her tent, or on the cliff of the mesa, or one of the other dozens of missed opportunities he'd had from the moment they'd met.

Holding her, kissing her, felt so right, so perfect, so exactly where he belonged for the first time in his whole life. He didn't care if he was the heir to the Thrones. He didn't care what happened after this moment. If anything, being a prince might actually give him a chance at a future with her. He was worthy of his princess, if not in nature, at least in title.

Thoughts of her and their future consumed his mind. No more drips, no more whispers. Just him and Isolde and her lips on his and their hands on each other and a warmth blossoming between them that was unlike anything he'd ever felt in his life. His forehead came to rest against hers. "I love you," he confessed into the breath between them. "I know we haven't known each other long, but I swear I knew the moment I met you. I was afraid, but I'm not anymore. I jumped into fire, and even that wasn't as scary as telling you this, but I can't hold it in any longer. I love you, Naabila."

She pulled back, again exploring the depths of his eyes as they reflected the shimmering stars above, giving her a thousand galaxies to explore. The smile missing from her face gave him cause for concern, but he couldn't take it back now. The truth was out.

Leaning to kiss him again, just once, soft and tender, she locked her golden gaze on his. *"Novi'tueor tuu mielu."*

Exhaling a huge sigh of relief, he pulled her into his chest. "All your yesterdays and all your tomorrows." He kissed her hair, her temple, her cheek. "I'm sorry I scared you. I'm so sorry, Naabila."

"Fortem." She squeezed him tighter.

"You're the brave one." He burrowed his face into the crevice of her neck, breathing in her familiar scent.

Over his shoulder, she glimpsed Griffin's distasteful expression. She loathed not honoring her brother. He would be the Naaba someday, and that meant something to her people. The thought of disappointing or defying him made her sick to her stomach, but she couldn't help it. Orion O'Connell was special. And she loved him. She too had felt their connection from the very moment she'd discovered him valiantly taking on a hive of nieda to rescue his friend. She couldn't imagine her heart ever feeling for anyone else the way it fluttered in his presence.

Griffin loved her. Surely he would put her happiness above his judgments. Eventually.

Jax cleared his throat to get everyone's attention.

Orion and Isolde separated and turned to face him, though their hands remained clasped as she leaned into him, resting her head on his shoulder. Iris joined Foxxglove and Alexander, followed closely by Declan. The rest gathered around to listen.

"Now that we're all here, we should get moving. It isn't safe to linger, especially since we didn't escape Ashgate undetected."

"Jax is right." Hector hobbled up next to his lieutenant. "The Warden will send guards out to look for us. He may even alert Sirena." His eyes shifted to Alexander, who gestured his agreement. Under his breath, Hector spoke so only Jax could hear. "Though you should have Vera look at that hand while the others pack up."

"Get packed quickly and let's move out." Jax rattled off a few extra instructions, ignoring Hector's suggestion. "Johnathan, make sure the horses and tryka have some water before we go. Orion, Raven, Declan—you should change and return your borrowed clothing to the guards. Everyone else, pack up, put out the fire, and get ready t—"

A vicious growl in the distance cut his sentence short. He spun, scanning the dim topography for the origin of the sound as he pulled his pistol from his hip. The faint moon had risen higher in the sky, casting the palest light across the frosty landscape.

Then the ground began to shake with the vibrations of a stampede, and growls and howls and ear-piercing screeches filled the air.

CHAPTER 37

DARK TIDINGS

"Something's coming." Jax pulled his eyes from the empty landscape to check his mag.

Isolde and Orion released each other and drew weapons. Orion looked at his pistol and sighed, eyeing the pile of bags a few *sylis* away where his preferred weaponry lay.

Declan had left his dagger in the door leading to the prison, but his pistol remained on his hip. Iris slid Thorn and Bloom from their scabbards, and Foxx nocked an arrow as Raven drew daggers from the chest sheath hidden beneath her shirt. Hector eyed her with playful reproach, and she shrugged. Avoiding any further conversation about it, she eyed the pile where she'd left her broadsword.

The others drew the weapons they had on hand, watching every direction and trying to discern where the sounds were coming from. As the creatures drew nearer, their size and number became more evident.

Orion said, "Sounds like there might be a lot of them."

"Maybe we should run." Jax looked to Orion, standing closest to him. When he nodded his agreement, Jax called Hector's name.

Needing no further convincing, Griffin motioned to his group, and Jovan, Crow, and Kwame rushed for the animals, scrambling to untie them. Leone and Vera helped the others round up the supplies.

Raven slid across the frosty ground and sliced through their prisoners' ties. "Now would be a fabulous time to flee, fellas." Without a word, the guards raced off into the night.

Everyone mounted, pairing up so they would all fit on twelve animals.

Then Jax ordered, "Ride!"

Galloping off, they rode east across rough terrain putting distance between them and the pursuing horde. They'd hoped if they got far enough away, the animals might give up and back off, but the rumble of whatever chased them remained unyielding.

Someone screamed.

Orion recognized Crow's voice, and Isolde confirmed this by shouting his name. Yanking the reins, he turned them around. The others slowed to circle back. Vera grabbed the reins of Crow's empty tryka before it ran off.

Leone yelled his name into the turbulent shadows above them, unable to bear his continuous screams of fear and pain. "What are they doing to him?"

Eyes searching the sky, Vera asked, "Griff? What now?"

"We're going to have to fight." Foxx raised her bow into the air. Seated in front of her, Alexander controlled the skewbald as she watched the sky, keeping her eyes alert for signs of men or monsters.

Isolde slid from the back of Orion's horse and hurried toward her brother, just as Crow violently collided with the ground at her feet. She cried his name and dropped to inspect him, holding her sword above her as a guard. He was alive but drenched in blood. Gashes tore through his arms, legs, and torso, as if multiple creatures had been gnawing on him at once. Severed flesh hung from gushing wounds.

Vera sprinted to Isolde and their fallen friend, leaping from her tryka and kneeling on Crow's opposite side. Raven slid from Hector's chestnut and lifted her broadsword in a defensive stance to shield them. Iris did the same, drawing her blades and guarding at Raven's back.

Johnathan took the reins of Crow and Vera's tryka and pulled them out of the way. The creatures had yet to descend from sky or ground, but one thing became painfully obvious to each of them: this wasn't a random attack of Crystavium wildlife.

They were being hunted.

Alexander shouted Jax's name.

"I'm here, Alexander." Remaining on guard, Jax made his way toward the Prince's voice. They'd fled the fire and hadn't sparked any torches. Clouds grew more dense above them, blocking out the faintest light of the moon.

"Take Seth away from here!"

"No!" Seth shouted from where he clung to Jax's waist.

Ignoring Seth's exclamation, Jax called back, "Leave you?"

When the soldier and the boy came into view, Alexander met Jax's surprised eyes and commanded, "Yes. Protect him."

The lieutenant's gaze slid to Hector, now stationed at his side. Though Alexander was the Prince, Hector was his commander.

Hector nodded. "Do it."

When he continued to hesitate, Raven shouted, "Get out of here, Jax!"

Seth called Iris' name and reached for her with one hand.

Soaking in his terrified expression, Iris promised, "I love you, Seth! I'll see you soon!"

"Hold on, Seth." Jax wrapped the reins tight around his arm, tucked into his dapple gray, and squeezed his heels. They shot off into the night, swallowed by the moonless dark.

All at once, the horde descended.

A beast from the sky swooped low on Foxx's right. She released an arrow into its shadow and heard the *thunk* of the arrowhead penetrating its body, followed by a *thud* as it crashed to the ground. Grabbing Alexander's shirt in her shock, she drew his attention to the downed creature. "Alexander, it's a mandrill!"

Alexander gaped. "Far worse than the ones we met in Sateen."

Misshapen fangs protruded from its cheeks and jaw at unnatural angles, long talons poked through the tips of its fingers, and membranous wings sprouted from its back like a giant bat.

Orion pulled his horse up next to them and shivered at the sight. "Verivaras?"

Alexander scanned the sky. "I don't think so. This is something else entirely." Leveling his brother with a concerned expression, he added, "There will be more. Watch your back."

A growl behind Orion had them turning to see a giant creature barreling their way. Two more followed close behind. Taller than a grizzly, the monsters towered over them on two legs, with shoulders that extended high on either side of their heads mimicking armored shoulder pads housing long, metal spikes.

The monsters spread out in different directions, but the first headed straight for Orion, Foxx, and Alexander. Orion yanked the reins, and his stallion reared up. When its hooves hit the ground, he found Griffin standing in front of them, fending off the beast with his gruesome bludgeon. Though its gorilla-like torso outmatched the Nabiiga in build, Griffin got the upper hand and forced it backward. The jaw of its bovine skull free of flesh snapped at him, attempting to catch his arm mid-blow.

A new cluster of monsters arrived: quadrupeds with the head and tail of a fennec fox. One hastened for Iris and Raven, wrapping its long, scaled body around their legs and knocking them to the ground before either had a chance to react. Untangling itself with ease, it slithered on top of Raven, holding her in place with reptilian feet. Razor-sharp canines gnawed into the flesh between her ribcage and hip bone. She cried out, and Iris rolled toward her, swiping at the creature with Thorn. Its body recoiled from the attack as a snake swimming in water, but it didn't release Raven's arms. It held her in place as it continued to twist its head back and forth, ripping through muscle. Stabbing her blade into the ground, Iris wrapped her arms around the creature's body and attempted to yank it away without success.

Raven at last managed to twist an arm free and snatch a thin blade from Iris' chest sheath. With a warrior's cry, she stabbed it into the creature's neck, splattering blood all over both of them. It released her and tumbled to the ground, its beady eyes remaining open.

No time to catch their breath, Raven returned the blade to Iris and both girls leapt to their feet. "Glad to have you back." Tears stung her eyes as she lifted her arm away from the wound bleeding down her hip to her thigh, but her layers made it impossible to see the severity of the damage.

Iris grinned. "I had a feeling you'd miss me."

Raven laughed and wiped her cheeks. "Let's not go that far."

Another fox appeared near Hector, rising up on its back legs as if readying to pounce. Iris whipped the blade in her hand, aiming for its skull. Instead, it struck between the shoulder blades, but the outcome was the same. Startled, Hector watched it tumble to the ground before looking up at Iris to find her own eyes wide in horror.

"Behind you!" she screamed.

Another mountainous monster came hurling into the scene and knocked Hector from his mare. On his way down, he fired off several shots into its shoulder, doing little damage. As he landed and rolled away, a long tongue slid from its mouth, wrapped around the horse's neck, and pushed it to the ground. Its jaw unhinged as it sank ivory teeth into the horse's ribcage, spraying blood everywhere as it tore flesh from bone.

The horse's whines drew everyone's attention to the plight. With a loud cry, Isolde swung her sword between the monster's shoulder plates and neck and removed the bovine skull from its body. It rolled away, landing at Hector's feet. Charcoal smoke seeped from empty eye sockets. The rest of its body slumped forward, laying dead across the slaughtered horse.

Isolde helped Hector to his feet before charging off toward Orion. When she arrived, he jumped from his horse, feeling more comfortable fighting on foot, and smacked the stallion's behind so it ran toward Hector. The commander caught the reins and swung himself onto the horse's back with a pained groan. His arms felt weak and his head fuzzy, but he kicked his heels into the horse and pressed on.

More devilish mandrills swooped from the sky, trying to attack Declan and Jovan. Jovan had scooped up Crow's felled bow and joined Foxx in her efforts to shoot them down.

Griffin and Leone fought off two more bovine giants with tongues dripping from their mouths, hovering next to their heads like a scorpion's tail. Vera had her bow aimed high, protecting them from above as they fought below.

Knowing his skill set would leave him more in the way than helpful, Johnathan lingered on the outskirts of the battle holding the reins of Crow and Vera's tryka. From the dark, a mandrill moved toward him, using the fingers at the top of its wings to propel it across the frosty ground in long strides. Johnathan shrieked, discharged his weapon, and missed. Just as the mandrill lunged, he yelled his brother's name. The monkey knocked him to the ground and his tryka fell with him, scrambling to regain its footing. He tried to clamber away, but the creature wrapped taloned fingers around one of his ankles and lifted him into the air. Hearing his screams, Declan and Kwame rushed over to find his tryka stumbling on an injured leg.

Declan hollered his name into the sky, desperate to rescue him from his agony. "Where is he?" he shouted, volleying between fear and anger. His eyes slipped to Crow's limp and bloodied form, and panic overwhelmed him as he yelled his brother's name into the dark.

Raven and Iris stood nearby fighting off their own monsters. When they heard Declan's mournful cries, Iris fought her way to him, leaving Raven to guard Crow.

"They have Johnathan," he told her.

Iris shouted his name into the sky, just as a huge form dropped from the darkness and landed on top of her.

"Johnathan!" Declan leapt from his horse to help his brother off Iris. Raven rushed over and took the reins. Climbing atop the animal, she paced between Johnathan and Crow, trying to guard them both.

Declan rolled Johnathan's body away from Iris and onto his back. Like Crow, the monsters flying above had treated his body like a buffet. His eyes were closed, but an ear to his mouth informed Declan that shallow breath endured.

Iris rose into a crouch. "Drag him over to Crow so we can cover them together. We don't want anyone trampling him." Declan lifted his brother into his arms, and Iris continued to guard them.

Another bear of a monster dropped by Griffin's hand. Felled mandrills and reptilian foxes littered the ground. The remaining mandrills began to flee, and Alexander and Foxx slaughtered the last of the quadrupeds. Orion and Isolde took down the final behemoth with a bludgeon to the head and a stab wound to the chest. Its fall sent a quiver through the ground. Foxx, Vera, and Jovan watched the skies. Declan and Iris stood back to back by the wounded men, with Raven and Hector circling them on horseback. Leone and Kwame roamed the perimeter.

The surrounding area seemed to fall silent but for the rapid breathing of the group and the hooves of circling riders. All eyes surveyed the dim landscape, waiting.

"I think that's the last of them." Orion wiped blood from his face with his shirt as he spun to survey the group. Blood splattered every one of them, and many nursed new injuries. Griffin's arm hung limp at his side, likely from when he'd been lifted off the ground and tossed by one of the big monsters. Raven clutched her side as it gushed blood. When Orion caught a glimpse of Declan kneeling next to Johnathan, he rushed over to them.

Isolde dropped to check on Crow. Orion followed instructions as she patched his and Johnathan's injuries as quickly as possible, hoping to block the blood flow until it clotted on its own. Declan watched and held his brother's hand but didn't offer to help. His eyes turned down with fear and exhaustion. Iris put a hand on his shoulder, and he looked up at her with a small smile.

"He's going to be okay," she promised.

Isolde nodded. "They both are."

Hector hopped from his horse to look at Raven's side. Blood soaked her uniform. As her adrenaline slowed, the pain of the injury increased considerably. When Vera returned from scouting the perimeter, she helped Hector wrap it up, stifling the bleeding until they knew they were safe and could examine it further.

Alexander and Foxx trotted to where the others had gathered. Leone and Kwame returned to tell everyone the coast appeared clear. Jovan held the reins of Griffin's tryka as he joined his sister's examination of the injured.

A new noise drew the group's attention in the direction Jax and Seth had gone. Expecting them to appear, Hector called out, "It's safe, Lieutenant!"

When neither Seth nor Jax replied, Orion stood to join Hector, and both men took a few steps in the direction of the sound. Foxx raised a nocked arrow as Alexander guided them closer.

Out of the dark, a large figure, tall and wider than three men, moved toward them, creeping smoothly across frozen ground.

Squinting, Hector said Jax's name.

As the creature took shape, those watching took an involuntary step back. Tentacles slithered across the earth, carrying the monster toward them. Atop the tentacles sat a slender body with wings tucked under like an insect's. Huge, oval eyes covered the majority of its triangular face, and appendages folded like the arms of a praying mantis clutched two bodies wriggling in its grasp. A tentacle wrapped around each of their heads, covering their mouths to muffle their screams.

Iris noticed the change in atmosphere and turned to see Seth's tear-filled eyes staring right at her. A wave of nausea crashed over her, and she jolted to her feet, blades raised.

Orion held out his hand. "Wait."

"What is it doing?" Hector whispered from Iris' opposite side.

Orion didn't drop his hand from blocking Iris' torso. "It'll squeeze the life from them if we attack. I'm not sure why it hasn't already."

"Like it's tormenting us," Hector agreed.

"So what do we do?" Iris' gaze found her sister's. "We can't just stand here and watch this."

The cry of a warrior rang out from behind them, and they turned to see Griffin barreling forward, his spike-embedded club held high. Foxx let an arrow fly, striking the creature in the chest just as Griffin swung.

Shifting Jax and Seth out of the way, it wrapped a tentacle around Griffin's ankle, yanking him to the ground and encasing him in squirming legs. A noise escaped Seth and Jax's throats, an indication of the monster's constricting grip.

Vera shot it with another arrow, though it didn't seem phased. Hector and Declan rushed from either side, firing several rounds into the bottom of the tentacles holding their friends. Stunned by the shots, the monster released Jax and Seth, and they tumbled to the ground. Jax scrambled to protect the boy, guarding him.

Tentacles released Griffin just enough to carry him upright. Both mantis arms wrapped taut around his chest.

"It's using his body to block our shots," Iris said.

"Then we must attack it hand-to-hand!" Isolde charged the monstrosity, ignoring Griffin's muffled warnings, and swung to strike the side of its torso. A tentacle grabbed her leg and wrenched her down so she missed, her sword slicing open air. She hit the ground hard, and her blade skittered away.

Helpless and lost at how to proceed, her eyes locked on Griffin to find his expression not one of fear but of great sorrow. A tear slipped down his cheek, landing on the tentacle encircling his face. Isolde whispered his name as a question, seeking guidance from a man she'd always looked up to, counted on, trusted.

The mantis' mouth opened and encompassed Griffin's entire head. Isolde longed to crawl closer, but fear had her cemented to the spot. As the creature yanked abruptly to one side, the sharp crack of shattering vertebrae echoed in the vast wilderness. Foxx cringed, and Iris looked away, covering her eyes.

Isolde let loose an excruciating wail.

Griffin's face fell forward free of its mouth, though his crown remained within the jaws of the insect. The others watched as it began to chew. Some considered attacking from afar but feared disfiguring Griffin's body more. Others assessed moving closer, but the precision tentacles kept them at bay.

The monster stared around at them with enormous eyes as it devoured the back of Griffin's head, rendering those watching transfixed and immobilized by the spectacle.

At last breaking free of the sight, Orion grabbed the hammer-head axe at his hip and ran for the creature, circling around its back. It reached for him, but he avoided its tentacles or chopped them off when he couldn't.

The creature tried to turn on him, but its continued feasting made its movements slow. Dodging one last tentacle, Orion plunged the axe into the back of its skull. It stiffened mid-gnaw until he yanked the axe free. Then it dropped Griffin into a crumbling heap and fell sideways, its body crashing to the ground with a tremor felt by all. Tentacles continued to twitch postmortem.

Isolde sobbed as she crawled to her brother and wrapped herself around him. Though scratches and bruises marred his face, it wasn't maimed like the back of his skull where the creature had crushed through bone and sucked away bits of brain beneath.

Orion knelt to comfort her, but she pushed him away. Vera cried behind them, though not quite so passionately.

Seth had curled into a ball on the ground, covering his eyes and sobbing quietly. Iris ran to him and wrapped him in her arms, her own eyes welling up from both his and Isolde's crippling emotions.

Hector rushed to Jax's side and helped him to his feet. "You good?"

The bandage around Jax's hand had loosened, and he tightened it, tucking the end underneath to hold it in place. "We need to get moving."

"I don't think this was a random attack. These monsters were sent to find us."

Alexander agreed with Hector as he and Foxx approached. "This might not be the end of it." Foxx slid from the horse to collect everyone's arrows. Alexander's attention caught on Isolde snared in a wailing mass on the ground. Then he looked at Orion watching over her from a distance. "Everyone," he called. Drawn from their horror by his commanding, princely tone, most gave him their attention. "I know you're hurting, but we need to go. There might be more coming."

Orion glared at him, but when their eyes met, he yielded.

"Alexander is right. Get mounted up." Returning his attention to Isolde, he crouched next to her and put a hand on her back.

"We cannot leave him," Isolde whispered through unfettered tears.

Orion nodded. "We won't. Jovan, Kwame, help me. Get my horse." Kwame hurried to retrieve the roan. "We're going to lift him up and tie him on. Then I'll climb up and you can tie him to me." Jovan acknowledged his command without argument, though he didn't move closer to Griffin's felled corpse, too afraid to disturb Isolde in her grief. It was only then that Orion noticed tears in Jovan's eyes, too.

Hector and Jax approached as Kwame returned with the horse. "What can we do?" Jovan gestured to Isolde and shrugged, feeling lost at how to proceed.

Rubbing her back, Orion spoke low to her. "Isolde, we need to get out of here. Let me help you. I need you to let go of Griffin." Vera appeared at his side, and Isolde lifted her eyes to him as he stood to give Vera room to speak to her. At last conceding to her friend's supplications, she allowed herself to be guided away from her brother. Vera held her princess' head on her lap while Orion, Jovan, and Kwame raised Griffin's lifeless body onto the back of the horse. Hector and Jax spotted them, making sure he didn't fall.

Foxx handed Orion a circle of rope from her bag, and Alexander pulled a blanket from his own to cover the body. Then the three men tied the desert Nabiiga firmly to the horse.

"Is there any more rope?" Orion looked at Foxx.

"Iris has some."

He turned and called her name, but Iris had already taken it from her bag and started toward them.

After handing it over, she put a hand on his shoulder. "It's going to be okay. Somehow, someway."

Nodding, he turned back to the men and handed Jovan the rope. "When I get up there, tie it around us both so he's secure." Orion mounted, and the others wrapped Griffin in the rope until they felt comfortable he would be safe. Then they fastened Crow to the back of Jovan's tryka, and Leone helped Kwame tie rope around them so Crow wouldn't fall if he stopped holding on. Others helped harness Johnathan on the back of Declan's palomino.

Hector and Raven claimed Griffin's tryka since Hector's horse had been killed. Jax and Iris helped Seth up onto Alexander and Foxx's horse, situating him in front of the Prince.

"It's going to be all right, buddy," Alexander assured him, but Seth didn't respond.

Jax took over watching Isolde so Vera could check on Johnathan's injured tryka. When she returned, she said, "I put her down. She was too injured to make it. Crow's male ran off as well."

"We can share." Iris passed over the reins someone had given her, though she didn't know everyone's name yet. "I'm Iris. Sorry about your friends."

"Vera. And thank you." Swinging herself up on the tryka, she scooted forward so Iris had room to hop on behind her.

Leone handed Jax the reins of the last available tryka and nodded to Isolde.

Cautiously, Jax knelt next to her and touched her shoulder. Sad eyes rose to meet his, and he extended a hand. "Come on Isolde. It's time to go home."

Orion watched the interaction intently, longing to be the one to comfort her but also not trusting anyone else to watch over Griffin's body. Isolde caught his eye and held his gaze. Then her eyes shifted behind him to the blanket covering her brother.

Returning her attention to Jax's outstretched hand, she let him help her to her feet and waited as he mounted the tryka. When she climbed on behind him, exhaustion had her slumping against his back.

All in place on five tryka and three horses, the group left the terrifying remains of felled beasts behind and rode off into the tundra of Crystavium.

CHAPTER 38

CALAMITY

Fatigued but eager to put distance between themselves and the prison, the group traveled through the starless night and into the following day with minimal stops. They stopped for a few hours on the second night but opted not to build a fire or hunt. Instead, they rationed what was left of their dried food and the produce harvested from Celestelvyra. It wasn't much, but it would hold them off until they reached the Wilds.

Sleeping for a few hours, the group was up and moving again long before sunrise. As the 6th of Reaping came and went with the moon reaching its peak, they'd crossed the border into the scorching desert. After sleeping another couple of hours, they left with the ghost of a crescent still visible on the horizon and reached Caritas before luncheon.

When they crossed the boundary of the village, their pace slowed as the security of being within the confines of civilization washed over them.

The villagers greeted them immediately, though it only took them moments to evaluate the warriors' melancholy and the mangled passengers. They cautiously examined the new faces in the crowd, marveling at the gorgeously scarred woman riding behind Prince Alexander.

As the riders began to dismount, a man realized Griffin's absence, and a woman quickly figured out that he must be the lump on the back of Orion's horse. Wails rang out through the crowd in a chorus of sorrow. Isolde tried to keep her head up, knowing the conduct required of the Naabila, the only living heir.

Orion gave the impression of a steady rock, positioned to withstand the crashing current of a river, but that didn't stop him from feeling the villagers' tangible grief in his core. He ached for every one of them, as if he, too, had lost someone exceptionally precious.

When Kaatachi heard they'd returned, he hurried out to greet his children only to discover what the other villagers already knew. The Naaba dropped to his knees. Isolde slid from the back of Jax's tryka and ran to him, wrapping her arms around his shoulders as he bawled. His excruciating cries were nearly more than Orion could take, but he remained silent and sturdy as the Naaba's sorrow welded with the villagers' lament. Gently, they untied the ropes and lifted their Nabiiga from Orion's horse, and when his body was at last taken away, Orion slid from the roan and allowed it to be escorted to the stables with the other animals.

The rest of the group existed beneath a storm cloud of misery and exhaustion. Vera helped Isolde and a few others get Kaatachi up and returned to his tent. Jovan, Kwame, and Leone dispersed to their own houses. Healers came to take Crow and Johnathan, and Raven, Jax, and Hector followed after them. Though Vera and Declan had stitched them up and wrapped them more efficiently since leaving Ashgate, they needed to truly clean the wounds and cover them in fresh bandages.

The rest of the visitors wished to give the villagers space to mourn outside the witness of strangers and decided the best thing for everyone would be to get some much needed rest. Orion wasn't sure he would be able to sleep, but the moment his body was horizontal, he drifted into the best sleep he'd had in weeks. No more whispers. No more nightmares.

Seth curled up with Iris, and Declan laid next to her. They hadn't yet discussed what the future held for them, but amid the chaos, they'd silently agreed to figure it out when things settled. A few of the villagers offered their homes up to Prince Alexander, insisting he deserved a bed off the floor, but he kindly declined, and he and Foxx slept on a rug in the sand like the rest of them. Jax and Hector were the last to pass out after a short conversation outside the tent regarding how devastating a war would be if their assailants in Crystavium were the kind of monsters they would be facing.

Everyone slept through the rest of the day and night, waking early with the sunrise. Despite the amount of sleep, most rose feeling only mildly refreshed. The emotions of the past few days weighed heavily on each of their shoulders.

C

Foxxglove woke first, followed immediately by Alexander, as he'd felt her moving next to him. Exiting the tent, they found the village silent and still, a stark contrast from when they'd arrived the previous day. A handful of people dallied outside their tents, but most remained within their property, reading and praying as they watched dawn's fingertips graze the sky.

The fires at the center of the village had all smoldered to ashes, but the smell of burning timbers lingered in the air.

Not wishing to disturb those in meditation with their Creator, Alexander and Foxx rounded the tent and idled in the open area on the southern side, out of sight from the village center. Standing hand-in-hand, they watched the sky brighten in the east. The still invisible sun shot shards of saffron through a pigmented expanse of lavender and pink peony, bedecked in wispy clouds.

Alexander turned to face her, taking her other hand and pulling her close. He leaned in and placed a tender kiss atop her scar, and though they'd already been awake for several minutes, he murmured, "Merry morning, love."

Her cheeks warmed at his affection, though she found herself entirely comfortable in his arms, as if there had never been a single shred of distance between them. Any hesitation present days ago had been cast down the waterfall with that first kiss. Alexander had chosen to stick by her side through all of her arrogant fighting, pushing, and painful failings. Not once had he given up on what he believed they would become. Since the moment they'd met, he'd clung to her and never let go.

Long before they'd ever laid eyes on one another, he'd fought to rescue them. He'd searched for them, pursued answers in their childhood home after their mother passed and their father had left. The day they considered the last day of an ordinary life became the beginning of his journey to find them. The inception of Ataraxia was just one example of his efforts to provide them sanctuary in a fallen world. How different their lives would have been if he'd succeeded.

Thinking back on the things they'd been through, she realized that even recollections of his secrets and lies provoked a warmth of understanding and affection. All the anger and pain she'd felt had washed away, leaving her with not one single question or concern about their future.

"Merry morning, Alexander." She pressed a kiss to his lips.

"How are you?"

Foxx thought for a moment. "I think I'm actually okay."

"Yeah?" He pulled her closer, matching her smile.

She lifted a shoulder. "I feel a little guilty about it, honestly. There is so much grief amongst us, but I just feel—" Alexander brought his lips to hers, sending a shockwave of pleasure through her before pulling away and leaving her floating on her tiptoes. "Yes," she breathed, letting her eyelids remain closed as she soaked in the moment. "Like that."

He chuckled, amused by her delight. "Me too. I have a feeling things are about to get very complicated, but at the moment…" He kissed her again, shooting sparks of excitement all the way down to the toes that curled inside her boots. "I'm feeling lighter than air. Like the wind could scoop me up and carry me away, and no matter where it took me, I'd be blissfully content as long as you were by my side." He tugged her closer for emphasis.

"How are you feeling about Orion?"

Alexander lifted his eyes to the sky, shifting his weight from his heels to the balls of his feet and back again. "I suppose I feel confident things will work out how they're meant to." She lifted a skeptical brow, and he added, "With a little bit of nervousness and a twinge of uncertainty mixed in there, too."

She chuckled as Orion and Jax rounded the outer edge of the tent. Orion raised an uneasy hand to them, and Alexander lifted his chin in greeting. Separating from Foxx, he kept hold of her hand as they turned to face the men.

"Morning," Orion said.

"How are you?" Foxx surprised Orion by looking directly at him for a response. They hadn't spoken much since he'd fallen from the sky in Celestelvyra, but the agony etched into the lines of his face and the dark circles beneath his eyes had her feeling sympathetic. She couldn't imagine losing Iris, especially in such a horrific way as Griffin had been taken. Watching Isolde mourn her brother had been heartbreaking, and if Orion felt anything for her, Foxx knew he must be hurting, too. "Physically, I mean. Did you sleep?"

Orion scratched the back of his head, displaying a mild anxiety at her attention. Foxx failed to stifle a grin, as it was the exact same tell Alexander exhibited when feeling anxious. She hadn't noticed the parallels before, but now with the knowledge of their bloodline, she found herself spotting all kinds of similarities in their mannerisms and appearance.

"I slept really well. I think Maeve took my—" Orion paused, realizing no one in the current group knew of his internal issues. His eyes flickered between them as they waited for him to finish his sentence. "Nightmares."

"That's great." Foxx smiled. "I'm sure you needed it." Her gaze slid to Jax, implying she was expecting an answer from him as well. His right eye had swollen completely shut, and a row of stitches held the skin together along his brow.

Jax didn't respond immediately, and Foxx saw the gears turning beneath his expression as he took in her and Alexander's clasped hands. Then he looked down at his own hand, bandaged and short two fingers. Vera had practically forced cauterization on him the first time they stopped after fleeing the monster carcasses. She and Jovan had started a small fire for the sole purpose of heating a blade.

"Both fingers severed from below the second knuckle." He held it up to show the ring and pinky fingers missing from his left hand. "My eye is beat, and I have a few other scrapes and bruises. Nothing to worry about. Prince Al—"

"Let's at the very least drop the *Prince* part, all right?" Alexander interrupted.

Jax's thick, black brow pinched in the middle, revealing his reluctance to be so informal. "Alexander, have you seen any of the villagers yet?"

"Not many. Just the few resting on the outskirts of their tents, as you probably saw when you came out."

Orion said, "Many are usually up by now, but I suppose they must be finding it hard to drag themselves from the dredges of sleep. It's going to be a very difficult day for everyone."

Glancing at Orion, Jax asked, "Is Maeve someone I should know?"

Orion shook his head. "She's a—you know, I am not actually sure what she is. We saw her in Celestelvyra. With the Creator."

Jax's eye widened in a mixture of awe and disbelief. "You actually met Him?"

"So we will hear no more of your skepticism," Alexander said seriously, though his expression revealed his raillery. Slipping the vial from his pocket, he held up the glistening Pyhä-ki as proof of prior claims and handed it over to Jax when he reached for it.

"This is really it?" Jax examined the vial close to his eye, twisting it back and forth to watch the particles dance and shimmer. "This is what we'll use to kill the Queen?"

Alexander grinned. "That's it."

Slowly but surely, more sounds could be heard in the surrounding tents, indicating the village was in the steady process of waking. Very soon they would be able to meet with Kaatachi and find out his needs and expectations.

Orion said Alexander's name and cleared his throat. "We should probably discuss things."

Alexander nodded. "When?"

"Not now. Maybe this afternoon. After we've all conferred about the next steps."

Jax glanced back and forth between both men. Returning the vial to Alexander, he asked, "Anything I need to be made aware of?"

Alexander looked at Orion before saying, "Eventually."

Foxx said, "So what do you think happens now? We go back to Jericho, I guess? Figure out what our next move is from there?" Her mind flashed to the mysterious Konungr: the man she'd seen in her visions, who'd winked at her during the revolution rally, and who was apparently like family to Alexander.

Jax nodded. "Yes, to Jericho to confer with Abram and the King and plan the next step in this revolution."

"We need to get this moving as quickly as we can. I hate that Avaline is in the castle while all this is going on." Alexander's eyes met Orion's, and it occurred to Foxx that they'd just realized Avaline was Orion's sister, too. Orion released a tired sigh and massaged his temples but said nothing. Alexander swallowed to refocus. "I hope Sirena hasn't taken her anger toward me out on her. She was furious when we entered Celestelvyra."

"I think we can leave for Jericho today once everyone is up and moving. We need to speak with Naaba Kaatachi, but I don't know how the people of Caritas deal with mourning." Jax's eyes slid to

Orion, as if he might know the answer, but he was looking at the ground in deep thought. "Maybe some of us can leave and others can stay behind if they need or want our help. Or maybe just one person can stay as an ambassador to communicate with us in Jericho."

"Let's wait and see if we're able to speak with him before we decide," Foxx suggested. "I also think we need to consider what Maeve said about not rushing into battle."

Before the others could respond, Hector, Declan, and Raven rounded the tent to join them. "Morning, all." Despite his smile, Hector seemed as downcast as the rest of them. Both he and Raven walked on unsteady legs, their injuries easily visible in their steps.

"Merry morning, Commander," Jax said.

"Is Iris still sleeping?" Foxx looked at Declan, though seeing him now in her rested form had her anger resurfacing in a way it hadn't when they'd first reunited. Alexander felt her tense and squeezed her hand.

"She's with Seth," Declan answered, oblivious to the tension. "He woke up crying. She's laying with him for a bit until he calms down." Foxx nodded but didn't respond further.

"Maybe you should go find Isolde?" Alexander's voice jolted Orion from his inward contemplation.

As if summoned by her name, Isolde appeared at the front of the tent. The top half of her face was painted black. "My father is ready to speak with you." She looked only at Alexander. Her glacial tone indicated her suppressed grief. "It will be too much for him to have everyone. Perhaps just a few of you. Whomever Prince Alexander chooses." Then she turned and left them without another word.

Jax said, "Orion should definitely go. He is in good standing with Kaatachi." Alexander looked at Orion in question, and his brother nodded.

"Yeah, Kaatachi seems to like him. If you can believe that." Hector's chuckle spawned a groan.

Orion shrugged and cracked a smile, but Foxx thought it felt forced.

"You should come, too, Commander," Alexander said.

Hector nodded. "Assuming everything we discuss is acceptable, we can leave for Jericho today."

"All right, just the three of us, then. We'll meet up with the rest of you in the visitor's tent when we're finished." Alexander bent to kiss Foxx on the forehead, and her cheeks flushed. Then he, Hector, and Orion headed off to see the Naaba.

C

Orion flinched at the sound of rattling beads as the men pushed through the doorway of the Naaba's tent. Standing in a row before him, they bowed at the waist in unison.

Though set up similar to Isolde's, Kaatachi's tent had far more possessions scattered about: animal skulls and stacks of colorful fabric, a branch holding strings of necklaces and bracelets, and a plethora of decorations hanging from the walls.

Crafted of petrified wood, as if a tree had grown into the shape of a chair and fossilized, a massive throne stood against the western wall. The lines in the bark twisted in a spiral to form the arms and legs, and branches stuck out over the top like antlers. Feathers, foxtails, and beads decorated the entire display.

When his visitors straightened, the Naaba greeted them from the throne, looking weary with mourning and restless sleep. Rather than his usual attire, he was draped in a robe dyed the deep purple of blackberry-stained fingertips, though he still held his staff in his left hand.

Isolde stood on the side opposite his staff, her hand resting loosely on her spear. Her expression could have chilled the bitter wind of Crystavium as she stared straight ahead. Another man stood at her side, and Orion recognized him as one of the warriors he'd met when he and Isolde had returned from Jericho, though he couldn't remember his name.

Speaking first, Alexander said, "Naaba Kaatachi, it's wonderful to see you again. I am terribly sorry it is under such duress." He respectfully dipped his head again. "Nabiiga Griffin was a great man. A powerful warrior and an exceptional son."

Kaatachi dropped his chin in return. "Thank you for your kind words, Prince Alexander. My Griffin was always fond of you."

It occurred to Orion then that Alexander not only knew of Naaba Kaatachi but knew him and his family on a personal level. They'd spent time together, perhaps more than royal customs would require. He tried not to feel bitter at the Naaba mentioning Griffin's fondness for Alexander and speculated whether people liking his brother more than him was to become a notion he would soon find very familiar.

"Naabila Isolde." Alexander dropped into another bow. "I am sorry for your tragic loss. I truly wish there was something I could do to ease your pain."

"When you destroy the Immortal Queen, it will be ease enough, Prince Alexander." Isolde barely turned her eyes to him as she spoke.

"You remember Peiskos, as well, Alexander." Kaatachi gestured to the man next to Isolde. "He is to be the next Abrafo."

Peiskos lowered himself before the Prince, his broad shoulders curling in as he dropped his head. "It is an honor to see you again, Your Highness." He stood and tossed a cluster of dreadlocks behind his back. "I believe I owe you a rematch in *juhta bola*."

Alexander chuckled. "You do, indeed, Peiskos. It's good to see you."

"You have grown much, Alexander," Kaatachi said. "Not just physically but in mind and heart. It will serve you well in what is to come."

Alexander smiled at the compliment. "I'm just sorry we lost such a fearsome warrior so early in the unraveling events. I've been told he led his team at Ashgate well, and then I personally witnessed as he sacrificed himself to save two of our own. One of them being the young boy traveling with my company. Seth is someone extremely important to me, and I can't express my gratitude enough."

The Naaba nodded, shifting his back against his throne. "Yes, yes, Isolde has told me everything. He gave his life as a true warrior does. The hero does not always survive the battle, but his death allows others to prosper."

"We will never let Seth forget his sacrifice. I promise he will know of the man who rescued him."

Hector added, "Lieutenant Blackmoor won't forget either. I'm sure it haunts him even now."

"It was no fault of anyone." Kaatachi couldn't hide the sheen in his eyes. "Griffin lived exactly as he meant to. And died exactly as he meant to."

Isolde muttered something under her breath that sounded like a curse. Kaatachi waved a hand dismissively at his daughter, and her face burned with anger.

"Will there be some kind of ceremony?" Orion's eyes flashed back and forth between the two royals.

Isolde tisked and turned her head from them to stare blankly at the other side of the room.

Kaatachi glanced at her, then back to the men apologetically. "You must forgive my daughter. She is grieving."

Alexander lifted his hands. "It's completely understandable."

Orion said, "Her brother was an exceptional man, loved by his people. He—"

"He hated you," Isolde snapped, cutting into his sentence like a serrated knife through stiff bread. Her head whipped toward him in a surprising fury. Orion eyed her curiously, feeling slapped by her harsh tone.

"Iso, my child. Calm now." Kaatachi soothed his daughter, his eyes heavy with exhaustion and bloodshot from shed tears. She huffed and looked away again.

Orion tried to recall what he might have done to make her so angry. He'd taken down the beast who killed her brother with his own hands; rode all the way back to Caritas with his corpse strapped to his back. She'd been short with Alexander, but she hadn't spoken with such wrath.

Peiskos took a step forward. "Our mourning is not long. We will hold the ceremony tomorrow at daybreak."

Hector said, "We need some of our people back in Jericho to meet with the Konungr and his commander, but we can leave some here to help with the arrangements. Or even as a go-between for the two nations. Whatever you need."

"Yes, yes, that will do." Kaatachi nodded, taking in all their words with a grateful exhale. "Leave one here for communication, and your injured boy as well so he may heal. Johnathan, I believe, young Declan's brother. After the ceremony, we will begin to prepare for war. You will send word when you know what you need from us."

"I was thinking." Alexander scratched his chin, eyes to the side in thought. "Naaba Kaatachi, your tents are easily moved, is that correct? You moved them all the way from Savanni at one point?"

Kaatachi eyed him with interest, trying to discern his reason for asking. "Yes, Caritas has moved a few times even in my lifetime. Why do you ask?"

"What if we move you closer to the Metsa Sateen barrier?"

Hector's eyes lit with understanding. "For easier communication."

"Yes. So we have a more direct route to you. But also to give you an easier escape route if needed. Sirena may know of Caritas' involvement in the prison heist, especially if your warriors were the ones causing the distraction outside the gate. I would hate to leave you out here in the desert with little protection. Being stationed right along a barrier seems an answer to both those needs."

"A brilliant plan, Alexander." Kaatachi tapped his stomach. "There is open land next to the vineyards. A perfect place to resettle. In fact, we have discussed making the move many times, but it never seemed worth the trouble. Perhaps now we have a valid reason. Let me discuss it with my daughter and the elders, and I will let you know what we decide before you depart today."

Hector said, "We can leave extra people behind to help with the moving process, if that is the decision you make. To help get things settled quickly, especially in the midst of your mourning."

"Thank you, Commander. I will talk to them now, and we will meet again before luncheon. Until then, go in peace."

Alexander, Hector, and Orion bowed before the man and then to Isolde and Peiskos. Orion sent a final concerned glance in her direction as they exited the tent, but she didn't return it. When the flap closed behind him, he heard her begin berating her father in Vetoräti. Kaatachi shut her down with a stern command and the tent went silent.

Alexander and Hector walked back to the visitor tent, but Orion lingered, hoping Isolde would come out so he could speak with her privately. Moments later, she stormed through the tent door, stopping short when she saw him a few paces away. Scoffing, she turned and stomped around the side of the tent.

He wasn't sure if this was an invitation to follow, but he did so anyway. He called her name as he rounded the corner, and Isolde turned an about face so abruptly, he nearly ran into her.

Glaring at him with molten irises, she snapped, "What is it, *herr* Orion?"

Taken aback by her jarring tone, he took a cautious step toward her. "When did we return to formalities?" She refused to meet his gaze, staring blankly into the air over his shoulder. "Isolde. Talk to me, please."

"I do not wish to speak with you." Her fingers stiffened around her spear, and her other hand grazed the hilt of the sword hanging at her hip. By her expression and attitude, he honestly wondered if she meant to draw it on him.

"Why? What have I done to deserve this treatment?" When she didn't respond, he empathized, "I know you are hurting, Isolde. Trust me, I understand."

"Have you lost a brother?" Her eyes finally locked on his, and the rage he felt from them turned his stomach with fear.

"No, I haven't. But I have lost a mother and a father and an entire life. More than once. I've lost more than you can imagine, Naabila, so trust me when I say, I can sympathize." He tried to hold the hand at her hip, but she slid it behind her back and out of reach. "What are you doing?" His voice began to tremble as his frustration grew, both from his lack of understanding and her unwillingness to explain. Days ago, they'd confessed their affections, but everything in her demeanor now shouted the complete opposite of love. "Isolde, I don't understand what's happening. I'm going to need you to spell it out for me."

Isolde cleared her throat. "What you said before. About my being the Naabila. An heir." He narrowed his eyes as she inhaled a sharp breath. "You were right."

A rock dropped heavily into his stomach. "About which part, exactly?"

"About you." Her eyes narrowed to match his, made more ominous by the black paint covering the top half of her face. "And me. Not being right for each other." Though she tried to conceal it, he could discern the teary stiffness scratching her throat.

Fighting to restrain the growl in his tone, he took another step toward her. "That hasn't seemed to matter this whole time, Isolde. What are you even talking about?"

She took a step back. Her wrapped knee gave out, leaving her unbalanced, and she left it bent. Orion looked at it, wanting to ask what had happened and if she was okay, but before he got the words out, she said, "You know what I am talking about." Her eyes glazed over with liquid as the words shot from her lips.

"Then what have we been doing this entire time?" he snarled, fear making him angry. Reining it in, he said, "I thought none of that mattered to you. You said it didn't matter."

"I did not think it did." She took a long, heavy breath and the seconds passed by like hours as he waited for her to continue. "But things have changed now. I have responsibilities to my people. The person standing beside me needs to be—"

"A prince?" His heart grew colder with every word she spoke.

Her glare turned steely as if he'd offended her with his assumption. "Someone who is prepared for the responsibilities."

"And all of a sudden that someone is no longer me?" He could hear his anger detonating in his tone, but he seemed unable to hinder it. The air around him felt hotter than usual as the boiling of his blood made him sweat. "Has nothing I've done in your presence made a difference? Have I proven nothing to you?"

Her eyes flitted from his, landing on the hand fiddling with her sword. "You have said it from the very beginning. I am sorry I did not want to listen. It was not my intention to give you mixed signals."

"Mixed signals?" he shouted. Then he inhaled, rubbing his temples with his thumb and index finger as he willed himself to calm down. "I can't believe I am hearing this." Stepping closer, he invaded her space as they often did to each other, and this time she didn't back away. He secured his eyes on hers, and she didn't shy from his gaze. "Isolde, don't do this. You've suffered a great loss. There is so much more coming. Let me help you through this. Let me stand by you. We can take on everything together." He grazed her arm with the tips of his fingers, wishing he could confess his love again, wishing to remind her of the truth behind his feelings, but he failed to force the words out. "Please, Isolde."

She stared at him for a long moment, searching the oceans of his eyes as she had done so many times before. Her expression revealed transparent sadness but not indecision. "No, *herr* Orion. I cannot." Then she turned from him and disappeared behind the tent.

He debated running after her. He considered pulling her back and making her see he could be worthy of her and the life she was destined to live. He hadn't believed he could be worthy of anything before, but that was changing—he was changing.

How could she leave before he had a chance to prove it?

He stood rooted to the ground, staring at the exact spot where she'd vanished from his view. Anxious thoughts coursed through his mind and rattled his heart. A noise behind him had him turning to find Alexander standing at the entrance to the aisle between the two tents.

Taking a step into the shaded alley, Alexander said, "I didn't mean to eavesdrop. I was coming to look for you, and I heard you talking. I didn't want to interrupt."

"It's fine." Orion ran his hands down his face in an effort to wipe away evidence of escaped tears. "What did you need?"

Alexander held his gaze for a long time, trying to get his thoughts in order. Then he said, "Tell her, Orion. Just tell her who you are."

"No."

Alexander's lack of understanding was revealed in his expression. "Why? Won't it change everything? She thinks she needs a prince, but she already has one."

"It won't make a difference." Again, Orion's words emerged harsher than intended. "The issue isn't my lack of title. It's my..." He paused, wondering what word would describe it efficiently. Biting back his habit of concealing insecurities, he finally settled on, "... my everything else." Then he pushed past Alexander, ignoring him when he called his name.

When he arrived at the front of the tent, a soldier riding a Jerichonian horse crossed the threshold at the entrance to the village shouting for Commander Kayvan.

Alexander stepped up next to Orion. "One of Hector's men. A new Reko Raptor.

"Wyatt Hearne," Orion said. "But what's he doing here?" They walked toward the rider as Hector and Jax emerged from the visitor's tent, responding to the sound of the commander's name.

The five men converged next to one of the unlit teepees, and Wyatt slid from the back of his horse, out of breath and sweating. "Commander Kayvan, Lieutenant Blackmoor." He put his hands on his knees as he fought to catch his breath. "I found you. I'm so glad you're here. I worried I should have crossed into Crystavium instead."

Hector put his hand on the Raptor's shoulder, drawing his eyes. "What is it, Wyatt? Why have you come? What's wrong?"

Still out of breath, Wyatt tried to get his answers out. "Abram sent me from Jericho. With a message. I barely stopped the entire way."

"What is the message?" Jax pressed.

"It's the Queen," he stammered between gasps. The title sent a surge of fear through the group. Finally, he rose to stand upright and put his hands on his hips, lifting his eyes to the sky. "As news spread about Jericho and the revolution, some of the more rebellious cities began fighting back. Rioting and spreading malcontent against the Legion soldiers stationed there." The mens' eyes widened in a mixture of fright and glee. "It's been happening all over. Except now the Queen is responding. She's been attacking towns. Decimating them."

Villagers who'd been alerted by the anxious rider began darkening the doorways of the tents surrounding them. Foxx and Raven exited the visitor's tent and began walking in their direction.

"Just in the past few days, she's not only destroying places that are rebelling, but her attacks seem almost random. Though I imagine they aren't."

"What towns?" Jax asked as Raven approached

Wyatt lifted his chin. "Hey Raven. Wow, you guys are a mess." For the first time since arriving, he took in the bandaged Raptors with a concerned expression. Raven nodded in greeting and asked what was going on.

"Uprisings and insurgence all over Arkaemor," Hector answered.

Wyatt said, "There doesn't seem to be a pattern. Lupene, Alta Herba, Sal, Ranta—"

Having just arrived after being stopped by one of the villagers, Foxx inhaled sharply and lifted her hand to her lips. "What happened in Ranta?"

"Sirena is decimating towns," Alexander said. "Ranta is where Foxx and Iris are from."

"She's attacking towns that are rebelling?" Raven asked for clarification.

"Among others." Hector took a step closer to her so their shoulders touched, and Raven slipped her hand into his.

Wyatt continued naming cities. "Falcon's Quarry, Norsukylä, Kesken Ala."

"No!" Alexander and Foxx gasped in unison.

"Werifesteria, Kalladem, and others. We don't know how many more." Wyatt exhaled another long breath. "It's been happening for about three weeks, pretty much within days of us declaring Jericho as the base of the revolution, but we didn't receive reports about it until after you left the city. Who knows how many more she's attacked since I left Jericho or how many haven't been able to get word to us at all."

"She isn't only hitting rebelling cities or cities with militaries." Hector began to pace as he processed the information.

Alexander said, "She's making it personal. The Belamour home, Werifesteria is near their mother's childhood home, Kesken Ala is where they stayed and hid from the Legion."

"Norsukylä was my mistake." Hector's eyes met Jax's. "My failure that led to my promotion. Though honestly, they were probably included on the list of rebelling towns, so maybe it had nothing to do with me. I wonder if she hit the city or the compound."

Wyatt shrugged. "I think she hit the city, but I don't know for sure."

Jax said, "Alta Herba has a small military and is known for housing rebels. Same with Sal, though Sal's military includes some of the Valentino's troops, too."

"I wonder how the other royals are responding," Orion said.

Suddenly in a panic, Alexander asked, "Did she hit near the Monastery in Metsa Sateen?"

Wyatt scrunched up his eyes as he tried to remember. "Yes, when they destroyed the Monastery, they also attacked some place nearby, I think."

"It wasn't a city though," Hector said.

"Oh, my goodness." Foxx's eyes filled with tears as they fell to the beaded bracelets on her wrist.

Alexander wrapped an arm around her, and she buried her face in his chest. "Ataraxia."

"Define *decimated*," Orion said.

"Obliterated, gone, destroyed. Turned to rubble." Wyatt used his hands to demonstrate. "If there are survivors it's because they fled in time."

"Kaen?" Jax asked.

"Many cities were attacked by the drakinferno, yes, as well as Legion soldiers. Others were assaulted by monsters."

Hector cursed and wiped his brow. "Not only is she trying to make a point, that she is stronger than us and can strike us where it hurts, but she's trying to wipe out anyone who might stand alongside us. They have a list of all the known rebel groups with information on size and location." Looking at Alexander, Hector added, "Caritas is on that list."

"Thanks to us," Jax said. "How can we protect them?"

"Alexander already suggested they relocate to the barrier. Kaatachi is discussing it with his elders now." Hector ran his hand down his face, scrambling to organize his thoughts.

Orion's eyes found Kaatachi's tent. Isolde stood at the doorway, watching the group from afar. "We should go talk to him."

When Foxx stepped away from Alexander to wipe her face, he clapped his hands together in front of him. "So, what's our next move?"

"We need to leave for Jericho right now." Hector looked at Orion, who took a step toward the Naaba's tent.

"I'll go talk to Kaatachi."

"We'll inform the others to pack up and prepare to head out," Alexander said. Foxx leaned in to whisper something in his ear, and he nodded in reply. Then she touched Raven's arm, and they both hurried off toward the visitors' tent.

Jax watched them go. "We need to decide who will stay and who will go. I'll go with Orion to talk to the Naaba."

"We're going to figure this out." Hector met eyes with each of them. "We have an army, one Sirena thinks she's destroying, but she's wrong. She's forcing growth with each attack. Any survivors will be angry and vengeful. Ready to fight."

Wyatt grinned and rubbed his palms together in excitement. "And we will show them how."

Hector nodded, and Alexander said, "And we now know people were rebelling before the attacks began. People on our side who will want to join our cause and stand with us."

Hector grinned, agreeing with Alexander's words. "That's right. We have Pyhä-ki to take down Sirena once and for all. We have the Konungr and his Guard on our side, and the Prince of Arkaemor, ready and willing." He put a hand on Alexander's shoulder and shook him for emphasis. Then a glimmer of electric hope sparkled in his eyes. "It's time to go to war."

Epilogue

In the Smoking Hollow on the outskirts of Inaravale, Queen Sirena arrived in a horse-drawn carriage. The steeds pulling the coach were blacker than night, with hair of deep ruby matching the hue of Sirena's dress. Golden, damask designs embellished the carriage, adorned with vines of ivalace ivy and crimson amaryllis blooms.

Accompanying Sirena was her recently appointed commander, Dagon Wraith, of the King's High Legion. He sat across from her within the coach, silently watching tree trunks pass by the window. The Queen's voice startled him from his meditation as they pulled up to an aged building of stone deep in the forest appearing no bigger than an outdoor privy.

"I believe we have arrived," she said. As the carriage slowed to a halt, Dagon pushed open the door and stepped out, extending an arm for the Queen to use for balance.

She exited the carriage without the use of his politeness, holding her dress away from her ankles so as not to stumble. With feet planted on the ground, she dropped the hem and gazed at the building with curiosity. "It's smaller than I remember, Commander Wraith. I do hope they aren't too squished together." The slight grin curling her lips revealed this to be a falsehood.

Dagon closed the carriage door. "Should we be concerned about the King following us?"

"Pollux is still under the impression I am trapped in my living quarters."

Dagon nodded, lifting a glass lantern from where it hung atop the carriage and turning toward the building. "Follow me."

Displeased by his ill-mannered demand, Sirena glared at the back of his head before trailing him to the wooden door. Turning the key in the padlock, he yanked it open and removed the locking mechanism, hooking it onto his belt as he tugged open the door with a loud creak. A gust of air escaped, smelling of feces and body odor.

Peeking over his shoulder, Sirena found the inside dark and seemingly empty. "What is this, Commander?"

Stepping aside to allow her full view of the space encased in layered stone, Dagon said, "Stairs, Your Majesty." He handed her the lantern, knowing she would want to be the first to enter.

Sirena descended the dusty staircase, discovering it opened into an underground cellar. Up against the far wall, crowded together in fear of the incoming intruder, sat a group of civilians. Dirty and disheveled, they quaked with fear. The Queen moved closer, holding the lantern above the people to get a better look.

"There are about thirty here now, but we're still gathering others. More are on their way as we speak. We brought a few men, but we're mostly taking women, as you requested."

Her eyes scanned the crowd. "No children?"

"We left the children for the Sasori Raj to round up. My men have sent correspondence to all the bosses letting them know where they can find their prey."

"Very good, Commander." Sirena smiled wickedly, making the people cower deeper into shadow. Stopping before a man with fair hair swept to one side, she held out a hand. "Rise, please."

Hardening his features, the man stood. Sirena scanned him from head to toe, running a hand over the muscles of his chest as she circled him. "Take this one, Commander. And her, too." She gestured to a woman sitting alone against the far wall. Wraith crossed the room and dragged the woman up by her arm. She fought his grip as he led her over, stilling in the Queen's presence with a sharp glare. Sirena touched the woman's chin, turning her face so she could see her better in the lantern light. "Yes, these will suit me just fine. Bind them and set them by the stairs until we finish here. They'll ride with us back to Castle Solís."

Neither the man nor the woman fought back as Dagon bound their hands in front of them and pulled them away.

Another man stood up from the crowd. Brave but cautious, he took a step toward her. "My Queen?" he croaked, his throat dry with dehydration. "Are you here to free us, Your Majesty?" His eyes flashed to the cuffed pair by the stairs.

Sirena surveyed the man, taking in his disheveled hair and soiled clothing. She grimaced at his appearance, though her voice came out soft, like a caring stranger discovering a lost child. "What is your name, sir?"

"Stefan, Your Majesty. Stefan Barlow."

"A pleasure to meet you, Stefan Barlow."

He bowed. "It is wonderful to meet Your Majesty in person."

Dagon said, "This is one of the ones you specifically requested. From Ranta."

"Interesting." The word lengthened in her enjoyment as she looked around the room at all the hopeful eyes gazing back at her. "I am here to free you, Stefan." A light sparked in his eyes as a murmur of relief spread through the crowd. Louder, so all could hear, the Queen said, "I am here to free all of you. Free you from the mundane lives you once led. Free you from pain and sorrow and all the heavy burdens weighing you down."

Stefan took an involuntary step back. Others in the room retreated toward the wall, but there was nowhere for them to go. Nowhere left for them to hide.

Gracefully, the Queen lifted her hand and slid the tips of her fingers down the side of Stefan's face. He quivered with fear at her touch. When her hand fell away and nothing happened, he exhaled, letting his eyelids fall closed with relief.

A moment of silence passed before a smile curled the Queen's lips. Stefan's eyes widened, excruciating dread registering at last. In the dark, underground bunker by the flickering glow of the lantern, Stefan Barlow began to change. Holding his hands out in front of his face, his arms and fingers stretched, elongating until they were lengthy and thin. The skin over his entire body turned gray as his cells died before his eyes. Then the skin on his face melted off to reveal smokey muscle stretched over a tarnished skull. His hair fell to the floor in clumps and the clothing he'd been wearing sagged atop a bony form until sliding completely off. His legs extended so he grew tall above them, his body needing to hunch over when it hit the ceiling.

Those crowded behind him cried noises of terror, willing themselves to become one with the shadows.

The being opened his mouth to release a silent scream, running his hands over his face as he expressed his last moment of human emotion. Then the entirety of his eyeballs clouded with inky black, and Stefan Barlow was gone.

C

The Great King and the Seer
Book 3 SNEAK PEEK...

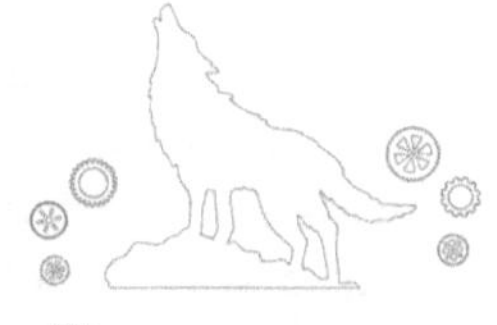

PROLOGUE

Ingrid traced delicate circles on Vali's chest with the tips of her fingers. Perched on his elbow at her side, he stared at her with absent eyes. His mind lay elsewhere, off in the desert with the company who'd departed several hours prior.

The Dróttning had managed to drag him to bed more than an hour ago, luring him from his brooding with kisses and playful banter. When they first arrived, he'd been eager to watch her change from evening-wear into her favorite wool robe, but he'd since faded back into trepidation.

She massaged the tense skin above his brow, smoothing away anxiety and compelling his attention. Plucking a grape from a cluster that slithered down from the viny canopy above the bed, Ingrid held it to his mouth.

Smile returned, he accepted the fruit, meeting her gaze as the grape slid between his lips. His hand slid beneath her robe, long ago untied and left open. Cool fingers roamed her curves, exploring the hills and valleys of which he was an expert traveler.

Tender touch fueling his passion, Vali embraced her with all the zeal he could muster.

Her hands perused his muscles, sliding up his arms and down his shoulder blades. As her fingers grazed the ridges of his ribcage, an arousing shiver tickled the back of his neck. When her hand found the clasp of his belt, he caught it with his own and pressed their palms together, interlocking their fingers.

"Not tonight, my Dróttning. I don't have it in me to give you the satisfaction you deserve." He kissed her temple and let his body rest heavier against the bed.

"You worry for them, but you have trained her well."

"The others don't yet know what she's capable of, and she and Alexander were at odds when they departed." He pressed a trail of kisses across her knuckles. "In a way, I feel I've sent her there all alone."

"We can leave now. Join them."

Vali shook his head. "Allegiance was claimed. Perhaps I worry for nothing. I only wish I could dispel this horrible feeling in the pit of my stomach."

With a small smile, Ingrid fixed the section of his hair flipped to the wrong side. "Hector seems a wise man. Alexander is keen and careful. Foxxglove is brave and clever. Perhaps you need to give them a little more credit."

"You and I both know the ruthless depths of Sirena's cruelty. If she gets the upper hand, it could turn the tide of this war before it's even begun."

Ingrid scooted closer to his warmth and settled deeper into the mattress. "Not this time. We have everything we need to ensure victory."

"We thought we had that with Amaryllis."

"Amaryllis was not Foxxglove. You have said so yourself. She will be far greater than her mother ever dreamed to be. She is the woman with the white hair. Do not lose sight of that, my love."

After a long moment, Vali conceded, "Hector is wise. I wouldn't have expected him to be the man who would lead the charge."

"Nor I. But Elohim works in peculiar and puzzling ways."

A frantic knock rattled the door to their outer chambers, and Vali stilled, silver eyes flashing with fear.

"Enter," Ingrid called as she pulled her robe closed and sat up.

The sound of keys twisting in the lock preceded the illumination of a torch filling the chamber outside their bedroom. Viggo's form appeared in the doorway, and a single glance at the leader of his Royal Guard had Vali leaping from the bed.

"What's happened?"

"It's Lady Foxxglove and her friend. The bad-tempered one." Viggo looked back and forth between the Konungr and Dróttning, eyes lit with panic. "They are in the throne room. And there is a lot of blood."

"They are alone?" Ingrid asked.

"Why are they in the throne room?" Vali asked.

"They're alone, yes, and as to why they are in the throne room, it is unclear. They seem to have appeared from nowhere."

Vali pushed past Viggo and hastened through the door. Ingrid sprung from the bed and hurried after him with his shirt in hand. When she caught up, she slipped it over his shoulders. Pushing his arms through the sleeves, he buttoned it up the front as he picked up speed.

C

Vali called Foxx's name before he crossed the threshold, but when her figure came into view, the sight stopped him in his tracks. Saturated clothing glistened with fresh blood, and crimson stained her arms from her elbows to the tips of her fingers. Her unbearable expression conveyed rage, terror, and inconceivable sadness. Orion stood behind her, eyes bulging and mouth slack. Blood coated his torso as if he'd bathed in it.

"What happened?" Vali closed the distance between them, and Foxx threw her arms around him as she crumbled into a fit of sobs. She went limp in his arms, and he dropped with her, catching her before her knees collided with the floor.

"Orion, can you tell us what's going on?" Ingrid asked, her voice serene enough to subdue a ravenous bear. Orion's eyes darted about the room as he tried to process his surroundings. She reached for him, gently touching his arm, and his attention snapped to her. Still, words failed him.

Vali rubbed Foxx's back as unbridled tears soaked his shirt. His gentle voice in her ear endeavored to soothe. "It's okay, Foxxglove. You're home now. Whatever happened, it's going to be fine." He pushed hair from her cheeks and held her face between his palms. With a rascally grin, he said, "You know, if you wanted to see the throne room this badly, it didn't require such theatrics."

Foxx let her forehead drop to his shoulder, too full of sorrow to be swayed by his attempt at humor.

Vali looked at Ingrid, finding her equally unsuccessful at getting information out of Orion. Returning his attention to Foxx, he created space between them and gripped her shoulders to hold her upright. "Foxxglove, I need you to tell me what happened. You are stronger than this. Calm down and speak to me. Now."

Foxx inhaled a deep breath and attempted to arrest her tears. Her chest continued to heave. "It was a trap. She took them." A new wave of sobs wracked her body as she fought to continue. "She took them, Vali, and I couldn't stop her. I couldn't save them."

Vali's eyes lifted to Orion, hoping he would clarify the story, but it seemed there was little to be gotten from either of them. To his wife he said, "Ingrid, get—"

"I will," she replied and hurried from the room before he could make his request.

Vali slid a hand beneath Foxx's legs and scooped her up into his arms. "Orion, I can't carry both of you, so you're going to have to walk on your own. Follow me."

Check back in 2026 to find out what happens next. Follow Jessica Pietro on social media or sign up for her newsletter for updates.

About the Author

Jessica Pietro has been enchanted by fantasy worlds her entire life. Though she dabbled in writing, she never anticipated being a published author.

In 2019, she started selling artwork and teaching under the name *Vellichor and More*. In 2021, she began writing *The Great King and the Seer*.

Not only is she passionate about art and stories, she also enjoys adventuring, board games, studying her bible, anime, gardening, music, hot beverages, camping, and spending time with her family.

Jessica resides in Pennsylvania, with her husband, their son, and their kitties. Find out more about her by connecting with her on social media.

Links to all of her sites can be found here:

www.vellichorandmore.com

C

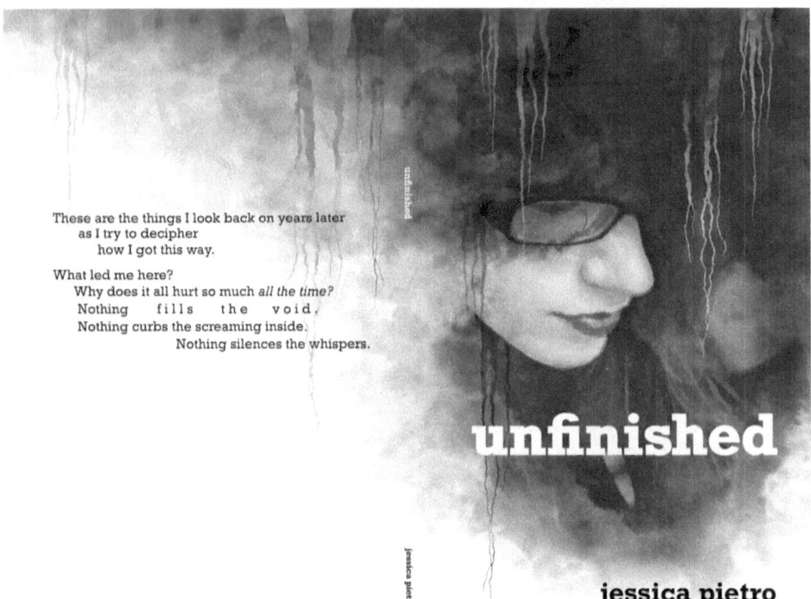
unfinished
These are the things I look back on years later
as I try to decipher
how I got this way.

What led me here?
Why does it all hurt so much *all the time?*
Nothing   fills   the   void.
Nothing curbs the screaming inside.
Nothing silences the whispers.

unfinished
jessica pietro

9 781962 891172